# Maureen Lee

## Mother of Pearl

## Nothing Lasts Forever

# Maureen Lee

## Mother of Pearl

## Nothing Lasts Forever

*Mother of Pearl*
First published in Great Britain by Orion in 2008

*Nothing Lasts Forever*
First published in Great Britain by Orion in 2009

This omnibus edition published in 2011
by Orion Books Ltd
Orion House, 5 Upper St Martin's Lane
London WC2H 9EA

An Hachette UK Company

A CIP catalogue record for this book is available from the British
Library.

ISBN 9781407234243

Printed and bound in Great Britain by Clays Ltd, St Ives plc

www.orionbooks.co.uk

# Mother *of* Pearl

For Richard
Just for being here

## Acknowledgments

Once again Norman Longmate's fascinating book, *How We Lived Then*, has proved invaluable while writing this novel, and Phil Thompson's scrupulously researched book on *The Cavern, The Best of Cellars*, is an essential tool for anyone interested in the recent history of Liverpool.

# Chapter 1

## April 1971
## Pearl

Hilda Dooley was reading aloud from the *Daily Mirror*. 'I see they're letting that Liverpool woman out of prison,' she announced.

There was a long pause. 'Which woman?' Audrey Steele enquired when it looked as if no one was going to say anything. Audrey was the oldest, and the kindest, of the teachers present, and Hilda was largely disliked.

'That Amy Patterson. She murdered her husband. Stabbed him in his heart, poor sod. It happened in nineteen fifty.' Hilda gave a disapproving sniff. 'Before she got married, she used to live in the next street to us in Bootle.'

'Did she?' This time a few heads were raised in interest. 'And where was that?'

'Agate Street. It's off Marsh Lane. I lived in Garnet Street; still do.' Hilda pursed her lips as if she wasn't exactly proud of this fact. 'She was about twelve years older than me. I used to see her at Mass. I can't remember her maiden name, but her husband was Barney Patterson. They had a daughter, who was about five at the time. I don't know what happened to her.'

'What was she like? The mother, that is.'

'Pretty,' Hilda said wistfully. A plain woman in her late thirties with buck teeth and thin hair, Hilda had never married, and lived with her widowed mother. 'Dead pretty.' Her voice changed, became hard. 'Personally, I think she should have been hanged by the neck until she was dead.'

'You mean the State should have murdered *her*?' said Louisa Sutton, who was a member of the Campaign for Nuclear

Disarmament and Amnesty. Louisa could always be relied on to promote the Liberal cause.

I held my coffee mug tightly in both hands, stared out of the window and pretended not to listen, although it was impossible to ignore Hilda's penetrating voice. Barney Patterson hadn't been stabbed in the heart, but in the stomach. It had said so in the newspapers at the time.

I wondered how Hilda would have reacted had she known that Amy Patterson's daughter was sitting only a few feet away. At the age of five I had hardly noticed when people began to call me by my mother's maiden name, Curran, instead of Patterson. And now my mother was about to be released from prison. My heart was performing cartwheels at the news.

'If you hold that mug much tighter, Pearl, you'll crack it!' remarked Nan Winters, who was sitting next to me. 'I'm glad it's not my neck.'

I managed to smile, loosened my grip on the mug and tried to think of something funny to say back, but couldn't. On a normal day at this hour, twenty to nine, the staff would have been in their classrooms waiting for the bell to go and the school day to begin, not gossiping in the staffroom. Today, though, it was raining too heavily for the pupils to play outside, so the playground helpers were looking after them indoors.

It had rained all week, and the weather was getting everyone down, especially the children. They became restless stuck inside all day. Very soon, St Kentigern's Roman Catholic Junior and Infant School in Seaforth would be occupied by more than two hundred and fifty young people brimming over with energy. Every window would be steamed up, and the floors would be wet and slippy. Shoes would squelch, skirts would drip, and some of the cheap canvas satchels would be soaked through, ruining homework.

It was all very depressing. The teachers were reluctant to leave the cosy staffroom until the last minute. But today was Friday — a very special Friday. At quarter past three we would break up for the Easter holiday. I visualized the weather changing drastically overnight: the sky turning blue, the sun shining, and daffodils popping up all over the place. This thought would have cheered me considerably had it not been for the disturbing news that Hilda had just read out.

I watched the children race from the gate to the school building. Only a few, mainly girls, made any attempt to avoid the numerous puddles, which had been getting bigger and bigger all week. It would be hell on earth in the cloakrooms while they hung up their wet coats and changed their Wellington boots for shoes. I really should be there, helping the little ones.

Gary Finnegan came through the gate holding his mother's hand. He had only started at the school in February. He wore a bright red anorak and red boots. The other boys made fun of the fact that, unlike the other mothers who left their kids at the gate, Gary's brought him inside and kissed him goodbye outside the classroom door. I couldn't get used to how cruel five-year-olds could be. I began to collect my equipment together. The first lesson today was reading.

An argument was raging between Hilda and Louisa over the pros and cons of capital punishment. No one else had bothered to join in. There were six teachers present including me. All were women. The only male, Brian Blundy, hadn't yet arrived or was elsewhere on the premises.

'Amy Patterson is about to be released from prison,' Hilda raged. 'It says here she's only forty-nine. She's got quite a few years ahead of her. She's got a daughter somewhere, but her poor husband is dead. It hardly seems fair.'

'She's spent twenty years behind bars,' Louisa said calmly. She knew what she was talking about: Hilda was merely blustering. 'I reckon she's paid for her crime. Anyroad, this country abolished the death penalty in nineteen sixty-five. The Government must have realized it was barbaric.'

Hilda looked sulky. Her lips twitched as she searched for a reply. The staffroom telephone rang and she reached for it. It was a way of escaping from an argument that she was losing. After a few short words, she put down the receiver and said to me, 'Miss Burns wants to see you in her office, Pearl.'

'Now?'

'Now,' Hilda confirmed. She picked up a stack of books and left the room. The other women followed suit.

I made my way to the headmistress's office at the rear of the building and knocked on the door.

'Come in!' Miss Burns shouted.

I sighed and went in. I knew why she wanted to see me.

'Good morning, Pearl. Sit down, dear.' Catherine Burns laid down her pen and picked up a packet of Marlboros. She shook one out, put it in her mouth and lit it with a silver lighter. Her hands were shaking slightly. A different newspaper, the *Guardian*, lay open on her desk. 'I expect you've guessed why I asked to see you?'

'It can only be because of my mother. Hilda Dooley was on about it in the staff room. Apparently it's in the *Daily Mirror*. I didn't know she was being released.'

'Neither did I. Does Charlie know?'

'He would have mentioned it if he had. I wonder if she'll come and live with us? I get the impression that Marion and my mother didn't get on.'

'They didn't.' Miss Burns shook her head. 'It wouldn't be fair on Charlie to have his sister and his wife under the same roof. But Amy knows she can always come and live with me. Your mother and I have been friends since we started school together at five.' She stubbed out the half-smoked cigarette and lit another. 'I'm chain-smoking,' she said apologetically. 'The news has upset me, but I can't think why. I'm only too pleased Amy is about to be released. I suppose it's brought back the horror of that time: the murder, the trial, Amy being sentenced to life imprisonment.'

'Hilda Dooley thinks she should have hanged. Did you know she lives in Garnet Street? She actually knew my mother before she got married.'

Miss Burns looked surprised. 'No, I didn't. My own family lived no distance away.' She chuckled. 'Let's hope Hilda doesn't put two and two together. The Burnses weren't exactly model citizens in those days.' This was hard to believe now. Catherine Burns, in her smart navy-blue costume and sensible blouse, with her grey-brown hair short and plainly styled, and her pleasant face devoid of make-up, gave the impression of rather dull respectability, though the chain-smoking was slightly at odds with this image. 'How do you feel about all this, Pearl?' she enquired. 'The news must have come as a bit of a shock.'

'I've no idea how I feel,' I said honestly. 'I might later, once I've got used to it. Now, all I feel is numb.'

I knew it had been bound to happen one day. People sentenced to life imprisonment weren't usually kept in until they died.

'I understand, dear.' Miss Burns nodded. Half an inch of ash fell off her cigarette and landed on her skirt; absent-mindedly she brushed it off. 'She's been a model prisoner.'

'I've never visited her, you know,' I said. 'I didn't even know she was in prison until I was fourteen. Charles and Marion told me she'd gone to Australia when my father died. And they said he'd been killed in a car crash.'

By the time I was twelve and had discovered Australia was on the same planet – a girl in my class and her family had actually gone to live there – I knew there must be something very odd about my mother never coming home. But I didn't ask Charlie and Marion about it. Perhaps I suspected there was a good reason for hiding the truth, and it was preferable that I didn't know.

'She expressly said she didn't want you to see her in prison, Pearl.'

I could understand that. It was another two years before Charles had told me the truth. He'd shown me a file full of newspaper cuttings of the trial, left it on a shelf under the stairs and told me I could look at it whenever I pleased. I'd read the contents quite a few times over the years. They never failed to horrify me. These were my parents I was reading about.

Miss Burns lit a third cigarette. 'I must stop this,' she muttered. 'You'd better go, Pearl. Don't hesitate to come and see me if you need someone to talk to. Call me at home if it's out of school hours.'

'Thank you, I might well do that.' But I knew I never would. I was always a little unsure of my relationship with the woman who was both head of the school where I taught and had been my mother's best friend. When I was little, Cathy Burns had been virtually a member of the family. She had nursed me on her knee, read to me, taught me how to play Snap and other card games. On Sundays, while my mother made the dinner, Aunt Cathy had taken me to Sefton Park to see the fairy glen – I'd lived in another part of Liverpool in those days. When we spoke nowadays, I tried to steer a course between being too friendly and not friendly enough.

Later that day, halfway through the chaos of a double craft lesson, Miss Burns's secretary came in and gave me a note in a sealed envelope. It read: 'Charlie phoned and asked to speak to you. I told him you already knew about Amy. He said he'll see you tonight.'

I was always the first to arrive home at my aunt and uncle's house in Aintree on the outskirts of Liverpool. Charles, my mother's brother, worked as a draughtsman for the English Electric Company on the East Lancashire Road. Marion, his wife, was a secretary in the same place. It was where they had met more than thirty years ago when they were teenagers. They'd never had children of their own.

As soon as I got in, the first thing I did was get the file from under the stairs, sit on the floor, and read everything in it. There were dozens of photographs of my extremely photogenic mother and equally attractive father, whom I was said to resemble. But when I looked closely at the photo of my parents' wedding in 1939, I could see no similarity whatsoever between the dark-haired young man and myself. My parents were grinning widely, as if the whole thing were a big joke. Three months after the photo had been taken, Barney Patterson had joined the Army and been sent to France.

'Barney Patterson, thirty-two, who spent nearly five years of the war in a German prisoner-of-war camp, was brutally murdered by his twenty-nine-year-old wife …' That was from the *Daily Sketch*.

Most of the papers said the same. Some referred to my father as a 'war hero', others claimed that he had been 'cruelly slain'. The fact that he had survived the fighting in France and the camp, only to die at the hands of his wife, was repeated more than once. There were calls for my mother to be hanged. A petition was launched in support and another against. Arguments raged in the letters pages between supporters and opponents of the death penalty.

The accused had refused to give an explanation for why she had thrust a bread knife into her husband's stomach. Her friend, Catherine Burns, testified that Barney Patterson continually accused his wife of having affairs with other men.

'Were you ever present when this happened?' the prosecuting counsel had asked.

'No, but Amy told me,' Miss Burns had replied. 'Once she had a big bump on her forehead and I just knew that Barney had done it.'

'Did you see Barney doing it?' the witness was asked.

'Well, no. I just knew.'

In what was described as a 'startling development', the victim's mother took the stand and announced that her daughter-in-law had been having a long-standing affair with her husband, Leo. Both the accused and Leo Patterson had 'hotly denied' the allegation. Nevertheless, it had been made, and the idea of Amy Patterson having had a relationship with her father-in-law while her young husband was away fighting for his country turned the feeling of the court against her. Until then I had got the impression that it had been relatively sympathetic.

The trial was over at Easter 1951 – almost twenty years ago to the very day that I was sitting on the floor in my uncle's house reading about it. Amy Patterson was sentenced to life imprisonment. The victim's mother said she thought her daughter-in-law had got off lightly. 'She deserved to be hanged,' Mrs Patterson said with tears in her eyes, according to the *Daily Express*.

There was a photograph in the *Evening Standard*, taken in 1961, of Amy Patterson at forty. It showed a nondescript, unrecognizable woman wearing a drab outfit that looked like a crossover pinny with sleeves.

I put everything back in the file and returned it to its place under the stairs. I don't know why, but I only read it when Charles and Marion weren't around.

In the kitchen, there was a note from Marion stuck to the fridge requesting that I turn on the oven at a quarter to five: 'There's a lamb casserole inside.' My watch showed it was now quarter past. Marion would be upset. She liked things to happen on time. I decided to tell her I'd arrived home late, rather than I'd been reading my mother's file, to save upsetting her. Marion was very easily upset.

I set the table and boiled water for tea, then went upstairs and took off the bottle-green sweater and beige skirt I'd worn to school, and put on my new flared trousers and cream blouse.

The trousers felt funny the way they flapped against my legs, but looked OK when I examined the effect in the mirror. I suited trousers. I was tall, verging on the skinny, and had my father's hair: dead straight and quite thick. I had also inherited his brown eyes, but my face was rounder and my features very different – at least, I thought so. Most people seemed to think I was good-looking – not pretty, or lovely, or beautiful. I never knew whether to be flattered or not.

Later, I was going to the pictures with my friend Trish to see *The Magic Christian*, starring Peter Sellers. We were only going because Ringo Starr had a part: we were still enthralled with the Beatles.

I put on a Simon and Garfunkel LP – I wasn't in the mood for rock 'n' roll – and lay flat on the bed with my hands tucked behind my head, listening to 'Bridge Over Troubled Water'. Soon, Trish would be leaving Liverpool for good. Ian, her fiancé, was shortly returning from Kuwait to work in London. In a month, they were getting married, and Trish would move to London to live with him. I would have to find a new friend – not so easy at twenty-five. Anyway, I was no good at 'finding' friends. The ones I'd had before had been made in the natural way that friends are usually made. I'd met Trish, for example, when we were eighteen and had passed our driving tests at the same time. We'd gone to a pub to celebrate. Now Trish was about to acquire a husband and eventually a family, just like my other friends. As for me, I had no intention of getting married. Look at what had happened to my mother and father! But did I really want to remain single and childless for my entire life? I wasn't sure about that, either.

The room was suddenly flooded with sunlight, lightening the dark mood that was threatening to engulf me – it always did when I thought about the future. The rain had stopped. I got off the bed and went to look out of the window. The wet leaves and the soaking grass glistened in the sunshine, so brightly it almost hurt my eyes. I felt my heart lift at the sight. Soon it would be spring, genuine spring, not just a date on the calendar when the season was judged to have started, even if there was no sign of it. I opened the window and could have sworn I could smell the flowers that had yet to grow and the blossom that was yet to appear on the trees.

Downstairs, the front door opened and Charles shouted, 'Are you there, love?'

'Yes.' I ran downstairs and kissed him. My uncle looked tired, but then he always did. He was a comfortable-looking man with worn good looks. Very soon, his hair would be completely grey, and the creases in his cheeks were getting deeper and deeper. I kissed him again. I loved my uncle every bit as much as if he were my father.

There'd been a lot of unpleasantness after my mother had gone away. Mrs Patterson, my grandmother on my father's side, had insisted she had the right to raise her son's child. 'I've lost my son and now I'm about to lose my only grandchild!' she had shouted. I had been sitting on the stairs in this very house listening, knowing what the discussion was about, terrified I might be sent to live with the beautiful, hot-eyed, hot-tempered person, whom my mother had hated according to Cathy Burns: 'and she had good reason to, Pearl.' By that, I assumed she meant the things that Grandma Patterson had said at the trial.

Charles had said courteously that Mrs Patterson was welcome to come and visit her granddaughter whenever she wanted, but that Pearl's mother had requested she be brought up by him and his wife: there was actually a legal document to prove it. Mrs Patterson had threatened to take the matter to court and Charles had replied that she wouldn't have a leg to stand on. At five this had seemed to me a strange thing to say.

In those days I'd called my mother Mummy.

'Mummy, can I have a drink of water?'

'Mummy, I want to do a painting.'

My mother would spread a newspaper on the table, fetch the paints and paper and a jar of water for me to dip the brush in.

'What are you going to paint, sweetheart?' she would ask.

'You, Mummy. I'm going to paint you.'

When I remembered how much I had loved my mother in those days, I would feel tears come to my eyes.

As Hilda Dooley had said that morning, she was pretty. She had a little rosebud mouth, blue eyes, a perfect nose, and clouds and clouds of fair, curly hair. Some people said she was 'chocolate box pretty'. I had used to think that flattering, but it wasn't until I grew older that I realized that it hinted there was no depth to my mother's looks, that she was shallow. Even so, everybody stared at her when we went out, particularly the men, who turned round and looked at her legs. In those days, I'd been mystified as to why men would want to stare at a woman's legs when her face was so much prettier and more interesting.

Charles held me close for a minute. He said, 'Marion won't be long. She picked up some dry-cleaning at lunch-time and she's just getting it out of the car.' He grinned. 'I can't be trusted to do it. Apparently, clumsy old me will only crease it.' He gave me an affectionate shake. 'We'll talk about you know what later.'

Marion appeared with two winter frocks over her arm. She was a handsome woman with aristocratic features and raven-black hair that she'd had dyed since the grey started to show. She was fifty-two, the same age as Charles. It was rare that she smiled. Tonight, she looked particularly cross, though there was unlikely to be much of a reason for it. The slightest thing could put her in a bad mood. 'Did you put that casserole in on time?' she asked.

'I'm sorry, but I had to stay behind at school so I was late,' I lied. 'It's the last day of term, you know, but it went in at quarter past.'

She sighed. 'Oh, well, I wouldn't mind a sit down and a cup of tea before we eat. That was a horrendous drive home. The traffic gets busier and busier all the time. Years ago, Charles and I used to cycle to and from work and it took less time than it does now in a car. I don't know why it's at its worst on Fridays.'

'People going home for the weekend, I expect,' Charles said mildly.

His wife gave him a glowering look, but Charles was used to glowering looks and merely smiled. Marion didn't mean it. Behind her rather sour exterior, she was very kind and was given to bouts of real tenderness. Although I might not be as fond of my aunt as I was of Charles, I hadn't gone short of love during the years I'd spent in the house in Aintree.

'Is there tea made?' Marion asked now.

'Well, the kettle's boiled. Sit down a minute and I'll make some.'

When I went into the lounge with the tea tray, Charles and Marion were discussing my mother.

Charles looked at me. 'Someone at work mentioned she was being released. They don't know I'm her brother. I telephoned Catherine Burns and she said you already knew.'

'One of the teachers read it out from the paper in the staff-room.'

'I suppose it came as a terrible shock,' Marion said kindly.

'I still feel numb. I can't imagine her being around – my own mother.'

Marion said quickly, 'She won't want to come and live here. Your mother and I never got on.'

Charles looked pained. 'She has nowhere else to go, dear.'

'I'm sure she'll find somewhere,' Marion said sourly. 'Amy made friends at the drop of a hat.'

'I think she should come and stay with us while she finds her feet, Marion.' Charles folded his arms and tightened his lips. 'Pearl and I are the only blood relatives she has in this country. Jacky and Biddy both live in Canada.'

Jacky and Biddy were my mother's sisters. All I could remember about them was they had lots of blonde hair and blue eyes rather like my mother, but they weren't quite so pretty. Both had married and had families of their own. They often wrote to Charles and sent cards at Christmas with photographs of the cousins I would probably never meet.

'Do you know when she's being released?' I asked. I hadn't

looked at the paper. Perhaps I should have. Maybe seeing it in black and white would convince me it was true. Right now, I wasn't sure if I believed it.

'I bought the paper myself. It said only that the release would be soon. It could be a few days, a few weeks – even months,' Charles replied. I'm sure she'll write and tell me when it is. If necessary, I'll take the day off work and fetch her home.'

Charles looked at Marion, who didn't say anything, but the perpetual frown she wore deepened.

After dinner, I went to meet Trish. We saw *The Magic Christian* but it didn't make sense. It wasn't the film's fault. I wasn't concentrating. Nor was I listening, according to Trish when we went for a coffee afterwards.

'You're miles away, Pearl. Is something wrong?'

'No.'

Charles had made me promise I would never tell a soul about my mother, however good a friend. 'It's our own private business, he'd said, 'and I'd sooner we kept it that way. I don't want to be known as the man whose sister murdered her husband. It would be even worse for you, Pearl. She's your mother. Some people will look upon you as a bit of a freak.'

So nobody knew my real name or the truth about my family. Hardly anyone ever asked why I lived with my aunt and uncle rather than my parents. If they did, I would just shrug and say my parents were dead.

When I arrived home, Charles and Marion were watching the ten o'clock news. Charles looked up and said, 'There's been nothing on about it.'

I just nodded and went to bed, refusing a hot drink. All of a sudden, I wanted to be by myself. At some time very soon, I would see my mother for the first time in twenty years. But I didn't want to. I really, really didn't want to. Would my mother expect to be kissed? Hugged? Be told I loved her and had missed her? I hadn't written her a single letter, mainly because I didn't know what to say.

Charles sent cards at appropriate times signed, 'From Charles, Marion and Pearl, with our fondest love.' It made Marion cross. 'How dare you send that woman my fondest love?' she'd asked once.

'I'd've thought you could spare a bit of love for someone in Amy's position,' Charles had said. 'You have her daughter, after all.'

'She couldn't expect to keep Pearl in prison.' Marion tossed her head, but didn't object when Charles put the card in an envelope and stamped it.

They were unable to have children of their own. My mother's loss had been their gain.

Two weeks later, on the day that I returned to school, the Easter holiday over, Charles received a letter from my mother saying she was about to be released from prison and was being collected by a friend with whom she would stay for a while. 'I have things to do over the next few weeks,' she wrote, 'but will be with you as soon as I can.'

'Typical,' Marion said with a sniff. 'I just hope she doesn't come here and start calling you Charlie again.'

## Chapter 2

### Easter 1939
## Amy

'I love Easter. I love Christmas, too, but with Christmas you know you've still got the worst of the winter to come. At Easter the summer stretches ahead, months and months of it, followed by autumn. I really like autumn, but it's the start of winter in a way, so if anyone asked what my favourite time of the year is, I'd have to go for Easter.'

'What the heck are you on about? Who wants to know what your favourite time of the year is? *I* don't. If the truth be known, I couldn't care less.' Cathy rolled her eyes and grinned.

Amy grinned back. 'I just thought you'd be interested, that's all. It's the weather. It's put a spell on me. It's the most beautiful day I can ever remember.'

'The sun only has to be out five minutes and it's the most beautiful day you can remember.'

'I love the sun,' Amy said with a throb in her voice. 'If I weren't a Catholic, I'd be a sun worshipper.'

'Where would you go to Mass?' Cathy asked.

'I dunno,' Amy had to concede. 'And who would hear our confessions?'

Cathy didn't answer.

The girls were on the train to Southport. It was an electric train. Amy preferred trains that puffed smoke, they looked and sounded nicer, but electric ones were miles cleaner. She was wearing her best summer dress – yellow with buttons like little faces – a white cardigan, and a white crocheted beret made by her mam. Cathy wore a similar beret except it was red. She had on the red jacket that belonged to one of her sisters and suspected had originally fallen off the back of a lorry. The sister, their Lily, had gone to Blackpool for the day, and Cathy hoped to get home before she did; either that, or after Lily had gone to bed.

It was Sunday – *Easter* Sunday – and Amy felt happy enough to bust. They'd caught the Southport train straight after Mass and only intended to wander up and down Lord Street, have a few goes on the fairground, buy some fish and chips for tea, then go to the pictures, but she just knew it was going to be a perfect day.

The winter was over. Through the window, she could see the countryside coming to life: the trees, gardens and fields were showing signs of what was to come – a scattering of leaves and buds, and rows and rows of tiny regimented plants. People were cutting grass, digging, weeding. A man was watering his garden with a hosepipe, something that appealed to Amy no end.

'I wish we had a garden,' she said emotionally, 'instead of just a yard. I'd plant roses. I'd have roses round the door – both doors – and climbing up the walls, and I'd like a rabbit in a hutch and a tortoise.'

'You don't want much,' Cathy sniffed.

'Roses, a rabbit and a tortoise *aren't* much. Last week, you only wanted to marry Clark Gable. My wants are far more reachable – is there such a word?'

'I wish you hadn't mentioned Clark Gable.' Cathy's eyes went all misty. 'Now I want to cry.'

'Don't be a soft girl,' Amy said scornfully. 'He's too old for you. Anyroad, I can't stand men with moustaches.'

She could tell Cathy was torn between making a joke or shedding a tear. In the end, she went for the joke. 'How about women with moustaches?' she asked.

'I can't stand them, either.'

They both giggled.

An elderly man on the other side of the carriage had been listening to the conversation. It was difficult not to listen: the youthful voices were loud and full of excitement. 'It must be nice to be young,' he remarked.

'Oh, it is,' Amy confirmed. 'But it must be nice to be old, too,' she added with the assurance of a seventeen-year-old who thought she knew everything. 'Every age must have its good points.'

'I'll try and remember what they are,' the man said, conscious of the pains in his joints, the difficulty he had breathing and the fact he could barely see out of his left eye.

The train drew into Southport station and everyone got off. The elderly man walked behind the girls and thought what a picture they made with their bright clothes and confident way of walking. You'd think they owned the whole bloody world. The blonde one was the prettiest by far, a regular bobby-dazzler. She was quite tall, with an hourglass figure but, forty years younger and given the choice, he'd go for the dark one. She'd be a safer bet. The blonde spelt trouble. Fellows wouldn't leave her alone, married or not, and he'd worry every minute she was out of sight. He could see them now, the men, staring at her lustfully, undressing her with their eyes, trying to imagine what she would look like with nothing on – he was doing the same thing himself. He couldn't remember when he'd last had these feelings, but it was a long, long time ago and they made him feel more breathless than ever.

Amy and Cathy made their way to Lord Street. The elegant street was crowded, mainly with day-trippers. The men wore sports jackets and open-necked shirts, and the women had discarded their coats for cardigans, although it was early April and there was a chill in the air. People had been seduced by the sun. The children carried buckets and spades. Some families had already been to the shore and had sand in their hair and on their bare legs. Everyone appeared to be particularly happy, as if, like Amy, they felt this was the end of the dark months and the beginning of summer. There was, of course, the threat of war in Europe where a chap called Hitler was making menacing noises, but it was only a threat and might not happen.

Amy and Cathy oohed and aahed noisily over the clothes in the windows of expensive shops – clothes which would take months, even years, of their wages to buy – variously annoying or amusing the people who happened to be within earshot. Amy earned seven and sixpence a week working in a canteen on the Dock Road, and Cathy a shilling more as a junior clerk in Woolworth's offices in town – she was good with figures. At school, she'd been top of the class for arithmetic. Amy hadn't come top in anything.

'Look at that frock!' Amy gasped. It was white crêpe with sequins around the neck and the cuffs of the long sleeves. The skirt was long and tight and resembled a mermaid's tail. 'I'd give my right arm for a frock like that,' she sighed.

'It'd look daft if you only had one arm. And it's fifteen pounds, nine and a tanner!' Cathy squeaked. 'Who in their right mind would pay that much for a frock?'

'*I* would.'

'Where would you wear it, girl? I mean, it's got a tail, for God's sake. It'd get filthy in no time.'

'That's not a tail, it's a train.'

'Tail or train, Amy, you'd have to get someone to carry it.' Cathy shook her head as if to emphasize her friend's lack of common sense. 'It's dead impractical.'

'All right then, I won't buy it.' Amy laughed. 'But I need to buy something. What shall I get?'

'Tea?' Cathy suggested. 'We can afford a pot between us.'

'Rightio. We'll go in the first café we come to, as long as it's not too posh.'

'What picture shall we go and see later?' Cathy asked when they were in an upstairs café with the tea in a white muggin pot. '*King of the Underworld* with Humphrey Bogart or *Algiers* with Charles Boyer?'

'I don't really mind. Shall we toss for it?'

Cathy took a halfpenny out of her purse. 'Heads for the first, tails for the second.' She tossed the coin and it came down tails. '*Algiers*,' she said.

Amy pulled a face. 'I'd sooner see the Humphrey Bogart one.'

'You always do that,' Cathy said crossly. 'Whenever I toss for something, you want whatever lost. You always win however it turns out. Why suggest we toss in the first place?'

'It's because it helps make up me mind.'

'No, it isn't. It's because you like being awkward.'

'OK, so it's because I like being awkward. Shall we go to the fairground when we've finished our tea?'

'Fine – unless you'd like to toss for it first.'

Amy's most outstanding feature was her hair. It was creamy-yellow, a mass of tiny ringlets, curls and waves. In the bright sunshine of that day in Southport, it shone and glittered as if it were made of pure gold. Her whole body was perfectly proportioned, her eyes blue with dark lashes, and her nose exactly the right length. Her bottom lip was possibly slightly bigger than the top so that, in repose, she looked as if she were pouting. Not many people noticed this because Amy's face normally wore a smile or a wide, wide grin that was quite captivating. Not everyone was captivated, though. Some claimed that a girl so pretty was not to be trusted, that she hadn't a brain in her head.

By contrast, her friend, Cathy, was very ordinary. Her long brown hair was inclined to be frizzy, but her sister, Frances, had ironed it that morning and it hung down her back like a length of brown satin. She also had a slight burn on her neck that was smarting horribly. Ironing a person's hair while it was still attached to the head was a risky business, and it was easy for the iron to slip. Cathy had grey eyes, a too-long nose and a too-wide mouth. She was a sensible, serious girl who was only inclined to be frivolous when she was with Amy.

When they arrived at the fairground, there was hardly room to move between the stalls. They looked at each other, took deep breaths, linked arms and plunged into the fray. Ignoring the likes of hoop-la and roll-a-penny, which were just a waste of money as they never won – had never even seen anyone win – they didn't stop until they reached the ghost train. They sat in the front seat and screamed their heads off when the skeletons and ghosts appeared – not to mention the coffin with an open lid in which a corpse sat doffing his top hat and inviting them to join him – though neither girl was the slightest bit frightened. The waltzer came next, Cathy's favourite. The young man who collected their money parked himself on their car and made it swing much faster than the others. Afterwards, they bought ice creams and took them on the big wheel.

Cathy was the first to feel sick. She suggested they sit quietly on the pier for a while with another cup of tea. It was one o'clock. The day had become warmer and a pleasant breeze blew. The girls removed their hats and tossed their heads, enjoying the feeling of the gentle wind blowing up their skirts and through their hair.

In the years ahead, Cathy often wondered how Amy's life would have turned out had they not visited the pier at that particular time. Say if they'd missed the train – they nearly had – and had arrived much later. Or if they hadn't stopped for a drink in Lord Street and been earlier. If only they'd managed to miss meeting the Patterson brothers, then her friend wouldn't have had to spend the best years of her life in prison.

Neither Cathy nor Amy had noticed the young men leaning over the rail of the pier, staring at the distant sea. They were extremely well dressed in flannels, blazers and straw trilbies. One blazer was dark-green, the other navy-blue, and both were liberally festooned with gold buttons. Their flannels were well pressed and their shoes polished.

They were handsome, healthy young men, brothers, with thick brown hair and brown eyes. The green-blazered one was the tallest and the slimmest. His hair was also the longest and his eyes the boldest. He had more swagger than his brother, and his movements were quicker, more assured. He was also the youngest.

'I'm thirsty,' he remarked, turning round. 'I wonder if there's a bar around here?' His gaze swept the pier. Suddenly, he gave his brother a nudge and remarked, 'Look at *that*!'

The other man saw the two young women giggling madly on a bench. He groaned. 'Oh, for Pete's sake, Barney, don't let's pick up a couple of girls. I'd far rather we spent the day by ourselves. You know I can never think of what to say. I'll feel uncomfortable if we have a meal and even more uncomfortable if we go to the pictures. We might even end up taking them home.' They'd come in Barney's car, and he knew he'd be stuck in the back with a girl he hardly knew and almost certainly wouldn't like.

'Don't be an old misery-guts, Harry. Those girls are special – at least, the blonde is. You can have the brown-haired one.

She doesn't look too bad. Come on, let's hope our luck's in today.'

'Your luck, Barney, not mine,' Harry muttered, following his brother to the bench. He hoped the girls would tell him to bugger off. They weren't tarts and appeared to be quite respectable.

Barney removed his hat and bowed politely. 'My brother and I wondered if you ladies would like an ice cream?' he enquired, addressing the question to the blonde.

'No, thank you.' The dark-haired girl edged away. The blonde said nothing, just stared at Barney, a dazed expression in her blue eyes.

To Harry's surprise, his brother sank down on to the bench beside her. 'Hello,' he said in a cracked voice. There was a look on his face that Harry had never seen before, a dopey sort of grin, as if all his senses had deserted him in the space of a few seconds.

'Hello.' The blonde girl spoke in little more than a whisper. 'My name's Amy Curran.'

'And I'm Barney Patterson. Pleased to meet you, Amy.'

And that, as they say, was that. It was a case of love at first sight.

For the rest of the day, Harry and the other girl – her name was Cathy – just trailed behind Amy and Barney. At one point they disappeared into a fortune-teller's kiosk without a word.

'I think they've forgotten we exist,' Cathy said dryly while she and Harry waited for them to come out.

'I think they have.' Harry stuffed his hands in his pockets and jiggled the coins inside while he tried to think of things to say.

'I'd go home, except it doesn't seem right to leave Amy. After all, she hardly knows your brother.' She frowned worriedly. 'I don't know what's got into her. She never normally acts like this. She's never had a proper boyfriend before – neither of us has.'

'Barney is behaving very oddly, too.' Very oddly indeed. 'Oh, he's got off with girls before, but he's never been so soppy about it.' He relaxed a little. He and Cathy appeared to be in the same boat. 'I say, would you like a cold drink? There's a café over there with tables outside so we can see the lovebirds come out.'

'I'd prefer tea, if you don't mind. To tell the truth, I feel a bit shaky.' She wrinkled her nose. 'Lovebirds! It sounds dead peculiar.'

Harry went in the café and paid for the tea. On impulse, he also ordered two buttered scones. The waitress promised to bring everything in a minute.

Cathy smiled when he returned to the table. Harry decided he quite liked her. She wasn't the least bit silly or flighty. He wished she didn't have such an ugly Liverpool accent, but that was all.

'Do you come from Southport?' she asked.

'No, Liverpool. Calderstones, to be exact.'

'Oh, the dead posh part. Me and Amy are from Bootle. Have you got any more brothers and sisters?'

'No, there's just Barney and me. What about you?'

'Me?' She laughed. 'I've got five brothers and four sisters. I'm the next to youngest. Our Dugald is the oldest: he's thirty-five.'

'Dugald is an unusual name.'

'It's old Irish. It means "dark stranger".'

The conversation was getting easier and easier. He asked what she did for a living and she told him she worked in Woolworth's accounts department. She asked what he did.

'I work in my father's factory in Skelmersdale,' Harry said. 'I'm the assistant manager. We make medical instruments and equipment.'

At this, she looked highly impressed. 'Is that where Barney works, too?'

He explained that Barney had finished university the year before. He'd read Classics. 'He's been in and out of the factory a few times,' he confided, 'but he intends to join the Forces if, when, the war starts.' He was beginning to think that war was unavoidable.

The waitress arrived with their order. Cathy thanked Harry profusely when she saw the scones. Apparently, she was starving. 'We went to Holy Communion this morning, which meant we had to fast, so all we've had to eat is a bar of chocolate between us on the train. We were saving our appetites for fish and chips later, but I doubt if Amy will want anything now. She's got other things on her mind.'

'You're Catholic?' Little particles of ice chased each other up and down Harry's spine. If it really turned out to be serious between Barney and this girl, if he took her home to meet their parents …

'Yes.' Cathy looked at him amused. 'Do you have any objection?'

'No,' Harry stammered. 'No, of course not.' But his mother would. Elizabeth Patterson was an Irish Protestant who hated Catholics with every bone in her body and every drop of blood in her veins.

'It's just that some people do.'

He swallowed nervously. 'Well, I'm not one of them.'

'I didn't think you were.' She tucked into the scone and ate it with such obvious enjoyment that he suggested she eat the other one as well. His own appetite had gone.

Barney and Amy came out of the fortune-teller's. They were holding hands. Harry gasped. He had never known that people could be as radiantly and wholeheartedly happy as his brother and Amy so obviously were. As if some mysterious inner light had been switched on, they quite literally glowed. It wasn't just their eyes, but their skin and their hair. It made Harry feel – he tried to think of the word – *incomplete*, a pale imitation of his brother. He knew he would never glow like that. He didn't possess an inner light. At twenty-one, Barney was younger than him by two years, but today Harry felt as if he were only half his brother's age.

Cathy said, stating the obvious, 'Harry and I are just having some tea and scones.' It made Harry feel better, as if he and Cathy had formed a little team between them, and his brother and her friend weren't the only ones who mattered.

Amy said, 'I'm hungry,' so Barney went and bought more tea and scones. Amy sat with her arms wrapped around her knees and stared dreamily at her feet until Barney re-appeared and, from then on, they only had eyes for one another. Even in the cinema – they went to see *King of the Underworld* with Humphrey Bogart – they sat with their arms around each other, never once looking at the screen.

★

It was dark when they got back to Bootle. Cathy hadn't been surprised that the Pattersons had a car. She couldn't imagine them using the train or the tram like ordinary people. It turned out that they had one each, but had come to Southport in Barney's.

'What sort is it?' she asked when she got in the back with Harry. 'It's just that if I say I've been in a car, our Kev will want to know the make.' Kevin was mad on cars.

'It's a Morris Eight Tourer with a sliding head. I've got an Austin Seven and Pa has a Bentley. But I think we might have to get rid of them if there's a war,' Harry said worriedly. 'They say petrol is likely to be rationed.'

In front, Amy and Barney didn't say a single word until they reached Bootle and Amy told him how to find Agate Street.

'Are you all right?' Cathy asked when she and Amy got out by the Currans' house and Barney drove away. It was a stupid question to ask, but Amy had been desperately odd that afternoon.

'I'm fine, ta,' Amy said. She leaned against the window sill and said, 'Fine' again in a preoccupied voice. 'How about you?'

'I had a nice time with Harry.' For her own sake, Cathy felt it was important to stress that the enjoyment hadn't only been on Amy's side, even if hers had been totally different. She'd genuinely liked Harry, though there was nothing romantic about it. When she was getting out of the car, he'd shaken her hand and said, 'I'm sure we'll meet again one day,' and she'd agreed. 'Can I come in?' she asked Amy, who showed no inclination to go inside. It was as if she'd forgotten where the door was or had no idea what her next move should be now that Barney had gone. Cathy usually had a cup of cocoa in the Currans' when they'd been out together. Her own house was full of noise, with people fighting or arguing in every room, and Mam throwing things. No one had a bedtime drink, as there was never any milk left. When the pubs closed, her dad would arrive home as drunk as a lord.

'I think I'd sooner go straight to bed,' Amy said, rubbing her eyes as if she were tired.

'All right then. I'll be round tomorrow at around midday.'

'What for?'

'It's Easter Monday: we're going to the sports day at the English

Electric with your Charlie and Marion.' There'd be stalls, games and competitions. Cathy was looking forward to it.

'Oh, I won't be going.' Amy shook her head as if the whole idea was nonsense and she'd had no intention of going in the first place. 'Barney's taking me to New Brighton. But you can go to the English Electric with our Charlie and Marion,' she said quickly, as if she'd only just cottoned on to the fact she was badly letting Cathy down.

'I'd sooner not. Marion doesn't like me.'

'She doesn't like me, either. I don't think she likes anyone, not even our Mam, though Mam thinks she's just shy.'

'I'd feel uncomfortable with her and Charlie on me own.' What was she supposed to do when they got there? Trail around after Marion and Charlie just as she'd done with Amy and Barney? She wouldn't even have Harry for company. 'It's all right,' she said, 'I'll find somewhere else to go instead.' She was deeply hurt. Amy had been her best friend since they were five and now she was being dropped like a hot brick because she'd met a chap. But it wasn't the real Amy who was being so casual with their friendship. This was an Amy she'd never known before. Something had happened to her while they were in Southport. She'd been mesmerized, put under a spell. Who knew when the old Amy would come back?

Her friend went inside and closed the door. Cathy was left alone in the otherwise empty street of small terraced houses, each one exactly the same as the next. They looked very bare and featureless in the semi-darkness, with their doors shut and not a light to be seen in any of the windows. There were no flowers and not a patch of grass: people stepped out of the houses on to the pavement.

Cathy sighed. She couldn't remember having felt so miserable before.

'This is the life,' Moira Curran murmured. She'd never thought the day would come when she had nothing else to do except sit in an armchair with a romantic novel in one hand and a ciggie in the other, while feeling pleasantly tiddly; she'd spent the evening playing cards with her best friend, Nellie Tyler, and they'd had a drop too much port and lemon.

Last summer, her youngest child, Biddy, had started work. With her son and three daughters now giving their mam a portion of their wages, Moira could take things easy at last. Since her husband, Joe, had died ten years ago of a heart attack, leaving her with four young children, Moira's life had become one of unremitting hard work. But her children were all she cared about, and she was prepared to labour on their behalf until she dropped.

It was nearly ten, according to the clock on the sideboard – a wedding present from Joe's mam and dad, both a long time dead. This time last year it would have been near closing time in the Green Man on Marsh Lane, and she'd be almost dead on her feet from exhaustion. Working in pubs was tiring, but the hours were convenient if you had kids at school. By then, Charlie had been old enough to keep his eye on his sisters while his mam was out. Mornings, she'd made a few extra bob by going in and doing the cleaning before the pub opened.

But now Moira had a relatively easy job as an afternoon waitress in the Flowers Café on Stanley Road. There were days when she didn't get up till as late as eight o'clock. Shopping was a leisurely pleasure when she'd been used to doing it in a desperate hurry. Some days, she actually went in the Flowers with Nellie for a morning pot of tea and was waited on for a change. Life was sweet indeed.

She'd been buying bits and pieces for the house. She'd bought the tan chenille tablecloth with a knobbly fringe in the New Year sales. She gave the fringe a little push with her finger, watched it swing and experienced a tiny thrill. How pathetic, she thought with a grin. It was just that she hadn't been able to afford luxuries like new tablecloths for an awful long time. If she'd had the energy, she'd have gone in the parlour and had a peek at the bronze satin cushion covers, which she'd made herself, and the dried yellow grass in the fireplace: she wasn't sure if the grass was real, but, along with the cloth, the cushion covers and the other odds and ends she'd bought, they gave her a lovely sense of satisfaction.

She was just thinking that her eldest daughter should have been home by now, when the front door opened and Amy came in. There was a look on her face that Moira had never seen before.

It was difficult to describe. A vacant look, sleepy almost, as if she were in the middle of a lovely dream.

'What's up with you, luv?' she asked suspiciously. 'You're not drunk, are you?'

'No, Mam. I'm not old enough to go in pubs, am I?'

'That doesn't normally stop people.' Nevertheless, she gave up on the idea. Amy was a good girl and had never given her a moment of worry. Mind you, she was fully aware of the effect Amy had on the opposite sex. She hadn't missed the leery looks and wolf whistles when she and Amy were out together. They had started when Amy was only thirteen or fourteen. Moira had been a bit of a bobby-dazzler herself when she was young – she wasn't so bad now, despite the years of hard work – but she hadn't been a patch on Amy. She wouldn't put it past some fiend to slip her lovely daughter a Mickey Finn in order to get his evil way. Moira had perhaps read too many novels – the steamier the better – since she had so much free time.

'Is our Charlie in?' Amy asked.

'He's in the parlour with Marion.' Moira sniffed. She wasn't sure if she liked her son's fiancée.

'When he comes out, tell him I'm not going to the English Electric tomorrow.'

'Why not?'

'Because I'm going somewhere else instead.' Amy made for the stairs. 'I'm off to bed now, Mam.'

'But where's the somewhere else you're going?' Moira hissed from the bottom of the stairs, not wanting to wake Jacky and Biddy, who had gone to bed ages ago and would be fast asleep by now.

'New Brighton. There'll be someone coming for me in a car at about ten o'clock.'

'In a car! And who will that—' But before she could finish the question, the front bedroom door closed with a snap.

Why hadn't Cathy come in for a cup of cocoa? Moira wondered. Perhaps the girls had had a row, and that was the reason for Amy's funny look. But it hadn't been a miserable funny look. She'd go round to Cathy's there and then and ask her outright, except her mother, Elsie Burns, frightened the living daylights out of her. Cathy apart, the Burnses were a violent family – two of their lads had been in prison – and their mother was the most violent of them all.

She looked in the cigarette packet: there was one left. Good! In a minute, she'd make a cup of cocoa, smoke the ciggie, then go to bed, though she supposed she'd best ask Charlie and Marion if they'd like a drink. She could hear them talking when she knocked on the parlour door and opened it just a crack in case they were up to something.

'Would you like a cup of cocoa in there?' She had no idea why she whispered.

'No, ta, Mam,' Charlie said in a normal voice. 'Marion is going home in a minute.'

'Goodnight, Marion.'

'Goodnight, Mrs Curran.'

Moira winced. Marion's tone was so unfriendly. Or was it just that she was shy? Whatever, she was a strange girl who lived in a Catholic hostel in Everton Valley. Prising information from her about her background was harder than removing teeth. According to Charlie, she was born in Dundalk on the east coast of Ireland, a place she had left for Liverpool when she was barely fourteen. Now she was twenty and, in the meantime, had managed to lose most of her Irish accent as well as learn to type and do shorthand.

'They're dead,' she'd snapped when Moira asked about her mam and dad. Moira hadn't liked to ask if she had any brothers or sisters and have her head bitten off a second time.

Furthermore – Moira was getting quite hot under the collar – she would have liked to impress upon Marion what a catch she was getting in Charlie Curran. There wasn't a young woman in the whole of Bootle who wouldn't have accepted him like a shot had he proposed. He was an apprentice draughtsman at the English Electric – actually had his own *drawing board* – and was the only man in the street who went to work in a suit.

Even more impressive, Charlie was buying his own house! It was in Aintree by the racecourse and had just finished being built along with a hundred or so others. He and Marion went every

Sunday to see how it was progressing. Moira had hardly met a person in her whole life who owned a house.

Oh, what the hell! Moira made the cocoa, sank into her armchair, lit the ciggie and picked up her book. She'd think about it tomorrow or the next day. Right now, she didn't really care. She'd forgotten to tell Charlie that Amy wasn't going to the sports day tomorrow, but she didn't care about that, either.

Cathy went in to find their Lily sitting on the stairs, apparently waiting for her to come home.

'You bitch!' Lily shrieked, launching herself at her sister. 'I was wondering where me red coat had gone.'

Cathy had forgotten she was wearing her sister's coat. 'I'm sorry, sis,' she began, but Lily wasn't prepared to listen to any explanation Cathy was able to think up on the spur of the moment. She grabbed a handful of hair and tugged hard. Cathy screamed and Mrs Burns came into the hall and banged the girls' heads together. They both screamed. Mrs Burns screamed, 'Grow up, the pair o'yis!' She slapped Cathy's face. 'That's for pinchin' your sister's coat.' Lily smirked, but not for long. 'And that's for pulling your sister's hair,' Mrs Burns snarled as she slapped her other daughter's face.

The front door opened and Mr Burns came in, witnessed the goings-on in the hall, and immediately went out again before his wife could have a go at him. He went round the back to sit in the lavatory in the yard until he felt sober and things had calmed down a bit.

'Jaysus!' Lily ran upstairs. 'I hate living in this bloody house.'

Cathy followed more slowly, nursing her head in one hand and her left cheek in the other. If only Amy had asked her in for a cup of cocoa. Lily would have been in bed by the time Cathy came home and hung the red coat at the back of the wardrobe. 'As far as I know, it's been there all the time,' she would have said tomorrow had Lily asked.

Cathy saw little of Amy over the next few weeks. It felt odd without her. For years they'd done everything together. Cathy had always realized the day would come when they'd both meet someone they'd want to marry, but had imagined it happening to them at about the same time: that they'd go out in a foursome, get married, have babies, their friendship continuing unbroken as the years went by.

She was pleased when, one Sunday, Amy called and suggested they go to Mass then spend the rest of the day together. It was the way their Sundays had always been spent in the past.

'We can walk along the Docky into town and have a cuppa in Lyons,' Amy said. It was May: the weather was getting warmer and the days longer.

The relationship with Barney must be cooling off, Cathy thought, but it turned out that it was Barney's dad's birthday and friends were coming for the day.

'Why weren't you invited?' Cathy enquired.

'Barney doesn't want me to meet his mam just yet. She'd throw a fit if she found out he was going to marry a Catholic.'

'You're getting married?' Cathy could scarcely believe her ears. It was three weeks ago to the very day that she and Amy had gone to Southport, and the last thought in either of their heads was of getting serious with a chap. Now here was Amy acting very distant and talking about marriage.

'Well, we're thinking about it, but don't say anything to me mam.' Amy refused to meet her eyes. 'Are you coming to church or not?' she asked.

'I won't be a mo: I'll just fetch me hat.'

They walked to St James's mainly in silence. Cathy had a thought that made her go all funny – she'd like to bet that Amy and Barney had *slept* together. There was just something about her friend, not just that she looked older, but she acted older. On that day in Southport, she'd stopped being a girl and become a woman.

After Mass they walked along the Docky into town, had a lemonade each in Lyons, then managed to scrape enough together for the front seats in the Scala where they saw *Captain Blood* with Errol Flynn and Olivia de Havilland. It was years old and they'd seen it before, but it was better than trying to talk to each other. Amy appeared to be lost in thought most of the time, and kept smiling secret little smiles. She responded when Cathy spoke to her, but it was as if she was being awakened from a delightful reverie. Cathy felt she was intruding, so gave up.

She was glad that the tram home was so crowded they couldn't sit next to each other. That night, she badly wanted to cry herself to sleep, but crying wasn't a practical proposition when she slept in the same bed as Lily, who was likely to give her a thump if woken. But she would never have another friend like Amy and it would seem she'd lost her for ever.

When she came home from work a few days later, Cathy found an anxious Mrs Curran hovering on the corner of Amethyst Street, apparently waiting for her. Cathy really liked Amy's mam. She was slim and pretty and always dressed nicely, even though all her clothes were second-hand. Today she wore a smart mauve dress with short sleeves and a pleated bodice. She asked Cathy if she wouldn't mind coming round to Agate Street after she'd had her tea. 'I'd like a word with you, luv. It's about our Amy.'

'Will she be there?'

'No, luv. She's going to see a show at the Princes Theatre in Birkenhead. She won't be home till all hours.'

Cathy was glad of something to do. Two of her sisters were married and the other two, Lily and Frances, were courting. They had no time for her. She'd been stuck for places to go and people to go with since Amy had met Barney Patterson.

After she'd eaten, she went round to the Currans'. Mrs Curran made a pot of tea, set everything nicely on a tray, including a plate of broken biscuits that included some Bourbon creams, Cathy's favourite.

'Help yourself, luv,' she said when they were seated in the parlour and she had lit a ciggie.

Cathy's evening meal had consisted of a piece of dry bread, as thick as a brick, soaked in watery mincemeat. She was still hungry and gratefully helped herself to the biscuits. Her mam didn't believe in puddings.

'It's about our Amy's birthday,' Mrs Curran began. 'As you

know, she'll be eighteen on the first of June. I was wondering what to do about a party.'

'Have you talked it over with Amy?'

'Not yet, no. It's awful hard to pin her down these days.'

'She might not want a party.' Cathy couldn't visualize tall, handsome Barney Patterson in the Currans' little house when he was used to a much bigger one in Calderstones.

Mrs Curran put her cup back in the saucer with a clatter. 'Oh, Cathy, luv,' she cried. 'I asked you here to talk about more than parties. It's this chap our Amy's knocking about with. What's he like? She refuses to bring him home. He used to pick her up and drop her off outside the house, but when I threatened to go out and introduce meself, he stopped coming. Amy must have told him to wait somewhere else. She won't even tell me what his name is or what he does for a living. I mean, is he a Catholic? What sort of family does he come from? Where does he live?' She began to cry, just as Jacky and Biddy came storming downstairs and shouted they were going out. 'Out where?' Mrs Curran shouted back.

The girls came into the room. They had Amy's hair, Amy's blue eyes, even Amy's features, yet there was something indefinable that prevented them from being as radiantly pretty as their elder sister. 'Hello, Cathy,' they chorused cheerfully. 'We're going to Stanley Park with Phyllis McNamara, Mam.'

'And what are you going to do there?' their mother demanded.

The girls looked at each other, puzzled. 'Just *talk*, Mam,' Jacky said after a while.

'That's right, Mam, we're just going to *talk*,' Biddy confirmed.

'All right, then, but don't be home late.'

'Why do they need to go all the way to Stanley Park just to talk?' Mrs Curran asked when the front door slammed. Cathy said she didn't know, but that it was what she and Amy had always done, at which Mrs Curran sniffed tearfully. 'I wish me and our Amy talked a bit more. She's become dead secretive. Jacky and Biddy have noticed and they're awful upset. Charlie's annoyed because she was rude to Marion the other day. It all dates back to

31

that Sunday when you both went to Southport. I take it she met this chap there. She was in a really funny mood when she came home.' She looked sorrowfully at Cathy, her eyes full of tears.

'His name's Barney Patterson,' Cathy said slowly. She tried to remember all the questions Mrs Curran had asked. 'He lives in Calderstones and he has a brother called Harry. His father has a factory in Skelmersdale that makes medical instruments. They're not Catholics,' she added. *His mam would throw a fit if she found out Barney was marrying a Catholic,* Amy had said. And Harry had looked a bit dismayed in Southport when she mentioned having been to Mass.

'Barney isn't working at the moment. He finished university last year and he's going to join the Forces.'

'University!' Mrs Curran said faintly. She'd gone quite pale. 'Our Amy's going out with a chap who has got a car and been to university? Where did they meet?'

'On Southport pier.' She wished she could have told Mrs Curran the way they'd so obviously felt about each other, but that wasn't really any of her business. Anyroad, she wasn't sure if she would be able to describe it. And it would be like telling tales if she said that Amy had actually mentioned marriage.

'Will she be all right, do you think? I mean, what sort of chap is he?'

'I don't really know,' Cathy confessed. 'He *seemed* all right. His brother, Harry, is really nice. I hardly spoke to Barney.' He'd been too wrapped up in Amy.

'What's going to come of it, Cathy?' Mrs Curran asked in a shaky voice. 'Let's hope it doesn't last, eh?'

She looked at Cathy for confirmation, but Cathy just smiled vaguely and said, 'We'll just have to see.'

Cathy called in at the Currans' every few days, more for Mrs Curran's sake than her own. She was too sensible and proud to allow herself to be miserable for long because her friend had dropped her. There were loads of girls at Woolworth's she could go with to the pictures or to a dance at the Rialto or the Floral Hall in Southport. She was fast making new friends, but promised

Mrs Curran that she would come round on Amy's eighteenth birthday, and bought a present – a box of embroidered hankies – in readiness.

'She's bringing Barney round – at last,' Mrs Curran said breathlessly on her most recent visit. 'It won't exactly be a party. Our Charlie and Marion will be here, Jacky and Biddy, and, of course, you, luv. I'll just make a few sarnies and a bun loaf, and get a bottle of sherry in.'

Cathy promised to come round at half past six. It turned out to be a day she would never forget.

The first of June was horrible. The sky was a thick blanket of dark grey clouds and, although it didn't rain, the air was full of moisture that stuck to the face like wet cobwebs.

Just before half past six, when Cathy was on her way to Agate Street, the sun came out just in time for Amy's party. Lucky old Amy, she thought. Everything seems to go right for her, even the weather.

When she turned the corner she saw that Barney's car was already outside the Currans' house. Cathy knocked and Biddy opened the door. She rolled her eyes and said in a voice that quivered with excitement, 'Now our Amy's really gone and done it!'

'What's happened?' Cathy asked, alarmed.

'She and that feller of hers only got married today, didn't they?' Biddy said with an enormous grin. 'Mum's doing her nut and our Charlie's awful annoyed. Me, I'm dead envious. I wish someone with a car would ask me to marry them.'

'There's plenty of time, Biddy,' Cathy assured her. She was only fourteen.

She went inside and found the entire family, apart from Marion, in the parlour. Barney was standing in front of the fireplace looking very much at home, while Amy and Charlie tried to comfort Mrs Curran, who was having a mild case of hysterics.

'How could you do this to me?' she wept. 'How could you? Me own daughter getting married without inviting her mam.'

'It was a private wedding,' Amy said half to Cathy and half to her mother. 'No one else was there. We asked two guests from another

33

wedding to be witnesses. Then we went to a photographer's shop and had our photies taken.'

'You must have known how much it would hurt your mam,' Cathy said coldly.

'You don't know the circumstances, Cathy,' Amy said, just as coldly.

For the first time, Cathy noticed her friend was wearing a lovely white silk frock that reminded her slightly of the one she'd hankered after in the window of the shop in Southport. It didn't have a tail, but looked just as expensive. Her hair was piled in a knot on top of her head from which little curls had escaped to perch on her forehead, around her ears and on her white, slender neck. Her hat comprised two white silk roses and a little scrap of white net. Cathy had never seen her look so beautiful.

And Barney hadn't been at the back of the queue when the Lord handed out good looks. He was as handsome as a film star in his dark suit and dazzling white shirt, a lock of brown hair hanging tantalizingly over one eye. He was smiling a really seductive smile and couldn't take his eyes off his new wife. Will anyone ever look at *me* like that? Cathy wondered with a pang.

Charlie patted his mother on the back and Amy gave her a little shake. 'Don't take on so, Mam. Me and Barney never dreamt you'd be so upset.'

'I just wanted to be at me own daughter's wedding,' Mrs Curran said pitifully, 'but not in one of them awful Register Office places, luv. It should have been in a Catholic church so you'd be married in the eyes of God.'

'Oh, Mam, things like that don't matter.'

'They matter to me, luv,' her mother cried. 'Does Barney's mam know you and him are married?'

'Not yet, Mrs Curran,' Barney replied.

Cathy wasn't sure what happened next. Looking back, she vaguely remembered that, like a magician, Barney had produced a bottle of champagne, a box of elegant fluted glasses, and a gold locket and chain for Mrs Curran. He then began kissing everyone in sight, including Cathy. He gave Jacky and Biddy a pound note each, thereby becoming their friend for life, and shook hands with

Charlie: a warm, extended shake that also involved squeezing Charlie's shoulder with his other hand. Amy's mother was still crying while she examined the locket that Amy promised would one day have her and Barney's photies inside, but the tears were more happy than sad. He'd charmed everybody.

Or so Cathy thought. She'd forgotten all about Marion. When she went into the living room, she was sitting at the table staring into space. 'Would you like some champagne?' Cathy asked. 'There's still some left.'

'No, thank you.' Marion was a sallow-skinned young woman with jet-black hair, an unnaturally thin nose and thick eyebrows that made her face appear rather mannish. Barely twenty, she looked a good twenty-five. She was also a bit of a snob and insisted on calling Charlie 'Charles'. They were getting married in September, but no one could understand what he saw in her.

'I don't know how Amy could do something like that to her mother,' she said bitterly. 'Charlie's told me how hard she worked for years and years to make sure her kids didn't go without, and look what she gets in return from her daughter! Me, I was put to work in the family business from the age of five. But diamond cut diamond, that's what my own mother always used to say.'

Cathy had never heard of the expression before. It turned out that it meant 'tit for tat'.

## Chapter 3

### April 1971
### Pearl

Miss Burns lit another cigarette. Her office smelt like a pub. The ashtray on her desk was already full of stubs and it was only lunchtime. 'Diamond cut diamond. Have you heard of that saying, Pearl?'

'Marion comes out with it all the time. It means getting your own back. Retribution. Something like that.'

'Tit for tat. It's what she said the day your mum and dad got married. She was the only person that your dad didn't charm the socks off. Pretty soon he had everyone eating out of his hand, even me. I had thought I didn't like him, which was most unfair: I hardly knew him until then. Can you remember much about him – your dad?'

'Not a great deal,' I confessed. He'd been a distant figure and I'd felt in awe of him, frightened even. He'd scared me the way he'd used to shout at my mother, calling her names. Sometimes he would tell me a story, making it up as he went along, neither of us knowing how it would end.

Since my mother had come out of prison a week ago and, according to the newspapers, gone to ground, Miss Burns had asked me into her office every day to discuss where she might be and who she was with. She spent half the lunch hour staring into space and reminiscing about her old friend.

'I telephoned Harry the other day in case he might know where she was, but he said he hadn't a clue,' she was saying now. 'It's surprising, in view of what happened, that he doesn't bear Amy a grudge and neither does his father. Mrs Patterson, on the other hand, loathed Amy. After the trial, she made a huge fuss, claiming she should have been hanged – she actually petitioned the Home Secretary about it.' She stubbed out her cigarette and lit another. I wondered if there was a time in the day when she didn't have a cigarette in her mouth or was about to light another. She blew smoke in the air and looked at it with disgust. 'You'll never believe this, Pearl, but when I was young I swore I'd never take up smoking. The trouble is everyone in the Forces did it during the war.'

I looked for a way of changing the subject from the past to the present. 'Perhaps the person who picked my mother up was someone she'd met in prison,' I suggested.

'I suppose it could have been that model she got friendly with – Nellie something-or-other.'

'I didn't answer. I'd never heard of Nellie something-or-other. Perhaps my silence got through to Miss Burns and she realized how sick I was of the whole subject – or perhaps she thought I was just hungry. She said, 'I'm taking up all your lunch hour, aren't I, dear? Perhaps we could go for a meal one night – my treat, naturally – and we could talk there.'

'That would be nice.' At least it would be better than her regularly phoning the staffroom to request that I come to her office. Hilda Dooley was becoming suspicious. Maybe she was worried that I, the youngest teacher in the school and the last to arrive, was about to be promoted.

That night, Charles wondered aloud where my mother might be. Marion was annoyed. 'Trust Amy to make a drama out of it,' she complained. 'I can understand her wanting to go into hiding, but not from *us*. Well, *you*,' she conceded when Charles gave her a funny look.

Reporters had waited outside Holloway the day Amy Patterson had been released, and they were still interested in her disappearance. There'd been photos in the paper of her speeding away from prison in a white Rolls-Royce that had turned out to be hired. Charles jumped every time the telephone rang or someone knocked on the door in case one of the newspapers had tracked him down. Aintree was miles away from Bootle, but it was still part of Liverpool.

'It's you they'll want to talk to more than anyone, Pearl,' he said. 'Amy's daughter. You'd be a real find.'

The uncertainty was getting me down. On Saturday, I did what I always did when I was feeling low: went into town and bought some clothes. I convinced myself I badly needed something that was both summery and sensible for school. As I wandered around the ladies' clothes departments in Lewis's and Owen Owen's, wishing I hadn't already bought an outfit for Trish's wedding so I could get one now, I tried to push anything that wasn't connected with clothes to the back of my mind. It proved quite easy after a while.

After trying on an assortment of frocks, blouses and skirts, I eventually chose a calf-length grey voile dress with a white collar in Owen Owen's. It had hardly been in my possession for a minute when I decided it was too dressy for school, so I bought a dark-blue linen skirt and a white broderie anglaise blouse as well.

I took everything up to the restaurant on the top floor and ordered a coffee. Tonight, I was going to dinner with Charles and Marion and would wear the dress then. I mentally went through my shoes: the dress would go perfectly with my white wedge-heeled sandals.

The waitress arrived with the coffee. As I stared into the brown depths, my mood changed. Charles and Marion were only going to dinner for my sake. It was Saturday. Trish had gone down to London to look at property for her and Ian, leaving me with absolutely nothing to do and nowhere to go on a Saturday night. Charles and Marion had taken pity on me.

I poured cream into the coffee and was stirring it when a small voice said, 'Hello, miss.' It was Gary Finnegan, the boy whose mother kissed him by the classroom door in front of everyone, causing the other kids to make fun of him. He was a gentle child with a lovely disposition. Teachers weren't supposed to have favourites, but I couldn't help liking Gary more than most of the other boys.

'Hello, Gary.' He stared at me, green eyes like saucers, as if he hadn't believed his teacher existed outside the four walls of the school. 'Where are your mum and dad?' I asked.

'Dad's over there; he's just coming.'

A harassed-looking man approached, struggling with several carrier bags. He was in his early thirties, tall and well built, with straight fair hair and a tough, good-natured face. He wore a light-weight grey suit and his skin bore the remains of a tan. I wondered why his brown eyes looked so sad.

'Come away, Gary. Don't bother people.' He smiled tiredly. 'I'm sorry. Sometimes, he can be over-friendly.'

'But, Dad,' Gary piped, 'it's miss from school.'

'We do know each other,' I explained.

'Oh, well, if that's the case …' One of the bags fell and he stooped to pick it up. 'I've been getting Gary some stuff for school: shorts and things.'

I wrinkled my nose. 'Shorts?'

'Is there something wrong with shorts?' He looked worried.

'Not if they're just for games.' I nodded at an empty chair. 'Sit down a minute, Mr Finnegan. I'm Pearl Curran, by the way. I teach the first-year pupils, and Gary's in my class.'

'Rob Finnegan. How do you do?' As we shook hands he dropped the rest of the bags. I helped stack them beneath the table and pulled a chair up for Gary, while Rob Finnegan sat down. A waitress came immediately. He looked at me. 'Do you mind if I order? Are you expecting someone?'

'Order away, I'm not expecting anyone.'

'Coffee, please, white, and a strawberry milkshake. What would you like to eat, son?'

'Sausage and chips, please, Dad.'

'What a nice, polite little boy,' the waitress remarked. 'I won't be long, luv.'

'So, what's wrong with shorts – do I call you Pearl or Miss Curran?' He ran his finger around the collar of his shirt and loosened the knot in his tie. He looked slightly less harassed.

'Call me Pearl. Shorts are a bit old-fashioned, apart from when they're worn for games.'

'Old-fashioned? But I wore shorts until I was eleven and went to big school.'

'That was then and this is now. Most little boys wear long trousers, usually jeans. Gary will stand out like a sore thumb in shorts.' I didn't like to suggest he ask his wife to leave their son outside the school gates in future.

'What about a short-sleeved shirt and a tie for summer?'

I shook my head. 'The school doesn't have a formal uniform policy. Miss Burns, the headmistress, prefers the pupils to wear casual clothes: the boys in jeans, the girls in plain skirts, with red T-shirts or sweatshirts on top.' Miss Burns didn't want to put the cost of clothes out of the reach of some families who might have to resort to jumble sales to dress their children. 'You should have had a letter telling you that before Gary started school.'

'I probably lost it. It was all a bit hectic in February, wasn't it, Gary?'

'*Really* hectic,' Gary agreed. 'We came back from Uganda, didn't we, Dad?'

'Uganda?' I was surprised.

'I was a policeman there,' he informed me, 'but there was a coup and a chap called Idi Amin came to power. We were advised to get out straight away. The guy's dangerous.'

'Where are you living now?'

'In Seaforth with my sister until we find a house of our own. She has a flat in Sandy Road.' He pulled a face. 'It's a bit cramped, but in the few years we've been away, house prices have shot up and I'm having a job finding something I can afford. And I don't have much time to look as I work nights for the Post Office. Once we're settled, I might rejoin the British police, though I'm wondering if it wouldn't be more sensible to go back abroad: Australia, maybe, or Canada. There are more opportunities there.'

'If we went to Australia, Dad, could I have a koala bear?'

'They're a protected species, Gary,' I pointed out. 'You can't have them as pets.'

The little boy looked disappointed. 'We had Jimmy in Uganda, but he would have had to stay in kennels in England for six whole months so we left him behind.'

'Is Jimmy a dog?'

'No, he's a cat.' Gary frowned earnestly. 'He has stripes, and I pretended he was a tiger.'

'Jimmy's very old,' Rob put in. 'We inherited him about a year ago from a family who were about to return to England. I doubt if he could have stuck it for six months in kennels. They're kept in cages, you know.'

'Did he go to live with someone as nice as you?' I asked Gary.

He nodded seriously. 'Even nicer, a girl called Petron ... what was she called, Dad?'

'Petronella.'

'She had long gold hair right down to her feet.'

'I think you're exaggerating a bit there, son. Petronella's hair only reached as far as her waist.' Rob's smile completely transformed his face. He was beginning to relax.

I wondered where his wife was. It was unusual for a father to go shopping for his child's clothes. I said, 'You can take those clothes back and change them for the right ones, you know.'

'Won't anyone mind?'

'Not if you've still got the receipts.'

'I've got them somewhere.' He fished in his pockets and produced a pile of crumpled paper.

The waitress arrived with their order. Rob asked if I'd like another cup of coffee and I said yes. I glanced around the crowded restaurant. If people were looking, they would assume we were just an ordinary family who'd come into town to do our shopping. I didn't know why this idea gave me a certain amount of pleasure. No one would know I wasn't the wife of the man and the mother of the child.

I noticed a flat WH Smith bag beneath the table. 'What records have you bought?'

'Jimi Hendrix, the Tremeloes, Pink Floyd's "Piper at the Gates of Dawn".' He picked up the bag and showed me the sleeves.

'I love them all,' I said delightedly. 'I've got the latest Simon and Garfunkel record – "Bridge Over Troubled Water". I play it all the time.'

'I got a bit behind with my record collection in Uganda.' He put the bag in a safer place. 'Tell you what, though, I was at Litherland town hall one night in nineteen sixty-one and saw these four dead scruffy lads play the sort of music I'd never heard before: they only turned out to be the Beatles.'

'I was there, too!' I cried. 'I was only fifteen.'

'I was only eighteen!'

'Where were you sitting?'

'Right at the front. I was the mate of a mate who knew Ringo Starr.'

'Me and my friend were right at the back.' I laughed. 'We weren't mates with anyone.'

'Well, if that's not a coincidence I don't know what is,' he marvelled. 'Both in the same place ten whole years ago.' All of a sudden, he looked years younger. He was only twenty-eight, not in his thirties as I'd thought.

'Dad plays music all the time,' Gary remarked solemnly. 'Bess moans because he's always using her gramophone. She likes ...' He frowned. 'What sort of music does Auntie Bess like, Dad?'

'Country and western, son,' his dad supplied. He turned to me and said in an appalled voice, 'Her favourite singer is Connie Francis!'

'Oh, dear!' I said sympathetically. 'How can anyone prefer country and western to rock 'n' roll?'

'Wonders will never cease,' Rob said, nodding.

'What sort of music does your mum like, Gary?' I asked.

'My mum's dead, miss,' he said simply. 'She drownded in Spain.'

I clapped my hands to my burning cheeks. I badly wanted the floor to open up and swallow me. 'I'm so sorry. I never dreamt ... I mean, I thought the lady who brought Gary to school was his mother.'

'No, that's Bess, my sister. Oh, look, here's your coffee.' He took the coffee off the waitress's tray and put it in front of me. I drank a mouthful and it scalded my tongue. 'Don't be embarrassed,' he said. 'How can you possibly have known? It happened three years ago. Gary and I talk about his mum quite openly.'

'She had green eyes,' Gary said. 'Just like me.'

'Did she?' I said in a stricken voice.

'And brown hair. It was curly like mine – only mine's not brown. Mine's the same colour as Dad's.'

'She sounds as if she was very pretty.'

'She was dead beautiful. We've got photos of her at home, haven't we, Dad?'

'Yes, Gary.' He ruffled his son's blond curls. They gave each other a look that seemed to say, 'We're in this together.' They shared a bond that didn't always exist between father and son.

'I must go.' I swallowed the rest of the coffee. It was still too hot and burnt my tongue again. I'd been about to offer to go back with them to the shops to change the clothes for the right ones. I really liked Rob Finnegan – had *allowed* myself to like him. I had been pleased to discover we shared the same taste in music and had both been to the first ever Beatles' concert. But it was because I had thought he was married and therefore unavailable. I kept strictly out of the way of single, available, attractive men because I was scared I might fall in love with one and end up getting married, a very dangerous thing to do.

Wasn't it?

I didn't know. I didn't know anything.


'Cathy Burns rang,' Charles said when I arrived home. 'I invited her to dinner with us tonight. I hope you don't mind. Will you feel awkward eating with the headmistress of the school where you work?'

'Not a bit,' I assured him.

'Marion's not very pleased. She thinks she'll want to talk about your mother all the time – and that she'll call me Charlie.' He grinned. 'These days, there's hardly anyone left to call me Charlie.'

I agreed that Miss Burns would almost certainly want to talk about my mother. 'She's desperate to know where she is.'

'Who isn't?' Charles said dryly. 'Still, I expect she'll turn up when she wants to. I'm off to have a bath. I've just cut the grass for the first time this year and I'm knackered. Marion's having her hair done: she'll be back in half an hour or so.' Marion had her hair set every Saturday afternoon without fail.

Charles went upstairs and I wandered into the garden to examine the lawn. It looked intensely green and had the lovely smell that was special to freshly cut grass. I sniffed appreciatively. It cheered

43

me that soon everything would be in full bloom and there would be a bouquet of wonderful scents. It was mainly Charles who had created the garden. The thick privet hedge and the swollen bushes had all grown from cuttings and the flowers from seed. It was his pride and joy.

The house had been bought in 1939 when it was rare for anyone who was working class to own a property. It was a redbrick semi with three good bedrooms, two reception rooms, a breakfast room, and a garage that had been added on over the years.

Charles said it had been amazingly cheap – 'It cost less than four figures,' he often boasted – and now it was worth five or six thousand pounds. He and Marion often looked at the houses for sale in the *Liverpool Echo* to check the prices, though they had no intention of moving. They even went to look at properties. It seemed to be a sort of hobby. The furniture had been expensive: solid wood bought to last a lifetime. They would never buy another thing, however much styles might change.

Marion came home, her hair intensely black and neatly set. She asked to see the clothes I'd bought. She always made a big show of admiring the style, feeling the material, commenting that the garment, or whatever it happened to be, appeared to be very good value. I didn't know if she was genuinely interested, or merely doing what she thought mothers were expected to do. My aunt wasn't interested in jewellery or clothes, possessing only her wedding ring and a tiny pair of pearl earrings that Charles had given her for a wedding present: she wore them all the time. She had two smart suits and a handful of plain dresses, skirts and tops, all in dark colours. She had never worn trousers in her life and refused to let Charles have jeans. 'I didn't marry a cowboy, did I?' she'd say.

We were eating in the Lonely Bell, a public house in Formby not far from the sands. Although we were early, Catherine Burns was already in the upstairs restaurant when we arrived. She wore a midnight-blue velvet trouser suit with a white frilly lace blouse underneath and a touch of make-up for a change. She looked very glamorous and considerably younger.

Marion half-groaned, 'Oh, sugar!' she whispered. 'She's smoking. You know I can't stand cigarette smoke, Charles.'

'It's not my fault she smokes,' Charles whispered back.

'You shouldn't have invited her.'

'I'd completely forgotten she smoked.'

Fortunately, Miss Burns stubbed out the cigarette when she saw us coming. She stood and kissed Marion, then Charles. 'Oh, come here, Pearl.' She kissed my cheek. 'You're the daughter of my very best friend in the world,' she said emotionally. Her breath smelled of alcohol.

'It's not much good having a best friend who's spent twenty years in prison,' Marion said as she sat. Her habit of speaking her mind could be embarrassing at times. 'It's even worse when the friend's released and completely disappears off the face of the earth. I mean,' she snorted, 'some friend!'

'Friendship, like generosity, covers a multitude of sins,' Miss Burns replied. She sounded more amused than annoyed.

Marion opened her mouth to say something else, but changed her mind, clamping her jaw shut. I reckoned that Charles had kicked her underneath the table.

'When did we last see each other?' Miss Burns wondered aloud.

'When Amy was sent back to Holloway,' Charles said. 'You and I turned up to see her at the same time. I think it was about three years ago.'

'You're right. And the last time I saw you, Marion, was at Pearl's twenty-first birthday party. We really should see each other more often.'

'Hear, hear,' Charles said. He gritted his teeth – Marion had kicked *him*, I could tell. I hoped the evening wouldn't be spent with Miss Burns and Marion blowing poisoned darts at each other, and Marion and Charles secretly kicking each other to death, but Charles ordered a bottle of red wine and one of white, and regularly refilled their glasses without asking. By the time the meal was finished, all was sweetness and light.

## Chapter 4

### September 1939
### Amy

Ever since they'd started work, Amy and Cathy had spent virtually all their pocket money at the pictures, sitting right at the front where the seats only cost a penny. They knew that not all girls led the same sort of lives as they did, had the same sort of jobs or lived in a place like Bootle. American films, for instance, showed young women starring in shows on Broadway, and, if they weren't on the stage, they were film stars, newspaper reporters, models or married to desperately rich men and living in desperately posh houses.

In her heart, Amy had known that her own future wouldn't offer the same choices. The best she could hope for was a husband that she loved and a slightly better house than the one in which she had been born and raised. There would, of course, be children: Amy fancied having four and Cathy said she'd like just two. Both girls were quite content with this vision of the future that awaited them.

But since the day Amy had met Barney Patterson on Southport pier, the life she'd always known had turned into one that was beyond the wildest of her dreams. She hadn't known it was possible to be as truly and wholeheartedly happy as she was with Barney: sleeping with him, being with him almost every minute of every day.

She had given up her job in the canteen and Barney was waiting for the war to start before he joined the Forces – the Army, the Navy, or the Air Force, he didn't mind which. At twenty-one, he was bound to be called up soon and there might be no need for him to volunteer. Amy kept expecting a letter to drop on the mat at any moment. But until then, their time was their own and they could do with it whatever they pleased. She prayed morning, noon and night that something miraculous would happen to prevent the war from starting, but Barney said it was too late for that.

'Things have gone too far,' he assured her. Gas masks had arrived; there was a stirrup pump in the hallway; the cellar would be used as an air raid shelter; blackout material had to be bought to make curtains, and tape stuck to the windows to prevent the glass from shattering in the event of a bomb dropping nearby.

A bomb! Had she allowed herself to dwell on such horrors, Amy was convinced she would have gone out of her mind. As it was, she managed to ignore everything that was happening outside the little flat in which she and Barney lived.

The flat was on the top floor of a four-storey house overlooking Newsham Park. It had a big living room with a window at each end, a moderately sized bedroom, and a tiny kitchen and bathroom. It was lovely not having to go down to the yard to use the lavatory, and to have a stove with four gas rings and an oven, rather than a kitchen range that took for ever to clean and polish with black lead.

Mornings, the sun shone directly into the bedroom, waking them with its brightness and its warmth. Evenings, it set right outside the living-room window so that they could watch the sky change colour as it slowly disappeared behind the nearby houses. The ceilings sloped so acutely in places that sometimes Barney banged his head. The latest bruise would be fading when he'd bang it again.

A silver-framed photograph of their wedding stood on the mantelpiece: just the two of them, smiling at each other. It had been the happiest day of Amy's life and she wished Mam hadn't been so upset about it. Mam hadn't spoiled things – nothing could have spoiled a day like that – but Amy had expected everyone to be as happy about the wedding as she and Barney. She seemed to have lost the knack of seeing things through anyone's eyes but her own.

A couple in their thirties, Clive and Veronica Stafford, lived on the floor below, and Mr and Mrs Porter, who were very elderly, on the floor below that. Captain Kirby-Greene, a bachelor who'd spent most of his life in the Royal Navy, lived in the bottom flat. They were all terribly posh. Clive and Veronica had invited Barney and Amy to dinner.

'But we'll have to invite them back and I can't cook for toffee,' Amy wailed. 'All I can make is scouse.'

'It doesn't matter, darling,' Barney said soothingly. 'I bet your scouse is nicer than anything Veronica could make.' They were lying on the settee. He nuzzled her neck. 'If you like, we can just say our kitchen is too small to cook in and that we'll take them out to dinner.'

For Barney, money was no object. When they'd first moved into the flat, he'd decided it was under-furnished so had gone out and bought a brown leather settee from George Henry Lee's. It had been delivered the following morning along with a heap of bedding, loads of other linen, a circular red rug and a radiogram. The next day, an engineer arrived to install a telephone. Amy now had enough frocks to wear a different one each day of the week.

Barney's grandparents on his father's side were dead and had left him and Harry a tidy sum of money each. Amy would have loved him just as much had he been penniless, yet she couldn't deny that his wealth only added to the magic of her fairytale existence. When he went into the Forces, the bank would pay the rent on the flat until he came home, as well as an allowance for his wife. She refused to talk about it when he brought up the subject. 'I don't want you to go away. I don't think I'll be able to stand it. I shall probably die,' she announced in a trembling voice. She'd sooner be dead than parted from Barney.

'Oh, Amy!' He would gather her in his arms, take her into the bedroom, and they would make love, no matter what time of day it was, even if they'd only just got up. Making love was unbelievable. Amy didn't know enough words to describe it. Anyroad, who would she describe it to? Only Barney, and he already knew.

When it was over, they would lie on the bed, wrapped so tightly in each other's arms that they could scarcely breathe. Barney would say how fortunate it was that he'd gone to Southport on Easter

Sunday. 'Just think,' he'd say, 'if I hadn't, we wouldn't have found each other.'

They would be silent for a long time, trying to imagine what life would have been like had they never met, but it was impossible. An angel had been watching over them that Sunday, or perhaps even God himself. Both were convinced that their marriage had been made in heaven and that other couples didn't love each other half as much as they did.

That summer the weather was glorious – or maybe it only seemed so to Amy and Barney, who were living in their own special little world. When they weren't making love, they spent the days driving into the countryside and calling in at pubs for a drink. Some days Barney took the car through the Mersey tunnel to places like New Brighton or Chester, or even as far as North Wales. They went to the pictures and the theatre, and ate most of their meals out, though Amy loved experimenting in the kitchen. She could already make a reasonable omelette and Barney adored her scouse, especially when it was covered with lashings of brown sauce.

'That's the way me dad used to like it,' she told him. 'Mam would get dead cross with him. She said he ended up with more sauce than scouse.'

'What did your dad do?' he asked.

'He drove a delivery van for Henderson's department store. Him and his mate were carrying a three-piece suite into someone's house when he had a heart attack. That was ten years ago. I still miss him; we all do. His name was Joseph, but everyone called him Joe.' She shed a few tears. She cried a lot nowadays, and not just when she was sad, which hardly ever happened, but when she felt as if she were the happiest woman on earth, like now.

Some days all she and Barney did was shop. He would insist on buying Amy's mam a present, such as gloves or jewellery or bottles of scent: Chanel No. 5 or Guerlain's Shalimar. Until then, Amy and her mother had used Evening in Paris or June: dead cheap in comparison. Mrs Curran was really sweet, Barney said, and as different from his own mother as chalk from cheese.

★

49

'Oh, you shouldn't, luv,' Mam cried the next time they went to see her, as she opened the box and found a silk scarf folded neatly inside. It was shell pink with a pattern of big, white flowers. Barney had chosen it. He'd bought jars of pot-pourri for Jacky and Biddy, who were mad about him, and chocolates for Charlie and Marion, although Marion didn't look the least bit pleased.

Amy said not to take any notice. 'She's a real sourpuss. No one can understand what our Charlie sees in her.'

Mam draped the scarf around her neck. 'It's dead pretty,' she said, blushing. 'I'll just go and change me shoes and put a bit of lippy on.' They were taking her for a ride in the car.

'There's no need to rush, ma-in-law,' Barney said with a smile. Mam loved being called that. Amy's heart always skipped a beat when Barney smiled because it made him look even more handsome than he already was. She still hadn't met Barney's mother.

'When am I going to meet her?' Amy had asked once. 'I mean, does she know we're married?' It disturbed her that she hadn't been introduced to his parents.

'She knows we're married, but you're never going to meet her,' Barney had said flatly. 'Never, never, never. She hates you.'

'*Hates* me! But why?' Amy had wanted to cry.

'Because you're a Catholic: she loathes Catholics. I've told you that before.'

'She might get to like me if we met.'

'I'd sooner not take a chance on that, darling.'

'How about your father?'

'Pa's OK. I'll just have to find a way of getting you two together. He doesn't like to go behind Ma's back, you see.'

One morning towards the end of August, Barney decided it was time he and Amy had a honeymoon. 'Otherwise, we might never have one, what with the war about to start and me likely to be called up any minute,' he said. 'Where shall we go? It's too late to go abroad. How about a few days in London? We'll go in the car.'

Amy, who had been thinking of Blackpool or Morecambe,

considered London a marvellous idea. 'But don't forget it's our Charlie and Marion's wedding on Saturday.'

'We'll buy them a wedding present while we're there and come back Friday afternoon. Today's Tuesday, so we'll still have two whole days to ourselves.' Seeing as how there was absolutely nothing to stop them and no need to tell anyone, Amy carefully chose two outfits to take with her – an emerald-green frock with cap sleeves and a Peter Pan collar, and a coarse cream linen costume with a brown blouse – put on her new black pleated skirt and white tailored blouse to travel in, helped Barney pack the suitcase, and they set off.

The weather was cool for August and the sky full of clouds; not black, heavy ones that promised rain, but the fluffy cotton wool sort that looked as if they'd break up any minute and reveal the sun.

It was pleasant driving through the little winding country roads in Cheshire and past the tall smoking chimneys of Stoke-on-Trent. Once they'd passed Birmingham, they stopped at a pub for something to eat. Amy loved the strangeness of it all, the different accents, the different smells, the fact that they were only about a hundred miles away from Liverpool, yet it felt as if they were on the other side of the world.

From then on the scenery became countrified again until they reached the outskirts of London, and eventually they drove down a pretty, tree-lined road that Barney said was called Park Lane. 'That's Hyde Park on our left,' he said. 'If I turn right down here, there's a little hotel where Pa always stays. Harry and I came with him once. It's small and very comfortable, not like these places.' They were passing a palace of a building that was called the Dorchester.

Their hotel was called Priests. It was quite ordinary and inconspicuous outside, but the inside was quietly luxurious with cream satin walls and beige carpets that were as thick as overgrown grass.

As soon as they were shown to their room, Amy threw herself on the bed. She bounced up and down a few times. 'It's lovely and soft,' she said.

Barney flung himself down beside her. 'So it is.' He slid his arms around her. 'Shall we make love now, or would you like to sleep first and we'll do it later?'

'Later.' Amy yawned. 'I'm awful tired.' They kicked off their shoes and fell asleep in each other's arms. An hour later, they woke up at exactly the same time and Barney began to undo the buttons of her white blouse while Amy did the same to the buttons of his shirt.

Their love-making had been wonderful right from the start but it seemed even more wonderful doing it in a hotel room in London. On a strange bed in a strange city it felt daring, exciting and slightly sinful.

Afterwards, Amy picked up the clothes that had been thrown so carelessly on to the floor, unpacked the suitcase, and put everything away in the wardrobe and the lavender-scented drawers, except for Barney's hairbrushes and the toiletries, which she left on top of the tallboy. She went into the bathroom – she'd been deeply impressed to find they had a bathroom to themselves – washed her face in the big white sink and dried it on a fluffy white towel, both actions inexplicably making her want to explode with happiness.

'Where are we going tonight?' she asked Barney when she came out.

'To the Theatre Royal to see Ivor Novello in *The Dancing Years*,' Barney replied. 'I asked the chap on reception to book us seats. He said there were plenty. It's the same in all the theatres. People are leaving London in their droves for somewhere safer.'

'Is London dangerous?' Why on earth had they come if it wasn't safe?

'It will be when the war starts,' Barney said ominously. 'It's one of the first places that'll be bombed; Liverpool's another.'

'*Shush!*' Amy stamped her foot and burst into tears. 'It still might not start. Why are people so sure it will?'

Barney came over and took her in his arms. 'Because everyone – except you, my darling girl – just knows that there's no going back. It's like a train going down a hill at full speed and the brakes don't work.'

'A miracle might happen,' Amy sobbed.

'I suppose it might,' he agreed, but she knew he was only saying it to make her feel better. 'Let's try and forget about it for the next few days,' he said gently. 'After all, this is our honeymoon.'

The theatre was more than half-empty. Before the curtain went up and the lights went out, Ivor Novello, the incredibly handsome star of the show, came on to the stage and asked the people at the back and in the gallery to come and sit at the front. Everybody clapped. Amy and Barney moved along their row to fill up the empty spaces and allow more people to sit in their row.

'I suppose this is how it's going to be from now on,' said the middle-aged woman wearing a pink satin evening dress sprinkled with sequins when Amy sat next to her. She wondered if she should buy an evening dress for herself.

'What do you mean?' she asked.

'Things won't be normal any more. Ordinarily, we at the front would be quite outraged if those from the gallery were allowed to join us. After all, our seats cost so much more than theirs. But now the war has virtually started, we're all in it together and we don't mind. Don't you think it feels much more friendly now we're all sitting together?' All the moving and shuffling about had stopped and everyone was waiting for the curtain to rise.

'I suppose it does,' Amy agreed.

There was a warmer atmosphere, but it was spoilt rather by the woman's talk of war.

There were more signs of war the next day: a gun battery in Hyde Park, for instance; notices in the big shops telling customers where to shelter if the air raid siren sounded; sandbags outside important buildings; and quite a few people already self-consciously carrying their gasmasks in boxes over their shoulders. One woman had crocheted a pretty cover for hers, with raised flowers on all six sides.

They wandered along Oxford Street and had coffee in Selfridges. Outside, Barney hailed a taxi that took them to Harrods – 'the most famous shop in England,' he said, 'and probably the most expensive.'

Amy nearly fainted when she saw the price of the clothes. Even Barney, who was incredibly generous, didn't offer to buy her anything, though he got a lovely canteen of cutlery in a black leather case with velvet lining as a present for Charlie and Marion.

'Even Marion is bound to like that,' Amy said. 'It just might bring a smile to her miserable face.'

'And what can I do to bring a smile to your face, Amy?' Barney whispered in her ear. Amy whispered something back and he said, 'Your wish is my command, Mrs Patterson.' With that, he hailed a taxi, and they returned to the hotel and didn't emerge until it was almost teatime.

Next morning, Thursday, when they came down to breakfast, a number of guests had gathered in the lounge and were listening to the wireless. Barney said he thought they should catch up on the latest news, but Amy said she wasn't interested in the news, not while she was in London. 'I'll order breakfast,' she said. 'What do you want?'

'Everything,' Barney said, 'and tell them I like my toast well done.' He had the appetite of a horse.

Minutes later, the pot of tea she'd asked for had arrived, but there was no sign of Barney. A couple in their sixties were seated at the next table. The woman said, 'I really think we should go home today, darling, so we can help Sally get the children ready to go to Aunt Alice's. She'll have a job seeing to the five of them on her own.'

'You're right, Flora. After we've finished eating, we'll pack and catch the first train out of Waterloo. It might be hell on earth tomorrow.'

Barney came back. He didn't say anything, just looked grim. Amy poured him tea. 'What's happening tomorrow?' she asked. 'The man on the next table said it might be hell on earth, but I think he was talking about the trains.'

'Do you really want to know?'

Amy sighed. 'Yes.' She couldn't very well ignore the war any longer. It was childish to pretend the threat didn't exist.

'The Government has ordered the evacuation of children to

54

begin in the morning.' Barney unfolded his linen napkin and spread it on his knee. 'It might not be a bad idea to set off then rather than wait until teatime. The roads could be very busy. It hasn't been much of a honeymoon has it, Amy?' he said ruefully. 'Tell you what.' His brown eyes brightened. 'One of these days we'll come back to London for a whole week. Or we could even go to Paris! We'll have a proper honeymoon, you'll see.'

They'd planned to spend the day sightseeing, but Amy had lost interest.

'We can do it another time. I'd sooner just walk around the shops than look at Buckingham Palace and the Houses of Parliament,' she said when they came out of the hotel. 'I'd like to buy a present for Mam and our Jacky and Biddy and your Harry – and Cathy.' She realized it was ages since she'd seen the friend she'd used to see every day of the week. 'I'll get her something really nice.'

Barney loved shopping almost as much as she did and he readily agreed. He said he'd quite like a new suit for Saturday's wedding. 'I fancy pale grey with a white stripe. Charlie isn't wearing morning dress, is he?'

'Good heavens, no!' she laughed. 'He's bought a new suit, too. It's plain dark blue.'

'Let's get your stuff first.' He tucked her arm inside his. 'Oh, and we must get you a present, darling, a souvenir of London. How about an engagement ring? I never got round to buying you one. I'm sorry, but our honeymoon is turning into a bit of a washout.'

'It's not. I've loved every minute. I'm really glad we came and I'd love an engagement ring.' They stopped in Park Lane for a long, lingering, tender kiss. They made a striking couple: Barney so tall and elegant in his brown summer suit, and Amy as pretty as a picture in emerald-green. Passers-by treated them to an amused smile or a disagreeable look, depending upon their mood. A few people wondered if they'd seen them before in a Hollywood film.

Four hours later they had lunch in John Lewis's restaurant on the top floor. Amy examined her ring, a solitary diamond, on the third finger of her left hand. She twisted her hand this way and that, admiring the way the facets of the jewel twinkled. Satisfied, she turned her attention to the things she had bought: a snakeskin handbag for Mam, two plain leather handbags for her sisters, and a really pretty ivory lace blouse for Cathy, which was dressy enough to go dancing in, but plain enough for work.

'What shall we get your Harry?' she asked. She genuinely liked her brother-in-law. They met in town for dinner every Sunday night.

After much discussion, they decided to get him a propelling pencil in its own little black box. It had a rubber concealed inside the screw-top and a supply of spare leads.

Amy insisted they catch a red bus back to the hotel to deposit their parcels. 'I've never been on a bus before. At home, we go everywhere on the tram.'

Barney bought the *Evening Standard* so they could look through the pictures and decide what to see that night, their last in London.

'The fleet's been mobilized, mate,' the newsvendor said. He was a heavily freckled young man barely five feet tall. 'It ain't in the paper yet; someone just told me.'

Amy's feet were aching. When they got to their room, she decided to have a bath while Barney read the paper. She emptied the little jar of complimentary bath salts into the steaming water, climbed in and immediately fell asleep.

When she woke, she wrapped herself in a giant white towel and found Barney had fallen asleep on the bed. He had removed his jacket and waistcoat, and loosened the collar of his shirt. He lay on his side, curled up like a baby, one hand spread on the pillow.

Amy lay beside him. She laced her fingers through his, but he didn't wake, just sighed. 'Oh, Barney,' she whispered. She loved him so much that it hurt, really hurt, making her throat ache – and her heart. There really was something called heartache.

He opened one eye – the other was hidden in the pillow – reached for the towel and dragged it off. They made love. It wasn't the least bit gentle, but fiercely passionate and full of bitter anger at what was going to happen tomorrow, or the next day, or the day after that. The world was about to turn upside-down and inside-out, not just for them, but for everyone in the country, and possibly the entire world.

'I don't feel like going to the pictures,' Amy said later when Barney began to read out the films showing in London that night. Not even *Mr Smith Goes to Washington* with James Stewart, her favourite actor, appealed. 'I wouldn't be able to concentrate. Let's go somewhere where we can talk.'

'We can talk while we walk,' Barney said with a grin.

They strolled along Park Lane until they reached Piccadilly, arms linked. At Piccadilly Circus, they watched the brightly coloured lights flash on and off, then they sat on the crowded steps of Eros and sang 'Keep the Home Fires Burning' and 'It's a Long Way to Tipperary' with an impromptu choir. Buses, cars and taxis circled slowly around them sounding their horns, as if that would some-how make the traffic go faster.

There were quite a few people in uniform, nearly all young. Very soon, Barney would have a uniform, possibly as early as next week. He'd vowed that if his call-up papers hadn't arrived by the time they got home, he'd call in at the recruitment office and volunteer. Amy clung to his arm. She wasn't being the least bit brave about things. All she wanted to do was cry.

Next morning, after an early breakfast, Amy and Barney stood outside the hotel with their luggage while they waited for the car to be brought. 'We'll come back one day,' Barney promised, kissing her nose when she got into the Morris beside him.

They'd only been going a matter of minutes when they realized they should have left sooner. The traffic was at an almost complete standstill. It took nearly half an hour, edging forward inches at a time, to reach the end of Park Lane. It would appear everyone was anxious to get away from London before the war officially began. Cars were piled high with luggage. The children in the car in front knelt on the back seat and made incredible faces at them, but Amy, who would have normally have enjoyed making faces back, just didn't have the heart.

It took almost three hours to reach the outskirts of the city where the traffic wasn't quite so heavy, but it was still heavy enough, as the cars were joined by coaches full of children being evacuated to the countryside.

'We should have gone home yesterday,' Barney said for the fifth or sixth time.

'Where are we?' Amy asked after about an hour.

'I've no idea.' He looked moidered. 'I reckon some of the road signs have been removed.'

Soon afterwards, they passed a train station and Amy asked him to stop because she badly needed a lavatory, having drunk far too much tea that morning. Barney must have drunk too much, too: he emerged from the station at the same time as she did.

'It's worse on the trains than on the roads,' he said when they set off again. 'Some chap just told me. Everyone's jammed together like sardines. At least we've got somewhere to sit.'

An hour later, they found themselves approaching Oxford, and Barney suggested they stop and have a drink and something to eat. 'There's a pub not far ahead. It should be open by now.'

Amy was longing for a break. It was a relief to turn off the busy road and stop outside the Malted Loaf, which had just opened for business. They took their drinks and a plate of ham sandwiches into the sunny garden, and sat on a bench beside a rough wooden table as far away from the sound of traffic as it was possible to be. They were the only customers. Close by, a bee buzzed noisily, and a man could be seen through a hawthorn hedge cutting grass with a scythe. It was such a peaceful scene that it was hard to believe the country was in such a state of panic.

Another couple came into the garden. The man waved and shouted, 'Have you heard? Hitler's invaded Poland. Warsaw has been bombed. To all intents and purposes, this country is at war with Germany.'

Khaki-painted lorries had joined the traffic, some packed with troops, adding to the chaos. There were occasions when everything ground to a halt and took ages to get started again because a vehicle had broken down ahead. Policemen on bikes pedalled through the lines of cars, lorries and coaches, trying to sort out the mess. Traffic was diverted down pretty minor roads lined with trees, barely wide enough for two vehicles to pass. At one point, a crowd of children picnicked on the grass verge while steam spurted from the bonnet of their coach. It was past teatime and some families had driven their vehicles into fields and erected tents, presumably to spend the night there.

'That's what we could do with,' Barney muttered, 'a tent. I can't see us getting to Liverpool tonight. We're only about half-way there. When we get to Coventry perhaps we should look for a hotel and stay till morning.'

'But what about our Charlie's wedding?' Amy cried.

'I'd forgotten about it.' He wiped his white, strained face on the sleeve of his shirt and sighed with exhaustion.

Amy's shoulders were aching badly. She would have loved to stay the night in a hotel, but couldn't possibly miss her only brother's wedding. Mam would be dead upset and Marion would never forgive her. She suggested that when they got to Coventry they stopped for a few hours. 'Let's have a proper meal,' she said more cheerfully than she felt. 'We can have a little rest afterwards. Surely the roads won't be all that busy when it's dark. Another few hours should do it.' She couldn't wait to get to their flat.

The fish and chip restaurant on the fringes of Coventry was a rough and ready place, but the food was delicious: the chips crisp outside and soft inside, the fish white and flaky, and the batter as light as air. They washed it down with mugs of milky tea.

Barney looked his old self again by the time they'd finished. Outside, they walked up and down for a few minutes to stretch their legs: Amy felt as if her knees were about to buckle. The traffic had lessened considerably while they'd been eating and it was rapidly growing dark; so dark that there was something unnatural, almost ghostly, about it. Amy noticed that there wasn't a light to be seen in any building and not even the street lamps had been turned on. The traffic crawled along, as headlamps were covered with black paper, leaving just a narrow slit for the light to shine through. She pointed this out to Barney, who put his hands to his face and groaned, 'Shit!'

'Barney!' She'd never known him swear before.

'Sorry, darling, but the blackout's started. I'd forgotten it was today. I should have made shields for the lights.'

'You mean we can't have the headlamps on properly?' They'd never be able to see where they were going. Even now, in a road full of shops and houses, the night was getting blacker and blacker, and it was hard to make out the outlines of the buildings against the dark sky. Once they reached the countryside it would be impossible. 'We'll find a hotel and stay the night,' she said flatly. 'If we start off really early in the morning, we might manage to get to the wedding on time. If we don't it's just too bad.'

Funny sort of families her children were marrying into, Moira thought as she sat in the taxi feeling a bit like the Queen of England. It was the first taxi ride of her life.

Amy had been married for almost three months and there'd been no suggestion of meeting Barney's mam and dad. Moira didn't like to push, but thought it would be nice if they were all friends together. They could ask each other round at Christmas, even if it was only for a drink, and celebrate their children's birthdays together. She hoped Amy wasn't ashamed of her mam.

Today had been Charlie's wedding – and what a lovely day it was for it, too: brilliantly sunny and the temperature perfect. She'd gone to the Holy Cross church in Scotland Road with Jacky and Biddy, expecting to meet at least a few members of Marion's family: her parents were dead, but surely she'd have a sister or other relatives. But the only guests were Charlie's family and a handful of people Marion worked with at the English Electric.

Moira would like to have invited both her sisters from Ireland to the wedding, and some of Joe's relatives she still saw. Her friend, Nellie Tyler, would have loved to come, and it would have been a friendly gesture to ask Cathy Burns – she was a lovely girl and Amy had badly let her down. She'd even envisaged Jacky and Biddy being bridesmaids, an expense she wouldn't have minded. But there'd been no suggestion of that, or of inviting more than Charlie's immediate family.

In the church, while worrying that the blue costume she got from Paddy's Market was too obviously second-hand and her blue hat was showing its age, despite having been freshened up with a yard of cream net, it gradually dawned on her that Amy and Barney weren't coming, and she began to worry about them as well, not to mention the war that she'd been worried about for months. Her daughter and lovely new son-in-law hadn't been seen for a few days, but that wasn't unusual. Surely they hadn't forgotten today was the day that Charlie was getting married? The wedding was turning into a nightmare.

The Nuptial Mass over, one of the friends took half a dozen photos, and everyone made their way to a restaurant in Scottie Road where a cold buffet awaited them in an upstairs room. Moira ate a few slices of tinned ham, drank a mouthful of wine, and informed the bride and groom that she was leaving.

'I'm dead worried about our Amy,' she said in a rush. 'Her and Barney might have had an accident in the car or something. I'll pop round to the flat and see if they're all right.'

'Pop round' was a bit of an understatement, as the flat was miles away on the other side of Liverpool.

Charlie squeezed her hand. 'To tell the truth, Mam, I'm a bit worried meself. I know Amy was looking forward to the wedding. But there's a phone box outside: why don't you telephone? I'll do it for you if you like.'

'I haven't got the number, luv.' She felt close to tears. 'Our Amy wrote it down on a piece of paper and put it behind the clock on the mantelpiece. I never thought to put it in me bag.'

'Give your mam half a crown, Charlie, so she can get a taxi,' Marion said kindly – so kindly that Moira wondered if she'd badly misjudged the woman who was now her daughter-in-law.

Now here she was stepping out of the black cab outside Amy's grand house by Newsham Park. She'd been there before quite a few times, but had never come unannounced. She gave the door-bell four rings to indicate it was the tenants at the top she'd come to see. Almost immediately, Captain Kirby-Greene, who lived on the ground floor, opened the door. He bowed courteously.

'Good afternoon, Mrs Curran. I saw you from the window. I thought I would let you in, save your daughter having to come all the way down.'

'Thank you, Mr ... Captain,' Moira stammered, amazed that he'd recognized her when they'd only met the once and then only for the time it took for Amy to introduce them. She was halfway upstairs when he said gruffly, 'Ahem,' and she turned.

'I hope you don't mind my saying, Mrs Curran,' he said shyly, 'but you look especially charming today.'

'Of course I don't mind, Captain.' She flushed with pleasure. He wasn't bad-looking for a man of his age – a good sixty, she reckoned. His hair was a lovely silver and there was plenty of it, though his obviously false teeth were too big for his mouth.

'Is that you, Mam?' Amy had come out onto the landing two floors above.

'Yes, luv, I'm just coming.' She waved tara to the captain and continued upstairs, aware his eyes were following her until she disappeared.

'Oh, Mam, I know we've missed our Charlie's wedding,' Amy cried when Moira arrived. 'I'm dead sorry, I was really looking forward to it.' She looked as if she'd been dragged through a hedge backwards and was still wearing her dressing gown. Her small white feet were bare. 'You wouldn't believe the day we had yesterday trying to get home from London. In the end, we had to give up altogether when we realized the blackout had started, so we stayed at some hotel – well, it was more a bed and breakfast place – and the woman wouldn't give us a hot drink before we went to bed: we offered to pay, but she said it was against the rules. Neither of us slept a wink all night long.' She was babbling now, the words tripping over each other as she tried to get them out. 'We left the minute it was light, then poor Barney felt really ill and we had to keep stopping so he could be sick at the side of the road. It must have been something he ate.'

'Where is he, luv?' Moira put her arm around her daughter's shoulders and they went into the flat.

'In bed, fast asleep. I wanted to get the doctor, but he wouldn't let me.' Amy paused for an anguished breath. 'And, oh Mam, you'll never guess. His call-up papers arrived while we were away. They want him in the Army. He was supposed to report somewhere today. He said he'll telephone when he feels better.'

'Can I have a peep at him?'

Amy nodded, and Moira opened the bedroom door a crack. All she could see was the top of Barney's head: the rest of him was buried beneath an untidy heap of bedclothes. His breathing sounded perfectly steady. She quietly closed the door. 'He's probably just tired now, Amy. When he wakes up, just give him plenty of water or weak tea. You can make him a bowl of bread and milk if he feels hungry. Now, if you don't mind, luv, I'm longing for a cuppa. I'll make it: you sit down and rest a minute.'

Her mother's presence must have calmed her. Amy sat on the leather settee facing the window. 'It's a lovely day,' she said, as if she'd only just noticed the way the sun shone on the slate roofs of the houses across the park, making them glisten like sheets of glass. 'How did the wedding go?' she asked when Moira came in with two cups of tea.

'All right.' Moira shrugged. 'There was hardly anyone there, only about a dozen of us altogether. Charlie and your sisters were really worried when you two didn't turn up. Marion hadn't asked any relatives, just friends from work. Her dress wasn't up to much,' she said in retrospect. 'To be frank, it looked as if it had cost about nineteen and elevenpence in Blackler's Bargain Basement. And she didn't carry a bouquet just a prayer book. As for the reception, it was pathetic: I mean, tinned ham at a wedding! And they're not going on honeymoon, but staying in the new house.' It was a bit late to feel indignant, but the whole thing had clearly been done on the cheap. She sniffed, feeling hard done by. 'I haven't been introduced to any of Marion's relatives, or Barney's, come to that. I'm beginning to think you and our Charlie are ashamed of your mam.'

Amy uttered a very unladylike snort. 'Don't be daft, Mam. It's more likely to be the other way round and Marion's ashamed of letting *her* family meet you. You look really smart in that costume. As for Barney's mam, I haven't met her, either: she's an Irish Protestant and can't stand Catholics.'

'Dear God in heaven, Amy,' Moira muttered, making the sign of the cross. 'What sort of crowd have you married into?'

'I married Barney, Mam, not his family.'

'I suppose so,' Moira conceded. She was feeling a bit better about herself. It wasn't only what Amy had said, but the way Captain Kirby-Greene had looked at her. And although the wedding had been done on the cheap, it was due to Marion that she'd come all this way in a taxi.

She felt even better when Amy produced the presents she had bought in London and gave her a snakeskin handbag. 'A real snake?' Moira stroked the pitted grey and black leather, and hoped the snake had died a peaceful death.

'Well, they wouldn't call it snakeskin if it didn't come from a real snake, Mam.' Amy managed a wan smile. 'We got our Jacky and Biddy handbags, too, and a lovely canteen of cutlery for Charlie and Marion. It's a pity I couldn't have got everything to you before the wedding.'

'Never mind, Amy; better late than never. I'll take all this stuff back with me in a taxi.' The journey had only cost ninepence and she'd given the driver a penny tip, so there was enough left out of the half crown to take her back to Bootle.

'In that case, you can take this blouse I got for Cathy as well.' Amy waved a pretty ivory lace blouse.

'I'd sooner not. It'd be better if you gave that to Cathy yourself.' Since her daughter had married Barney Patterson, her brains had turned to feathers and she seemed to have forgotten Cathy's existence. Barney was just as bad. Moira couldn't think of anything dafter that skipping off to London when they both knew the war was likely to start any time soon.

At teatime, Barney got up, saying he felt a bit better. He had a bath, but refused bread and milk when it was offered, pretending to gag and saying it could well make him sick again. 'Anyway, before I do anything else I want to sort out the matter of my call-up,' he added.

'There won't be anyone there,' said Amy. 'It's Saturday afternoon.'

'My darling girl, there's almost a war on. I can assure you the phone will be manned at the other end.'

He was right. When he dialled the number it was answered immediately. Amy went into the tiny kitchen and tried not to

64

listen as he arranged to report to somewhere near Chester at nine o'clock on Tuesday morning. 'It means I'll have to leave on Monday,' he said when he'd finished.

'Will you go in the car?' she asked, surprised that she was able to pose a perfectly sane and sensible question.

'No. It would be best if I went by train. I'll leave the car where it is, outside in the road. Harry will see to it if it has to be laid up, darling. It depends on how long this damn war lasts.' He took her in his arms, his face sober. 'How will I live without you, eh?'

'I wish I knew,' Amy said with a sob, 'because then I might know how *I* will live without *you*!'

They decided not to go out to dinner, and had an early night instead.


On Sunday, Amy went to Mass for the first time since she'd married Barney – Mam would have a fit if she knew she'd been missing Mass for months – and he went to tell his family that he was leaving the following day. 'I might be sent back,' he said before leaving for Calderstones. 'They might not need me yet, or I might not pass the medical.'

But both he and Amy knew he would be needed straight away, and there wasn't a chance in a million he would fail the medical, a fine, healthy young man like him.

In church, she prayed a miracle would happen and war would be avoided – it was still possible – but when she arrived home Captain Kirby-Greene came out of his room and told her the Prime Minister, Neville Chamberlain, had just been on the wireless and announced that war had been declared on Germany.

'And about time, too,' he said indignantly. 'We should have done something about that Hitler chappie long before now. A bloody good hiding might bring him to his senses.' He bowed majestically. 'I hope you will excuse my French, Mrs Patterson.'

'Of course, Captain,' she said quietly.

She ran upstairs, rushed into the flat and burst into tears.


Barney came home looking very serious. His mother had taken the news badly. 'She hasn't been feeling well lately.'

65

'Poor thing!' Amy said sympathetically. 'Would it help if I went to see her?'

'No, it would only make her feel even worse.'

He'd bought a packet of twenty Senior Service while he was out, although he only smoked occasionally. Amy had tried, but hated it. Now, he smoked incessantly while they packed the suitcase, trying to think of every single thing he was likely to need, as if once he had closed the door of the flat behind him, he would never again have the opportunity to buy razors or hankies or a comb.

They didn't make love that night, just curled up in bed together. Barney lay on his side with Amy tucked against him, held there by the weight of his arm on her waist. At some time during the night he removed his arm, kissed her and climbed out of bed. Amy came to for a moment, gave a little cry and immediately went back to sleep.

Next morning, when she woke up, the suitcase had gone and so had Barney. He left a note saying he just couldn't bear the idea of saying goodbye: 'I love you too much, my darling. I'm taking the coward's way out. I'm sure you'll soon realize this is the simplest way for us both.'

He was right. The worst of it, the parting, was over. Now she was left with only half a life, and she had no alternative but to get on with it, like all the other women in the country whose men were being called upon to fight.

# Chapter 5

## April–May 1971
## Pearl

'After we've finished our tea, I'd like us to discuss having the hall, stairs and landing decorated,' Marion announced on Monday. 'So don't leave the table, either of you.'

'No, miss.' Charles winked at me. 'Shall I take the minutes?' he asked with mock seriousness. 'And may I suggest that Pearl chairs the meeting?'

'This isn't a joke, Charles,' Marion chided. 'The three of us live in this house together, and it's only right and proper that we come to a decision regarding what is to be done that will suit us all. It's called democracy,' she finished primly.

Charles could hardly contain his amusement. At least once a year Marion would call what he referred to a 'board meeting' to discuss the decoration she had planned. Her mind was already made up, but Charles and I were allowed to put forward suggestions, which would then be so politely and tactfully rejected that we weren't aware it was happening and could end up thinking we'd had our own way. At least, that's what used to happen, but these days we were wise to Marion's manipulative ways and regarded the whole procedure as an entertaining charade.

The discussion always took place while we were seated at the table, not in armchairs; perhaps Marion thought this added gravitas to the occasion. Tonight, as soon as the meal was over, she produced a shorthand notebook and a pencil, and announced she was open to suggestions.

'Brown and cream,' Charles said immediately. 'Brown at the bottom and cream at the top with a narrow border in between.'

'And what colour would the border be?' Marion enquired.

'Why, a mixture of brown and cream, dear.'

Marion gave him a sharp look, but his face was completely straight. 'What about you, Pearl?'

'I'd quite like brown and cream, too.'

'Mmm.' Marion made notes. 'I quite like that colour combination. Would either of you mind if we got a pinkish cream and a reddish brown?'

'No,' Charles and I said together. It appeared the matter was going to take less time than usual.

'I wonder,' Marion said thoughtfully, 'what you think of the idea of having *two* borders – a wide one between the colours and a narrow one adjacent to the ceiling? We could get them in cream and brown as Charles suggested.'

'Or pinkish cream and reddish brown. That would look even better, dear.'

Marion frowned. 'Are you making fun of me, Charles Curran?'

'As if I would, dear.'

The telephone rang and Marion went to answer it.

Charles said, 'She knows I'm making fun, and she knows that I know that she knows I'm making fun, but neither of us minds.'

'Am I in the way?' I asked, taking even myself by surprise, but it had suddenly occurred to me that my aunt and uncle might have even more fun if they had the house to themselves.

Charles's jaw dropped. 'What a silly question, Pearl! Of course you're not in the way. You've blessed our lives. I don't know what Marion and I would have done without you.'

'Did you want children of your own?'

'Of course we did, but it just didn't happen.' Charles shrugged. 'But even if we'd had children, we would still have wanted you.' He smiled at me tenderly. 'You were a real little charmer, and you still are, though not so little now. We both loved you long before the accident.' He always referred to my father's death as 'the accident'. He squeezed my hand. 'What's brought this on, eh?'

'I was wondering if I'd outstayed my welcome,' I said in a small voice. 'I'm twenty-five. By now, most women are married. You and Marion could be having a better time without me.'

'That's ridiculous,' Charles said warmly. 'Most people never want their children to leave – and that's how we think of you, as ours. What we would like more than anything is for you to stay and look after Marion and me in our old age: give us our medicine and wipe our chins.'

I laughed, feeling relieved. 'At the rate I'm going, I probably will.'

'If it comes to the stage where we can't wipe our own bottoms, then you must put us in a home.'

Marion came in. 'That was Harry Patterson on the phone. He's invited us to dinner on Wednesday. He wanted to know if we all liked Chinese food and I said we did. It seems there's a new restaurant in Bold Street. Is everyone happy with that? I can always ring him back if you have other plans.'

'It suits me fine,' Charles said.

'Me too.' Trish was getting married next week. Once she'd gone, I was most unlikely to have 'other plans' apart from parents' evenings and various school events. It really was time I seriously considered what to do with the rest of my life, otherwise I *would* end up looking after Charles and Marion in their old age, though I balked at the idea of having to wipe their bottoms.

Harry Patterson had never married. I visualized him having met a girl during the war who had been killed or had married someone else. Like his brother, Barney, Harry had joined the Army and been sent to France. The brothers had belonged to different regiments and Harry had never become an officer, but they had actually met on the road to Dunkirk when they'd passed each other, Harry on his way towards the boats that were taking the fleeing troops back to England, and my father returning to hold the enemy at bay while his comrades, including his brother, got away on one of the flotilla of boats that had come to rescue them.

'At the time, I thought I'd never see your dad again,' Harry told me when I was about fourteen and suddenly found myself with loads of unanswered questions.

'But you did, didn't you?' I asked anxiously, as if Harry could change history by denying it. I tried to imagine my youthful father bravely pushing his way back through the departing troops. Did he feel lonely all on his own? It was years later before it struck me that he hadn't fought a lone battle, that he would have other soldiers with him.

'Of course. Your dad came back safe and sound, but it was a long time after me, not until the war was over.'

'And you were with him when you met my mum?'

'Yes, Pearl, we met your mum on Southport pier – and Aunt Cathy. Do you call her Aunt Cathy?'

'Auntie Cathy.' Cathy, Miss Burns – nowadays I didn't know what to call her – had always come to my birthday parties along with Grandma Curran, who was my mother's mother. She was really sweet, and one of the few people in the world that Marion liked. My other grandma only sent a card and a postal order. Marion said she was an 'evil old hag'. I think it was the only thing on which Marion and my mother agreed.

Both grandmas had died in 1960 within a few months of each other, leaving me with a grandpa I only saw a few times a year, two uncles and an aunt. I didn't count the two aunts I could hardly remember, Jacky and Biddy, who'd gone to Canada after my mother's trial, or the five Canadian cousins I'd never even seen. I would have loved to have had more relatives of my own age, but the ones I had were all that God had intended, and I would just have to put up with it.

Uncle Harry was already in the restaurant when we arrived. He was fifty-four, a distinguished-looking man with brown eyes, and dark hair sprinkled with grey. He worked for the medical instrument company that belonged to his father, Leo Patterson.

'Hello, there.' He seemed delighted to see us, kissing Marion and me, and shaking hands with Charles. He wore a charcoal-grey suit with the very palest of blue shirts and a navy-blue tie with a gold crest. Marion said his ties were pure silk and his suits hand-tailored, although I was unable to tell. 'You're all looking very fit,' he said.

'I could say the same for you, Harry,' Charles said jovially. The two men got on well together. 'Have you just had a holiday?'

'A fortnight in Morocco,' Harry replied. His face was brown from the sun. 'Pa's making plans to go to Paris soon; says he feels like a break. He won't leave the company in anyone else's hands but mine.' This was said with childish pride.

'It's not like Leo to take a holiday. How old is he now?'

'An extremely healthy seventy-five. He and my mother were barely out of their teens when they got married. I can't help but wonder what he intends getting up to in Paris,' he said with an amused twinkle. 'By the way, has anyone heard from Amy?'

'Not a word,' Charles replied. 'We have no idea where she is.'

There followed a discussion as to where my mother could be and who had collected her from prison, to which neither Marion nor I contributed a word.

'I had a reporter call me the other day,' Harry said self-importantly. I suspected he had a gigantic inferiority complex, what with a hugely successful father and a brother who'd been superior to him in every possible way (or so I'd been given to understand). 'I professed total ignorance as to Amy's whereabouts, which is true, and told him that so far as I knew, all her relatives lived abroad, I knew not where.'

The waiter came with the menus and there was silence for a few minutes while we chose the food. I wasn't an adventurous eater. I ordered curried prawns and rice, while the others ordered a whole range of exotic dishes to share.

Fifteen minutes later, the table was groaning with food. On top of my own meal, I was encouraged to try a bit of this or a slice of that until I began to feel sick. They probably didn't realize, but they were fussing over me as if I were a small child, paying me far too much attention. I couldn't wait to get home and feel grown-up again. I wondered if I was destined to go to dinner with old people for the rest of my life.

On Thursday, Trish and I went to see Robert Mitchum in *Ryan's Daughter*. It was too long and neither of us enjoyed it much. Trish was off to London the next day for the second weekend in a row. She'd been dismayed by the high rents charged in the capital. 'Even a bedsit with a shared kitchen and bathroom can be as much as fifteen pounds a week,' she told me. 'This time I shall search further afield.'

We were in a pub in Whitechapel drinking shandy. Trish was small, plump and cuddly with feathery blonde hair and a little snub nose. She looked at me fondly. 'Gosh, Pearl, I'll miss you when I go.'

'And I'll miss *you*,' I assured her. What would I do on Saturday, for instance? I'd better think of something before Charles and Marion and arranged another meal.

Trish said sadly, 'There's a place I would have loved to have gone before I left Liverpool for ever, and that's the Cavern. There was a time when we virtually lived there, but we haven't been for ages. Now there isn't time before the wedding.'

'You're not leaving Liverpool for ever,' I said comfortingly. 'Anyroad, it's different sort of music in the Cavern. These days, it's more heavy metal than rock 'n' roll.'

Trish grimaced. 'It frightens me that I'm leaving so much behind. London is so big and impersonal compared to Liverpool.'

'You'll soon get used to it.'

*That's* where I could go on Saturday: the Cavern. It was the sort of place where no one would notice if you were by yourself.

On Saturday night at half past eight, I stood outside the Cavern club in Mathew Street, wearing my black flared trousers and a white polo-necked sweater. I'd never heard of the groups that were playing: Mushroom and Confucius. Now that I was there, I wasn't sure if I could bring myself to go in. A few men had entered by themselves, but not a single woman went in on her own. They all looked much younger than me, still in their teens. I wasn't much good at communicating with strangers. If someone spoke to me, I'd be stuck for words. If no one spoke, the chances were I'd sit there all night without so much as opening my mouth, which didn't exactly appeal.

The first time I'd come to the Cavern had been with a crowd of girls from school. We were only fourteen, four years before I met Trish.

No, I wouldn't go in. I'd go home instead. But I couldn't do that – it wasn't all that long since I'd left. Charles and Marion would be watching television and I'd told them I was going out with one of the teachers from school – 'Hilda Dooley,' I'd lied when Marion had asked the teacher's name.

The pictures. I'd go to the pictures. It didn't matter what I saw or if I missed some of the film. It was just somewhere to sit until it was time to go home and say I'd been to the Cavern. If necessary, I'd say I was going to the Cavern every Saturday for the rest of my life, rather than have my aunt and uncle take me to dinner in order to get their twenty-five-year-old niece out of the house.

I turned on my heel and collided with a man in a suede jacket, check shirt and jeans. 'Fancy meeting you here,' he said.

'Hello,' I stammered. It was Rob Finnegan, Gary's dad. 'What are you doing here?' It was a stupid question. Why else would he have come except to listen to Mushroom and Confucius?

'My sister, Bess, and her boyfriend decided to have a night in. They're babysitting Gary, so I thought I'd go out for a change. Saturday is the only night I have off from the Post Office.' He looked affectionately at the grimy, run-down building. 'I haven't been here for years.'

'Neither have I.'

'Are you going in?'

'No.' I shook my head as if going in had been the last thing on my mind. 'I've just been to the pictures with a friend and thought I'd walk down Mathew Street on my way to the car park to see what the place looks like.' I hoped he wouldn't ask what picture I'd seen.

'It looks pretty much the same to me.'

'And me.'

A crowd of boys came down the street kicking a tin can to each other. They went into the club.

Rob said, 'They look like kids. All of a sudden I feel desperately old.'

There was a short silence. I wondered if it was time I announced I was going home, though felt strangely reluctant. Rob stuffed his hands in his pockets and jiggled back and forth on his heels. 'It's only half eight. Do you fancy a coffee?'

I was about to refuse, but that would have been another lie, as I really did fancy having a coffee with him, not because it was *him*, Rob Finnegan, but because he was another human being and I didn't want to be alone.

'Yes, please,' I said stiffly. 'I'd love a coffee.'

'I could never get used to the heat in Uganda,' he said. 'I would have come back before, but Gary loved it there. We lived in a detached bungalow – there were about twenty altogether, all occupied by Brits. We had a communal pool and a nursery for the kids, so I didn't have to worry about having him looked after when I went to work.'

'What made you decide to go there in the first place?' I asked.

'After Jenny died, I felt the need to get away from familiar surroundings, and I thought it might help Gary get over it. He was only two, but he really missed his mum. Trouble is,' he said with a shrug, 'we're pretty short of relatives. Jenny's folks are dead and so is my dad. My mother married again, but I've never got on with my stepdad.'

'And did Uganda help Gary get over it?'

'Yes, it did. And it helped me, too, despite the heat.'

I leaned back to allow the waitress to remove my empty mug, which was big enough to hold at least half a pint of coffee. Rob ordered two more. The basement café was only a few hundred yards away from the Cavern. It had the same rough brick walls and musty smell and was called Le Beats, an anagram of Beatles. We'd been there nearly two hours. Rob was easy to talk to. We'd discussed music and films, and shared our memories of the Cavern, after which he'd told me about life in Uganda.

'How is Gary settling in at school?' he asked now.

'He's a bit shy,' I admitted. 'It didn't help that he came after the start of the second term when all the children already knew each other and had made friends.'

'When I ask if he likes school, he goes very quiet.' His eyes clouded with concern. 'Is he being bullied?'

'Not in the classroom. I'm afraid I don't know what goes on in the playground.' I'd find out on Monday. 'I hope you don't mind my mentioning this,' I said hesitantly, 'but would you please ask your sister to leave him outside the school gates? She brings him as far as the classroom, and it makes the other boys think he's a cissy.'

'I'll speak to Bess about it,' he promised.

'Who picks him up after school?' I asked.

'I do, except on the occasions I have a job interview, when the lady next door does it for me.'

'It must be difficult fitting everything in,' I remarked.

'Extremely difficult.' He rolled his eyes. 'I don't suppose Gary's much good at games?'

'Not really.'

'Even when he was tiny, Jenny used to say he had two left feet. He was always tripping over himself.' He smiled wryly. 'I don't like to boast, but I was a star at games at school. In Uganda, I captained the police football team. The Brits had a league, and our team was always top. Thank you,' he said when the waitress brought our drinks.

'I won't sleep tonight,' I murmured. 'All this coffee!'

Rob put sugar in his and stirred it. 'Do you like being a teacher?' he asked.

'I love it,' I said fervently. 'I love children, but ...' I paused.

'But what?'

'I don't really know. I think I should be doing more, like teaching in a Third World country.' I was putting vague thoughts I'd recently had into words. In some places, education was in short supply and considered very precious. Would I feel happier if I was teaching deprived children in makeshift classrooms or even outdoors?

'There's a guy I knew in Uganda who's trying to fix me up with a job in Canada,' Rob said. 'Mind you, I wouldn't mind going back to Africa despite the heat. The pay's much better and you don't have to worry about accommodation. That's probably a hard-nosed way of looking at it, but my main concern in life is making sure Gary's happy.'

'Me, I'll think about it,' I said.

\*

That night, I dreamt about my father. It often happened, but I could never remember what he looked like when I woke up. I could recall parts of the dream, but not his face: he always seemed to be turned away, standing behind me, or in another room. His voice was muffled and slow.

The dream took place in the bungalow by Sefton Park where we were living when my father had his 'accident'. It had been late afternoon and must have been winter, as it was dark outside yet it wasn't time for bed.

I was lying on my stomach on the living-room floor in front of the coal fire, and drawing a face with a black crayon on a large pad. In the kitchen, my mother and father were arguing, shouting at each other. None of it made sense. It was something to do with the roof. Someone was stealing the tiles. Mum wanted Dad to tie them down.

'You don't tie down tiles, Amy.'

'I'll buy some ribbon tomorrow. Shall I get pink or blue?'

I listened for a few seconds then returned to my drawing. To my surprise, there was a bloodstain on the pad. It had fallen on the face's mouth. I raised my head to see where it had come from. Nowhere, it seemed, but when I looked back, there was another red stain bigger than the first, blotting out the face's eyes.

'Would you prefer yellow ribbon?' my mother asked.

'I told you: you can't tie down tiles. They have to be nailed.'

There was more blood on my pad. I sat back on my heels and watched the red spots fall until the entire page was soaked in blood. I began to scream.

'Is that you, Pearl?' my father shouted.

'I'm frightened, Dad!' I screamed.

'I'm coming, Scrap.'

But he didn't come. I could hear him racing around the house, opening doors, shouting my name, but he never came into *my* room. I became more and more frightened. I realized he couldn't find me because we were in different houses, but that only terrified me more because he sounded so near. There was a hardly discernible crackling in the air that made the hairs on my neck stand on end. I shivered.

I was still shivering when I woke up, and felt unnaturally cold. The dream was perfectly clear and fresh in my mind. I'd forgotten my father had called me Scrap. I wondered why.

Downstairs, I heard the sound of water running. Marion or Charles was putting the kettle on for the first cup of tea of the day. I got out of bed, drew back the curtains and breathed a sigh of relief. It was morning. Weak sunlight shone on the roofs of the houses and the sky was a watery grey. There was even someone up; the old man who lived a few houses away was pottering about in his greenhouse. Marion knew his wife and she said he couldn't sleep.

I threw on my dressing gown and went downstairs.

# Chapter 6

## October 1939
## Amy

Barney had been in Surrey for a month when he was allowed five days' leave. For most of the time, he and Amy hardly left the flat, just sat and talked about what they would do when the war was over. He wanted to do something more exciting than work for his father. He seemed a bit down and confessed he regretted having been in such a hurry to volunteer.

'I miss you so much, Amy,' he said miserably. Even the fact that he was being sent on an officer training course didn't cheer him. 'The uniform's more comfortable than for other ranks, but that's about all,' he sighed.

He asked if they could visit her mother. They went one night to find Mam over the moon having discovered she could get a job in a factory for an unbelievable four pounds, ten shillings a week.

'It's working on a big machine called a lathe,' she said vaguely. 'I'm going for an interview next week. It's in some place not far from the Philharmonic Hall.'

Jacky and Biddy stopped staring adoringly at their brother-in-law for a minute to announce their intention of joining the Women's Air Force, but Amy told the pair of them not to be so daft. 'You're much too young,' she said.

Amy had already been to see Charlie and Marion's new house in Aintree with its modern kitchen and lovely big rooms. She described it to Barney and they began to design their own house, the one they would live in when their lives returned to normal, actually drawing it on paper and making a list of the colours for each room. They discussed what sort of furniture they would buy and the flowers they would plant in the garden. Now they were applying the finishing touches, choosing the ornaments, the crockery, the cutlery, the front door.

'I'd like one with a stained-glass window,' Amy mused.

'Then a stained-glass window you shall have,' Barney said generously. 'Two, if you prefer.'

'One will do, and I'd want it varnished, not painted – the door, that is, not the window.'

'Your wish is my command, madam. And where will it be, this house of ours?' he asked.

'Anywhere,' Amy said simply. 'Anywhere in the world. As long as I'm with you, I don't care.'

As before, Barney left in the middle of the night without saying goodbye. This time, Amy only pretended to be asleep. After the door had closed, she got up and knelt on the floor by the window in the lounge where they watched the sun set, and rested her arms on the sill. She barely heard him go down the stairs. Then, in the moonlight, she saw his tall, lonely figure pass like a ghost along the road until it was swallowed up in the black shadows of the house next door.

Not long afterwards, she heard a car start. Had he ordered a taxi? she wondered. Or arranged for Harry to pick him up?

What did it matter? What did anything matter now that he had gone?

Amy had been buying the *Liverpool Echo* for weeks to see what jobs were available when she realized she might be pregnant. She'd missed a period, which happened sometimes, but now the next one was late. She sat down with a calendar on her knee and counted the days: it was nine weeks and a day since her last period.

How did she feel about having a baby? Pleased. *Really* pleased. She looked at herself in the long mirror on the wardrobe. Her stomach looked as flat as a pancake, but she was unlikely to show when she was barely a couple of months gone.

'I'll write to Barney and let him know,' she said aloud. She fetched the writing pad, but changed her mind before the letter was even started. She wouldn't tell him until it had been confirmed. Women in Mam's part of Bootle consulted Mrs O'Dwyer, who lived in Coral Street, about their 'personal' problems, but Amy reckoned Barney would sooner she saw a proper doctor. He'd actually mentioned a doctor once. He was a family friend, but she couldn't remember his name.

She put the pad to one side and went to kneel by the window, something she'd been doing a lot since Barney had gone away for the second time. She didn't want to miss seeing him if he paid a surprise visit home.

Had she got the nerve to go and see Mrs Patterson to ask the name of the family doctor? The woman was her mother-in-law, after all. Her son was the father of the baby Amy was almost certainly carrying. He or she would be her first grandchild. Surely she wouldn't turn her away. There was a good chance that Barney had exaggerated about his mother. She understood her not liking Catholics – a lot of people Amy knew couldn't stand Protestants – but surely that sort of prejudice didn't apply to your own flesh and blood, to your *grandchildren?*

'I won't go today,' Amy said aloud. 'I'll give it six more days, when I'll be ten weeks late, and I'll go then.' She'd also wait to tell her own mam until she knew for certain that she was pregnant. Mam would be desperately excited, and Amy didn't want her disappointed if it weren't true.

Six days later, she lay in the bath and drew circles on her stomach with her finger. It didn't look quite so flat today. There was a slight bulge in the middle and she imagined a tiny, perfect baby curled up inside. It might even have its tiny hands pressed together and be using them as a pillow or be sucking its thumb.

'Hello, baby,' she whispered. She imagined her baby smiling back and whispering, 'Hello, Mammy.'

As soon as she'd had her bath, she'd go and see Mrs Patterson. She climbed out, dried herself and looked through the wardrobe for something nice to wear. She chose the blue dress that Barney liked best and a short, off-white jacket.

He'd once driven her to Calderstones, shown her the dead posh road and house where his family lived, but she had no idea how to get there on her own. As far as she knew, it wasn't the sort of place that you could catch a tram to. There was nothing for it: she'd have to take a taxi, something else that, like wearing silk stockings, she'd never imagined doing. She telephoned and requested a taxi in ten minutes' time. While she was waiting, she made a cup of strong tea to steady her nerves.

Less than half an hour later, Amy climbed out of the taxi outside the Pattersons' house. It looked hundreds of years old, but Barney said it had only been built just before the Great War, using old bricks and beams from a genuine Tudor mansion in Chester that had been demolished. The man the Pattersons had bought it from was an industrialist who'd been honoured with a knighthood and gone to live in London.

Amy approached the front door – there were *two*, shaped like an arch. She pulled the bell that dangled by the side. As the taxi drove away, she wondered if she should have asked the driver to wait until she'd made sure there was someone in.

A woman opened one half of the door. She was plump and cheerful-looking, and wore a dark-green overall.

'Mrs Patterson?' Amy asked hopefully.

'No, luv, she's upstairs. I'll give her a shout, shall I? Who will I say it is?'

'Amy. Amy Patterson. I'm her daughter-in-law.'

The woman's smile faded. After a minute's hesitation, as if she wasn't sure what to do, she invited Amy inside and asked her to wait in the hall. She went upstairs, having decided for some reason not to give her employer a shout.

She reappeared almost straight away and said, 'Mrs Patterson will be with you in a minute.' She gave Amy a look that she couldn't quite define – it might have been pitying or it might not – and went to the back of the house. Somewhere, a door closed, and the sound was followed by a silence that lasted for an unnaturally long time, broken only by the loud ticking of the grandfather clock in the hall.

Quite out of the blue, Amy felt a painful, dragging sensation in her stomach, as if she were about to have a very heavy period. She shifted uncomfortably from foot to foot. Apart from the ticking clock, the hall contained a little table with a telephone on top and a glass-fronted cabinet full of ornaments, but nowhere to sit. She badly wanted to sit down.

There was another sound, as if someone had trodden on a creaking stair. When she looked up, Amy saw a woman standing at the top of the stairs staring down at her. How long had she been there?

The woman, aware that she'd been spotted, began to descend the stairs slowly, her hand clutching the banister so tightly that the knuckles shone white. Amy got the impression she didn't need the banister's support, but that it was absorbing all the pent-up strain and anger in her body. She knew then that she shouldn't have come. She'd made a really big mistake.

She hadn't even tried to think what Barney's mother would be like, but hadn't expected her to look quite so young or be quite so lovely. She wore a black velvet gown that buttoned down the front and black velvet mules with high heels and a diamanté buckle on the toes. Her hair was a glorious red, very long, and fell over her narrow shoulders in deep, natural waves. With her perfect bone structure and flawless skin, Mrs Patterson could have been a film star if it hadn't been for the expression in her dark-green eyes: as she got closer Amy could see that she wasn't quite sane.

'Yes?' she drawled when she reached the bottom of the stairs. She managed to put a great deal of feeling into the one-syllable word. Amy was left in no doubt that she wasn't welcome in her mother-in-law's house.

But she was determined not to be intimidated. 'I'm Barney's wife,' she said, tossing her head. 'I came to tell you I'm expecting a baby, but I won't stop. I can tell I'm not wanted. Tara.'

She opened the door and was about to leave, when a beautifully manicured hand was laid on her arm. 'You're right: you're not wanted. I never want to see you in this house again. My son was crazy to marry you. And how can he be sure the baby is his? It could be anybody's.' The harsh voice with its broad Irish accent was close to her ear. 'Catholic whore,' Mrs Patterson hissed.

Amy fled. The woman was genuinely mad. She stumbled down the path, cursing herself for letting the taxi go.

It was a long walk to the end of the road, where she prayed she'd find a tram or a bus that would take her home. The dragging sensation in her stomach had become stronger and more painful. If only she were in Bootle, a place she knew like the back of her hand, rather than the south side of Liverpool, which she hardly knew at all.

She came to a road called Menlove Avenue that had tramlines running down the middle and asked a woman how to get to Newsham Park. 'There's a tram coming along now, luv. Get off at Lodge Lane and ask someone to put you on to the one to Sheil Road,' she was told. 'I can't remember the number. Do you feel all right, girl?' the woman added worriedly. 'You don't look a bit well.'

'I just need to sit down.' It didn't help that she was freezing; the autumn day had turned cold. As soon as she got home, she'd make a cup of tea and go to bed. The tram came to a stop and she scrambled on.

She badly wanted her mam, but this week her mother was on the afternoon shift at the factory and wouldn't be home until nearly eleven. But the person she wanted most was Cathy. She could tell Cathy things that she couldn't tell Mam. Mam must never know about Mrs Patterson, but Cathy could well make a joke about it and they'd end up laughing. She realized she hadn't seen her friend since before the war began. Somewhere in the flat was the ivory lace blouse she'd bought in London and hadn't got round to giving her.

The conductor shouted, 'Lodge Lane,' so Amy got off and boarded another tram to Sheil Road via Newsham Park. After she'd got home, had the tea and was in bed, she'd have a really good cry with her head buried underneath the clothes so no one could hear. She hoped Barney would never find out she'd been to see his mother and the horrible way she'd behaved. He wouldn't say, 'Serve you right, darling,' or anything like that, but he would think it.

At last she was unlocking the door of the house, praying Captain

Kirby-Greene wouldn't emerge from his flat and want to engage in conversation. Fortunately, he must have been out, so Amy managed to reach her own flat without interruption, though her footsteps got slower and slower, and, by the time she reached the final flight of stairs, she found it hard to drag one foot after the other. She already had a horrible suspicion what might be happening, but was trying not to think about it.

After forcing her wobbly legs to carry her across the threshold of the flat, she almost fell on to the leather settee, laid her head on the arm and instantly fell asleep. She dreamed a ginger cat with green eyes was scratching her. The cat was hissing loudly, and angrily flicking its tail as it circled around her. A furry paw shot out and scratched her leg, tearing her stockings, drawing blood. Then it leapt upon her knee and began to scratch her arms, long painful scratches that stung and left little bubbles of blood.

It was trying to get at her face, her eyes, when Amy woke. But it wasn't the cat that had woken her, but the pain in her stomach, a monstrous, agonizing pain that was wrenching at her guts. She screamed and tried to stand, but instead slid off the settee on to the floor where she blessedly fainted.

'Amy, Amy!'

Amy shook her head. Her cheeks were being slapped, only softly and it didn't hurt in the least, but she found it irritating.

'Amy, open your eyes, there's a good girl.' More slapping, a bit harder now.

So Amy opened her eyes and saw a strange man bending over her about to slap her again. She was lying on her bed and he was sitting on the edge of it.

'Ah, so there you are,' he said jovially. 'Welcome back to the human race.'

'Who are you?' she croaked. He was a stout individual with a very red face, kind eyes and a mass of white hair. She felt more surprised than frightened.

'I'm Doctor Sheard. How do you feel, dear?'

'All right, I think.' The pain had gone and she felt empty and washed out, as if her entire body had been fed through a mangle.

'I'm very much afraid you've lost your baby,' he said gently. 'You've just had a miscarriage.'

Tears began to pour down her cheeks, so quickly that they must have been waiting behind her eyes ready to fall. 'Was it a boy or a girl?' In her heart of hearts she'd suspected she was losing the baby.

'It was too early to tell, dear.' Her shoulder was gently squeezed.

She tried to push herself into a sitting position, but didn't have the energy. 'How did you get here? I mean, how did you know I needed a doctor?' She remembered screaming. Perhaps someone in the house had heard and called him. What had happened to the baby? She decided she didn't want to know.

'Leo found you,' Doctor Sheard said. 'He telephoned and I came straight away.'

'Leo?' She didn't know anyone called Leo.

'Leo Patterson, Barney's father.'

Had he come to repeat his wife's demand that she never darken their door again? 'Where is he?'

'In the other room, making a drink.' He raised his head and bellowed. 'Is that tea ready yet, old chap?'

'It won't be a minute.' At least Mr Patterson had a nice, pleasant voice, unlike his wife, and his Irish accent wasn't as broad as hers.

'I'll not be staying for a drink,' the doctor said. 'It's time I went home, had my tea and got ready for evening surgery. But before I go I'd like you to take these.' He helped her sit up and picked up two tablets off the bedside cabinet. 'Open.' Amy dutifully opened her mouth and he popped the tablets inside, then handed her a glass of water. 'How does your tummy feel?'

'Numb,' she replied.

'It could well start hurting later. I've left two more tablets for you to take before you go to sleep.'

'Thank you.'

He got to his feet, picked up a shabby, black leather bag and made for the door, where he paused. 'You'll probably feel as right as rain by tomorrow, but give me a call if there's anything wrong. Here's my card.' He came back and put a white card on the table beside the tablets. 'I'm sorry about the baby, dear, but you're a healthy young woman and there'll be plenty of time to start a family once Barney comes home. Goodbye.'

'Tara, doctor,' she murmured.

'Are you off now, Bob?' the pleasant voice enquired. It was just like Barney's, she thought.

'That's right. The patient will be fine after a good night's sleep. Try to make her stay in bed if you can manage it. Bye, old chap. See you soon.'

The front door closed at the same time as the bedroom door opened and Leo Patterson came in. Just as she hadn't expected Barney's mother to look so young, she hadn't expected his father to be so much like him. Leo was an older version of his youngest son: the same height, the same dark brown hair, if a little shorter, the same lovely brown eyes. His face was harder and there were tiny wrinkles around his eyes, but it made Amy feel peculiar, as if a quarter of a century had passed and she was seeing her husband as he would be in the future.

'Hello,' he said, smiling warmly. 'I'm sorry about what happened. What do you think brought it on?'

The smile came as a relief: at least he was going to be nice to her. 'I don't know,' she said.

His brown creased in an angry frown. 'Was it Elizabeth's fault? Did she upset you?'

So Barney's mother was called Elizabeth. It was one of Amy's favourite names. 'She did upset me – what she said would have upset anyone – but I had the pains before I met her.'

Nevertheless, it might have helped had she been asked to sit down. And if a doctor had been called straight away, there was a chance the baby might have been saved.

'That's good – well, no, it isn't good.' He flushed slightly at his lack of tact. 'But you know what I mean. Elizabeth would never have forgiven herself if she'd been responsible for the loss of your baby – our first grandchild.'

Amy didn't believe Elizabeth would have given a damn.

'Have you been eating properly? You look desperately thin.'

She hadn't been eating properly. She'd been doing what she'd done when Barney went away the first time – having nothing to eat except jam butties washed down with gallons of tea, while lying in bed listening to music. 'I've been eating fine,' she lied. She doubted if too many jam butties would cause a miscarriage. Once again her eyes filled with tears at the enormity of what had taken place that afternoon: she'd lost the little human being who'd been asleep in her tummy.

'Don't tell Barney about the baby,' she sniffed. 'I was going to tell him when it had been confirmed.' She swallowed hard, not wanting Barney's father to see her cry.

'Indeed I won't, Amy. Look, I've made some tea. Do you take sugar?'

'Two teaspoons, please.' She'd like to bet it wasn't often he made anyone a cup of tea: he looked far too important.

'If I were you, I'd try getting used to having it without sugar. They say it's going to be rationed soon.'

He disappeared. It was only then that Amy realized she was wearing a nightie. Who had removed her clothes? She prayed it was Dr Sheard, not Leo. And someone had carried her into the bedroom. Had there been a mess in the living room where she'd had the miscarriage? Best not to think about it. It was too embarrassing for words.

'How did you get in?' she asked when the cause of her embarrassment returned with two cups of tea on a tray. Was she supposed to call him Leo or Mr Patterson?

'You left the door ajar.' He put the tray on the floor, gave her one of the teas, and seated himself on the little embroidered stool by the dressing table where Barney often sat and watched her dress.

'Mrs Aspell – she's our housekeeper – phoned me at work, told me that you'd called and what Elizabeth had said. She thought I should know what had gone on. I came round straight away. I was worried you'd think I felt the same as Elizabeth.' He shrugged and eyed her keenly. 'You probably think she's crazy, but she has a good reason for hating Catholics. She was fifteen when the car her mother was driving was blown up by a Fenian bomb. Her little brother, Piers, was in the back. Both were killed outright. It was a mistake. Her father was the real target. He was in the Royal Irish Constabulary.'

'That's desperately sad,' Amy said bluntly, 'but it's no reason to hate *me*. It wasn't *me* that blew up the car. It's dead silly to hate all Catholics because of that.'

He blinked. Her bluntness had surprised him. 'Unless you'd lost your own mother and brother that way, you wouldn't know how a person would feel.'

But Amy wasn't prepared to mince her words. She considered her mother-in-law an out-and-out bitch. 'I *know* I wouldn't speak to someone the way your wife spoke to me,' she said, adding as a way of changing the subject, 'Thank you for helping me.'

'Well, it's about time we met, isn't it? I just wish it had been under different circumstances. I've been meaning to come and see you, but ... well, you'll understand that it was a bit difficult for me. I kept putting it off.'

Amy took this to mean his wife wouldn't have approved. 'Will you tell Mrs Patterson that you've been to see me?' she asked.

'No,' he said abruptly.

She was about to tell him to get home quick or she'd have his guts for garters, but it wouldn't do to be offensive. Anyway, he didn't look the sort of man who'd take much nonsense from a woman, even if she were his wife. He'd probably found it 'difficult' because he didn't want to hurt her or have a row.

He got to his feet. 'I'll come again soon,' he said. 'I don't like the idea of you living here alone. Say if I hadn't come along today? What would have happened then?'

'I suppose I would have come to of me own accord and phoned for an ambulance.' She resented the idea that he found it necessary to watch over her.

'I'd like to keep an eye on you for Barney's sake. You're my daughter-in-law. It's a pity you couldn't come and live with us.'

Amy shuddered at the very idea of living under the same roof as Elizabeth Patterson. 'That would have been nice,' she said.

He grinned. He looked so much like Barney that her heart missed a beat. 'Are you being sarcastic or polite?' he asked.

'Polite.'

Now Amy was on her own. She couldn't get over the fact that the baby had been alive that morning, but was now dead. There'd been no time to think about a name, or where she would live when the baby was born – the top floor of a four-storey house was hardly practical.

Amy slid down the bed. All of a sudden she felt enormously tired. She fell asleep in an instant and when she woke up it was morning, the sun was shining and the trees in Newsham Park were full of twittering birds. She hadn't thought or remembered to take the tablets that Dr Sheard had left.

She remembered how cold it had been yesterday and realized that she didn't have a really warm coat – she'd married Barney in June and there hadn't been the need to buy one. Later on, she'd go into town and do some shopping, but first she had an overwhelming urge to go to Bootle and see her mam, though she wouldn't tell her about the baby because it would really upset her. Oh, and she'd take that blouse for Cathy and leave it with Mrs Burns along with a message asking Cathy to come and see her when she had the time. Cinemas had been allowed to open, and perhaps they could go to the pictures together, as they used to.

To Amy's astonishment, when she knocked at the door of the Burnses' house in Amethyst Street, it was Cathy who opened it.

'Hello, Amy,' she said brightly. 'Come on in. I've just finished packing.'

'Packing!' Amy felt even more astonished.

Cathy took her into the living room where a warm fire burned and the fireguard was draped with drying socks as well as an assortment of stockings and knickers, which poked through the wire mesh. The room ponged more than a bit. The girls sat on easy chairs on either side of the fireplace.

Cathy looked extremely pleased with herself. 'I've joined the Auxiliary Territorial Service: the A.T.S. Didn't your mam tell you? I thought you'd come to wish me tara. I'm off to Yorkshire first thing in the morning, to a place called Keighley.'

'You've had your hair cut!' Cathy's long, straight hair now

reached just below her ears. 'You suit a fringe,' Amy said. 'It makes your eyes look bigger.'

'Ta.' Cathy tossed her head. 'I didn't fancy one of those sausage roll hair-dos sticking out from under me cap. They're all the rage at the moment. Shall I make some tea?'

'Yes, please. What are you going to do in the A.T.S?' Amy shouted when Cathy went into the kitchen.

'I'm only going to be a clerk, but it'll be far more interesting than Woolies'. I might even get sent abroad. I'm really looking forward to it.'

'I bet you are,' Amy said enviously.

'What are you doing for the war effort?' Cathy stood in the doorway while she waited for the kettle to boil. 'You'll get bored stupid sitting in that flat all on your own – although your mam said it's really nice.'

'I've been looking round for something to do,' Amy said vaguely. 'I'd join the Forces like you, except I'd hardly ever see Barney.'

'You could always get a job in a factory like your mam,' Cathy suggested. 'Someone at work said single women and married women without children will be forced to go to work whether they want to or not. If I were you, Amy, I'd get meself a job while you've got the choice, otherwise you might get sent somewhere dead horrible.'

Maybe it was the words 'married women without children', that made Amy burst into tears.

Cathy gasped, 'What on earth's the matter, luv?' and knelt beside her, making Amy only cry more.

'I lost a baby yesterday,' she sobbed. 'I was ten weeks pregnant. And I went to see Barney's mam and she was so awful she made me flesh creep. She called me a Catholic whore.'

'*What?*' Cathy gasped. 'Jaysus, Mary and Joseph, Amy, what sort of a family have you married into? She sounds like a nut-case to me.'

'She is, she is, but Barney's dad's as nice as his wife is horrible. He's dead good-looking, too. And Harry's all right – well, you already know that.'

Cathy said sternly, 'You shouldn't be up and about when you

only had a miscarriage yesterday. I thought you looked a bit off colour when I opened the door. And have you no warmer clothes than that?' Amy was wearing the white jacket over a slightly thicker frock.

'I haven't got a winter coat. I was going to buy one this avvy. And I feel all right, Cathy, honest.' Actually, she didn't. Her legs were still a bit wobbly and she wanted to be sick.

'What happened to that nice dark-green coat you used to have?' Cathy asked. 'You got it from Paddy's Market at the same time as I got my navy-blue skirt. It looked in perfectly good condition the last time you wore it.'

'It's still at home – I mean, in our mam's house.' She'd forgotten for the moment that the house in Agate Street was no longer home. 'I left most of me old clothes behind when I moved,' she explained. 'I suppose that'll do until I get a new one.' On reflection, she didn't fancy going into town today. She'd be better off spending the afternoon in bed. 'I'll pick it up later when I see Mam. She's on afternoons this week: she must have gone to do a bit of shopping as she was out when I called.'

'Is that the only reason you came to see me, because your mam was out?' Cathy gave a dry smile. 'You just wanted somewhere to keep out of the cold until she came back.'

'Mam never leaves the back door locked, does she?' Amy wasn't sure whether to be indignant or bawl her head off. 'I could have easily waited inside if I'd wanted. And I didn't know you'd be home, did I? I thought you'd be at work, and I was going to leave this with your mam.'

'Leave what?'

Amy produced the Selfridges' carrier bag containing the blouse. 'I bought it in London, but I kept forgetting to give it you. I don't suppose it'll be of much use in the Forces.'

'Oh, Amy, it's lovely!' Cathy held up the blouse by the shoulders. 'I can take it with me. I don't have to wear uniform all the time.' Her face went pink and she looked as if she were about to cry herself. 'I'm sorry I said that about you only coming because your mam wasn't in.'

'It's me that should be sorry,' Amy said in a small voice. 'I was even more horrible, just dropping you like that when I met Barney. I couldn't think about anyone else but him, you see.'

'Do you still feel the same?'

'Yes, but he's not here any longer,' Amy said plaintively. 'I can think about him, but I can't *be* with him. I've got to find something else to do with me time, but all I do is lie in bed and eat jam butties.'

Cathy gave her a little hug and Amy knew they were friends again. 'I bet that kettle's boiled dry,' she said. 'I'd forgotten I was supposed to be making tea. Look, tonight we're all going for a drink at the Green Man on Marsh Lane – where your mam used to work. It's just to wish me luck. Why don't you come along if you feel up to it? The change might do you good, as they say.'

'I will,' Amy promised.

After a while she went back to Agate Street, by which time Mam had returned from the shops and was really pleased to see her, though remarked she was looking a bit peaky. More coal was added to the fire so Amy could sit in front of it with a big mug of cocoa. It was lovely being fussed over. She didn't mention the miscarriage. Cathy had promised not to breathe a word about it.

At one o'clock, Mam left for work and Amy went upstairs to look for her green coat. She found it in the wardrobe in Charlie's old room, took it out and hung it on a hanger behind the door. It looked perfectly respectable and would do until she found the energy to buy a new one.

Charlie's bed was made, and she couldn't resist lying down with the eiderdown wrapped around her. She spent the afternoon half asleep and half awake, and gave her sisters the fright of their lives when they returned from work together and they heard her coming downstairs. She was as pleased to see them as they were her.

After they'd shared the scouse Mam had left in a pan ready to be heated up, Amy had a good wash, put on the green coat and made her way back to Cathy's.

The Green Man had sawdust on the floor and a spittoon in the corner. An out-of-tune piano was being played by a man with his cap on back to front and a ciggie stuck to his bottom lip. Everyone was singing at the tops of their voices.

Amy realized she'd forgotten her roots. Bootle was the place where she had been born and raised, where she truly belonged, not in a big house by Newsham Park with a retired Royal Navy captain living on the ground floor. But she would keep on living in the big house because it was where she had spent the happiest days of her life with Barney: days that she would never forget if she lived to be a hundred. It was where she would be when Barney came home for good.

# Chapter 7

## May 1971
## Pearl

'I thought that picture was the gear,' Hilda Dooley said when we came out of the cinema. 'I wouldn't mind seeing it again some-time.'

I agreed. 'Neither would I.'

'Normally I don't like car chases, but that one was dead excit-ing.'

'It certainly was. Would you like a coffee?' I would have pre-ferred to go home. Hilda was getting on my nerves, but I'd known that would happen. I'd never liked her, but it was only fair that I see the evening out, not cut and run immediately after we'd seen the film: *The French Connection* with Gene Hackman.

'I'd *love* a coffee,' Hilda breathed. 'Where shall we go?'

'I know a place.' I led the way to Le Beats, the coffee bar by the Cavern where Rob Finnegan had taken me last Saturday. Now it was another Saturday and I'd taken pity on Hilda when she'd re-marked wistfully in the staffroom yesterday how much she fancied seeing *The French Connection*.

'I quite fancy it, too,' I said.

'Shall we go tomorrow?' Hilda had said eagerly.

'All right.' I knew I would come to regret my hasty suggestion, yet welcomed the idea of having a date, even if it was with a woman. I was taking pity on myself, not just Hilda. There was something about Saturday night that made me feel I *had* to have somewhere to go, that staying in put me down as a social failure. I *was* a social failure, but was trying to disguise the fact by going out with a woman I couldn't abide.

'It's nice here,' Hilda remarked when we were in Le Beats with its rough brick walls and the same musty smell as the Cavern. 'We could be somewhere like Paris. Have you ever been abroad, Pearl?'

'No. Have you?'

'I went to Spain once with me mam. It was awful hot, and Mam got food poisoning. She spent most of the time on the lavatory. We had a lousy time.' To my surprise, Hilda giggled, displaying huge, wet teeth. 'You've got to laugh, haven't you, else you'd only cry?' She dabbed her eyes as if she were about to cry now. 'How old were you when your mam passed away, Pearl?'

'Five,' I replied. 'I don't remember much about her,' I added quickly, hoping this would prevent her from asking more questions.

One of these days, I thought, I'm going to start telling people the truth. I wasn't ashamed of my mother. I wasn't about to shout from the rooftops that she was a murderer, but I wasn't prepared to continue lying either. I remembered Hilda saying that my mother should have hanged. On her own, she wasn't anything like as loud and pushy as she was at school.

'Perhaps one day we could go abroad together?' she said shyly.

'Perhaps.' I smiled vaguely. The idea horrified me. But what was I afraid of? Was it because being seen with someone as pathetic as Hilda was another sign of failure, of an inability to find friends my own age, let alone a man? Not that I wanted a man, I reminded myself. At least, I didn't think so.

'You still live with your aunt and uncle, don't you?' I nodded and Hilda continued. 'Don't you ever think about getting a place of your own?'

'I'm quite happy where I am.' Surely Hilda wasn't going to suggest we live together!

'I'd love to leave home,' Hilda said longingly. 'I'd love to live by meself, go out whenever I felt like it, make me own meals, that sort of thing. Me mam's a bit demanding.' She sniffed. 'Well, a lot demanding. She looks upon me as her best mate. She had a real go at me tonight for leaving her on her own, yet it's not as if she'd have wanted to see *The French Connection*. She only likes pictures that make her laugh.'

'I'm sorry,' I said, meaning it. 'Is she very old, your mother?'

'Only sixty and she's as healthy as a horse.' Hilda sniffed again.

'Seeing as your mother's capable of looking after herself, there's no reason why you shouldn't leave home,' I said encouragingly. All of a sudden, it seemed important for Hilda to get some happiness out of life. 'If you want, I'll help you find somewhere to live.'

'*Would* you?' Hilda looked delighted.

'I'll come with you to look at flats – I take it it's a flat you're after, not a house? I expect they're advertised in the *Echo*.'

'Well, yes. I sometimes read the adverts. I could easily afford to rent a flat: better still, I could buy one. I'll look in the paper on Monday. Mind you, Mam won't be very pleased. The last time I suggested leaving home she virtually exploded.'

'Hello,' said a voice. 'I had a feeling you'd be here.'

I looked up. Rob Finnegan was staring down at me. I was so pleased to see him that I blushed, then prayed it wasn't noticeable. Had he actually been looking for me? *I had a feeling you'd be here.* 'Sit down,' I said, then to Hilda, 'You don't mind, do you?'

'No,' Hilda said stiffly, clearly annoyed. Perhaps she thought I'd been expecting to meet Rob all along, that she'd been used in some way.

I hastily introduced them. 'Hilda, this is Rob Finnegan: his little boy, Gary, is in my class. We met in Owen Owen's a few weeks ago when Rob was buying Gary's uniform and again last week outside the Cavern.' Rob extended his hand. 'Hilda teaches class three at St Kentigern's,' I told him.

Hilda appeared mollified as the two shook hands. 'It's nice to meet you,' she said with a smile.

'Same here.' The smile was returned with genuine warmth.

Why, he's really nice, I thought. Tonight he wore jeans and a thick grey sweater over a navy-blue shirt, no jacket. 'I've just been to the Cavern,' he announced.

'Who was playing?' I asked.

'Kansas Hook and Perfumed Garden: they weren't exactly the

Beatles, but they were OK. Would you both like another coffee?' he asked.

'Yes, please,' I said promptly.

Hilda shook her head. 'No more coffee, thank you. I'll be off in a minute.'

'Are you sure?' Rob looked at his watch. 'It isn't quite ten o'clock. Ah, go on,' he said with another warm smile. 'Have a coffee.'

'All right.' Now Hilda was blushing. I think she was worried she'd be in the way.

Rob left to order the coffees. As soon as he was out of earshot, Hilda hissed, 'He's nice. Has he got a wife?'

'No. He's a widower.'

'He likes you, I can tell. Don't let him get away.'

I laughed. 'You make him sound like a wild animal I've managed to trap. I hardly know the man.' I didn't know if I was interested in Rob Finnegan or not. I'd been pleased to see him, yet didn't want to get involved.

He came back and said the waitress would bring the coffees in a minute. 'Where have you two been?' he asked.

I left it to Hilda to describe *The French Connection* as one of the best films she'd ever seen. Rob remarked he must see it one day soon. I asked where Gary was.

'Bess, my sister, stayed in – she has a cold – so I thought I'd have another Saturday night out on the town,' he explained.

We sat and talked for another half-hour until Hilda said she really would have to go. 'I'm later than I said I'd be. Mam'll be doing her nut.'

Rob walked with us to our cars. I was more than a bit irked when it turned out that mine was the first car we came to. I'd parked in St John's Market whereas Hilda was much further away in Mount Pleasant. It meant I was left behind while Rob and Hilda walked away together.

I'd been keeping an eye on Gary Finnegan when the children went out to play at lunchtime. As far as I could see, no one bothered him, but no one spoke to him, either. He seemed to hang around at the edge of things being ignored. He looked very downcast and stared longingly at the other boys, who were playing football or just standing round in little groups talking and pushing each other about.

The same thing happened at break-times, I assumed – I was unable to watch as I was usually in the classroom preparing for the next lesson – but I was shocked the following Monday when Gary came in after lunch and I saw that his lip was bleeding. I could tell he'd been crying.

I didn't say anything until the bell rang for going-home time, then I called, 'Gary Finnegan, will you stay behind, please?'

As soon as the other children had left, I went and sat in the chair next to his. 'What happened to your lip, Gary?' I asked.

He refused to meet my eyes. 'Nothing, miss.' He sniffed and looked as if he were about to cry again.

'Then why is it bleeding?' I asked softly. I gently patted his lip with a paper handkerchief.

'I don't know.' He looked up. 'Oh, miss, I don't half wish my mum hadn't drownded in Spain.' He dropped his head on his arms and began to cry.

I stroked his head. 'So do I, darling.' My heart went out to this gentle little boy who'd lost his mother. I'd ask Joan Flynn, who looked after the children in the mornings, to watch out for him in future. I longed to pick him up and nurse him on my knee, kiss him better, but it was against the rules for a teacher to become that involved with a pupil, and also very stupid. If the rest of the class noticed that Gary had become the teacher's pet, his life wouldn't be worth living. 'Who's picking you up after school today?' I asked.

'The lady upstairs is collecting me,' he whispered. 'My dad's gone to Manchester to buy a house.'

'Has he?' Rob hadn't said anything about looking for a house when we'd met on Saturday. 'Tomorrow, will you ask him to come and see me?'

'Yes, miss,' he said with a sigh. He stood and walked away, shoulders drooping, as if he had all the cares in the world on his young shoulders. When I'd been his age, my mother had been on trial for killing my father. Life can be unreasonably hard for some people, even when they are only five years old.

My mother's release from prison and subsequent disappearance had brought the people who'd known her together. Normally, Charles and Marion saw Catherine Burns once every few years; the same went for Harry Patterson, but now all four were meeting for dinner again on Saturday.

I was washing the dishes after tea and could hear Marion telling Charles that it wasn't up to him to pay the restaurant bill for the four of them.

'I'm not going to avoid it,' Charles replied heatedly. 'Harry paid last time, remember?'

'Yes, but he invited us, didn't he?' Marion argued. 'It's only right that he should pay. Why should we have to buy Cathy Burns another dinner?'

'She wanted to pay the night we went to Formby,' Charles pointed out.

'Yes, but she let you pay in the end.'

'Only because I insisted,' Charles snapped. I could tell he was about to lose his temper, something that happened only rarely. 'Honestly, Marion, it's not often we go out for a meal and I'm not going to sit there all night worrying about who will pay the bill. You'd think we were hard up or something.'

'We're not exactly made of money.'

'We're not poor, either.'

'Yes, but ...' The door closed. One of them must have realized I might be listening.

I felt tempted to creep into the hall and listen some more, but couldn't be bothered. Marion was always more conscious of money than Charles. She could be quite mean, whereas he was over-generous. That wasn't the only big difference between them. Sometimes, I wondered why they'd married each other.

I'd been invited to the dinner on Saturday, but had something more important to do. On Saturday Trish was getting married, and I was going to the wedding.

★

I was at the back of the crowded church. Fifty-eight guests had been invited, and about half that many children. The organist began to play 'Here Comes the Bride', we all stood up and Trish came in on her father's arm. I smiled at her, but she didn't see me, just sailed past looking beautiful and very nervous. At the top of the aisle, her fiancé, Ian, who I'd only met twice, was scratching his head, as if he were wondering what he'd done with the rings.

Although I could only see the people from behind, it dawned on me that, apart from the bridal couple, the only guests I knew were Trish's parents and her younger sister, Jane, who was married with two children. What's more, there didn't appear to be any other young women on their own. The day changed. I began to suspect I'd feel like a fish out of water.

I'd bought a new outfit: an off-white suit with a fitted jacket and an ankle-length flared skirt. My pillbox hat matched the suit, and my bag, shoes and gloves were rusty brown. When I'd left the house, I'd felt quite pleased with myself, but my smart new clothes now seemed over the top.

At the reception, people wanted to know who I was and which of the men there was my husband – 'Your boyfriend, then,' said one of Trish's widowed aunts after I told her I wasn't married. She seemed to find it inconceivable that I had come on my own.

'Don't tell me you're not married, a pretty young girl like you,' remarked one of Trish's uncles feigning amazement, making me feel like a freak to have reached the grand old age of twenty-five and still be single.

The day was torture. I was asked to dance by men who grinned sheepishly at their wives as we jigged past, as if they were doing something terribly daring.

At five o'clock, Trish and Ian left for their honeymoon in Jersey. Trish whispered, 'Stand behind me, Pearl, so when I toss my bouquet you can catch it. It means the next wedding you go to could be your own.'

I stood behind her, but deliberately missed the bouquet. I didn't know what I wanted. I knew I didn't want to stay at the wedding any longer, but it was too early to go home, as Charles and Marion weren't leaving until half past seven and I didn't want to go to dinner with them, either.

A few days later, on the Tuesday, I went with Hilda after school to view a flat for sale in Norris Green. It was in a tall building with its own car park where we'd arranged to meet. I arrived first and sat in the car waiting for Hilda. I disliked the building straight away. It had ten storeys and was situated on the corner of two very busy roads. There was something soulless about it.

Hilda drove her grey Mini into the car park and parked it beside my red Volkswagen Beetle. She waved and made a face, both at the same time. I suspected the face was because there was a woman in the passenger seat who must surely be her mother.

'Mam insisted on coming with me,' she said through gritted teeth when I approached. Her mother was getting out of the other side of the car. 'Mam, this is Pearl Curran; she's a teacher from school.'

Mrs Dooley was much better-looking than her daughter. She had loads of rather nice brown hair without a hint of grey, which made her appear much younger than her sixty years. But her expression when we shook hands was sour.

'I don't know what's got into our Hilda,' she said in a surly voice. 'There's no need for her to go to the expense of buying a flat when she's got a perfectly good home as it is. She doesn't realize which side her bread is buttered.' She gave her daughter a filthy look. 'You'll soon come running back, girl, when you find you've got a bed to make, washing and cleaning to do, and there isn't a meal waiting for you when you get home from school.'

Hilda just rolled her eyes and made no response. She said, 'The flat's on the fourth floor, but Mr Hanley, the owner, is away at the moment. A chap on the second floor is going to show us around.'

We walked in silence to the entrance: the older woman clearly had a cob on. Hilda rang the bell for flat 2B and a voice floated out of an oval-shaped grill and asked if that was Miss Dooley.

'Yes,' Hilda confirmed.

'I'll come down and let you in.'

'It's like bloody *Star Trek*,' Mrs Dooley sneered.

'You didn't have to come, Mam,' Hilda said. 'You should have stayed at home and watched *Coronation Street*. Now you'll moan at me all night long because you missed it.'

'I came to give you moral support, girl,' her mother snorted. 'Knowing you, if left to your own devices, you'd be stupid enough to be talked into buying a place you don't want.'

'That's why Pearl came with me.' Hilda sounded quite proud of the fact.

It was my turn to be treated to a filthy look.

A man of about forty-five wearing a business suit opened the door. He had neat brown hair and twinkly eyes. 'I'm Clifford Thompson,' he informed us.

We all shook hands and were ushered into a lift. Mrs Dooley's ill temper vanished like magic and she became all coy and girlish. It was quite sickening.

'When our Hilda tells people I'm her mother it makes me feel terribly old,' she simpered.

'I must admit I was surprised,' the man said gallantly. 'I'd thought you were her sister.'

'Everyone thinks that.' Mrs Dooley gave her hair a little pat and puckered her lips as if she were about to kiss him there and then, or was hoping he would kiss her. It made me feel even more sorry for Hilda.

The lift stopped and we got out. Clifford Thompson unlocked a door that, like all the others on the floor, had been painted dark brown, and indicated for us to go inside. The first thing I noticed was the view from the window. It was most unattractive, just lots of houses and traffic. There was a crossroads directly outside and the sound of engines racing and horns blaring was quite loud.

Despite the modern kitchen and bathroom, the flat itself reminded me of a prison with its square, plain rooms. There was nothing remotely unusual or nice about it. It would suit a man, I thought, who didn't want to be bothered with fancy skirtings or picture rails or any sort of embellishments on the doors and ceilings.

Hilda obviously thought the same. 'I don't think so,' she said after merely glancing inside the bedroom. 'I'm sorry, but I'm not interested. Will you tell Mr Hanley for me, please?'

'Of course. The architect didn't show much imagination when he designed these flats,' Clifford Thompson said ruefully. 'I wish I lived in a place with a bit more character.'

'That's what I want.' Hilda nodded enthusiastically. 'A place with character.'

'There's a top floor, one-bedroom flat going in Waterloo overlooking the river,' the man told her. 'I don't know the address, but I'll find out for you if you like.'

'Oh, would you!' Hilda's plain face lit up. 'I'll give you my telephone number and you can give me a ring.'

'That was all a ruse,' Mrs Dooley said when we were outside.

'What was a ruse, Mam?'

'Him going on about that flat in Waterloo. I bet it doesn't exist. He only did it to get our telephone number. He really fancied me, I could tell.' She smacked her lips. 'He'll be ringing up to ask me out before the end of the week.'

I cringed. The woman was *sixty*, for God's sake.

It turned out that the flat in Waterloo really did exist. Clifford Thompson telephoned Hilda a few days later and offered to take her there. Hilda fell in love with it straight away. The next morning she told me about the lovely ceilings, the old-fashioned bathroom and the pretty Victorian fireplace in the lounge.

'The bedroom isn't very big, but there's room for a bed settee in the lounge so I can have people to stay if I want.' Her face glowed. Afterwards, she went on to tell me, Clifford had taken her for a drink while they discussed whether or not she should buy the flat. He'd then invited her to the pictures on Saturday.

'Did you accept?' I asked.

'Well, yes,' she said dazedly, as if she couldn't quite believe what had happened. 'He's got two teenage kids and is divorced. His wife was having an affair with this chap and they've since got married.'

'Good luck, Hilda,' I said, meaning it. I'd only got to know her a little better, but found I quite liked her after all, particularly since meeting her awful mother. But now I'd have to find someone else to spend my Saturdays with.

# Chapter 8

## November–December 1939
## Amy

After the miscarriage, Amy stayed at her mother's house in Agate Street for two more nights. It would have been the gear to stay longer. She hadn't realized just how much she'd missed her mother and her sisters' light-hearted chatter – not that she'd missed them while Barney had been home, and it was him she missed more than anyone.

But it was imperative that she went back to Newsham Park soon. Captain Kirby-Greene would have already started wondering why the Pattersons' milk hadn't been taken in. Knowing him, he could well inform the police she was missing. More importantly, there might be a letter from Barney.

Before she left – in her old green coat, which was lovely and warm on what was a cold, damp November day – Mam impressed upon her that Charlie's bedroom was hers any time she wanted. 'Whether it's for a day, a week, or for ever, there'll always be a bed for you in this house, girl,' she was told.

'Ta, Mam.' She embraced her mother lovingly. It was no wonder Barney had grown so fond of her. She was as different from his own mother as chalk from cheese.

It was mid-afternoon when she entered the flat. It felt cold and unused, as if she'd been away for months, not just a few days. She shivered. It also looked very bare without a single holy picture or statue, and none of the little knick-knacks and ornaments that covered every ledge and shelf in her mother's house.

One of the reasons it looked so bare, she realized after a while, was because the red rug that Barney had bought had disappeared. She spent quite a few minutes wondering where on earth it could possibly be before recalling that the last time she'd seen it was on her return from her fateful visit to the Pattersons' house. She had a feeling she'd collapsed on the damn thing. It must be where she'd had the miscarriage and her father-in-law had sent it to be cleaned – or thrown away.

There was also a horrid smell that she traced to the kitchen, where she found a jug of milk turned to lumps and a loaf covered with green spots. She emptied the jug down the sink, wrapped the bread in newspaper and placed it outside the door to take downstairs and put in the bin.

One of the bottles of milk that had been left outside was also on the turn. She'd sort it out later, she thought as she put the kettle on for a drink, and buy some groceries. From now on, she was going to eat properly and get a job, preferably something to do with the war. She hadn't minded being a lady of leisure while Barney was home, but it was boring when he was away.

The kettle boiled and the doorbell gave four short rings both at the same time. Amy made the tea and went to let in whoever it was. There were voices downstairs: Captain Kirby-Greene had got there before her, which he had a habit of doing. She recognized his voice and that of Leo Patterson, her father-in-law.

'I've only just arrived back myself,' the captain was saying, 'but I noticed the milk had been taken so I reckon Mrs Patterson must be home at last.'

'Good,' Leo said crisply. 'Thank you for letting me in.'

But the captain wasn't going let him escape quite so easily. 'I've just been to the Royal Navy recruitment offices,' he said proudly. 'Thought it was about time I offered my services to help get rid of that scoundrel Hitler. They said they'd get in touch if they need someone with my vast experience.'

'I hope they do.' There was a touch of impatience in her father-in-law's voice. And what did the captain mean by saying Mrs Patterson must be home *at last*? It sounded as if this wasn't the first time someone had come looking for her.

'Is that you, Mr Patterson?' Amy called. 'Come on up.'

He mounted the stairs with as much agility as his son. He wore a business suit, a long navy-blue overcoat, which she could tell had cost an awful lot of money, and carried a grey trilby with a navy-blue band. 'I thought we'd decided that you call me Leo,' he said as he bounded up the last few steps. Amy couldn't remember having decided any such thing. Once inside the flat, he asked, 'Is the captain always such a nuisance?'

'*I* don't find him a nuisance and neither does Barney.' They both really liked the captain. 'He's just a lonely old man with no one to talk to. It doesn't hurt to stop and chat for a few minutes.'

'You and Barney had nothing else to do with your time,' Leo replied, clearly irritated. 'I've got more important things to do with mine.'

'Then what are you doing here? Shouldn't you be at work doing these important things?'

He looked at her, astounded. Amy was almost as astounded at herself. A year ago, had she met someone like Leo Patterson, she would have been over-awed and stuck for words. She would have done her best not to show it, but she wouldn't have been up to treating him as an equal. Having Barney fall in love with her had done her confidence the world of good.

He laughed. 'You don't mince your words, do you?'

'Do you?'

'I'm not going to bother answering that.' He gave her a withering look. 'The reason I'm here is I've been worried about you. You had a miscarriage a few days ago and I left you in bed because you were too weak to walk. I telephoned next day to see how you were, but there was no reply. I telephoned again and again, but still no reply.' He began to stride up and down the room as if it were a way of containing his anger. 'I came round and the captain let me into the house, but he wasn't able to let me in the flat, naturally. I wondered how long it would be before I felt obliged to break in. Anyway, how are you feeling?'

'I felt better the next day.' It hadn't crossed her mind that he would worry about her. Perhaps she should have left a note stuck to the front door or told Captain Kirby Greene where she was going. Mind you, she hadn't planned on staying with her mother for so long. She went into the kitchen and poured two cups of tea. 'Do you take sugar?' she shouted.

'No, thank you,' he said tersely.

She came out and put the tea on the little round table where Leo was seated. While she'd been gone, he'd removed his coat and hung it behind the door. 'Me and your son have been married for six months,' she said very slowly and deliberately. 'Since then, you've made no attempt to get to know me. I could have died in me sleep or been murdered in me bed and you'd never have known. Now all of a sudden I can't stay with me mam for a few days without you making a to-do about it.' She wasn't angry. In fact, she was quite enjoying ticking him off. 'It's none of your business where I go or what I do,' she finished.

Leo frowned. 'Is that where you've been, at your mother's?' he asked, as if he'd suspected she'd been up to no good.

'Yes.'

'Do you realize I don't know where your mother lives?'

'You don't know an awful lot of things about me.'

'Before I leave, can I have your mother's address?'

'You can.'

They both picked up their tea. Quite out of the blue, his entire demeanour changed.

'I'm sorry I've neglected you for so long,' he said abjectly. 'Elizabeth and I thought Barney was mad, marrying a girl he hardly knew. When he said she came from Bootle, we were worried that she'd be incredibly ...' He paused to find the right word.

'Common?' Amy said helpfully. 'A scrubber? Vulgar?'

Leo's lips twitched with amusement. 'Possibly common.'

'Perhaps I am common, Mr Patterson – Leo,' she said coldly, 'but never in all my life have I called anyone a whore. I don't quite know what that makes your wife.'

'I said we were worried you might be common, Amy. Now that I've met you I know that you're not.' He treated her to Barney's glorious smile. Amy knew if she blurred her eyes it would be easy to believe it was Barney sitting with her at the table. 'In fact,' Leo went on, 'you're quite the little lady, and I'm glad my son married you. As for my wife, I'm afraid she's sick. One of these days, she might get better: all I can do is hope. I'm truly sorry for the names she called you.' He extended his hand. 'Can we put the past behind us and be friends?'

'I'd like that.' Amy shook the proffered hand. After a shaky start, she was confident that they understood each other and she could regard him as a friend.

He stayed much longer than she'd expected, until darkness had fallen and a shadowy moon had appeared in the sky. She told him about Mam, about her brother Charlie's strange new wife, how much Jacky and Biddy wanted to do war work.

'They were talking about giving false ages and joining the Forces like me best mate, Cathy. Biddy's only fifteen.'

'I admire that,' he said.

Amy kept wanting to ask why he wasn't attending to all the important things he had to do, but reminded herself they were now friends and it would be best if she kept her mouth shut.

A letter arrived from Barney the following day. He wrote saying that he might well have enjoyed officer training had he not been missing her so much. He went on to explain in precise detail exactly what it was he was missing, making her blush to the roots of her hair.

A few days later, Harry Patterson called at the flat to say he had received his call-up papers and would be joining his brother in the Army.

'Wouldn't it be nice if you went to the same place as Barney to be trained as an officer?' Amy remarked. She hoped so; she really liked Harry.

He pulled a face. 'I doubt if they'll regard me as officer material. Unlike Barney, I didn't go to university so haven't got a degree. I'll just be a common or garden private like most of the other men. Anyway, I'd prefer to be a private in the Army. Even if they offered me a single stripe I'd turn it down.'

He looked a bit doleful. It occurred to Amy that on both of the occasions she'd met Leo, not once had he mentioned his eldest son, though he'd had a great deal to say about Barney, of whom he was clearly extremely proud.

'Cathy's joined the Army,' she told Harry. 'She's been posted to somewhere in Yorkshire.'

His eyes brightened. 'It'd be nice to see Cathy again,' he said.

Amy and Barney had always meant to get Cathy and Harry together. It was obvious they'd taken to each other the day they'd all met on Southport pier. Neither had done anything further about it, but perhaps all they needed was a little nudge.

'Shall we ask Cathy and Harry to come, too?' Amy would often suggest when they were about to go for a meal or a drive into the countryside on Sunday.

'Why not?' Barney would say vaguely, but neither had got round to offering an invitation. They'd sooner be by themselves. Even Amy's best friend and Barney's brother would have been an intrusion into the glorious time they spent together.

Now, Amy kissed Harry and wished him all the luck in the world. He might be much happier in the Army than his brother, she thought, as he had no one to love and therefore no one to miss.

The next time Amy went to see her mother, she was dumbfounded to discover that Leo Patterson had visited and offered her sisters jobs in his factory in Skelmersdale.

'I didn't realize he knew our address,' her mother said, still flustered, although it was two days since Leo had been. He had thoroughly charmed her, just as his son had done.

'He asked for your address last week. And I told him Jacky and Biddy were keen to change their jobs for some sort of war work.' Amy frowned. 'Working in a medical instrument factory is hardly war work.'

'That's what I thought, but he managed to convince the girls it was,' her mother told her. 'Apparently, he's just been given a Government contract, some of his workers have been called up, and he's badly in need of more staff. I suppose it *is* war work in a sort of way. He didn't seem to mind that the girls were so young, and they're thrilled to pieces. Jacky's in the packing department and Biddy's in the post room. Have you done anything about getting yourself a job, luv?'

'Not yet.' Amy couldn't make up her mind what she wanted to do. 'I'm torn between becoming a postwoman or a conductress on the trams,' she confessed.

'Mmm,' Mam said thoughtfully. 'With one, you'd have to be up at the crack of dawn: with the other, you'd be worked to death running up and down the stairs a million times a day – *and* you might have to be up at the crack of dawn an' all. If I were you, I'd go for the postwoman.'

'I'll think about it.' It was already December. It might not be a bad idea to leave it until after Christmas and start the New Year with a new job. Just imagine if Barney got a few days' leave over the holiday and they couldn't spend it together! Yes, Amy decided, she'd leave getting a job until the New Year.

Perhaps she would have done so had she not arranged to meet Charlie in town the following Saturday to buy Christmas presents for Mam and their sisters. They met in Lyons' first for a cup of tea. It was one of the coldest days she'd ever known and she wore her new dark-brown velour coat and fur-lined boots.

'I have a feeling this will be the last Christmas in a while when there'll be much to buy in the shops,' Charlie said gloomily. 'The longer this bloody war lasts, the worse things will get.'

'I thought Marion didn't approve of swearing.'

'Marion isn't here, is she? I'll swear as much as I bloody well like.'

'No, she isn't.' Amy nearly added, 'I'm pleased to say,' but thought better of it. Marion was Charlie's choice. He hadn't been forced to marry her. 'What did you mean,' she asked, 'by the longer the war lasts, the worse things will get?'

'It stands to sense, doesn't it?' He looked at her as if she were an idiot. 'There's already a shortage of tea and sugar. We can't expect seamen to risk their lives on a daily basis just so the population can treat itself to endless cuppas. Pretty soon, there'll be a shortage of every damn thing that has to be imported.' Charlie folded his arms and looked even gloomier. 'Not only that; factories will stop producing stuff that doesn't go towards the war effort. Marion wants an umbrella for Christmas before they stop making 'em.

D'you think Mam would like one, too?' he asked hopefully.

'She's already got one – Barney bought it her before he went away.'

'What about a nice handbag?'

'I brought her a lovely one back from London – and Jacky and Biddy, too.'

Charlie heaved a sigh of annoyance. 'Can you think of anything she wants?'

'Slippers. I know,' Amy cried, 'you get her slippers and I'll get her a dressing gown. We'll get them from the same shop so we can make sure the colours match. As for Jacky and Biddy, they'd like make-up; any sort. You can buy them really pretty make-up bags, and I'll get the stuff to go in them.' She was conscious that her usually good-humoured brother wasn't himself today. In fact, she'd never known him so clearly dejected. 'What's wrong, Charlie?' She squeezed his fingers.

'Marion just doesn't understand,' he said glumly.

'Understand what?' Amy enquired when he went no further.

'That I don't want to be in a reserved occupation. I want to join the Forces, to *do* something towards the war, not sit behind a bloody drawing board for the next who-knows-how-many years. People'll think I'm a coward or an invalid – I'm not sure which I'd hate the most.' Charlie worked in the fusegear department of the English Electric. His job was important to the war effort and had been categorized as a reserved occupation, meaning he wouldn't be called up. 'When I told Marion how fed up I was being a civilian, she took it personally and was dead offended. She thinks I should consider meself lucky not having to leave home. What do you think, sis? Did you mind Barney going away?'

'Of course I did.' But she hadn't been remotely offended that Barney had wanted to join the Forces, and it hadn't crossed her mind to try to persuade him to stay. She thought Marion was being selfish and unreasonable, but loved her brother too much to say so.

They got Mam a lovely blue quilted dressing gown and slippers to match in C&A Modes. The make-up for their sisters was bought in Owen Owen's. While they were there, Amy picked a pretty enamel brooch for Charlie to buy her, and he chose a shirt as her present to him.

Amy felt pleased with their purchases, but Charlie was still a bit low. She treated him to a beer and a beef sarnie in the Fatted Calf in Tithebarn Street. She had one herself and a glass of white wine. She listened while he forecast that very soon the breweries would have to start producing munitions and by the time next Christmas came along beer would be just a pleasant memory. Two men sitting nearby regarded him with horror.

'Oh, don't be daft, Charlie.' She poked him in the ribs with her elbow.

The beer and wine drunk and the sarnies eaten, she walked back with him to Exchange station, an easy place to get a taxi. By now, there was snow in the air and it was even colder. Charlie considered a taxi a monstrous extravagance and didn't hesitate to say so. 'You've become too bloody snooty to travel on trains and buses like ordinary people.'

Amy just shrugged and grinned.

At the entrance to the station, her attention was drawn to a large notice headed 'London, Midland and Scottish Railways.' It announced that the company was desperately short of staff: 'There are vacancies for drivers, stokers, porters, ticket collectors, office workers, guards, restaurant car attendants and cleaners. Interested persons should apply at the station master's office next to left luggage.' In very small letters at the bottom were the rather grudging words: 'Some of these positions are open to women.'

'I quite fancy going to and from London every day in the restaurant car,' Amy said.

'It'd be dead boring – and being a woman you'd probably end up a cleaner.'

'Oh, Charlie, luv, don't be such a misery-guts,' she chided. 'If I were Marion, I'd be only too pleased to see the back of you in this mood.'

It seemed that nothing on earth would make Charlie cheer up today. 'Tara,' he said grumpily; allowed her to kiss him, and made for the train, muttering something about how Marion would think he'd left home.

Amy read the notice again. If she stuck to her other choices, it meant finding addresses, sending for forms, whereas a job with L.M.S. merely required walking across the station and knocking at a door.

If she hadn't had the wine she might not have been quite so impulsive, or if Charlie had stayed he might have talked her out of it, but Charlie had gone, the wine had been drunk and, to Amy, right now, the idea of working on the railways seemed extremely appealing.

The snow hadn't stopped since the day she'd met Charlie in town to buy Christmas presents. That was over a week ago and it was getting even thicker. She'd told L.M.S. she didn't want to start work until after Christmas, but her patriotism had been questioned, making her feel so awful that she'd agreed to start straight away.

'Next week will do,' she'd been told curtly, not by the station master – he was too busy to interview a nobody like her – but by a gruff individual with a beard and a disagreeable manner whose name was Osbert Edwards.

Now it was half past eleven on Monday morning and she was on a steam train with Mr Edwards, going she knew not where because he refused to tell her.

'You'll see when we get there,' he'd said enigmatically through his thick black beard. He also had thick black hair and wasn't wearing a uniform, just an ordinary suit.

The names of the stations the train had stopped at had been familiar until it drew up in Fazakerley, a place she'd never heard of, or Kirkby, the station that came next. Hardly anyone got on or off. The train must be virtually empty, she thought. The scenery was flat and desolate, and everywhere was covered with a thick layer of snow. There was hardly a building in sight, just the occasional isolated house. The further away they got from civilization, the more miserable Amy felt.

'Next stop's us,' said Mr Edwards. He put on his bowler hat and pulled on a pair of darned black gloves. He would have made a perfect undertaker. Amy could visualize him walking in front of the hearse with a mournful expression on his long, thin face.

The train braked and a few minutes later came to a stop at Pond Wood, another station she'd never known existed. Mr Edwards opened the door and got out, but made no attempt to give Amy a hand down.

'Thanks,' she said sarcastically, but he either didn't hear or took no notice.

The engine driver, his face black with soot, waved and shouted, 'See you, Ossie,' and the guard called, 'Are we picking you up on the way back, Os?'

'Depends on how long this takes, Cyril.'

The train puffed away, the smoke mingling with the falling snow so that it was hard to tell which was which. What did he mean by, *Depends on how long this takes?* Amy wondered.

The narrow platform on which they stood contained a small waiting room and two strange, lumpy objects, which she eventually realized were benches, hidden beneath a pile of snow. The snow on the ground looked trampled, indicating that people had used the train that morning. A footpath led up to a curved, brown stone bridge, and another path sloped down to the platform on the other side.

Amy expected Mr Edwards to make for the path. Instead, he walked to where the platform petered away, and she saw there was a narrow walkway across the railway lines that had been cleared of snow, across which an elderly man in a peaked hat was slowly making progress. He disappeared into a building on the platform opposite which had a ticket office, a slightly bigger waiting room, ladies' and gents' toilets, and more snow-covered benches.

They crossed and entered the ticket office, which was dimly lit by a low-wattage electric bulb. A fire burned in the grate and the elderly gentleman was sitting in a shabby armchair. He got to his feet, removed his cap, to reveal a head as pink and smooth as a baby's bottom, and said respectfully, 'Good morning, Mr Edwards, sir. Is this the young lady you was on about?'

'Yes, Maxwell, this is Miss Patterson. She's starting today.'

Amy was too startled to remind the man she was a married woman. What was she starting today? What was she doing here?

'I'll show her the ropes and I would be grateful if you could make us a cup of tea if you have any.'

'No tea, sir, but plenty of milk that I can heat on my little camping stove. You can have that with a bit of cocoa if it's to your liking, though there's not much cocoa left.'

'Cocoa would be very welcome, Maxwell. What about you, Miss Patterson?'

'*Mrs* Patterson. Yes, Mr Maxwell, I'd love a cup of cocoa if there's enough.'

While the cocoa was being made, it became clear to Amy that she was being put in charge of Pond Wood station. Twenty years ago, it had been Mr Maxwell's job but he had retired when he reached the grand old age of sixty-five. He'd returned when the most recent incumbent had left to work in a munitions factory for three times the wages. Now eighty-five, the old man had found the job too much for him. Also, he was neglecting the garden that he loved.

'Not that I can get much gardening done in this weather,' he said sadly. 'Never known snow like it, that I haven't.'

Amy was shown how to issue tickets, how to make sense of the timetable, how the stove worked, how to use the telephone – as if she didn't already know – when to blow the whistle to indicate a train could leave the station – only when every single door had been closed, as if she were likely to blow it when they were open – where the forms were kept to order things like refund books, more tickets, pens, pencils and ink, where the broom was kept to sweep the platform, the Harpic for the lavatories, the key to wind the station clock, and the ladder with which to reach it, the coal for the fire, the safe where the money was kept at night, and so on until her head felt dizzy at the amount of information she was expected to take in.

'At any other time, you'd have been given at least a month's training, but training's gone out the window since the war started,' she was told.

The train on which she'd arrived returned, having been to and from Wigan. Mr Edwards departed on it after shaking her hand and wishing her luck in her 'new employment'. It was the last sort of employment Amy had wanted. She'd been looking forward to being a tram conductress or a postwoman, becoming a familiar face to hundreds of people, making loads of new friends. Here, she would hardly get to know anyone. Not every train, she discovered, stopped at Pond Wood. Some went straight through, and she had to make sure, when one was expected, that there weren't any children in the vicinity intent on playing dangerous games, or on the bridge with stones to throw at the driver.

'You've got to have your wits about you, girl,' William impressed upon her, his old face creased earnestly. (He said he preferred to be called William rather than Mr Maxwell.) 'You can't get lost in a book, else you might miss what's going on outside. Once or twice, when me wife took over – me being poorly like – she used to bring her knitting.'

'What do *you* do while you're here?' Amy enquired faintly.

'Me? Oh, I just sit and think about me garden. 'Stead of a clock or a watch when I retired, they bought me a little greenhouse, and I sit and think about that an' all, like how me tomatoes are doing, and me marrows, and whether me roses will win first prize at the summer fair next year.'

'I see,' Amy said, even more faintly. No matter how hard she tried, she couldn't imagine it ever being summer again. At twenty past six, she would lock up the ticket office and catch the 6.27 p.m. train back to Liverpool. She couldn't wait. No more trains would stop at Pond Wood station until the following morning when she arrived on the 7.15 a.m. from Liverpool and opened up.

William left just after one. 'Elspeth'll have me dinner ready, but I'll pop back later and see how you're getting on,' he said as he put on a thick, shabby overcoat and woolly hat with a tatty bobble. 'I advise you to look in the timetable and make a note of the trains from Lime Street station to London Euston. Mr Cookson from the Red House rings at least once a day to ask. There was a time when he'd walk up from Exchange station to Lime Street every Monday then come back again on the Friday, having spent five days in London where he worked for an Oriental bank. He hasn't done it for quite a while, poor chap. His mind's long gone.'

Amy said she'd make a note of the trains straight away.

''Nother thing,' the old man continued, 'Miss Cookson – she's Mr Cookson's sister – went to Wigan today to see her friend Miss Everett, who's been a bit poorly of late. They met on a cruise in eighteen ninety-eight when they were just girls. She'll probably arrive home on the two twenty-seven – she doesn't like being out in the dark. She's a nice woman, Miss Cookson, but if you let her, she'll keep you talking till the cows come home, so try and get rid of her, but do it politely.'

'I'm never anything else,' Amy assured him.

He left the office and closed the door. Seconds later, his face appeared at the little window where the tickets were sold. 'Oh, and Susan Conway's taken her little-uns to Liverpool to see her mam. She'll be back on the three forty-five so you'll need to be ready to give a hand with the pram. The baby had a bit of a cough this morning so the less time he's in the cold the better. There'll be some school kids on the same train: Ronnie and Myra McCarthy. The school lets them off early. Myra's a nice girl, but Ronnie's a proper little scoundrel. Don't forget you're the station master now and make sure you don't take any nonsense off him. And don't forget either that the one forty-five's due in three-quarters of an hour. You should hear it coming if you keep your ear out. You've to go on the other platform for that: you can either walk across the lines or over the bridge. I'd say the bridge was safer in this weather. If you slipped on the lines you might catch your foot or summat and the train'd never have time enough to stop before it mowed you down. If any passengers attempt to cross the lines, tell them it's an offence and they'll be up in court before they know it.'

After William had gone, Amy made up her mind that when she got home she would collapse on the stairs making a loud noise. Captain Kirby-Greene would call an ambulance, she'd be taken to hospital and tomorrow she would ask one of the nurses to telephone Mr Edwards to tell him she'd had an accident and would have to leave her job with L.M.S. railways.

This was probably the most boring job in the entire world. An afternoon of unrelieved dreariness stretched ahead – and unrelieved hunger. She hadn't thought to bring anything to eat, having assumed they'd either feed her, or that there'd be food available to buy. The trouble was she'd been expecting to be sent somewhere civilized, not to a place she'd never heard of situated in the back of beyond. She poured the remainder of the milk into a pan and heated it on the stove. There was no cocoa left but it was better than nothing.

The 1.45 p.m. gave a loud hoot as it approached the station. Feeling numb, Amy reached for the cap and jacket hanging behind the door. She was expected to wear them when a train came in. Both were much too big for her.

She crossed the bridge and had only just reached the other platform when the train stopped. A woman wearing a beautiful fur coat, a fur hat to match, and soft brown leather boots alighted, gave Amy her ticket and an indifferent nod, and made her way up the path. The driver and the stoker gave Amy appreciative looks and asked her name. The guard waved and deposited a wooden box on the platform. Amy checked that the doors were closed, blew her whistle, raised her arm, and the train chuffed away.

She picked up the wooden box. It had a wire lid and contained about twenty fluffy, newborn chicks, which were cheeping and falling over each other because the box wasn't nearly big enough to hold them comfortably. A label attached to the lid showed they were for a Mr P. Alton. Amy wrapped her arms around the box, as if this would keep the chicks warm, then staggered with it over the lines and into the lobby. The woman who'd got off the train was standing inside, clearly waiting for someone to collect her.

Amy fell to her knees, still holding the box. 'Ah!' she wailed when she saw the chicks were sprinkled with snow.

'What's the matter?' the woman asked, coming over. Her face was perfectly made up, though nothing could hide the wrinkles around her chin and under her eyes.

'It's these chicks,' Amy said tearfully. 'They look so tiny and helpless.'

The woman had brought with her the scent of Chanel No. 5, Amy's favourite perfume. She looked down at the box. 'They do, don't they?' she said in a hollow voice. 'They're like us humans in a way; we're just as helpless. Sometimes I feel as if I'm being carted around in a box, that I have no say in my own destiny.' The look in her brown eyes was full of despair. 'Don't you sometimes feel like that?' she whispered, fixing her tragic gaze on Amy.

'Not really,' Amy whispered back.

A car drew up outside and the woman stepped out into the snow without a word. 'Hello, my darling,' Amy heard her say. A door slammed and the car drove away.

She carried the chicks into the ticket office and put them near the fire. She felt tempted to take them out one by one and give them a little cuddle, but before she could the door opened to admit a woman wearing the same overcoat and woolly hat as William had gone home in. She was carrying an earthenware pot covered with a tea towel. Her face was as red as a beetroot, her eyes bright blue, and the hair that stuck out from underneath the hat was like cream straw. The mouth-watering smell coming from the pot was ten times nicer than Chanel No. 5.

'Brought you some stew, poppet,' she said cheerfully. 'Willie said you'd brought nowt with you to eat. This has got a dumpling in. Are you partial to barley?'

'I love barley,' Amy breathed, though she'd never given barley a thought before today.

'Sit down then, poppet. Here's a spoon. Eat it up quickly before it goes cold like. As you might have guessed, I'm Elspeth, Willie's wife. How are you getting on?' She didn't pause for breath, let alone wait for an answer. 'I saw the one forty-five go chuffing past, so you obviously saw that off safely. Don't forget the two twenty-seven isn't far off, and you'll need to keep an eye out for Miss Cookson and make sure she doesn't capture you for too long. I expect Willie told you Susan Conway will be along later: she's been to Liverpool to see her mam. Poor thing, she's lived in Pond Wood five years, but she's still homesick. Goes to see her mam in Scotland Road every Monday and Friday. Was that Mrs Shawcross what got in the car just now? I was too far away to see proper.'

'I don't know who it was. She was wearing a lovely fur coat.'

'That'll be Mrs Shawcross then – the coat's mink. Lost three babies, she did, poor lamb. The fourth lived, but was killed in the

Great War. All that money, but not a penny's worth of happiness out of it.'

There was a noise in the lobby and someone tapped on the window. 'I understand my chicks have been sent from Wigan,' said a voice with a Lancashire accent, 'but there's no sign of them.'

'They're in here in the warm,' Amy called.

Elspeth opened the door to admit a nice-looking young man about six feet tall. He was wearing a green mackintosh, stout boots and a tweed hat with a narrow brim. He blushed when he saw Amy and nervously shuffled his feet.

'Hello, Peter,' Elspeth said.

Peter merely swallowed and continued to shuffle his feet. He snatched off his hat and fed the brim in circles through his fingers.

'I put the chicks by the fire to keep warm,' Amy told him. 'Are you taking them in a car?'

'I came in the lorry,' he stammered.

'Well, you must put them in the cab so they don't get cold,' she said sternly. 'Have you got a blanket to put over them?'

'No, but I can use some sacks.' He seemed very anxious to please.

'I suppose sacks will do.'

'That young man badly needs a wife,' Elspeth said when Peter and the chicks had gone. 'I don't suppose you're interested? Oh, now I remember, Willie said you're already married.'

'My husband's in the Army,' Amy told her.

The afternoon passed more quickly than she expected. Elspeth hadn't been gone long, when the 2.27 p.m. arrived from Wigan. Miss Cookson proved as garrulous as William had said. Perhaps another time Amy might have minded, but today it helped pass a few minutes.

She helped Susan Conway push the pram containing two small children and a baby up the footpath towards the bridge. The ground was becoming perilously slippy. 'Can I come and talk to you about Liverpool some day when I've got a minute?' Susan asked. 'I really miss the pictures and the dance halls since I married John.'

'Come any time you want,' Amy told her.

Myra McCarthy and her scoundrel brother Ronnie must have missed the train, and didn't arrive until 5.45 p.m. Perhaps by then Ronnie was too cold and hungry to misbehave. Both children went racing up the path and Amy returned to the ticket office, her work done for the day, apart from a phone call from a man requesting the times of the trains from Lime Street station to Euston – she took it for granted that was Mr Cookson – and a lady buying a return ticket to Liverpool.

'I'm going to the theatre with my friend and staying the night,' she told Amy.

Amy put the money in the safe, raked the fire, locked the door and went to wait for the 6.27 p.m. to Liverpool.

Captain Kirby-Greene emerged from his flat as soon as Amy came in. 'What was it like?' he enquired.

Awful, Amy wanted to say, boring, I hated every minute. Instead, much to her own surprise, she replied, 'It was all right. I'm a station master.'

That, she realized, had been holding her together throughout the day, had stopped her getting on the first Liverpool train and coming home. She was a station master. Station mistress just didn't sound the same. Master was so much better. As soon as she'd had something to eat, she'd write and tell Barney.

# Chapter 9

## May 1971
## Pearl

'A what?' I gasped.

'A station master.' Charles laughed. 'Didn't you know? I thought someone would have told you.'

'No.' I had no idea that my mother had been a station master during the war. I imagined station masters as unsmiling, middle-aged men, possibly with whiskers and half-moon glasses, not pretty young women with tons of blonde hair. 'How old was she then?' I asked.

It was evening, and Charles and I were weeding the garden. Weeds were the bane of his life and he hated them more than anything. I was kneeling on the grass digging up the dratted things with an old spoon when a fierce tug wasn't fierce enough to budge them. It being Wednesday, Marion had stayed behind at work to play badminton. She'd been playing for years and was still hopeless at it.

'Awfully young,' Charles replied. 'Only eighteen.'

'Shouldn't it be station mistress?'

'She preferred master. The thing is,' he continued, 'we eventually discovered she'd not long had a miscarriage, but she threw herself heart and soul into the job. She started in December, and it was the worst winter anyone had ever known. It didn't stop snowing until March. Every day, she'd light the fire in the ticket office, sweep the snow off the platform, wind the clock …' He smiled fondly. 'She used to write long, long letters to your dad—'

'Has anyone got them?' I asked, butting in. They might have ended up with Uncle Harry or Grandad Patterson. 'I'd love to read them.'

'Not that I know of, love.'

'Was she there for the whole war?'

'No, only for about nine months. She made friends with every-one. Pond Wood wasn't exactly a village; it had hardly more than a few dozen houses, a few farms. The summer she was there the station was a picture, full of flowers. We used to go and see her. We'd go on the train – me and Mam, Jacky and Biddy, some sea captain who lived in the same house as she did. Marion went just the once.' His lips tightened and he said scornfully, 'As you know, she and your mother never got on.' I was surprised: it wasn't often he was critical of Marion. 'That's where Jacky met her husband, Peter, on Pond Wood station. I think he'd been sweet on your mam, but she was already married to your dad.'

'I knew about the miscarriage.' It had been in the newspaper reports of the trial.

'She never told anyone at the time. Damn!' he swore. 'That thorn's drawn blood.' He sucked his finger.

'You should wear gloves like I do.'

'Only cissies wear gloves for gardening – and women. Do you know,' he went on, 'every day, your mother used to take a taxi to and from Exchange station to get to work and home again? It must have cost her more in taxis than she got in wages.' All of a sudden his eyes were moist. 'I wish you'd known your mother then, Pearl. She was so full of life.'

It was more than three weeks since my mother had written to Charles saying she'd 'be in touch soon.' Cathy Burns thought she might be in hospital, 'having something done that she didn't want done in prison.'

'Such as?' I asked. I'd been summoned when I had a free period on Thursday afternoon. My class was taking singing in the gym and my presence wasn't required.

There was a long pause until Cathy admitted that all she could think of was a hysterectomy, and it would have been silly to wait until she came out. 'What would you do, Pearl, if you'd just got out of prison after twenty years?'

'I think I'd like to get rid of the smell of prison,' I said. 'The *feel* of it. I'd want to buy loads of clothes and make-up, get my hair done. Things like that,' I finished lamely. It sounded very trite.

'It wouldn't have taken very long to do those sort of things. It wouldn't need three and a half weeks.'

'Perhaps she fancied a holiday,' I suggested.

Cathy Burns was far more preoccupied with my mother's non-appearance than anyone else. Charles was quite laidback about it. 'Knowing Amy, she'll turn up when she feels like it,' he'd said.

Harry was equally unconcerned. 'As long as she's safe. I'm sure we would have heard if something had happened.'

'I wonder if she went to see Jacky and Biddy?' the headmistress mused. 'She might be in Canada.'

'She would have told people if she was going to Canada. There would have been no need to keep it to herself.'

'I suppose you're right.'

I noticed there were only three cigarette stubs in the ashtray. At least she'd cut down on smoking, despite the fact her friend hadn't come home. Perhaps she was getting used to the idea.


Gary Finnegan limped into the classroom the next morning. I saw that there was blood on his right sock. I beckoned him over. 'How did you do that, Gary?'

'I tripped, miss.'

Like the last time I had spoken to him about his lip, he refused to meet my eyes. He looked so miserable that I resolved something had to be done. I just knew he hadn't fallen over. I'd asked Joan Flynn to keep an eye on him and she reported that the other children left him alone.

'*Too* alone, in my view,' she'd said, 'but you can't force kids to play with each other. It'd only make things worse. One of these days he'll be accepted – hopefully before the end of term. By then, he'll be a familiar face.'

I rolled down his grey sock. His ankle was swollen and bleeding badly. I was convinced it was the result of a kick. I went outside and grabbed one of the older girls in the corridor who was on her way to her own class. 'Will you take this little boy to Mrs Miller's office, please, and ask her to put some TCP and a plaster on his ankle?'

'All right, miss,' the girl sang. Sarah Miller was the school secretary and the First Aid box was in her office.

I told Gary to come back straight away, then I began the lesson. It was Art. There were no longer desks in the classroom as there'd been when I went to school, but four tables painted different colours – red, blue, yellow and green – with seven or eight children seated at each. I gave every child a large sheet of drawing paper, glue, chalk, little squares of coloured cardboard, plastic scissors, and other odds and ends, and told them to glue the squares to the paper to make a house and fill in the background with chalk.

'I made this one last night.' I held up the house I'd done the night before. I always had to stop myself from making things too skilfully in case it put the children off. 'I've made the roof red, but you can have any colour you like. You can draw trees, or children playing, as well as clouds and the sun in the sky.'

'Can I draw a car outside like me dad's?'

'Yes, Barry.'

'Can I have a swing in the garden? We've got a swing in *our* garden.'

'Of course you can, Heather.' Little show-off, I thought.

I walked around the room. I was continually surprised, and upset, by how quickly and cleverly some of the children got to work using the cardboard as bricks and sticking them to the paper, while others seemed totally bemused. I made suggestions in a roundabout way so they would think the ideas came from themselves.

My watch said half past nine. Gary should have come back by now. Perhaps Sarah Miller had been busy and he'd had to wait. I couldn't stop looking at my watch. A few minutes later, I left the classroom with the door open and sped round to the secretary's office, which was next to Miss Burns's. There was no sign of Gary when I opened the door.

'Have you seen to Gary Finnegan?' I asked. Sarah was a lovely, grandmotherly woman with pure silver hair. Everybody liked her.

'Yes, ages ago. I took him round to your classroom, but just pointed to the door and told him to go in. My telephone was ringing, you see, and I had to rush back. Don't tell me he didn't arrive?' she groaned. It must have been obvious from my face.

'No. Look, can you check the boys' lavatories and anywhere else you can think of. I'll have to get back to my class before a riot breaks out.'

'Straight away.' She rushed out of the room, while I sped back to my class, who were as quiet as mice, heads bent over their work. I doubted if any had noticed I'd been away.

It wasn't long before the conclusion was reached that Gary Finnegan was nowhere on the premises. Cupboards had been searched, as well as the staffroom, the storage space under the stage in the assembly hall, the girls' and boys' lavatories, the boiler room and the coal house, which was now used to store cleaning equipment.

When Sarah Miller reported this, I asked her to tell the head-mistress. In no time, Cathy Burns came hurrying along to the classroom. An air of quiet panic prevailed.

'Where do you think he can be?' she asked. Her brown eyes were scared. I was praying that Gary had come to no harm.

'I expect he's at home,' I said. 'If he ran he'd be there by now.'

'Sarah's rung his home, but the line is engaged.'

I wanted to weep at the idea of the little boy going home by himself, his ankle hurting. He must have been terribly unhappy to run away. No doubt he just wanted his dad and didn't care about the consequences.

'He wasn't happy at school,' I said. 'I think he was being phys-ically bullied.' I felt really guilty. 'I should have looked into it when it happened the first time.'

'When was that?'

'Only last week. I asked Joan Flynn to watch out for him.' I'd also told Gary I'd like a word with his dad, but he mustn't have passed the message on.

'Don't blame yourself, Pearl,' Cathy said kindly. 'You have thirty children to look after. You can't give special treatment to every single one.'

'No, but ...' I didn't go on. This wasn't the time to explain about Gary's circumstances. Rob Finnegan might not have told the school that his son didn't have a mother.

Sarah Miller came into the classroom with Gary's address, and Cathy said she'd go round there straight away.

'Can I go, please?' I put my hand on her arm.

'Miss?'

'Yes, Heather?' I'd forgotten all about my class. I did my best to keep the impatience out of my voice.

'Do I *have* to draw smoke coming out of the chimney? We don't have smoke coming out of *our* chimney: *we've* got central heating in *our* house.'

'You don't have to draw anything you don't want to, Heather.' I turned to Cathy. 'Can I go round to Gary's house?' I asked again. 'I've met his father more than once. I sort of know him.'

'If you want, dear. I'll look after the class. Ah, I see you're all making houses.' She smiled brightly at the children and began to walk from table to table making admiring comments. She was a wonderful, inspired teacher. 'Hurry, Pearl,' she urged. 'If he's not at home, let me know and I'll call the police.'

Someone was likely to call the police if they saw me driving. I drove like a maniac round to Gary's house in Sandy Lane. It was an old semi with two bells on a panel beside the door. The bottom bell was for Miss E. Finnegan. I pressed it twice. Almost immediately, Rob Finnegan opened the door. He was holding Gary in his arms. The little boy's eyes were red and swollen. When he saw me, he buried his head in his father's shoulder.

'Yes?' Rob said shortly. His expression was hard and unfriendly.

'You know why I'm here.' I hadn't realized it was possible to feel faint with relief. I had to hold the doorframe for support. 'Can I use your phone to tell Miss Burns that Gary's safe? Everyone is worried about him.'

'It's a bit late for that.' He stood aside. 'You can use the phone. It's in the front room.'

The room was obviously a sitting room. There was a sideboard with a television on top, a bookcase and a small table with three chairs, as well as a bed settee that was still unfolded, the duvet in a heap in the middle. I remembered that Rob worked nights and must have been asleep when his son came home. A bright red phone stood on the mantelpiece, the receiver lying upside down beside it – that's why the line had been engaged. I dialled the number of the school and Sarah Miller answered. I told her Gary was all right. 'Safe and sound,' I said.

'Thank the Lord for that,' she breathed. I promised I'd be back as soon as I could and she said, 'I'm sure Miss Burns would want you to take all the time that's necessary.'

I said goodbye and turned to see that Rob was lying Gary on the bed. The child's eyes were blinking with tiredness. The morning's events had worn him out.

Rob tucked the clothes around him, put his finger to his lips and nodded towards the door. I followed him back into the hallway and he entered an untidy kitchen with unwashed dishes on the draining board. I stood in the doorway.

'Excuse the mess,' he said briefly. 'I wasn't expecting visitors.' He picked up the kettle. 'Would you like some tea? Please don't think I'm being sociable, it's just that I'm desperate for a cup myself and it would be rude not to offer you one. I'd ask you to go except I want to know what happened. Why wasn't someone keeping an eye on my son? He was in a right old state when he got home. How did he manage to leave and get all the way home without anyone noticing? Needless to say, I won't be sending him to that school again.'

It was as if a shutter had been closed between us. We'd got on well, were becoming friends, but now I was the enemy.

I explained what had happened. 'You could hardly call Mrs Miller neglectful. She brought Gary back to the classroom, just didn't open the door. As soon as we realized he'd gone, the premises were searched. When he couldn't be found, we phoned here but the line was engaged.'

'I take the receiver off so I won't be bothered with wrong numbers and people trying to sell me things when I'm trying to sleep.' I just nodded. I didn't want him to think I was blaming him for not answering his phone. 'What happened to Gary's ankle?' he asked.

'I think someone kicked him. Last week, his lip was bleeding. When I asked how it was done, he said he'd fallen over.'

'He told me the same thing – about the lip, that is. We still haven't discussed the ankle. The other week, he had a bad bruise on his shoulder. He said he'd banged it on a door. He's not prepared to tell tales on another lad and get him into trouble. Christ!' His eyes were hot with anger. 'He's had a bloody awful life. First his mum dies, then we have to leave Uganda, which he loved. We're squashed in this damn place, making life hell for my sister because I don't want to waste money on rent when it might be needed to buy a house one day soon, and now he's being bullied at school. I mean, the kid's only five. How much is he supposed to put up with?'

Just then I had a vision. It was the vision of a little girl standing in a doorway, just as I was now, but her arms were hanging at her sides, her mouth was open, and she was bawling her head off. She was also five and she was crying because she couldn't understand anything, because she was terrified. She couldn't understand why life was being so cruel. She'd been taught about God, but didn't think about him while she cried and cried and cried, until she felt sick from crying, until her throat ached from it. No one could console her. People kept trying to pick her up, but she pushed them away. There were only two people in the world she wanted: her mum and dad. But apparently her dad was dead and her mum had gone away.

'What's the matter?'

I'd forgotten where I was. I blinked and found myself in a strange house with a strange man, who was looking at me curiously. 'Nothing,' I muttered. The man, I realized, was Rob Finnegan and the part of the house we were in belonged to his sister, Beth. For some reason I noticed that his feet were bare, his fair hair was tousled and his jeans and white T-shirt were crumpled. He no longer looked angry.

'You're crying,' he said.

'Am I?' I rubbed my cheeks with the back of my hand. 'I was thinking about something.'

'It must have been something pretty bloody awful. I've never seen such a look of misery on anyone's face before.'

There was weariness in his tone. He had enough on his plate without being landed with his son's neurotic teacher. 'I'd better go,' I mumbled. 'I'm sorry about Gary. If you send him back to school tomorrow, I promise we'll never let him out of our sight. And I'll sort out the bullying.'

'Don't go.' I was halfway down the hall when he caught my arm. 'You're not in a fit state to drive – you look awful. Stay and have a cup of tea. See, the kettle's boiled. We can have it in the garden, as there's nowhere else to sit, only Beth's bedroom. Come on,' he urged, giving my arm a tug when I just stood there, not knowing what to do.

He led me into an old garden with old trees and over-grown bushes. The rough grass had recently been cut. The hedge was thick with May blossom as white as snow. There was a wooden table, black with age, with benches attached, directly outside the back door. When I'd left the house that morning it had been a beautiful day and it still was. I just hadn't noticed the hours in between. The trees made lacy, shimmering shadows on the grass. I liked it much more than Charles's garden with its neat lawn and scalloped borders, which looked as if they had been cut with a knife. My uncle pruned, weeded and trimmed everywhere regularly. The garden was his creation. This looked completely natural, as if it belonged to God himself.

'If we sit here, I'll be able to hear if Gary wakes up,' Rob said. 'I won't be a minute with the tea.' He made sure I was sitting down before going back inside the house. His former antagonism had completely disappeared, and he was being very kind, very patient.

He had hardly been away a minute before returning with the tea in bright orange mugs. 'I assume you don't take sugar as you don't have it in coffee?'

'That's right. It looks lovely and strong.' I took a sip. 'Thank you.'

'What was wrong back there?' he asked. 'I hope it wasn't because of me letting off steam. I shouldn't have got on to you like that about Gary. It wasn't your fault he came home – I don't suppose it was anyone's fault. He just saw the opportunity and took it. But he's obviously unhappy there. Normally, he's a very good little boy.'

'Very good,' I concurred.

'You've never told me anything about yourself,' he said. 'Not that there's been much opportunity. The first time we met, all we talked about was the school uniform, the second time it was the Cavern and rock 'n' roll, and the third time you were with your friend, you'd just been to the pictures, and we talked about films. You've mentioned a Charles and a woman – I can't remember her name – that you lived with. I assumed they were your parents and that you called them by their first names; some people do.'

'Charles and Marion are my aunt and uncle. But, look, just because …' I didn't know how to put it, 'because I lost control back there, it doesn't mean you have to do anything about it. I'm really sorry. You've got enough to cope with as it is.' I was beginning to feel embarrassed, as if I'd accidentally appeared naked in front of him.

'Gary and I have been through a lot together and we'll come through this,' he said with conviction. 'Trouble is, if someone hurts him, he isn't aggressive enough to hurt them back.'

There was a cry from indoors: 'Dad,' then more loudly, 'Dad?'

'Coming, son.' Rob hurried inside.

I got up and walked down the garden. It wasn't very big, but the trees gave it the appearance of a small park. I stood under the leaves and looked at the sun, the way it sifted through, losing most of its brightness. I threw back my shoulders in order to shake off the heaviness I felt after recalling the little girl: me at five, sobbing my heart out. In the end, Charles had picked me up, wrapped me in his arms. I'd clung to him – I had to cling to someone.

A black-and-white football lay on the grass. I kicked it at a tree trunk. It bounced back and I kicked it again. I was still kicking it when Rob appeared. He had white trainers on his feet.

'I've put Gary in the bath,' he said. 'He was all hot and sticky. He's playing with his plastic duck at the moment.' He grinned. 'Actually, it's mine, but I let him borrow it. I'll go back in a minute. Here, let me have that?'

I kicked the ball towards him. He seemed to dance with it for a while, bouncing it from one knee to the other, to his head, and back to his knees again.

It was then I had this really wonderful idea ...

# Chapter 10

## Amy

No more than a few dozen people went every day from Pond Wood to Liverpool, or stations on the way, and even fewer travelled in the other direction to Wigan. A special bus took children to school in Upholland, but for everyone else in the tiny village who didn't have a car, the only way of getting anywhere was on the train. But now car owners were finding they couldn't manage on the meagre petrol ration, so the number of passengers was fast increasing.

Mornings, Amy caught the quarter past seven train from Exchange station. When she got off at Pond Wood half an hour later, there'd be a few people waiting on platform two for the same train to take them to Wigan. It was always snowing, about to snow, or had just stopped. As the ticket office wasn't open at such an early hour, tickets had been bought the day before or paid for at the other end. Some people had a contract.

By 8.27 a.m., a small crowd of passengers would be sheltering in the waiting room on platform one for the next train to Liverpool, among them Mr Clegg, a stockbroker, who wore a bowler hat and carried a rolled umbrella, and Miss Feathers, a secretary with the Liverpool Victoria Friendly Society. The rest were mainly young girls and a few boys, who worked in the big Liverpool shops or offices. There were also Ronnie and Myra McCarthy, who got off at Sandhills and caught another train to their secondary schools in Waterloo, and best friends Benny Carter and Andrew Woods, who only went as far as the next stop, Kirkby, where they worked in a munitions factory.

During the rest of the morning, more people would appear, mainly women, some with small children, who were off to the city shops, Wigan market, or to see relatives. Amy would give the children a sweet and help lift the prams into the guard's van.

On Saturday, the trains were mainly occupied by men going to football or rugby matches and young people off to a tea dance at Reece's ballroom or to a cinema matinée. The last Liverpool train to stop at Pond Wood left Exchange station at quarter past five. It was possible to catch a much later train to Kirkby and walk the remaining three miles, but even those willing to face a late-night hike balked at the idea of the doing it in the middle of the inevitable snow storm or trudging through huge drifts.

There wasn't a pub in the vicinity. By the time Amy left for home, most people were tucked up in their houses and there wasn't a chink of light to be seen. Pond Wood had become a miniature ghost town, eerily beautiful in the moonlight. In all the time she was there, she never ventured far in case there was an urgent telephone call. It was only from hearsay that she knew the houses in the village ranged from tiny, thatched cottages that had hardly been improved since they were built in the last century, to large detached houses set in their own grounds, with more modest houses in between. There were also a few isolated farmhouses.

When she went home, she always left the waiting rooms unlocked because William Maxwell told her courting couples sometimes used them. She hadn't so far discovered any evidence that anyone had been there, which wasn't surprising considering the weather.

The station was closed on Sundays – Amy's only day off. She lay in bed until it was time for the last Mass, then went to Agate Street for her dinner, leaving early to go home, tidy the flat and do a bit of washing. Apart from Saturday nights, when her father-in-law sometimes picked her up from Exchange station and took her to dinner, this was now the pattern of her life, and she assumed Barney's was just as unexciting.

Three weeks passed. She learnt every passenger's name, and they knew hers. As the weather grew colder and the snow became thicker, she invited them into the ticket office to wait for the train in front of the fire – lighting it was the first thing she did when she arrived. William said that in winters before the war, fires had also been lit in both waiting rooms, but now there wasn't the fuel. Amy was relieved. She'd never lit fires before, and lighting one was enough, let alone three.

Susan Conway, who'd married a farm worker and lived in a tied cottage, called at the station at least once a day with the baby for a chat. She missed Liverpool with all her heart, and liked nothing better than to talk about it, exclaiming, 'Isn't that a coincidence!' when she discovered she and Amy had once been to the same cinema or walked down the same street, as if Liverpool was a hundred miles long and a hundred miles wide, and the odds against them having been to the same places were hundreds to one.

Barney wouldn't be coming home for Christmas. He was getting a forty-eight hour pass, but attempting to get from Aldershot, where he was now stationed, to Liverpool and back again in the space of two days, with the weather as it was, wasn't even worth thinking about. Amy knew as much as anyone the difficulty trains were having, what with the snow-bound tracks, the blocked-up tunnels, and the signals and points that were too frozen to move.

Some roads were impassable. It had been known in Liverpool for snowdrifts to reach the top of ground-floor windows overnight, making people feel as if they were living in an igloo when they drew back the curtains the next morning.

Amy's own trains were often late (she was inclined to think of the trains that passed through the station as 'hers').

'Anyway,' she wrote to Barney, 'it seems the station has to open on Christmas Day, though I can't imagine people using it. I can leave a bit earlier, on the 4.27 p.m. instead of the 6.27 p.m., but that's all. Elspeth, William's wife, is bringing me some turkey. I've never had turkey before and I'm really looking forward to it.'

She couldn't stop thinking that, if she hadn't been a station master, she could have gone to Surrey, met Barney, and it wouldn't have mattered if it had taken an entire week for her to get back to Liverpool.

The present he sent was a tiny gold watch with an expanding strap. It looked incredibly expensive. 'It's a cocktail watch,' his letter said. Amy wore it all the time, though wondered if it should be kept for cocktail parties. She bought him a pair of leather gloves with fur lining and slid a tiny roll of paper into each finger saying how much she loved him. She started to knit him a scarf – Mam was showing her how. He promised to try and telephone on Christmas Day, but had no idea what time it would be.

Cathy wrote from Keighley in Yorkshire to say she was having a wonderful time. She was in the finance office and learning to type: '... The girls I'm billeted with are a scream. We go to the pub most nights, except for Saturdays when there's a dance on the base. Soldiers are bussed in from miles away and there are usually ten men for every girl. But the thing I like most is having a bed to myself. Honestly, Amy, it really is the gear sleeping on my own ...'

Harry had completed his basic training and was now at a camp just outside Leeds. Rumour had it that after Christmas his company was being sent to France.

Amy looked at the faded map pinned to the ticket office wall and discovered Keighley and Leeds weren't all that far from each other. She'd got the impression that Harry wasn't too happy in the Army, so she wrote and told him where Cathy was stationed. If he was interested, he could always seek her out.

She arrived at Pond Wood on Christmas Day in a snowstorm to find parcels waiting for her outside the ticket office door. Miss Feathers had knitted her a lovely warm tea cosy, Andrew Carter and Benny Roberts had bought her a box of Cadbury's chocolates, and Elsie Paddick, who went to Reece's tea dance every week, had left a bottle of Evening in Paris. Amy didn't use cheap scents like Evening in Paris any more and resolved to give it to one of her sisters, but quickly changed her mind. It was such a sweet, generous gesture: how could she possibly give the scent away? She sprinkled herself with it liberally before she went to light the fire and wind the clock.

Later in the morning, the sun came out and, for a brief while,

Pond Wood sparkled in its brilliance. More gifts arrived. Mr Clegg, looking strange in a balaclava helmet instead of a bowler hat, brought a bottle of port; Myra McCarthy presented her with a slice of Christmas cake; and a woman she didn't recognize came with an orange. 'You always give my granddaughter a sweet when her mother takes her to hospital,' she said. 'I'm very grateful.'

Susan Conway, her husband and children arrived in time to catch the 12.27 p.m. to Sandhills. 'We're having Christmas dinner at me mam's,' Susan whispered when she bought the tickets. 'I've managed to persuade John to stay the night. I'm *so* excited.' John was a weather-beaten individual of about thirty, who seemed to have been struck dumb by the sight of a female station master.

Amy sold more tickets than she'd expected to people who were off to visit relatives. At one o'clock Elspeth came with her dinner: roast turkey, roast spuds, and all the trimmings.

'I only picked them sprouts this morning,' Elspeth said. She sat in the armchair and relayed all the local gossip while Amy ate. Gladys Planter was having a baby, but Doris Sparrow wasn't. 'Everyone thought she was, but she's just putting on weight. She'll end up as big as a house if she's not careful. Oh, and Peter Alton had one of his hens pinched. He reckons someone from Kirkby took it for their Christmas dinner.'

As soon as Amy had finished, Elspeth said she'd better be getting back to Willie. She took the plate and departed, humming happily.

What did they do with their lives? Amy wondered. They had no children, didn't possess a wireless, their cottage had neither gas nor electricity, and she'd never known either use the train. Elspeth cooked a lot and William took care of their large garden, but that was all she knew. Did they read, play cards, sing hymns? Did they have any sort of social life? Just thinking about it made her feel depressed.

The 3.45 p.m. arrived from Liverpool, and Amy could have sworn she could hear the excited chatter before the train had even stopped, so she wasn't all that surprised to see her sisters get off, though felt terribly moved. Fancy them coming all this way to see her on Christmas Day! They wore almost identical hat, glove and scarf sets, knitted in a pretty, complicated Fair Isle pattern.

'Barney sent them us for Christmas,' Biddy explained. 'And sent Mam a lovely enamelled compact and lipstick case to match. Every time you look at her, she's powdering her nose and putting on more lippy.'

'She invited some awful chap from work to dinner,' Jacky cried. 'His name's Billy Martin. We just had to get out the way.'

'He never stops talking,' Biddy exclaimed, a case of the kettle calling the pot black if ever there was one.

Jacky giggled. 'He offered us *ciggies*!'

'He's staying to tea an' all,' Biddy declared. 'I think he's got the hots for her.'

'The what?' Amy demanded. Barney and Mam apart, she couldn't have been more pleased to see anyone.

'The hots – it means he fancies her something rotten,' Biddy explained. 'Lord, Amy, isn't this place *depressing*! It's like the end of the earth.'

'Let's go into the ticket office, on the other platform. It's lovely and warm.' In another three-quarters of an hour they would all catch the 4.27 p.m back to Liverpool, but there was still time to have a bit of a party.

She opened the port and the chocolates, and broke the cake into three pieces. She hardly drank at all – to be in charge of a station while under the influence of alcohol would be irresponsible.

They were singing 'Jingle Bells' when there was a knock on the door. Amy opened it to find Peter Alton outside. He wore a black hat with a wide brim, an ankle-length tweed overcoat and Wellington boots.

'I've brought you some eggs.' He handed her a cardboard box. 'Happy Christmas, Amy,' he gulped.

'Eggs!' Amy said faintly. The egg ration was one a week and the box felt heavy enough to have a dozen inside. 'Thank you. Thank you very much. These are my sisters, Jacky and Biddy,' she said, waving towards the girls, who were squashed together in the armchair, mouths open having stopped singing mid-carol. 'This is

Peter Alton: he's a farmer. Come in, Peter. Would you like a glass of port?'

'Yes, please.' He appeared glad to be asked. 'It's a bit dull at home. My sister and brother-in-law have brought slides of their holiday in Greece to show us.'

'It sounds dead boring,' Jacky said sympathetically. She was looking at Peter as if she'd like to eat him. 'Sit down,' she said, patting the arm of the chair.

The telephone rang, the sound so loud and penetrating that everyone jumped. Amy prayed it wasn't a message to say that the 4.27 p.m. would be late, but it was her father-in-law announcing that it was his intention to collect her from Exchange station and take her to dinner.

'What about the Adelphi? Are you up to it?'

'I would have been up to it, but Barney said he'd telephone today and I don't want to miss him.' For the same reason she wouldn't go and see her mother. She wondered what Elizabeth Patterson was doing on Christmas Day that left the entire evening free for her husband to take someone else to dinner.

'Then I shall bring dinner to you,' he said in a voice that brooked no argument.

She rang off. Jacky and Peter appeared to be getting on like a house on fire: Biddy looked a bit peeved. In the distance, Amy heard the signal click to indicate the train was coming.

Jacky was saying to Peter, 'Why don't you come back with us? You can always sleep in our Charlie's bed – he got married in September and left home,' she hastily explained.

Amy began to tidy up. She told the girls to put their coats on. Peter asked if he could use the telephone. He told the person who answered that he wouldn't be home until tomorrow, quickly replacing the receiver before questions could be asked as to where exactly he would be.

'Come on, everybody.' She ushered them outside and locked the door. Minutes later, the train puffed into the station. When it stopped, she could hear the telephone ringing in the ticket office, but there wasn't time to answer it now. It could be someone demanding to know what Peter was up to, it could be Mr Cookson asking for the time of the next train to London, or it could be Barney.

If it were Barney, he would call her at home tonight. Right now, she didn't care about the others.

Harry Patterson was disinclined to mix with his fellow soldiers. It wasn't that he was snobbish, but they had little in common with him and he had no idea what to say to them apart from to remark on the frightful weather. They'd stopped inviting him to come for a drink, as he always refused, convinced that his constitution wouldn't stand it: they seemed able to drink themselves to a standstill and wake up the next morning as fit as fiddles.

He had made a friend, though – a good one. Jack Wilkinson was twenty-five, two years older than he was. He had little in common with him, either. In fact, Jack made him feel like an ignorant oaf. Having left school at thirteen, he was self-taught, had fought on the side of the Socialists in the Spanish Civil War, and had read Darwin's *Origin of the Species*, Marx's *Das Kapital*, Hitler's *Mein Kampf*, and lots of other important books.

Harry claimed to have started some of the books, but had never found the time to finish. In fact, his favourite authors were Raymond Chandler and Dashiel Hammett, both thriller writers.

Jack was a bag of bones. His narrow face was drawn and lined, he looked twice his age, and it was hard to believe he'd had a decent meal in his life. He was already going thin on top. Yet women seemed to find him enormously attractive, whereas Harry, who had an enviable head of thick brown hair and was quietly handsome, was rarely given a second look by most women.

On Christmas Day, the men ate together in the mess and discussed the state of the war so far. Harry thought Hitler was likely to give up when he realized what the British had in store for him, but Jack just smiled and said that was most unlikely.

'We haven't yet had a taste of the German military might. It'll take more than what this country's got to offer at the present time to put off a chap like Hitler,' he said darkly. 'Would you like to go for a drink tonight, mate?'

'Well, actually, Jack,' Harry replied, a trifle embarrassed, 'I put my name down on the list to go to that dance in Keighley. A friend of my sister-in-law is based there: she's in the A.T.S. I thought it would be nice to look her up.'

'That's an excellent idea,' Jack said with enthusiasm. 'I'm a terror at the tango. Do you mind if I come with you?'

'Not at all.' Harry had visualized Jack only being interested in intellectual pursuits. For the life of him, he couldn't imagine him doing the tango.

The dance was being held in the mess. It wasn't a very big room and was already crammed to capacity when the troops arrived from Leeds. Red and green paper chains were looped around the walls, and there was a Christmas tree in the corner. Harry was already worn out after standing in the back of a draughty lorry and being thrown all over the place for what had seemed like hours. Jack asked a woman in civvies to dance and led her on to the floor with a dramatic flourish. The band were playing 'You, the Night and the Music' ...

Harry walked around the room twice in search of Cathy, but there was no sign. He left the mess and stood outside, wondering which way to go. He would never get used to the blackout: there was something genuinely creepy about crowds of invisible people walking past yet being able to hear their voices and snatches of their conversation.

Perhaps Cathy was still at work in the finance office. It seemed unlikely but it was the obvious place to try. He asked the next faceless person who came along where it might be found.

'Second right, first left,' he was told.

It sounded so easy, 'second right, first left', but even though the short journey was helped by the fact that the paths had been cleared and the snow was piled on what he assumed were grass verges, it was still a good fifteen minutes before Harry found the wooden building that served as the finance office. Like every other building on the camp, it was in total darkness, but he could hear voices, laughter and music inside. After a short search, he found the door and knocked loudly.

The door was opened an inch and a male voice said, 'Sorry,

mate, but this is a private party.'

The door closed and Harry banged on it even more loudly. 'I'm looking for Cathy Burns,' he shouted.

There was a shuffling noise inside and once again the door was opened a crack. 'Harry!' hissed another voice, a female one this time. 'Harry Patterson!' A hand reached out and dragged him into a dimly-lit room where desks had been pushed against the wall and three couples were dancing to 'Whispering Grass', the music issuing from a portable radiogram on one of the desks. Arms were thrown around his neck and his cheek was kissed. 'How lovely to see you, Harry,' said Cathy Burns.

She looked very different from how she had seemed on Southport pier. Could it really be only eight months ago? She was more grown up – *much* more grown up. Could she possibly be taller? He'd liked her, but she'd seemed an insignificant little thing, completely over-shadowed by her beautiful friend, just as Harry had lived his life in the shadow of his charming brother. Now they were both privates in the Army, and Amy and Barney were nowhere in sight.

'There's refreshments in the next room, though there's not much left,' Cathy said. She wore a pretty cream blouse and a tweed skirt. Harry wished he wasn't wearing his uniform. 'Just enough to fill a corner.' She took his hand and they went into another office where she gave him a paper plate. Harry helped himself to a sausage roll, a sardine sandwich and a jam tart. 'Would you like some wine?' Cathy asked. 'We could only get red.'

'Great,' Harry muttered, a sardine sandwich already in his mouth. This was all very civilized, very different from how life had been since he'd joined the Army. He had a feeling he was about to enjoy himself.

Cathy introduced him to the crowd – there were about twenty of them there. 'This is Harry,' she shouted. 'We knew each other in Liverpool. I won't bother telling him your names; he'll never remember.'

The women were very emancipated, asking the men to dance, talking to them without any hint of flirtatiousness. They discussed the war, their work, politics. No one mentioned the awful weather.

He'd been there for about an hour when the radiogram was turned off and a young man, who sounded very like Bing Crosby, sang 'Two Sleepy People', 'We'll Meet Again', and 'There's a Boy Coming Home on Leave'.

Harry never forgot that young man. He only looked about sixteen, but there was something about his young face and wonderful voice that seemed to express all the horror and emotion of the war: the sense of loss, the feeling of helplessness when everything went wrong, and the joy when things went right.

At half past eleven, when it was time for him to leave, Harry felt extraordinarily fond of everyone, particularly Cathy. They'd danced together several times. She'd put her arms around his neck, rested her head on his shoulder, while his hands were spread protectively over her back.

'I don't want to go,' he whispered.

'I wish you could stay,' she whispered back. 'Maybe you could come and see us again one day.'

'I will if I can.' He had no idea if transport to the camp was regularly available. If not, he'd find out if he could cadge a lift. 'We're being sent to France any minute.'

'I'll miss you.' She laughed huskily. 'That's a joke: we've only met once before.'

'I should have got in touch with you a long time ago.'

'I'd always hoped you would.'

Harry reached for his greatcoat. 'I really must go.'

Cathy came with him to where the lorry was parked outside the mess. 'Merry Christmas,' she said, kissing him.

'And a Happy New Year.' He kissed her back. They were both nearly bowled over by a group of soldiers, very much the worse for wear, who were making for the lorry.

'Tara, Harry.' She held his hand for a few seconds before letting go.

'Bye, Cathy.' Harry wished it were daylight so he could see her properly. He wished he wasn't stationed so very far away. He wished there wasn't a war on.

But if wishes were horses, then beggars would ride, he thought sadly.

He discovered the lorry was taking the men to Keighley for another dance on New Year's Eve, so put his name down, and wrote and told Cathy to expect him. Jack had thoroughly enjoyed himself and put his name down, too. But on the Wednesday, four days before New Year's Eve, the men were ordered to get their kits together and to be ready to leave for France the following morning.

On New Year's Eve, Harry and Jack were sitting in a French café in the middle of nowhere with a jug of wine between them. The café was packed with British troops, and there wasn't a single female present. The French were either keeping their women safely out of the way of the Army, or they were forbidden to enter bars.

Either way, it was a good thing, Harry thought primly. He wouldn't have wanted a female relative of his mixing with this baying mob. They were like animals, stewed to their eyebrows on cheap wine. He said as much to Jack.

'Oh, they're all right,' Jack said easily. 'Someone's only got to shout, "Let's drink to King and country", and they'll be on their feet like a shot, as sober as judges. Right now, they're just releasing their feelings.' He gave Harry a keen look. 'You could do with releasing a few feelings, mate. You hold yourself as tight as a Gurkha's foreskin.'

'It must be the way I was brought up.' Harry laughed, making a joke of it, though Jack was probably right. The men began to sing 'La Marseillaise'. Behind the bar, the staff were standing to attention, no doubt resenting such a rowdy rendition of their national anthem.

Harry felt deeply depressed. He would never be able to let go like his fellow soldiers. He was no good for anything, he thought miserably. The feelings he had for Cathy were nothing like those his brother had for Amy. He would make a very half-hearted lover. For Cathy's sake, he wouldn't continue the correspondence he'd started back in England. He had written her a sort of love letter, only one. It was very mild, not the least bit spontaneous. He'd had to write it four times before he could get it right – well, sort of right.

Later, when he was lying on the floor of the church that the Army had commandeered as living quarters for the lower ranks, listening to the tossing and turning, the snoring and groaning, and all the other noises the men were making in their sleep, Harry had the horrible feeling that the few hours he'd spent in Keighley with Cathy Burns could well turn out to be the high point of his life, that he would never again enjoy himself quite so much.

The snow melted, as everyone had known it would. The grass beneath was revealed to be an exceptionally vivid green and the soil a rich, chocolaty brown. The streets looked as if they'd been given a good wash with soapsuds.

Snowdrops and, later, bluebells appeared on the banks of Pond Wood station. William Maxwell had brought daffodil and tulip bulbs, and planted them in the wooden boxes that Amy was surprised to discover were attached to the waiting-room windows, having been hidden underneath the snow all this time. It was as if a magician had waved his wand and transformed the station – the entire country – into this astonishingly vibrant place where it would have been wonderful to live had it not been for the war.

The sight of everything bursting into life all around her reminded Amy of the baby she had lost. If she hadn't had the miscarriage, her baby would soon have been born. By now, she would have bought the cot and all the other things a small baby needed, and Mam would have knitted loads of clothes. She could well have left the flat and be living somewhere more suitable for a mother with a child, having never heard of Pond Wood and its station.

She scrubbed and polished the waiting rooms, put jars of flowers on the mantelpieces, and never told a soul how miserable she felt. She felt ten times worse when Barney telephoned late one night, long after she'd gone to bed, to say that he was being sent to France.

'You never know, I might meet up with Harry,' he sighed.

'But we haven't seen each other for ages,' Amy protested. She was sitting in her nightie on the padded telephone seat and doing her utmost to hold back the tears. The last time she'd seen him was from the window, a dark figure passing along the moonlit road until he'd vanished into the shadows. Just imagine if she never saw him again. What if they'd kissed for the very last time?

'I know, darling,' he said gruffly.

'Look after yourself, Barney.' She almost wished there were no such things as telephones. There was something horrible about hearing his voice while knowing he was miles and miles away and she could neither see nor touch him. All she could do was remember the way his brown eyes had looked at her and the feeling of his lips against hers.

They didn't even say goodbye because the line suddenly went dead. He'd warned her he didn't have much change, but it still came as a shock. She shouted, 'Barney, Barney,' several times, but it didn't bring him back.

In April, Hitler invaded Norway and Denmark. A month later, his armies marched through Holland and Belgium on their way towards France. At the same time, Neville Chamberlain, the Prime Minister, lost a vote of confidence in his government, and was replaced by Winston Churchill.

Until Barney went away, Amy had never bothered to read the newspapers, but now she bought the *Daily Express* on Exchange station every day and read it on the train to Pond Wood. At night, when she was getting ready for bed, she turned on the wireless for the nine o'clock news. Until then, she'd only put it on for the music.

She listened with horror to the accounts of Hitler's troops advancing triumphantly across France. She heard Churchill's first speech to the population since he'd become Prime Minister: 'The British and French peoples have advanced to rescue not only Europe, but mankind from the foulest and most soul-destroying tyranny which has ever darkened and stained the pages of history.'

The words made her feel as if the world was about to end. What if Germany won the war? It was something she hadn't thought possible before.

By the end of May the German Blitzkrieg had forced thousands of British troops to abandon their equipment and retreat to Dunkirk on the French coast where hundreds of boats, large and small, had assembled to take them back to England.

The rescue effort went on for days. Amy would jump whenever the phone rang in the ticket office or at home, her heart lifting, convinced it was Barney to say he'd arrived back safely and would see her in a few days – and to wish her happy birthday, because in another few days she would be nineteen.

The telephone was ringing in the ticket office when she returned after waving off the 9.45 a.m. to Wigan one morning. It was Leo Patterson. For the briefest second, she thought it was Barney because their voices were so alike, but he didn't have his father's broad Irish accent.

'Harry's back,' he told her. 'He's just phoned from Dover, safe and sound.'

Amy said she was really pleased, which she was, but couldn't help wishing that it was her husband, not his brother, who was home. 'I don't suppose he saw anything of Barney,' she asked hopefully.

There was a pause. 'It so happens that he did.' She could tell from the pause, and the way the words were said, that the news wasn't good. 'They met on the road to Dunkirk. Harry was on his way to the rescue boats, but Barney was heading back the way he'd come. His unit is staying behind to try and stop the Germans from reaching the coast … Are you all right, Amy? *Amy!*' he shouted when she didn't answer.

She found her voice. 'Thank you for calling, Leo,' she said politely. 'I shall have to go. Someone wants to buy a ticket.'

Afterwards, she was glad the news had come while she was at work. It was essential she get on with things, not just lie down and stare at the ceiling as she would have done at home in the flat. There were trains to see to, tickets to sell and rather less important telephone calls that had to be dealt with.

When Harry arrived home he told her exactly what had occurred on the road to Dunkirk. He looked excessively weary and was limping badly, not because he'd been injured, but because his feet were full of sores and blisters after tramping for miles in ill-fitting boots and socks that were full of holes.

'I was struggling along with my good friend, Jack Wilkinson,' he said tiredly. 'Jack had sprained his ankle and was having a job walking. All of a sudden a horn sounded and went on and on and on. I never dreamt it was someone trying to attract my attention until I heard a voice yell, "Harry, Harry Patterson. Look over here, you blithering idiot," and I realized it was Barney.'

Amy gasped. The mere mention of his name had brought him closer to her.

'He was driving a lorry,' Harry went on. 'Naturally, we stopped and had a long chat. He'd just transported a bunch of wounded men to Dunkirk to be taken home, and was on his way back to rejoin his unit. Jack and I, we still had a couple of miles to go. Barney said he wished he could have turned round and taken us, but he'd already been gone much longer than expected. The roads were packed with refugees,' Harry explained. 'Poor buggers, most of them had lost everything. All they wanted was to get out of the way of the Germans. Anyway, Barney and I shook hands and off we went, him to the north and me to the south. I tell you what though, Amy,' he said in a dead voice. 'I've never felt worse in my life than when I watched him drive away: my brother to face the enemy; me on my way home.'

Could Barney actually *die*? Amy had said so many prayers that she'd made herself believe he would never be killed. It terrified her to think how vulnerable he would be in a foreign country surrounded by enemy troops.

Harry continued, 'I told myself that if it weren't for Jack, if he hadn't needed me so badly, I would have jumped in the lorry and gone with Barney, but that's probably not true. The truth is, Amy, I'm a coward. If it had been me in the lorry, I think I would have abandoned it and come home. I'm sure I could have thought up a plausible explanation. It was so chaotic over there.'

'If you'd gone with Barney,' Amy said, 'if the two of you hadn't come back, then your mam and dad would have been twice as upset.'

'I don't think so,' Harry said bitterly. 'They both make it obvious they'd sooner it was Barney who'd come home. They never made much secret of the fact they preferred him to me. I know you'd sooner have Barney sitting here, it's understandable, but for my own mother and father to make it so bloody obvious doesn't do much for a chap's self-esteem.'

'I'm sure that's not true, Harry,' Amy said, though she thought it almost certainly was.

Harry was home for five days. The June weather was fine and sunny, and she invited him to Pond Wood station to experience the life of a station master for a day, then took him to Agate Street for Sunday dinner, as he'd never met her family. The same night, she went with him to the pictures to see *Adventure in Manhattan* with Joel McCrea, and he treated her to dinner in Southport on Monday evening. For Harry's sake, Amy made herself smile and appear to be enjoying herself, but all she could think about was Barney.

He told her about meeting Cathy on Christmas Day, and she told him that Cathy had described their meeting in a letter.

'My mate, Jack,' he said, 'is going back to Leeds until his ankle gets better. He's promised to look up Cathy for me.'

The next day Harry himself would go by train to a base in Colchester, and reckoned his eventual destination would be North Africa. 'France is bound to capitulate any minute,' he said. 'The next battle will be fought in the desert.'

Amy didn't ask what would happen to Barney if France capitulated. Harry was no more likely to know than she was.

Harry had only been gone a few days when she heard that eight thousand British troops, along with many more of their French comrades, had been taken prisoner in a place called St Valery en Caux. Even the general in charge had been captured.

A whole month passed without a word. Amy was convinced that Barney was still alive otherwise she would have received one of the dreaded orange telegrams saying he'd been killed in action. She positively refused to allow herself to think any other way.

July had turned into August when she had a letter from the War Office to say that her husband had been taken prisoner. It ended: 'You will be advised of his location when information is received from the German authorities via the Red Cross.'

Some people had said the war would only last six months, but it was almost a year since it had started and there was no sign of an end. How long would it be before she saw her husband again? Amy wondered. Surely war wouldn't continue for yet another year. It hardly seemed possible. She was happy that he was no longer fighting but she desperately wanted to see him.

At the end of August, Pond Wood had its annual summer fair. Amy was almost moved to tears when she discovered that, purely for her sake, it was being held in the field next to the station rather than its usual place at least a mile away. It was Mr Clegg, chairman of the summer fair committee, who told her. 'You're one of us now, Amy. How can we possibly enjoy ourselves while you're stuck here, away from all the excitement?'

'They should have had it by the station before,' said Susan Conway when she heard. 'Me mam's always wanted to come, but it was too far to walk.'

Amy's own mam made two jam sponges for the cake stall, the eggs supplied by Peter Alton, who was now Jacky's official boy-friend, much to Biddy's chagrin. Captain Kirby-Greene had tidied his wardrobe and donated a beautiful velvet dressing gown for the second-hand clothes stall. He was very much looking forward to being there.

The day, a Saturday, started off cloudy. Tables for the stalls arrived on a horse and cart, the horse sporting a pink bow for the occasion. Shortly after the stalls had been erected and two tents had been put up for the refreshments and for the flower and vegetable displays, a trickle of people began to arrive, most of whom Amy had never seen before. Some of the older women looked as if they belonged in the last century with their white cotton bonnets and lacy shoulder shawls, and skirts right down to their ankles. The sun came out like a blessing, warming the earth and melting the jellies in the refreshment tent.

Quite a few more people arrived on the 12.27 p.m. train from Wigan, and even more on the 1.45 p.m. from Liverpool, including Amy's mam, both her sisters and, much to her surprise, Charlie and Marion. Captain Kirby-Greene alighted, resplendent in a navy-blue blazer with glittering brass buttons, white shirt and colourful cravat. With a flamboyant gesture, he held out his arm for Amy's mother to take. She looked embarrassed, but allowed herself to be escorted on to the field. Later, they did the three-legged race together and came third.

The area of the station, usually so quiet between trains, was today a froth of voices. Apart from the stalls, there was a baby show, a knobbly knees competition, a fancy dress contest, a prize for the biggest hen, and a dog obedience test, which was accompanied by a great deal of barking. William Maxwell's roses and carrots each won a first prize, and he'd also grown the biggest marrow.

Amy had plenty of time between trains to have turns on the roll-a-penny, the hoop-la and the coconut shy that used empty tins instead of coconuts. By some miracle, she hit the bull on the darts and made the highest score so far, possibly worthy of a prize, and dropped three pennies in the barrel full of water in the hope one would land on the half-crown piece at the bottom, but none went anywhere near.

The brass band arrived from Wigan on the 2.27 p.m., wearing royal-blue uniforms decorated with gold braid. They played 'Alexander's Ragtime Band', 'You Are My Sunshine' and other stirring marches, finishing with 'We Saw the Sea' from a Fred Astaire picture – one of the first Amy had ever seen. She'd gone with Cathy, and the memory of those carefree days when war had been an unimaginable horror made her feel very sad and very old.

Even today, in the heart of the peaceful countryside, there was no getting away from the reality of war. There were reminders on the stalls that the money raised by the fair would be donated to the Pond Wood Spitfire Fund.

The day wore on and the air became cooler. People started to wander home along the fragrant, dusty lanes, or catch trains to their various destinations. The brass band left after drinking gallons of tea. When Amy returned to the ticket office, she found an elderly gentleman in a panama hat studying the timetable on the wall. 'Can I help you?' she enquired.

'I was just looking up the time of the next train to London,' he explained.

'It's the twenty-seven minutes past six. You have to change at Exchange station for the seven-thirty from Lime Street to Euston,' Amy told him gently. She'd often wondered what Mr Cookson looked like.

'Thank you, miss,' he said, courteously raising his hat and smiling at her sweetly.

Tables were being folded and stacked on the back of the cart. The horse made soft snuffling sounds, as if it understood it would shortly be going home.

Amy went to find Mr Clegg and thank him for a wonderful day. All the Currans had enjoyed themselves. Nearly everyone had won a prize, and even Marion, usually so difficult to please, was thrilled to bits, having bought the captain's dressing gown with the intention of turning it into a coat.

Mr Clegg warmly shook Amy's hand and said she had been an adornment to the fair. 'And your two beautiful sisters and even more beautiful mother. I'll see you on Monday morning, my dear. Let's hope this lovely weather continues over the weekend.'

The lovely weather did continue, but Amy didn't see Mr Clegg on Monday morning, because by then Pond Wood station no longer existed. Apart from Sheila Conway, who became a good friend, she never saw anyone from the village again.


The bombs had started to fall in June, landing in fields on the outskirts of the city. In July the raids were more frequent. With August came the first fatalities and raids on the enemy's main target, Liverpool Docks.

Amy always got out of bed when the siren went, a terrifying, spine-chilling sound. She would make tea and sit in the dark with the curtains pulled back, watching the strange green glow where incendiary bombs had fallen. During these times she felt wretchedly lonely, as if she were the only person in the world. She badly wanted Barney, but didn't even have an address to write to. It was a relief when the All Clear would go and she could return to bed.

★

On the Monday after the Pond Wood fair, Amy arrived at Lime Street station and was surprised to see a hastily chalked notice announcing that the Wigan train would only go as far as Kirkby.

'What's this all about?' she asked Paddy Fahey who collected the tickets. Paddy was another L.M.S. employee who'd retired and returned to work because his country needed him. This morning he looked extremely grave, and his old, thin face was devoid of its usual cheery smile.

'Ah, Amy, luv,' he said, 'Ossie Edwards wants to see you.'

'Why?' Amy demanded.

'I'll tell you, luv, if you'll give me a chance. On Saturday night, a bomb dropped on Pond Wood station. The lines are up, the bridge is damaged, both the waiting rooms are rubble and there's a crater big enough to bury a double-decker bus. You best go and see Ossie, luv. I expect he's already got something else lined up for you to do.'

# Chapter 11

## May 1971
## Pearl

Gary Finnegan watched his father's skilful play with the ball, the way he transferred it from knee to head and from head to knee, making it look so simple. Rob wore a black-and-white football strip and his movements were very graceful, balletic almost. There was a look of awe on his son's face, as if he were just as impressed as the other kids in classes one and two – girls as well as boys.

The children were sitting on the grass by the north end goal, and I was kneeling a few feet behind. 'Is that really your dad, Gary?' I heard Matthew Watts ask. Matthew was a hefty lad from class two who could be a bit of a bully if not closely watched.

'Yes.' I was touched by the amount of pride that Gary managed to convey in this single-syllable word. 'He was the team captain back in Uganda.'

'Where's Uganda?' one of the girls asked.

'In Africa,' Gary replied.

'You used to live in Africa?' Matthew was impressed. 'Isn't that on the other side of the world?'

'Almost,' Gary said simply.

'He's the gear, your dad,' another boy said admiringly.

Cathy Burns came over. She wore the navy-blue suit I had seen numerous times, but it looked different somehow. It took a while for me to realize there was no longer any grey in her hair: she must have had it tinted. It made her look younger. 'He's extremely professional,' she said. 'That was a really good idea you had, Pearl, inviting him. Do you think he'd mind coming again to do it for the older children?'

'I'm sure he wouldn't mind a bit.' I was convinced Rob would do anything if he thought it would help Gary settle in school. He'd asked the children to gather around him in a circle and was gently heading the ball to each in turn. They were totally absorbed.

'He's an awfully nice young man,' she said. 'It's a pity about his wife. Where did you say you met him?'

'Owen Owen's. He'd been buying clothes for Gary, all the wrong things. I suggested he return them and buy the right ones.' Looking back, it seemed quite touching, the idea of Rob taking over his dead wife's role. I wondered if it would seem just as touching for a widow to be seen buying parts for a car.

'When he's finished, perhaps he'd like a cup of tea in my office. You must come too, Pearl. Sarah can look after your class for a while.'

'I'll be there,' I said.

'Good.' She gave me knowing smile. 'Is it serious between you two?'

I gasped. 'It isn't *anything* between us. You couldn't even call us friends.' That wasn't quite true.

'What a pity!' She winked in a way I could only describe as lewd. 'If I were twenty years younger or he were twenty years older, I'd be over the moon if there was something between him and me.'

I remember someone saying once – it could only have been Charles or Marion, or possibly Uncle Harry – that Cathy Burns had had a bit of reputation when she was in the Army. 'She was a proper flirt,' the person had said. I recalled now it was Granny Curran who'd said it, but only in a nice, jokey way. She'd been very fond of Cathy.

On reflection, I thought it a terrible pity that flirtatious Cathy Burns had ended up as the sober and respectable Miss Burns, head-mistress of St Kentigern's. Had the first Cathy been happier than the second? I wondered. Or was it the other way around?

Rob said he would be pleased to come again. We were in Cathy Burns's office, and he'd changed into jeans and a white T-shirt. Not only that, he would come twice so the top classes could have separate demonstrations. 'I work nights, so early mornings would be best, and I can then grab a few hours' sleep in the afternoon.'

It was arranged he would be there the next two Mondays at half past nine. He said it didn't matter if it was raining as he could manage almost as well in the gym as outside.

'That would be wonderful,' Cathy said as she poured the tea. 'We haven't got a sports or P.E. instructor. Each form teacher just does the best he or she can. We have a single male teacher here, but he's less interested in sport than the women. It's nice to have an expert for a change.'

'I'm glad I can be of help,' Rob said politely, while stressing he wasn't exactly an expert.

I took my own tea and watched him through lowered lids, trying to work out how I felt about him. This was the fifth time we'd met. I must have an opinion of some sort by now. He felt familiar to me, as if I'd known him for a very long time and was someone I could rely on. I liked and trusted him. He was easy to be with. Even the last occasion when we'd met and he'd been angry because Gary had come home hurt from school, somehow I had known that we wouldn't fall out – and we hadn't. It was as if we were very slowly growing on each other until one day we would realize we knew each other very well. I had no idea what would happen then.

He was discussing football with Cathy. 'My dad,' she was saying, 'was an Everton supporter and he worshipped the ground that Dixie Dean walked on. He used to cross himself every time his name was mentioned. I'm not exaggerating.'

'Dixie Dean,' Rob said in a voice tight with awe, 'scored more goals in one season than any other footballer – sixty altogether. No one's come anywhere near that number either before or since. But Alan Ball is doing his utmost. He's probably the best player Everton's had since Dixie.'

They chatted about the World Cup that England had won five years ago. I had nothing to say about it. I had grown up in a house where sport was rarely discussed. Charles was neither a participant nor a spectator. In addition to her badminton Marion watched the tennis from Wimbledon for two weeks of the year, but that was all. When they'd first moved to the house in Aintree, my aunt and uncle told me they had watched the Grand National from an upstairs window, but only because they could do it for free and it was something to boast about at work. I remember meeting Trish on World Cup Final day: England had been playing Germany and the centre of Liverpool was a ghost town.

The tea finished and the subject of football exhausted, Cathy asked if I would walk Rob to his car. I expected him to insist there was no need, but he didn't. Should I be flattered? I wondered.

'I think that went very well,' he said when we were outside.

'Oh, it did,' I assured him. 'I'm sure it's done Gary loads of good.'

He raised his eyebrows. 'You think so?'

'Lots of the kids will want to be mates with him because you're his dad.'

We'd reached his car, an old grey Morris Minor that had seen better days. He opened the door – it creaked mightily – and leaned on the roof. 'You know when you were at the flat last week,' he said, 'and you looked so broken-hearted that I asked what was wrong? You didn't tell me because Gary woke up and then you had to go back to school. Why don't I take you to dinner on Saturday if I can persuade Bess to babysit? We can talk – about you for a change, rather than Gary and me and our problems.'

'You've got more problems than I have,' I said. 'Mine are all in the past.'

I thought then about my mother, who could come home any minute after spending twenty years in prison for murdering my father, and supposed that some of my problems existed now.

'I'm all right,' I added as an afterthought, though I wasn't, never had been and probably never would be.

'Will it be all right for Saturday, then? If Bess can't do it, I'll try to think of something else we can do, but it would have to be with Gary,' he said apologetically.

'Both would be fine with me.'

Cathy was waiting by the back entrance to the school when I returned. 'Have you noticed my hair?' she asked. I'd thought she'd been waiting to say something about Rob.

'Yes, of course I have. You've had it tinted; all your grey has gone.'

'Is it noticeable? So far, no one's said a word.' She ran her fingers through the hair to fluff it out. She sounded hurt.

'They're not likely to, are they? You're the headmistress. No one's going to make personal remarks about your appearance.' I hoped *that* remark wasn't too personal, but I had known her all my life, after all. 'Your hair looks very nice,' I said. It was smooth and brown and very silky.

'Thank you. I was thinking of having a shaggy perm.' She fluffed the hair again. 'Do you know anything about them?'

'No. I've never had a perm, and neither has Marion.'

She chuckled. 'Your mother gave me a home perm when I came back after the war. She had to cut it all off, as my hair bent rather than curled. It looked awful.' She opened the door for me to go inside. 'When we were very young,' she said chattily as we walked along the corridor, 'Amy and me had enormous fun with make-up. We were forever getting chased out of Woolies' for trying on the lipsticks – that was before I went to work there. I remember, when we were at school, we attempted to colour our eyelashes with black ink. It's a wonder we didn't go blind.' She chuckled again, but this time it was followed by a sigh. 'Oh, Pearl, I do wish I could have those times back. Not just with your mum, but the war years, too. I think it was only then that I felt truly alive.'

A different person, someone a bit more grown up, would have made an appropriate comment and squeezed her hand. Instead I tried frantically to think of a suitable reply, and came up with a pathetic, 'Oh, dear!'

Charles and Marion had stopped getting along. In the twenty years I'd lived with them, I'd never known them have a major row. Marion usually triggered the minor ones over something trivial like Charles forgetting to return his library books on time and incurring a fine, leaving a tap dripping, or slopping puddles of tea on the worktop.

Lately, though, it was Charles who was annoyed. 'But what have I *done*?' I heard Marion wail on more than one occasion.

To be honest, it was all rather childish and put me in mind of the arguments the children had at school. Perhaps I was being unreasonable to think it served Marion right to be on the receiving end for a change.

I eavesdropped shamelessly. It had started when I was very small. My parents had fought endlessly in our bungalow by Sefton Park. Despite the door being closed, I could hear every word that was said as my father accused my mother of sleeping with virtually every man in Liverpool while he'd been away. In those days, I couldn't understand what was wrong with sleeping with another person, even if it was a man.

'You *whore*!' he would shout. 'Dirty, filthy whore!'

'Barney,' my mother would say tiredly. 'Darling ...'

'Don't darling me – *whore*!'

Sometimes, the rows would end with my father bursting into tears and my mother comforting him. 'Tell me what's wrong, darling, please. Maybe I can make things right again.'

'You can't, you can't,' my dad would weep. 'No one can do anything.'

There were nights when I would fall asleep to the sound of my father's frantic voice and my mother's gentle replies. Next morning, I could never be sure if the words I'd heard had been real or if I had dreamed them.

Anyway, I was so used to listening to adult conversations that I continued the practice when I came to live with Charles and Marion, mainly because, at first, a lot of the discussions were about me. Should Marion cut down her hours at the English Electric or arrange for someone to pick me up from school? Would Grandma Curran do it? 'Of course she would,' Charles had said. 'She adores Pearl.' What were they going to do about Grandma Patterson? 'Amy doesn't want that woman anywhere near her daughter,' Charles would say; they had the same conversations many times. I'd used to wonder why my mother had gone away if she was so concerned for my welfare.

This particular row took place twenty years later when Charles and Marion were in the lounge and I was in the breakfast room preparing the next day's lessons.

'But what have I done?' Marion hissed for what must have been the sixth or seventh time.

'You haven't done anything,' Charles replied. I visualized him giving an indifferent shrug.

'Then why are you being so ... so *cold* with me?'

'I'm not aware I'm being cold.'

'Well, you are, and it's not fair, Charles. You have no right to behave like this and refuse to tell me why.'

'That's because there isn't a why.'

'Oh, don't be stupid. I'm going to bed.'

'Goodnight,' Charles said indifferently.

'Good*night*.' Marion slammed the door.

I told Rob about the ongoing quarrel on Saturday night. We went to the Chinese restaurant in Bold Street where I'd been with Uncle Harry. The food and wine were just as good, and there was a nice atmosphere. I had my usual curried prawns and rice; Rob was more adventurous and chose mini-portions of six different things.

We chatted about school; Cathy Burns had fascinated him. 'She looks like a typical headmistress, yet she's got this look in her eye ...' He left the sentence unfinished. I didn't tell him that she had been just as fascinated with him.

I said that, since Monday, Gary had been basking in the glow of his father's magnificent exhibition of ball control. 'He's been invited to two parties. Has he told you?'

'Yes.' He looked worried. 'What am I supposed to do? Buy presents, obviously, but do I send cakes and stuff?' He pulled a horrified face. 'I won't be expected to stay and help with the games, will I?'

I assured him a present was quite enough and that he wouldn't have to stay. I asked when it was Gary's birthday, and he said he would be six in January.

'I wonder where we'll be then?' He stared at his plate, as if the future was mapped out there. 'I'm in two minds about going back to the police. It's a good job, the pay's decent, but the hours are lousy if you're a single parent. I still fancy going abroad, but so far nothing's come up that would suit me. I still have hopes of Canada.'

'Gary said you went to look at a house in Manchester.'

He wrinkled his nose. 'I must have been mad. I'd seen a job advertised, but the wages were hopeless. Common sense dawned on the train there, and I came straight home again. Trouble is, I truly don't know what to do with the rest of my life – and Gary's life.'

We'd reached the pudding stage. I said I couldn't eat any more, and Rob declared himself full. He ordered coffee, and as soon as it arrived he looked at me expectantly. I duly told him the story of my life.

When I finished, he looked so stunned that it was a while before he could bring himself to speak. When he did, it was to admit that he didn't know what to say, 'Other than I'm flabbergasted. Struck all of a heap, as my mother would have said.'

'I've brought a photo.' I took out of my bag the photograph from the file. 'This is of my parents at their wedding. The newspapers used it during the trial.' They'd gone straight from the wedding to a photographer's. They were standing stiffly, linking arms, yet the wide grins on both their faces were wildly at odds with their formal pose.

'Wow!' Rob said. 'They look happy.'

'Don't they! My mother was only eighteen and my father twenty-one. They got married without telling anyone.'

'They look like a Hollywood couple. I can see where you get your looks from: you're the spitting image of your dad.'

'Everyone says that.' I sighed. I'd much rather take after my mother. 'Have you got a photo of Jenny?'

He brought out a wallet and showed me a small photograph. 'I took this the day before she drowned. We were on a beach near Barcelona. They thought it was cramp'

The photo showed a pretty, brown-haired girl wearing a gold Alice band, a bright red halter-top and white shorts. Unlike my photo, it was in colour. She was kneeling on the sand with two-year-old Gary leaning against her. I remembered him saying his mum's eyes were green, but this wasn't apparent from the photo.

The woman was smiling directly at the camera – presumably at Rob, her husband – and looked as if she hadn't a care in the world.

'She looks happy, too,' I said.

'The world would be a pretty terrible place if we knew what was in store for us,' Rob said. 'Fortunately, Jenny didn't know she'd be dead less than twenty-four hours after that was taken.'

And my parents didn't know that the day would eventually come when one would murder the other.

The night out with Rob couldn't really be described as enjoyable, but it wasn't disagreeable either. I suppose 'cathartic' was the right word. It was the first time in my life that I'd told another person about the tragedy of my parents, and I felt better afterwards. I don't think I could have confided in a more understanding person, and that helped a lot.

We'd come to Liverpool in our own cars and had agreed to leave them in the car park in St John's Market, though they were on different floors. Rob walked with me to mine. When we reached it, he shook my hand and said he'd had a nice time. I wasn't sure whether to be glad or sorry that he hadn't kissed me, but then he pulled me towards him and kissed my cheek. I still wasn't sure how I felt. Would I ever?

He said he was taking Gary to Southport tomorrow afternoon and would I care to come with them? 'I expect you won't want to,' he added hurriedly. 'After all, you're dealing with other people's kids all week long. Weekends, you'll be glad to see the back of them.'

'I really like Gary,' I said. 'I'd love to see both of you tomorrow.'

'Good.' He looked pleased. 'Shall I pick you up at about one? I'd planned to go earlier, but I promised I'd give Bess a hand with the garden after Mass.'

'I hope you're not cutting down trees or anything like that,' I said. 'It's the nicest garden I've ever been in.'

'No, but it needs weeding; next door have complained about them coming through the fence.'

'That'll all right then. I'd better give you my address.' I had a letter from Trish in my bag (she hated London and longed to be back in Liverpool). I gave the envelope to Rob.

'See you tomorrow,' he said, taking it.

I too had something to do after Mass. Hilda Dooley's flat purchase was progressing like a dream. It belonged to an old lady, Mrs Edmunds, who had already gone to live with her daughter, and as Hilda didn't have a property to sell and had already been offered a mortgage, there was nothing to hold up the proceedings.

Mrs Edmunds had even let her have the key, and she invited me to have a look at the place. 'I can have any furniture that I want,' Hilda told me as she showed me round, 'so I said I'd have the lot. It really suits the place, much better than modern stuff would. Everything's just as I want it.'

Clifford Thompson and Mrs Dooley were already there. Almost owning her own home and having a boyfriend had done Hilda the world of good. Everyone in school kept remarking on how well she looked. Somehow her thin hair looked thicker and even her buck teeth didn't seem to stick out quite so much.

Mrs Dooley wore a slinky black frock and black lace tights, which made her look like mutton dressed up as lamb.

I marvelled at how well Hilda and Clifford were getting on. I'm pretty certain they'd slept together: there was an intimacy between them, their hands touched a lot, and they exchanged quick little glances. You'd think they'd known each other for ever.

The flat was lovely. It looked Victorian inside as well as out. I loved the fancy tiled fireplace in the odd-shaped lounge that wasn't quite square and the ancient bathroom with its arched window. Normally, I didn't like old-fashioned furniture – it was often too big and cumbersome – but the top floor of the old house had low ceilings and narrow stairs and could only accommodate furniture I would describe as 'bijou'. The tiny kitchen needed a complete overhaul, but Hilda was leaving it until she'd saved enough to have it done.

She was obviously revelling in her role as hostess and soon-to-be-owner of a property in one of the best positions in Liverpool. From the living-room window, the River Mersey could be seen twinkling less than a mile away.

I soon understood why Hilda had invited her mother. She was making up for all the years her mother had made her feel small. Now *she* was the one on top, the one with the handsome boyfriend and the lovely home. I wouldn't be a bit surprised if Hilda and Clifford didn't announce they were shortly getting married. Perversely, I couldn't help but feel sorry for Mrs Dooley. She looked really pathetic in her sexy clothes, and didn't open her mouth once.

I told Charles and Marion when I got home that someone was coming to collect me and we were going to Southport. 'It's one of the fathers from school with his little boy,' I said.

Charles raised an eyebrow. 'And what about the father from school's wife?'

'She's dead.'

'How old is he? He sounds old.'

'He's twenty-eight,' I said. 'Only three years older than me.'

'Do you like him?'

'Am I likely to go to Southport with someone I didn't like?'

'I suppose not,' Charles conceded. 'Can I be doing something outside when he comes, like cutting the hedge, so I have a good look at him?'

'If you want.'

So, when Rob and Gary arrived, Charles was snipping away at the privet hedge that had been trimmed over the years to a perfect wavy line. I often saw people admiring Charles's hedge, and wondered if some came from quite far away. Perhaps the hedge had become a tourist attraction.

Rob had the window down, and Charles bent and wished him good morning. Rob said, 'Hello, there.' I opened the passenger door. It made even more noise than the one on the other side and I saw it only had one hinge. I don't know why I giggled. Everyone else I knew had perfectly respectable cars.

It was a lovely day out. We played football on the shore, had turns on some of the milder fairground rides, and walked up and down the pier. It was where my mother and father had met and

I couldn't help but wonder where exactly the spot was. Had my mother been sitting on a bench or leaning on the railings looking down at the water? I pictured her walking along with Cathy, both carrying ice creams.

We had afternoon tea in Lord Street, then went to the pictures to see Woody Allen in *Bananas*. Gary didn't understand a word of it, but laughed himself sick, and Rob and I weren't far behind. In view of Rob being so hard up, I insisted on paying for a meal when we came out.

'It's not right,' Rob complained.

'Don't be daft,' I snorted. I took hold of Gary's hand and entered a classy-looking restaurant, leaving his father with no alternative but to follow. 'It's ludicrous and dead old-fashioned you paying for everything just because you're a man,' I said after we were seated. 'I pay a pittance for my keep, so have most of my wages for myself. Haven't you heard of feminism?'

'I have, yes, but I've never met a feminist – unless you're one.'

I confessed I didn't know if I was or not.


On the way home, Gary fell asleep in the back seat, by which time it had grown dark. I felt conscious of Rob's bare arm touching mine whenever he changed gear.

'It's been a good day,' he said. I agreed that it had. He went on, 'Perhaps we could do it again one day soon?' I agreed to that as well and he suggested the following Saturday. 'We could go to Chester Zoo. Gary would love it.'

I said, 'OK', not caring that being free two Saturdays in a row indicated I led a pretty lousy social life. 'Would your feelings be hurt if we went in my car?' I asked.

Rob said he'd be cut to the quick, but if I was worried about being seen in his pile of junk, then we'd go in mine. 'You can pick me up. What sort of car have you got?'

'A Volkswagen Beetle, bright red: it's only two years old.' I was buying it on hire purchase. It had been Charles's idea because it was an interest-free loan or something.

'Wow!' Rob was impressed.

'I told you I wasn't short of a few bob.'

'Back in Uganda, I drove a brand-new jeep. I bought this for a hundred and fifty quid just to get me around while I sorted myself out.' He slapped the steering wheel of the Morris.

He stopped outside the house in Aintree and once again kissed my cheek. 'Like I said, it's been a good day,' he murmured.

I went indoors to find Marion in bed and Charles waiting for me to come in so he could have a good moan. That was the day when it seemed their marriage had broken down, possibly for ever. Apparently, it was all the fault of Rob's car.

## Chapter 12

### 1940
## Barney and Amy

Barney never forgot the sense of total desolation and despair he felt as he watched his brother and his brother's friend hobble away in the direction of Dunkirk. With a sigh, he started up the engine of the lorry. He could think of plenty of reasons for turning around and going with the two men: he'd misunderstood his orders, he could say; the lorry had broken down; he'd had an accident, been knocked unconscious and, when he came to, found himself on the boat to England without any idea of how he'd got there. He'd already lost his driver, who'd caught a bullet in the shoulder when he'd got out to relieve himself and the convoy had been strafed. He'd been left in Dunkirk with the other injured men, and now Barney had to make his way back to his unit on his own.

He wouldn't be at all surprised to find it had been sent elsewhere by the time he arrived at St Valéry-en-Caux where it had been heading when he was appointed to take a dozen badly injured men to Dunkirk. St Valéry-en-Caux was about a hundred miles away, and all sorts of different orders might have been issued in his absence. What was he supposed to do then?

It didn't help that the journey was taking for ever. The road was packed with refugees going in the opposite direction, from the very young to the very old, getting as far away as they could from the advancing German Army. He could only edge along, not prepared to sound his horn and distress these already wretched people even more. Until recently, most had led quite ordinary lives. Now they were carrying their most precious possessions stuffed in suitcases or sacks, tiny children clutching their hands or held in their arms.

Horses strained to pull carts with far too many passengers. Prams were laden with parcels of bedding and clothes.

The way he had to crawl along, stopping and starting, reminded him of coming back from London that time with Amy. Then he'd cursed the traffic, called it all the names under the sun, but it was nothing compared to this. At least he'd been heading for home – and he'd had Amy at his side.

He remembered arriving at the flat, feeling sick, Amy helping him into bed, bathing his brow, making him tea, lying beside him and reminding him of how much she loved him.

Amy! Barney turned the lorry into a narrow country lane that was entirely devoid of traffic. He braked and his shoulders sagged. It was as if he'd moved from a relatively peaceful world into a cruel, violent one with different standards, where human life had lost all its value.

'Phew!' he said, very loudly. He withdrew from the breast pocket of his shirt a fountain pen and a little notebook with a bright red cover. At least a quarter of the pages were full of his tiny, neat print. It was a diary, and one of these days he would send it to Amy.

He wrote the date in the side column, followed by: 'Delivered twelve injured men to Dunkirk to be taken to England. Met Harry and his friend, Jack, on way back. Feel sad. Very hungry.' He chewed the pen for a minute, then wrote: 'Very thirsty. Love you more than all the tea in China, my darling Amy.' He was aware that the last bit didn't make sense, but she would know what he meant.

It was stupid, but the act of stopping the lorry had made him feel light-headed and dizzy. He really was exceptionally hungry and thirsty, having given all the supplies to the injured men. What's more, he hadn't slept since yesterday morning.

All he had on him was a packet of Senior Service. A cigarette wouldn't help with his hunger or his thirst, but it would soothe his nerves. But the cab of the lorry was too hot. He climbed out and sat at the side of the road in the shade of a bright green hedge covered with white blossom. It smelt tangy and fresh, and felt cool when he leant against it. It was quiet here and possible to forget – or pretend to forget – where he was and what was happening in this part of the world.

He didn't hear the plane approach. It appeared out of nowhere, its engine deafening as it swooped over him, barely twelve feet above his head before he had time to move. There was a series of spitting noises followed by screams, then the plane roared away, having done what it had set out to.

Barney took a final puff of the cigarette and threw it away. He would never, no matter how long he lived, understand the mentality of the Gerry pilots, who were capable of strafing helpless refugees.

He climbed back into the lorry's cab. A line of bullets had punctured the canvas awning, and one had gone right through the jacket that he'd left on the driver's seat. Had he not got out to have a smoke, he would be dead.

The screaming persisted. The road behind would be stained with blood: people would have been killed and injured. This couldn't be true. It wasn't real. It could only be part of the worst nightmare he'd ever had. Numbly, he jumped out of the lorry again and went to help.

By late afternoon, the procession of refugees had been reduced to a few stragglers. Barney was able to get up a moderate speed, but noticed that the lorry would very soon need petrol. If it ran out altogether, it would be a good reason to get out and make for Dunkirk on foot, except he'd been given the order to rejoin his unit and it was immaterial how he got there: it didn't matter if he drove or walked, hopped or flew.

He came to a crossroads with three or four houses on each corner and stopped. It was a desolate place without any sign of life, but perhaps there was somewhere he could get a drink: a well maybe, or an outside tap. His mouth was as dry as a bone; there was very little he wouldn't have traded for a glass of cold water.

His tired eyes rested on a single-storey building and he wondered if what he was seeing really existed, or if it was a mirage, the sort of thing people saw when they were lost in the desert and the need for a drink made them hallucinate. The small building had the word 'Bar' painted on the window, the door was wide open, and in the gravelled forecourt there was a petrol pump.

Barney parked the lorry beside the pump and climbed out. His legs nearly failed him when he tried to stand, but he managed to stagger towards the open door, almost grinning because he reminded himself of Charles Laughton in *The Hunchback of Notre Dame*. Once inside the bar, he stood upright with the aid of a chair.

It was a miserable place, with just four small tables, an assortment of chairs and benches, and a wooden counter that served as a bar. He shouted, 'Is anyone here?' but there was no reply. Behind the bar, not only were the shelves crammed with bottles of wine, but there was also a dripping tap that made lovely plopping sounds when the water landed in a deep, brown earthenware sink.

Barney wasn't interested in the wine. He turned the tap full on, seized a mug and filled it. Water had never tasted so delicious. He drank mug after mug before going outside to fill the tank with petrol. Having done this, he drove the lorry round to the rear of the building; he had no intention of leaving the place until he'd had his fill of water and had searched for food.

He found a room behind the bar where the owner might well have lived. It had a narrow bunk built underneath the window, a small table, a single chair, and a dresser that took up almost an entire wall. The floor was stone-flagged and the walls were rough, unpainted plaster. Everywhere was surprisingly clean. Despite Barney's longing for food, he briefly stopped to study the fifty or more books that were stacked tightly on the dresser shelves: Balzac, Flaubert, Verlaine, the works of Shakespeare translated into French, all of Dickens, again in French, some Russian authors. What sort of man had lived in this depressing place, running a bar and spending his free time reading great works?

He found a lump of rock-hard bread in one of the dresser cupboards, a piece of cheese, two hard-boiled eggs and a jar of pickled onions. He sat on the bed and ate everything, twice falling asleep with his mouth full. When he'd finished, he lay down, his thirst quenched and his stomach satisfied. Now all he needed was a little nap – forty winks, Amy would have said – then he would continue his journey.

The noise in the bar woke him, not surprisingly, as it was quite a racket: shouting, singing, the stamping of feet and the clink of bottles.

The language being spoken was German.

Barney heard everything, but didn't open his eyes. His heart thudded painfully in his chest as he tried to remember the geography of the room. Where was the back door? Could he escape through it before he was discovered? He could hide somewhere until the troops – they could only be troops – went away. He hoped they hadn't noticed the lorry.

Slowly, cautiously, he let his eyes open the merest slit and saw a German soldier standing just inside the door with his rifle pointing directly at him. Barney opened his eyes properly, slowly lifted his hands above his head in a gesture of surrender, while letting his feet swing on to the floor. Just as slowly he got to his feet, not wanting to frighten the soldier with a sudden movement that might cause him to fire the gun. Neither he nor the soldier, who looked no more than eighteen, spoke, though Barney was aware of the thunderous beating of his heart. The youngster gestured with his rifle towards the bar.

Barney nodded obediently and shuffled towards the door, keeping his eyes fixed on the rifle, as if staring at it would prevent it from being fired.

The soldier gave him a poke in the ribs with the barrel of the gun, and they entered the bar where about a dozen enemy troops had removed their helmets and jackets, thrown their rifles in a heap just inside the door, and were drinking wine from bottles, heads thrown back. Empty bottles stood on the counter and rolled along the floor. They must have been there quite a while; he'd been too fast asleep to hear.

The soldier who'd captured him shouted something and the men stopped drinking, saw Barney and started to laugh. One came forward, seized his collar at the back and flung him face down on to the floor. When he tried to rise, a foot was placed none too gently on his head. He lay there, thinking of Amy the first time they met, Amy laughing, Amy crying, holding her in his arms, making love, all the time waiting for a bullet or bayonet to enter his body and finish him off, so he would become just a memory to his wife, his family and everyone else he knew.

But instead of a bullet or a bayonet, he felt warm liquid spilling over him, soaking his legs, his arms, his back, every part of him. The foot was removed and the liquid poured over his head.

They were peeing on him! The smell of it made him want to puke. They were laughing while they did it. One of them – he couldn't see their faces – kicked his leg, another kick was aimed at his hip, and he was beginning to think it was his fate to be kicked to death, when a harsh voice clapped out an order – Barney couldn't speak German, but it sounded like an order – and the men stopped peeing and kicking, and stood to attention, their boots making such a terrible clatter on the stone floor that it made his head ring.

Seconds passed. Barney didn't look up. Footsteps approached and stopped right by his ear. A voice said pleasantly, 'Stand up.'

He stood, urine dripping from his hair. He tried to wipe it away with his sleeve, but his shirt was soaked. The speaker was a handsome man of about forty wearing the grey uniform of an officer and highly polished black boots. He removed his cap and tucked it underneath his arm, revealing corn-coloured hair. His eyes were a penetrating blue and his lips so thin they were scarcely visible.

'What is your name and and number?' he asked courteously. After Barney had given this information, he was asked where he was heading.

'I am not obliged to tell you,' he mumbled. Under the Geneva Convention, name and number were all that a prisoner was obliged to give.

The officer smiled. 'If you were on your way to St Valéry-en-Caux, then your journey would have been a wasted one, Lieutenant Patterson. Today, the German Army took eight thousand British troops prisoner, including their general and their officers, together with about three times that many Frenchmen.' He snapped an order in his own language and the soldiers grabbed their helmets, jackets and rifles, and pushed and shoved their way out of the bar. Then he called, 'Oscar,' and a middle-aged man wearing wire-framed spectacles marched in and saluted briskly. He regarded Barney with expressionless eyes.

The officer spoke, Oscar nodded, saluted again, barked, 'Ja, Mein Herr,' and left the bar. Now there were only Barney and the officer left. The older man said, 'My name is Frederick Toller. I am a colonel in the Seventh Panzer Division of our glorious German Army. If you are wondering why my English is so good, in the twenties I took a Ph.D. in Ancient Greek at Cambridge University. I was a History professor at Leipzig University when the war broke out and I gave up the post to fight for my country. Did you go to university, Lieutenant?'

'I took a Classics degree at Oxford.' Barney saw no harm in revealing such an insignificant fact.

'I thought as much. You can always tell. A good degree gives a man a certain bearing.' He went over to the bar, picked up a wine bottle, and held it against the light to see how much was in it. Apparently satisfied, he rinsed one of the stone mugs under the tap and half-filled it. 'Would you like some, Lieutenant?' he enquired.

Barney shook his head. 'No thank you, but I would like to get out of these clothes. Your men clearly have no idea how to treat a prisoner of war.' He said this with a confidence he didn't feel. It just seemed time he asserted himself in front of this senior officer.

'I apologize for my men,' Colonel Toller said. He genuinely sounded sorry. 'They will be told how to behave in future. I hadn't forgotten about your clothes. It so happens that I am on my way to Rouen and have a suitcase in my car. Oscar will shortly bring in a change of clothing and arrange for what you are wearing to be laundered.'

Oscar arrived at that very moment and put the clothes on a chair: a pair of white trousers, a white shirt and underwear. He placed a pair of white tennis shoes on the floor and left the bar without a word.

Barney removed his shirt and singlet, put them in the sink, and let the water run over them. The red notebook was completely ruined. He held it between finger and thumb and threw it on the floor. It didn't hold any military secrets. Anyway, the ink would have run and the writing would be illegible. He rinsed his hair and splashed himself from the waist up using his hands. Three rags that might have been tea towels were hanging on hooks inside the bar. He took one and dried himself as best as he could, then fetched the chair with the clean clothes so it was close to hand.

At this point, Colonel Toller strolled into the room behind, while Barney removed his trousers and placed a leg at a time beneath the tap. What he would have liked was to stand underneath a steaming shower with a lump of carbolic soap and scrub himself until he was confident every trace of urine had gone.

The colonel shouted, 'Whoever lived here was quite a reader. What do you think of Tolstoy, Lieutenant Patterson?'

'His books are too long,' Barney shouted back. 'At least, that's what I thought when I was seventeen. I might not be so impatient now.'

'You are a very honest young man. How old are you?'

'Twenty-two,' Barney replied. It was another piece of information that didn't seem all that important, and the colonel had told him enough about himself.

'Are you married?'

'Yes.'

'Children?'

'Not yet, no.'

'I have five: three boys and two girls. My wife is English. Her name is Helena and she comes from Brighton. Are you decent, Lieutenant? Can I come in?'

'I'm decent,' said Barney. The trousers were too big around the waist and the shoes were too small although the shirt and underwear fitted more or less. He felt much better, but could still smell urine.

The colonel returned, smoking a cigarette. He still had the silver case in his hand and offered one to Barney, who took one gratefully, murmuring, 'Thank you,' when it was lit with a matching silver lighter.

'Leave your soiled clothes – Oscar will collect them,' the colonel said. 'Now, Lieutenant Patterson, you and I will travel together in a staff car to Rouen. We will have a civilized conversation – about literature, say?' He raised his fine eyebrows questioningly. 'I will put you on your honour not to try to escape, though the door on your side will be locked just in case you are not as honourable as you seem – I would be quite blatantly dishonourable were I in your position. I shall find out where the men who were captured this morning are being held and arrange for you to join them, though not until your clothes have been cleaned and dried and you have enjoyed a good meal.' He bowed and gestured to Barney to precede him from the bar. 'After you, Lieutenant. I think in different times we would have become good friends. But now the times are such that, as from this moment, you are officially a prisoner of war.'

People weren't allowed to change their jobs in wartime unless they were transferring to one of equal importance. Amy didn't want to stay with London, Midland and Scottish Railways. She couldn't think of anything she could do that compared favourably with being the station master at Pond Wood. The line was in use again, but the station was closed for the foreseeable future. She didn't want to sell tickets, answer phones or stand behind the desk in Enquiries. She was neither big nor strong enough to become a porter, something she wouldn't have done anyway even had she been six feet tall and as strong as Samson.

'I want to get away from railways and do something completely different,' she told Leo, who immediately offered her a job in his factory in Skelmersdale. 'In a position of authority,' he promised.

'Is there a vacancy or are you going to invent one?' She knew he didn't want his daughter-in-law doing something menial. He hadn't been keen on the job in Pond Wood, but she'd refused to be talked out of it. If she weren't careful, Leo would take control of her life. He actually had the nerve to be cross if she wasn't in when he telephoned or turned up unexpectedly. She told him bluntly she wasn't prepared to be at his beck and call: 'I'll go out whenever I want, Leo, to wherever I like.'

She turned down the job in Skelmersdale, not wanting to be answerable to him in any way. He came up with another: a friend of his was opening an Army, Navy and Air Force club in the basement of a building in Water Street and wanted a receptionist.

'I told him about you and he's really keen. It'd mean getting dressed up to the nines every night. There's plenty of time to buy some pretty evening frocks before clothes are rationed.' His dark eyes danced with mischief. He knew it would appeal to her.

Amy was sorely tempted. It was the sort of job she'd love. Buying clothes was her favourite occupation. She was about to accept when Leo revealed the club would be for officers only: other ranks wouldn't be allowed in.

'That means Harry, your own son, would be banned,' she said, and told him she wasn't prepared to go near the place. 'The privates and corporals are just as important to the war as the officers.'

'I didn't know you were a socialist, Amy,' he said.

She eyed him suspiciously, having no idea what the word meant. 'Well, I am,' she said stoutly, hoping she wasn't making a fool of herself.

In the end, Amy went to work in the canteen of the Mulholland Car Manufacturing Company in Speke after seeing the job advertised in the *Echo*. The only cars turned out nowadays were for the Forces. She'd worked in a canteen before and had the right experience. Buses left from various parts of Liverpool to collect the workers: one stopped in Sheil Road, only a short walk from the flat. She would work shifts: from 6 a.m. until 2 p.m., and from 2 p.m. until 10 p.m. alternate weeks. The morning shift went in on Saturdays; the afternoon one had Saturday off.

Leo said she was wasted in the job. She asked him what was so special about her. 'I'm just an ordinary person like everyone else,' she said.

'No, you're not, Amy,' he said quite seriously, without his usual grin. 'You really are special.'

The words worried her. She had tried valiantly not to think the unthinkable, but after he'd said that she found it impossible not to be concerned that Leo Patterson was attracted to her. Even worse, instead of being shocked, she felt flattered. He was without doubt an extremely attractive man. Her sisters thought he was the bee's knees, even Jacky, who was now madly in love with Peter Alton.

★

Amy's first day at Mulholland's was an afternoon shift, and that morning she received her first letter from Barney in months.

He was in a prisoner of war camp in Germany in an area called Bavaria. It wasn't a very long letter. He'd write to her again, he promised, as soon as he'd settled in, and tell her what had happened over the last few months.

Amy had a thick wad of letters waiting to send to him via the Red Cross as she'd been writing nearly every day without having anywhere to send them. Parts of Barney's letter had been crossed out. Leo said the censor had done it – she'd let him read most of the letter apart from the last page where Barney told her how much he loved and missed her. 'He or she must have considered it sensitive information,' Leo said.

'Cheek!' Amy snorted. 'What a terrible job to have, reading other people's letters and crossing bits out.'

'Some people might find it interesting.'

'They're nothing but nosy-parkers. It's worse than being a spy.'

So, it was a much happier Amy who turned up in Mulholland's canteen that afternoon. The four other women who worked there – Gladys, Em, Tossie and Joan, whose ages ranged from twenty-five to sixty – weren't exactly taken with the pretty young woman in her smart red linen frock and black patent, high-heeled shoes, who looked as if she hadn't done a hard day's work in her entire life.

As Em, the twenty-five-year-old, explained later, 'We thought you were some posh bitch who was showing off to her friends by working with the riff-raff.'

'I forgot to get changed,' Amy confessed with a tinkling laugh when she first got there, and Gladys, aged sixty, asked gruffly if she was sure she'd come to the right place.

'The cocktail lounge is upstairs,' she said with a loud sniff.

The women's rude words and contemptuous glances went over Amy's head. She'd had a letter from Barney and nothing else mattered.

'I heard from my husband this morning for the first time in ages,' she explained excitedly. 'I was told he'd been taken prisoner not long after Dunkirk and I've been waiting desperately for a letter ever since. Oh, what sort of urn is that? The canteen where I worked before had a gas one, but it was forever blowing out: it was awful dangerous. Every time it was lit, we expected the place to blow up. Is that one electric?'

The fact that Amy's husband was a prisoner of war would have been enough to make the women take her to their hearts, but that she had worked in a canteen before and made no claim to be better than they were only made them like her more. Before the day was out they were the best of friends.

Amy went home at ten o'clock, every part of her body throbbing painfully, even though Joan, who seemed to be in charge, had found her a sitting-down job – rolling out several miles of short-cut pastry and cutting it into circles for jam tarts. She had learned that Joan's husband was in the Merchant Navy and that she was having terrible trouble with her fifteen-year-old daughter, who was going out with a chap twice her age.

Em, unmarried, looked after two very elderly aunts, and Tossie was a widow in her thirties who, due to the war, was having the time of her life. 'I never thought the day would come when I'd go dancing again,' she told Amy when they were having their mid-afternoon break. 'I'm earning more money than I've ever known in me life. I get me hair done every week. If me husband were alive, he'd bloody kill me. He hated me having a good time, did Ron.'

Gladys was a grumpy soul who only saw the black side of life. Yet it was obvious the other women were extremely fond of her. They made fun of her gloomy face and ill humour.

When she got home, Amy lay in the bath and let the throbbing ebb away until she felt numb instead. Tomorrow, she could sleep in as late as she liked – or she could get up early and go shopping. She could do with a pair of flat shoes. Was it possible to get really *smart* flat shoes?

She boiled milk for cocoa, and read Barney's letter again. The cocoa drunk, she climbed into bed clutching the letter. Barney had actually *touched* it. She pressed the sheets against her lips. 'Barney,' she whispered. 'Oh, Barney.'

Amy was working much harder than she'd done in Pond Wood, yet she had more free time. She had forgotten what it was like to shop leisurely, go to the pictures or out for a meal. All sorts of wonderful films had come out while she'd been buried in Pond Wood: *Dark Victory* and *The Old Maid* with Bette Davis; *Ninotchka* with Greta Garbo; and the most wonderful film that had ever been made, *Gone With the Wind*, starring Clark Gable and Vivien Leigh and loads of other famous stars. Amy went to see them all with Em, who was mad on the pictures and familiar with the life story of every famous film star.

'My friend Cathy had a big crush on Clark Gable,' she said to Em when they came out of the picture house. 'I must write and ask if she's seen *Gone With the Wind*: she'd love it.'

Cathy wrote back to say she'd seen the film, but no longer had a crush on Clark Gable. 'I was only young then,' she wrote, as if, at nineteen, she was as old as the hills. 'He's dead handsome, but I prefer real flesh and blood men, not the celluloid sort.'

The air raids began to get more and more frequent. Captain Kirby-Greene and Mr and Mrs Porter, the elderly couple who lived on the first floor of the house in Newsham Park, had turned the spacious cellar into a shelter fit for royalty. Armchairs had appeared like magic, as well as a coffee table, a battery wireless that could still function if the electricity supply was lost, a camping stove for making hot drinks, an assortment of books, the provision of which had been taken over by the captain, who haunted second-hand bookshops for tales with a nautical bent. There were two biographies of Nelson and detailed descriptions of sea battles going back hundreds of years.

The Porters made their way down to the cellar at around eight o'clock every evening, that's if the air raid siren hadn't already sounded: she armed with her knitting and he with an assortment of newspapers to read, including the 'damned Socialist' ones. 'I don't suppose it hurts to get the other person's point of view,' he would say grudgingly in defence of his purchase of such left-wing trash.

The captain, always anxious for someone to talk to, would be listening for the click of the cellar door rather than the siren, and would immediately follow.

Clive and Veronica Stafford, who lived on the second floor, were both tall and bony with insipid features and pale blue eyes. They could easily have been taken for brother and sister, a likeness helped by the fact that both wore rimless glasses. They nearly always arrived in the middle of an argument over something that Clive considered was Veronica's fault: he'd forgotten to take a handkerchief to work; he'd been too hot, or cold, in bed the night before; his fountain pen had run out of ink; one of his shoelaces had snapped – Veronica should have noticed it was beginning to fray.

Veronica would point out that the shoe had been on his foot, not hers; he was the last to use the pen, and how on earth was she supposed to keep track of the ink? He should have noticed there wasn't a handkerchief in his jacket pocket; she had been asleep when he had been too hot, or cold, in bed, and therefore there was nothing she could have done about it.

'You should be more alert, Vee.' Clive didn't like to lose an argument.

'I'll do my best in future,' Veronica would say, or something like it, a tinge of sarcasm in her voice that her husband didn't notice. She would also make a hideous face behind his back as soon as he turned away. She told Amy that she hoped Clive would be called up one day. 'He needs to learn that there are more important things to worry about than missing hankies and frayed shoelaces,' she said.


Mrs Curran and Amy worked the same shifts. Sometimes, Amy went straight from Mulholland's to Agate Street and spent the afternoon with her mam, or they went shopping together in Strand Road, Bootle, or South Road in Waterloo.

It was late October when Amy arrived at her own home and found, for the first time ever, Mam waiting for her. She'd been captured by Captain Kirby-Greene and was in his living room drinking very strong tea and eating fig biscuits when Amy went in.

'He must have used up all his tea ration,' Mam whispered as she and Amy went upstairs, the captain very reluctant to let her go. 'I wonder where he got the fig biscuits from? They've always been me favourite.

'I suppose you can guess what's happened,' she said a few minutes later when she was having a cup of very weak tea provided by Amy, who didn't have a single biscuit in the flat. When Amy confessed she hadn't the faintest idea what had happened, she went on. 'Our Jacky and Peter only want to get married. Trouble is, he isn't a Catholic, though he's perfectly willing to change. His mam and dad don't mind – I've already met them and they're really nice.'

'Then what's the problem?'

'They want to get married straight away, that's the problem.' Mam sighed. 'Jacky's only seventeen and she needs my permission to get married. She can't do it behind me back like you did. I'm sorry, luv, but it's true, isn't it?' she said when her daughter opened her mouth to argue.

'I suppose so,' Amy was obliged to concede. She'd waited until her eighteenth birthday, but Jacky had a whole year to go before she was eighteen.

'There's no suppose about it, Amy, but we won't go into that right now: it's all over and done with. All I'm concerned about is our Jacky. Peter would've been called up ages ago except his dad needed him on the farm, but, at Peter's insistence, his dad got someone else to help, leaving him free to join the Forces. I don't know,' Mrs Curran said irritably. 'None of me kids get married normally. Our Charlie married a really weird woman who hasn't got a single relative in the world, you married a Protestant in one of them heathen Register Office places, and now our Jacky's about to do the same. There isn't time for Peter to take instruction and become a Catholic. What the hell am I supposed to do, Amy? Should I let her get married or not?' She put the cup and saucer on the floor and lit a cigarette. 'I'm smoking meself silly,' she said. 'I should be smoking less, not more. The last time I bought a pack of ciggies I had virtually to prostrate meself on the floor in front of Ernie McIlvanny before he'd sell me them.' Ernie McIlvanny ran the sweet and tobacconist's shop on the corner of Agate Street and

Marsh Lane. 'Once the war's over, I shall never go near his bloody shop again.'

'Let them get married,' Amy said promptly. 'Our Jacky would never forgive you if Peter was killed and they hadn't been able to marry.' There was a sure-fire way of making her mother give permission. 'Just imagine if Peter went away and Jacky found she was pregnant!'

'Jaysus, Mary and Joseph!' Her mother crossed herself. 'That'd never do. Oh, all right then. I'll tell the pair of 'em to go ahead,' she sighed. Amy suspected she'd been resigned to the marriage all along and had known Amy would back her up.

Jacky Curran became Mrs Peter Alton on the final Saturday in 1940. During the nights leading up to Christmas, tons of bombs had fallen on Liverpool: incendiary and high explosives, and mines. At times it had appeared as if the entire city was on fire, the flames reaching into the sky and turning it a sinister blood-red. Hundreds of people were killed and many famous Liverpool landmarks were destroyed or damaged.

After so much carnage and horror, it was with a sense of relief that the residents of Agate Street turned out to watch Jacky Curran leave the house to get married to a lovely young man who'd just joined the Royal Navy. She looked so young and pretty in her blue tweed costume and little feathered hat. It was a brave thing to do, taking on a husband in the middle of a terrible war, perhaps even starting a family. Jacky wasn't getting married in a church as she would have in normal times. But times were anything but normal, and the young couple were keen to get married in a hurry. God wouldn't mind that they would only be wed in the eyes of the law and not in His.

Nowadays, everything had to be done in a hurry. A person couldn't go to bed and expect to be alive the next morning. If you left your house, you couldn't be sure it would still be standing when you got back. Nothing was certain any more. The only certainty lay in the present, so you had to live for the moment just in case tomorrow never came – at least, not for you.

★

Cathy came home the day after the wedding. She'd been hoping to be there in time, but the trains had been all over the place and she'd spent the night in the ladies' waiting room at Preston station. She came to Agate Street wearing civvies, as her mam was pressing her uniform in readiness for her to go back. Mrs Burns was desperately proud of her youngest daughter, who'd been promoted to lance corporal and boasted a stripe on the sleeves of her khaki jacket.

Mrs Curran provided a lovely tea with leftovers from the reception and a tin of ham. The house seemed strange without Jacky, who was on honeymoon with Peter in the Lake District. Poor Biddy looked so lost that Amy invited her to come to the pictures with her and Cathy that night.

'Thank you, sis,' Biddy said with a pathetic sniff.

After that, Amy and Cathy went into the parlour to catch up. They wrote often, but the last time they'd seen each other was right after Amy had lost her baby.

'I still think about it,' Amy said sadly. 'He or she would be nine months old by now. Every time I see a baby I wish it were mine.'

'There'll be plenty of time to have another.' Cathy's eyes were full of warmth, and Amy thought what a good friend she was – always had been.

'How's Jack?' she asked.

'He's in North Africa with Harry Patterson.'

'Of course, I'd forgotten they were friends.'

'Comrades, Jack calls them. Comrades in arms.' Cathy smiled shyly. 'I haven't told you yet, but we're engaged. I haven't got a ring, but we're going to get married as soon as he comes home.'

'Oh, Cathy, I'm dead pleased,' Amy cried. 'But why didn't you get married while he was still in England?'

'We didn't realize how much we meant to each other until he was in Africa,' Cathy said dreamily. 'He proposed to me in a letter.'

'For a while, I thought you might end up with Harry Patterson. I remember you said he came to see you the Christmas before last and you got on really well.'

'We did.' Cathy looked puzzled. 'I've always liked Harry, ever since the day we met on Southport pier, and I liked him even better after he came to see me in Keighley. Afterwards, he sent me a sort of love letter and I wrote back, but then I never heard from him again. Not that it matters,' she sighed joyfully. 'It's Jack I love, not Harry.'

Amy felt very emotional. 'Wouldn't it be the gear if we both had babies at the same time?' Her face fell. 'Though the chances of you seeing Jack are much better than the chances of me seeing Barney. It could be years and years before this stupid war is over and he comes home.'

'You never know, Amy: miracles can happen.'

Amy managed half a smile. 'Can I be a bridesmaid at your wedding?'

'You can be matron of honour.' Cathy gave no hint at how hurt she'd been when Amy had married Barney without saying a word to her – her best friend. That was in the past, and she'd never been one to cry over spilt milk.

Harry Patterson lay stretched out and completely still on the canvas bed. He was lying on top of the bedclothes, and all he wore was a pair of cotton underpants. Despite this, perspiration was dribbling out of every pore, and he felt unpleasantly and uncomfortably damp.

The hot weather didn't agree with him. It was something he hadn't realized until he arrived in North Africa in August and experienced temperatures unknown in the British Isles. He'd discovered he was susceptible to the sun and burnt horribly if he got too much of it, his skin erupting in ugly blisters. Fortunately, the Army was sympathetic and he was allowed to work under canvas for most of the time. This meant he had peeled an awful lot of spuds, as the men called them, and washed an awful lot of dishes. He wondered what his father would say if he knew. Would he care that one of his sons was engaged in such menial tasks? Harry somehow doubted it. Dad might care if it were Barney, but not him.

Trouble with nights like this, when sleep was impossible and he found it hard to breathe, he couldn't stop himself from thinking dark thoughts. The darkest of them all was wondering why on earth he'd told Jack Wilkinson that he wasn't interested in Cathy Burns.

'She's a nice girl,' he'd said. 'I really like her, but it's not serious.'

It had happened just after Dunkirk. While Harry kicked his heels in Essex, Jack had been sent back to Leeds to have his ankle seen to. At first, it was thought to be broken, but it had turned out to be just a bad sprain. Jack had written to him: 'Remember that girl you met in Keighley at Christmas, Cathy something? Is it serious between you two? There's a dance over there on Saturday, but at the moment I can only dance on one leg. I'm not looking to seduce her, but I remember you saying you had loads to talk about and it would be great to meet a girl I can hold a conversation with …'

'Cathy and I are just friends,' Harry wrote back. Her surname is Burns and she's in the finance office. I'm sure she'll be pleased to see you.'

Jack didn't write again, and Harry got the shock of his life when his friend had rejoined his unit, now in Cyrenaica, his ankle mended and with the news that he thought he was in love with Cathy Burns.

'She's a cracking girl,' he said, rubbing his thin hands together joyfully. He punched Harry's shoulder so hard that Harry winced. 'Thanks, old chap. That's the biggest favour anyone's ever done for me. I'll be grateful to you for the rest of me life.'

In the tent that he shared with three other men, Harry flexed his toes: he was getting cramp on top of his other miseries. Behind him, Jack was peacefully asleep. A few weeks ago he'd proposed to Cathy in a letter and she'd accepted. He had no idea when they would meet again, but when they did they would get married.

Harry groaned. Even the fact they were winning the war wasn't enough to make him happy. The Brits and their allies had taken Sidi Barrani, Sollum and Fort Capuzzo, along with thousands of Italian prisoners. Right now, he was too hot, his head ached and he had cramp in both feet, but the worst pain of all was in his heart because Jack and Cathy had fallen in love. It was his own fault: he'd virtually handed Cathy to Jack on a plate, and there was no one to blame but himself.

# Chapter 13

## May 1971
## Pearl

I went to bed early because I could tell Charles and Marion were itching for a row. I didn't try to sleep, it was too early, but sat up reading a book. I'd hardly left the room before my aunt and uncle were at it hammer and tongs.

Rather reluctantly, I'd closed the bedroom door, but I could hear them even with it closed. To tell the truth, it really upset me. Marion was inclined to let Charles lead a bit of a dog's life, but he'd never seemed to mind. In fact, he usually made a joke of her constant criticism and bad moods. But now it appeared he'd decided he wasn't prepared to put up with it any longer. I wondered why.

'Why are you like this, Charles?' Marion must have been asking herself the same thing.

Charles's laugh was more like a bark. 'You mean why am I fed up to the teeth with your complete lack of charity, your mean-mindedness, your obsession with what the neighbours think, and a hundred and one other things?'

'You've never minded before,' Marion said. I gritted my teeth at this rather unfortunate remark.

Charles must have thought so too. 'Ha!' he barked again. 'So you agree you *are* uncharitable, mean-minded and obsessed with the neighbours?'

'No, no, of course not.' She sounded so confused that I felt sorry for her, though I was usually on Charles's side in the event of an argument. Mind you, I'd never joined in, or offered an opinion, even if one had been asked for. With wisdom beyond my years, I had vowed at an early age to stay neutral.

'I'm sorry if I'm making you unhappy, Charles,' Marion said humbly. It was the first time I'd ever known her apologize for anything serious.

'My name is *Charlie*,' my uncle said furiously. 'Everyone used to call me Charlie, my mam and dad, my sisters and my friends, until you came along and decided I had to be Charles because it sounded better. I remember the way you used to be annoyed with Mam whenever she called me Charlie.'

'I always liked your mother, Charles. It's just that Charlie is so common.'

'Charlie Chaplin mustn't have thought so. Oh, and lucky old Mam – you *liked* her. There's a turn-up for the books. That's another thing – I'm supposed to refer to her in public as Mother, not Mam. Who the hell do you think you are? Royalty? Lady Muck? The Queen of Sheba?' I winced. He was sneering now. He didn't sound a bit like the Charles I'd always known. I wouldn't be surprised if he hadn't been bottling up all this stuff for years and years. 'If I remember rightly, *your* mam and dad were gypsies who lived in a filthy old caravan and made their living selling rubbish from door to door. As for you, you didn't wear knickers until you were twelve.'

'Charles!' Marion gasped.

There was a pause. I suspected he regretted that. He eventually said he was sorry, but didn't sound it. 'I never tried to change you, Marion, but you set your mind on changing me. Personally, I didn't think I was all that bad.'

'You're a wonderful man, Charles,' Marion said with a throb in her voice, but he wasn't in the mood to be influenced by soft words.

'We've been married for over thirty years, but do you realize that's the first time you've ever said anything like that?'

There was another pause, longer than the first one. Marion said, 'Why are you behaving as if you hate me?'

'I don't hate you.' He sounded tired, as if all his anger had gone. 'Sometimes, though, I dislike you. I didn't like you saying Amy wouldn't be welcome in this house. Amy is my sister and I love her. She's been in prison for twenty years and you are so devoid of pity and human kindness that you'd actually refuse to let her into our home.' I imagined him pacing the room, hands in his pockets or waving his arms. 'Then you complained about paying for Cathy Burns's meal. I mean, *Cathy*! Can't you remember the way she stuck by Amy after Barney came back from the war?' There was a bang, as if Charles had kicked something: the sideboard, maybe. 'The last straw was you moaning about Pearl's boyfriend's car. Honestly, Marion, I didn't think that even you could be so petty. It's a rust box, a banger, but who gives a shit what the neighbours think? Pearl told us the lad's position: that he's looking for a job and if he doesn't get one soon he's going back abroad. Buying a cheap car seems a wise move to me. If you're so ashamed of it being outside our house for half a minute, then go and live in another house.'

Marion gasped. 'Do you really mean that, Charles?'

'Yes, Marion. Yes, I think I do.'

Then the phone rang. At that point I slid down the bed and pulled the pillow over my head. I didn't want to hear any more. When I emerged there were no sounds downstairs. I wondered if they'd gone to bed together, or if one was sleeping in the spare room.

For about half an hour, I tossed and turned. When sleep seemed impossible, I crept downstairs for a glass of water. On my way back, I passed the cupboard where my mother's file was kept. Just then, I badly wanted to look at a picture of my father, the man who'd become a monster. I took the file and was about to go back upstairs when a voice said, 'Is that you, Pearl?'

I went into the lounge where Charles was sitting on the settee without the light on. The curtains had been pulled back and the full moon, together with the street lamp outside, illuminated the room to the extent that Charles was clearly visible.

'What are you up to?' he asked.

'I was thirsty and couldn't sleep,' I explained. 'And I just thought I'd like to look at my mother's file.'

'Were you listening to what was being said down here?'

'I couldn't help it. I closed the door, but I could still hear you. Eventually, I hid under the pillow.' I should have hidden under the pillow at the start of the row, not near the end.

'I'm sorry, love.' He patted the space beside him on the settee. 'Come and sit here a minute.'

I sank on to the settee and leaned against him. 'I'm sorry about Rob's car.'

It had been the 'last straw' according to Charles. If Rob hadn't come to collect me on Sunday the recent fight might not have taken place, though I suspect some other insignificant detail could have sparked it off.

'Don't be daft,' he said bluntly. 'It's a car. Marion's probably one of the only women in the world who'd give a shit about it being parked outside the house.' Tonight was the first time I'd known my uncle use a four-letter word. He nodded towards the file on my knee. 'Do you often read that?'

'No. Just now, I wanted to look at my father's picture.'

'He was a remarkably handsome young man, your dad. You're very like him.'

I sniffed. 'I'd sooner not be handsome.'

Charles laughed. 'You're not handsome, Pearl: you're very pretty. You've got your dad's features, but in feminine form. Does that make sense?' I agreed that it did and he went on. 'Don't believe a lot of the stuff in there. Your mum never had affairs, not with Leo Patterson, not with anyone. She was a wonderful wife. Lots of women wouldn't have tolerated your dad for five minutes, yet your mother stuck by him for six whole years.'

'I used to hear him swear at her,' I said. 'He called her a whore. I didn't know what a whore was in those days. I looked it up years later.'

'Do you remember much about your father?' Charles asked curiously.

A car passed and its headlights flashed around the walls.

I confessed that I wasn't sure if some of the things I remembered were real or part of a dream. 'After he died, I was told it was in a car accident, yet I knew he'd been in the house that night because he'd been shouting that he wanted to kill my mother and I didn't hear him go out.'

I felt Charles stiffen beside me. 'Christ Almighty, Pearl,' he said in a shocked voice. 'I didn't realize you remembered all this.

You've never mentioned it before.'

'It comes and goes.' I shrugged. 'Anyroad, when it happened I had chicken pox and was terribly feverish so it could have been a dream. The police came as well as Grannie Curran. She wrapped me in a blanket and took me in a taxi back to Agate Street.' I shivered. It had been an awful time. 'I don't think I ever saw my mother again.'

'It's all so bloody sad.' Charles removed my mother's file from my knee. 'I'd sooner you didn't read this right now. And I think it's about time we changed the subject.' He cleared his throat. 'Regarding your young man: are you likely to go abroad with him if he can't find a job here?'

'I hardly know him, Charles,' I muttered.

'Why not invite him to come with us to Southport on Thursday? That was Leo Patterson on the phone earlier. He's invited us to dinner along with Cathy and Harry. Let us meet this Rob. Knowing your granddad, he could well offer him a job. He's probably best mates with the chief constable of Lancashire.'

'I'll ask him,' I promised. 'It depends if he can take the night off from the Post Office and get his sister to look after Gary. I'll give him a ring tomorrow.' Such a grand occasion called for a new dress. I'd go straight after school and buy something suitable for dinner in Southport with my granddad.


My friend, Trish, had met Granddad when she was about twenty and he was in his late sixties – he might even have been seventy – and she'd considered him desperately attractive.

I couldn't get over it. 'But he's really *old*,' I exclaimed.

'I don't care.' Trish rolled her eyes extravagantly. 'I really fancy him. He's dead sexy.'

My granddad had a lot of iron-grey hair, straight and sort of floppy, quite long for an old age pensioner. I wouldn't have been at all surprised if one day he turned up wearing an earring. He was very slim and straight-backed with a craggy face and twinkly brown eyes. Apparently, my father and I had inherited his brown eyes, though mine didn't twinkle all that often; I don't know about my father's.

The Carlyle Hotel in Southport was where we met the following Thursday. It was opulently old-fashioned with thick red carpets and lots of gilt. The tablecloths were so white they hurt the eyes, and the silverware gleamed. In the corner, a woman in an emerald-green evening dress was seated at a grand piano playing 'The Warsaw Concerto'.

There was something about the place that made me feel as if I'd been transported back to before the war or even Edwardian times. It wasn't just the hotel that was old-fashioned, but the clientele: there were lots of women with stiffly-set grey hair and strings of pearls, and quite a few of the men wore evening suits.

Granddad, Uncle Harry and Cathy were already there. Rob had come with us in Charles's car and left his rusty old banger outside the house – Charles's idea. He clearly didn't care if Marion minded.

Granddad got up and gave me a ferocious hug. He wore black trousers, a black corduroy jacket and a white silky shirt with a high neck – the sort of thing worn by Russian Cossacks. I introduced him to Rob, who'd managed to get the night off, feeling quite proud that I had a sexy granddad who didn't need a walking stick, a hearing aid or even a pair of spectacles: he had to squint at the menu, but only a bit. He was probably the hippest person in the room.

'Pleased to meet you, Rob,' he said, shaking his hand vigorously. 'Pearl tells me you worked in Uganda. Smart of you to get out before the coup, I must say. That chap Idi Amin sounds a bit of a stinker.' He still had an Irish accent despite spending most of his life in England. 'Have you found another job yet?'

Rob explained the problem he would have with Gary if he rejoined the police force. 'The hours are long and unpredictable, and there's no one to look after him. But even if I went abroad, I doubt if I'll ever come across as good a set-up as we had in Uganda.'

'You and Pearl should get married,' my granddad actually said, nodding wisely like an old sage. I felt the blood rush to my face. Rob looked distinctly uncomfortable. 'I understand she teaches your boy at school,' my outrageously tactless grandparent went on. 'That would be an even better set-up than you had in Uganda. Houses in Liverpool aren't all that expensive. Let me know if you ever want to buy one. I'm friendly with quite a few estate agents and I could get you a bargain.'

Cathy Burns winked at me across the table. 'You're an old rogue, Leo,' she said bluntly. 'You've just made Pearl and Rob feel dead embarrassed.'

'Have I?' His brown eyes twinkled. 'I was just pointing out the blindingly obvious.'

'Anyroad,' Cathy went on, 'why should Pearl give up her job to look after Gary? Why can't the man do it for a change? That reminds me.' She turned to Rob. 'Gary has won second prize in an art competition with his painting of a tree. You know the one, Pearl. It was organised by the *Crosby Herald* for all first year pupils in the area. I had a phone call just as I was leaving this afternoon.'

'That's great.' Rob looked pleased. 'Can I tell him in the morning?'

'If you like. I'll announce it on Monday at assembly.'

A waiter came and took the starter and main course orders, then another waiter brought the wine and began to fill our glasses.

'I'd like to make a toast,' Granddad said. 'There's no need to stand, but I'd like to drink to the health of Pearl's mother, who is also Charlie's sister, Cathy's friend, Harry's sister-in-law and my daughter-in-law.' He held the glass high. 'To Amy Patterson.'

'Amy Patterson.' We all clinked our glasses together. I wasn't sure if I just imagined Marion whispering, 'And jailbird.'

'What was it like in Paris, Leo?' Charles asked.

'Very nice, very relaxing,' Leo said affably. 'I was there for just over a fortnight and the weather was perfect. I think I might retire and do more travelling. I quite fancy visiting the States.'

At this, Harry's eyes gleamed hopefully. He was longing to take over the business from his father.

Cathy said excitedly. 'I've just thought of something. It's Amy's birthday next week. I wonder if that's when she'll come home, on her birthday.'

'Isn't that unnecessarily dramatic?' Marion said coldly. 'Are you suggesting she's hiding somewhere until the first of June when she'll jump out of a cake?'

Cathy laughed. 'Something like that. What do you think, Charlie?'

'Nothing Amy did would surprise me,' Charles said.

The starters arrived. Cathy described a whole series of wonderful and surprising things that my mother had done, which I knew was only to get up Marion's nose for being so sour. Charles kept nodding and smiling, which I knew was only to get up Marion's nose, too.

Rob was being very quiet beside me. 'Are you all right?' I whispered.

'I'm fine. I really am fine,' he insisted when he saw my worried look. I was beginning to wish I hadn't invited him. 'I always enjoy family gatherings, but only when it's someone else's family. It's like watching a play.'

'I'm sorry.' Marion was the only one who was spoiling things, though Granddad's suggestion that we get married hadn't helped.

'Don't be. I'd have to pay good money for this in a theatre.'

I hadn't realized he had a sense of humour. In fact, I thought, there were an awful lot of things I didn't know about him.

Cathy Burns was really enjoying herself. She wore a pretty blue voile frock with a frilly collar and cuffs. Her short hair, usually flat, looked thick and bouncy, and her little stud earrings sparkled when she moved her head; I wondered if they were real diamonds. The staff at school would be amazed if they could see her now, looking ten years younger and so very different to the primly dressed, almost drab headmistress that they saw every day.

My own ankle-length dress was pastel flowered crêpe with a deep square neck, long bishop sleeves and a high waistline. When I'd put it on earlier, I worried it looked like a maternity dress, but Marion assured me it looked perfectly all right.

Marion hadn't bothered to get changed out of her plain grey blouse and darker grey skirt when she came home from work. I would have thought most women in her position – on bad terms with her husband – would have made an effort to look nice tonight. But then Marion wasn't like other women. I don't think she was capable of guile or trying to look nice just to please Charles, just as she wasn't capable of pretending to make a toast to my mother when she didn't want to. I suppose in her own way she was rather admirable. I badly wanted to know more about her being a gypsy, and hoped I'd have the opportunity to ask Charles one day.

I looked up and found Granddad, who was sitting on my left, staring at me thoughtfully. I smiled and he smiled back. 'You're awfully like your father, Pearl,' he said.

'Am I? Would you sooner I was your grandson and not your granddaughter?'

'No, darling. It would be too weird to have another Barney.' His face changed and he looked terribly sad. It came to me how awful it must have been to have your son murdered by his wife. Yet he'd stayed friends with the wife, my mother, and had even been to see her regularly in prison.

The main meals arrived along with more wine. I wasn't used to drinking much and already felt a little bit tipsy, but I didn't have to worry about driving back, unlike Rob, who had refused the wine. I wished I'd suggested Charles pick him up from Seaforth and take him home. Cathy announced she'd come in a taxi and could drink all she liked. She signalled to the waiter to refill her glass.

Cathy was sitting on Granddad's other side with Charles next to her and Marion next to him. As Marion seemed to have been struck dumb, poor Uncle Harry was left with no one to talk to, as the person on his left side was Rob, who I was doing my best to entertain. I was almost glad when I was captured by Granddad, and Rob and Harry struck up a conversation about football. Both had watched England beat Germany in The World Cup in 1966 and could remember every ball of the match. They took turns giving a running commentary.

It would have been a cheerful occasion if it hadn't been for Marion, who was really spoiling things. Then Granddad said in a loud voice, 'And how is life treating you, Marion?'

'Oh!' she stammered, attempting to smile. No one would dream of being rude to Leo Patterson. 'All right, I suppose.'

'Are you still working in the same job? Where is it – the English Electric?'

'Yes, Leo.'

'How long have you been there now?'

'Thirty-three years.' Marion licked her lips. She looked nervous for some reason. I guess she understood that Granddad speaking to her like this was a sort of rebuke for the way she'd been behaving. 'I started in the typing pool in nineteen thirty-eight.'

'And what about that lovely garden of yours?' Leo said effusively. 'I remember visiting your house a few times and being deeply impressed. It was a work of art.'

'Well, it's Charles who does all the work. All I do is a bit of tidying.'

'And where are you and Charles off to on holiday this year, my dear?'

'We haven't booked yet, but we thought we might go to one of the Greek islands – or perhaps more than one. Do a cruise, maybe.'

'I went to Rhodes last year and it was lovely,' Cathy remarked. 'But don't go at the height of summer: it can get too hot.'

All of a sudden, before Marion knew it, she had been forced into a conversation about holidays that eventually turned into one about the cost of hotel telephone calls abroad and then into one about cameras. Granddad kept the conversations going like a stoker with a fire, and Marion wasn't allowed to retreat into an intimidating silence again.

We'd nearly finished eating when Granddad, grinning like a Cheshire cat, ordered a magnum of champagne. He was up to something, I could tell. 'I've got a surprise for you,' he said.

'What is it, Dad?' Harry asked, but Granddad just shook his head mysteriously.

A woman had come into the room and was approaching our table. She stopped and stood a few feet away, watching us. She wasn't young, but she was extremely pretty with brown curly hair and incredibly blue eyes. Her black dress fitted her shapely figure like a stocking.

My brown eyes met her blue ones. She smiled wistfully and said, 'Hello, love.'

Cathy screamed, 'Amy! Oh, Amy,' and nearly knocked over her

chair as she struggled to her feet. 'What on earth have you done to your hair?'

Granddad continued to grin as if he'd just pulled a rabbit out of a hat.

Charles's jaw dropped. 'Well, I'll be damned,' he gasped. 'If it isn't our Amy.'

'Amy!' was all Harry said, but he was obviously delighted to see her.

I have no idea how Marion reacted. Just then, I wasn't interested. I can't remember getting up, but I must have done because the next minute I was throwing myself into my mother's arms and sobbing my heart out, while she was patting my back and saying, 'There, there, darling. There, there.'

I was only half-conscious that the restaurant had fallen strangely silent except for the noise at our table. Afterwards, I realized everyone had stopped eating to watch us.

'There, there,' my mother kept saying. 'Don't cry, love. I'm home now.'

And I was wishing that I'd gone to see her, that I'd written to her, sent her birthday cards, and told her I loved her, because, twenty years too late, I knew that I did.

## Chapter 14

### 1940
### Barney

The journey from France to Germany could have been far worse. The officers had been kept together, were reasonably fed, and it hadn't been too crowded on the trains that had transported them through the sunny French countryside. The only deprivation was the lack of cigarettes, from which some suffered more than others and some not at all.

From what everyone could understand, they were being taken to Bavaria, to a monastery that hadn't been lived in for some years and was in the process of being turned into a prison for officers captured in the war. It must have been the reason why they travelled so leisurely, sleeping overnight on three occasions in well-guarded hotels: their prison wasn't yet ready.

In Rouen, Colonel Toller had passed Barney on to the German authorities and he'd found himself with a Scottish regiment, the Highland Rangers, who'd been captured at St Valéry-en-Caux. The bulk of the Lancashire Rifles, Barney's regiment, had managed to escape, although a handful of men and three officers had been captured. The men had been bundled into lorries and driven away, no one knew where, and the officers were Barney, Captain William King – a tall, pale-faced man with jet-black hair and magnificent eyebrows who put Barney in mind of a pantomime villain – and Lieutenant Edward Fairfax, whom Barney had known at Oxford and had met again in the camp in Surrey.

'Poor old Eddie', as the other chaps at Oxford had referred to him, was a year older than Barney and more senior by one rank. He was small and plump with light-blue eyes and slightly receding hair. He was also, as Amy would have put it, 'as thick as two short planks.' How he had managed to get into Oxford was a mystery. It could only be due to the influence of his distinguished father. Much had rested on Eddie Fairfax's chubby shoulders. In order for the honour of the Fairfax family to be sustained, it was essential that he did better, or at least as well as his esteemed father. Fortunately for Eddie, he had a winning disposition and was extremely popular. His father expected too much of him so the other chaps quite shamelessly helped him to cheat. Even so, he only managed to scrape through with a Third.

Perhaps it was as punishment for letting the family side down that Eddie was immediately sent to Sandhurst to be trained as an officer in the Army. When he and Barney had met up again on the journey to Bavaria, he'd latched on to the younger man immediately. Barney had always liked the chap, but if there was one member of the Lancashire Rifles that he would have preferred not to meet when he became a prisoner of war, it was Eddie. He was no longer the sunny individual he'd been at Oxford, but fretful, almost tearful at times. He complained that his men didn't respect him and considered him a figure of fun, and that the other officers held more or less the same opinion.

Eddie clung to his old university chum and sat by him on every train. Barney longed to tell him to go to hell, but was prevented by his own inherent good nature. He felt sorry for the man and had enough sensitivity to imagine what it must be like being Eddie Fairfax.

They crossed the border into Germany about ten days after Barney's encounter with Colonel Toller in the bar.

Now they were in Bavaria, someone said. There were fifty officers altogether. A general had been taken prisoner, but his whereabouts were unknown. The officers had sorted themselves out and the most senior, Colonel Campbell, was in charge.

Barney resented this. He didn't see why anyone should be in charge when they were prisoners. When they'd stopped for the night in Reims, Colonel Campbell had taken it upon himself to order an inspection.

'Where is your jacket, Patterson?' he'd demanded after Barney had reeled off his name and number.

'I wasn't wearing my jacket when I was captured, sir.'

'And your cap?'

'I wasn't wearing that, either – sir.' Both cap and jacket had been in the lorry parked behind the bar.

'Well, we shall have to see about getting you replacements.'

'Thank you, sir.' Barney didn't feel the least bit grateful. Unusually for him, he wasn't in a very good mood. How long would it take before this damn war ended? He doubted if he could stand being a prisoner, yet it would seem there was no stopping Hitler, who had taken over most of Europe. At this moment in time, victory for Britain and the Allies looked distinctly hopeless.

Their prison was reached after a long drive in trucks up a steep, unmade road that sliced through a forest. It was obviously an old castle, with towering walls built of huge stone blocks, and thick wooden doors. Even the inside walls were stone. At some time the slit windows had been filled with glass. Most of the rooms were small, barely large enough to take two men, and they learned that most recently it had been a monastery. A monk's room was called a cell, appropriately.

On the ground floor was a large room with a high ceiling. No doubt Masses had been held there when the building had been a monastery, and banquets during its time as a castle. It would seem the room was to be used for eating again now the building was a prison, as it held a large number of wooden tables with benches each side. When they arrived, one of the tables had been taken over by two clerks in German Army uniform who were registering the new arrivals and allocating accommodation.

After standing in a queue for almost half an hour, Barney was handed a piece of paper listing meal times and other information. He discovered he would be sleeping on the third floor in room ten. Unlike the other men, he had no kit to take with him up the two flights of curved stone stairs. He was struck by how cold the building was on a relatively hot June day, and could see no form of heating. If it were like this in summer, he thought, what would it be like in winter?

The contents of room ten comprised bunk beds, a table, two hard chairs and a cupboard. A young man with a heavily freckled face and ginger hair was sitting on one of the chairs. He leapt to his feet when Barney went in, and they shook hands.

'Hello, there. I'm James Griffiths, Second Lieutenant, Highland Rangers. Everyone calls me Jay. I've put my stuff on the bottom bunk, but I'll sleep on top if you prefer.'

To Barney's surprise, Jay Griffiths had a broad Lancashire accent, despite his regiment. Barney introduced himself, said he'd much prefer the top bunk, described the nature of his capture and the reason he had no kit.

'That was hard luck,' Jay commiserated when he'd finished. He glanced around the bare room with its bare walls and single narrow window. 'This is a bit of a hole, isn't it? I wonder how long we'll be stuck here?'

'As long as it's not for ever,' Barney said. The two men laughed.

'At least we're lucky to be alive,' Jay said. 'I lost my cousin in the recent shenanigans. He was the same age as me.'

'Christ, I'm sorry. I came across my brother on his way to Dunkirk. I keep hoping he got home safely.'

'I hope so, too.'

Barney strolled across to the window and looked out. 'That's some view!' he commented. He felt as if he were perched on the very top of the world. The castle stood on a plateau, which finished about thirty feet away at the thick wall that encircled the entire building. From there it fell steeply over a vast area covered with fir trees, a forest so dense it looked more like a dark-green carpet. The trees stretched as far as the eye could see. He noticed the wall had the addition of a barbed-wire fence into which a number of birds had flown and been unable to disentangle themselves. Their small carcases hung from the wire like tiny scarecrows, feathers flapping.

'I wonder if there's any chance of escaping from here?' he said to his room-mate.

'I can't think of a way at the moment. Even if the wall could be scaled, a person could easily get lost in that forest.'

A few chaps were strolling around the plateau. 'Do you fancy a walk?' Barney asked. It wouldn't feel so much like a prison outside.

'Wouldn't say no. I could do with a breath of fresh air.'

The young men went down the winding stairs and into the open air, which had a lovely fresh scent. James said it was pine. He told Barney he'd joined a Scottish regiment to please his mother who was a Scot.

The more they talked, the more they discovered how much they had in common. Jay had a degree, but his was in Entomology. 'The study of insects,' he explained when Barney looked blank. Both preferred football to rugby, had been married for just over a year, had an aversion to thunderstorms, and couldn't abide green vegetables of any sort.

'Particularly cabbage,' Barney said.

Jay pretended to be sick. 'I wouldn't be surprised if we weren't given lots of cabbage in this place. What's sauerkraut all about?'

'I don't know, but it sounds vile and definitely cabbagy.'

They came across a little group of men sitting on a stone bench playing cards and watched for a while. It would seem their prison had already been given a nickname: the Beehive. Barney thought he wouldn't mind being in the Beehive if it weren't for very long. He was enormously relieved that it appeared he'd got rid of Eddie Fairfax in exchange for Jay Griffiths, whom he really liked. Some other poor chap was being forced to share a room – a cell – with Eddie.

It would shortly be time for the evening meal. 'Do we get washed?' Jay asked as they returned inside. 'Or are such niceties dispensed with when we're prisoners of war?'

Barney raised an eyebrow. 'Do we change into dinner jackets?'

'I hope the maid has polished the silver properly.'

'If there's one thing I cannot abide it's badly polished silver.'

They raced each other upstairs – it was a draw – and went into their cell. Captain King was standing by the window looking out. He turned when the two men came in. 'Ah, Patterson,' he said jovially, 'I'm afraid we've got a problem on our hands that only you can solve.'

Barney had a premonition what the problem might be and felt his stomach shrink. 'It's that little twerp, Fairfax,' the captain continued. 'Apparently, he can't share a room with anyone else but you. He nearly had kittens downstairs, made quite a scene when he discovered he had to share with a stranger. In my humble opinion what the bugger needs is a psychiatrist – either that, or a good kick up the behind. Ordinarily, I'd order him to shut up and get on with it – he's in the Army, not one of the ladies' services – but these aren't ordinary circumstances, are they? I'll send him up, shall I? Griffiths here can take himself down to room fourteen on the floor below.'

'Do I have a choice, sir?'

'Well, no, Patterson, you haven't. I'm asking nicely rather than giving an order, but the answer must be in the affirmative.'

'In that case, sir, send him up,' Barney said tiredly.

'Your enthusiasm does you credit, Patterson.' The captain left with a grin.

'Shit,' Barney swore.

'That's a pity.' Jay began to collect his stuff together. 'Who is this chap Fairfax, anyway?'

'We were at Oxford together. He should never have joined the Army.' Barney scowled and aimed a kick at the cupboard. 'Trouble is, you can't help being sorry for the chap.'

'Well, as my mother always says, "You'll get your reward in heaven."' He squeezed Barney's elbow. 'It would have been nice for us to stay together.' He chuckled. 'If I went to room fourteen and made a bigger scene than Fairfax, do you think they'd send me back?'

'I doubt it.' He shook the other man's hand. 'Bye, Jay.'

'Bye, Barney.'

It wasn't Fairfax who needed a psychiatrist, it's me, Barney thought that night, as he lay face down on the top bunk, listening to his unwanted friend drone on.

'Are you sure you're all right, Barney?' Eddie asked solicitously from below. 'You've been awfully quiet all night.'

'I'm tired. If you want someone to talk to go downstairs.' The dining room doubled as a mess. 'There'll be loads of fellows there.'

'I wouldn't dream of leaving you alone, old chap, while you're feeling a bit off.'

'I'm not feeling the least bit off, Fairfax. I feel tired – *dead* tired, if you must know.'

'If I go down there by myself, no one will talk to me.'

'Why not take the notepaper we were given and write a letter home?' Barney snapped. He would have gone down to the mess himself, but the idea of Fairfax trailing two steps behind him down the winding staircase made him want to puke. He was longing to write to Amy, but only when he was alone, so he could think clearly while he poured out his heart.

'I'm not in the mood to write a letter,' Fairfax said in a hurt voice.

Barney didn't answer.

Five days later, the camp commandant arrived. His name was Frederick Hofacker and he held the rank of colonel. His arrival wasn't witnessed, but it was impossible not to be aware of the noise made by the small motorcade that brought him, the loud click of boots on stone floors and the barked orders.

Rules, which until then had been non-existent, were put into force. Prisoners were expected to be up by seven and in bed by ten when the lights would go out, after which time there would be no talking. Outdoor exercise must be taken for at least two hours a day. They had to wash their own dishes after meals and make their own beds. Latecomers to meals would not be served and insubordination dealt with by the culprit being banished to the cellar and put on a diet of bread and water for three days. Anyone caught trying to escape would be shot. The last bit was underlined twice.

On Sundays, they were also informed, there would be a Catholic Mass in the mess, following a service conducted by a Lutheran pastor for those of other faiths, which covered every religion in the world.

'It doesn't sound too bad,' Barney said when he read the stencilled sheet.

'But two hours of outdoor exercise, Barney,' Fairfax complained. '*Every day!*'

'I wonder how our other ranks are doing?' Barney said meaningfully. 'I bet they're sleeping in a crowded dormitory rather than two to a room, and I'd be surprised if they're being fed as decently as us.'

Fairfax ignored this. These days, the only person he cared about was himself. 'Do we have to go to church?'

'It doesn't say. I shall be going to the Catholic service.'

'I didn't know you were a Catholic, Barney.'

'I'm not, but my wife is. I shall be doing it for her.' It was the perfect place to pray for Amy, think about her in peace, feel closer. He tried to imagine the expression on his mother's face if she ever found out he'd been to a Catholic Mass, but it was impossible.

Colonel Hofacker had been at the camp a week when he appeared before the prisoners one morning when they were outside. The men came running, limping, or simply walking, having made their way ten times around the Beehive.

Barney was the first to arrive at the finishing line – two upturned buckets – and the first to notice the tall, immaculately turned-out German officer who was walking up and down – a few feet one way, a few feet the other – one hand behind his back, the other clutching a small stick that was tucked underneath his arm. Two soldiers armed with rifles seemed to be providing a loose sort of guard. It was a warm day and Barney estimated it must be stifling in the tight-fitting grey uniform with the high neck, breeches and highly polished boots.

'You always win,' Jay remarked as he came jogging up.

'I'm the fittest, that's why.' Barney ran on the spot, lifting his knees and waving his arms in the air as if he were drowning. Had the circumstances been different, he would have found it exhilarating to run in the fresh, pine-scented air. He wore a khaki singlet, shorts and plimsolls, which Colonel Campbell had managed to obtain for him. He'd also been provided with a replacement jacket, cap and greatcoat, all of which were much too big, but it was better than being too small. He didn't ask, but suspected he was wearing a dead man's clothes.

Captain MacDermott of the Highland Rangers came strolling up, having walked around the plateau a couple of times. He was the smallest prisoner in the Beehive, even smaller than Eddie, being no more than 5ft 5in tall, with an infectious sense of humour. 'We shall have to have a wee cup made for you, Patterson, with your name carved on,' he drawled. 'I say, I do believe that's Colonel Hofacker over there. Bit of a fop, if you ask me: Beau Brummell will never be dead while he's alive.'

He signalled to Clive Cousins, a second lieutenant, to bring the junior officers to attention. Cousins had been training to be an auctioneer before the war and had a foghorn voice. He bellowed an order and the men formed into two lines and shuffled into position, just as Eddie Fairfax came panting up, his face moist with perspiration. 'I think I must have run round eleven times instead of ten,' he gasped as he joined the end of the front line. No one believed him.

'At ease,' Cousins boomed.

At this point, the commandant marched over and stood in front of Captain MacDermott, towering over the much smaller man. The two men saluted, the German clicking his heels and raising his arm in a stiff, mechanical way so that it quivered with tension.

'Heil Hitler,' he barked. There were a few titters.

At first, Captain MacDermott appeared nonplussed. 'God save the King,' he said mildly.

A young German officer stepped forward and gave a little bow. He was effeminate with small puckered lips. 'I shall translate for Colonel Hofacker,' he said in a soft voice with just a hint of a German accent. 'He requests that you bring your men back to attention as he would like to inspect them.'

'Atten*shun*!' Cousins screamed. There were more titters. Captain MacDermott frowned and gave an almost imperceptible shake of his head. He was indicating that it wouldn't do to aggravate the enemy unnecessarily. From then on, there was no more laughter.

Colonel Hofacker walked slowly along the front line of men,

stopping for the briefest of seconds in front of each and staring at him, as if he were trying to commit every face to memory. Close up, he proved to be an unattractive individual of at least fifty, with badly pock-marked skin and an unnaturally flat and slightly twisted nose. Barney imagined a fist landing on it with considerable force a long time ago, destroying its shape for ever. Despite his unprepossessing looks, the colonel clearly though very highly of himself. 'The bee's knees', Amy would have said. It was obvious from the arrogant expression in his small eyes and the way he strutted along with his powerful shoulders thrown back. At the same time, he looked sickly. The whites of his eyes were distinctly yellow.

Barney, in the second line of men, felt an unease that quickly turned to revulsion when the man stood in front of him for much longer than a few seconds, the small eyes boring into his own. He fixed his eyes on the back of someone's head and tried to pretend the colonel was invisible.

Hofacker finished his inspection. '*Danke schön,*' he said to Captain MacDermott, bowing stiffly. With that, he marched away, followed by the translator and the armed guards.

A few days later, Eddie Fairfax fell ill. It started with a temperature and a headache that kept him awake groaning for most of the night – and Barney awake with him. Next morning, Captain King managed to track down some Aspros, but they didn't help. As the day wore on, Eddie only got worse. He lost consciousness and his breathing became loud and laboured.

As there was no one with medical knowledge among the prisoners and the sick bay on the ground floor was not yet manned, Colonel Campbell went to see the commandant to request a doctor for the invalid. He returned fifteen minutes later seething with anger. He'd been told that Colonel Hofacker was too busy to see him.

'I spoke to that interpreter chappie and he said he'd pass the message on. I told him if nothing was done, his bloody commandant would be reported for not abiding by the Geneva Convention on the treatment of prisoners of war.' The colonel snorted. 'The chap just looked at me vacantly. He knew as well as I did that right now the chances of my reporting anything that happens in this bloody place to a person in authority are less than nil.'

'I didn't like the look of Colonel Hofacker from the start,' said Captain King.

This conversation had taken place outside Barney and Eddie's room. Barney listened with a heavy heart. In a way he would never understand, he was fond of Eddie – no, not fond, more that he felt responsibility for him. Right now Barney was the only person that Eddie had to get him through life.

'Patterson,' the colonel said, 'you'd better find yourself somewhere else to sleep tonight. Whatever Fairfax has got might be catching.'

'If that's the case, sir, then I've probably already caught it. I'll stay, if you don't mind, in case Fairfax needs something.'

'Good chap, Patterson. But I insist you come down to dinner. I'll arrange for someone to keep an eye on the patient while you're absent.'


It wasn't Eddie's groans and heavy breathing that kept Barney awake during the night, but his silence. He lay like a corpse on the bed, not moving, hardly making a sound. Barney looked over the side of his bunk repeatedly to make sure he was still alive, and was relieved to see his eyelids flicker or the blanket move the smallest fraction of an inch as proof that he was still breathing.

The last time this happened, having satisfied himself that Eddie was still in the land of the living, Barney didn't bother to lie down. From the phosphorous hands of his watch, he could see it was quarter to three. The silence could almost be felt. He sat on the bed, leant his head against the wall and contemplated life. He missed Amy so much it hurt. He imagined her asleep in the double bed in the little flat where they had spent a mere four months together, yet it had been the most important and amazing part of his life. He closed his eyes and touched her hair, her cheeks, the curve of her chin, her gleaming shoulders. Then he pulled back the covers and saw her nightdress was twisted around her legs ...

'Excuse me.'

Barney was so startled he uttered a little yelp. 'Yes?' he asked when he saw the German translator had come into the room.

'I'm sorry to have frightened you, but I was worried if I knocked I might wake your friend,' the man said apologetically in his soft voice.

'What do you want?' His irritation was held in check by having to speak in a whisper.

'The commandant would like to see you.'

'Now?' He looked at his watch again. 'It's three o'clock in the morning.'

'Now. Will you come, please?' The man indicated that he should get up.

Barney didn't move. 'What does the commandant want to see me for?'

'He will tell you. I think it is something to do with your friend.' The man's eyes slid down to Eddie.

'Rightio.' It was a strange request at a strange hour, but Barney didn't hesitate. He climbed out of the bunk, put on his clothes, and followed the translator out of the room, quietly closing the door behind him.

They went down to the hushed dining room, usually so full of noise and voices, but now deserted, and along a corridor he'd never seen before. His guide opened a door and they went into a small room that held two desks, both equipped with a typewriter and a telephone. He knocked on a door in the corner and, without waiting for an answer, gestured for Barney to enter, then closed the door behind him.

It was like a different world. Barney blinked in disbelief at the rich tapestries and colourful oil paintings that covered the stone walls; the writing desk, sideboard, circular table and chairs in black and gold; the half-dozen brightly patterned rugs. There was a bowl of flowers on the table, their scent overpowering in the over-heated room. A log fire burned in the open fireplace.

On a crimson upholstered couch in the middle of the room, Colonel Hofacker, the commandant of the Beehive, half-sat, half-lay, smoking a cigarette in an ivory holder. He wore a black silk dressing gown over matching pyjamas. One of his black-slippered feet rested on a rug, the other on the couch. His hair was thick and black and longer than a normal Army haircut. He looked at Barney and smiled. Barney didn't smile back. There was something about the man – he couldn't think of the word … Decadent! That was it. And he looked surprisingly ill, as if his skin was being eaten away.

'What do you want?' he asked courteously, remembering he'd been taken to see the man because of Eddie and it wouldn't do to be rude.

'Sit down, Lieutenant.'

'I'd prefer to stand, thank you.'

'As you wish.' The commandant shrugged.

'I thought you couldn't speak English.'

'One hears quite interesting conversations if people think you don't know what they're saying.' There was a pause and he said, 'You are a very beautiful young man, Lieutenant Patterson.'

'Eh?' It was the very last thing Barney had expected to hear. To his horror, he felt himself blush.

'I have a weakness for beautiful young men,' the colonel continued in a silky voice. 'Are you prepared to accommodate my weakness, Lieutenant?'

'Christ Almighty, *no!*' Barney spluttered. He retreated a few steps in order to increase the distance between them.

'Not even to help your friend?' The man was smiling again. He put the cigarette to his lips and blew out a cloud of smoke.

'*No,*' Barney gasped. 'Not for any reason on earth.'

'Should you change your mind, then a doctor will attend to Lieutenant Fairfax within half an hour.' He reached for the ashtray on the seat beside him and stubbed out the cigarette. 'There is a good man in the nearest village and I will arrange for a car to be sent for him.'

'I can assure you I won't be changing my mind.'

When Barney got back, Eddie's breathing had changed. The breaths were very short and accompanied by a rasping, choking noise. Was that a death rattle? Barney wondered, horrified. What if Eddie died and he could have saved him? He wasn't exactly a stranger to homosexual behaviour. He'd never participated himself, but it had gone on quite a bit at Oxford. With some chaps, it was their nature; with others, it was a bit of a lark.

Eddie seemed to stop breathing altogether and uttered a terrible choking sound. Barney knelt beside the bed and felt for his pulse, but there was nothing. A minute later, Eddie made another choking sound.

'Oh, *God*!' Was a man's life worth less than another man's temporary humiliation?

*No.*

Barney rushed down the stairs to the commandant's quarters. When he opened the door of the little office the translator was seated behind one of the desks writing on a pad. 'Tell Colonel Hofacker I'll do what he wants, *after* the doctor has seen to my friend – and only if the doctor makes him better. He can have my word on that.'

'I'll tell him now.' The man got to his feet. His little pink mouth twisted in a dry smile. 'He thought you would come back. That's why he told me to wait.'

Barney stayed downstairs. There was nothing he could do to save Eddie's life if he decided to die in his absence. He sat by one of the long tables in the dining room and longed for a cigarette. After what seemed an age, he heard a car leave and the sound of the engine fade to nothing in the stillness of the night. After another age, the car returned. The translator came and answered the door before the driver had time to ring the jangling bell and wake everybody up. It was he who took the doctor – a stout, red-faced man with salt-and-pepper hair and a full beard – up to see Eddie. He came back a couple of minutes later.

'One of your officers, Captain King, must have heard the car,' he said to Barney, 'and he came to see what was going on.' He sat on the other side of the table. 'It seems he and the doctor can speak French so they can converse with each other.'

'What did you tell the captain?' Barney asked quickly.

'That Lieutenant Fairfax's condition had worsened and you had insisted we send for a doctor, and that the commandant had complied.'

'Thank you.'

'Would you like a cigarette?' He produced from his pocket a shiny black cigarette case with the initials F.J. engraved in silver. 'My name is Franz Jaeger,' he said. 'I used to work in the London office of Mercedes-Benz. Our showroom was in Mayfair, just around the corner from the American Embassy.'

Barney gratefully took a cigarette and the other man lit it. 'Thank you,' he murmured.

'I'm sorry about everything,' Franz Jaeger said.

'What do you mean?' Barney asked. He wished the translator would go away, he would sooner be left alone.

The man spread his small white hands in a gesture almost of despair. 'The war, the deaths on both sides, the commandant.'

'So why did you join up?'

'My father joined me up,' he said gloomily. 'I came back to Germany because my mother was ill, intending only to stay a few weeks. She died, the Führer invaded Poland, Great Britain declared war and I was stranded. Given the choice, I would have remained in London, even if it meant being interned as an alien on the Isle of Man with my alien friends. I understand it is a very attractive holiday resort, preferable to a prisoner of war camp in Bavaria. I feel just as much a prisoner here as you.'

Barney had never been to the Isle of Man, but felt sure he would also sooner be there than in Bavaria.

'When this stupid war is over,' Franz Jaeger continued, 'I shall return to London.' He threw the cigarette stub on to the floor, took another out of the case and offered it to Barney.

Barney flicked his stub across the room and took a second cigarette. Franz Jaeger was about to put the case back in his pocket. Instead, he emptied the contents on the table. 'Take them. I can get plenty more.'

'Thanks.' Barney put the cigarettes in the breast pocket of his outsize jacket.

'He's dying, the commandant,' the other man said in a distant voice. 'He is riddled with cancer. He won't bother you for very long.'

'Right,' Barney said. Colonel Hofacker was unlikely to die

before tomorrow night, but there was always a chance Eddie Fairfax would, and then he wouldn't have to keep the promise he had made.

Eddie didn't die. It turned out he had pneumonia and should have been sitting upright rather than lying on his back. 'So the fluid can drain,' Captain King said vaguely. 'The doctor gave him some medicine. I don't know the name, it's German.'

'He already looks a bit better,' Barney remarked. Eddie was sitting up, propped against half a dozen pillows. He was fast asleep, but there was a hint of colour in his cheeks and he was breathing normally.

Days passed. The doctor visited every day and Eddie continued to improve. A week later he was talking and his appetite was almost back, though he felt very weak and could only walk a few steps.

Colonel Hofacker amazed everybody, except Barney, by sending up little treats for the patient: breast of chicken, pork chops, marzipan cakes, the sort of food the prisoners never saw.

'We clearly misjudged the chap,' Colonel Campbell remarked.

Another week, and there was nothing about Eddie Fairfax to suggest he'd ever been ill.

Barney, unable to sleep, wasn't surprised to have a visit from Franz Jaeger. It was an unearthly hour and the Beehive was as quiet as a grave.

'The commandant is waiting for you,' he whispered.

Barney grabbed his greatcoat, shoved his feet into shoes and followed the man downstairs. When they reached the hall where the prisoners ate, Barney pulled out a chair and said, 'Let's sit down a minute.' The big room was freezing. What little heating there was had been turned off, and his hands were like blocks of ice.

The translator looked surprised, but took a seat at the other side of the table.

'I've no intention of going near the commandant,' Barney said. 'I would be pleased if you would tell him that.'

'But you promised, Lieutenant.' The man frowned slightly. 'You gave your word.'

'Most people would,' Barney said bluntly. 'My friend was dying and it was an unreasonable thing to ask. Lieutenant Fairfax was entitled to a doctor without the colonel expecting anything in return.'

'True,' the translator conceded, 'but I'm afraid the colonel isn't a reasonable man. He thought you might renege on your promise and said to tell you that if you did, in the very near future one of your comrades would be shot trying to escape. It would be a simple matter to shoot a man who was outside on his own and claim he was trying to cut through the wire fence.'

'He couldn't do that!' Barney gasped. A feeling of terror rose in his chest.

'I'm afraid he could – and he would.' There was sympathy in the man's tone. 'He doesn't give a damn what he does or what anyone thinks. As I told you before, he is dying, and his last wish on earth is to have you.'

What was that line at the end of *A Tale of Two Cities*? Barney wondered as, a few minutes later, he made his way to the commandant's room. 'It is a far, far better thing that I do, than I have ever done …' Something like that.

Eddie Fairfax would never know what his friend had done for him.

Colonel Hofacker disappeared a few days before Christmas. Rumour had it that he'd gone into hospital. On New Year's Day it was announced that he had died.

'You have no idea what he was really like,' Barney wanted to shout when he heard people say that the colonel had been a decent sort of chap. Under him, there'd been an easygoing atmosphere in the Beehive. The rules he'd made were fair and the guards hardly bothered the prisoners. And look what he'd done for Eddie Fairfax when he'd been ill!

The new commandant, Major von Waldau, kept a low profile. Once a week, he met Colonel Campbell, the senior officer, and they discussed matters pertaining to the prisoners and the conditions in which they were kept. The conditions worsened early in the New Year when a hundred more prisoners arrived and they had to live four to a room.

Gradually it dawned on the captives that it would be a long time before they returned to their homes and families.

It turned out that more than four years would pass until they were free. The years were boring and monotonous, but kept bearable by the strength of the human spirit to triumph over adversity. A drama society was formed, a library, clubs for this and clubs for that. Lectures were given, poetry read, sports days held, books written, shoes mended, socks darned, and myriad other ways to pass the time were found.

But Barney Patterson was never able to forget what he'd done to save Eddie Fairfax's life. It had unsettled him to the degree that his personality suffered a marked change, and the memory of that night would haunt him for the rest of his days.

# Chapter 15

## May 1971
## Pearl

I was angling for an invitation to Hilda's flat in Waterloo. She still hadn't signed the final contract, but she had a key. 'I'd like to have another look at your bathroom,' I told her when we collected our handbags and other paraphernalia from the staffroom at the end of the day – the day after my mother had put in an unexpected appearance at the Carlyle Hotel in Southport. 'My aunt's thinking of having our bathroom decorated and I remembered how much I liked the colour of yours.'

I had no idea what colour her bathroom was. I just wanted an excuse not to go home because my mother was there, even if I was only delaying it for a couple of hours. It wasn't all that long since I'd loathed Hilda: if she'd had her way, my mother would have hanged twenty years ago. Now I regarded her as a friend, though there was no suggestion her views on the death penalty had altered during the intervening weeks.

She looked surprised. 'You must be the only person, apart from me, who likes pale green and dark green together. Mam says when I move in I should paint it different colours.'

'I thought the two greens went very well together,' I lied, adding indignantly, 'It's your flat, Hilda, not your mother's. It's up to you what colours you have in your bathroom.'

'I know, that's what I keep telling her. To tell you the truth, Pearl,' Hilda said confidentially, 'I'm meeting Clifford outside the Odeon at half past seven: we're going to see *Kelly's Heroes* with Clint Eastwood. I thought I'd go into town straight from school and do a bit of shopping in order to avoid me mam. She goes on and on about moving into the flat with me.'

'Flippin' heck, Hilda!' I was horrified. 'There's only one bedroom.'

'That's what I said, but she pointed out there was such a thing as twin beds. I didn't exactly tell her to get stuffed, but as much as.' Hilda grinned, an unusual sight, but she'd been doing it quite a lot lately. 'Tell you what, come Monday night after school and you can see the bathroom then.'

'Thanks.' I'd forgotten it was Friday. I supposed that I'd still want to get away from my mother on Monday, but I wanted a reason not to go home right now. I considered going into town myself, but it seemed a bit extreme. I'd felt really odd all day. Now it was time to go home and I felt even odder.

Hilda and I left the school and made our way to the back of the building where the staff parked their cars. It was a cloudy day, but quite warm. A few children were still in the playground waiting to be collected, and a group of mothers with prams had gathered outside the gate, where they were having an impromptu meeting.

Hilda was in no hurry and I was rather childishly taking my time when a voice behind said, 'Hello, there.'

I jumped and dropped my bag, so Hilda was the first to turn.

'Oh, hello, Rob,' I heard her say.

I felt myself blushing, Lord knows why. Rob Finnegan was coming towards us holding Gary's hand. 'Hello,' I mumbled. I don't know why I mumbled, either.

'I'll love you and leave you.' Hilda waved and walked away.

'I wondered how you were.' He looked at me keenly. 'Last night you were really upset.'

'I'm still upset.' I sniffed loudly and quite unnecessarily. 'I'm sorry about what happened. It must have been awful for you.'

'It was anything but awful.' He shook his head. 'It was one of the most interesting nights of my life. Your mother's a bobby-dazzler, as my dad used to say – and your granddad's right out of Hollywood. My family are a very ordinary crowd compared to yours. I've got a granddad in Ireland who wears felt slippers instead of shoes, striped braces and smokes a revolting pipe.'

'Granddad's nice,' Gary chipped in. 'His toenails are really, really long. He has to take his feet to a man who cuts them.' He tugged his father's hand. 'What's the man called, Dad?'

'A chiropodist.'

'He's got a girlfriend,' Gary continued.

'The chiropodist or your granddad?' I asked.

The little boy giggled. 'No, Granddad, silly. She's got a glass eye and a wooden leg.'

'Granddad was only joking when he said that, son.'

'Your granddad sounds fun, Gary.' It wasn't really on for a pupil to call his teacher silly, but the more I got to know his father, the more familiar Gary was likely to become. Having learnt he'd come second in the art competition, the little boy had been excited and giggly all day.

Rob said he was taking Gary to the barber's to get his hair cut in readiness for the photographer from the *Crosby Herald*, who was coming to the school on Monday to take his picture. 'I might have a trim at the same time,' he added.

'You don't need a trim.' He didn't exactly have a short back and sides, but almost. During the last decade, loads of young men, inspired by the Beatles, the Rolling Stones and other pop groups, had grown their hair long. Although Rob liked their music, he hadn't copied their style. I couldn't imagine him letting his hair grow as far as his collar.

'Don't I?' He stroked the back of his head. 'It feels long. It comes from having been a policeman. I'm used to having it closely cropped.'

'I'm sorry. It's none of my business, is it?' I had no right to interfere.

'If you think it looks OK, I won't have it cut. What do you say?' He twisted his head so I could see the back.

'If I were you, I'd leave it as it is.' I felt the urge to put my hand on the nape of his neck and stroke it, which alarmed me.

Gary was looking at us as if he were at a tennis match, his eyes moving from left to right and from right to left when either of us spoke. I had the sensation of this being a significant moment between his father and me. To offer my advice on the length of Rob's hair and for him to take it was moving our relationship on to a different, more personal level.

'I won't bother having mine cut then,' he said, 'just Gary's.'

Gary's eyes swung back to me as he waited for an answer.

'Good.' The match was over.

'I'll see you tomorrow at about eleven,' Rob said as I got in the car, and he and Gary backed away. 'We were going to Chester Zoo,' he explained in response to my look of incomprehension.

'I'd forgotten all about it.'

'That's understandable. It doesn't matter. I'll take Gary on my own.'

'There's no need for that,' I said hurriedly. 'I'll come with you. I'd *sooner* come with you than stay home.'

Gary tugged at his father's leg, and Rob backed away some more. 'Are you sure?'

'Really, really sure.'


Charles had taken the day off work. When I got home, he was in the back garden with my mother. They were seated on white metal chairs at a white metal table. Both were drinking wine and their conversation must have been hilarious because they were laughing fit to bust. I found myself smiling as I watched them through the kitchen window.

Charles looked young and carefree in his baggy gardening trousers and an open-necked shirt. I couldn't remember seeing him so happy. My mother said something and slapped his knee, and they laughed again.

She looked beautiful in a dark-green dress made from fine, silky material that was slightly sheer so the shape of her legs was visible. I'd known she was lovely. I knew it from the photographs of her wedding, the ones in the newspaper during the trial, and from things Charles and Cathy Burns had said. Yet there was that other photo, the one taken in prison when she was forty and unrecognizable as the woman she'd once been.

I'd been expecting someone old to come out of prison, a person who looked more than forty-nine, not considerably less. She'd spent three weeks in a health farm in Suffolk, she'd told us last night, 'Recuperating'.

'Recuperating from what?' Marion had asked sourly.

'From my time spent as a guest of Her Majesty the Queen,' she'd replied with a throaty laugh. 'It did me the world of good – the health farm, that is.'

I'd also not expected the woman who emerged from prison to be able to laugh quite so heartily. The health farm had been followed by a week in Paris with Granddad, buying clothes and other 'bits and pieces'. I suppose she meant jewellery and handbags. I felt pretty sure that would help me recuperate from virtually anything, however unpleasant.

In the garden, my mother got to her feet and began to head indoors. I raced upstairs and shut myself in the bathroom. I was dreading seeing her again. Since I'd known she was about to be released, I'd more or less prepared myself to meet her, but hadn't dreamt I'd burst out crying and fall into her arms. I sat on the lavatory with the lid down and relived the embarrassing experience for the umpteenth time that day.

I hadn't realized how much I'd missed her: I hadn't realized I'd missed her at all. I had imagined us meeting and me being slightly cold, in time becoming a little bit warmer, because she was, after all, my mother.

I heard her shout, 'Would you like more wine, Charlie?'

Charles must have said that he would, because she then shouted, 'Red or white? Have you got any crisps?'

I could have told her that we hadn't. Marion didn't approve of crisps. She said they were unhealthy, full of salt and a sheer waste of money. Some of the children brought crisp sandwiches to school for their lunch. I'd always fancied one.

'What time does my little girl get home?'

I winced. I'd never been called that before.

I heard her go back outside. I left the bathroom and went into my bedroom. I peered through the net curtain and saw her put two glasses of red wine on the table. Charles took a sip of his, said something and came indoors. I held my breath when I heard him come galloping upstairs – most unusually for him, as he went about things like climbing stairs in a calm and sober way. I expected him to go straight into the bathroom, unaware I was in the house.

Instead, he walked into the bedroom. I couldn't tell if he was annoyed or amused when he saw me stationed by the window almost certainly looking guilty – I *felt* guilty.

'She won't bite, you know,' he said. 'I heard your car so I knew you were home. Is it your intention to stay up here for the rest of the day?'

'Of course not.'

'She loves you. She's always loved you. She was really touched when you hugged her last night. She was worried you might not want to see her.'

'I didn't want to see her.' I felt tears come to my eyes. 'I don't know what came over me. I must have missed her without knowing it, and now I feel dead stupid.'

'That's silly, Pearl.' He came over and put his arm around my shoulder, and I laid my head on his. My forehead rubbed against his unshaven chin; he was really letting himself go today. 'You behaved in a perfectly natural way. That's good, much better than holding yourself in all the time like Marion.'

'Where is Marion?'

'At work. Where else?'

'I thought she might have taken the day off like you.'

He snorted loudly. I think he was a bit drunk. 'Then you thought wrong. There's not much that would make Marion have time off work, and your mother coming home is at the very bottom of the list.'

I moved away and sat on the bed. 'Why are you and Marion getting on so badly? It's really upsetting.'

Instead of being sympathetic, Charles made one of the really ugly faces that had used to cheer me up when I was upset as a child. They'd always made me laugh, and I laughed now. 'You mustn't have noticed, but round about every seven years your aunt gets me down. It doesn't take long for me to get over it. You shouldn't let it upset you, Pearl, because the rest of the time it's *me* who gets *her* down.' He raised his eyebrows. 'Don't tell me you haven't noticed *that*?'

'She does nag a bit,' I admitted.

'More than a bit.'

'What's going on here?' My mother sort of floated into the room, reminding me of an actress coming on stage for the first time and expecting a round of applause from the audience. 'Why am I being left out?'

'You're not being left out, Amy,' Charles assured her. 'Pearl has just arrived home. She was about to change into something more comfortable and come downstairs.'

My mother sat on the other side of the bed and leaned against the headboard with her legs stretched out. 'It's getting a bit chilly outside.' She chuckled. 'This reminds me, Charlie, of when our Jacky, Biddy and I were little and sleeping three to a bed. You'd come in mornings when we were still asleep and jump all over us.'

'And who used to put cockroaches in *my* bed? One night I found six. I had to shake the sheets out of the window before I dared get in.' He shuddered. 'I can't stand insects. The lavvy in the yard was full of them.'

'That was our Biddy. Me, I wouldn't touch a cockroach to save me life. She used to collect them in a matchbox.'

'It's a good job she went to Canada.' Charles plonked himself at the foot of the bed where he half-sat, half-lay. 'She had a narrow escape, that girl.'

After a while, I became like little Gary Finnegan, my gaze flickering from my mother to my uncle as they talked about life in Agate Street when they were young. In those days, they hadn't quite appreciated how hard their mother had worked after their dad died – they referred to her as 'Mam'.

'I used to get annoyed that I had to look after you lot while she was at the pub,' Charles said. 'Later, I felt dead ashamed of wanting to be with me mates.'

'I used her lippy and face powder when she was out,' my mother confessed. 'I could cry when I think about it now. She couldn't afford to buy more stuff.'

They said 'me' instead of 'my', talked about lavvies and butties. My mother spoke of walking along the Docky – I assumed she meant the Dock Road.

The time flew by and we were all surprised when Marion

appeared in the doorway, struck dumb by the sight of the three of us on my bed. This was a conventional household where people sat on chairs downstairs when they wanted to talk.

'Hello, darling.' Charles overdid the effusiveness to the extent it was obvious he didn't mean it. 'There's no tea made, but that's because Leo and Harry are coming later and bringing some pizza with them.'

'I am perfectly capable of making food for our guests, Charles.' Marion looked as if she'd spent the last half-hour in a freezer. 'There's no need for anyone to bring their own. What's more, you know I can't stand pizza.'

I hadn't known that Granddad and Uncle Harry were coming. I slid off the bed and muttered that I would make some tea. I was glad we were having visitors. I hummed 'Can't Buy Me Love' while I filled the kettle.

'I like that tune,' my mother said, coming in.

'Could you listen to music in prison?' I'd broken the ice and asked a question.

'We used to watch *Top of the Pops*. Some of the women would dance.'

'Did you have a favourite group?'

'I liked the Bee Gees best, and that chap who sang about going to San Francisco with flowers in his hair.'

'Scott McKenzie.'

'That's right.' Her pink lips twisted sadly. 'I vowed I'd wear flowers in my hair one day, but I don't think they do it any longer.'

'Flower power came to an end when the Vietnam War started, but you can still wear them.'

'Of course I can.' Her face split into a dazzling smile. 'Does our Charlie still have roses in the garden?'

'Lovely red ones, yes.'

'Then I shall pinch one of his roses when they come out.'

I was pleased that we were talking to each other quite easily. I had this silly idea of people going into prison and losing all contact with the outside world. I liked the Bee Gees, too, and Scott McKenzie. It meant we could talk about music.

She leaned against the sink and folded her arms. 'I was thinking earlier that it would probably be best if you called me Amy. Not now,' she said hurriedly, 'but one of these days, when you get used to the idea.'

I made a noise that was impossible to describe. I'd far sooner continue with our previous conversation. I said, 'I've got loads of records and a record player upstairs. You can play them whenever you want.'

'Thank you, though I doubt if I'll be here for much longer. It upsets Marion, poor thing. She likes to have our Charlie to herself.'

'But Charlie – Charles – loves having you here.' It had been obvious earlier.

'I can stay with Cathy, and he can come round whenever he likes.'

Marion wouldn't have Charles to herself if he was at Cathy Burns's house, but I didn't bother to point that out.

Granddad and Uncle Harry arrived about an hour later with pizzas and wine. It was so unusual to be having so many visitors, as well as my first ever takeaway meal, that I felt childishly excited. Not long afterwards, Cathy Burns came, and we sat around the table in the dining room eating and laughing rowdily.

Marion rather pointedly made a cheese sandwich for herself and kept glancing at the communal wall as if she was worried that the people next door would hear us.

My mother – Amy – said she'd telephoned her sisters in Canada that afternoon, and both had been thrilled to hear from her. 'Biddy's eldest daughter is starting university in September and Jacky's girl is just finishing. She's going to be a biologist.'

'If you'd rung after six it would have been much cheaper.' Marion sounded more upset than annoyed at the idea of wasting money.

'When she finished, she asked the operator how much the calls had cost and gave me the money,' Charles said sarcastically. 'We're not out of pocket, darling.'

Anyone else would have looked uncomfortable, but Marion merely nodded approvingly. 'That's good.'

We sat round the table talking for ages – well, I didn't talk, just listened while they remembered some of the strange and funny things that had happened during the war, though I knew desperately sad things had happened, too.

Cathy told us her mother had come home from the shelter one morning to find a strange man asleep underneath the living-room table. 'He'd come in the back way thinking it was his own house. Mam chased him out with the yard brush, though it was a perfectly understandable mistake in the blackout.'

The blackout had been responsible for all sorts of confusion. Granddad and Grandma Patterson had gone to the theatre one night, but lost each other when they came out. 'We had to get separate tramcars home,' Leo said.

'I can't imagine you using a tramcar, Granddad,' I said. He was much too posh.

'The war was a great leveller, Pearl,' he said. 'Petrol was rationed whether you were a pauper or a millionaire.'

'You could get things on the black market,' Amy said. 'Our mam bought a wireless, but she could never get it to switch on. She felt so guilty for buying it that she didn't mind when it turned out not to have any bits inside.'

Uncle Harry said that as far as he was concerned, the war had been nothing but a bloody tragedy – 'Sorry about the language, ladies' – from beginning to end, and he hadn't enjoyed a single minute. 'I lost my best friend in the world.'

'So did I.' Cathy looked at him, and a flash of understanding passed between them. I wondered why.

'Out here,' Charles said, 'we were just spectators. We cycled to and from work every day, and nothing exciting happened. During the really bad air raids, we had Mam and my sisters come and stay. We'd watch the sky over Liverpool turn red, as if the entire city was on fire. We felt as if we were in a different world.'

'Elizabeth and I spent some of the worst nights in the factory in Skelmersdale,' Granddad admitted.

'Where did you stay during the raids, Amy?' Cathy Burns asked. I remembered she'd joined the Army and had spent most of the war years in Yorkshire.

'In the cellar of the house by Newsham Park,' my mother answered. 'We used to have fun down there. Does anyone remember Captain Kirby-Greene? He lived on the ground floor.'

'He was a damn nuisance,' Granddad grumbled. 'Every time I went to the place, he'd nab me in the hallway.'

'I quite liked him,' Marion said, speaking for the first time. 'I only met him the once at that fête by Pond Wood Station. He seemed quite keen on your mother, Charles.'

'He was mad about her. She quite liked him, but not in *that* way.' Charles smiled ruefully. 'I think the only man Mam ever wanted was our dad. There was some chap she worked with wanted to marry her, but she refused.'

'Anyway,' Amy said, 'Captain Kirby-Greene elected himself entertainments organizer for when we had an air raid. He used to spend nearly all his time in the cellar getting things ready for when the siren went. If it didn't, he'd be really disappointed. On Christmas Eve, the second of the war, the raids were really terrible. They'd been like that for days: heavy bombing every night lasting for hours. I remember us singing "Silent Night" and me wondering if Barney was singing it in the prisoner-of-war camp in Bavaria ...'

# Chapter 16

## 1941–5
## Amy

'… all is calm, all is bright,' Amy sang at the top of her voice. 'Round yon Virgin, Mother and Child …' Her voice was doing something to her ears, making them tingle. The louder she sang, the more she managed to drown out the sound of bombs exploding all over Liverpool, making the building shudder and the foundations groan. Any minute, she expected the house to collapse on top of them. It had been the same every night this week. Even tonight, on Christmas Eve, there was no let-up.

'Holy Infant so tender and mild,' she yelled. It was a German carol and she wondered if Barney might be singing it right now in the camp. In the cellar, they were putting their hearts and souls into it: Amy, Clive and Veronica Stafford, Mr and Mrs Porter, and, of course, the captain, as they tried to blot out the reality of what was going on outside.

She remembered when she, Charlie and her sisters were little they'd used to sing 'While Shepherds Wash their Socks at Night', and Mam and Dad would be really annoyed, particularly if they were in church. It wasn't often she thought about her father, and the memory of him brought a fond smile to her lips.

This was the second Christmas since she and Barney had married, and they'd spent both of them apart. What was it like in the prisoner-of-war camp? The camp wasn't in a field with tents as she'd always imagined a camp to be, but in a real castle that was very cold. Barney said he had to wear his greatcoat all the time. It wasn't his original greatcoat, the one he'd been issued with, because he'd lost nearly all his kit in France. This was someone else's coat and he'd found a handkerchief in the pocket with an embroidered W in the corner. 'It must have belonged to a William,' Barney had written, 'or a Walter or a Wilfred.'

Captain Kirby-Greene was conducting the carol-singing with a wooden ruler. He was making dead peculiar faces, twitching his nose and raising his eyebrows, as if he were conducting a genuine choir. Amy longed to laugh, but didn't like to hurt his feelings.

'Sleep in heavenly peace,' everybody chorused, 'Slee-eep in hea-ven-ly peace.'

The ensuing silence, though expected, took them by surprise, and they blinked at each other, until a bomb fell close by, shattering the silence and making them gasp. The house rocked and Amy crossed herself. Captain Kirby-Greene merely looked supercilious. He had steeled himself not to react to the air raids, no matter how bad they were. He considered himself their leader and that it was up to him to stay strong.

'Shall we pause for refreshments?' he suggested. 'It's nearly midnight.'

'That's not a bad idea.' Mrs Porter had made a plate of sandwiches.

As it was Christmas, they were having mince pies. 'There wasn't a jar of mincemeat to be had anywhere in Liverpool,' Mrs Porter said apologetically. 'It's just raisins mixed with blackberry jam, but,' she added, a note of triumph entering her voice, 'we've got egg sandwiches. Amy got the eggs from her brother-in-law's relatives, who live in the countryside.'

'Good-oh!' Clive Stafford licked his lips. He was terribly greedy and would eat far more than his share if he wasn't watched. Veronica made a face at him behind his back.

The captain was looking at his watch. 'It's midnight,' he announced. 'Merry Christmas everyone.'

'Merry Christmas.' They all kissed each other. Clive Stafford kissed Amy with rather more enthusiasm than was necessary.

Life was dead peculiar. Amy had nothing in common with the Porters, the Staffords or Captain Kirby-Greene. She liked them, but their backgrounds were totally different from hers. Yet here she was, spending night after night with these five strange people in a place where any minute they might die. It might be one of their faces, not Barney's or anyone who was really close to her, that she would see before she took her last breath.

What a miserable thought to have within the first few minutes of Christmas Day!

In Keighley, at exactly the same time, Cathy Burns was as happy as it was possible to be in wartime. Just like last year, a party was being held in the finance office. Sandwiches had been made and someone had donated a Christmas cake they'd won in a raffle. There were a dozen bottles of Guinness and plenty of wine.

For the women, it was miles better than going to the dance in the mess and being pawed over by troops, who acted as if they hadn't seen or touched a woman for years, and for the men it meant not having to fight for a dance partner. What's more, they all worked in close proximity and were comfortable with each other.

Reggie Short, who owned the radiogram, had bought some new records for the occasion: 'When You Wish Upon a Star' from *Pinnochio*, Judy Garland singing 'Over the Rainbow' and 'East of the Sun and West of the Moon' by Frank Sinatra.

Reggie asked Cathy to dance. He was an exceptionally handsome young man with blond curly hair and the features of a Greek god. When the war started, he'd been a newly qualified dentist but had discarded dentistry straight away to join the Forces. To his intense disappointment, he found himself still a dentist: the Army had no intention of turning such a highly trained individual into a fighter when he was more valuable to them as he was. Reggie's surgery was next to the doctor's, which was next to the finance office.

Cathy and Reggie had slept together when they'd first met just over a year ago. Cathy, eager to throw off the restraints that had bound her back in Liverpool, was only too willing to go to bed with him when he'd asked. A few weeks later, she'd changed her mind. Reggie was clearly taking the relationship seriously, and Cathy realized she shouldn't just throw away her virtue at the drop of a hat. Even if it had already gone, she was determined that the next time she slept with a man it would be for a better reason.

For a while, she'd thought Harry Patterson might provide the better reason. She'd always liked him and guessed he felt the same. She had even more reason to think that last Christmas when he'd turned up unexpectedly. They'd got on extremely well and he'd written to her afterwards, a lovely letter that made her suspect her feelings were reciprocated. But she'd not heard from him again. She'd been less disappointed than she'd imagined.

Then, not long after Dunkirk, Jack Wilkinson had appeared on the scene. He was dead skinny and not even faintly good-looking, but there was a mischievous twinkle in his dark-grey eyes that Cathy found immensely appealing. Within the space of just a few minutes she was longing to be kissed by his thin, curved lips.

'Me old mate, Harry Patterson, said it would be all right to contact you,' he said when they'd first met. It was June. Cathy had finished work for the day and was sitting in the sun on the grass behind her office. Jack had a Cockney accent and a really wicked grin that made her heart turn over. 'I've come in the lorry from Leeds for the dance in the mess. Trouble is, I can't dance, I've done something to me ankle, see.' He limped a few feet to show how badly he'd been injured – they both knew he was putting it on – 'and Harry said you're a good conversationalist. I'm badly in need of a good conversation with a pretty young woman right now.'

They'd talked all evening, covering life and death, religion and politics, the weather, marriage and other topics that Cathy had trouble remembering later, until the sky had grown dark and the lorry was due to return to Leeds, by which time they were in love. He was the cleverest man she'd ever known, though he'd left school at fourteen, the same as she had. She had never dreamt that being in love was so intense, that your whole being was wrapped up in that one person every minute of every day.

From then on, they saw each other whenever they could. Jack kept an eye out for any sort of transport going to Keighley and cadged a lift, twice coming on the back of a motorbike.

Cathy found it less easy to get away, though managed to get to Leeds a few times where they booked a room in a hotel, not even bothering to pretend they were married. They did the same thing in Keighley, and in neither place did the management appear to care. There was, after all, a war on, and morals, along with quite a few other things, had gone out of the window. Six weeks later, Jack's ankle had healed and he was sent to join Harry Patterson in Egypt. They wrote to each other frequently. Jack's letters were long and thoughtful, and Cathy's neatly typed and full of jokes, describing the funny incidents that had happened on the base.

She thought about him now as she danced with Reggie, wishing a miracle would happen and he would turn into Jack. She wasn't like her friend, Amy. She didn't think her relationship with Jack was made in heaven, or that she would die if she lost him, or that she missed him a hundred times more than other women missed their men. All she knew was that she loved him with all her heart and wanted them to spend the rest of their lives together.

The telephone on the desk in the other room rang and someone answered. 'It's for you, Cathy,' the someone shouted.

Amy was the only person she could imagine telephoning late on Christmas Eve. Cathy abandoned Reggie, went into the other room and picked up the phone.

'Hello, darlin',' said the dearest voice in the whole wide world.

'Jack!' she screamed, then more quietly, 'Oh, Jack. Where are you?'

'Egypt. I'm in this British pub and there's a phone, the sort you put money in. It's taken all night to get through and I've got about a hundred quid with me in small change.'

'A hundred!' she gasped. She didn't notice the room empty and the door quietly close.

'Well, more like five,' he conceded. 'How are you? I thought you'd be having a party in your office.'

'I'm fine – even finer now I'm talking to you.' Her voice dropped to throbbing whisper. 'But, oh, Jack, I do wish you were here.'

'So do I, darlin'.' She heard him put more money in at the other end, in Egypt. It would be really hot there. She looked out of the window and saw frost on the ground. The sky was navy-blue and the stars looked very close and unnaturally bright.

'I suppose it's cold there,' he said.

'Really cold. It looks as if it might snow.'

'I love you, Cath,' he said. More money clanked into the box.

'I love you. Why are we talking about the weather?' She knew when she put the phone down she'd think of loads of things she should have said.

'I love you and I miss you, and, Cath, I really want you.' There was a tiny pause. 'Right now, right this minute, I want you more than anything I've ever wanted in this world.'

Before Cathy could answer, the phone went dead. She stared at the receiver, willing Jack to come back and imagined him in Egypt doing the same thing. She said, 'Jack, where are you?' just in case he was still there, but he wasn't.

After a while, there was a knock on the door and Reggie poked his head inside. 'Have you finished?' Cathy nodded but didn't speak. 'It's Christmas Day and we've just cut the cake. Do you want a slice?'

'Yes, please. I'm just coming.' She'd actually managed to speak to Jack, yet there must be loads and loads of women whose boy-friends and husbands were thousands of miles away in a strange part of the world and who had no chance of hearing from them. She felt dead lucky.


Barney was writing a letter to Amy. He was sitting by the table in his room with his greatcoat on and the eiderdown wrapped around his shoulders. It covered most of his body, but he still felt cold. There were no curtains on the small window so it was impossible to hide the swirling snow that had been falling thickly for days.

It was Christmas Eve and the prisoners were being allowed to stay up until one o'clock. It wasn't long since the guards had stopped throwing snowballs at each other outside, despite the howling wind and the temperature that must be below zero. Now all he could hear were the prisoners singing carols in the mess downstairs, where he should have been himself, not shut in his room alone on such a night.

He'd already told Amy how much he loved her and thanked her for the Christmas parcel that had arrived through the Red Cross:

the chocolates, the biscuits, the novels, the writing pad and envelopes, and a set of pencils and a sharpener instead of a bottle of ink (which might have spilled and ruined everything), the Christmas cards and little gifts from all the Currans as well as the other people living in the house by Newsham Park. Amy had knitted him a scarf and he was wearing it as he wrote. It had numerous dropped stitches and quite a few knots, but it only made him love her more as he imagined her head bent over the needles, biting her lip as she usually did when trying to concentrate on something.

'You'll never guess, darling,' he continued, 'but Eddie Fairfax is no longer my room-mate. He thinks I don't know that he arranged for a Polish officer to move in with me so he could move out. Since then, a couple of Frenchies have arrived and we feel like sardines. Apparently, Eddie was fed up with me. I was bad-tempered all the time and wouldn't listen to him. Both are true, but it was what I did for Eddie that makes me bad-tempered. I can't get it out of my head. I feel as if everyone is able to read my mind and know what I did and hate me for it. I wonder if Franz Jaeger has let it be known and it's being spread around?'

Barney raised his head from the letter. 'People know: I can see it in their eyes,' he said aloud before lighting one of the cigarettes that Franz Jaeger gave him whenever he could. He was a decent bloke and it was unfair not to trust him. He breathed in the smoke and could feel it warming his insides.

There was laughter from down below, and he remembered they were having a concert. One of the best turns was two of the chaps imitating Greta Garbo and Marlene Dietrich singing a medley of songs, most of them funny, but the finale, 'Keep the Home Fires Burning', was quite touching. The laughter, the fact that he wasn't a part of it, made him feel very alone. It wasn't something Barney was used to – he'd always been a very popular chap. But nowadays he was on the outside looking in.

He returned to Amy's letter. 'I quite like my new room-mates,' he wrote. 'As I can't speak Polish or French and they can't speak English, we have nothing to say to each other, which suits me right down to the ground.' It was also fortunate that none smoked so he didn't feel obliged to share the cigarettes.

He finished by telling her how much he missed her, adding, 'Some people here, more expert than me, are saying that 1942 will see the end of this damn war. Hopefully, by the time next Christmas Eve comes round, we will be spending it together.'

Barney didn't bother to sign the letter. He tore the sheets out of the pad and ripped them in half. Then he did the same with the halves, ripping the bits until they got smaller and smaller and the letter was a heap of confetti on the table.

Then he opened the window and threw his letter to Amy to the icy wind, watching the pieces being blown away until he could see them no more.

Then he started another letter that would be much shorter than the first. As if he could tell her all those things. As if he could ever tell anyone.


The air raids continued, causing much loss of life and terrible damage, until the beginning of May when there was a heavy, week-long blitz that made everyone in Liverpool wonder if Hitler was trying to wipe their city off the face of the earth.

Hour after hour, night after night, the bombs fell. In the morning, people would emerge from their houses to find craters where entire streets had once been, and friends they'd had for most of their lives lost for ever. Churches, schools, theatres and landmarks were destroyed, not to mention thousands of houses.

Amy went with her mother and sisters to sleep in Charlie's house in Aintree where the carnage could be seen and heard, but only an occasional bomb fell. Mr and Mrs Porter went to stay with their daughter in Southport and the Staffords to Veronica's sister, who lived in Formby.

Captain Kirby-Greene was invited to stay at any of these places until the terrible raids ceased, but he opted to remain in Newsham Park, 'To look after the place', he bravely claimed.

He was found one morning in the cellar. Slumped in his chair, he had succumbed to a fatal heart attack during the night. But there was a smile on his face and the wooden ruler was in his hand, as if he'd been conducting an invisible choir.

★

Another Christmas Eve came, but there was no sign of the war reaching an end. The air raids had petered out but things were still very black. The British had been driven out of Greece and were losing in North Africa where once they had been winning. On Christmas Day, Hong Kong fell to the Japanese, followed a few weeks later by the loss of Singapore. At least Britain had gained another ally in the war after the Japanese had destroyed the American fleet in Pearl Harbor and Germany declared war on the United States. Weeks later, the Yanks began to arrive on British shores, causing many a young woman's heart to twitter.

Months before, Germany had invaded Russia, the biggest mistake Hitler was to make, as his army wasn't prepared for the savage winter and it meant his attention had drifted away from Great Britain. A stalemate seemed to have been reached, with neither side progressing as the months passed.

At home, 1942 saw rationing bite even harder and there was a shortage of virtually everything. Amy was far more put out by having to use coupons for clothes than for food. She wasn't as particular about what she ate as she was about what she wore.

It had become a ritual. It brought them luck, Harry claimed, convinced he wouldn't survive if Jack weren't around to shake hands with before they went into battle.

They grasped each other's hands now, using both hands to make the gesture more heartfelt. It was four o'clock on a still, warm morning in El Alamein, not far from Alexandria. The sky was dark with a eerie purple glow, and the sand was like powder: if you didn't tread lightly it would almost swallow your feet. No one spoke as the men advanced in uneven lines behind a row of tanks, sand spurting from under the treads like smoke, so that all they could see were the backs of the half-hidden tanks.

The enemy was ahead and supposedly retreating, although, every now and then, a bullet would whiz past or a shell explode nearby.

Jack marched slightly in front of Harry, loosely clutching his rifle, a grin on his face. He'd lost his socks and his boots were too big on his scrawny feet. He was incapable of taking anything seriously. He genuinely thought the world was mad and the people in charge were the maddest of all, yet good-naturedly went along with the craziness, never complaining.

In the two years that Harry had known him, Jack had become more of a brother than Barney had ever been. That was no reflection on Barney: just that they hadn't shared the same dangers, taken the same risks. If there was one person in the world Harry would be happy to see marry Cathy Burns, then it was Jack Wilkinson. He had already agreed to be best man at their wedding, whenever that would happen.

A red line had appeared on the horizon: the sun was about to rise. Harry hoped the fight would be over before it got too hot. If he stayed in Egypt for the rest of his life, he would never get used to the heat.

He felt like part of a ghost army as they shuffled along, making hardly any sound on the sand. A shell landed behind one of the tanks and another in front. Then there was another explosion that threw him to the ground with considerable force. He lay there for a minute, stunned, and when he raised his head he saw at least half a dozen other men had also been floored. Dazed, he struggled to his feet, relieved to find he was unhurt, but considerably shaken. The other men had also managed to stand and were trying to get their breath back, apart from one lying flat on his back with a hole in his stomach as big as a football while his life blood gushed out on to the sand, staining it scarlet.

'*Jack!*' Harry knelt beside his friend and shook him, though there wasn't a chance on earth that he was alive. 'Jack!'

There was a shout. 'Get a move on, Patterson.'

'But, Sarge – it's Jack,' Harry screamed. He could feel tears streaming down his cheeks.

'I know who it is, Patterson. Get a fucking move on the lot of you. The medics will see to Wilkinson. They're not far behind.'

It should have been me, Harry thought furiously as he looked into his friend's lifeless brown eyes for the very last time before tipping his battered hat over his face. *It should have been me.*

★

Eighteen months later, Harry Patterson was one of the first soldiers to storm on to Gold Beach in France as part of the D-Day landings. Harry would never be promoted, win a medal or be Mentioned in Despatches. He was just an average soldier who had fought diligently, never complained or answered back, and had always obeyed orders, no matter how stupid he considered them to be. Men like him were the backbone of the British Army, and without them the war against Germany would never have been won.

After D-Day, the population breathed a sigh of relief, as it looked as if the conflict might soon be over, though in fact it was to be another eleven months before the war in Europe came to an end.

During that time, Amy moved out of the flat by Newsham Park into a bungalow in Woolton, an ancient part of Liverpool with a pretty clock tower. The bungalow was on a little lane no distance from the centre of the village, but Amy felt as though she were in the middle of the countryside.

Leo Patterson arranged everything. 'Barney needs to come home to somewhere better than that pokey little flat,' he proclaimed.

Amy wasn't sure. They couldn't have been happier than they'd been in the pokey little flat, but she let Leo overrule her for once: perhaps this time he knew best. It was Leo who managed to furnish the new place, no easy task in wartime when factories had more important things to do than make chairs and tables and beds.

He laughed when she referred to the furnishings as 'second-hand'. 'They're antiques,' he informed her.

'They're still second-hand,' Amy argued.

'This wee desk cost a fortune,' he said. It was rather a nice little desk, white and kidney-shaped with elegantly curved legs at the front.

'I thought it was a dressing table,' Amy said. 'Why do we need a desk?'

'You can sit at it to write letters.'

'I always write letters on me knee.'

Leo grinned. She had no idea why some of the things she said amused him. 'Well, now you can do it at a desk. Oh, by the way,' he continued casually, 'Elizabeth has invited you to dinner.'

'Huh!' Amy snorted. 'You can tell Elizabeth to go and jump in the lake. I've met her once and that was enough.'

'That was more than five years ago.' He frowned as if she were being childishly stubborn. 'I think normal relations between the family should begin when Barney comes home, don't you?'

'It depends what Barney wants, not you, me or Elizabeth.' She mustn't have a very forgiving nature because her natural instinct was never to see her mother-in-law again. She changed the subject. 'Isn't it the gear to be able to say, "When Barney comes home", and know that it won't be long?' It was almost Christmas and this time people knew for sure it would be the last of the war. Amy hugged herself. 'I'm longing to see him, yet dreading it, too.' She bit her lip. 'It's been so long …'

'You're bound to feel strange for a while.'

'Am I – are we?'

'Yes.' Leo patted her shoulder. He was very easy to talk to.

'Thank you,' she said.

He looked at her, eyebrows raised. 'What for?'

'For coming round that day when I lost the baby, for getting us this house, and all the things in between.' He'd been an enormous help. Without him, she would have been desperately lonely.

'Don't mention it.' His face softened. 'Do you ever think about the baby?'

'A day never goes by when I don't.' Amy's lips twisted. 'I wish I'd known whether it had been a boy or a girl so I could have given it a name, then he or she would seem more real. Just imagine if Barney had a little boy or girl to come home to!'

'Just imagine,' Leo echoed. 'Wouldn't it have been great?'

Cathy Burns now had two stripes on her sleeves, having been promoted to corporal. Mrs Burns told everyone she met about it. 'I always knew there was something special about our Cathy,' she said to Mr Burns more than once.

In March, with the Allies approaching Berlin and only weeks before the war would end, Cathy met Reggie Short in a hotel in the centre of London. Cathy had spent two years in Ipswich and the last year in Portsmouth, while Reggie had remained in Keighley for the entire period of the war. They met for dinner in the Bonnington Hotel in Holborn every few months.

'What are you going to do when it's all over, Cath?' Reggie enquired while they waited for the first course. She knew he would always regret informing the Army he was a dentist. Had he claimed to have left school at fourteen and worked in a shop he would have had a far more interesting war.

'Go to college and train to be a teacher,' Cathy replied promptly. The course was open to ex-service men and women as long as they could pass the entry exam. 'What about you?'

'What do you think?' Reggie made a face. 'Just carry on being a dentist. I think I'd like to set up a practice in a nice little village, get married and have half a dozen kids.'

'Good luck!' Cathy raised her wine.

'The same to you. Are you serious about being a teacher?' Reggie looked at her appealingly. 'Would it be possible to talk you into marrying a dentist who wants half a dozen kids? I'll reduce the kids to two if it would please you.'

Cathy visualized the nice little village, the children, a comfortable life, but didn't feel vaguely tempted. 'I'm deadly serious, Reg – though really touched that you want to marry me.' She loved him, but not nearly enough. 'You know why I can't.'

'Is it Jack?' Cathy nodded, and he continued earnestly, 'You can't spend the rest of your life pining for him, Cath.'

'I'm not pining for him,' Cathy said flatly. 'He's dead and I accept it completely. It's just that I don't want to marry anybody else if I can't marry him.'

'Will you think about it, though?'

Cathy promised that she would, knowing her answer would always be the same.

'Is there any more lemonade?' Moira Curran asked of no one in particular when she went into the house in Agate Street, closely followed by her friend, Nellie Tyler.

'Dunno, Mam,' replied Jacky, her middle daughter.

'Do you want us to go and buy some?' Biddy asked.

'No, ta, luv. If ours has gone, someone else is bound to have some.'

'It's all gone, Moira,' Nellie shouted from the kitchen.

'Would you and Nellie like a glass of sherry, Mam?' asked Amy.

'I wouldn't say no, luv. How about you, Nellie?'

Nellie grinned a trifle drunkenly. 'I wouldn't say no, either.'

The street was having a party to celebrate the end of the war and today, 8 May, was a Bank Holiday. With no work to go to, the sisters had gathered around the table in their mother's house for a chat. It was a long time since the three of them had been together for any length of time. Jacky spent most of her weekends with Peter's family in Pond Wood, and Biddy's fiancé, Derek O'Rourke, a trainee fireman, lived over the water in Birkenhead. They were getting married at the end of June.

'We'd like a baby as soon as possible,' Jacky said after her mother and Nellie Tyler had left the house rather more tipsy than when they'd come in. 'We're going to try for one as soon as Peter is demobbed.' Since Peter had joined the Navy, they'd managed to see each other every few months.

'I would, too.' No matter how hard she tried, Amy couldn't imagine Barney being home. She could say it, the words tripped off her tongue quite easily, but Barney *being* there was another thing altogether.

There was an air of quiet satisfaction between them. Mulholland's was no longer making vehicles for the Army, and Amy had been allowed to leave. She wanted to be home full-time when Barney eventually returned. As Jacky pointed out, the war had ended: the air raids were over; no more ships would be sunk or planes shot down; no more servicemen and women would be killed.

'That's not true,' Amy reminded her. 'Only the war in Europe is over. The war in Japan has yet to be won.'

'I forgot,' Jacky said gloomily. Snatches of song kept drifting into the house through the open front door. 'When the lights go on again, all over the world', they were singing now. It was a glorious day, sunny and warm – as glorious, Amy pointed out, as the day war had been declared nearly six long years ago.

'Would you two like a cup of tea?' Biddy enquired.

'I'd love one,' Amy said, 'but has Mam got enough tea? And what about milk?'

'There's plenty of both. I brought some tea with me, and our Jacky brought the milk.'

'It's fresh milk, straight from the cow. I got it at the farm this morning.'

Amy winced. 'I never remember to bring anything.'

'We've noticed that, haven't we, Jacky?' Biddy said sternly.

Jacky smiled. 'It doesn't matter, sis. Your Christmas prezzies more than make up for milk and tea and stuff like that. That brooch you gave us last year has been admired by all and sundry, and people still stare at the bag you brought from London all those years ago.'

Biddy nodded. 'So you can have a cuppa without feeling guilty.'

Amy stood. 'OK, but I'll make it, seeing as how I haven't brought anything towards it.'

She was in the kitchen quietly singing, 'Yours till the stars lose their glory' along with the rowdy crowd outside when her sisters came in.

'There's someone to see you,' Jacky said.

'We've put him in the parlour where it's private,' Biddy told her.

Amy still hadn't properly understood when she opened the parlour door. She thought they might have meant Leo – though both her sisters knew him well and were unlikely to put him in the parlour – so she wasn't really prepared for the person who was there.

'*Barney*!' It came out half a groan and half a gasp.

When she'd thought about this impossible thing happening, Barney coming home, she had envisaged him wearing a uniform of sorts, possibly even the greatcoat that had belonged to the person whose name began with W, but he had on a smart dark-grey suit, a cream shirt and a maroon tie. She stared at this stranger; a pale and hollow-eyed Barney stared back at her. He lifted his arms. It was a limp gesture and his arms barely reached the level of his waist, but it was enough for Amy, who flung herself at him.

'Oh, *Barney*!' She clung to him, sobbing into his neck, wetting the maroon tie and the collar of his shirt. His arms slid around her and he held her so tightly that she could hardly breathe. Then he began to cry, too.

Amy had no idea how long they stayed in the parlour, hardly speaking, just holding each other. People came in and out of the house, and the party outside got rowdier, the singing noisier. Two men had a fight, a football was kicked against the wall for a good ten minutes, feet clattered loudly on the pavement as revellers danced an Irish jig.

And still they sat, Amy and Barney, hardly able to believe the war was over, that they were back together at long last. They would have to get to know each other all over again, and Amy had a feeling that would be far more difficult than the first time.

It was almost June and on the first it would be Amy's birthday: she would be twenty-four. Barney suggested they went somewhere special to celebrate.

'I can't think of anywhere special,' Amy said, 'unless we have a late honeymoon in London.' He'd promised to take her again when their first – and last – visit had had to be cut short.

'We'll go to London one day,' Barney declared, 'but not just yet. Dad's still showing me how the business works.' He'd gone to work for his father, having forgotten or changed his mind about doing something exciting after the war. 'This week I'm in the glass-blowing department. It's fascinating to watch.'

'Are you learning to blow glass?' Amy hoped that wasn't a stupid question.

'No, just to see how it's done,' he replied impatiently, as if it *had* been a stupid thing to ask. 'Glass-blowing is a trade. It takes ages to learn. Tell you what, let's go to Southport – to the pier where we met that Easter Sunday. It seems a lifetime ago.'

'I'd love that.' She was willing to do anything that might make their relationship normal again, stop him being so distant and cold. Only in bed, in the dark and under the covers, was he the old Barney. Even then, it was only while they made love. Before and after he didn't say a word, just grabbed her and let her go without saying a word. He smoked heavily and never spoke about his time in the prisoner-of-war camp.

It was Amy who started every conversation – at least, until Barney had come up with the idea of going somewhere special on her birthday.

'It's a pity Harry won't be here,' she said. 'Cathy's home for a few days and it would be nice if all four of us could go. We could get the train.' It could be months or years before petrol was available and people could use their cars again.

'Hmm,' Barney murmured in a uninterested way.

It so happened that, a few days before her birthday, Harry returned to England for the first time since D-Day and was granted five days' leave.


The weather was horribly cold for June. A chill wind blew across the flat sands of Southport, penetrating the clothes of the few hardy souls who were strolling along the pier. This time, it seemed to be Cathy and Harry who wanted to be alone together, while Amy and Barney tagged along behind with hardly a word to say to each other.

Cathy and Harry hadn't met since the party in the finance office in Keighley the first Christmas of the war. So much had happened since, the most important being that Cathy had met Jack, who had died at Harry's side in Egypt. They were desperate to share their memories of the man who had been the lover of one and the dearest friend of the other.

Amy wished that she and Barney had come on their own. The presence of the other couple only seemed to emphasize how badly they were getting on. She was quite pleased when he grabbed her arm and said, 'Let's walk to the end of the pier. Come on.'

It was a desolate sight, the Irish Sea in the far distance glistening dully like pewter, while the sand stretched before them, wet and unwelcoming. There wasn't a soul in sight. Barney breathed in and let the breath out again with a satisfied sigh. Very slowly, he let his eyes sweep the horizon. 'That looks good,' he said. 'I wish I could live here for the rest of my life. I wish you hadn't given up the flat, Amy,' he added petulantly.

He hated the bungalow. The rooms were too small, the windows too dark because of the thick hedge surrounding the property, whereas from the windows of their flat there'd been no limit to the view, just the roofs of the nearby houses and endless blue sky. The new house made him feel as if he were still in prison.

'Let's look for somewhere else,' Amy suggested.

She wasn't all that keen on the bungalow, either. She would have been only too willing to move elsewhere, but Barney was being awkward. 'It doesn't matter,' he'd say sulkily. 'This place will grow on me, I suppose.'

Standing at the end of Southport pier, he suddenly put his arm around her shoulders. 'I'm sorry, darling. I used to dream about coming home, but now I have and I can't get used to it. I can't get used to four walls. I feel I want to live in the open air – on top of a mountain where I can walk in any direction with nothing to stop me.'

Amy kissed his chin. She was expecting too much of him. He'd been confined for five long years and it would be a long time before he became adjusted to freedom. Until then, she would just have to be patient.

'Are you two looking to catch pneumonia?' Cathy and Harry had followed them to the end of the pier. Both wore civvies. There was nothing to show that either had spent the last six years in uniform. Cathy had a headscarf on her neat brown hair, hands stuffed in the pockets of her warm tweed coat, the collar turned up. 'I wish I'd put me mink coat on,' she laughed. 'Could we please go somewhere for a nice hot drink?'

By now, there were more people about. Half a dozen boys were racing each other from bench to bench; two men were fishing; an elderly couple, wearing matching knitted cardigans, were throwing bread to the seagulls.

Barney took charge. 'Let's have some tea in the place we went to last time, then go for a wander along Lord Street and have a meal. Does anyone know what films are showing this week?'

'*Double Indemnity* with Barbara Stanwyck and Fred MacMurray, and *The Lost Weekend* with Ray Milland,' Cathy said promptly, adding, 'I looked in the *Echo* last night.'

Barney looked from face to face. 'Which one shall we see?'

'Let's take a vote on it,' Harry suggested.

'What happens if each film gets two votes?' Barney asked.

'Then we'll ask Amy to toss for it and she'll want to see whichever picture loses,' Cathy said. 'It's a habit of hers,' she explained when the men gave her a puzzled look. 'At least, it used to be.'

Amy remembered the last time she'd done it was in Southport, in a café in Lord Street where she and Cathy had had a pot of tea. She couldn't remember the names of the pictures, but Charles Boyer had been in one and Humphrey Bogart in the other. They tossed and Charles Boyer had won, but she'd wanted to see Humphrey Bogart so Cathy had given in. She'd never dreamt that when she went to see the film some hours later it would be with Barney. That was the day that her life had changed for ever.

Today it was still changing. Perhaps they should come back, the four of them, in another six years. She wondered what would have happened by then.

## Chapter 17

### *June 1971*
### Pearl

I'd forgotten how much I hated zoos. If Rob suggested we come again I'd tell him to take Gary on his own. There was something hideously cruel about wild animals being kept in cages. One of the few things I could remember about my father was that he felt the same. I suppose it was something to do with being in the prisoner-of-war camp for so long.

It was a relief when Gary had seen everything. Rob asked if he'd like to go round a second time, but he declined. 'I'm hungry,' he announced. 'I'm hungry for sausage and chips.'

We drove into Chester – we'd come in Rob's car – and looked for a suitable restaurant where I ordered cod and chips. It was quite a treat, because Marion considered fried food unhealthy; she never made chips, and batter was a dirty word in the house.

Today, I felt as if I were split in two. One half of me wanted to be with Rob, the other half longed to be with my mother. My feelings had completely changed since yesterday. I'd never thought we'd get on so well together. Already I was feeling protective towards her, and it really hurt to think she'd spent all those years in prison. Today was her birthday – she was fifty – but had insisted she didn't want a fuss. 'We can have a party when I'm fifty-one. By then, I might be in the mood.'

One of these days, when there was just the two of us, I wanted to talk to her about my father. I'd been remembering the furious rows they'd used to have – the fury always on his side. Her voice was consistently quiet, patient and, reasonable, as she tried to calm him. But that only made him worse. 'Whore!' he would scream.

Once, he'd said, '*I really would like to kill* you.' It had terrified me. I'd wanted to stop him, but didn't know how. Anyway, my mother had killed him first.

'Penny for them,' Rob said.

I stared at him vacantly. 'Pardon?'

'I said, "Penny for them." I've asked twice if you'd like a pudding.'

'I wouldn't, thank you, but I'd love some tea. I'm sorry,' I added apologetically. 'I was miles away.' I thought of a simple way to be with Rob and my mother at the same time. 'Would you like to come home with me so Gary can meet Amy?' At least I could call her Amy when she wasn't there, though I doubted if I'd ever do it to her face. 'If you think that's all right,' I added hurriedly. Not everyone would be keen on the idea of his or her child having contact with a murderer, however pretty and charming she might be.

'That'd be great,' Rob said.

'Where are we going?' Gary asked.

'To see Pearl's mother.'

The little boy looked at me in surprise. 'Have you got a mummy, miss?'

'Yes, Gary, I have.' I didn't discourage him from calling me 'miss': I didn't want him referring to me as 'Pearl' in class.

'Do all teachers have mothers?'

'They do indeed,' I told him.

He considered this for a while, frowning, then shrugging as if he found it very mysterious. 'And dads, too?'

'And dads, too,' I confirmed.

Within the space of a few minutes, Amy had totally bewitched him. She and Charles were in the garden; Marion had her usual Saturday appointment at the hairdresser's. 'My, aren't you handsome!' she said admiringly. She patted the empty chair next to her. 'My name is Amy. Would you like to sit down and tell me all about yourself?'

Gary was only too happy to oblige. He described the picture he'd painted that had come second in the competition: 'It's an orange and lemon tree, and rabbits live in the roots. I drew their house. What's it called, Dad, a rabbit's house?'

'A warren, son.'

'I drew a warren with curtains on the window. The man from the paper said it showed I had a good – what was it the man said, Dad?'

'That you had a good imagination.'

'The man said I had a good imagination. And I'm getting a prize. It's a painting set in a wooden box, and the paints are in tubs, not squares.'

'Tubes, darling, not tubs.'

'I'll really enjoy squeezing the tubes,' Gary said seriously. 'You can't squeeze squares. Would you like me to paint you a picture when I get the tubes?'

'Yes, please. I'd love that. And will you do one for my brother? His name is Charlie, and this is him here.'

Charles smiled benignly.

'Yes, I will, Amy, but I'll do a different sort of tree.'

'You,' Amy said, 'are a truly delightful young man. Would you like to come indoors and I'll make you an ice cream cornet?'

'Yes, please.' He trotted beside her into the house, and I wondered why my mother hadn't had more children when she so obviously adored them.

Half an hour later, Marion returned, her hair short, smooth and black. I was worried she'd be put out to find we had more visitors, and was ready to be annoyed if she were: it wasn't often I brought people home. But she was as nice as it was possible for Marion to be. I remembered Rob's old banger of a car was outside and it was only the other day that she'd complained to Charles about it. But she showed no sign of having noticed: if she had, she was pretending not to care.

She made quite a fuss of Gary, but he was too enamoured of my mother for it to make much of an impression. I don't know if Amy had picked him up, or he'd managed to wriggle on to her knee unasked, but they were sitting companionably together on one of the garden chairs while he ate his ice cream cornet.

I suppose it was inevitable that Cathy Burns would turn up,

irritating Marion and astonishing Gary, whose ideas about teachers were being turned upside down.

Rob and Gary stayed for tea. I went inside and helped Marion prepare it. She told me my mother was moving into Cathy Burns's house tomorrow, Sunday. I wished Marion were different so she could stay. I would really miss her when she'd gone, which was ridiculous when you thought about it. I'd spent most of my life without her and it hadn't bothered me, yet she'd only been home a couple of days and I didn't want her to go.

After tea, Rob and Gary went home, Cathy Burns and my mother returned to the garden with a bottle of wine, and Marion and Charles went into the front room to watch television. I reckoned Charles would far sooner have stayed outside – I did. I could watch television any day.

That night, their wartime reminiscences developed into a singsong. The neighbours and their guests in the conservatory next door came out and joined in with 'When They Begin the Beguine', 'Goodnight Sweetheart' and songs I'd never heard of. Conversations were conducted over the hedge regarding what to sing next. Perhaps it was because Marion had brought me up that I felt so embarrassed. I imagined the singing passing from garden to garden until the whole block was involved.

Marion poked her head out of the back door and shouted that there was a phone call for me. 'What's going on out there?' she asked.

When I went inside, I told her to go back to her television programme, adding, 'It's best you don't know.' It must have been a really interesting programme because she did.

To my surprise, the caller was Hilda Dooley. Even more surprisingly, she was crying. 'I need to talk to you,' she wept.

'Where are you, Hilda?'

'In town. I'm in a phone box at Lime Street station.'

'Can you come here?' I couldn't go to her as I'd had too much wine. 'You know where I live, don't you?'

'Yes, I came once to collect some jumble. You couldn't fit it into the boot of your car.'

'That's right.' The irritating thing about a Volkswagen was that the engine was at the back and the boot at the front, so it hardly held anything.

'I'll see you in about twenty or thirty minutes.'

I wondered what was wrong, then thought it could only be something to do with Clifford.

I put the kettle on in readiness for when Hilda arrived, and returned to the garden where everyone was singing 'Roll Out the Barrel', a horrible song in my view. I made my point by not joining in.

When Hilda arrived, I made tea and took her into what Marion referred to as the 'breakfast room', more an alcove with a table and built-in wooden benches. It was situated between the kitchen and the hallway.

'What's wrong?' I asked once we were sitting down. Hilda's eyes were bloodshot and her powdered face was streaked with tears.

'It's Clifford,' she said.

'What's he done?'

'Asked me to marry him,' Hilda said dolefully.

I was confused. 'Is that a bad thing?'

Hilda sniffed and wiped her nose with the back of her hand. I hurried into the kitchen and fetched half a dozen paper hankies. 'It is when it turned out that flat he lives in doesn't belong to him, and he wants to move in with me.' She sniffed again, but this time it was more indignant than pathetic. 'I can't help but think he only wants to marry me so he'll have somewhere to live where he doesn't have to pay rent.'

'I thought he owned the flat in Norris Green,' I said.

'So did I, but apparently he only rents it. He doesn't like it there – remember he said that when he showed us the one for sale? And he definitely gave the impression that he owned it. Oh, Pearl!' She began to cry again, big, droopy tears that followed the shiny tracks of the tears she'd shed before. 'I thought it was too good to be true, that he was attracted to me when he was so good-looking.'

'Don't be daft,' I said, though I'd been a bit surprised myself. 'Did you agree to marry him?'

'Yes,' she groaned. 'I feel a real idiot. He asked over dinner and after I'd said yes, we started to talk about the future. I suggested we use some of the money from the sale of his flat for a new kitchen in mine. It was only then he admitted he didn't have a flat to sell.'

Amy came into the kitchen singing 'Yours Till the Stars Lose their Glory', and Hilda looked as if she were about to cry again. 'I'm sorry. Are you having a party? I've disturbed you, haven't I? I'm sorry.' She stumbled to her feet to leave.

'There you are, Pearl,' said my mother. 'I wondered where you'd gone.' She gave us both a dazzling smile. 'How do you do?' she said to Hilda. 'I'm Amy.' She looked really gorgeous today in a bright red dress with a straight skirt and short sleeves and a white frill around the neck. She wore white sandals with straps no broader than shoelaces.

'This is Hilda,' I said. 'She teaches at St Kentigern's.'

I wondered if Hilda would recognize the woman she used to see at Mass all those years ago, despite the long blonde hair being short and brown. I didn't care if she did or not. Never again would I tell anyone that my mother was dead. From now on, I'd tell people the truth and nothing but the truth.

Amy sat on my side of the table and shoved me along with her hip. She took hold of the Hilda's big red hands in her small white ones. My mother had spent the last twenty years in prison, yet Hilda's hands looked as if she'd been in a chain gang breaking rocks.

'What's wrong, dear?' Amy asked. 'You're obviously upset about something.'

Hilda didn't look up to going through the whole thing again, so it was left to me to explain why she was so upset. 'She feels she's been taken for a ride,' I finished.

'Perhaps you have, perhaps you haven't,' Amy said enigmatically. 'If I were you, I'd tell Clifford I'd changed my mind; that I didn't want to marry him – at least, not for a while. If he genuinely loves you, he'll hang on. If he doesn't, he'll take off.'

'The thing is, Amy,' Hilda whispered, 'I don't want him to take off. He's the first man who's wanted to marry me and I'd sooner keep him.'

'Which would you prefer, Hilda: to be Mrs Clifford whatever-his-name-is, unsure if your husband really loves you; or a single, independent woman with a good job and your own flat?'

For a few seconds, Hilda seemed confused. Then she nodded a few times and said, slightly shamefaced, 'You'll be shocked, but I'd sooner be married any day than single, whether Clifford loves me or not. And I've always wanted children. I'm only thirty-seven: there's still time.'

Amy didn't appear the least bit shocked. 'In that case, next time you see Clifford, tell *him* you want children. You can't raise a family in a one-bedroom flat. You'd have to buy a house and he'd have to take out a mortgage. See what he thinks about that.' She squeezed Hilda's hands. 'I came in for another bottle of wine,' she said. 'Cathy will think I've gone all the way to Spain to fetch it.'

'She's nice,' Hilda remarked when my mother had gone. 'Is she a relative?'

'She's my mother,' I said. 'Her name's Amy Patterson and she's not long out of prison.'

It was Sunday and Charles had taken my mother's belongings to Cathy's house. They consisted of a large, expensive suitcase full of lovely clothes, most of which had been bought in Paris. My mother had gone to lunch with Uncle Harry. I felt quite pleased about it.

'Is there a chance they'll get together?' I asked Charles. 'After all, he's her brother-in-law. She met him at the same time as she met my father.'

'No chance at all,' Charles said dismissively. 'If Harry was going to get together with anyone, it'd be Cathy.'

'Cathy!' I gasped.

'They had something going during the war – or at least, they nearly did. I'm not exactly sure what happened, but it was before she met Jack.'

'Who's Jack?'

'Cathy's fiancé: he died at El Alamein.'

'Why haven't you told me all this before?' I said crossly. 'It's so *fascinating*. What was Jack like?'

Charles shrugged. 'I don't know, I never met him, but ask your Uncle Harry next time you see him. Jack was his best friend.'

'Damn!' I muttered. I hated not knowing things.

That afternoon Marion said, 'Pearl, your mother's left her cardigan behind, the blue one. Did you say you were going to Southport this afternoon with Rob?'

'Yes. I'm picking him and Gary up at half two. Do you want me to drop the cardigan off at Cathy's on the way?' She probably wanted rid of it so my mother wouldn't have an excuse to come back.

'If you don't mind.'

Actually, Cathy lived in Crosby and it wasn't on my way, but Gary would love to see Amy if she were back by then.

Cathy Burns lived in a small, tree-lined cul-de-sac of small detached houses that had been built about twenty years before. As expected, Charles's car, a dark-green Cortina, was parked outside the one covered with red ivy, which looked lovely in the summer, but not so nice in winter when the leaves disappeared, leaving the branches crawling all over the walls.

'I don't think my mother's there,' I said to Rob, 'otherwise Uncle Harry's car would be outside, too. He wouldn't just drop her off and go away again.'

I got out of the car and promised I wouldn't be a minute.

The first thing I noticed when I walked down the path was that the curtains downstairs were closed, which I thought was rather strange on such a lovely sunny day. A really perverse, truly horrible suspicion entered my mind, and when I arrived at the front door I felt reluctant to knock.

I stood there, hugging the cardigan and wondering what to do. I went around the back – *that's* where they would be, in the garden. Why hadn't I thought about that before? But if they were, they were being awfully quiet. Charles and Cathy weren't in the garden, and when I looked through the kitchen and dining-room windows they weren't there, either.

'Perhaps they've gone for a walk,' Rob said later when I told him. 'Or a drink.' He laughed. 'You've got a dirty mind, Pearl.'

'I must have, mustn't I?'

'What did you do with the cardy?'

'I left it on the back step.' But when I did, I'm pretty sure I heard a woman's laugh inside the house.


On Monday I'd hardly been home five minutes when the telephone rang. I guessed somehow it would be my mother.

'What are you doing tonight?' she enquired. She was calling from a phone box.

'Nothing in particular.' I just had to prepare tomorrow's lessons.

'How do you fancy going to the Cavern?' There was an undercurrent of excitement in her voice.

'The Cavern! Why? Do you want to see what it's like?' She was the sort of person who would have loved the Cavern. It was a shame that she'd missed it when Liverpool was the most important city on the earth.

'I'm meeting a friend. Her name is Susan Conway and her son is playing there tonight. He's a guitarist.'

'I'd love to go.' My interest increased. 'What's the name of the group?'

'The Umbrella Men. Have you heard of them?'

All I knew was that they'd played at the Cavern before. 'Yes,' I told her.

She said she was calling from George Henry Lee's, and would do a bit more shopping before meeting Susan Conway at six for a meal. I promised to be at the Cavern by eight and to drive her home. She muttered something about buying a car and rang off.

I hadn't remembered she could drive, and wondered where the money would come from to buy a car. We'd been quite well off when I was little. I suppose there'd have been money mounting up in the bank all this time. Even if there weren't, I felt sure Granddad wouldn't let her go short.

Marion sniffed disapprovingly when I came downstairs that night in my new blue jeans and flared black top. I tied my hair back for a change and told myself I looked like a Beatnik. It was a bit late in the day for that, but my friend Trish used to say I dressed too conventionally. I was reminded that I hadn't heard from her in ages and made a mental vow to give her a ring soon. I wondered how London was treating her.

Amy and her friend, Susan, looked old enough to be everybody's mother when I met them later in the Cavern. Susan wore outsize Crimplene trousers and a beige nylon jumper on her ample frame, and my mother had chosen a simple peasant dress in flowered cotton. It appeared she had met Susan during the war and they had remained in contact ever since. In those days, the Umbrella Men's guitarist had been a mere babe in arms. He was now thirty-one.

'Me other two kids have been married for years and have kids of their own, but our Steven's had more girlfriends than hot dinners and shows no sign of settling down,' his mother snorted, though I could tell from her shining eyes she was extremely proud of her youngest son. When she'd got married, she told me, she'd gone to live in a little village called Pond Wood not far from Kirkby, but had moved back to Bootle to live with her mam when her husband had died a few years ago.

'Pond Wood's where I met your mam,' she said. 'She worked on the station. As soon as I read in the paper about what had happened with your dad, I knew there must have been a good reason for it. Your mam's a lovely person: she wouldn't hurt a fly.'

My mother looked embarrassed. A voice from the past screamed, '*Whore!*' I wondered if she would ever explain to me exactly what had gone on the night my father had died.

There were three groups on the bill; the Umbrella Men were second. I thought the first one perfectly OK, but Susan and my mother kept looking at each other and rolling their eyes at their apparent awfulness.

The Umbrella Men comprised two guitarists, a drummer and a pianist. The lead guitarist stationed himself behind the microphone and searched the audience with his eyes until they rested on Susan, whereupon he gave a wide smile. Susan dug me sharply in the ribs, saying, 'That's him, that's our Steven.'

Steven's gaze transferred to me and he smiled again. A warm sensation washed over me, as if in some way I had been uniquely blessed. I stared at him hard, hoping for another smile, but he was busy tuning his guitar and telling the audience what to expect – 'A couple of songs written by Pete here on drums and Alf on piano, some Jerry Lee Lewis numbers, followed by a couple more from our very own Jerry on base and yours truly.' There was a cheer from Susan. 'Thanks, Ma.' The audience laughed and he continued, 'There won't be a pause between numbers, so's there's no need to clap until we finish.'

He was completely at home on stage, at ease with the mike. His accent was more Lancashire than Liverpool. Stepping back, he started to play and I studied him. He wasn't very tall, about 5ft 10in, I reckoned, and wore a scruffy black leather jacket, black jeans and T-shirt. A gold earring glittered in his left ear, and golden-brown hair tumbled on to his shoulders in untidy waves and curls. He was boyishly handsome and looked more in his early twenties than thirty-one. To be frank, he wasn't the sort of man I was usually attracted to. *Was* I attracted to him? In the past, I stayed well clear of men like him – I was too shy and they were too extrovert.

I didn't know what to think. I'd been told that when my mother met my father it had been love at first sight, that it had happened, 'just like that'. Whoever it was had clicked their fingers: *Just like that.*

It was Uncle Harry! He'd actually been there. I was about sixteen. It was his birthday and he'd had a bit too much to drink. I remember how sad he'd been, but, drunk or sober, Uncle Harry had never seemed truly happy.

Steven Conway was singing about being lost. He was alone and couldn't find his way out of the darkness, was searching for a light. His voice was soft and mournful. All of a sudden, the audience were applauding and there were shouts of appreciation. I'd hardly heard a thing. Susan was clapping so hard it must be hurting her hands.

The Umbrella Men left the stage and there was an interval. We left and made our way along Mathew Street to Le Beats, the coffee bar where Steven would shortly join us. I'd completely forgotten about Rob while we were in the Cavern, yet normally he was rarely far from my thoughts.

My mother asked if the Umbrella Men were able to live off their music or if they had daytime jobs.

'They're in and out of work like yo-yos,' Susan replied. She sounded quite pleased about it, as if she liked the idea of having an unconventional son. 'They drop everything if they get a gig in another part of the country or an audition, which are nearly always in London. Some firms will stand for it, but others won't. If just one or two of them are working, they support the others till they get a job.'

The door opened and Steven Conway came in with his guitar on his back. He gave a smile that took in every single person there, then sat in a chair slightly behind me, bent his head until I could feel his breath on my ear, and said, 'Hi.'

'Hello,' I stammered. 'I mean, hi.'

'And who are you?' he asked.

His mother heard. She said, 'This is Pearl, Amy's girl. She's a schoolteacher.'

'I bet you could teach me a few things,' Steven said.

I swallowed nervously. 'I doubt it.' I couldn't think of a single thing he could be taught – well, not by me. There was a girl on the next table with creamy blonde hair, the skirt of her A-line dress halfway up her thighs. She was much more his type. I'd like to bet *she* could teach him a thing or two.

As in the Cavern, time seemed to pass without my noticing. All I was aware of was Steven's face close to mine. He asked me questions about my work and my favourite music, and told me about the places he'd been with the Umbrella Men – places like Australia and Canada and Germany – how they'd *nearly* got a record contract once, but the guy who'd auditioned them had got the sack the following day.

My mother and Susan were chatting away, but every now and then I caught my mother looking at me worriedly – at least, I think I did.

The warm sensation I'd had earlier was still there. I was breathing a little faster than usual and was conscious of the beating of my heart. I think I could have sat there for ever, never moving, listening to Steven, except it wasn't possible. Life had to move on.

The others got to their feet and I followed. Outside, my mother and Susan walked in front. Steven asked me out; I accepted. He was playing in the Cavern at lunchtime on Saturday and again in the evening. We would go somewhere in between. I didn't ask where.

He didn't come with me to my car, but went off with his mother while I insisted on taking mine home.

'Did Steven ask you out?' she asked, as I was driving out of the car park.

'Yes.' I half-expected her to give me a lecture or advise me to be careful, but she said no more.

We were going through Bootle when I asked if she would always live with Auntie Cathy.

'Goodness gracious me, no. I love Cathy to bits, but she drives me mad: never stops talking.' She looked out of the window at the sun that was setting in the summer-blue sky. 'No, Pearl. I've no idea where I'm going to live or what I'm going to do once I get used to being out of prison.'

'Does that mean you might leave Liverpool?' I found the idea upsetting.

'I honestly don't know, Pearl. Look,' she said turning towards me, 'while there's just the two of us, would you like to ask questions about your father?'

'Not just now.' I'd sooner do it when I wasn't driving and we were somewhere quiet. And I wasn't prepared. Try as I might, I was unable to think of a single question apart from, 'Why did my father call you a whore?' Charles had said there was no reason for it, but I would still have liked to ask.

## Chapter 18

### 1945–51
### Amy

Barney was almost his old self again by the time Pearl was born. He had adjusted to life in the bungalow and spent a lot of time digging the long garden. He never planted anything, just spent hours turning over the soil. When he finished, he'd turn over the same soil again.

Pearl was such a good baby right from the start. Amy would lie her in her cot then sit on the white padded chair in the nursery and watch her beautiful little girl gradually fall asleep, her eyes blinking until they stayed closed, her long dark lashes resting, quivering ever so slightly, on her creamy cheeks.

When Barney came home from work, he would sit on the white chair while Amy made their tea. 'It's ready, love,' she would come in and whisper, pleased to be snatching another glimpse of Pearl before they went to eat.

Amy could tell that Barney was secretly delighted his daughter was so like him. He'd expected their child to be blonde and blue-eyed like his wife, but Pearl's blue eyes had eventually turned the same rich brown as his, and she had the same smooth brown hair. A photo of him as a baby showed he'd once had a little pointed chin and snub nose, too.

It was Barney who had accidentally chosen the name. Amy had leapt upon it: anything to please him and subdue the bitterness and bad temper with which he had viewed the world when he first came back from Germany and which she prayed would never return.

'Pearl' hadn't been included on the mental list of male and female names she'd had in mind, but Barney had appeared in the maternity ward of the private hospital in Princes Park and remarked that the new baby, with her creamy, lustrous skin, reminded him of a pearl.

'That's what we'll call her: Pearl,' Amy said quickly. She quite liked the name. It was unusual, but not so unusual that people would remark on it. A woman in the hospital who'd had a daughter at the same time had called her Scarlett, after Scarlett O'Hara in *Gone With the Wind*.

'Poor child,' people had observed. 'Everyone will know where it came from.'

'Pearl' was perfect.

For eighteen months after Pearl was born, life was as normal as it would ever be. Amy and her mother-in-law called a truce. It was a very reluctant truce on Amy's side and may well have been on Mrs Patterson's: they never discussed the matter. Amy always made an effort to prevent them being alone together, not trusting either of them to hold their tongues. Leo, well aware of the situation, did his best to make sure the atmosphere stayed calm.

It wasn't really surprising that Elizabeth Patterson refused to come to Pearl's christening. To see her one and only grandchild baptised a Catholic was asking too much of a woman who was a Protestant through and through.

It was, however, a pleasure to Moira Curran, Pearl's other grandmother, as proof that life was returning to normality after the war. Moira had emerged from the conflict six years older and with three of her four children married with homes of their own. Biddy was also married, but she and her husband were living with Moira until they found a place.

Soon, Moira would live alone in the house in Agate Street, a situation for which she was fully prepared. During the war, she had received three proposals of marriage from three different men. She had turned them all down. She had only loved one man in her life and he had died when her children were small. Now she had a really nice job in the gas showroom on Stanley Road and the rest of her life would be spent with the spirit of the man she had loved and the grandchildren that would eventually appear.

Barney was working for his father's company in Skelmersdale, but was worried Harry was being sidelined. 'Dad has no faith in him. He treats him like an idiot,' he said to Amy one night.

Much to her surprise, Amy seemed to be the only person that Leo Patterson would listen to. 'If Barney's noticed,' she remonstrated, 'so will other people. That won't do Harry's confidence much good.'

'I want Harry and Barney to be directors of the company,' he growled, 'but Harry doesn't show much initiative: he's very slow at catching on.'

'Harry,' Amy said in an angry voice, 'was in the war from when it started until well after the end when he was demobbed. He was at Dunkirk *and* took part in the D-Day landings. He fought in the desert *and* all the way across Europe until the Germans surrendered. You should be proud of him, not complain. He's a sticker. He does what he sets out to do. If he's slow at catching on it really doesn't matter, because he'll do it in the end.'

Leo laughed. 'You, Mrs Patterson, are a typical example of an old head on young shoulders. I'll remember what you said and treat Harry with more respect from now on.'

She glared at him, unsure whether he was joking or not. 'I jolly well hope so,' she said threateningly, and he laughed again.

Everything was going swimmingly until the night the man came to see Barney. Until then, their lives had assumed a sort of pattern: dinner with Barney's family and tea with Amy's on alternate weekends. Petrol was still rationed, but drivers were allowed a basic amount. Cars were retrieved from the garages and gardens where they had been laid up for the duration of the war and made fit to drive again. Every few weeks Barney drove to Pond Wood where Jacky and Peter lived in a small cottage with their own newborn son, taking Amy's mother with them. Occasionally, they went to see Charlie and Marion in Aintree, though Marion never made them feel welcome.

It was September when the man came, a strange day early in autumn when a poisonous yellow fog gripped Liverpool and the air smelled as if fires were burning somewhere close but out of sight. It was teatime when Amy answered the door to the visitor. He was beautifully dressed in a camel overcoat and nut-brown trilby hat. He looked about thirty years of age and was quite handsome, albeit in an effeminate way.

'Is this the home of Barney Patterson?' he enquired politely, removing his hat. He had a foreign accent, only faintly discernible.

Amy acknowledged that it was. She put him in the parlour, apologizing for the fact it wasn't very warm, but saying that she was feeding their toddler in the living room. Pearl was inclined to make a great game out of being fed with a spoon, and the visitor was likely to be splashed with mashed carrots or apple purée.

When she got back, Barney had already started on the feed, a tea towel tucked underneath his chin. He was pretending the spoon was an aeroplane – or it might have been a wasp – making it fly through the air with a buzzing sound until the contents came in contact with Pearl's mouth, when she might eat it or she might not.

'There's someone to see you,' Amy said. 'He's in the parlour.'

'What's his name?'

'I didn't ask, I'm sorry. Here, shall I do that and you can see to him?' She took the spoon, removed the tea towel and set about giving Pearl the rest of her tea, little knowing that something was happening in the parlour that would change her life for ever.

The man was sitting on the edge of the linen-covered settee, his hat beside him, leaning against the tapestry cushions that had been a present from Barney's mother the Christmas before last. He jumped to his feet when Barney entered and came towards him, hand extended, a broad smile on his face. 'Hello, old chap. We can greet each other in a more civilized way now that the damn war is over.'

It was Franz Jaeger, the translator from the castle in Bavaria. Barney blinked, convinced that he must be seeing things or that this was just a dream. But the man was real. He closed the parlour door in case Amy could hear. 'What are you doing here?' he croaked, ignoring the man's outstretched hand.

'I thought I would look you up. This is a social call.' He seemed rather put out that his hand hadn't been taken. 'I think I told you I was employed by Mercedes-Benz in Mayfair before the war?' He looked at Barney, as if waiting for affirmation of this fact, but none came. 'When the war ended, I returned to London, not to the same job, but only too happy to be back.'

'I asked what you were doing here?' Barney's voice was thick with rage.

'I've already said – I thought I would look you up. I'm on my way to Ireland with some friends and passing through Liverpool. I remembered you lived here and found your address in the telephone directory.' He frowned, clearly hurt. 'I had thought we were friends. I kept you well provided with cigarettes during the unfortunate time we were thrown together. I hated the war as much as you.'

Barney collapsed on one of the blue linen armchairs. He could have done with a cigarette right then, but had cut down drastically and there were none in the house. 'After what happened, you are the last person I want to see.'

'What happened? You mean that business with the commandant? But why should that upset you? He told me later that you appeared not to mind a bit, that you actually enjoyed it.'

Barney felt as if every drop of blood had drained from his body. 'How ridiculous!' It was a limp word to use, but on the spur of the moment he'd been unable to think of anything stronger. Outrageous would have been better.

'Look,' the visitor said reasonably, 'I have a taxi waiting outside. My friends are in the bar of the Adelphi Hotel. Why don't you come and we can all have a drink together?'

'Are your friends homosexual?'

Franz Jaeger's eyes narrowed and he looked thoughtful. 'Yes, they are, as a matter of fact – like me and like you, only you refuse to acknowledge it. That's why you're so upset to see me, isn't it?'

'I have a wife and a child,' Barney said harshly. 'In no way am I like you and your friends.'

'It is possible to love both men and women. Colonel Hofacker had a wife.' The man got to his feet. He looked very regretful. 'I

264

am so sorry. I wouldn't have dreamed of coming had I known the way you felt. I sincerely apologize and hope you will be happy with your wife and child.' He picked up his hat. '*Auf wiedersehen*, Lieutenant. I will leave my card just in case you wish to contact me one day.' He waved Barney down when he made a move to stand. 'Don't worry, I'll see myself out.'

He left the room and a few seconds later the front door closed. Barney reached for the little white card on the mantelpiece and tore it to pieces, then threw the pieces on to the fire that had been neatly set by the cleaning woman, Mrs MacKay, so all it needed was a match when visitors were expected.

Then he went back to Amy and Pearl.


The silences were preferable, the moody silences that could go on for days, even weeks. Amy talked far too much to fill in the long hushed periods during which she was over-conscious of the ticking of the clock, her breathing and the little squeaking sounds from outside when it was growing dark and the birds were settling down to sleep.

The rages could also go on for weeks. Amy could do or say nothing right. The food was too hot or too cold, too well done or not done enough. If she tried to calm him, she used the wrong words. She was relieved some nights when he drove into town and had dinner on his own. She always tried to be in bed by the time he came home, and pretended to be asleep when he joined her. They hardly ever made love and when they did there was an awkwardness about it, as if they were strangers.

Then there were the times when he was so sorry for having lost his temper, for saying this or saying that. He didn't know what had got into him. He was sorry, so very, very sorry, and would never behave that way again. Would she forgive him?

Amy always did, but it didn't stop Barney from going through the same routine again: the silences, the rages, the pleas for forgiveness. He had started to smoke heavily, too: at least sixty a day.

He flatly refused to see a doctor. Leo consulted his friend, Dr Sheard, who in turn consulted a psychiatrist, who said he couldn't pass an opinion without speaking to Barney. At a guess, he could only assume the years spent in captivity had done something to his mind, twisted it in some way. 'He suggested Barney is more mentally fragile than we'd thought,' Dr Sheard reported.

'I'd never have believed it.' Leo shook his head in astonishment.

Amy had never given a thought to Barney's mental state – or anybody else's come to that. To her, he'd always seemed very strong in every way, though she remembered the times during the war when he'd crept out of the house at the dead of night rather than wish her goodbye. Did that mean he was mentally fragile?

He snapped out of one of his long silent periods by accusing her of sleeping with other men. It was the first time he'd suggested such a thing.

'Barney!' she cried. 'What a terrible thing to say.'

'It's true, though, isn't it?' His eyes burnt into hers. 'You're a whore.'

'How dare you say that?' It was what his mother had called her when they'd first met. 'I've never been unfaithful to you – and never will.'

He contemplated her answer for at least half a minute. She knew he was trying to think of a reason for his accusation. 'I can't believe you didn't sleep with other men when I was away all that time,' he said sulkily.

'You can believe whatever you like, Barney, but I know I didn't.' She usually put up with his bad temper, but now she was really angry. 'If you say anything like that again, I'll take Pearl and go and live with Mam.'

He was instantly apologetic. 'But I can't live without you,' he groaned. 'I'll die if you're not here. I need you, darling. I need you more than I've ever done before.'

'Of course I won't leave,' she assured him. She took him in her arms and could feel him trembling. He was ill, very ill, and she'd vowed to stay with him in sickness and in health. She could never bring herself to desert her beloved Barney.

★

Cathy Burns finished her course at Kirkby teacher training college and emerged a fully qualified teacher. She bought a car and rented a small flat in Upper Parliament Street. Her first job was at a school in Toxteth and she frequently called on Amy after she had finished work.

Amy had never appreciated her friend more. Most days she managed to get out of the house for a few hours, but there were the days when Pearl had a cold, or she didn't feel well herself, or it was raining. It was such a joy to see Cathy after hours spent in the house with just a toddler for company. Mind you, Pearl was becoming more interesting the older she grew, but Amy couldn't exactly discuss with her whatever accusation her father had thrown at her the night before or tell her that she suspected he was seeing another woman.

'Jaysus!' Cathy gasped when Amy confided in her. 'What makes you think that?' She looked very smart in a black costume with a cream jumper underneath, her hair stylishly short.

Amy told her every little thing that Barney had said or done. It helped to have someone to talk to who would understand. Leo was the only other person she confided in, and there were certain things you couldn't tell a man. He telephoned nearly every day to see how she was and impressed upon her he would come at the drop of a hat if needed, though she didn't see him nearly as much as she'd done during the war.

'Three times this week he didn't come home from work until half eight or nine o'clock,' Amy told her friend, 'but Leo says he always leaves at about half five. When he did arrive, he smelled of cheap scent.'

'Where does he say he's been?'

'In a pub, drinking; he has whiskey or brandy on his breath.' Amy shrugged wearily. 'I don't know the difference.' She didn't really believe Barney was seeing someone else. The cheap scent probably came from a woman he'd sat close to in the pub. She didn't know what to do or to say to make the old Barney come back.

One Saturday morning, he woke up in a fuming temper. Amy, in the kitchen setting the table for breakfast, could hear him slamming the wardrobe doors and closing drawers with a terrific bang.

'Good morning,' she said brightly when he came in.

He didn't answer, just picked up the tea when she put it in front of him. Then he put the cup in the saucer and seemed to wilt in front of her. His head and shoulders drooped, and his hands and arms went limp.

'Oh, Barney, love, what's the matter?' She laid her hand lightly on his neck. He was still her Barney, the man she had fallen in love with on Southport pier nearly ten years ago. She recalled the wonderful times they'd had in the flat by Newsham Park and their 'honeymoon' in London. How could those times have been reduced to this?

Pearl came running in, stopping short when she saw her father, who'd usually gone to work by the time she had her breakfast. She edged around to the other side of the table and took hold of her mother's skirt. Amy had never known her do that before. Barney had never laid a finger on his little girl, but she was obviously afraid of him.

He jerked upright, dislodging her hand. 'Nothing's the matter. Leave me alone.' He got up abruptly and left the room. A few minutes later, the front door slammed. He couldn't be going to work as the factory didn't open on Saturdays.

Amy fed herself and her daughter, washed the dishes, then telephoned for a taxi. Mrs MacKay, who did the rough work, didn't come weekends. 'I've had enough of this,' she said to Pearl. 'Let's have a day out.'

Not long ago in Paris, Christian Dior had unveiled the New Look. Women who could afford to were thrilled to wear long, flared skirts, narrow waists and bunchy petticoats after the plain, utilitarian styles of the war.

But Amy's clothes allowance was hardly touched these days. She found it difficult to go shopping alone. Her mother was always willing to look after Pearl, but she worked full-time and was only free on Saturday afternoon when Barney didn't go to work either and Amy felt obliged to stay at home. She had a few New Look outfits, but not nearly enough!

Today, she didn't care that she had to take Pearl with her into town. It was about time her daughter had a few new outfits, too, but Barney, even though he wasn't there, cast a shadow over the day and it never felt quite right.

For a child who wasn't quite four, Pearl took fashion very seriously. She insisted on trying on the frocks and coats before they were bought and looked at herself in the mirror, turning this way and that to make sure the garment looked good from every angle.

'Isn't she a scream?' whispered the assistant in George Henry Lee's while she and Amy watched the little girl put on a chocolate-brown winter frock with a lace collar and cuffs. She examined her reflection. 'Can I have new shoes, Mummy?'

'If you want, love. Maybe we could get cream ones to match the lace.'

Pearl looked at her small feet in the mirror. 'Cream ones would be nice.'

'We'll look in the shoe department in a minute. Shall I buy you that frock?'

'Yes, please.' She pulled the frock carefully over her head and stood there in her little white silk petticoat and white socks. Her dark-brown hair was tied in bunches with white ribbons. 'I like you buying me clothes, Mummy.'

'And I like buying them for you, Pearl.' They smiled at each other in perfect understanding. Amy had never felt so close to her daughter. 'Always remember this love: a new frock is the finest medicine a woman can have if she's not feeling her best.'

'Hear, hear,' said the young assistant, 'though me, I can only afford C & A's prices, not George Henry Lee's.'

'Oh, it's dead lovely,' Moira Curran gasped when Amy showed her the light cream tweed suit with self-coloured embroidery on the collar of the jacket and around the hem of the flared skirt.

'I got a pale-blue blouse to go with it.' Amy held up the blouse by the shoulders. 'What do you think?' It was heavy crêpe with a satin collar and cuffs.

'That's lovely, too,' Moira said admiringly.

'I hoped you'd like it, because I bought you one, too, except yours is pink.'

Pearl chipped in. 'Can I give it to Grandma?'

'Of course, love.' Amy handed the George Henry Lee's bag to Pearl, who slipped off her chair and gravely gave it to Moira, who said it was the prettiest blouse she'd ever had in her life. 'I bought a new frock too, as well as shoes and a handbag.' She lifted up the grey and white check frock by the shoulders. It had a black patent leather belt that exactly matched the court shoes and handbag.

'What's brought this on, luv?' Moira asked.

'What's brought what on?'

'The shopping spree. It's a long time since you bought new clothes.'

Amy was carefully folding the frock before putting it back in the bag. 'That's probably the reason, because it's such a long time since I bought anything new.'

'Why didn't Barney go with you? He always used to. I remember him saying once how much he enjoyed helping you buy clothes.'

'Barney went out somewhere,' she said casually.

'What's wrong, Amy, luv?'

Amy turned and looked at her mother wide-eyed. 'There's nothing wrong, Mam.'

'Would you like to come in the kitchen and help me make a cup of tea? Pearl will be quite happy here with her new drawing book, won't you, pet?'

'Yes, Grandma.' Pearl was busy colouring a strawberry with a red crayon.

'Of course there's something wrong,' Moira hissed when she and her daughter were in the kitchen. 'There's been something wrong for ages. It's obvious. When you were putting them clothes away your hands were really shaking. Have you met another feller? Is that it?'

'No, Mam,' Amy said exasperatedly, 'I haven't met another feller. Oh, all right,' she conceded. It was no use denying something had gone wrong with her marriage any longer. 'Barney and I aren't getting on as well as we used to, that's all. Being in that camp badly affected him. It'll work itself out in the end.' She tried to sound confident. 'These things always do.'

'I hope so, luv. You haven't looked very happy in a long time, and Pearl looks dead tired. Isn't she sleeping well?'

'I've noticed she looks tired, too, but whenever I check on her during the night she's fast asleep.' She went to the kitchen door and watched Pearl, who was now holding a green crayon as she filled in an apple, and chose that very moment to rub her eyes with the back of her hand and yawn at the same time. Amy always made sure the nursery door was firmly closed so Pearl wouldn't hear her father accusing her mother of sleeping with other men and the other crimes that she had supposedly committed.

It was lovely and peaceful at her mother's. Amy really appreciated not having to listen to Barney when he was in a bad mood, or sit through one of his long periods of silence, trying to think of things to say or wondering whether it would be best if she didn't say anything.

It was ten o'clock. Pearl was fast asleep upstairs in her grandma's bed and, for the last hour, Amy had been trying to raise the energy to walk as far as Marsh Lane and telephone for a taxi. Barney would almost certainly be home by now and was bound to guess she was at her mother's. She should have left him a note, except she'd had no intention of coming to Agate Street when she'd left the house this morning – and Barney never bothered to tell *her* if he was going to be late home from work.

'Can I stay the night?' she asked her mother. She'd still have to phone Barney and say she wasn't coming home.

'Of course, love. Would you like some cocoa?'

'I'd love some. Ta, Mam.' She'd telephone Barney when she'd drunk it.

Her mother had just brought in the cocoa when there was a knock on the door, but not just an ordinary knock, more a loud hammering. Moira put the cups on the table and hurriedly went to answer it.

'Hello, ma-in-law,' Barney said cheerfully. 'I've come to collect my wife and daughter – I take it they're here?'

'Yes, but we weren't expecting you, luv.' Her mother's voice shook ever so slightly. Perhaps she, like Amy, recognized the cheerfulness wasn't genuine. 'Come in. Pearl's fast asleep upstairs.'

'Then I'll leave Pearl and collect her tomorrow. But I'd like to take Amy home if you don't mind.'

'It's not up to me to mind, is it, luv?'

'No, Moira, it isn't.'

Barney came into the living room, his overcoat billowing out like a cape, bringing with him a rush of cold air. He was followed by a worried Moira, who asked if he would like some cocoa. 'No, thank you,' he said with exquisite politeness. 'Are you ready, Amy?'

'Yes.' She began to collect the shopping together, but Barney scooped everything up in a bundle and took it out to the car.

Before her mother could come out of the house to say tara, he had driven away.


They didn't exchange a single word on the way home. Amy got out of the car leaving Barney to drive it into the garage. She had a feeling something awful was going to happen, that they were going to have a really bad row, and was glad Pearl had been left at her mother's.

She wasn't prepared for what actually happened, for Barney to come storming into the house, stand in front of her and say, 'Don't you ever dare do that again,' and slap her face with such force that she fell sideways and banged her head on the wooden arm of the easy chair. She screamed, and Barney fell to his knees beside her and burst into tears.


He'd been terrified when he got home and found she wasn't there. He thought she'd left him and knew he couldn't live without her – he'd told her that before. Without his wife and daughter he would go insane.

Amy, her head throbbing and her left ear feeling as if it had swollen to twice its size, wondered if he were already insane. And perhaps she was insane, too, for whatever Barney did, however badly he behaved, nothing in this world would stop her from loving him, at least not while he was like this, sobbing like a baby in her arms.

'Shush,' she said tenderly. 'Shush, now.'

In September, when Pearl was four and a half, she went to a convent school in Brownlow Hill. She wore a uniform: a tiny navy-blue gymslip, a white blouse and tie, a blazer and a velour hat with a striped band.

'You look *adorable*,' Amy cried on Pearl's first day when she was dressed and ready to leave, a perfect miniature schoolgirl, although she was tall for her age and surprisingly strong. She badly wanted to cry at the idea of not seeing her daughter again until half past three.

She had recently passed her driving test and drove Pearl to Brownlow Hill in the new Morris Minor. It was a crisp sunny day and the leaves on some of the trees were already gold. Back in the house, she felt as if a corner had been turned. Pearl starting school was the start of a new phase in their lives. Barney had been relatively normal of late, and she'd had the impression he was thinking deeply about something. An eternal optimist, Amy got the impression that, from now on, everything was going to be all right. When it was, she'd like to try for another baby. They rarely made love, but perhaps that might soon be all right, too.

It was for a while. Then one day Pearl came home from school with a temperature and complained of feeling sick. Amy tucked her up in bed and she immediately fell asleep. She telephoned Dr Sheard and he promised to come in half an hour. When Barney arrived, he sat on his daughter's bed and bathed her burning forehead with a cold flannel. Amy sat on the other side and waited for the doctor to come. Pearl had always been very healthy; this was the first time she'd been seriously ill.

'Chicken pox!' Dr Sheard announced after a brief examination of the patient. 'There's a lot of it about. Just dab the spots when they come with calamine lotion from time to time, give her plenty to drink and keep her in bed. She'll feel better in a few days. Oh, and put some gloves on her. If she scratches the spots, they'll leave scars that she'll have for the rest of her life.'

Amy thanked him and showed him the bathroom so he could wash his hands.

'This is a nice little place,' he said, glancing around when he came out into the hall. 'I've never been here before. The only other time I've seen you out of surgery hours was in that flat of yours when you had the miscarriage.'

'What miscarriage?' Barney asked when the doctor had gone. They were back in Pearl's bedroom, sitting on either side of her bed. She'd been hoping he hadn't heard. She'd never told him about the miscarriage or the way his mother had behaved, not wanting him to be upset and worried while he was away. It had seemed pointless to tell him when he came back years later.

'It happened in the November after you went away,' she said. 'I was ten weeks pregnant, but I lost the baby.'

'How? Where? Why didn't you let me know?' He cross-examined her, wanting to know every tiny detail. Had Dr Sheard known she was pregnant?

'No.' She explained she had gone to see his mother. 'I know you said she wouldn't like me for being a Catholic, but I thought she'd be glad to know I was having a baby.'

'What did she say?' he asked.

'She wasn't very pleased to see me.' Elizabeth Patterson had called her a Catholic whore, but she didn't think it would improve Barney's mood if she told him that.

'How did you know to call Doctor Sheard? You'd never met him.' She didn't like the probing way he asked the questions, as if he were trying to trip her up. It made her feel she'd done something terribly wrong.

'I didn't call him: your father did. A woman at your house phoned and told him I'd been to see your mother and he came to the flat. It was a good thing he did, because by then I'd lost the baby.'

Neither of them spoke for a while, until Barney said, nodding at Pearl, 'Will she be all right?'

'I'm sure she will. I had chicken pox when I was little, and so did Jacky and Biddy.'

He stood up so abruptly that it disturbed Pearl, who coughed and turned her head the other way. 'I'm just going out for a while. I won't be long.'

'But where are you going?'

Barney didn't answer, just opened the front door and left the house.

Pearl woke up wanting to use the lavatory. She refused the chamber pot and insisted on walking unsteadily to the bathroom, Amy hovering anxiously behind her. 'I feel dizzy,' she complained. Afterwards she was tucked up in bed, and went back to sleep immediately.

Amy made a pot of tea and remembered they'd had nothing to eat that night. She peeled potatoes and put them on to boil. When Barney came back, she'd make corned beef hash. He'd never had it before they got married, and, covered with brown sauce, it was one of his favourite meals.

She wondered where he had gone, and suspected it was to see his mother. She prayed there wouldn't be a row. The miscarriage had happened ten years ago – no, eleven – and it would be silly to rake things up after all this time. Her relationship with Elizabeth Patterson was brittle and could easily be broken.

Barney returned about three hours later, by which time it was almost half past nine and pitch-black outside. Amy offered him the corned beef hash, but he refused. She made tea, but he refused that, too. She got the butter and a jar of strawberry jam out of the cupboard and cut two slices of bread, seeing this as an ideal excuse to have her favourite meal – bread and jam – for her own tea, but Barney said in a dull, rather distant voice, 'I have something to say to you, Amy. Would you mind sitting down?'

Her heart sank as she followed him into the living room where a small fire burned behind a brass fireguard. Amy removed the fireguard and was about to shovel coal from the scuttle on to the flames when Barney said in the same dull voice, 'Leave that for now.'

'But the fire will go out,' she protested.

'I said leave it!'

She felt like hitting him with the shovel. 'What's the matter with you?' she demanded, flinging the shovel on to the tiled hearth, regretting it immediately when it made a terrible clatter that could well have woken Pearl. This must be something to do with the miscarriage and his mother. What had she said to him? Right now, Pearl was sick and Amy felt very short of patience. She sat down on one of the easy chairs, noticing it was the one she'd fallen against when he'd knocked her to the floor that time.

'I've been to see my mother,' he said. 'And she tells me that you and my father had an affair during the war – that you are probably still having one now.' He looked at her slyly. In the past, the accusations had been invented, but now he had a real one – or so he thought, because it had come from his mother. Why was he so pleased about it?

Amy closed her eyes and didn't reply.

'She thinks that my father is in love with you.'

Still Amy didn't utter a word.

'Have you nothing to say for yourself?' he asked coldly.

'There is nothing to say to such nonsense.' She got up. 'I'm going to get a cup of tea. I've no intention of sitting here all night listening to you. You're mad and your mother is mad.' How could she love a man who spoke to her like that? Tomorrow, she'd take Pearl and go to Agate Street and live with her mother. This time, Barney had gone too far.

He pushed her back on to the chair. 'Is it true?'

'No, Barney, it isn't true. I haven't had an affair with your father. Why has your mother waited so long to say this? She's just trying to cause trouble. Barney!' She tried to get up, but his hand was pressed against her chest. 'You're hurting me.'

'How many times have you slept together, you and my father? Dozens? Hundreds?' he whispered, his mouth against her ear. 'Was it him who was the father of the baby?'

Had his mother actually suggested that? 'I can't be bothered with this, Barney. It's too ridiculous for words.' She turned her face away, determined not to answer another of his stupid questions.

His hand moved to her throat and he pressed hard. She choked and managed to kick him in the shin, feeling frightened. Apart from that one incident, he'd never been violent. The pressure on her throat eased.

'Mother said he was at the flat all the time, that he used to take you to dinner. Is that true?' He sat back in his own chair, but edged it forward until their knees almost touched.

'He used to come and see me, to make sure I was all right,' she agreed. 'I never counted how many times, and yes, he used to take me to dinner. But that doesn't mean we had an affair.' How long did he intend to keep her there, trapped in the chair, unable to move? She hadn't closed the curtains and could see the trees in the back garden swaying like ghosts against the dark sky. There must have been a strong wind blowing. In the bedroom, Pearl's bed creaked as she turned over and she coughed hoarsely. Amy shivered, feeling cold. The fire was barely flickering. Very soon it would go out.

Looking thoughtful, Barney reached over the fireguard and picked up the brass-handled poker. He sat with it on his knee. He said, 'There was a chap in the paper the other day, an ex-serviceman, who discovered his wife had been having an affair with a neighbour while he was away fighting for his country. He beat her to death, but only got five years. The judge said he'd been provoked. I wonder what he'd have to say about a wife sleeping with her father-in-law?'

'Nothing, because it isn't true,' she said quietly. She didn't believe he'd kill her with the poker. He was playing a game, a really ugly game, and she wished he would stop.

He looked at her and there were tears in his eyes. 'You know, darling, I really would like to kill you. Then I wouldn't have to sleep with you any more.'

'Barney, you don't *have* to sleep with me now.' What a strange thing to say. 'We can get twin beds, or we can turn the box room into a bedroom and one of us can sleep there.'

'That mightn't be a bad idea. Oh, Amy, darling, I'm so tired.' His head flopped sideways and at first she thought he'd fainted, but he'd actually fallen asleep. She leaned forward and tenderly stroked his forehead. Her feelings for him swung wildly from something approaching hatred to pure and simple love.

Amy stood, took the poker off his knee and put it in one of the cupboards beside the fireplace. She checked Pearl was asleep – she was, but seemed very restless – took a pile of bedding and a pillow from out of the airing cupboard and threw them on to the settee in the parlour. She'd sleep there tonight and let Barney sleep by himself. Maybe tomorrow, if he felt himself again, he'd explain why he didn't want to sleep with her any more.

In a minute she'd get undressed, but for now she sat on the settee, laid her head on the arm, and pulled a blanket over her – it was chillier here than in the living room. At the same time it was a relief to get away from Barney: her heart was thudding. Tomorrow, she'd absolutely insist he saw one of those psychiatrist people, and would threaten to leave him if he refused. They couldn't go on like this any longer. She must telephone Leo and tell him what Elizabeth had said.

Leo Patterson drove quickly through the dimly-lit Liverpool streets. He could scarcely believe what Amy had just told him. 'I'll be there as soon as I can,' he'd promised.

'Where are you going?' Elizabeth had asked when he'd picked up the car keys and made for the door.

'I have to see someone,' he said tersely. He didn't know his son had been there earlier that night.

'But it's half past ten!' she protested. 'You've only just come in.'

'It's an emergency.'

'Is it one of your women? Is that who you're going to see – a woman?' She could lose her temper in an instant. She came over and put her long white hands on his arms. The nails were perfectly shaped and painted glossy white, reminding him of a corpse's hands. He hadn't said anything to Amy, but Barney's state of mind was exactly the same as his mother's. The deaths of her own mother and brother as a result of a terrorist bomb had tipped her mind over the edge, just as the prisoner-of-war camp had done to Barney's. 'I told you, it's an emergency,' he said patiently, removing her clinging hands.

He'd had other women, dozens of them. It had been necessary

for his own sanity to escape from Elizabeth from time to time into the softer, more yielding flesh of another woman. Amy, his son's wife, was such a woman, yet there was nothing on this earth that would have persuaded Leo to lay a finger on her, though he was in love with her and had been since the day they'd first met. She belonged to his son, and that was that.

He drew up outside the house. When he looked, Amy was waiting for him in the open doorway. The trees around the house were swishing angrily in the gale. He walked up the path towards her, and she reached for him and led him inside.

'Leo!' she said in a deep, agitated voice. 'Come in here.'

She walked in front of him to the parlour where his son was sitting on the settee with a bread knife protruding from his stomach. The red stain on Barney's white shirt seemed to be getting bigger and bigger as Leo watched. His eyes were half-open and he looked quite peaceful, both hands palms upwards as if he'd been holding something when he died. There was no need to send for a doctor or an ambulance: Barney was quite clearly dead.

'Christ Almighty!' Leo groaned. He was torn between the desire to be sick and the desire to burst into tears. 'How did it happen?'

Amy shook her head and walked quickly out of the room. Her face was paper-white and she looked about forty years old.

Leo followed. 'Why did you kill him?' His voice rose. 'What did he do that made you kill him?'

'I didn't.' She swayed, and he managed to catch her before she fell. 'It was Pearl.'

'I'd fallen asleep on the settee,' she told Leo when they were in the kitchen waiting for the police to arrive. The brandy he'd given her had made her head swirl. She tried to take in what had happened – no, she'd already done that. Now she had to accept it, live with it, knowing that she would never see Barney again.

'Pearl has chicken pox,' she said in another woman's voice; it didn't sound faintly like her own. 'I called Doctor Sheard. He mentioned the miscarriage, but Barney knew nothing about it. For some reason, it really disturbed him. He went racing off to see his mother and it was then that she told him that we – you and I – had been having an affair since the beginning of the war.'

Leo used an expletive, a really foul one, but Amy took no notice. 'The woman's crazy,' he muttered.

'He came back in a terrible state,' Amy went on. 'He threatened to kill me. Then he fell asleep. I went into the parlour and sat on the settee. It was so peaceful there and I fell asleep too. When I woke up, Barney was shaking me: he was angry again. I began to scream. I just couldn't stand it any more. Next minute, Pearl came running in ... she climbed on to the settee between us. She was shouting, "Leave Mummy alone, Daddy. Don't you dare kill her." By then, Barney had stopped shaking me.' Amy began to cry wildly. 'I'm not sure what happened then, only that Barney looked shocked and reached to hug Pearl, pulling her to his body. Perhaps she made him realize how badly he was behaving. He obviously hadn't seen the bread knife in her hand. Then he fell backwards and I saw the knife sticking out of his stomach. She must have got it from here.' Amy laid her hand on the table next to the bread she'd cut earlier, the butter and the strawberry jam. 'It was an accident, a complete accident. She really didn't intend to kill him: She loved her daddy.'

'What happened then, darlin',' Leo asked gently.

'She ran out of the room crying. She never saw the knife in Barney's stomach. She didn't know she had killed him. I followed her. Her nightie had blood on it, so I changed it and put her back to bed. She's delirious, so I just hope and pray she never remembers what happened.' Amy stood and left the kitchen.

'Where are you going?' Leo called.

'To pull the knife out so my fingerprints will be on it. When the police come, I shall tell them it was me. What sort of life would Pearl have if it became known she'd killed her father? I don't want her to so much as see a policeman, let alone have one question her.' She threw back her head and looked defiantly at Leo. 'I *never* want her to know.'

Leo looked at her in horror. 'But Amy, it was an accident! You can't take the blame for something that was no one's fault,' he said, pleading with her.

'No Leo. I won't have Pearl growing up with that knowledge staining her heart. Accident or not, she would know that it was her hand that held the knife. Enough, I've made up my mind.'

'He was tormenting me,' she told the police, a young constable who didn't open his mouth once and a bland-faced sergeant, heavily overweight, whose podgy fingers trembled while he made notes in a little black book. Amy wondered if he was drunk. 'My husband threatened to kill me and I killed him first.'

She was living a nightmare that was too horrible to be real. She said, 'I have to look at my daughter, see if she's all right.'

'Is she?' the sergeant asked when she came back.

'She's got chicken pox.'

Pearl had been fast asleep, completely relaxed. Her little girl had only been trying to protect her mother, she thought distantly. It wasn't something a child of her age should be expected to do.

With hindsight, it was silly to be surprised when she was taken to the police station, leaving a stunned Leo sitting with his head in his hands. The sergeant couldn't say when she would be allowed back home. As she climbed into the police car, Amy looked at the bungalow and wondered if she would ever see it again. She never did.

It was amazing how someone's life could change so drastically in the space of just a few hours.


Moira Curran noticed that the living room and Pearl's bedroom shared a chimney, and every word said in one room could be heard in the next. Moira had given up her job and had been living in the bungalow looking after Pearl since Amy had been on remand in Strangeways Prison, Manchester.

She was tidying Pearl's bedroom. The little girl was in the living room and began to talk to one of her dolls. She asked the doll when her mummy was coming back, her voice as clear as a bell in the next room. Moira, terrified, had actually glanced at the chimney, half-expecting her granddaughter to be there.

That night, she mentioned it to Leo Patterson, who called every day on his way home from Skelmersdale. Pearl was being kept away from school until the whole horrible business was over. Then she would start somewhere else under a different name.

Leo imagined his granddaughter in bed listening to her father rail at her mother until the night he told her that he wanted to kill her. What sort of thoughts had gone through the little girl's head when she'd heard those words? Thankfully, she appeared to have no memory of the incident.

Moira and Leo sat in silence for a while contemplating the terrifying reality that had blighted their very ordinary lives. Apart from Amy, they were the only people who knew the truth about Barney's death.

A London solicitor was engaged, Bruce Hayward, the best there was, as was the barrister, Sir William Ireton. Both reckoned that Amy would be sent to prison for between five and seven years.

'There are witnesses who will say her husband had been mentally abusing her for years, yet she had never considered leaving him, that she had the patience of a saint,' Bruce Hayward said. He met frequently with Amy, and the two had become friends.

It was Easter when the trial took place in a blaze of publicity at the Liverpool Assizes in St George's Hall. The photograph of the handsome victim, sometimes referred to as a 'war hero', and his pretty wife on their wedding day was published in every newspaper in the land, and some abroad.

It was hard to detect which way the sympathy of the court lay. 'I think our side has the edge,' Leo told Moira Curran. Amy was an excellent defendant. She spoke with obvious truth and without exaggeration when describing the way Barney had treated her – the accusations and the threats to kill her – yet she made excuses for him. 'Something bad must have happened to him when he was a prisoner of war,' she testified. 'When he came back he was a different man.' Cathy Burns also made a good impression, so clearly honest and anxious to protect her friend.

This was how things stood until the day Amy's mother-in-law took the stand.

★

A surprise witness, she'd been called by the Prosecution. Amy wondered what on earth she'd have to say. Across the room she saw Leo frown.

'What do you think of your daughter-in-law, Mrs Patterson?' the opposing counsel asked.

'I hate her,' Elizabeth Patterson replied in a steady voice. 'I hate her because she and my husband have been having an affair ever since my Barney went away. Her green eyes were full of tears. It was hard to doubt the sincerity of her belief. 'He used to take her out to dinner. He was always at her flat.'

It was a brilliantly sunny spring day. Particles of dust danced madly in the sunbeams that slanted across the crowded courtroom. The judge, who always looked asleep, opened his eyes and peered over his half-moon glasses at the attractive, red-haired woman in her leopard-skin coat and matching hat. He opened his mouth to say something, but must have had second thoughts.

The change in the court was palpable. From that moment on, Amy was damned, even though Leo swore on oath that they hadn't had an affair. 'There's no smoke without fire,' people said.

There was talk of a death sentence, that if – when – she was found guilty, Amy Patterson should hang. Her mother-in-law was one of the leading proponents of this view.

'I'll tell,' Moira said to Leo. She didn't attend the court, staying in the bungalow with Pearl, the front curtains drawn, leaving only when it was dark to take Pearl for a walk and get some exercise herself. 'I'll tell the truth. There's no way I'd see our Amy swing for something she didn't do.' Her blood turned to ice. 'But who'd believe us now?' It was too late for the truth. 'Everyone would think we were making it up.'

With a feeling of dread, Leo agreed. Amy had made sure her fingerprints were on the knife. It was much, much too late for the truth.

Amy Patterson was sentenced to life imprisonment for the brutal murder of her husband. Next day, it was the main headline on every major newspaper. Leo brought them to the bungalow, and Moira spread them on the floor. Her daughter's lovely face stared back at her from every angle. There were photos of her other daughters, too: Jacky and Biddy had attended court every single day. Charlie hadn't been at all, but there was a good reason for that.

'Tell me, Amy, if there is anything I can do,' Leo said the first time he went to see her in Holloway Prison, London, where she was now confined. '*Any*thing,' he stressed. 'Anything at all.' She was the strongest and bravest person he had ever known. He had always loved her and now he loved her even more. She'd cried for Pearl, for her mother and the rest of her family, but never for herself. He had a job holding back his own tears, but if Amy could then so could he.

'Yes, there is.' Her face had lost its glow and her eyes their warmth. Her lips were hard and grim with determination. 'I want you to give Jacky and Biddy and their families enough money out of my account to go and live abroad somewhere – Canada, say, or Australia – so they can start afresh without anyone knowing their sister is a murderer. Have I much money left, Leo?'

'Loads, darling,' Leo replied. He had paid her legal fees and there was plenty of money in her account. It had been Barney's money and now it was hers.

'Good. Another thing: Charlie and Marion are going to have Pearl. That's why I asked Charlie not to come to court, so the newspapers wouldn't know where he lived. He and Marion have been married nearly twelve years and are unlikely to have a baby of their own now. Pearl will be their only child and have all their love. I've never liked Marion, but she'll make a good mother, and our Charlie will be a great dad.'

'I'll see to it,' Leo promised. 'I think you should put it in writing – get Bruce Hayward to do it. Oh, and Amy,' he said anxiously, 'I'd like to play a part in Pearl's life. I can't see Harry getting married, so it looks as if she'll be the only grandchild I'll ever have.'

'Of course you must play a part,' Amy said fiercely. 'Our Charlie will realize that. You and Mam, Harry and Cathy will be her family – oh, and tell Harry the truth, will you? I'd sooner he didn't think I killed his brother. Charlie already knows, Mam told him, but he's promised not to tell Marion – I wouldn't trust her not to let it slip to Pearl one day.'

'What about Cathy?'

'The fewer people who know the better. Cathy doesn't blame me for anything.' At that point, her iron control almost faltered. 'Does Pearl know her father is dead?'

'Yes, darlin'. She thinks he was killed in a car accident.'

'And that I have gone a long way away?'

Leo nodded. 'She thinks you're in Australia.'

'Good.' She pursed her lips, satisfied. 'Charlie will tell her where I really am – and why – when he considers she's old enough to cope with the information. And I've told him that under no circumstances is she to visit me. I don't want my daughter to see her mother in prison.'

Minutes later, she disappeared into the dark interior of the building, where she expected to spend the rest of her life.

## Chapter 19

### June 1971
### Pearl

When I got home from school the next day I discovered Marion had arrived before me. Something very serious must have happened to make her leave work early. She only reluctantly took annual leave, and on one occasion, when she was forced to stay home with a severe dose of flu, her boss, Mr London, dictated some important letters over the phone. Despite having a temperature of over a hundred, Marion had typed them on her portable typewriter and someone had come round in a car to collect them.

'What's wrong?' I asked when I went indoors and found her sitting in the breakfast room with a big pot of tea. She wore an unflattering grey cotton blouse and a maroon skirt that was neither short enough nor long enough to be fashionable.

'Nothing.' She looked surprised that I should be surprised. 'I just felt like a few hours off, that's all.'

I put my hand on her forehead.

'Why are you doing that?' she asked.

'To see if you're feverish.'

'I'm perfectly all right.' I'd expected her to snap my head off, but she sounded quite mild. 'Are you going out tonight?'

'I might pop round and see my mother later. She's having a friend to tea, Susan Conway. They met when she was a station master during the war.'

Marion's lips twisted and she half-smiled. 'Only your mother could get a job as a station master – and make such a success of it. She was friends with the whole village by the time she left, and that was only because the station was destroyed by a bomb.'

'Yes, Charles told me.' Marion's comments had sounded suspiciously like admiration.

'Charles is going round there later as well.' She looked a bit lost. 'I should have known everyone would want to be where Amy is. People always were attracted to her like flies to jam. I wish now she'd stayed here. I didn't say I wanted shot of her, you know: she just assumed I did. I wouldn't have minded if she'd stayed a bit longer.'

'Why don't you ask her to come back?'

'That would look a bit obvious, wouldn't it? You know the people next door?' I nodded, though I hardly knew them at all. 'We've not said much to each other over the years, but on Saturday night your mother had them all singing together. Sunday, the woman asked me who she was. I didn't tell her who she *really* was, just that she was my sister-in-law, and she said what a nice woman she seemed and when was she likely to come back.'

I fetched a cup and poured myself some tea. 'Why don't you come with me tonight?'

'I don't think so, Pearl. I'd feel a bit daft.' She hunched her shoulders and sighed. 'I expect you wish your mother had brought you up, not me.'

'Now you really are being daft.' I regarded her fondly. 'Even if I did wish that, which I don't, she wasn't around to bring me up, was she?'

'No, but I wish you'd had more fun. I mean, we don't laugh much, do we? Charles and I, that is. And I think he'd laugh much more if it weren't for me. I mean,' she said, warming to her theme, 'there's been more laughter in this house since your mother came home than there's been in all the time Charles and I have lived here.'

'I think you're exaggerating just a bit, Marion,' I told her. I picked up the teapot: it was empty, so I went into the kitchen and put the kettle on. 'You make this place sound like a morgue,' I said when I came back. 'We laugh more sedately, that's all.'

'And your mother puts all her heart and soul into it. Can you imagine, Pearl, coming out of prison after twenty years and laughing the way she does? Most people would be hard put to raise a smile.'

'What's brought this on?' I asked. 'I hope you don't mind my saying, but I thought you disliked my mother?'

'I do – I did. Oh, where's that damn tea.' She disappeared into the kitchen just as the kettle switched itself off. A minute later she came back with the pot. 'I stirred it a bit so we don't have to wait for it to brew.' I put milk in both cups and she filled them. 'About your mother,' she said. 'I expected her to be cowed and pale and afraid of her own shadow, but she hasn't changed a bit. There's another thing: I should never have let you know how I felt about your mother. That was really bad of me, Pearl.'

'I've always been happy here,' I protested.

'You could have been happier,' Marion said miserably.

'I suspect all of us think we could have been happier when we look back.' I felt uneasy with this rueful, conscience-stricken Marion, and would have far preferred the tart, plain-spoken woman I'd always known.

'Until I met Charles I led a pretty awful life, Pearl.' She didn't look at me, but began to draw circles on the table with her finger. 'I've never told you this before, but my family were gypsies. We lived in Ireland and, if I'm being completely honest with you, I have no idea how many brothers and sisters I had – still have, I expect. As soon as they were old enough, they took off. I was the youngest.' The circles had become figures of eight and her fingernail was leaving marks on the tablecloth. 'One of my earliest memories is of knocking on doors and offering sprays of heather to buy. Hardly anybody bought them, and that meant we wouldn't eat that night unless one of us managed to pinch something.' She smoothed her hand over the table to remove the marks, still not looking at me. 'I won't go on about it: those times are long gone. At thirteen, it was my turn to run away. I came to Liverpool, got a job, learnt to do shorthand and typing, got rid of my accent. I was nineteen when I met Charles and I felt I was the luckiest woman alive when he fell in love with me.'

'Any woman would feel lucky with Charles,' I muttered. I was finding this embarrassing, but at the same time it was helping me to understand my aunt.

'The only fly in the ointment was your mum,' Marion said with a sigh. 'Everything seemed to fall into her lap without any effort on her part. She didn't care how much she hurt her mother. Oh, I *am* going on about it, aren't I?' She put her hands together on her knee. 'I won't say any more. Anyway, that's the reason I never liked your mum – I suppose the correct word for it is jealousy.'

We sat in silence for a while. That night, I didn't go and see my mother, but stayed in and talked to Marion.


On Saturday afternoon at the Cavern, I only half-listened to the Umbrella Men. I couldn't help wondering if Rob Finnegan and Gary were enjoying the film they had gone to see at the Odeon – it was only a few minutes' walk away.

The other day, when Rob collected Gary from school, he'd asked if I'd like to go to the pictures with them. 'It's on in town, *Bedknobs and Broomsticks,*' he said. 'It got very good reviews. They said it was suitable for adults as well as children – adults with a mental age of less than ten,' he added with a grin. 'I love all kids' films, so I don't know where that puts me. Afterwards, we could have a meal, then go back to Beth's flat and listen to records. She's going out and I've got the Hollies' *I Can't Let Go* LP and an old Yardbirds album I wanted years ago but never got round to buying.'

At that point, he'd made a face. 'I'm sorry, it's not very exciting, is it? I wish I could take you to some dead posh hotel for dinner, but it's just not on when I have Gary. Next time Beth stays in perhaps we could go somewhere like that.'

I didn't bother pointing out that he couldn't afford it. Besides which, I thought the invitation on offer sounded extremely appealing and regretted having to turn it down. I loved the Hollies.

'Sorry, I've got something on,' I mumbled. I didn't say what it was, that I was seeing another man because I thought he might be more exciting. Anyroad, Rob and I weren't committed to each other in any way, but I wouldn't have liked him going out with another woman. I felt awful when he appeared disappointed.

All of sudden, everyone was applauding the Umbrella Men and I'd hardly heard a thing. Steven came and said they were all going to the pub, so I followed him outside. It was drizzling. The three other members of the group were there with three girls. Steven just said, 'This is Pearl,' and they all smiled and said, 'Hi, Pearl.'

'Hi.' I sort of waved and felt very foolish.

The pub was crowded and there were no empty seats. We had to stand and hold our drinks. I had a shandy. Steven put his arm around me and nuzzled my neck. I felt a thrill, but was also scared. It was an awfully forward thing to do and I was worried he'd want to make love on our first date. I'd made love before to a boy in the Sixth Form when we were both seventeen, but I was probably the most inexperienced non-virgin in the world. I felt out of my depth.

The pub closed at three o'clock and we returned to Mathew Street, past the Cavern, to a large white van badly in need of cleaning. It was half-parked on the pavement. The drummer and his girlfriend climbed into the front and the rest of us got into the back where there were no seats and we had to sit on the floor. It was very dark once the doors were closed. As the van began to move, the other two couples lay down and began to kiss each other passionately. I dreaded Steven might want to do the same, but he seemed happy just to put his arm around me again and talk. He wanted to know what I thought of his group; I said they were first class.

'First class!' He sounded amused. 'No one's ever said that before.'

'Where are we going?' I asked. I could hardly see his face, let alone the direction the van was taking.

'To Moll's place,' he said vaguely.

Moll's place turned out to be the basement of a house in Myrtle Street underneath a shop selling camping equipment. There were already about ten people sitting on the numerous armchairs, large settee and the floor. The walls were full of film and show posters. The music was so loud we'd been able to hear it in the van before it had stopped. It was the Moody Blues, a group I really liked, but not when played at such a deafening pitch, making the room shake and vibrations travel through my shoes and up my legs until my whole body was quivering. I felt like a giant electric drill.

A woman of about fifty, dressed entirely in black and wearing a copious amount of make-up, including false eyelashes, shouted, 'So, you're Steven's latest?' and asked me what I wanted to drink. I assumed this was Moll.

'A cup of tea, please,' I screamed.

'I meant in the way of booze, dear,' she screamed back.

'Oh! A glass of white wine, then.'

'When I said booze, it's a choice between Guinness, lager or brown ale.'

'Do you have water?'

'There's a whole tank somewhere. Find yourself a spot to sit and I'll fetch some.'

For a long time I sat on the very edge of the settee without talking to anyone. People were passing hand-rolled cigarettes to each other, and I suspected they didn't have ordinary tobacco inside. One was given to me. I took it gingerly, too scared to puff, and handed it to the next person.

Steven had disappeared. Moll brought the water and I kept thinking I was wasting my time here and could be at home doing something useful like tidying my room or ironing. Or in the Odeon watching *Bedknobs and Broomsticks* with Rob and Gary.

Then Steven came, sat behind me on the arm of the settee and cupped his hands over my breasts. I nearly died of embarrassment. No one had ever done that to me in public.

'You're beautiful, do you know that?' he bellowed in my ear.

Despite the noise, several discussions were taking place close by: should the United Kingdom take part in the war in Vietnam? Most people on the settee seemed to think definitely not. A woman on the floor asked if anyone had seen that new telly programme, *Monty Python's Flying Circus*. Most people had, apart from me, and they said it was a scream. Marion hadn't liked the look of it and refused to have it on. I must ask my aunt, still strangely subdued, if we could see it next week.

The noise was having a serious effect on my ears. Strange sounds were coming from the furniture and I suspected it was moving around by itself. Moll came round with plates of meat paste sandwiches and I asked Steven who she was.

'That's Pete's mum.' He released my right breast to take a

sandwich. 'She likes having people here. Before she married Pete's dad, she was on the stage. When the shop upstairs is closed we sometimes rehearse in here. Trouble is the acoustics are crap.'

A few hours later, about a dozen of us went back to the Cavern for the Umbrella Men's evening performance. By now, it was raining heavily. We all squashed into the van. It seemed terribly dangerous for us all virtually to be sitting on top of each other, but no one seemed to care.

Suddenly I realized I had nothing in common with these people. We dressed differently, spoke differently, even smelled differently. There wasn't another person present wearing steam-pressed jeans, highly polished sandals or Coty L'Aimant. No one else had such neat hair, and my eyes must have looked curiously naked without eyeliner and shadow. I felt colourless and uninteresting.

We all filed into the Cavern and the group disappeared. The girls talked amongst themselves, and I was ignored. When we'd left Moll's, Steven had said to her, 'See you later, alligator.' I wondered what would we do afterwards. Sit around listening to deafening music again while we screamed at each other and smoked dodgy cigarettes? And then? I had a strong suspicion what would happen then, and didn't fancy it a bit.

This afternoon had been a new experience for me and I was glad I'd had it, but once was enough. I wasn't Steven's type and he wasn't mine. I could sit for ages doing nothing but stare at the moon or a spectacular sunset, but spending time in Moll's flat had been a complete waste of time.

Steven was singing one of his own compositions. He had a nice voice, could play the guitar really well and was terribly attractive, but he didn't make me feel nice inside like Rob Finnegan did.

I left the Cavern. It was almost nine o'clock, the rain had stopped and it was a lovely summer night. The setting sun was a huge fiery ball in the fading blue sky. I collected my car from St John's car park and drove to Cathy Burns's house. I badly wanted to see my mother, but not for any particular reason. And I wondered if there was time to go to Rob's house – I badly wanted to see him, too.

*

There were already four cars parked outside: Leo's Mercedes, Harry's BMW, Charles's Cortina and – I could hardly believe my eyes – Rob's old Morris Minor. What on earth was *that* doing there? I wondered. I parked my own car, went down the path and could hear voices coming from the garden. My mother seemed to prefer to be in the open air after the years in prison.

For a while, I stood by the gate, unnoticed, and watched my mother nurse a sleeping Gary in her arms like a baby while Cathy Burns, Uncle Harry and Charles, all standing, laughed mightily over something, and Granddad and Rob sat together on a bench discussing something that must have been of great importance if the expressions on their faces were anything to go by. There was no sign of Marion, who must have been at home in Aintree by herself.

Rob was the first person to see me. He stopped talking, got to his feet and came towards me. I could tell by his eyes and the look on his face that he was really pleased I'd come, and I wondered if I looked the same. I took a few stumbling steps forward and fell into his arms and it was the warmest, most comfortable place I'd ever been in my life.

'I love you,' he whispered.

'And I love you,' I whispered back.

'I've got a job: it's in Canada. Will you come with me? We'll get married first, of course.'

'Yes, I'll come with you, and yes, we'll get married.' I looked over his shoulder and saw my mother looking at us with tears in her eyes. I wanted to cry too, because she'd hardly been home five minutes and now I was about to go away.

It turned out that last Saturday Gary had told my mother of his longing for an Everton football kit, so this afternoon she'd gone into town with Cathy and bought one. When they got home, Cathy had found Rob's sister's telephone number, and my mother had rung and invited Rob and Gary to tea. The telephone had been ringing when they arrived home after seeing *Bedknobs and Broomsticks*, Rob said.

'Anyway,' my mother said later, 'I felt really sorry for him

– Rob, that is – you deserting him for another man. How did you get on with Steven Conway?'

'It was dead boring,' I told her. 'I felt like a fish out of water.'

'You'll be safe with Rob, love.' She squeezed my hand. Across the garden, Rob was helping Gary climb down a tree. 'You'd never know where you were with Steven. Oh, and don't forget you've got two aunties in Canada – Jacky and Biddy – as well as two uncles and five cousins – three boys and two girls. I've promised to stay with them over Christmas. They all live in British Columbia where Rob's job is.'

The job was head of security in an electronics factory that had just opened on Vancouver Island. The offer had come from a Canadian friend who'd worked with Rob in Uganda. The factory belonged to his brother.

By now, everyone knew that Rob and I were getting married, even Gary, who wanted to know if he still had to call me 'Miss'.

I said I wanted to be called Pearl, knowing I would never replace his mother.

My mother asked if I would do her a favour. 'Give Marion a ring and tell her you're marrying Rob. It wouldn't look good for you or Charles to blurt it out when you got home. Poor old thing, she can't stand me. I never liked her, either, but I managed not to make a song and dance about it. Tell you what: invite her over. Charles has gone to buy champagne for a toast and she should be part of it.'

'All right.' I turned to leave, but remembered there was something I had to know. 'Are Charles and Cathy having an affair?' I asked as quietly as I could.

Her jaw dropped a mile. 'Of course not. What on earth gave you that idea?'

I explained about bringing her blue cardigan round last Sunday and all the curtains being closed. 'Charles was here, his car was outside.'

'So it was you who left the cardigan on the step! We thought it was Marion – it was the sort of thing she'd do.' She laughed. 'No, love, Cathy and Charles were watching a science fiction film: they mustn't have heard you knock. You know how much Marion hates them – cowboy films, too – and refuses to have them on in the house. Charles is easy-going to a fault and lets her get away with it, silly man. It's about time he put his foot down.'

I telephoned Marion and she said she'd come over. She sounded very emotional, so I was glad I'd rung. She arrived about twenty minutes after Charles had returned with the champagne. Cathy didn't have any champagne glasses, but nobody cared.

We stood in a circle in the garden and Granddad made the toast: 'To Pearl and Rob. May they enjoy everlasting happiness, and provide a plentiful supply of brothers and sisters for little Gary here.'

'Pearl and Rob!' Glasses were raised, champagne drunk, and everyone began to sing 'Auld Lang Syne', I don't know why.

'I want three brothers and three sisters,' Gary announced when the singing stopped.

I told Hilda my news when I arrived at school on Monday. We both drove in at the same time and parked our cars next to each other.

'Congratulations,' she said warmly. 'When will it be?'

She was really thrilled to be able to attend my wedding. 'Towards the end of July. My mother's going to the church this morning to see what dates are free. It won't be a big affair. You're invited, of course.'

'Thank you. Your mother is a lovely person,' Hilda said sincerely. 'I'm sorry for the things I said that time. You build up a picture in your mind of what people are like, and I couldn't have been more wrong in your mother's case. I suppose even the nicest people can do things on the spur of the moment that they'll always regret.'

'What's happening with Clifford?' I asked, changing the subject.

'Clifford said he doesn't want any more children. He has two from his first marriage, and they're enough for him.' She kicked a football back to its owner with rather more force than was necessary. 'I think it's fair to say he's only marrying me to get a roof over his head.'

'I'm sorry, Hilda.' She really was due some happiness in her life.

'There's no need to be sorry. I'm still going to marry him,' she said surprisingly. 'I'm pretty certain that I'm pregnant. By the time he finds out, we'll be married and if he wants to leave he can. I won't care because I'll be a married woman and pretty soon I'll be a mother, which is all I've ever wanted out of life.'

Now that there were two weddings about to take place, it was no surprise when it turned out there would be another. Cathy Burns called me into her office at lunchtime and announced she and Uncle Harry were to be married.

'We've always got on well together ever since we met on Southport pier: it was the day your mother met your dad,' she said. She was pink and flushed and pretty, and I could suddenly imagine what she must have been like as a young woman during the war. 'That was thirty-two years ago. If it hadn't been for Harry, I would never have met Jack, who was the love of my life.'

'I'm really, really glad,' I said. Next to my own wedding, it was the best news I could have had. 'I'm glad Uncle Harry proposed at last.'

'He didn't, Pearl: I proposed to him.' She laughed so loudly and with such gusto I thought it would be heard all over the school. 'Left to himself, he would never have found the nerve. He accepted like a shot. We're going on a world cruise for our honeymoon. Leo is putting back his retirement until we return and I'm taking a year's leave. I'm so happy, Pearl, I could bust a gut.' She laughed again. 'That's not a very headmistressy thing to say, is it? But I don't care!'

'Oh, Charles, I don't want us to lose our little girl,' Marion wept.

Her voice was so full of misery that I wanted to cry myself. They were in the living room, and I don't think they realized I was in the breakfast room and could hear every word.

'We won't be losing her, sweetheart,' Charles said soothingly. 'She'll always be our little girl. And we can go to Canada and see her at Christmas. Isn't our Amy arranging a great big do?'

'But she won't be *here*, in this house with us. She won't bring home her new clothes for me to see. There won't be a pot of tea waiting when we get back from work. She won't be *here*, Charles.'

'I know, sweetheart, but I'll always be here for you and you for me.'

'Will you, Charles?' Marion asked tearfully.

'You know I will, sweetheart.'

I went into the kitchen, not wanting to hear any more, but glad they were getting on again. Charles and Marion had never realized how thin the walls were in their house. They must have been even thinner in the bungalow where I'd lived with my mother and father. I remember that I could clearly hear everything that was said when I was in bed, even though the door to my room had been closed. I used to pull the clothes over my head, but the words never went away. Even now, all these years later, I could hear them still in my dreams. One dream in particular often came back to haunt me. A voice was saying, 'I really would like to kill you,' and my mother was crying. A little girl – it could only be me – shouted, 'Leave Mummy alone …' I'd wanted to get out of bed to save her, but my body felt too heavy to move …

It was there that the dream ended, but I wondered if there was another, different ending and it would come to me one day.

# Chapter 20

## 1971–2
## Amy

Nellie Shadwick sat in the back of the Rolls-Royce, which was parked at the side of the road, and drummed her heels against the floor.

'What's that?' asked the driver, who was also her brother. 'An S.O.S.?'

'I'm fed up waiting,' Nellie complained.

'That's because you consider your own time so important you resent wasting it on other people.'

'Is that such a bad thing, Ducky?' Ducky wasn't a term of endearment, but the name by which her brother David had been known since he was a baby. No one had any idea why.

Ducky thought earnestly for a few minutes before saying it wasn't such a bad thing to want, except it was impossible not to waste time. 'You have to depend on so many other things being on time, too: buses and trains and taxis, fr'instance. Then there's folks falling ill at the last minute, snapped shoelaces, not being able to find stuff, all sorts of accidents, the weather, including the occasional meteorite—'

'All right, all right,' Nellie said testily. She stretched out her long, slim legs, which were encased in sheer black nylon tights. 'Do these look forty years old to you, Ducky?'

Ducky turned round. 'D'you mean your legs, your feet or your shoes, gal?'

'Me legs, of course.'

Ducky shook his curly head. 'They look more like a good fifty to me.'

She leaned forward and cuffed him lightly on the side of his head. 'Don't be so bleedin' cheeky, Ducky Shadwick. Where would you be without your sister?'

'Dead, probably,' Ducky said solemnly. 'Or banged up doing life or begging on the streets. I'd probably have had all me teeth knocked out by now and there'd be scars all over me body.' Reflecting that there was a good chance at least one, probably more, of these things really could have happened if their Nellie hadn't made good, he added, 'Actually, Nell, your legs only look twenty-one.'

'Are you sure?'

'Sure I'm sure.'

Nellie looked at her ludicrously expensive watch: it was a minute to nine. She buttoned up her black quilted coat and pulled the hood over her head.

'Are you intending to rob a bank?' enquired her brother, watching her now in the rear-view mirror.

'I don't want to be recognized, do I? That's why I hired a car, so no bleeder can track the registration back to yours truly.' She stared intently at the door of the grim building across the road. Scarcely a minute passed before the door opened and a small, insipid-looking woman came out carrying a suitcase. Nellie nearly fell out of the car. 'She's here. Oh, look, there she is, there she is.' She began to run.

As she got closer, she could see that the woman seemed taller than she'd first appeared, and it was obvious she'd once been very pretty. Nellie continued across the road, her clumpy high heels clattering, jewellery jingling, arms waving. 'Amy,' she yelled, 'Amy, gal. It's me: Nellie.'

Amy gasped when she stepped out of Holloway Prison and was caught up in the sails of what looked like a human windmill wearing a black hooded coat. Nellie kissed her cheeks, her forehead, her nose, and the air around her head as if Amy were wearing a halo.

'It's lovely to see you, Nell,' she said, wanting to burst into tears. She was free! She could walk any way she liked along the road in which she was standing. If she had wings, she could fly up into the sky, which was full of black clouds, not that she cared.

'The car's over here.' As if Amy could have missed the gleaming Rolls-Royce parked across the way. As Nellie dragged her towards it, a pack of young men, about ten strong, began to run in her direction waving notebooks and cameras and yelling that they wanted a photo and an interview. The driver of Nellie's car jumped out and bundled the two women and the suitcase into the back, and a minute later the car sped away.

Amy looked out of the rear window and saw the pack racing towards their own cars, but it was too late. They were out of sight in no time.

'This is Ducky,' Nellie said breathlessly, waving at the driver's back. 'He's me youngest brother. Ducky, this is me friend, Amy.'

'How do you do, Amy?' Ducky nodded at the rear-view mirror in which Amy could see herself. 'I've heard an awful lot about you.'

'Shurrup, Ducky.' Nellie closed the glass partition. 'I don't want big ears listening to everything we say. Don't forget to put your seat-belt on, gal.'

Amy confessed she'd never come across a seat-belt before and would Nellie kindly show her what to do. 'Where are we going?' she enquired.

'Constable country,' Nellie replied, fastening the belt. 'Suffolk,' she added in response to Amy's look of incomprehension. 'At least, that's what it said in the brochure. It's where some painter called Constable did most of his stuff. The health farm is called Butterflies and it's in a house that belonged to some lord or other. I've booked you in for three weeks under the name of Curran 'stead o' Patterson, like you asked. Me, I can only stay a week. You'll be all right on your own for the rest of the time, won't you, gal?'

'I will. Let me know how much it's costing, won't you, Nellie? I'll settle up while we're there.'

'It's not costing you a bleedin' penny, Amy. No, no,' she waved away Amy's protestations that she really must pay her share. 'If you hadn't got hold of me by the scruff of me flamin' neck eighteen

300

years ago and told me I could make something of meself, I'd still be struttin' me stuff on the streets, wouldn't I?'

It was the third time Nellie Shadwick had been sent to Holloway for soliciting that she'd met Amy, who recognized straight away that although Nellie – who had inherited her creamy, coffee-coloured skin and exotic eyes from her father, who was half-Jamaican and half-Chinese, and her dark red hair from her Irish mother – wasn't even faintly beautiful, there was something quite extraordinary and outlandish about her that nobody had yet spotted. Her hard life had done nothing to diminish her blazing good spirits and sense of humour.

'Have you ever thought of becoming a model, Nellie?' she had asked.

'A model?' Nellie squawked. 'A bleedin' model? No, Amy, I ain't ever thought of becoming a model.'

'Well, you should.'

For the six weeks of her sentence, in her free time and under Amy's tuition, Nellie walked up and down the prison library with a copy of James Joyce's *Finnegans Wake* on her head until she could do it quite elegantly. Amy advised her not to squawk quite so much and cut down on the swearing. 'It might put people off,' she warned.

Nellie left Holloway promising she would do her very best not to come back. Amy arranged for Leo to send her fifty pounds to buy some decent clothes and get her hair cut, and Nellie was taken on by the first model agency she went to. Her name was changed to Ellie and she became an overnight sensation, a model who had 'picked herself out of the gutter and done well for herself and her three younger brothers', according to the gossip columnists. She stopped squawking and swearing, at least in public, but still retained her broad Cockney accent and was well liked by everyone she met. Five years ago, she had retired from modelling and married a minor member of the aristocracy, who was extremely rich. She'd visited Amy frequently over the years.

Amy had asked for her name never to be mentioned in connection with her friend. 'For my family's sake I'd sooner everyone forgot about me,' she said. 'Anyroad, it wouldn't do you much good to be linked with me,' at which Nellie had squawked she didn't give a damn what anyone thought.

'Why did they let you out now?' she asked now.

'I think they were sick of the sight of me,' Amy replied.

In fact, women given life for murder were usually freed earlier, but her crime, and the circumstances surrounding it, were regarded as more despicable than most.

She felt too overwhelmed to talk. All she wanted was to look out of the window and let the fact that she was out of prison sink in. She had eaten her last meal behind bars, slept there for the final time, would never have to wear prison clothes again. Nellie must have realized how she felt, as they had been travelling in silence for at least an hour when Amy looked out at the flat countryside and asked, 'Where are we now?'

'Essex, gal; shortly coming up to Chelmsford. By the way, I've bought you some clothes, just a few bits and bobs for the health farm: leisure things like tracksuits and towelling robes and shorts. Oh, and there's a leotard and a couple of playsuits.'

'What's a playsuit?'

'Sort of very smart pyjamas you wouldn't dream of wearing in bed.'

'It's awfully kind of you, Nellie. Thanks.' Amy felt quite choked. Cathy had sent the clothes she was wearing now – the plain black skirt, black jacket and frilly white blouse from Marks & Spencer, along with some pretty underwear. 'I doubt if I would have come through without my friends,' she said now to Nellie. 'No matter which prison I was in, there was hardly a weekend when someone didn't come to see me: Leo, Cathy, our Charlie, Harry, you! Mam came regularly until she died.' Mam dying so suddenly of heart failure had been an appalling shock. 'My solicitor visited often, too.' It was due to Bruce Hayward's tireless efforts on her behalf that she'd been unexpectedly released.

There was silence again as Nellie appeared to doze off. Amy concentrated on the level fields and little villages of Essex until they passed a sign announcing they were now in Suffolk. It was late spring and everywhere looked as if it were covered with a lacy blanket of green. The sky was still a mass of heavy, dramatic black clouds.

She was free! At last the dark days were over. No longer would she have to steer a careful course through the minefield that was prison life: avoiding cliques and being nice to everyone, even the most violent prisoners – truly terrifying women, who beat other women up in the showers for no reason at all, as far as Amy could see. One morning, not long after she'd first arrived in Holloway, she'd witnessed a stabbing; the woman had almost died.

'I never saw a thing,' she told the governor afterwards when there was an investigation. It was a cowardly thing to do, but she wanted to stay alive, even if she had no real future to look forward to.

She was generally popular with the other prisoners. Many had suffered at the hands of men – their pimps, boyfriends, husbands, fathers – and she was considered something of a heroine for having had the courage to kill the man who was abusing her. No one doubted that he deserved it.

Next morning in Butterflies it was barely light when Amy woke up. She had a shower, luxuriating in the softness of the white towels and sweet-smelling soap. Having no idea of the programme for the day, she pulled on a pair of loose white cotton trousers – she'd read enough fashion magazines in prison to know they were no longer referred to as 'slacks' – and a loose top to match, then stared at her reflection in the mirror. She looked jaded and pale, but a trifle better than she'd looked yesterday. It must be due to a good night's sleep that her cheeks had a tinge of pink. By the time she was ready to leave Butterflies in three weeks, she was determined to look as good as she had before she'd entered prison, apart from being twenty years older.

She left the room and went downstairs. It was a beautiful old house, light and airy, with pale walls and polished floors. The clink of dishes could be heard coming from the kitchen, but there wasn't a soul to be seen.

She opened French windows leading to a paved area with benches and tables, and sat down, not minding that the air felt damp and chilly. A glimmer of light had appeared in the east and the grey sky was becoming brighter. An occasional bird sang and dew glistened like teardrops on the lawn, which sloped away to a small copse reminding her of Pond Wood.

There was a small village to her left, the only sign of life a spiral of smoke coming from the chimney of a cottage with a thatched roof. Maybe that was the village with the pub. Nellie had wanted to go last night, but Amy said she really wasn't up to it.

'I need time to adjust, Nell,' she'd explained.

Nellie had apologized for being a really thick cow and promised to follow wherever Amy led in future.

It was too much too soon, Amy thought. There were too many people, the scenery was too vast and this place too luxurious. Last night, she'd slept in a bed with cream satin covers in a room with a cream carpet and lace frills on the windows. The contrast between that and a prison cell was hard to deal with.

A woman appeared wearing a flowered towelling outfit. Was it a playsuit? She sat beside Amy and proceeded to ask loads of probing questions. Amy was forced to invent an imaginary life for herself. Then more guests came, Nellie among them. She looked spectacular in a purple leotard and black tights. She was immediately recognized, and all the attention switched to her, much to Amy's relief.

Later on, Nellie produced a bundle of newspapers. 'There's something about you in all of these,' she said. 'They say you've gone to ground. Do you want to read them?'

'No thanks.' Amy never read about herself in the press. It was bad enough hearing what people had to say, let alone reading it as well.

Over the following weeks, her body was massaged, squeezed, pummelled and tweaked. Her legs were waxed; her nails manicured and painted Blushing Pink. She was introduced to a sauna, but came out straight away, terrified of being shut in a small, hot room and finding herself unable to get out. She swam daily in the sparkling little indoor pool – she'd learnt to swim in Bootle baths with Cathy before the war. Clad in a leotard, she joined in exercises before breakfast, attempted Yoga, went for long walks in the persistent rain with Nellie, usually ending up in the village pub, the Cock and Bull, where they stuffed themselves with steak and kidney pie and chips. The food at Butterflies consisted mainly of salad and boiled fish.

On the first Friday, the day before most women were due to leave and a new batch arrive, she sat in front of the mirror in the hairdressing salon and was thrilled by how much better she looked. With each day, she could sense her body responding to the pampering. Her skin was no longer grey and her eyes no longer drooped. She was beginning to feel as if she belonged to the human race again. Her hair was at that very minute being combed out after being set in giant rollers. She had kept it long in prison, cutting it herself, not really caring that she was beginning to go grey.

But now it had been cut, styled and tinted, so it looked like brand-new hair. The waves and curls were back, and once again they were a gleaming golden blonde, if not as natural as they had once been.

'I'm almost myself again,' Amy told herself. 'At least, I am on the outside, if not in my head.'

Over the next two weeks, without Nellie, Amy had a lazy time, breakfasting in bed and getting up late, reading a lot, strolling or cycling slowly around the grounds, usually by herself. The weather had improved. She had facials, a few gentle massages, more Yoga. She lay on the floor with her arms stretched out while a gentle voice encouraged her to relax every single part of her body while breathing in the scent of a score of flickering candles.

On the morning of the day she was due to leave, she had her hair done again. That afternoon, Leo was coming to fetch her. On Friday she was getting a passport, and on Monday they would go to Paris.

Leo Patterson had always been a charming and exceptionally good-looking man. Amy had been conscious of it from the day they'd met, just as she had been conscious of the fact that he was attracted to her, his son's wife. It had never crossed her mind to encourage him, and if Leo had made a pass she would have been horrified and had nothing more to do with him.

Now things were different. Barney was dead and so was Elizabeth, who had died alone in the house in Calderstones that had been built from old bricks and old beams. Leo had left for good after her testimony at Amy's trial had nearly resulted in a death sentence.

But Amy's feelings for Leo hadn't changed. He was still Barney's father, and any sort of relationship with him other than friendship would have felt incestuous. However, she wanted to look her best for him, see the admiration in his eyes, and would like to bet that he had the same effect on most women.

She was in the lounge reading a novel, wearing the black skirt and white blouse that Cathy had sent, when Leo was shown in. For a man in his seventies he looked remarkably handsome with his lean face and dark grey hair. Not many older men could – or would – have worn such narrow, well-fitting jeans topped by a smart silver-grey jumper. He blew Amy a kiss and stopped to speak to the receptionist.

'So,' the woman sitting beside her said in a low voice, 'it was true after all.' She was about Amy's age, beautifully dressed and exquisitely made up, but nothing could disguise the sadness in her eyes. She'd only arrived at Butterflies the day before, and her name was Audrey.

'I beg your pardon?'

'You were having an affair with your father-in-law after all.'

Amy felt all the colour drain from her cheeks. 'I was doing no such thing,' she stammered.

'It doesn't matter to me whether you were or not.' The woman shook her head dismissively. 'I remember admiring you very much at the time. I read about you in all the papers and saw you in the news at the cinema.'

'Admired me?'

'You had the courage to get rid of your bastard husband. I was too frightened. We're still together after all this time.' Amy couldn't think of a single thing to say to this. She had never been so stuck for words. The woman continued, 'You look surprised, Mrs Patterson. See, I know your name and that your first name is

306

Amy. You had a little girl called Pearl. If you don't want people to recognize you, I suggest you do something with your hair. It was the first thing I noticed.'

'Thank you,' Amy said stiffly.

The woman said something, but Amy didn't hear because Leo came up and told her she looked like a million dollars. She stood up and he gave her a hug.

'Would you mind hanging on for a bit?' she asked. 'I want to see if the hairdresser is free.' She didn't want people pointing at her in restaurants or as she walked down the street. Although she had no intention of hiding her identity, she didn't want to advertise it.

'I'd like to buy a dress this afternoon,' Amy said to Leo. They were sitting in a pavement café in the Champs Élysées drinking coffee, watching the traffic pass and listening to the drivers impatiently sounding their horns. It was a lovely May day, neither cold nor warm, and brilliantly sunny. Leo was half-reading *The Times* and wearing the funny little glasses that John Lennon had made famous. It was more or less all they'd done since they got to Paris: drink coffee and stroll up and down the leafy boulevards. Oh, and shop!

'Have you seen the one you want?' Leo enquired.

'I saw it yesterday in the Place de la Republique.'

'The blue one or the green one?' He was very interested in everything she bought, just as Barney used to be. Although they were in Paris, she was paying little more for clothes than she would have done back home. But they all had that extra bit of *chic*, in particular the shoes.

'The green one – I think.' She found it hard to make up her mind about anything. Until recently, almost every decision had been made for her, the days and weeks ahead rigidly mapped out. All she'd had to think about was which book to read next or what to put in the letters she wrote to people. She still woke mornings expecting to find herself in a prison cell. She would never know any greater joy than when she realized she was as free as the wind. 'I'm dying to see Pearl,' she said. 'See what she really looks like, not just in a photograph.' She'd asked for just one photograph a year, enough to remind her that her daughter was no longer the five-year-old tot she'd left behind.

Leo let the glasses slide to the end of his nose. 'That was a lovely one taken on her twenty-first.'

'She looked dead pretty,' Amy said tenderly. She had a record of Pearl's First Holy Communion, her Confirmation, the day she'd left teacher training college. It was Cathy who'd overseen Pearl's career when she expressed the desire to become a teacher.

A young couple came and sat at the table in front of them. They immediately wrapped their arms around each other and began to kiss. A waiter came and stood, smiling slightly, until they'd finished. They ordered, looked deeply into each other's eyes, and kissed again.

Watching, Amy felt a pang of envy. 'Barney once suggested we come to Paris for our honeymoon when the war was over,' she said. If she'd been with Barney now – the old Barney – they might well have sat on the Champs Élysées and kissed. 'But he wasn't in the mood for honeymoons when he came back from the prisoner-of-war camp.' The thought reminded her of the bungalow where they'd lived and she asked Leo what had happened to it.

'It was only rented,' Leo told her. 'I've no idea who moved in after you.'

Soon, Amy would have to find somewhere to live. For the first time in her life she would be on her own and it wouldn't be enough just to be out of prison: she'd want more than that. In a matter of days she would be fifty and would have to decide what to do with the rest of her life.

Leo had come up with the idea of Amy appearing at a dinner party where the Pattersons, the Currans and Cathy Burns would be present, giving them a really big surprise.

'Isn't that a bit theatrical?' She didn't think much of the idea. 'Do they need to be surprised? Why can't they just be told I'll be there?'

'It wouldn't be the same. Ah, go on, Amy,' he said coaxingly. 'I like giving people surprises.'

To please Leo, who'd been so marvellous over the years, she agreed. She paid five times as much as she had for her other clothes for a plain black fitted dress from Galleries Lafayette. It had a high neck and long sleeves, and the thin material clung to every curve of her slim body.

The following day they flew home from Paris, the holiday over.

She was in the ladies' room of the Carlyle Hotel in Southport. It was all highly dramatic. In a minute, she was to wait outside and a waiter would tell her when Mr Patterson had ordered champagne and it was time for her to cross to his table. She knew where the table was, but had only seen it from the distance.

Her nose was shining. She powdered it, renewed her lipstick, patted her short brown hair. Did it really matter that when she saw her daughter for the first time she looked like a film star? It does to me, she thought. I've always been concerned with my appearance, perhaps too much. But it's the way I am.

She went over to the door and raised her hand to open it when she had a wish that completely took her breath away. What she wished – wished with every single part of her, so hard that it swiftly became an ache – was that when she opened the door in all her finery, Barney would be waiting for her: a fifty-two-year-old Barney, as handsome as ever in his best suit.

'Ah, there you are, darling,' he would say, reaching for her hand. 'Would you like a drink before we eat?'

But it was a wasted wish. Now she was trembling and her heart raced. She left the cloakroom and a waiter approached. 'Are you ready, madam?'

Amy nodded and followed the man across the room to where her daughter would be with a young man called Rob, whom Leo had never met.

And there she was, Pearl, so like Barney with her smooth skin and dark brown hair. She had a quiet face – could a person have a quiet face? Then Pearl looked up, caught her staring, and Amy said, 'Hello, love,' and her daughter burst into tears and threw herself into Amy's arms, and Amy was saying, 'There, there, love. There, there. Don't cry, I'm home now.'

After a few days Amy had lunch in the Adelphi with Harry, while Charlie took her things to Cathy's house where she intended to stay. Barney's brother had always been perfectly turned out in the old days. Today, he wore a pale-grey suit, a white shirt and a silver tie, the sort of man who could have been taken for a friendly bank manager or the family solicitor. You would never have dreamt he'd once been a soldier who'd stoically fought his way through the war. This was the first time they'd been alone together.

He told her she looked fantastic. 'I'd expected you to turn up hollow-eyed like Susan Hayward in that picture, *I Want to Live*. Have you seen it?'

'If that's the one when she's in prison, then no, Harry, I didn't see it because I happened to be in prison myself. Didn't she go to the gas chamber in the end?'

'Yes,' he said mournfully. 'Have I just put my foot in it?'

'Yes, but I don't mind.' She gave him a forgiving smile.

'What do you think of your daughter?' he asked.

'She's lovely. I think she's decided she quite likes me, after all. I'd been expecting coldness, indifference, even rudeness, but she's been very nice, if a bit shy.'

'In view of the circumstances, it would be a bit blooming ironic if she was anything else but nice,' Harry puffed.

'Harry, love,' Amy said patiently, 'Pearl thinks I murdered her father.'

'I know, I know. But she's aware there were mitigating circumstances.'

'Mitigating circumstances or not, to stab someone to death is a pretty extreme thing to do, particularly when it's your husband.' A waiter came and removed their plates; she hoped he hadn't heard the last remark.

'Do you think Pearl will ever remember she did it?'

Amy shuddered. 'I pray not. But if she does, I hope that by then she'll be happily married to that nice boyfriend of hers with the lovely little son.' For some strange reason, Gary, with his innocent eyes and sweet nature, had moved her more than anything since she'd come home.

Harry spent the rest of the meal talking about Cathy. 'I wish I saw more of her,' he said, mournful again.

'Why don't you ask her out next time you meet?' He'd been hankering after Cathy since the day they'd met in Southport all those years ago.

He sniffed miserably. 'She wouldn't want to be bothered with an old codger like me.'

'For goodness' sake, Harry. You're only fifty-five. That's not exactly ancient.'

'I'm fifty-four, actually,' he said quickly.

'That's even less ancient.' She felt like hitting him with a spoon. 'When we go back to Cathy's you can ask her then.'

'I might.'

Amy woke up in the middle of a dream that she couldn't remember, just that it had been one of those heavy, sad dreams that make everything feel hopeless. It was only quarter to six. She lay there, crying quietly, not wanting to disturb Cathy, who eventually got up, had a shower, then knocked on Amy's door and said her name.

Amy didn't answer. She heard Cathy make tea and hoped she wouldn't bring her up a cup, but she must have decided to leave her friend to sleep. Downstairs, the radio went on and Amy began to cry properly, sobbing uncontrollably into the pillow. She thought she'd been coping wonderfully, had actually felt quite proud of herself. She'd been impressed with the conversation she'd had with Harry yesterday. It had been civil, pertinent and faintly amusing. But that was yesterday and this was today, and she felt really despondent, as if there were no point in being alive any more.

It was stupid, but she wished Gary were there, sitting at the foot of the bed and looking at her with his green eyes, talking about his 'tubs' of paint and the cat he'd had in Uganda. He was the same age as Pearl had been when Amy had gone into prison, and he made her feel she'd missed so much.

Was it too late for her to become a teacher?

It was such an outrageously stupid idea that she stopped crying and laughed hysterically. Oh, yes, she'd be snapped up. Someone who'd been in prison for murder would make an excellent teacher.

It would appear she'd stopped crying – until the next time. She put on the lilac dressing gown that Nellie had bought her and went downstairs.

'Ah, there you are!' Cathy looked delighted to see her. Could anyone have had a better friend?

'Why aren't you at school?' Amy enquired.

'Because it's Saturday and we're going into town later. Had you forgotten? You wanted to buy an Everton football shirt for Gary. Would you like some tea?'

'Several cups, please.' She already felt better. It wasn't just Cathy, but the thought of going shopping. She followed her friend into the kitchen. 'I think I'll buy another handbag. I've only got the one.'

'I wouldn't mind another bag, either. It's ages since I bought one.'

'I'll buy one for you,' Amy promised.

'There's no need for that,' protested Cathy.

'If I bought one made of solid gold it wouldn't make up for all you've done for me, Cathy,' Amy said with a throb in her voice.

'Don't get all maudlin on me, girl.' Cathy looked embarrassed.

Amy pulled herself together. If she weren't careful, she'd start crying again.

It rained for most of the time in town. They rushed from shop to shop: from Lewis's to Owen Owen's to George Henry Lee's where they had lunch. She kept thinking about Pearl, who was going out with Steven Conway today, and hoped she wasn't doing anything foolish. She said as much to Cathy, who assured her that Pearl had her head screwed on the right way.

'She's a sensible girl. Stop worrying.'

'I can't help it. I hope Rob doesn't find out she's with another man. Perhaps I should have a word with her before she goes to meet Steven. I'll ring our Charlie.'

'Look at you!' Cathy hooted. 'Not home five minutes and you're already an interfering mother.'

'Oh, all right; I won't ring.'

She wasn't the least bit surprised when, not long after tea, Leo and Harry turned up, as they did virtually every night. Harry still hadn't invited Cathy out.

'What did you all do with yourselves before I came home?' she asked.

Leo said, as it was Saturday, he'd be doing something at the Rotary Club. 'There's usually a function of some sort.'

Harry said he'd be propping up the bar in his golf club after a hard day's play.

Amy raised her eyebrows. 'In the rain?'

'Especially in the rain: *real* golfers prefer to play when it's raining.'

Cathy, busy putting on a Frank Sinatra LP, claimed if Amy weren't there she'd be at the theatre with friends. 'Any number of friends that I've been neglecting since you reappeared on the scene, Amy Patterson.'

'Very soon we'll get fed up with you,' Leo warned. 'You'll be pleading with us to come and see you.'

Amy conceded that that would almost certainly be the case.

Later, she suggested that they invite Rob and Gary over. She was longing to give the little boy the Everton top. 'Do you know their telephone number?' she asked Cathy.

Cathy didn't, but knew Rob lived with his sister in Seaforth. An E. Finnegan was found in the telephone directory living in Sandy Lane, and a surprised Rob promised to come shortly.

'What happens if Pearl brings Steven Conway back and Rob's still here?' Cathy asked.

'Oh, Lord! I didn't think of that! But Steven's playing at the Cavern tonight, so it would be really late by then and Rob will have gone.'

Gary was full of the picture they'd been to see: *Bedknobs and Broomsticks*. Amy said it sounded fascinating. Afterwards, he and his dad had their tea in a Wimpy. 'I had a beefburger with sauce on,' he announced, 'and little thin chips and pink ice cream.'

'I'd love to have had a tea like that.'

'My dad will take you there next week if you want,' the little boy said generously. 'We won't have left for Canada by then, will we, Dad?'

'No, son. Not for weeks yet.' Rob turned to the others, his face shining with good news. 'I got a letter this morning,' he explained. 'It was from this chap I worked with in Uganda. His dad's taken over an electronics firm on Vancouver Island and they want me as head of security, to start in August.'

There was a chorus of congratulations. Leo shook Rob's hand and patted him on the shoulder. Amy wondered where this left Pearl. Would Rob want her to go with him? Would she go if he did? Or had she just decided that Steven was the man for her? Maybe she didn't want either of them.

She gave Gary the Everton top. He said solemnly, 'Thank you very much, Amy.' She helped him put it on there and then, and he asked if he could please play in the garden.

'It's raining, love,' she told him.

'No, the sun's just come out.'

'So it has!' She took his hand. 'We'll go out there, shall we?'

Cathy's garden was mainly paved with a border of small shrubs and trees. Amy fetched a canvas chair from the garage and watched Gary kick around an invisible football and score loads of goals in an invisible net.

The earth smelled fresh and the paving stones were already acquiring dry patches that seemed to be growing bigger by the second. The sun was fiery red and there was scarcely a cloud in the dusky blue sky. It had become a different world than it had been all day, and there was no one there who appreciated it more than she did, or was as strongly aware of the sights and the smells and the wonderful taste of freedom.

Rob and Leo came out, and she told them where the chairs were. Cathy turned up the music – by now Tony Bennett had taken the place of Frank Sinatra – and emerged from the house accompanied by Harry. Amy was surprised when they started to dance. Cathy couldn't stop giggling.

Charlie turned up, looking a bit put out that they were having

314

a good time without him. 'You know you're always welcome, Charlie,' Cathy told him. 'You don't have to wait for an invitation. Where's Marion?'

'Busy.' Charles shrugged.

Gary said he was tired, and Amy pulled him on to her knee and buried her face in the blue Everton top. He was badly in need of a mother.

Then, all of a sudden, much earlier than expected, Pearl appeared, having come down the side of the house and stood by the entrance to the garden. Amy held her breath. She had a feeling that something momentous was about to happen – and it did.

Rob got to his feet and walked towards her daughter, and a light seemed to go on in Pearl's eyes as she waited for him to come. Their arms went around each other, Rob whispered something, Pearl whispered something back, and Amy knew that everything was going to be all right.

Three weddings.

Cathy's was the first. She wore blue lace and a picture hat; Harry a biscuit-coloured suit. They were married in a Register Office, because Cathy didn't think getting married in a Catholic church mattered much these days. Her four sisters and five brothers came, along with their spouses and a good proportion of the twenty-four children they had between them. It was a triumph for feminism, Amy thought, the bride proposing to the bridegroom. The couple left immediately for a cruise around the world. A temporary headmistress was taking Cathy's place until she came back.

She wasn't sure if Hilda Dooley's marriage to Clifford Thompson was an even greater triumph for feminism, or a complete forfeiture of women's rights. As far as she could gather, Clifford was marrying Hilda in order to have somewhere to live, and she was marrying him to have the title of Mrs. Oh, and she was also pregnant, but Clifford didn't know!

Pearl and Rob got married in the last week of July. Amy would never forget the sight of her lovely daughter as she walked down the aisle of the Holy Rosary church on Charlie's arm to where Rob waited to take her hand in marriage. It made up for everything that had happened before: her loss of her freedom; the misery she had born; the ignominy that had been heaped upon her; the shame she had felt for a crime she didn't commit.

They didn't have a honeymoon, as there wasn't time before they left for Canada. Instead, when the reception was over, the newly married couple, and Gary, came back to Cathy's house where Amy was living alone, to spend their last few days in England.

And now a taxi was waiting at the end of the path; it was time for them to go. Leo, Charlie and Marion were there to say goodbye. The men shook hands and hugged briefly. Gary flitted from one person to the next demanding kisses, particularly from Amy, whom he really loved. Pearl threw her arms around Marion and then Charlie, who led his wife indoors when she began to cry uncontrollably.

Why are we doing this to each other? Amy asked herself. Why don't we all stay under the one roof and never part?

Pearl said goodbye to her granddad. 'Goodbye, darling,' Leo said gruffly.

'Mum …' The word made Amy immediately want to cry, but it was Pearl who was sobbing her heart out. 'Oh, Mum. I've only just got you back and now I'm going away.'

'But we'll see each other again at Christmas, love. We'll all see each other again. There's no need to cry.'

'Bye, Mum.'

'Bye, love.'

Rob helped his new wife into the taxi where a beaming Gary waited.

'I didn't want her to cry,' Amy sighed as she watched the taxi drive away. 'I didn't want her to cry, not so much.'

'Amy, darling,' Leo said, 'after what you did for Pearl, she could cry a million tears and it wouldn't be enough.'

# Epilogue

## January 1972
## Mrs da Silva

It was a spectacular view, beautiful beyond belief, but it made Amy's head swim. It was too much. She could see for miles and miles, had no idea how many: hundreds perhaps. Yet there wasn't a human being in sight, just the endless Pacific Ocean, which was gradually changing from glittering silver to blood-red as it began to reflect the dying sun.

Amy shifted in her seat. The drone of the plane's engine managed to be both disturbing and hypnotic. This was only the second time she'd flown, and she was just a hair's breadth away from panic. She concentrated on the view, but the sheer vastness of it was making her heart race and her stomach feel queasy.

The sky was an artist's palette of colours, bleeding into each other to make paler, brighter, duller, darker colours. The sun was melting like a golden jelly, its shape changing by the second. She longed to close her eyes against the terrifying magnificence of the sight, but she might never witness anything like this again in her life. It made her feel very small and unimportant, no more than the tiniest speck on the face of the earth.

Then, all of a sudden, the sun vanished, as if an impatient God had thought it was time it stopped dawdling and got a move on, dragging it below the horizon. Amy gasped as night fell in an instant over her portion of the world, leaving merely a silver glow where the sun had been. But then the glow disappeared and there was just dark sky and dark water, and no indication that there'd ever been anything else.

The man sitting beside her gave her a gentle nudge. 'She wants to know if you would like a drink,' he said. He had a Canadian accent.

A pretty stewardess was waiting to take Amy's order.

'Just a cup of tea, please,' she said, and allowed her eyes to close at last.

It was January and she was on her way home from Canada. The splendid sunset was a fitting finale to the last four wonderful weeks. She'd met her sisters, their husbands and their families for the first time in twenty years. Jacky had had two more children since she'd come to Canada, and Biddy one. She'd stayed a week with Jacky and a week with Biddy, then moved into a hotel to be near Pearl – who was expecting a baby – Rob and Gary, and Leo. To everyone's amazement, Charlie had managed to persuade Marion to join them. Cathy and Harry had interrupted their world cruise and flown all the way from New Zealand.

Amy could almost believe that the years in prison had been worth it in return for the dizzying months since she'd been released, culminating in the time spent in Vancouver. So many highs after years of nothingness, so much love.

She could easily have believed that, before she had died or before the girls had gone to Canada, Mam had told her sisters the truth about Barney's death. Their affection for her hadn't changed: they seemed to understand that she had been driven to killing her husband, which was awful because Barney hadn't deserved to die. But there was something else, a look in their eyes – of understanding, admiration, and more love than she merited if she really had been guilty of such a brutal crime.

Her neighbour gave her another gentle nudge. 'Your tea is here.' He pulled down the little table from the back of the seat in front so that the stewardess could put down the tray.

'Thank you.' Amy smiled at them both, without really seeing them. She turned and stared out of the window where it was too black to see anything, but she didn't want to be distracted and let the memory of the holiday fade away.

Oh, Lord! Now she was thinking about Barney. If she did that for too long, she would burst into tears and have everyone on the plane staring at her. It really was time she let him go, stopped thinking about him and wishing he were there, wondering what he would look like now, remembering his smile, imagining the things he would say. It was so real in her mind that she'd think of things to say back.

New Year's Eve, a week ago, had held an undercurrent of sadness. Amy imagined everyone had felt as she did, that this joining together was the experience of a lifetime, that it was most unlikely all of them would be together again: all the Currans and all the Pattersons. The gathering had been difficult to arrange. Marion had had to take time off work, Pearl might not be able to get away with a small baby, Leo was an old man, Harry had a company to look after and Cathy a school.

Amy was definitely going back. She had just spent a week with Pearl in her comfy little house on Vancouver Island. Her daughter was expecting the baby in the spring and she'd promised to be there. And Jacky and Biddy were definitely coming to Liverpool to stay with their sister once she found a house of her own. Until then, she would live in Cathy's house.

It had been a truly wonderful holiday. But now it had come to an end and she wasn't sure if she could bear it.

She reached for the tea, but her hand trembled so much that the liquid spilled on to the saucer. She quickly replaced the cup.

'Are you all right?' Her neighbour placed his hand on her arm. She looked at him. He was a tough-looking man with a crew-cut, a grizzled face, and very dark, grey eyes, who somehow gave the impression of finding life rather amusing.

'Yes. Oh, but why is everything so sad? Why do really wonderful things have to come to an end?' Her eyes were full of tears.

'So even more wonderful things can happen,' he said gently.

She almost laughed. 'That's a very clever answer!'

'I have clever answers for everything.' He looked into her eyes, as if forcing her to take notice, to see him properly. 'My name is Frank da Silva. What's yours?'

# Nothing Lasts Forever

For Fenella and Dusty Miller.

*Prologue*

# Diana

## September 1999

'So, you see, Di, luv,' Michelle O'Sullivan said plaintively, 'it really is time I had a break. I was only twenty when I had you. Then our Damian came along, then Jason, then Garth. And it wasn't long after Garth was born when your dad did a runner.'

This was doing Diana's dad a grave injustice. Publicly, he had divorced his wife on account of their marriage having irretrievably broken down. There was no mention in the divorce papers that the breakdown was due to her adultery with four different men and that it had come to the point when he wasn't sure which of the children, Diana apart, were his. Jim O'Sullivan had then disappeared into thin air.

'Now you're eighteen, it wouldn't hurt for you to take on a bit of responsibility, so your poor mum can have a rest, like,' Michelle continued, her voice wobbling. 'Warren's a really nice chap, but he's a bit younger than me and it's not fair to ask him to move in and support another man's kids.'

Diana wouldn't have dreamed of saying it took Warren all his time to support himself – he was more often out of work than in.

Pausing for breath, Michelle took a long puff on her ciggie and looked appealingly at her daughter, her big blue eyes moist with tears. In her black jeans and red top decorated with a sequinned heart, she could have passed for a woman considerably younger than thirty-eight. She wore sandals with four-inch heels – the red nail polish had worn off the little toes on both feet.

'So, luv,' she went on with a theatrical sigh, 'I thought it'd be nice if I moved out for a while so me and Warren could have some time together, just the two of us, while you looked after your brothers. Him and me could get a little place of our own. In fact, Warren already knows of somewhere in Melling Village no distance from Liverpool; a little cottage with just one bedroom. Oh, but, Di, it's got a dead pretty tree in the garden: Warren said it's cherry.' She threw the half-smoked cigarette on to the hearth and glanced with disgust through the window at the minuscule back yard, the walls of which had needed painting for as long as Diana could remember. The row of houses behind was no more than a few metres away. At the front, the property ended at the door through which you stepped right on to the pavement. 'A tree, Di! Can you imagine – looking out at a tree?'

Diana smiled sympathetically. Her mother had never expressed a desire to see fields, trees, baby lambs, flowers or anything else to do with nature, but her own nature was so sweet and trusting that it didn't cross her mind she might not be telling the truth. 'When will you be leaving, Mam?' she asked.

'I thought I'd go this 'avvy,' her mother said casually, as if abandoning four children at a few hours' notice on a Saturday afternoon wasn't at all unreasonable. 'I'll make a stew before I go so there'll be something to eat for the lads when they get back from the footy. You might need to buy stuff from the supermarket tomorrow. Once me and Warren are settled, I'll make sure you get the Child Benefit for the lads.' All three boys were still at school. She reached for her bag. 'I'll leave you a few bob to be getting on with, shall I?'

'There's no need, Mum. I've got enough money of me own.'

For a moment, Michelle's eyes filled with real tears,

4

knowing she was taking advantage of Diana's soft heart. Not many girls of eighteen would so willingly have agreed to look after three rowdy lads for an unspecified length of time, but her daughter hadn't hesitated. It wasn't the first time, either. Diana had played mother on and off since she was about twelve.

For the umpteenth time, for Di's sake, Michelle wished her daughter hadn't taken after her dad. Jim had been such a clumsy bugger, always tripping over things and bumping into doors. Di was just the same – tall and gangly with giant feet and long white hands. She'd been born the day of Charles and Diana's wedding, hence the name. Thinking about it now, her Diana bore more than a passing resemblance to the late Princess of Wales, God bless her. They even had the same soft heart.

# Brodie

## October 2004

'Just think,' Colin said, getting into bed, 'there'll be no more need for us to lie awake till all hours waiting to hear her key in the front door. Tomorrow, we can sleep in late and go to midday Mass.'

Brodie didn't say anything, but thought that *she* would probably lie awake for the entire night wondering if Maisie, their daughter, was fast asleep in her bed at the university campus where her parents had left her earlier that very day.

Colin tucked his arm around her waist and pulled her against him. 'When we make love, you can be as noisy as you like,' he said.

'Noisy?'

He kissed her shoulder. 'Before we had the kids, you used to scream your head off when we had sex.'

'I did no such thing,' Brodie said indignantly.

'You did, darling.' He pulled her even closer. 'It's a good job this is a detached house, otherwise the neighbours would have complained.'

'You're exaggerating.' Thinking about it, she realized she had missed letting rip when she came to a climax. 'You don't seem a bit upset that we've lost Maisie,' she told him.

'I'm devastated,' he said simply. 'I'll miss her like mad, but let's look on the bright side: we haven't *lost* her any more than we've lost Josh. I'm proud our two kids are at university. Now we can begin to live like we're just a couple again, as if we'd just got married, starting with you making one helluva row when we make love. The next few weeks are going to be like a second honeymoon.'

'Oh, shut up!' She wriggled and he held her tighter.

'You'll never get away,' he whispered. He kissed her neck, then her shoulder and his hand moved up to her breasts. 'Why are you wearing a nightie? Is it in case one of the children might cry during the night and you'll have to get up? If I remember rightly, that was the reason you gave when you stopped coming to bed with nothing on.'

He had managed the seemingly impossible: making her angry at the same time as turning her on. She wasn't sure which emotion to give way to. On reflection, the second would have a much more enjoyable outcome than the first. She pushed the duvet away and began to remove her nightdress.

She woke up at precisely quarter past seven when a long strip of daylight was just beginning to show through the gap in the curtains. Her nightdress was on the floor where it had been thrown the night before.

Brodie got up, put the nightdress on, and sat on the edge of the bed watching Colin, who was lying on his side, snoring softly. He was forty-four, but looked younger than his age, even more so while relaxed in sleep. His brown, dead straight hair, slightly mussed, showed no sign of thinning and there wasn't a grey strand to be seen, unlike Brodie who had scores. Same with wrinkles. Despite being three years younger, she had acquired a few around her eyes, but Colin's boyish face was quite smooth. Awake, he frowned a lot, as if the world and everyone in it was the cause of perpetual surprise. Asleep, the frown had disappeared and his brow was smooth.

She felt tempted to rouse him with a kiss, but was too tired for what would inevitably follow – wonderful though it had been last night. Yesterday had been exhausting, driving to

London, with the boot full of Maisie's stuff and the back seat taken up with Maisie herself and even more stuff. Brodie had ended up with the hi-fi on her knees. It had been a most uncomfortable journey.

They'd stayed with Maisie until four o'clock, Brodie making the bed in the tiny room where her daughter would now live, putting her clothes away in the minute built-in wardrobe and drawers. The toiletries she arranged on the window sill, which seemed to be the only place for them, and the towels she hung under the sink.

While she did all this, Maisie was in the crowded corridor making friends, something she was very good at. Her voice, with its Liverpool accent, was distinguishable amidst a jumble of others.

'There's boys out there as well,' Brodie remarked. 'Will both sexes be living on the same corridor? I'd've thought they'd be kept separate.'

Colin had plugged in the hi-fi and was arranging the speakers. 'They were when I went to university, but things have changed since then.'

'I think they're arranging to go to a club in the West End tonight.' Brodie stopped unpacking and stood behind the open door where she could hear better.

'Don't eavesdrop!' He turned on the radio and New Orleans jazz filled the tiny room. 'Now, that's something worth listening to, not teenagers arranging their illicit affairs.'

Had Maisie gone to a London club? Brodie wondered now. She felt tempted to ring her mobile and find out, but common sense told her it would be a daft thing to do. Sad though it was – heartbreaking, in fact – she had to let her daughter get on with her own life.

She left Colin to sleep, put on her slippers, grabbed a dressing gown and went downstairs. The sky was a watery grey and it was impossible to tell what sort of day it would be – they'd missed the weather forecast the day before. She made tea, put everything on a tray, and took it into the front room where she switched on a lamp and settled herself in a corner of the settee.

The sideboard on the opposite wall held an assortment of photographs: Brodie and Colin's wedding, other weddings, the children at various stages of their lives, from birth till now. Maisie was making a funny face in her photos – either that or grinning madly from ear to ear – while Josh, their son, looked as serious as a baby as he did at twenty. He'd never been all that liberal with his smiles. When he'd left for university in Norwich, Brodie had been upset, naturally, but not worried. Josh was too sensible to get into trouble and had immediately got a job in a supermarket. Now in his final year, he had never asked his parents for money. Brodie imagined Maisie asking regularly.

The sun came out and her eyes were drawn towards the garden where a scattering of leaves had fallen on the neat lawn. As soon as Colin saw them, he would sweep them up. The garden was his pride and joy, but then so was the house, as were his wife and children. He loved his job as Head of English in a city centre school and appeared to be contented with his lot. She couldn't ever recall him wishing for something that was beyond his reach. He'd recently bought a 1974 Triumph Spitfire that he was looking forward to restoring to its original condition.

Should I look for a job? she asked herself. Until now, she'd been perfectly happy being a full-time wife and mother. Something interesting and part-time. She was fully computer-literate.

There were footsteps on the stairs and Colin came in wearing jeans and a T-shirt. His feet were bare. He looked so young and handsome that it took her breath away. 'Ah, there you are!' he said jovially. 'Is there any tea in that pot?'

Brodie gave the pot a shake. 'Plenty, but you need to fetch a mug.'

9

'I was thinking about getting a job,' she said when he came back. 'A part-time one.'

'Have a rest first, darling,' he advised, as if she'd been toiling away in a wash-house or down a mine for the last twenty years. 'Take it easy, do some shopping, go to lunch with your mum. Use some of the money from the house.' Years ago, when Brodie's mother had moved into a flat, she had given her daughter – her only child – the family home in Blundellsands: Chestnuts. It had been let ever since.

'Tell you what.' Colin clapped his hands. 'Let's go to that café on the way to Southport where they serve slap-up breakfasts. We can leave Mass till afterwards. Oh, and I'd like to drop in my folks this afternoon, see if Mum is still sane after having had Dad home for a whole fortnight.' Colin's obnoxious father had recently retired and his wife, Eileen, had been dreading it. 'Before anything,' Colin concluded, 'I'll just go and sweep those leaves off the lawn.'

Later, Brodie watched him tidy the garden. He was singing, but she couldn't make out the tune. She quite fancied the idea of a second honeymoon. Once she got used to the house without Maisie, life would be perfect. Well, almost perfect. Perfection was perhaps too much to expect.

# Vanessa

### Easter Saturday 2005

Vanessa sat on the settee in her mother's house making a list.

'What are you doing?' Amanda, her sister, asked with a frown.

'Something to do with work,' Vanessa mumbled.

'For Pete's sake, Vannie, it's your wedding day. Nobody *works* on their wedding day.'

'*I* do.' Vanessa turned over a page and continued to write. 'These are the people who will be interviewed tomorrow and Easter Monday.' She worked for Siren Radio, setting up interviews with local dignitaries and any celebrities who might be in Liverpool. It was a job she loved quite passionately.

'But you'll be on your honeymoon from tonight,' Amanda protested. 'Why should you care?'

'This is for Clare Johnson; she'll be at the wedding.' Vanessa finished writing and signed it with a flourish. 'She's taking over my job while I'm away – and I want it done properly.'

Amanda shuddered. 'I'd hate to work for you, sis.'

Vanessa said with mock severity, 'If a job's worth doing, it's worth doing well.'

Their mother came in wearing a smart blue silk suit, the effect entirely ruined by a pair of massive fur slippers with tiger faces. 'You used to say that when you were a child,' she commented. 'I longed to slap your little priggish face, though I never did.' She exchanged smiles with both her daughters.

'I bet you're taking your laptop on your honeymoon,' Amanda said.

'It so happens that I am.' Vanessa couldn't see anything wrong with it. She and William had been living together for three years. Making love wouldn't exactly be a new experience. 'I'm taking the laptop in case I get any ideas and can make a note of them.'

Amanda guffawed. 'I bet William won't want *his* ideas put on a computer.'

Their mother sat down and kicked off the tiger slippers. 'Would someone please help me on with these shoes? They cost seventy-five quid, but they'll probably never be on me feet again after today.'

Vanessa knelt in front of her mother and picked up a blue shoe with an incredibly high heel, the upper part consisting of a few narrow straps. 'You should have bought something more practical, Mam. These are all for show.'

'I liked the look of them,' her mother said stubbornly. 'Even if I never wear them again, at some time in the future, if I'm ever stuck in a wheelchair, I can look at your wedding photos with a magnifying glass and marvel that I'd once been able to wear dead gorgeous shoes like these – I'll ask your dad to take a photo of just me legs. It'll buck me up no end.' The shoes on, she stuck out her feet. 'Don't they look the gear?'

'Great, Mam,' her daughters agreed.

Vanessa wouldn't have dreamed of buying clothes for just one occasion. For her wedding, she wore a simple white crêpe frock with shoestring straps and a matching bolero. Unlike a proper wedding dress, it could be worn afterwards for all sorts of occasions, even work. Instead of a hat – she hated hats – the hairdresser had coiled her long blonde hair into a chignon that was sprinkled with tiny white rosebuds.

Even Amanda, who had argued she should buy a proper wedding dress, had said she looked absolutely fantastic.

'Every inch the bride,' she conceded.

Vanessa folded the list and asked Amanda to keep it in her handbag to give to Clare Johnson at the reception.

'I'll make sure you don't forget, sis,' Amanda promised.

'I'm not likely to forget something as important as *that*.'

Amanda laughed. 'I just thought, you know, with you just having got *married*, you'd have more interesting things on your mind than work.' She looked curiously at her sister. 'Doesn't today have at least a little bit of magic for you?'

'Of course it does,' Vanessa said irritably. 'But in a way, the wedding is a bit of an anti-climax.'

Amanda mouthed, 'An anti-climax' at her mother, and both women rolled their eyes at each other.

Vanessa's mobile rang and William's name showed on the screen. 'Hello, William,' she said in a crisp tone. 'You should have left for the church by now.' He was coming from their flat in Hunt's Cross where he and the best man had spent the night. And why did they have the television on? It was sport of some sort; she could hear the raucous cheering. If he was late for the wedding . . .

'I can't find my cufflinks,' he groaned.

'They're on the bedside cabinet on your side of the bed,' Vanessa snapped. 'I showed you where they were before I left last night.'

'I know you did, but they're not there now.' The sound of the television faded as he walked around the flat. 'Oh! Here they are, where you said. But they're not in the box,' he said accusingly. 'I was looking for the little red box.'

'You're an idiot, William,' she exclaimed. 'Is that all you've got to worry about?'

'Yes, darling.'

'Then I'll see you in church.' Without saying goodbye, she turned the phone off, annoyed. Honestly, sometimes it was like looking after a child. She found most men much the same.

Her mother had got to her feet, wobbling slightly on the too-high heels. 'Poor William,' she said softly.

'What d'you mean, Mam?'

'I don't know.' She shrugged. Vanessa was a lovely girl, but she was too sure of herself by a mile. That was no way to speak to anyone, let alone the man who was about to become your husband. One of these days her daughter would come down to earth with a bump. She just hoped it wouldn't hurt too much.

# Rachel

## Christmas 2005

Rachel and Tyler stared down at the baby they had made, hardly able to believe she was real. There was a Christmas tree in the corner of the ward and tinsel pinned around the door. Five other women were there, all with new babies and all fast asleep.

'She's awesome,' Tyler whispered. 'What shall we call her?' He was tall and skinny and wore large horn-rimmed spectacles that made him look incredibly studious, which indeed he was.

'Poppy,' Rachel replied. 'It's me favourite name.' She was almost as studious, but her studies had been interrupted of late, mainly by arguments with her mother over the expected baby's future.

'Cool,' said Tyler. 'Poppy's cool.'

Poppy, not yet an hour old, waved her arms and blew her first raspberry.

'I think she likes us.' Rachel, nursing her daughter in her arms, gingerly touched her chin as if worried she might break.

Tyler sighed. 'I wish I'd got here earlier.' He'd not long arrived at the hospital.

Rachel looked grim. 'So do I! It didn't half hurt. You could have held me hand or something. Did you manage to get out the house without anyone noticing?'

'Yeah, I kept the mobile under my pillow. When you called, I phoned for a cab, then snuck outside to wait for it.'

He wanted to pick up Rachel and their baby and fly them away to an uninhabited island with golden sands and trees full of exotic fruit. They would live happily ever after in a grass hut by the sea. 'What about you?'

'I did the same,' Rachel told him in her little pale voice. 'It was nearly midnight when I had the first contraction. Me mam was asleep by then. I told the taxi driver number twenty instead of number ten, so he didn't stop outside our house.'

'You should have called me then, honey,' Tyler said.

'Yes, but it might've taken hours and hours for the baby to come and you've got school in the morning.' He was taking his GCSEs in the summer.

'Jeez!' Tyler sighed again. 'It's the last day of term.' He wouldn't tell anyone that he'd become a father overnight, even though he felt inordinately proud. If the news got through to Pop, he'd insist Tyler went back to New York to live with his mother and there'd be one helluva row because Tyler would refuse to go. It was his intention to stay with Rachel and their baby for the rest of his life.

A nurse arrived. 'I think it's about time you two went to sleep,' she said, nodding at the new mother and her child. She half-smiled, half-frowned at Tyler. 'As for you, young man, you'd better get yourself home.' She clearly had no idea what to make of them. The girl claimed to be sixteen, but didn't look it, and at first she'd thought the young man was her brother, but the way he acted with the girl wasn't brotherly in the least.

They'd met, Rachel and Tyler, in Virgin Records in Liverpool, reaching for an Amy Winehouse CD at exactly the same time. Rachel's CD had nearly landed on the floor, but Tyler had managed to catch it just in time.

'My grandpa used to collect old-fashioned records,' he said as he handed her the CD. 'If you dropped one, it'd break into a million pieces.' His voice had started to break and the words were a mixture of high and low notes, which all sounded a bit rusty.

'Honest?' She waved the CD. 'Thanks, anyroad,' she said, 'for catching it.'

They stared at each other for a very long time. She was barely fourteen and he was almost exactly one year older. Rachel couldn't understand the feelings she was having at that particular moment, but suspected they'd come unnaturally early, that they were the sort of feelings people had when they were eighteen or even older. Some people might never have them in their entire lives.

'Would you like a Coke?' Tyler had asked.

'I wouldn't say no.' She couldn't have said 'no' to save her life.

She'd hardly started her periods when they'd stopped and she realized she was pregnant. She told her mother, who danced around the room in her glitzy lime-green shellsuit, screaming and yelling at her to have an abortion.

Rachel refused.

'In that case,' her mother said in her hard-as-nails voice, 'you can have the bloody thing adopted. Don't think you can just go back to school and leave it with me.'

'I've no intention of leaving me baby with you, Mam,' Rachel said haughtily. 'And I'm not going back to school, either. Me and Tyler are getting married as soon as I'm six-teen.'

'Tyler?' her mother spat. 'Is he that bloody Yank you brought round once?'

'That's right.' She'd never brought him again, ashamed of her mother's crude ways and foul mouth.

'It was a Yank who was the undoing of me Auntie Thelma during the war,' her mother snarled. 'As for you, my girl, I've

17

got to sign something, giving you permission like, before you can get married at sixteen.'

'If you won't, then we'll just have to wait till I'm eighteen. Or I could ask me dad to sign whatever-it-is.'

'If you could get a hold of him when he isn't pissed rotten; most of the time he can hardly remember his name.' She sniffed disdainfully, but there was something incredibly sad about it. 'And if you think that chap of yours is going to hang around for another three years, you've got another think coming.' She burst into tears. They were genuine, Rachel could tell, but she couldn't find it in herself to feel sympathetic. Meeting Tyler and having his baby were the best things that had happened in all her life.

'You're the only kid I've had that I've felt proud of,' her mother wailed. 'You were doing so well at school, you said you wanted to be a teacher.' Rachel's two brothers had been in prison for thieving, and her sister was being investigated for benefit fraud.

'I still want to be a teacher,' she insisted. 'Having a baby won't stop me. Five years and him or her will be at school themselves. You still can be proud of me, Mam,' she said awkwardly, but her mother just shrugged, as if she didn't believe it for a minute.

And now Poppy had been born. Rachel glanced longingly at the door through which the nurse had taken her baby daughter. She wanted her back. She wanted to hold the tiny body against her own and never let go. Very soon, she'd have to return home, where Mam was dead set against her keeping the baby. She'd threatened to fetch social workers who would take her away. Rachel knew it happened. She'd read about in the papers and seen it on telly, the way a person in authority could just pluck a baby out of its mother's arms and give it to someone else.

She dreaded the future. Just thinking about it made her

feel physically sick. Even though Tyler had plenty of money, they wouldn't be allowed to set up house together. Rachel slid under the bedclothes and began to cry.

*March–April 2006*

# Chapter 1

Diana stood with her back against the door, arms outspread, as if she were glued to it, worried that if she took another step it would be a sign of her commitment to live there. The room was big and square with tall, floor-length windows. Outside, the sun shone so brightly that everywhere was drenched in a bright golden light, revealing the high ornamental ceiling to be badly in need of a good clean, as well as a coat of emulsion. The furniture was covered with fine dust.

There was an old-fashioned wardrobe and chest of drawers to match, a single bed, a piano, a table and two chairs, and two mainly beige tapestry armchairs. The carpet was pale brown with a border of over-blown roses. It was a pleasant, comfortable room. If one of her brothers had chosen to live there – Jason often spoke about getting his own place – she would have thoroughly approved.

But did she want it for herself?

Over the years, Diana had envisaged all sorts of terrible things happening in the world that would destroy life as she knew it; bird flu, terrorism, weapons of mass destruction, global warming, the central heating boiler exploding, killing them all, that's if escaping gas hadn't done it first. It wasn't for herself that she was worried, but for her brothers.

Since the day her mother had left seven years ago to live with Warren, Diana had devoted herself completely to the care of Damian, Jason and Garth. People told her that she was silly, that it was time she had a life of her own, found a boyfriend, thought about marriage.

Diana ignored them. All she wanted was to look after the lads until they were old enough to look after themselves. One of these days they would leave home, get married, start families, and she would be left alone in the little terraced house in Coral Street, Bootle, where the four O'Sullivan children had been born. It was only then, with her brothers gone and hopefully happy, that she would start to think about herself, about getting married to someone really nice and having three boys of her own.

This vision of the future suited her perfectly. Apart from the ever-present worry over bird flu and terrorism and other horrors, Diana had been extremely happy with her life.

There was one horror, though, that had never remotely crossed her mind – and that was of becoming homeless, of having to leave the house in Coral Street because *she wasn't needed any more*. Since last Christmas, when Emma had moved in, Diana had become surplus to requirements.

She took a tentative step into the room. She tried to imagine sleeping there rather than in the box room into which she'd felt obliged to move so that Damian and Emma could have the middle bedroom with the double bed. There was nowhere in the box room to keep her clothes, and she had to remember to get next day's outfit out of the wardrobe in what was now Damian and Emma's room before she went to bed. Nor was there space for the portable television that she'd watched when she woke up early, unless she wanted to put it on the floor or perch it on her feet.

There was plenty of space in this room for one of those giant plasma screens – not that she wanted one – as well as all her clothes and other possessions, but she wouldn't be able to hear Garth giving a commentary on a football match in his sleep while Jason turned restlessly in his. Could she bear it? On the other hand, she wouldn't hear what Damian and

Emma got up to in Mam's old bed, the bed that had been Diana's for the last seven years. It wasn't that she disapproved, but she found it a bit distracting.

She took another step into the room. The cream curtains could do with a good wash – a ladder would be necessary to get them down. She'd need bedding and towels. How would she get everything, a duvet included, out of Coral Street without anyone noticing? She didn't want them to know she was going until she'd gone in case they tried to talk her into staying. If they succeeded things would only continue in the same unsatisfactory way.

She sat on the bed. It had an old-fashioned spring that creaked a bit, but was very comfortable. Next, she tried one of the tapestry armchairs. The arms were wide and well padded, ideal for draping her legs over while she read or watched television.

A movement in the garden caught her eye and she gasped at the sight of a squirrel racing along the branches of a tree. She watched entranced as another squirrel sat on the grass and chewed something held in its paws. The scene was like an illustration out of a children's book.

The house was the last at the end of a short cul-de-sac not far from Blundellsands Station – the railway track was hidden behind a grassy bank about thirty metres away. At that very minute, a train passed along the lines and the house vibrated slightly until it had gone.

The squirrels had gone, too, disappearing into the leaves or the long untidy grass. The house had been built well back from the road and was hidden behind a row of old trees – she could tell they were old because of the size of the trunks. At first, she'd thought it was someone's garden and the man in the paint shop had made a mistake when he'd told her where the place was. It wasn't until she glimpsed the windows glinting through the branches, the creamy bricks, and the faded lilac front door with the name 'Chestnuts' in dull brass letters, that she realized there was a house. It was charming and slightly mysterious, she thought as she'd opened the gate and walked down the brick path, as if it belonged in another place, or another time, even another country, like the American deep South. It would be an unusual spot in which to live. She could lie in bed, watch the squirrels and see the trees change colour as the months passed by.

Oh, but she didn't want to live here! She rested her forehead on the cool window and closed her eyes. She'd sooner stay in Coral Street any day where squirrels were unknown and she couldn't recall the whereabouts of the nearest tree. She remembered Mam had shown an unexpected fondness for trees when she'd gone to live in Melling Village with Warren; perhaps it ran in the family.

What was she going to *do*? She was trying to unravel her tangled thoughts when the front door opened and someone came in.

Diana went into the square hallway, which was about as big as the main room of the house in Coral Street. The patterns on the stained-glass windows on each side of the door were smudgily reflected on the black-and-white tiled floor. A woman of about forty had entered. She had neat brown hair and a kind face. She jumped when she saw Diana. 'I didn't know anyone was here,' she gasped.

'The man in the paint shop gave me the key and said I was the first person to see the house,' Diana explained. 'He had a card in the window and he said I could pick any room I liked.'

'The man in the paint shop?' The woman looked puzzled. Then her expression cleared. 'Oh, you mean Leonard; he sells artists' materials. He wasn't supposed to put a card in his window yet. I'm having a new kitchen installed and the plumbing needs a good seeing-to. Everywhere wants a thorough clean before it can be let. Didn't he tell you that?'

'No.' This rather disappointing news only made Diana

26

change her mind; she *did* want to live in Chestnuts. She might well be unhappy there, but she couldn't possibly be unhappier than she'd been over the last few months. 'When will it be ready?'

'In about a fortnight or so.' She looked anxiously at Diana. 'I hope you're not desperate. Have you got somewhere to live in the meantime?'

'Oh, yes.' Diana sighed. 'Will you be living here, too?' The woman seemed exceptionally nice and her presence would make the move from the only home she'd ever known more bearable.

'I'm not sure.' The woman went into the room that Diana had just vacated. 'I'd forgotten how high the ceilings were.'

Diana followed. 'Have you been here before?'

'It's my house,' the woman said surprisingly. 'My mother gave it to me.' She tugged at a cream curtain and it gave off a cloud of dust. 'These need sending to the cleaners,' she muttered. She turned to Diana. 'My name is Brodie Logan, by the way.'

'I'm Diana O'Sullivan. Your mother gave you a *house*?'

'Ages and ages ago, yes. It was let fully furnished on a twenty-five-year lease to the Slattery sisters. There were four of them, all in their fifties. The lease ran out last month. By then, three of the sisters had died and the one who was left went in a home. Saturday was the first time I've been here since I got married and, do you know, hardly a thing has changed.' She touched the lid of the piano. 'I wonder if this needs tuning? My mother let me have it so I would avoid Inheritance Tax when she died — the house that is. The Slatterys left the piano behind.'

'Really.' Diana had never heard of Inheritance Tax. There was no one in the world likely to leave her a rabbit hutch, let alone a lovely big house. Before he went away, her dad had bought the house in Coral Street, but there was still a mortgage to be paid.

27

'I was born in this house and lived here until I got married.'

'Why didn't you stay here?' Diana asked.

'Because my husband and I already had another house, and Mum had bought herself a flat down by the river. She's a widow; my father died not long after I was born.' Brodie opened one of the windows and stepped outside, Diana trailing behind. Everywhere smelled earthy and fresh, as if they were in the depths of the countryside. 'I used to play out here when I was little,' Brodie went on. 'I loved it. The trains didn't bother me and I used to chase the squirrels, hoping I would catch one. I imagined dressing it up in dolls' clothes and taking it to bed with me.' She smiled and dimples appeared in both cheeks. Close up, she was very pretty with a little turned-up nose and full lips. She wore a dark green corduroy suit with a flowered blouse underneath.

'I saw two squirrels earlier,' Diana informed her.

'Mum used to buy them nuts and seed for the birds, then sit just inside the window and watch.' Diana resolved to do the same as soon as she could. 'Would you like a drink?' Brodie asked. 'I've just been to Sainsbury's for the groceries so there's milk, coffee and tea in the car.'

'I'd love a cup of tea, ta.'

'Let's hope we can find mugs and a kettle in the kitchen.' They went back into the house. Brodie told Diana where the kitchen was, and went to collect her shopping from the car.

The kitchen was surprisingly small. It was ridiculous, Diana thought, for such an important room to be a quarter of the size of the hall. It was also very old-fashioned, with a chipped enamel sink, a series of run-down cupboards, an ancient fridge, and what looked like the first microwave ever made. The marble-patterned linoleum had been completely worn away in places to reveal a crumbling concrete floor. There was no sign of a washing machine or tumble dryer.

She thought of the kitchen in Coral Street. It was actually bigger than this, though not by much. Since her mother left,

Diana had gradually modernized it, buying appliances on hire purchase, having units fitted and some very superior linoleum laid, painting the walls rose-pink – she'd done them herself – while the lads had helped with the tiling. Her heart lifted with pleasure every time she went in and saw everything glittering and gleaming, particularly when she switched on the light.

But now the kitchen was out of bounds, taken over by Emma, making Diana feel as if she were no use at all.

The thought of being reduced to using this stone age kitchen after the lovely one she'd created for herself, the sheer misery of life since Christmas, made worse by the fact she'd lost her job on top of everything else, was enough to make her burst into tears, which she promptly did. Tears that had been threatening to fall on numerous occasions, but had remained unshed, gushed forth, streaming down Diana's pale cheeks and landing in miniature puddles on her boots and on the floor.

'Oh, my dear girl! What on earth's the matter?' Brodie cried when she came in with the groceries.

'Everything's the matter,' Diana sobbed. '*Everything.*'

'Let's sit down and you can tell me all about it.' Although they'd only just met, Brodie could see that Diana O'Sullivan was a very unhappy young woman. It was obvious from the eyes that never lit up, the turned-down mouth, and the fact that she seemed to have lost the knack of smiling. She wondered if her own eyes and face sent out a similar message to the world.

'It's Emma,' Diana said in a cracked voice when they were seated on the tapestry armchairs. 'She's our Damian's girl-friend; she's expecting a baby in August. They're not getting married until afterwards so she can wear a dead glamorous wedding dress. She moved in at Christmas and she doesn't go to work, so she does all the things I used to do: the cooking, the washing and ironing, the cleaning. The only thing she doesn't do is darn socks; instead, she just throws them away and buys new ones. I used to love darning socks, but nowadays I can't find any.'

'I don't understand, dear,' Brodie said gently. 'Who is Damian?'

'Me brother,' Diana wept. 'He's twenty-three and the oldest. Jason's twenty, and our Garth is seventeen and still at school.' Now the tears were dripping on her knees rather than her feet. She produced a handkerchief from her sleeve and began to mop her eyes. 'When Mam left, she asked me to look after them. And I did. But now when I get home from work, instead of me making the tea, Emma's already made it. She insists on washing and drying the dishes an' all, so there's absolutely nothing for me to do. She even does my washing as well as the lads', though I've asked her not to.' The tears were replaced with indignation. 'And she irons *everything*: tea towels, pillow cases, hankies, even underpants. Me, I didn't have the time.'

'Of course you didn't, dear.' Brodie had loads of time, but wouldn't have dreamed of ironing underpants.

'She won't let me do *anything*,' Diana wailed. 'If I get up to go into the kitchen, she gets there before me and wants to know what I want. But it's *my* kitchen.' She wrung her hands and looked at Brodie with bloodshot eyes. 'And I don't know where to *sit*. The downstairs rooms have been knocked into one, so if Jason and Garth go out, I feel in the way. But I can't go upstairs because I sleep in the box room where it's as miserable as sin and there's no room for a telly or even a chair. Where can I go?' she asked tragically.

'Out?' Brodie suggested. 'Couldn't you go out? Haven't you got friends?'

'All the friends I had at school are married. Anyroad, I was too busy with the lads and the house to make friends; there was always something to do.'

Brodie gathered together her nicest smile. 'Have you tried having a word with Emma?'

'I've tried, but she won't listen. The thing is . . .'

'What?' Brodie prompted when there was a long pause.

'She's *lovely*,' Diana said despairingly. 'She only wants to help. She thinks I like being waited on hand and foot. "Sit down, Di, and take the weight off your feet," she'll say the minute I come in. She even does the shopping.' She got up and began to wander around the room. 'That's why, when I saw the card in that shop window, I thought I'd come and have a look. The rent is awful cheap.'

'That's because I'm not interested in making a profit. I thought I'd let the rooms for a year or so while I decide what to do with the place; keep it as an investment, or sell it and put the money in the bank.'

'Really?' Diana seemed bemused. Brodie reckoned property and investments were way beyond the world as she knew it.

Her outburst appeared to be over. Brodie patted her hand. 'You sit there, dear, while I make some tea.'

'Thank you, Brodie . . . isn't Brodie a man's name?'

'It's Irish and can be a man or a woman's. Do you take milk and sugar?'

'Just milk, thank you. I was called after Princess Diana. She married Prince Charles on the day I was born.'

'Diana is a lovely name – it suits you.' Brodie left for the kitchen. She let the water run for a while before filling the kettle. She found two mugs in the cupboard under the sink, washed them and put a teabag in each. Diana, poor girl, was out of her depth. She wondered if Emma was really as harmless as she made out, or a very clever young woman who was intent on appropriating the house for herself? Maybe she was surreptitiously trying to edge Diana out – successfully, it would seem.

The kettle boiled, she made the tea, and took it into the room that her mother had called 'the parlour'. Brodie had always thought the light shone through the windows with a slightly greenish tinge as a result of the sun being filtered through the leaves. Diana was sitting staring into space. 'Here you are, dear.'

'Ta.' The girl came to with a jolt and leaned forward to take the cup in her long white fingers. She wore an outfit that Brodie guessed came from a charity shop; a badly knitted orange sweater, a grey pencil skirt, and black ankle boots with wedge heels. On Diana, they acquired a sort of elegance. Although the girl's movements were jerky, they had a youthful grace. Everything about her was long and thin; her face, body, arms and legs. Her blue eyes were the most innocent and trusting that she'd ever seen on anyone apart from a child – they were the colour of bluebells. She might well look and act like a teenager, but must be older if she'd been taking care of her brothers for such a long time. Was the mother still around? she wondered. She felt angry, not only with the mother, but with Emma, too, for treating this incredibly nice young woman so uncaringly.

'Where do you work?' she asked.

'In a call centre till last week, when it closed down and moved to India,' Diana said disapprovingly. 'They pay the staff much less over there. That's the reason why I'm not at work on a Monday. I'm starting another job next week in a refugee centre off Cazneau Street. I'm really looking forward to it.'

Brodie carried her mug to the window and looked out on the garden where she'd played as a child. 'Do you think you'd like living here, Diana?' she asked.

The girl sighed. 'I couldn't dislike it more than where I am now. That sounds awful because I love me brothers more than anything in the world, but it's not the same any more.' She came and stood next to the older woman, almost half a head taller. 'It's so pretty here. In Coral Street, the window in the box room where I sleep looks out on to the box room next door.' For the first time, she smiled, though rather sadly.

'At least I'll be at peace. Oh, that makes me sound as if I want to die!' She ran her fingers through the thick brown hair that flew all over the place. 'It's just that at home I feel in turmoil, as if there's a war raging in me stomach.'

'I always loved it here,' Brodie told her.

'It's very nice. Trouble is, I keep changing me mind. Right now, it seems a really good idea to move; five minutes ago, I hated the thought. It was the kitchen that put me off,' she said, adding tactlessly, 'It's really horrible.'

'As I told you, there's going to be a new kitchen. The builders are starting on it tomorrow.'

Diana looked doubtful. 'There isn't room for a washing machine or a tumble-dryer.'

'They're at the back. Look, shall I show you around?' Brodie offered. 'The room next to this is exactly the same and there are two identical rooms directly above. They're the only ones I shall let. There are some much smaller rooms that can be used for storage and a bathroom big enough to hold a dance in. There's a lavatory downstairs as well as up. Come on, I'll show you the laundry room. It's a bit depressing out there, but I'm having it decorated – nearly everywhere is getting a fresh coat of paint.'

The laundry room was fitted with a washing machine and a tumble-dryer, both relatively modern, an ironing board and a clothes maiden on which hung three stockings, none of which matched. The walls were the colour of mud and at least half the paint was flaking off.

Next to it was a conservatory with a glass roof and windows on three sides, mostly covered with untidy tendrils of ivy. It contained an old cane three-piece, with faded flowered cushions, and a small round table. Brodie said it was where her father had smoked his pipe. 'In summer, it gets unbearably hot, but it's as cold as a fridge in winter. My dad actually sat on that very same settee, on the very same cushions.' She touched the cushions and looked at Diana, wide-eyed. 'Gosh, that feels awfully strange. I can't remember anything about him.'

Diana touched the cushions and said it felt strange to her, too. 'What's that?' She pointed to an orange splodge on top of the glass roof.

Brodie laughed. 'That's a ginger cat. I reckon he's a male because he's so huge. I don't know what his name is or which house he belongs to. He was there when I came on Saturday.'

They went upstairs. Brodie asked Diana if she would prefer to live in one of the first-floor rooms, but she said she'd already got used to the downstairs one. 'And I like the idea of having a piano.'

'Can you play?' She had long hands, perfect for a pianist.

'No, but I can read music a bit – they taught us at school – and I wouldn't mind trying to play with one finger. Will you let me know when the decorators are finished so I can move in? I wish it could have been today,' she said wistfully. 'I don't know what to do with meself at home with Emma there. That's why I was wandering around Waterloo. I'd walked all the way from Bootle.'

'We'll make it today if you like.' It was odd, she'd only known the girl five minutes, but Brodie already felt quite fond of her. Since her own children had left home, she'd missed having young people in her life. Josh, twenty-two, had finished university with an average degree and had moved to London. He now lived in a squat off the Holloway Road. She'd sooner not think about Maisie just now. 'If you don't mind the mess,' she said to Diana, 'you can stay in one of the other rooms while yours is being done up – I'll ask the builders to start on it first. Mind you, there might not always be electricity and there'll be quite a lot of noise, so you're not likely to get much peace.'

'Move in today!' Diana looked quite thrilled at the idea and smiled properly for the first time. 'I'd love to move in today.'

'Will you be bringing your things in a car? There's plenty of room in the road to park.'

When the girl said she didn't have a car and couldn't drive anyway, Brodie offered to collect her and her possessions there and then and bring them to the house. 'We'll go now, if you like.'

'Now would be the gear. Afternoons, Emma usually goes to see her sister in Walton Vale and she's out until about three o'clock. I don't want anyone to know I'm leaving, but I'll write a note telling them where I am.'

It took hardly any time for Diana to throw her clothes into a few plastic bags and stuff the bedding in another. Her few bits of jewellery and make-up had of late been downgraded from the top of her mother's dressing table to a drawer in the sideboard. She emptied everything into a smaller bag. She decided to leave her books behind – she could always borrow some from the library – but she'd take her CDs and the CD player, plus the portable television and the DVD player that were now in Damian and Emma's bedroom. They never watched either, having more important things to do in bed.

She didn't feel as sad as she'd expected as she went round the house a final time, though when she went into the big bedroom where Jason and Garth slept, she tenderly stroked their pillows and hoped they wouldn't miss her too much. She said as much in the note she wrote and tucked behind the clock. She put that she didn't want anyone to think she was going away because she was unhappy, but perhaps her presence was no longer necessary now that Emma was there to look after them. She finished: 'My address is Chestnuts, Elm Road, Blundellsands. Come and see me whenever you want. Di.'

On the way back, Brodie asked for her mobile number. 'I'll give you mine in case we need to contact each other for some reason.'

'I haven't got a mobile,' Diana told her. 'I kept meaning to buy one, but never seemed to get round to it.'

'I see you haven't brought a computer with you.'

'We only had the one and the lads would be gutted if I'd taken it. Anyroad, all I did was play card games. I never learned to use it properly.'

'Well, there's a phone in Chestnuts; it's in the hall and it's still connected. I can ring there if necessary.'

'That's fine,' Diana said sunnily. She seemed different now, much happier. 'Have you got children, Brodie?'

'Two, Joseph – he's called Josh – and Maisie. They're both grown up and live in London.'

Well, Maisie was still in London the last time they'd heard from her, but Brodie had no idea where she might be now.

What a refreshing young woman; she belonged not just in the last century, but the one before, Brodie thought as she drove to Crosby after helping Diana unload her belongings in Chestnuts.

She drove rather faster than she should, having forgotten about the groceries in the boot. By now the frozen stuff would be frozen no more.

Before they'd parted, Diana had asked if it really was her intention to move in. 'Earlier, when I asked, you said you weren't sure.'

'I'm still not sure. I'm like you; things are happening at home that are beyond my control. I'm very unhappy a lot of the time.'

'I'm sorry,' Diana said sincerely. 'I hope you don't think I'm awful for wanting you to come, but I can't help it. It would be the gear if you were living in the room next to mine.'

I'll see what happens over the next few days, Brodie decided as she carried bags of food into the house. She knew you weren't supposed to put food that had melted back in the freezer, but she put it there all the same; it was unlikely to kill anyone.

Emma had been back in the house in Coral Street for more than an hour before she noticed the note behind the clock. When she read it, she couldn't resist a little smile of triumph.

Since before she'd even moved into the house, Damian had been quite firm about her stay being temporary. 'Our Di won't mind you being there, but it can only be until the baby's born and then we'll have to look for a place of our own.'

That had seemed a bit unfair, Emma thought. Di was a single woman, while she was almost married and expecting a baby. If anyone should look for a place of their own, it should be Diana. She hadn't told Damian how she felt; he and his brothers thought the world of their sister and wouldn't hear a word said against her.

So Emma began a campaign to make herself indispensable. She kept the house spotless, did the laundry every day, and made large, nourishing meals – she'd been good at Cookery at school, though it had seemed a waste of time when it was so much easier to open a tin or a packet. Garth had slightly broken ranks and said he didn't know what they'd do without her when she and Damian left. 'Our Di never made such nice food – and she didn't always make the beds, either,' he said.

At this, Damian had nearly bitten his head off. 'Di was out at work all day, that's why,' he snapped. 'And she only didn't always make the beds because some of us were still in them when she left for work. She looked after us when we were all at school,' he told Emma.

At this, Garth had blushed and said he was sorry. Emma realized she would have to tread carefully if she wanted to get rid of Di.

She could tell from the hurt in Di's big blue eyes that she missed taking care of her brothers, so did her utmost to make her feel worse. It was a really horrible thing to do, because she liked Di very much, but the world was a horrible place and you had to put yourself first. If nice people like Di got trampled on in the process, then it was just too bad. A different woman would have told Emma to eff off, but Di was too soft and gentle.

Emma took the note from behind the clock and screwed it into a ball. The longer their sister was away, the more the lads would realize it was possible to live without her. Otherwise, once they knew where she'd gone, they'd be round to this Blundellsands place pleading with her to come back.

But she was bound to turn up one day and swear she'd left a note behind the clock and Emma would be suspected of having removed it. Best keep it and put it in a place like . . . like . . . underneath the fridge! If it ever came to light, everyone would assume it had fallen there accidentally. She smoothed the paper out, took it into the kitchen, and slid it into its hiding place.

She stood in the middle of the room and thought how much she admired it. She loved the way the lights went on underneath the wall cupboards, the frilly lace blind on the window, and the little corner shelves that each held a red wine glass. Damian said Di had got them from Argos and they were called goblets: 'At Christmas, she puts them on the table with nightlights in. They look dead pretty.'

Emma's sister, Sophie, had two kids and lived in a crappy flat in Walton Vale. The cooker in the shared kitchen looked as if it came out of the ark and the washing machine only worked when it felt like it. It was useless trying to get the landlord to do anything about it. Sophie was in and out of the launderette like a yo-yo – and it cost the earth.

Damian would never let Emma and his own kid live in such a dump, but whatever sort of place he found it wouldn't have a kitchen like this. She ran her hand along the mottled cream top. Most women would die for such a kitchen.

'Our Di's late,' Jason remarked that night when they sat down to eat.

'Perhaps she's stayed behind at work for something,' Emma suggested.

'She never has before.' Damian didn't look too concerned, but by the time the meal was over and Di still hadn't appeared he was obviously worried. 'She would have rung if she'd been held up for some reason.'

An hour later, there was still no sign. Jason went upstairs to play on the computer and came down almost straight away his face as white as a sheet. 'The door to the box room's open and the things have gone off our Di's bed.'

'What?' Damian went upstairs to check for himself. He returned saying he'd looked in the wardrobe and Di's clothes had disappeared, too. 'What's the number of that place where she works?'

'It's seven o'clock, it'll be closed,' Garth said.

'It's a call centre, idiot. It's open till midnight.' Damian picked up the telephone book that Di had filled in with her incredibly neat writing and dialled the number. It was answered immediately. 'I see . . . yeah . . . OK, mate, ta.' He rang off and looked seriously at his brothers. 'That was a guy from British Telecom. The call centre closed last week and they're taking out the lines. Why didn't our Di tell us she was leaving?' he demanded angrily.

'She did,' Jason said. He was the shyest and quietest of the lads. 'But no one took any notice, only me. She got another job somewhere in town.'

'Somewhere in town!' Damian sneered. 'That's a great help.'

Jason shrugged. 'You didn't even know that much. Any-road, our Di wouldn't go anywhere without leaving a note. When she's had to leave a note before, she always puts it behind the clock on the mantelpiece.'

A hunt began for Di's note. It was clearly not behind the clock, so Jason started to look under the furniture, 'Just in case it got carried there in a draught.' The other lads went upstairs to look. Emma got a really horrible sickly feeling in her stomach and her heart began to thump unnaturally fast. What if Jason looked under the fridge? It was a daft place to have put the stupid note. She would have gone into the kitchen and eaten it if Damian hadn't come charging downstairs and got there before her.

'I thought she might have stuck something on the fridge with a magnet,' he said, but fortunately he didn't look underneath.

In Coral Street, you never felt on your own. The lads might be out, but next door's kids would be playing in the yard, televisions blaring in the houses either side, the man behind using his electric saw, cars and motorbikes revving, voices raised. There was noise everywhere.

In Chestnuts it was as silent as the grave, yet Diana didn't mind. It was the first time in her life that she'd been completely by herself, without another human being close at hand and a sound of some sort or another in the background. Inside the house, the trains could be more felt than heard – a slight vibration underneath her feet. As Elm Road was a cul-de-sac trains were the only passing traffic. She wandered from room to room, hoping the decorators wouldn't paint over the faded wallpaper that had a lovely satin finish, that they'd just clean, not replace, the even more faded carpets, and that none of the old-fashioned furniture would be taken away.

She really admired the tall lamps with fringed shades, the big, dark wardrobes and chests of drawers as high as herself. The piano was mottled grey and black and the keys deep cream, Diana played a few notes and the sound echoed through the old house.

Kitchens apart, Diana liked old things; not just houses, but films, music, books. She'd lost count of the times she'd watched *It's a Wonderful Life* and *This Happy Breed* on DVD. The Kaiser Chiefs and Arctic Monkeys' CDs rubbed shoulders with those of Al Bowlly and Rudy Vallee, and the novels of Jane Austen mingled with Maeve Binchy's on the bookshelf in the lounge in Coral Street.

She loved this house with its 1930s aura of tea parties and sing-songs around the piano. In the summer, the windows would have been left open for people to wander in and out. Children, who would now be much older than Brodie was now, would have played underneath the trees.

Diana had no illusions that she would have been one of these people. Until recently, what was left of Mam's family had lived for at least a century in the area of Coral Street in Bootle, and her dad was working-class Irish. Had she had any connection with Chestnuts, it would have been as a servant. She would have been slaving away in that disgusting kitchen, not wandering in and out of windows.

It gave her a sense of satisfaction that *her* kitchen was superior to the kitchen here. It just showed how much the world had changed for the better over the last hundred years, forgetting about weapons of mass destruction and other such stuff, that is.

At around sixish, she heated up the Marks & Spencer's cottage pie that Brodie had given her on discovering she'd forgotten to bring food, ate the trifle from the same source, and made a cup of coffee. She ate in the room next to the one that she intended to occupy once it was decorated, plugged in the television and watched the news followed by a holiday programme, followed by *EastEnders*.

Not long afterwards, feeling sleepy, she ventured out to get washed, but decided to leave it until morning because everywhere was a bit scary in the fading light. There were disquieting creaking noises coming from places unseen, and dark shadows flitted across the top of the stairs. It was possible that three of the Slattery sisters had died on the premises, as well as other people whose names she didn't know.

She used the downstairs toilet, then bolted the door of her room and splashed her face in the little corner sink. She went to bed and fell asleep almost straight away. It did cross her mind that her brothers hadn't been to see her, but no doubt they'd come tomorrow.

## Chapter 2

'Coo-ee! Diana, are you up, darlin'? It's only me, Megan. I'm just about to put the kettle on.'

It didn't take long for Diana to remember where she was, but she couldn't for the life of her imagine why a woman called Megan who spoke with a half-Liverpool and half-Irish accent was calling to her from the other side of the door. She supposed she'd better get up and find out. 'I'm getting dressed,' she shouted as she struggled into the clothes she'd had on the day before.

'Do you take sugar, darlin'?' the mysterious Megan wanted to know.

'No, ta.' Diana pulled back the heavy curtains and daylight seemed to tumble into the room. Only a patch of the garden was in sunlight. Birds were perched in an orderly row on the roof of an old shed that she hadn't noticed yesterday.

'That's good, because there isn't any.'

Megan had sounded like a young woman, but turned out to be an old one, Diana found when she went into the kitchen where the kettle had just begun to boil.

'Do you think there's ever been a more convenient invention than teabags — in the line of food, that is?' the woman asked. She looked slim and fit and full of energy. Her short, cropped hair was the most beautiful silver, and eyes the same blue as Brodie's twinkled in her heavily creased face. Of course, this must be Brodie's mother, the one who'd given her the house. She must have had her late in life because she looked almost old enough to be her grandma. She was dressed smartly in a long red skirt with a fluted hem and a black sweater with red piping and, like Brodie, was much shorter than Diana.

'Loads of things, I expect,' Diana replied. 'Sliced bread?' Was she supposed to address the woman as 'Megan'?

'Yes, you're right, of course. Then there's frozen chips and you can buy pastry already made. I always loathed making pastry, the way it got stuck under my fingernails. Have I asked if you take sugar?'

'Yes, and I said I didn't, and then you said that was good because you didn't have any.'

'Did you? Did I? My memory's like a sieve,' she said, rolling her eyes. 'Please, God, don't let me get Alzheimer's.' She picked up the mugs of tea. 'Shall we drink these in the garden? It's quite summery out there considering we're still in March. Later, perhaps you can help me take everything out of the kitchen before the builders smash the place to pieces.'

Diana promised that she would. She followed the woman through the conservatory into a sunlit part of the garden. An iron table with four matching chairs and a sturdy wooden bench had been placed beneath a huge spreading tree with leaves like plates. Dew dripped from the trees and sparkled like little diamonds on the grass. Diana shivered. It might look summery, but it felt quite chilly, and she could feel the dampness of the bench through her skirt. 'What time is it?' she asked.

'Quarter to eight, darlin'. I can never stay in bed once the sun's out.'

'Do you live far?'

'Burbo Bank Road.' Diana had never heard of it and was no wiser. 'It's no distance away. I have a flat with a view over the river. Oh, and call me Megan.' She squeezed Diana's knee with a thin, bony hand. 'Megan Sylvester.'

'Megan,' Diana said experimentally. It was a name she'd never used before. She'd never sat in a garden that was like a little wood before, either. Although she felt cold, she didn't mind. There was something very new about it, almost daring. Even the tea tasted different. She wriggled her shoulders happily. A giant cat, half-ginger, half-white, strolled into the garden looking as if it owned the place. It completely ignored them and stretched out on the grass in front of the shed and began to thoughtfully study the birds. Diana remembered the orange splodge on the conservatory roof. The cat obviously liked it here.

'The workmen will be here at eight to start on the house,' Megan informed her. 'Brodie can't make up her mind what colour to have the kitchen done. She's having new units fitted, light oak, but she hasn't ordered the tiles yet or paint for the walls.'

'Will there be a new fridge?' Diana asked.

'Oh, definitely. She's got one on order. It's half-fridge, half-freezer. And there'll be a new cooker, too, one with a ceramic hob. It looks very easy to keep clean.'

Diana nodded her approval. She knew all about cookers with ceramic hobs, having bought one for the kitchen in Coral Street.

There was a rustling sound above them. When Diana looked, two squirrels were racing along one of the branches. They dropped to the ground, paused for a moment, as if to establish their whereabouts, then, quick as a flash, shot up another tree and disappeared into the leaves.

'Oh!' Diana breathed, enthralled. 'Aren't they lovely?'

'They look nice, but they're greedy little buggers,' Megan said disdainfully. 'Mind you, I used to feed them daily when I lived here. You know, darlin',' she gave Diana's knee another squeeze, 'our Brodie called last night and told me all about you. We both wondered what had happened to your mother?'

'She lives in Nottingham with her second husband, Warren. We don't see them all that often. They've got two little boys.' Diana had sometimes imagined she'd end up looking after them, too. She wouldn't have minded.

Brodie was wondering whether to put on jeans and a sweatshirt or something pretty. She intended driving over to Chestnuts soon and everywhere would be in a state if the workmen had arrived, but it was they, not her, who'd be doing the cleaning and decorating. She would keep well out of the way.

Good! She'd never liked jeans. She reached in the wardrobe for a black-and-white check frock with buttons down the front and laid it carefully on the bed, took clean underwear and tights out of the drawer, chose which earrings to wear, then went into the shower.

As usual, Colin had thrown the towel in the bath after his own shower and it lay in a damp heap. Brodie retrieved it, put it in the laundry basket, and took another out of the airing cupboard.

She thought about Colin while she stood under the warm spray and wondered if their marriage would ever return to its former happy state. She remembered the passion at the start, the wonder and excitement when the children were born, the mutual contentment of the years in between then and now; they'd been harmonious years.

Climbing out of the shower, she dried herself roughly, rubbing the skin until it hurt. It was unlikely to recover, the marriage. They differed so widely over one, crucially important thing – the first real crisis in their lives. From now on, no matter what might happen, no matter how bad it might be, she couldn't rely on Colin to feel the same as she did about anything. In his misery, he'd turned his back on her. He preferred to be with his odious father, who told silly jokes and treated him like a teenager.

She was about to hang the towel behind the bathroom door when the telephone rang. She draped the towel modestly around her small, shapely body, even though she was alone in the house, and hurried into the bedroom where she picked up the extension. Her heart had begun to beat slightly faster.

'Hello, Mum. How's things?'

'The same as ever, love.' She sank on to the bed and put her hand over her heart, as if trying to make it slow down. She was bitterly disappointed it was Josh, though she loved her son with all her heart. The trouble was she was always expecting a call from someone else.

'Is it OK if I come home this weekend with this guy, Murdoch? His dad's crazy about old cars and Murd would like to take some photos of the Triumph to send him.'

'Of course it's OK.' She longed to see him. 'Will you be staying overnight?'

'Over two nights, if you don't mind, Mum.'

'This is still your home, Josh,' she told him warmly, 'and you know you can always bring your friends.' She would enjoy buying groceries for them both. 'Is Murdoch his first name or his surname?'

'Dunno,' Josh said vaguely. 'He's a Scot,' he added, as if this explained everything.

Brodie established that Murdoch wasn't a vegetarian or on a strange diet that required special food and that he wasn't averse to wine. Josh asked after his father. She told him about Chestnuts and Diana: 'I'm going over there shortly to see how she is. The workmen are coming today to start on the kitchen.'

Josh said he'd like to have a look at the house that weekend. Until now he had only seen it from the outside.

'How's the latest business?' Brodie enquired. He must have told her what it was, but she couldn't remember. Josh, a budding and so far unsuccessful entrepreneur, was doing his

47

utmost to make his living without actually going to work in a conventional job. He had started numerous small businesses that had so far failed.

'I've been selling books on ebay,' he told her. 'I'm not doing so badly, but I don't make nearly enough to live on.'

'You will one day.' Brodie tried to sound encouraging. She just wished her son would get an ordinary job like the sons of all the other women she knew.

'Has there been any news of Maisie?' Josh asked finally. Brodie could tell from the tone of his voice that he'd been saving the question until last because he was afraid of the answer, which could only be bad, as his mother would have told him straight away had it been otherwise.

'There's been no news at all,' she said.

Not long afterwards, Josh rang off.

Still wearing the towel, she went into Maisie's room and stood at the window overlooking the back garden. The house in Crosby had just been built when they'd moved in, the garden merely a patch of red earth. Now it was a sea of green, the small trees and bushes ripe and swollen as if they couldn't wait to burst into bloom. The grass looked ready to be cut for the first time this year.

The children's slide and climbing frame had been given away a long time ago, but the swing was still there. Maisie had insisted they keep it. She liked to sit in the dark, swinging gently, musing about life and things in general, she told Brodie whenever she asked. 'I plan my future there,' she said once.

Brodie gasped. She put her fist to her mouth and bit her knuckles. Maisie couldn't possibly have planned what had actually happened. She threw herself face down on the narrow bed with its buttercup yellow cover and began to cry.

*My twenty-year-old daughter is a drug addict. I don't know where she is. I don't know how she gets the money to buy the drugs.*

All she could do was imagine the worst.

And Colin was no help. He'd been upset at first, but had quickly given up. 'It's something Maisie has to sort out for herself,' he said, his expression hard and unyielding. 'There's nothing we can do about it.' He flatly refused to discuss the matter further. Maisie and her troubles could no longer reach him.

At first, Brodie had sent her cheques, but they hadn't been cashed when she examined the bank statements. Then she started to send cash. Colin had told her she was mad. 'She'll only spend it on drugs,' he said coldly.

'I'd sooner she got the money from us – from me,' Brodie argued. She dreaded to think in what way her sweet and pretty daughter would get money if it didn't come from her mother.

Just before Christmas, the latest envelope had been returned from Camden marked 'No longer at this address'. There'd been no more news of her daughter since. Brodie had no idea where she had gone. She'd written to the only person in London, a friend of Maisie's, who might have knowledge of her whereabouts, but Colleen knew nothing. Colleen and Maisie had started university at the same time. 'I've been doing my best to stay in touch,' Colleen wrote, 'but she'd disappeared when I last went round to that dump in Willesden . . .' Brodie hadn't known her daughter was living in Willesden – and in a dump!

Josh had searched for months for his sister, without success.

Downstairs, someone entered the house through the back door. George, her father-in-law, had arrived to work on his son's car. Colin was renovating the Triumph with a passion that had once been reserved for his wife and children. Nothing was too good for it, no expense spared when having new parts made, and virtually all his free time was spent in the garage where the Triumph was kept. His and Brodie's cars were parked in the drive.

Brodie slipped into her own bedroom and quickly got

dressed. She creamed and powdered her face, making sure her eyes didn't look puffy. She didn't want George to know that she'd been crying.

'Morning,' he said brusquely when she went into the kitchen. He was pouring water into a mug that contained a teabag. He was approaching seventy, a good-looking man with iron-grey hair, only slightly thinning on top, and a strong, arrogant face. He'd been foreman in a car manufacturing plant over the water in Birkenhead and was reputed to be a terror to work for.

'Morning,' Brodie replied, gritting her teeth. George never knocked, just came in and out as if the house were his. He didn't ask if it was all right to make tea. She was probably being unreasonable, expecting her father-in-law to behave in a way she herself would have behaved in his house. She couldn't stand him.

She wasn't alone. George's wife, Eileen, had left him after more than forty years of marriage when he retired. She couldn't face being under the same roof as him for twenty-four hours a day. George was a bully who always considered himself right and positively refused to lose an argument no matter how ridiculous his position might be. He insisted on accompanying Eileen when she went to the supermarket, completely taking over, choosing the cheapest meat and vegetables, refusing to buy anything organic, returning Eileen's favourite washing power to the shelf in favour of another he knew nothing about, as if he wanted his wife to know that from now on things would be done *his* way.

'He's never washed or cooked anything in his life,' Eileen said to Brodie, her daughter-in-law, in a choked voice – they were the best of friends. 'I've looked after him and four children for all these years, yet it counts for nothing as far as George is concerned. Another thing – he refuses to set foot in the supermarket café when the shopping's done. That was always one of my favourite treats: a coffee and a cream cake before going home. There were women there I used to meet regularly when I went on Friday mornings.'

Last year, unable to stand life with George any longer, Eileen had gone to live in London with her widowed sister, Mary. The pair had spent the winter in Goa where the weather was fine and the cost of living a fraction of what it was at home.

'Where's the sugar?' George grunted now.

'Where it always is – in that red jar with "sugar" on the side.' She wouldn't have been so sarcastic had he bothered to say 'please'.

He put three large spoonfuls in his mug and plonked himself on a chair by the kitchen table, rather pointedly, Brodie thought, as if he knew it would annoy her.

She'd planned to have a drink herself before she left. Instead she took a pint of milk out of the fridge and said goodbye to George more politely than he deserved. Then she went outside, got in her Yaris, and drove to Blundellsands. Had the relationship between herself and Colin not been so dire, they would have laughed together at his awful father. Instead, it only added to the distance between them.


There was a van outside Chestnuts when she arrived, with 'F. Peterson & Sons, Painting, Decorating, Plumbing and General Building Work' on the side. Leonard Gosling, her mother's friend, had recommended them. They'd decorated his flat beautifully, he reported. As Leonard was incredibly fussy, they must be all right.

Some very destructive noises were coming from inside, as if the place was being attacked with a sledgehammer. Brodie winced.

Her mother and Diana were in the garden seated on a bench, both clutching mugs. They waved when they saw her.

'It sounds as if they've started work with a vengeance,'

Brodie remarked. 'Are the water and electricity still turned on? I'm dying for a cuppa. I've brought some milk in case there wasn't any left.'

Mum said she'd filled a clean bucket with water so there'd be plenty enough for the day. She had no idea whether the electricity was on or off.

'I'll go and see,' Brodie said.

Diana jumped to her feet and collected the used mugs. 'You sit down: I'll get the tea for you. Here, Brodie, give us that milk.'

'Isn't she lovely?' Brodie sank on to the bench beside her mother. 'I told you she was nice, didn't I?'

'You did indeed. I like her very much.' Megan endorsed Diana with an approving wave of her hand. 'Oh, and she's a Catholic so we can all go to Mass together. By the way, it seems the mother has married again and lives in Nottingham. She's had another two boys. And her father sounds a good egg – he bought the house off the landlord before he did a bunk, so there's just a small mortgage payment every month.' Her expression changed, became sad. 'I wish your dad and I had had more children. I would have loved a big family, but three of my babies died before I had you, and then didn't your poor dad go and die before we could try again?' She smiled toughly. Her mother was the strongest and most positive person Brodie had ever known. 'But I'm lucky to have you, darlin', and two gorgeous grandchildren as well. Have you heard from them recently?'

'Josh rang this morning. He's coming for the weekend with a friend. You must come round for a meal, Mum. As for Maisie,' Brodie lied, 'she's got a new young man.' She'd kept the news about Maisie away from her mother, not wanting to upset her – or perhaps because she was deeply ashamed. 'She's probably too wrapped up in him to bother with her family just now.'

*

'Would you like a cup of tea?' Diana asked the Peterson brothers, Russell and Leo. Their dad was tied up in Everton Valley fixing someone's toilet and would be along later, Leo explained. The kitchen units had been torn away, leaving the walls badly pockmarked and looking like they were suffering from a terrible disease. Only the taps and the sink remained. Shelves had been removed and everything was piled in the middle of the room, as if ready for a bonfire.

'Wouldn't say no,' Russell said. He was a strapping lad of about twenty with straight, jet-black hair and ferociously bushy eyebrows. He wore a sleeveless vest and had barbed wire tattoos on both arms.

Leo was older, slighter and tattooless. His hair was also jet-black, but very curly, and his eyebrows were tidier than his brother's. Diana liked him the best. He smiled shyly, 'I wouldn't say no, either.'

Diana filled the kettle – the water hadn't been turned off and nor had the electricity. While waiting for the kettle to boil, she fetched five mugs and teabags out of the conservatory where the things had been put. She felt like more tea and she felt sure Megan would too.

Russell said, 'The sink'll be the next to go. I've never seen such an old-fashioned one before. That's a real antique, that is.' The sink was white, deep and square, the sort in which a couple of sheets could be left to soak.

'Do either of you take sugar?'

Russell did and Leo didn't.

Ten minutes later, the women were in the garden and the lads must have finished their tea because the banging in the kitchen had begun again. Megan said it reminded her of the Blitz during the war. 'It's like being in an air raid,' she remarked, 'except there's no danger of being killed.'

At midday, Diana let herself into the house in Coral Street. She shouted, 'Hello, it's only me,' just in case Emma was there but, as expected, there was no response. Emma was paying her daily visit to her sister in Walton Vale.

The note Diana had left the day before had gone from behind the clock, but that was only to be expected, too. She looked around to see if she could find it – it would have been kept, surely, so the lads would know her address. Perhaps one of them had kept it, she thought when she couldn't see it anywhere, probably Damian.

She wasn't sure if it was just her imagination, but the house wasn't quite as tidy as Emma usually kept it, as if, with Diana not there, she was already letting things slide. 'But I've hardly been gone twenty-four hours,' she said to herself. Even so, there were dishes in the sink waiting to be washed and the beds hadn't been made when she went upstairs.

In the living room, there was a strange smell and an ashtray on the hearth containing two unnaturally big dog ends. Diana picked one up and sniffed it.

'Grass!' she said aloud. She felt slightly sick. She'd always been dead set against drugs. Her brothers had been lectured to the point of boredom on how they ruined lives. 'If one of you becomes a drug addict,' she'd told them sternly, 'then it's not just you who'll suffer, but the whole family.' She'd always felt quite pleased that, until now at least, they'd listened.

She took the ashtray into the yard and emptied it in the bin, washed the dishes and made the beds. When Emma came home, she'd realize Diana was still around. As for the drugs, Diana didn't know what to do. Grass wasn't as serious as heroin or cocaine. She wasn't about to move back home and sleep in the box room just so she could keep an eye on her brothers. Anyroad, she was really hurt they hadn't bothered to come and see her. Perhaps they were only too glad to see the back of their bossy older sister.

It was really ghostly, Emma thought when she got back and found the dishes washed and the beds made. It could only have been Diana, but it still felt weird. That morning, she'd taken it easy for a change, ignoring the housework and smoking a few spliffs while watching telly. Damian would have a fit if he knew what she was smoking when she was expecting his kid. The ashtray had been emptied, but Diana was too bloody stupid to know what a spliff was, so there was no chance of her telling Damian when eventually they met again. Di's note was still under the fridge and, as far as Emma was concerned, it could stay there.

Damian O'Sullivan racked his brains as he tried to think of the names of people his sister had worked with at the call centre, but couldn't remember a single one, although the name 'Murphy' rang a bell, a chap who lived in the next street. Bill Murphy, Phil Murphy, something like that.

He looked up Murphy in the telephone directory and found a G. Murphy in Garnet Street. He dialled the number and a man answered. Damian asked if he had worked at the call centre and, if so, had he known Diana O'Sullivan.

The man agreed on both counts. 'I remember Di, nice kid. Everybody liked her. I've got a feeling she lived in Bootle same as me.'

'Do you know where she's working now?'

'Haven't a clue, mate. Maybe she hasn't got another job yet, like me. But then, I'm fifty-six, not a youngster like Di. Are you one of her brothers? I know she had three. She was always on about them. Dead proud of them she was.'

'No, I'm just a friend.' Damian was too ashamed admit he was a brother who didn't know the whereabouts of the sister who was so proud of him.

'Well, if you find her, tell her Gil Murphy was asking after her.'

'I'll do that. Oh, by the way, Gordon's, the factory outlet shop on the Dock Road, are looking for more staff: they prefer the over-fifties.'

He rang off before the man could thank him. Damian worked in a Job Centre. He would never have had such an important and responsible job had Di not encouraged him to do his homework so that he left school with eight GCSEs and two A-levels.

He *had* to find her.


When Diana got back to Chestnuts, there was no sign of Megan and Brodie, and the kitchen had been gutted. All that remained were a few pipes and cables sticking out of the wall. The units had been thrown in a heap in the front garden along with the sink and the ancient cooker, the sides of which had been hidden from view for an unknowable number of years and were revealed to be filthy and covered in grease. What remained of the marble-patterned linoleum had been torn to shreds.

Inside, Russell and Leo were plastering a wall each while an older man was on a ladder painting the ceiling.

'Oh, it looks lovely,' Diana marvelled.

'Are you having us on, miss?' the man on the ladder enquired. He must be F. Peterson, the boys' father. 'It's not nearly finished.'

'But it looks much better than before.' The room appeared to be twice as big as well as light and airy.

'You're easily pleased. You won't be able to contain yourself once it's finished,' Mr Peterson said drily.

Diana agreed. 'I probably won't.'

'Do you know what colour missus wants the walls painting?'

'No, but if it was me I'd have them mustard with bright red tiles and a rich brown floor.' She could see it in her mind's eye.

'That's an unusual combination.'

'It sounds the gear to me,' Leo put in. He had a smear of plaster on his nose. Russell was wearing headphones and hadn't noticed Diana was there – or at least he'd given no sign.

The water had been turned off, but Mr Peterson promised it would be on again before they left for the day.

Using Megan's bucket of water, Diana made everyone a cup of tea, then retired to the privacy of her room – or what she really hoped would be Brodie's room one day soon. Poor Brodie looked awful unhappy: there must be something really horrible happening at home. Diana knew the feeling.

The Petersons shouted, 'Tara, luv' and 'Goodnight, Diana' when it was time for them to leave, and silence fell upon the big house. Diana turned on the television and began to eat the sarnies Brodie had brought for her. There was a chippy on College Road, not far away. She might go and buy some chips later. But that would mean coming back to a totally quiet house. And anyroad, she might miss her brothers if they came.

Superficially, they got on well, she and Colin. A teacher, he was already at home when Brodie returned after spending the afternoon with her mother helping to tidy the part of the garden that belonged to her flat. He came out of the garage smiling and kissed her on the cheek. Apart from a few grey hairs, recently arrived, he had lost none of his boyish good looks or the toothy grin he'd had when they first met.

'Hello, love. Had a nice day?'

'Yes, thank you.' They were exquisitely polite to each other, but Brodie only had to mention Maisie or criticize his father and the smile would vanish. He would become brusque and rude. 'How was your day?' she enquired.

He made a face. 'Things got a bit rough at dinnertime. A couple of fourteen-year-old lads came to blows over a girl. One had his nose broken and had to go to hospital.'

'How awful,' Brodie said sympathetically. Teaching was tough these days and she could understand his obsession with the Triumph. It took his mind off things. 'There's quiche and salad for tea. It'll be ready in no time.'

He patted his stomach. 'Good, I'm starving. Oh, and don't forget Dad doesn't like salad. Perhaps you could do him some chips.'

'I didn't realize he was staying to tea.'

A tiny furrow appeared on his brow. 'You know darn well he always stays for his tea these days, Brodie.'

Brodie didn't answer. She went into the house and Colin followed. When they reached the kitchen, he glowered at her from the door. 'Do you have any objection to my father eating with us?'

'I've been looking forward to it all day.' Why oh why couldn't she keep her mouth shut? Lately, she'd been exhibiting a sarcastic streak she hadn't known she possessed.

'He's a lonely old man. If it wasn't for us, he'd go home to an empty house.'

She wanted to say she didn't care, ask why it was only Colin out of the four Logan children who felt the need to take their father under their wing, that he wouldn't be a lonely old man living in an otherwise empty house if he wasn't so thoroughly objectionable that he'd driven his wife away. She would have also liked to know why he had so much patience with his father when he had none at all with his daughter.

But she didn't ask any of these things. She'd asked before and it was a waste of time, making the atmosphere between them even worse. She took the quiche out of the fridge, started to prepare the salad, and switched on the oven for the chips. Wordlessly, Colin went back to the garage. The evening had already got off to a bad start, but then most evenings did. George might even decide to stay and watch television and then he'd sneer at *EastEnders*, a programme that Brodie really liked. She'd end up watching it upstairs.

It got even worse over the meal. For the umpteenth time, George expressed his approval of the war in Iraq, despite another British soldier having been killed that day. 'And as far as that Saddam Hussein is concerned, it's good riddance to bad rubbish.'

He knew perfectly well that his son and his wife were opposed to the war. They'd actually been on the famous two-million-strong march through London that took place two years before Maisie went to university and during Josh's second year. Eileen had yet to leave George and, despite the desperate problems in the world, life for Brodie and Colin held only the promise of better things to come. They'd had all sorts of plans as to what they would do in the summer holidays after the children had left home; buy a little property in France, perhaps, or travel to Australia to see Lucy, Brodie's best friend from school who'd gone to live there. They'd discussed working in an orphanage in India.

Life had seemed so good then. Why had everything gone so wrong? As she listened to her father-in-law's rants Brodie was unable to answer her own question.

She thought about Chestnuts, trying to imagine how it would look when it had a new kitchen and the ceilings had been painted, the walls sponged, the curtains washed – she'd already taken the curtains out of Diana's room to the laundry. She thought about living in the house with Diana in the next room and other women living upstairs. (She'd decided that she wouldn't take a male tenant and possibly end up with someone like George, determined to run things.)

The idea was vastly appealing. Things couldn't possibly be worse than they were now. She had an idea that Diana had said something similar.

Years ago, Megan had begun to wonder when she closed her eyes at night, if she would open them again next morning. The notion terrified her, yet it would be a peaceful death and she wouldn't have known anything about it. It was a hundred times better than rotting away, her mind gone, in an old people's home with poor Brodie feeling obliged to visit every Sunday. Knowing Brodie, she'd come every day.

Yes, passing away in your sleep was a blessing. There was much to recommend it. It was a shock for relatives, but preferable to watching a loved one die slowly and painfully.

She snuggled under the clothes. The electric blanket was switched on, despite it being almost April, and she was still using the winter duvet. There were some comforts you never stopped enjoying, no matter what age you reached. When she'd lived in Ireland the children had gone to bed in winter equipped with stone hot water bottles. She'd always hated feeling cold in bed.

She'd had a lovely childhood. Even earlier, when they'd lived in Liverpool, life had been good, though she'd made her mother's life a misery moaning about the uncomfortable bed and other things. She, Mam and Brodie had taken turns to sleep at the bottom, and Megan had made a huge fuss, complaining how much she hated it, as if Mam could produce another bed and another room out of thin air for her to sleep in.

Oh, God! She wished she hadn't thought about Brodie, *that* Brodie, her sister. Now, she'd never go to sleep. Megan felt herself cringe with shame at the memory, sixty years old, of the terrible thing she'd done to her sister. She'd been so much in love and couldn't help it – if it were possible to go back in time she wouldn't have changed a thing. Louis had insisted on calling their daughter Brodie. Perhaps he'd felt guilty, too.

The other Brodie, her daughter, didn't know she had an aunt of the same name who could still be alive, as well as two uncles, Tom and Jim. The other Brodie had always thought her mother was, like her, an only child, yet there was a whole army of relatives over in Ireland.

Every now and then Megan would punish herself in little ways for her sin. Now, she got out of bed and looked through the window at the flat, silvery-black expanse of the River Mersey. It looked desolate, with not a ship in sight and no sign of a light. She stood there, shivering in the cold night air, her feet like blocks of ice. When she felt that she'd been punished enough, she got back into bed, conscious of the bones creaking in her legs and shoulders. It was such a treat to get under the warm duvet that she was glad she'd got out in the first place. It hadn't been a punishment after all.

Ten days later the house was almost finished. Brodie was appalled one day to turn up and find the kitchen decorated in the most ghastly colours, the walls mustard with tomato-red tiles that didn't match, though the brown flooring didn't look too bad.

Diana confessed it was all her fault. 'I said I thought those colours would look nice, but I expected Mr Peterson to ask you first before he did anything.'

Brodie said she couldn't be bothered having the work done again. 'I suppose I'll get used to it eventually. I was going to suggest pink and cream.'

'The kitchen in Coral Street is pink and cream,' Diana said tactlessly.

'Lucky old you.' Brodie laughed, but felt just as tactless when Diana said she might never see that kitchen again. Her brothers hadn't been to see her and she was deeply upset, though her new job in the refugee centre was really interesting. She loved it there and it took her mind off things.

The walls of the four big rooms that were to be let had been sponged down and the satin wallpaper gleamed. The ceilings were now brilliant white. Elsewhere, the hallway had been painted a deep, buttery cream, all the windows had been cleaned and the garden tidied. The front door had been painted the same shade of lilac as before. Brodie had requested only a little of the ivy covering the conservatory be cut off. 'It's pretty and I don't want it spoilt,' she told Diana. 'Mum

61

said Dad was very fond of that ivy. He'd sit and stare at it while smoking his pipe.'

Leonard Gosling, who owned the art shop, had been asked to put the postcard back in his window. If no one noticed it, Brodie said she'd put an advert in the *Liverpool Echo*, although she wasn't in any hurry.

She had made up her mind to move into the room next to Diana's and had yet to convey this news to Colin.

'*What!*' he gasped the night she told him of her decision. 'You mean you're leaving me?' He looked totally astonished, as well he might.

'Not exactly,' Brodie said. 'I'm leaving you *and* your father.'

It was Sunday morning and George had yet to arrive. They were in the living room that she'd always loved. It was long and wide with windows at each end that caught the sun in the morning and evening. This was where the drama of their lives had been enacted, where the children had played, where Colin had taught them to read, where they'd done their homework. It was on the cherry-coloured settee that she and Colin had sat companionably holding hands while they watched television before Josh and Maisie were born, and later after the children had gone to bed, sometimes falling asleep if the programme wasn't very gripping. Whoever woke up first would make the cocoa.

Now Colin said dismissively, 'Don't be so bloody stupid, Brodie,' as if he didn't believe a word of it.

'Your mother left, didn't she? Doesn't that make you think?' It probably just reminded him there were two stupidly unreasonable women in the world, not one. 'I'll only be living in Blundellsands,' she reminded him gently, suddenly aware that it was possible she *was* being stupidly unreasonable. 'It's not exactly a million miles away. You can come and see me whenever you like, and I'll still be coming back for clothes and stuff. That's if you'll let me in.' It was a funny way of leaving someone. She grinned, but Colin didn't grin back.

'As if I'd shut you out,' he said stiffly. His voice was always stiff, these days – stiff, or cold or hard. 'You belong here, with me. Dad won't be here for ever. Mum might come back one day.'

'I don't think so, Colin. I reckon your mother's left your father for good. And it's not just because of him that I'm going,' she said in a rush. 'I find it upsetting that I can't talk to you about Maisie. Mum doesn't know and I can't very well ring Josh every day to discuss his sister.'

His boyish face twisted in a scowl. 'Maisie made her bed and now she can lie in it.'

'Now who's being bloody stupid?' she cried. If she weren't careful, she'd burst into tears. 'It's our daughter we're talking about, Colin. Our own little girl, the one you cried over the day she was born.'

'That girl is dead,' he said stubbornly. 'She's become some-one else and I don't want to know her.'

'And you thinking like that, Colin, is the real reason I'm leaving.'

## Chapter 3

Diana was in the basement where Tinker had sent her to sort out bags of clothes handed in for the refugees. She emptied a large John Lewis bag on to the floor and picked up a black satin strapless ballgown with a heavily boned bodice.

'I can't imagine anyone wanting this,' she said to Tinker, who came in at that very moment.

He regarded the garment, green eyes sparkling. He was only an inch or so taller than she was and reminded her of a mischievous imp with his curly red hair and fantastic smile. He grabbed the dress and held it against his skinny body. 'I wouldn't mind that meself. What do you think?' He began to dance around the room still holding the frock and grabbing Diana on the way so she had no alternative but to dance with him.

She burst out laughing. She wasn't sure if Tinker was gay or just pretending. He was too outrageous to be real. 'It suits you,' she managed to gasp.

'Tinker, you're wanted upstairs, son,' Alan shouted. Alan was a volunteer who came to the centre three afternoons a week. He was a retired boxer, old now, with cauliflower ears.

'Coming, sweetie.' Tinker tap-danced out of the room. Alan hated being called sweetie, dear heart, precious, beloved, or any of the other endearments that Tinker bestowed on just about everybody. It confused the refugees no end.

Left alone, Diana folded the black gown and put it in a bag

to go to a charity shop. Someone might buy it and alter it – it would look nice with sequin straps. Or it might be of use to a dramatic society.

She had never dreamed that the call centre's move to India would prove to be as lucky as it had for her. The refugee centre was a really gear place to work. Instead of being harangued all day by extremely irritable people about their incorrect, or so they claimed, gas and electricity bills – Diana was inclined to believe them – here there were only real flesh and blood people. Most couldn't speak English, but she was getting quite good at sign language.

Tinker, who lived on the premises, got up early to make breakfast for the twenty or thirty people likely to turn up. Diana, who came at nine o'clock, would start her day in reception with a cup of tea and a bacon butty. Around ten-ish, breakfast over, she would wash the dishes and get things ready for a light lunch, which was served between twelve and two – only simple things like beans, spaghetti rings or eggs on toast, sarnies or baked potatoes, with an assortment of fillings, and cakes for afters. No more meals were served that day, but tea, coffee and light refreshments were available until the centre closed at seven, by which time Diana had gone home.

She looked at her watch and was surprised to find it was past four o'clock. Here, time just flew by; in her old job it had crawled.

The centre was run by a charity and supported by Liverpool Corporation with a grant. Tinker held fund-raising events once a month that were open to the public. On Saturday, Leo Peterson was bringing his pop group, The Little Dead Riding Hoods, to the centre to give a concert; Diana had arranged it. Leo played the drums. He and Diana had been out together five times since he'd worked on Chestnuts. As he was twenty-two and Diana two and a half years older, she felt a bit uneasy and had so far refused to let him kiss her. She knew she was being ridiculous, but it was a bit like going

out with one of her brothers, from whom she still hadn't
heard despite it being three weeks since she'd left Coral
Street. It was very upsetting, but right now life was too
interesting for it to get her down. She hadn't been back to
the house again as she didn't want to come face to face with
Emma, although it was bound to happen one of these days.

She emptied the last bag of clothes, which were terribly
creased, and put them on wire hangers on the racks. There
were three racks, one each for men, women and children.
Later, if she had time, she'd give everything a quick iron. It
was bad enough being a refugee and having to wear other
people's cast-offs without the things looking as if they'd been
rolled up in a ball for the last ten years.

Diana bought most of her own clothes from charity shops,
though it was different for her because she didn't *have* to. She
only did it because she didn't like modern fashions and
thought old clothes were more interesting. Today, she wore
a patchwork skirt that had actually been stitched together by
hand, and a shiny wrap around blouse that looked brown
from one angle and green from another.

'Have you finished down there yet, luv?' Alan called.

'Nearly.'

'Rosa's just making us a cuppa.'

'I'll be there in a minute.'

Diana put the shoes in pairs under the appropriate racks and
went upstairs. The stout, three-storey building had once been
a chapel for some obscure religion. Downstairs had been
divided into four separate rooms now used as an office-cum-
reception – Diana could hear Tinker inside on the telephone
– a lounge with a television, a restaurant and a kitchen. The
first floor was just one large room where The Little Dead
Riding Hoods would play on Saturday night. There was a
dartboard up there and a snooker table. It was where the
young men tended to collect and Diana could hear the click

of the balls right now. A playgroup was held there in the mornings. Tinker's flat was on the top floor.

Everywhere was very rundown and there was a strange sort of smell that she'd been told was woodworm, but the walls were painted bright colours and the effect was cheerful and inviting. Tinker, who was in charge of everything, did a wonderful job trying to make everyone feel at home.

In the lounge, furnished with a variety of armchairs from the relatively modern to the extremely old, the television was on and an elderly woman in a long black gown, a scarf covering her hair, was watching a programme about buying holiday homes in Spain. A young woman, similarly dressed, was chatting to another who wore jeans and a sweatshirt. Two men slept soundly in chairs turned away from the television. They'd been there every day since Diana had started. She suspected they slept rough and Tinker let them in very early in the morning; he wasn't allowed to let anyone stay overnight. The men came from Zimbabwe where they'd been tortured for demonstrating against the president.

None of the women was a refugee. The older one, Mrs Sharma, was an interpreter; Diana found it amazing how many languages some countries had. Sarita and Wendy helped run the playgroup.

Four men wearing what seemed to be a uniform for the young – jeans and black leather jackets – were sitting on the stairs arguing passionately in a language she didn't recognize.

The restaurant was half full. Alan was seated at a table with a big pot of tea and an assortment of cups and saucers that didn't match. Nothing in the room matched. All the tables were different styles and different sizes, and no two dining chairs were the same. Diana thought the room had a higgledy-piggledy sort of charm. The walls were covered with posters of extremely photogenic dogs and cats. Through the hatch, Rosa Rosetti could be seen in the kitchen. She was Alan's partner and came the same afternoons as he did. Some volunteers merely popped in every other day to do the washing; others came for the whole day or even the whole weekend. Diana and Tinker were the only full-time paid employees. The wages were less than she'd earned in the call centre, but she didn't mind.

Alan patted the chair beside him. He had broad shoulders, a mighty chest and a battered face. His fists were as big as footballs. 'Sit down, luv. Take the weight off your feet, like.' His voice was high-pitched and gentle.

'Thanks.' Diana sat in a chair with a wicker seat that had a frayed hole. There was a radio in the kitchen and Gerry Marsden was singing 'You'll Never Walk Alone'.

Rosa poked her head through the hatch. 'Hi, Di.' She was half-Irish and half-Italian. Her grey ponytail was tied with a frilly red ribbon. Once, she'd told Diana, her hair had been coal-black and people had said she looked like Elizabeth Taylor in *Cleopatra*.

'Hi, Rosa. I'll come and wash the dishes when I finish this.'

'Righteo, luv. I've already cleaned the pans. I'll just see if anyone wants their cups refilling, then I'll come and join you.' She circled the room topping up tea and coffee cups, then came and sat down next to Alan. 'Phew!' She fanned herself with her hand. 'It's been a busy day, but I've enjoyed it. Did you see that young woman with the little boy, Di? Lovely little chap he was, just gone twelve months old. I think they're from Romania.'

Diana confessed she hadn't seen the woman because she'd been in basement for quite a while.

'Her hubby's gone to Norfolk to work on a farm and her bloody landlord only tries to get in her room every night.' She snorted with outrage. 'There's no lock and she has to jam a chair underneath the handle to keep the bugger out. Tinker's going round later to put a bolt on and give the landlord a piece of his mind at the same time; tell him if he doesn't behave himself, he'll call the coppers.'

'Quite right, too,' Diana said indignantly.

'I'd be willing to give him a good going-over,' Alan offered.

Rosa patted his hand. 'I know you would, Al, but you might end up killing the bugger.'

After Diana had finished the dishes, she went into the office and Tinker gave her another lesson on how to use the computer. She was really sorry now that she'd never learned to use the one at home properly.

She sat in front of the monitor and Tinker put his arm along the back of the chair. She could feel his warm breath on her neck. He showed her how to write and send emails – he could type like the wind with two fingers – and how to search the Internet using Google. 'All you have to do is ask a question,' he explained. 'Say if we get someone from Ethiopia, it helps to know a bit about the place, like if there's a war going on, what the political situation is. Me, I'm pretty wired up about most places, but how much do you know about the world outside the British Isles, Di?'

'Not much,' Diana confessed. She'd always been too busy to read the papers, and the lads wouldn't have dreamed of watching the news on telly. But now she could read and watch whatever she liked. She wanted to impress Tinker, with whom she suspected she was a little bit in love, gay or not.

There was a small, purple car parked in the drive when Diana arrived home, and a woman climbed out as she approached. She was extremely overweight and wore a loose black top, black trousers and gold sandals. Her hair was long, blonde and very beautiful. It fell in curls and ringlets halfway down her back. On anyone else the hair would have looked striking, but it only made this woman appear freakish.

'Hello,' Diana smiled.

The woman scowled. 'Brodie Logan told me to come. She said she'd be along later. If you're Diana, you're to show me the upstairs rooms.'

'Of course, luv.' Diana unlocked the front door. The house still smelled of fresh paint. The hall with its black-and-white tiled floor and cream walls looked extremely smart. She felt quite proud of it. 'I'm Diana O'Sullivan,' she said.

'Vanessa Dear,' the woman almost snarled.

'What a lovely name. Would you like a hand upstairs?'

She looked considerably put out. 'I can climb stairs by myself, thanks all the same.'

'I didn't know Brodie had put an advert in the *Echo*,' Diana said chattily. 'She's been meaning to do it for ages.'

Vanessa was making hard work of the stairs. They were only halfway up and she was breathless. Diana slowed down in sympathy.

'It was in last night's paper. I telephoned straight away and she promised to keep a room until I could see it. Apparently there's two. She sounds nice, Mrs Logan,' she said grudgingly.

'Oh, Brodie's lovely,' Diana enthused. 'And Megan's lovely, too. Megan's her mum. My Mum lives in Nottingham and I haven't seen her for ages.'

'Really?' Diana couldn't tell from the tone if Vanessa was bored, being sarcastic, or just plain fed up.

Three days later, Vanessa had more or less settled in her upstairs room. She'd taken the first one she'd gone into, not bothering to look at the other. Something had to be done, she'd decided a couple of weeks ago when she'd got up one morning, stood on the scales, and realized that if her weight increased at its current rate then by this time next week she would be eighteen stone.

It was no good going on another diet. Anyway, she reckoned she must have tried virtually every single one. She'd gone without fat, without carbohydrates, eaten nothing but pineapple, drunk nothing but low calorie milkshakes, tried to exist on a thousand calories a day, considered having her teeth wired together or her stomach stapled, exercised, had hypnotherapy, done yoga, listened to CDs urging her not to eat, and watched DVDs telling her the same.

Nothing worked. While Vanessa did all of these things – some at the same time – she only put on more weight, no doubt due to the tasty little morsels she indulged in between the items on the diet. She'd even joined a group of women determined to celebrate the fact that they were overweight. But that didn't work, either, at least not for Vanessa. She admired them, but didn't share their sentiments.

Twelve months ago, she'd been ten and a half stone and size fourteen. She'd never exactly been sylph-like, but she had no complaints with how she looked. Then *it* had happened, making her so unhappy she'd just let rip, eating everything in sight.

At first, it had made her feel better. Food was compensation for the thing she'd lost. She hadn't taken much notice when her skirts became too tight and she couldn't get her trousers on any more. She'd just moved up a size, then another, until, all of a sudden, she was size twenty. It was then she went on the first diet, during which time she put on a further stone and ended up size twenty-two. She'd put on more weight since and had probably gone up another size.

Her gloomy chain of thought was interrupted by the sound of laughter outside. She went over to the window. It was a pleasant April evening and three women were in the garden seated underneath a tree; Diana, who'd let her in the other day; Brodie Logan, who owned the house, and Megan, Brodie's mother, whom Vanessa hadn't yet spoken to. She could hear music, that 1920s or 1930s sort that she didn't like. A man with a very sad voice was singing, 'Every time it rains, it rains pennies from heaven.' It was terribly depressing.

Megan reminded Vanessa of her grandmother on her

father's side. She had two grandmothers and when *it* had happened, they'd vied with each other to be the most scathing.

'That bloody William. I never trusted him as far as I could throw him,' Granny Dear said at the wedding – at the *non*-wedding. Her hat looked as if it could receive Sky television.

'He had a sly face,' Granny Harper said grimly.

'And a mean one.'

'The bugger needs castrating, that's what I say.'

It was her sister, Amanda, who was the first to put Vanessa's dread into words. 'It looks as if William isn't going to turn up, luv.' She'd spoken hesitantly after they'd been waiting at the church for a good twenty minutes, as if she didn't quite believe what she was saying. They were words that she'd never expected to say in her lifetime, particularly to her own sister at her wedding.

By then, guests had started to arrive at the church for the wedding after Vanessa's. She and her sisters were in the porch. Vanessa wished she'd remained in the car, but it was a bit late for that; the car had gone. How on earth was she supposed to know that William wasn't coming to his own wedding? There was no sign of the best man, Wayne Gibbs, but that wasn't surprising, seeing as he and William were supposed to come together.

She hadn't known whether to scream or burst into tears. Most of all, she would have liked to faint and leave her parents and sisters to cope with what was left of the day while she came to a week later to find all the presents had been given back and the fact that Vanessa Dear had been jilted at the altar was no longer a hot topic of conversation in any part of Liverpool, or at Siren Radio where she worked.

But she didn't faint. She didn't scream or burst into tears, either. It would have been undignified. She was hurt, deeply hurt, more hurt than she'd imagined being in her entire life, but she kept her head held high, determined to retain her self-respect when people started coming to the back of the church to see what was wrong. William's mother was absolutely distraught and his father was so angry he could hardly speak. The guests for the next wedding stood outside and regarded the rejected bride with a mixture of curiosity and pity. She looked so beautiful in her simple white outfit, the white roses nestling in her natural blonde hair.

The reception had been held – or at least the food had been eaten. As Mrs Dear said at the time, 'It would be a shame to waste it.' The jazz quartet who'd been hired to play later were paid and told to go home. Vanessa had no idea what happened to the wedding cake. She'd returned home with her sisters, Amanda and Sonia.

At thirty-one, Vanessa was the eldest and the only sister who wasn't married and didn't have children. She had never actually considered herself a feminist, more that she was any man's equal. She would get married when it suited her, have children at her convenience, then go back to work and continue with her career while some other woman looked after them.

But on what should have been the day of her wedding to William James Lunt, Vanessa's confidence turned to dust. She felt old, unattractive, as undesirable as hell. Would she ever hold up her head again? Was she destined to become an old maid? Never have children? Did she care? Could she bring herself to go back to work in two weeks' time after what should have been her and William's honeymoon in the Canaries? (Most of the staff at Siren Radio had been invited to the wedding and had actually witnessed her ordeal.)

Come to that, what was she to do with herself over the next fortnight? Stay at home with her mum and dad? She'd sooner have died than go back to the flat in Hunts Cross that she and William had been buying for the last three years. What if they came face to face?

Fortunately, it was she who had booked the holiday in the

73

Canaries and had the tickets. She managed to persuade her parents to use them. Just as Vanessa had wanted to faint until the fuss had died down, or at least partially died down, her mother was anxious to avoid, for a little while at least, the disgrace of having one of her daughters so publicly humiliated.

'It would have to be you with your posh job and everything,' she complained bitterly. 'I've been blowing your trumpet so loud for so long that people are sick to death of hearing about you. There's some folk out there who are probably rubbing their hands with glee.'

So her parents went on Vanessa and William's honeymoon while she remained at home. She slept in her old room and ate and ate and ate. She'd always had a healthy appetite, but now it went into overdrive.

There was a knock on the door of her new room and she opened it to Megan, who was as thin as a lath with not a spare ounce of flesh on her. Nowadays, it was people's sizes that she noticed first, not their faces or their clothes.

'Hello, darlin'. Would you like to come and sit with us in the garden? We're only having a cup of tea and a gossip, but we forgot you were upstairs on your own.'

'Actually, I thought I'd go to bed early.' She didn't feel the least bit sociable and had always thought gossiping a waste of time. Where did it get you? People, apart from her immediate family, didn't much interest her. 'And I've still got some unpacking to do.'

'All right then, darlin',' Megan said warmly. 'But if you ever feel like a natter, don't hesitate to come down. Afterwards, we're going to watch a DVD in Diana's room – *Grand Hotel* with Greta Garbo and John Barrymore.' She chuckled. 'I was only six when it came out. I'll tell her to keep the sound down in case it keeps you awake.'

'I'm sure it won't.' The memory of her failed wedding day still kept her awake most nights anyway.

Megan wished her goodnight and Vanessa closed the door. Then her mobile rang. It was Amanda.

'How are you getting on, sis?' she asked. She sounded worried.

'All right. It's very nice here. The room's lovely.' Much better than Vanessa had expected. She'd imagined house shares to be rather sordid, makeshift places, but her room was gracious and beautifully decorated. 'The bed's really comfortable and there's a brand-new kitchen downstairs,' she said. 'The garden's what estate agents call "mature".'

'You haven't given me your address – and Mum said she hasn't got it, either.'

'I'm not going to, Mandy. I don't want anyone to know where I am.'

'Oh, but, sis!' Amanda wailed.

'I'll be back in touch about this time next year.' By then, she anticipated having reduced her weight to what it used to be.

'Next *year*?'

'I'm going to switch off my mobile for good when I finish this call.' Vanessa felt ruthless and powerful. 'I've got to do this, Mandy,' she went on in a softer voice. 'I need to.'

Amanda sighed. 'I think I understand. I can't even begin to imagine what you've been going through. But, sis,' she said, as if she'd just remembered something, 'we can always get in touch with you at work.'

'I've left,' Vanessa said bluntly. 'I gave my notice in last week.' It should have been a month's notice, but she didn't care – and neither did Siren's manager, Richard Freeman. Vanessa hadn't been the most agreeable of employees over the last year. He was probably pleased to see the back of her.

'But you worked so hard in that job!'

'I know.' Vanessa hadn't told her family that she'd been moved sideways months ago. She'd been hell to work for and the people underneath her had complained. Richard had

75

transferred her to overseas accounts where there was just enough work for one person, but not enough to keep her as busy as she'd been before. She and Richard were old friends and she reckoned if it had been anyone else he would have sacked them.

'Are you going to get another job?' Amanda asked.

'You mean go for interviews looking like I do?' Vanessa snorted. 'No chance.'

'But will you have enough to live on?'

'I've plenty in the bank and William sent back the money I'd paid on the mortgage for the flat.' She'd earned far more than her father and her sisters' husbands. And William.

Amanda groaned. 'But what will you *do* with yourself all day, Vanessa?'

'Exercise and diet.' And try not to think about William – and food.

'Oh, God, sis!' Amanda said, distraught. 'Does it mean when this call is over we'll not speak to each other again for a whole year?'

'I'm afraid it does. Bye, Mandy.' Vanessa turned the mobile off and the screen went blank. It seemed the best way to finish the conversation, not continue while Amanda – and Vanessa – became more and more upset.


She'd had Special K for breakfast, cottage cheese, a tomato and a cream cracker for lunch, and sardines on a wafer-thin piece of toast for tea. She felt very pleased with herself, but after finishing the telephone conversation with her sister, hunger came upon her like a curse and she could have eaten the furniture.

For a good half-hour, she paced the floor, but it only made the hunger worse. She gnawed her knuckles, but it didn't help. In the end, she went out and toured the streets in the car looking for a take-away, a chip shop, a pizza parlour, any-where that would sell her something to eat.

In the end, she bought a medium-sized Hawaii pizza and ate it in the car, pushing huge chunks into her mouth, not even chewing it properly. When she had finished, she wiped her hands and started up the engine. Eating had been bliss, but now she felt totally dispirited, like a sack stuffed with sawdust, hating herself for giving in.

Oh, well. At least she'd bought a medium pizza, not a large one.

The thought didn't help much.

In the middle of the night, she woke with indigestion and imagined doughy lumps of pizza lodged in various parts of her body. She burped loudly. It hurt.

The house was completely silent, but outside she could hear the trees rustle in a slight wind. A strip of moonlight showed between the curtains, which she hadn't closed properly.

She sat up, lodged a pillow behind her back, and burped again. Oh, God! She felt so miserable. Achingly, whole-heartedly miserable. How could William, who she had genuinely loved, who she had thought loved her in return, have done this to her? She recalled, word for word, the letter he had sent. It had arrived on the Tuesday after the 'wedding' when she was in the house on her own.

*Vanessa,*
*As you can imagine, I feel terrible about this.* [Not nearly as terrible as *I* do, Vanessa had thought when she'd read the letter for the first time.] *On Saturday morning, I felt a strange reluctance to leave for church.* [Oh, really!]
*The truth is that you make all the decisions about how our lives are run and I'm not prepared to put up with it any longer. It was you decided when we should buy the flat and when it would be time to buy a house – and where the flat and the house would be. You informed me when you planned to have children*

*and that it was your intention to leave them with a childminder when you do.*

*I have not been consulted on any these matters. For me, the most important is the last one. <u>I am sorry, but I do not want our children left with strangers</u>. As you earn more than I do, something I am not allowed to forget, then I would be happy to leave work and look after them. However, I can't bring myself to suggest this. You would call me a wimp — you have done before.*

*On Saturday, it was right after I phoned you — I couldn't find my cufflinks, remember? — that I decided I would sooner not marry a woman who thinks so little of me, who, in fact, regards me with contempt.*

*I don't quite know how to finish this letter except to say how sorry I am and to wish you luck in the future. I shall arrange for all you have paid into the mortgage to be transferred to your account.*

*With regards,*
*William.*

'Bastard!' Vanessa whispered hoarsely. 'You *are* a wimp. You're the biggest wimp in the world.' She wondered if he knew how much weight she'd put on. He worked in Manchester and they hadn't had any mutual friends, but Wayne, his best man, had once dated Fiona, Siren's receptionist. That's how she'd met William, when Wayne and Fiona had thrown a party. They no longer dated, but if they still saw each other then William would know his ex-fiancée was almost twice as big as she used to be.

Another three days passed and Vanessa found herself dreaming endlessly about food; soft, crumbly chocolate cake thick with fresh cream, cartons of ginger ice-cream; prawns in curry sauce with rice and sweet chutney; egg and chips sprinkled with vinegar; roast beef and potatoes with crispy Yorkshire pudding; lamb chops and mint sauce; boxes of chocolates, sausage and mash; fresh croissants heaped with butter and strawberry jam; hot dogs with mustard . . . In her sleep, Vanessa would consume entire banquets and not put on an ounce of weight.

These imaginary meals were pleasant, but she needed the food in her stomach, not in her dreams. With not a shred of willpower left, Vanessa would drive somewhere late at night and gorge on fish and chips or pizza.

She felt at the end of her tether. What sort of life was this? She hardly felt like living any more.


Colin was sulking. She was daft, Brodie thought, walking out on her husband then going back to see him two or three times a week. It was a ridiculous situation and she didn't blame Colin for sulking. The poor man didn't know where he was.

She only went in the evenings when George wouldn't be there, first looking to see what was on television to make sure it wasn't a football match, or one of those films in which hordes of people spent two hours massacring each other, which he could well have stayed to watch with his darling son.

When she turned up on Sunday Colin was watching a DVD of Peter Sellers in one of the Pink Panther films and didn't turn the sound down when she went in. 'There's some letters for you,' he snapped.

'Are they real letters or junk mail?' she enquired.

'Don't know, didn't look. You know,' he said nastily, 'you can fill in a form and the Post Office will redirect your post to wherever you happen to be living now.'

'I know.' She thought about the words for a while, feeling desperately sad. Eventually, she said, 'Why has everything turned so sour, Colin? We used to get on really well.'

'Things change, people change, life changes,' he muttered, staring at the screen. 'Nothing lasts for ever.'

'Things haven't changed so much that we have to hate each other.'

'I don't hate you.' He switched the television off and turned to face her. He looked haggard and so unhappy that she wanted to take him in her arms and assure him everything was all right. Except it wasn't. It wasn't even faintly all right. His father was merely a fly in the ointment. It was his attitude to their daughter that Brodie despised, so much so that she couldn't bear to live with him under the same roof. It was strange, but that was what his mother had said about his father, yet the two men were totally different. He sighed. 'Of course I don't hate you, Brodie.'

'I don't hate you, either.' She sat in her old armchair on the right in front of the fireplace. He had the gas fire turned on low. The fire, the kerb and everything else in the room was covered with dust. She didn't want to clean up in front of him, as if she was trying to make some sort of point, but if she came when he was at school, then George would be here. She'd like to bet Colin wasn't washing his shirts and would soon run out of socks even if he had about fifty pairs – it never crossed Josh's mind that his father wouldn't want anything other than socks at Christmas or on birthdays. The collar on his shirt didn't look too clean. It struck her that he must be feeling extraordinarily low to wear a grubby shirt when he was usually so particular about his appearance.

They sat in silence for quite some time, but not the comfortable, laid-back silence they'd once enjoyed. Brodie was trying to think of things to say, and perhaps Colin was doing the same. Or maybe he was wishing she'd go away so he could continue watching the film.

'Do you mind if I take the computer?' she asked. He'd never learned to use it, relying on her to type his notes and look up things on Google. 'I've had Broadband installed at Chestnuts. You can always let me know if you want work done. You can bring it round and look at the house, see what it's like now.'

'Take whatever you like.'

'OK.' She nodded sadly.

'What are you living on?' he asked after another long silence. There was something unpleasant about it – not the question, but the sharp way in which he asked it.

'What do you mean?'

'I mean money. How do you support yourself?'

'With money from our joint account, of course,' Brodie explained. 'The tenants each pay two hundred pounds a month rent and I'm expecting a third tenant tomorrow, the last one, but there won't be much over, if anything, once I've paid the bills. The council tax is horrendous on a big house like that, and water, gas and electricity are going up all the time. Now spring's here, the garden's getting very overgrown again and I'll have to get someone in to tidy it.' Until recently, the rent from Chestnuts had gone into the joint account. Now, though, Brodie wasn't contributing a single penny.

'A very large amount has recently been taken out of our joint account, which I assume is what you paid to have the house done up. Do you think it fair,' Colin went on in the same sharp voice, 'that, under the circumstances, I should continue to support you?'

'The circum . . . oh, you mean because I've left you?' Brodie felt herself go cold. Had it really come to this?

'Exactly. You are only a young woman, Brodie, you could easily get a job.' Halfway through the sentence, he wavered a little, as if he was finding it hard to stick to his guns.

'I wanted to get a job when Maisie went to university, but you talked me out of it.' Brodie got to her feet. 'I'll start looking for one tomorrow. You must change the account so that it's in your name only and I'll start one of my own.'

'I didn't mean straight away.' Now he looked regretful,

ashamed. Perhaps he hadn't expected her to agree quite so quickly, thought she'd put up some sort of argument. But what was there to argue about?

'I'd better go,' she said with a sigh. 'Where are the letters?'

'In the letter rack on the sideboard.'

They'd bought the wire letter rack on holiday in Greece. They'd hardly been married a year and Brodie hadn't known she was expecting Josh. It held four letters. Two were from charities, and one was from the Labour Party pleading with her to rejoin. 'Did you get one of these?' she asked Colin. He nodded. They'd both resigned from the party after the night they'd watched Baghdad being bombed. It had seemed a strange way of turning Iraq into a democracy.

The fourth letter had a London postmark and her name and address were neatly written with a purple felt-tip pen. She had a premonition it was to do with Maisie. She tore the envelope open. The letter inside was quite short.

> Dear Mrs Logan,
> I was on the bus on my way to uni the other day and it went down Dodge Street off Holloway Road. There was a traffic hold-up, as usual. I was just looking out the window, when a girl who was the image of your Maisie came out of one of the houses. I took a photo on my mobile and had this picture made. I would have got off the bus and spoken to her, but I was already late.
> I hope you are well.
> Colleen Short

Colleen, Maisie's friend. Brodie looked in the envelope. She saw the photograph but could hardly bear to touch it. Somewhat gingerly, she took hold of it between her finger and thumb and pulled it out.

'Oh, God!' she groaned.

It wasn't a very good photo, but it was clear enough to see

that her beautiful daughter had been reduced to skin and bone, that her eyes had sunk so deeply into the sockets they looked barely human. Oh, and she looked so tired, so weary, as she left the house, her hand on the doorknob to pull it shut. Brodie could just about make out the number three on the door.

Number three Dodge Street, off Holloway Road. She'd go tomorrow.

'What's the matter?' Colin asked tetchily.

'Nothing,' she said abruptly. She wasn't prepared to tell him about the letter, listen to his criticisms. Maisie may well have brought this on herself, but she was their daughter. So far, Brodie's attempts to rescue her had failed, but she was determined to try again.


Vanessa was enjoying her early-morning walk on the deserted beach. It gave her a sense of well-being to breathe in the fresh salty air and take long strides on the wet sand – she could feel the moistness through her canvas shoes. A cool breeze penetrated her grey stretchy trousers and matching sweatshirt. She'd only brought two outfits with her to Chestnuts; a black cotton top and trousers; and what she was wearing now, which looked like a babygro and was about as unflattering as a garment could be.

The waters of Liverpool Bay were calm. Overhead, gulls swooped as if they could see a multitude of fish floating on the placid surface. They squawked, possibly in frustration, when they found nothing but bits of seaweed and the flotsam and jetsam of today's world.

She was walking too fast and was beginning to flag. She turned round and retraced her steps. By the time she arrived at Chestnuts she was panting for breath and her sense of well-being had faded, but she was glad she'd gone. It was bound to have done her good, though being overweight put a strain on the heart. She knew that without having to see a doctor. She was dying for her breakfast; half a grapefruit sprinkled with pretend sugar, a Ryvita smeared with low-calorie butter and tea with skimmed milk.

She'd been carrying her shoulder bag across her chest like a soldier and fished inside for her keys; the front door key and her car keys were on the same ring. After a few minutes of fishing, she realized she had forgotten them. In fact, she could see them in her mind's eye on the table where she'd thrown them last night when she'd brought home a double serving of curried prawns and rice.

Vanessa rang the doorbell, which made an old-fashioned buzzing sound. Diana would probably have left for work by now, but Brodie would still be around. But although she rang the bell several more times, the door remained stubbornly closed.

She peered through the letterbox, though it was a silly thing to do. If there was no one in to answer the door, who or what did she expect to see?

What was she supposed to do now? Stand on the doorstep until somebody appeared? Diana wouldn't be home for ages and Brodie could have gone to see her mother and mightn't be home for ages, either.

To her relief, she remembered that Brodie had given her her mobile number and the one for the telephone in the hall. 'You never know, you might need them one of these days,' she'd said.

Vanessa's mobile was in her bag. It had been switched off since her conversation with her sister. She switched it on and found fourteen messages waiting to be read. She ignored them and dialled Brodie's mobile.

It was answered straight away. 'Hello, sorry about the background noise, but I'm on a train,' Brodie said.

Vanessa came straight to the point and explained that she'd locked herself out. 'Will you be long?'

'I'm on my way to London and I won't be home until very

late. I might even stay overnight. It depends how things go.'
Brodie's voice was very faint. A much louder male voice was
announcing that drinks and sandwiches were available in the
restaurant car. 'Oh, dear, you can't ask Mum, either, she's
gone to North Wales with her friend Gwen.'

'What about Diana? Do you know where she works?'

'Only that it's a refugee centre somewhere in town. Oh, I
know. Leonard Gosling has a key. Do you know the artists'
materials shop in Crosby Road?'

'No, but I'll find it.' Vanessa was getting impatient even
though Brodie was doing her best to help. It wasn't *her* fault
that her tenant had left her key on the table upstairs.

'I can't remember the number of the shop, but it's by a
school. It doesn't take more than five minutes to get there in a
car. Leonard is a friend of my mother's. Tell him that I sent
you. He loves helping damsels in distress.' The phone went
dead; the train must have gone into a tunnel.

Vanessa set off. The keys to her car were upstairs with the
key to the front door, so she'd have to walk. As she came
from the south side of Liverpool and this was the north,
she had no idea where Crosby Road was and would just
have to ask people. Her feet were freezing in the wet shoes.
She was dying for a cup of tea. If William James Lunt could
have heard the names his ex-fiancée called him as she trudged
towards what she hoped was Crosby Road, his ears would
have burned right through his head.

# Chapter 4

'Oh, my dear young lady. Oh, dear, oh, dear.'

Having collapsed in a chair behind the counter, Vanessa was being vigorously fanned by Leonard Gosling, who was using a large artist's pad. She'd arrived at his shop exhausted, thoroughly out of sorts and, she suspected, just a little bit smelly. She could feel her hair hanging around her shoulders in damp clumps. She wished she were wearing virtually any other garment on earth rather than the stretchy grey babygro.

'How do you feel now?' Leonard enquired solicitously. He was a small, dapper gentleman of around seventy with a full head of wavy brown hair and a pink complexion. She suspected the hair was dyed. He wore pale grey trousers and a lilac shirt with a darker lilac tie. His voice was like that of an actor, loud and very grand without a trace of Liverpool accent.

'Much better,' Vanessa gasped. 'I've nearly got my breath back.'

'Good, good.' He stopped fanning, slightly out of breath himself. 'It's a long way to walk from Elm Road.'

'I walked for miles. I kept turning the wrong way and having to walk back.' Her brain mustn't have been working properly; when she asked people the way their directions didn't make sense. It crossed her mind, much too late, that she could have phoned for a taxi. It was as if some malevolent being had cast a spell on her and she was destined never to be happy again.

'Would you like a glass of water?'

'Please.' Unusually for her, she was enjoying being fussed over.

He went into the back of the shop and returned with a glass of water containing a slice of lemon. 'What did you say your name was?'

'Vanessa Dear.'

'I'm Leonard Gosling,' he said rather shyly, 'but I suppose Megan told you.'

'It was Brodie, actually. I'd locked myself out and she said you'd have a key. Brodie was on a train and Megan's gone to North Wales with a friend.'

'That's right, I'd forgotten. You must call me Leonard and I'll call you Vanessa. Is that all right?'

'Fine.' It was the sort of conversation, going nowhere, that normally Vanessa found intensely irritating, but just now didn't mind. In fact, it was quite soothing. No one was trying to get one over on her and she didn't have to appear clever or business-like or even think very hard. 'This is an interesting shop,' she remarked. It was double-fronted, but quite narrow, no more than about four metres wide. On one wall was a large area of pigeonholes containing tubes of paint, pencils, crayons, brushes and artists' pads from the very small to the very large. Other shelves were full of books – how to paint, how to draw, how to do all sorts of crafts – as well as books on famous artists such as Van Gogh, Picasso, Degas, Monet. A full-sized easel stood just inside the door holding a painting that Vanessa could only see the back of. There was a stack of frames in one corner and a stack of canvases in another.

She'd been good at art at school. Since leaving, she'd often had a vague urge to take up painting, but there never seemed to be the time. Well, now she had all the time in the world. Before she left, she'd buy a couple of canvasses and some oil paints, although the one thing she wouldn't do was a self-portrait.

Leonard beamed. 'It *is* interesting, isn't it? I've been running it for nearly ten years – the lease comes up for renewal soon. I don't exactly make a fortune, but I love it.'

'What did you do before?'

He beamed even more. 'I was an actor. I appeared on television quite a few times. I was in *Z Cars* and *Maigret* – I was only a young whippersnapper in those days – and some lesser-known programmes, but I always preferred the stage. When my wife died, I decided to retire and make a permanent home for myself in the city where I was born. I live in the flat upstairs.'

'I'm so sorry – about your wife, that is,' Vanessa said sincerely. 'Whereabouts in Liverpool do you come from?'

'Knotty Ash.' He smiled. 'Where the Diddy Men live.'

If Vanessa didn't have a hot drink soon, she'd collapse. She said, 'Look, I don't like to take up any more of your time. If you could let me have the key to Chestnuts, then I'll go home.'

'My dear,' he said with old-fashioned gallantry, 'as if I minded my time being taken up by such a charming young lady. Have you had breakfast?'

'No.' Her heart began to beat a trifle quicker. Perhaps he had a stove in the back and would offer to rustle up a cup of tea or coffee.

'Then shall we go across the road to that delightful pâtisserie and partake of *petit déjeuner*? They do a delicious hot chocolate heaped with fresh cream, and their croissants . . .' He kissed his fingers and threw the kiss into the air. Vanessa knew exactly what he meant.

'Why not?' It wasn't usually until evening that her diet went for a burton. Today, she must make sure it didn't go for a burton twice. 'What happens if someone comes to the shop?'

'We can sit in the window and I can keep an eye on things. I rarely have customers this early.' He held out his arm. 'Come along, my dear, let's party.'

Brodie walked past number three Dodge Street, eyeing it keenly, trying to see through the windows, which were badly in need of a good polish. It was a dingy terraced house, three storeys high, with a tiny garden containing half a plastic bucket, a collection of empty crisp packets, and hundreds of cigarette butts. It looked as if people regularly emptied their ashtrays there.

It was only a short street with eight identical houses on either side, pubs on two of the corners, and a boarded-up shop and a launderette on the others. Most of the houses were badly rundown and had been turned into flats with numbered buzzers on the walls outside.

Brodie walked up and down the street a few times before plucking up the courage to approach number three. It had a bell, but she couldn't hear anything when she pressed it, so she used the knocker as well.

She had a strong feeling no one would answer, so was surprised when the door was suddenly opened by a tall black man wearing the bottom half of a scarlet tracksuit and nothing else. 'What you want, man?' he growled. 'I see you walking past and past. Are you the pigs?'

'I'm looking for Maisie Logan, my daughter. I was told she lived here.'

'Then you was told wrong, lady. No Maisie live here. No woman live here, all men.'

'But she's been here,' Brodie argued. She reached into her bag. 'See, I have a photo of her coming out of this very house.'

The man scowled. 'No Maisie here, no woman. Go 'way, lady.' The door was slammed in her face.

Brodie stepped back into the street. She was disappointed,

but not all that much. She hadn't really expected Maisie to be there, but there'd always been the chance. It would have gone against the grain not to have followed up on Colleen's letter. Did Maisie live in this area? she wondered. Or had she come to the house on the underground, by bus or even in a car? And what had she been doing there?

She was walking back the way she'd come with the intention of catching the tube to Euston and going home. Josh had gone to Brighton 'on business', so they couldn't meet – anyroad, she had always refused to visit him in his squat. Had the circumstances been different, she would have gone to the West End for lunch, then to the big Marks & Spencer by Marble Arch to do some shopping. But shopping was out – lunch, too – now that she had to watch the pennies until she got a job. What sort of job? Where? Brodie had no idea.

'Excuse me?'

Brodie broke out of her thoughts. A young woman in a plain black suit, white blouse and sensible shoes had stopped in front of her and was holding up a badge.

'WPC Karen Grant,' the woman announced. 'Can I have a word with you?'

'What about?' Brodie had never committed anything vaguely resembling a crime in her life, but immediately felt guilty.

'I would like to know why you just knocked on number three?' Karen Grant looked almost half Brodie's age, but Brodie envied her air of authority.

'Why?' Her voice wobbled. 'Because I thought someone I know might live there.'

'Can I please have the name of that person?'

Brodie thought before saying abruptly, 'No. No, you can't have her name. Why do you want it, anyroad? What's it got to do with you?' She felt pretty close to tears.

Karen Grant must have noticed. She was rather a nice young woman with pale curly hair and not a trace of make-up on her pleasant, very determined face. She put a firm hand on Brodie's arm. 'Look, there's a café around the corner. I really would like to talk to you. The person you're looking for won't get into trouble. I promise.'

'Oh, all right.' She supposed she had no choice but to talk to a policewoman.

'Am I allowed to know your name?'

'Brodie Logan,' she replied, a touch sullenly.

The café smelt of fried food and made her feel hungry; she'd had nothing to eat so far that day. It was a featureless place with a chalked menu on a blackboard in the window and an old man serving behind the counter. Not a single thing had been done to make it look attractive. The walls were bare and faintly dirty, and the customers, mainly elderly, sat at plain wooden tables, chewing mindlessly, looking lost. No one spoke to each other. The meals came with mountains of chips.

Brodie sat down while Karen Grant went straight to the counter. She returned with a pot of tea and a plate of cheese sandwiches.

'I'm afraid, being lunchtime, there's a minimum charge, so I bought us these. Would you like sauce or pickle?'

'No, thank you.' Lunchtime? Brodie looked at her watch. It was just going on for one o'clock. She'd thought it much earlier. 'Shall I pour the tea?'

'Please,' Karen picked up a sandwich. 'Do you know what number three Dodge Street is?' she asked.

'Only that it's a house.' Brodie shrugged.

'It's a crack house. It's where drug addicts go to buy crack cocaine. I'm from the drugs squad, by the way.'

The teapot nearly fell from Brodie's hand. She quickly put it back on the table, wanting to be sick. Her beautiful, laughing, clever daughter had been to a crack house. How many times? How much did the drugs cost? Where did she get the money from?

'Who is it that you thought might live there?' Karen asked.

'My daughter,' Brodie whispered. 'Maisie. She's only twenty. She was at university in London and then – oh, I don't know what went wrong. She stopped coming to see us, stopped phoning.' A university counsellor had telephoned to ask if Maisie was at home. When an astounded Colin had denied this, he was informed his daughter had disappeared. A few days later, the same counsellor had phoned with the shocking news that Maisie was on drugs. It was at that point that the bottom had dropped out of their world. Maisie had, quite literally, vanished from their lives, but only physically. Brodie thought about her all the time.

'What made you come here, to Dodge Street?'

Brodie gave her the photograph. 'Maisie's friend sent this. She took it on her mobile and told me the name of the street. I only got it yesterday.'

Karen looked at the photograph. 'Maisie Logan,' she said thoughtfully.

'You're not going to arrest her, are you?' Brodie felt alarmed. She didn't like the police knowing her name, knowing Maisie's name, knowing Maisie was a drug addict. She felt exposed and vulnerable, as if she had put her daughter in danger. 'Does it mean that Maisie's taking crack cocaine?' She understood that was the worst drug of all.

'Not necessarily. Crack houses don't just stick to crack; they sell other drugs as well.'

'If you know what that place is, why don't you close it down?' Brodie asked crossly. 'Isn't that what the police are for?'

'Because if we did, another crack house would open somewhere else and it could be a while before we knew where it was,' the young woman explained patiently, as if it was a question she was often called upon to answer. 'At least we can keep an eye on this place. Can I keep the photo?'

'What for?' Brodie asked guardedly. She imagined enlarged

versions of Maisie's face pinned to noticeboards in police stations all over the country with 'Wanted' underneath.

'Well, one reason is that if I ever come across your daughter, I could let you know where she is – if you are willing to give me your address and telephone number, that is.' She looked slightly amused. 'Why are you so suspicious of the police, Mrs Logan?'

Brodie denied she was suspicious. 'Not in the least.'

'Getting information from you is like pulling teeth. You were reluctant even to give your name.'

'I suppose I'm terrified of getting Maisie into trouble,' Brodie admitted. 'My husband would have a fit if she ended up in jail. Not that I care about him.' She twisted her lips contemptuously. 'He's disowned Maisie. He doesn't know I'm here.'

'Have you got other children?'

'A son, Josh. He lives not far from here. He's in Brighton on business.' It made Josh sound important – if she didn't mention the squat, or the fact that he had never had a proper job. She remembered something. 'My grandfather was a sergeant in the Liverpool police force. According to my mother, he was killed in the line of duty in nineteen thirty.'

'Really?' Karen Grant's brown eyes widened with interest. 'What happened? Do you know his name?'

'Thomas Ryan. He came across two men robbing a bank at the dead of night and one shot him.'

'I'll see if I can find out about him on the Internet. Oh, good, this tea looks nice and strong. You haven't touched yours yet, and please take a sandwich.' She leaned across the table and squeezed both of Brodie's hands. 'I hope I haven't been too abrupt with you, Mrs Logan. My elder brother died of an overdose when he was only seventeen. I hate drug-dealers. It's why I became a policewoman. If I had my way, every single dealer would be put in prison to rot for the rest of their miserable lives.' Her lips tightened. 'I'm going to find your daughter for you. Now, tell me something about her? Where did she used to live? What was she studying at university? And what's this nonsense about your husband disowning his own flesh and blood?'

Brodie told her. It was cathartic to get every single one of her worries off her chest, things that until now she'd never told a soul.

Afterwards, Karen drove her to Euston and Brodie returned to Liverpool feeling much happier than when she'd come. All right, she hadn't found her daughter, but she felt positive that Karen soon would, and somehow persuade her to come home.


Vanessa had bought two canvases, a box of paints and a packet of assorted brushes. She put everything under the bed and had a short sleep, having found the early morning's events quite exhausting, though the Leonard Gosling part had been relatively pleasant, in particular the breakfast. The hot chocolate with cream and the warm croissant and homemade strawberry jam had been delicious. She licked her lips and could taste them again.

When she woke and opened her eyes, she was reminded what an attractive room this was, with its old-fashioned, solid furniture and faded brocade curtains. The walls were shell-pink with a slight sheen. Over the fireplace hung a delightful painting of fairies playing in a circle of flowers. By the door there was another painting of the same fairies flying through a wood. She really should be happy in a room like this. Hopefully, she would be – as soon as she started losing weight.

She read the text messages on her mobile and listened to the voicemail. Amanda and Sonia had sent some of both, all saying more or less the same thing. Did she really have to cut herself off from her family? For a whole year? Wasn't she being just a little bit silly? Overly dramatic? 'All you're doing is drawing attention to yourself,' Sonia texted. 'And not for the first time.' She'd never got on as well with Sonia as she had with Amanda.

Vanessa couldn't see how disappearing out of sight for twelve whole months could be taken as drawing attention to herself, more the opposite.

'What on earth am I to *tell* people if they ask how you are?' her mother sobbed. Her father told her cheerfully to look after herself. Someone from Siren informed her an interview had been arranged with Wayne Rooney. Someone else said they were sorry to hear she was leaving. There was a message to say she'd won a holiday in Spain. To her annoyance, there was a voicemail from William. Amanda had told him what she was up to and he warned her not to do anything silly.

Anything silly! What did that mean? Did he seriously think she was likely to commit suicide because of *him*? Huh!

The house was empty. Diana was still at work, Brodie out somewhere. Vanessa had a lazy bath. When she got back to her room, she weighed herself and the needle swung past eighteen stone.

Suicide didn't seem all that bad an option, she thought wearily.

At around six o'clock, Vanessa heard Diana come home from work. Within minutes, she had put on a CD, one of those stupid Stone Age numbers she was so fond of. 'Are the stars out tonight?' a man with a plaintive voice whimpered. 'I don't know if it's cloudy or bright.'

'Hello, puss.'

Diana had gone into the garden. She spent a lot of time there, even when it was dark and sometimes cold. Vanessa watched the girl from the window. In her weird, old-fashioned clothes and wedge-heeled boots, she looked like a model in a retro photo from a fashion magazine. She was speaking to a ginger cat that had jumped out of a tree. It came and rubbed itself against her legs. She bent down and stroked it. 'What have you been doing with yourself today, puss?'

Vanessa rolled her eyes. She'd always had poor relationships with cats. Did Diana really expect the animal to answer? The girl wasn't exactly the Brain of Britain, but she couldn't be *that* stupid. She turned away from the window in disgust. She couldn't stand Diana. It was nothing to do with the fact that she was envious of her beanpole figure and air of natural elegance, more that she was lacking in basic intelligence.

Half an hour later, the doorbell rang and Diana let someone in. There were footsteps on the stairs. Vanessa tensed, praying that her whereabouts hadn't been discovered and it was someone coming to see her. Another part of her prayed exactly the opposite; that there'd be a knock on her door and she'd open it to a familiar face – any face apart from William's. She was in urgent need of company just then. A comforting hand, a friendly kiss, even a nice smile would do.

But the footsteps went into the room next door. The new – and last – tenant must have arrived.

Diana said, 'Brodie told me to expect you at about six. I'll fetch the rest of your stuff up. Would you like me to make you a cup of tea?'

The person must have accepted the offer, because Diana said, 'I won't be a minute.'

Vanessa hoped that didn't mean it was someone old, because *she* had no intention of making tea and waiting on them. She had enough to do looking after herself.

She lay on the bed, dozed off again, and woke to the sound of a baby crying. It was just her luck, she thought wretchedly, to find she was living in a haunted house.

Brodie knocked on Diana's door as soon as she came in. 'Has Rachel arrived?' she enquired. Rachel was the new tenant. She'd been to the house a few days before and paid a deposit on the room. She looked awfully young, but had assured Brodie that she was sixteen.

'I don't get on with me mam at home,' she'd told her.

'Will you be able to afford the room?' Brodie enquired. It was a question she didn't like asking. It made her look like a greedy, grasping landlady, but she needed the money. Rachel had assured her she could afford the rent and had paid a month in advance and a month's deposit, there and then, all in cash.

'She seems really nice,' Diana said. She said exactly the same about everybody, even Vanessa, whom Brodie didn't think was very nice at all. She wasn't happy, either – but not unhappy like Diana, or Brodie herself, because of the behaviour of other people. Poor Vanessa was unhappy with herself. 'But I didn't know', Diana went on, 'that Rachel had a baby.'

Neither did Brodie. There'd been no mention of a baby the other day. The girl had taken the room under false pretences. The elation Brodie had felt when leaving London had already dissipated. She'd arrived in Liverpool worried and sick at heart. It was an easy move from this to intense anger at the idea that she'd been fooled. She ran upstairs and knocked sharply on the rear bedroom door. Rachel opened it, a fearful expression on her heavily freckled face. She was tiny, no more than five feet tall, and very slight. Her eyes were almost hidden behind a thick, brown fringe. She reminded Brodie of a doll she'd had as a child.

'You've got a baby!' she said accusingly. As if in confirmation, a little chirrup came from inside the room.

'Yes.' Rachel hung her head and looked ashamed.

All Brodie's anger fled. 'Why didn't you tell me?' she asked limply.

'Because I didn't think you'd let me have the room.'

'I wouldn't have turned you away, not with a baby, but I don't like being misled.'

'I'm sorry.' The girl sniffed pathetically. 'Other people did.'

Brodie remembered that she adored babies and it would be lovely to have one on the premises. 'Is it a boy or a girl?'

'A girl. Her name is Poppy.'

'Can I see her?'

'Of course.' The girl stood aside, a touch reluctantly, Brodie thought.

She crept into the room and across to a large, very expensive three-wheeled pushchair with massive tyres in which lay a pink-clad baby staring into space, her eyelashes twitching ever so slightly now and then.

'She's beautiful,' Brodie breathed. 'How old is she?'

'Three months.'

'If you ever want any help,' Brodie whispered, 'don't hesitate to ask. I have two children, but they're grown up.' It was hard to believe that Josh and Maisie had once been so small and looked so helpless.

'Thank you.'

Brodie sensed Rachel wanted shot of her. She left the room after repeating her offer of assistance should it ever be needed.

She was in the kitchen making her tea when Diana came in. Together, they wondered if the baby's father knew he had a daughter.

'And how old is *he*?' Diana mused. 'Rachel only looks about fourteen.'

'Does she?' Brodie felt concerned. 'She assured me she was sixteen.'

'Are you allowed to leave home when you're under sixteen?' Diana asked. 'I mean, can you be forced to go back to your parents?'

'I hope not.' Brodie shuddered, suddenly worried she'd be prosecuted for harbouring a minor.

That aside, she felt happy with her three tenants. Diana was one of the nicest people she'd ever known. She suspected something horrible had happened to Vanessa and Chestnuts provided sanctuary of a sort while she recovered. As for little Rachel and her daughter, Poppy, they needed looking after, and Brodie would make sure that they were.

Diana mentioned that she'd met a reporter from the *Liverpool Echo* at work that afternoon. 'He's writing an article about the centre. He asked what I did. Oh, and he brought a photographer who took all our photos.'

'When will it be in the *Echo*?' Brodie enquired.

'Tomorrow, I think.'

'I must make sure I buy a copy.'

The next day, Garth O'Sullivan, who was in his last year at Liverpool College and about to take his A-levels, caught the train home from Central Station. He sat next to a woman in a bright red coat who smelled of disinfectant, though it might have been dead expensive scent. She was reading the evening paper. Being a woman, she wasn't reading the sports' pages, but the local news, which Garth knew would be dead boring. He glanced at the open pages and turned away in disgust.

He wished their Di would be there when he got home. He was fed up with Emma's cooking. It was the same old horrible stuff every stupid day: mincemeat fried, mincemeat boiled, mincemeat baked in the oven. He couldn't remember their Di making mincemeat, except when she did it curried with rice and chutney. *That* was one of his favourites.

Emma had stopped making the beds every day an' all – there hadn't been any clean bedding since Di had gone. He and Jason had tried to work out what Emma did with herself all day, but couldn't come up with anything, apart from going to see her sister in Walton Vale.

Or shopping. Jason swore she wore different clothes every single day. 'And earrings,' he added. 'She must have a couple of hundred pairs.'

Both the lads were very anti-Emma these days. They had a feeling that if it hadn't been for her, their Di might not have done a bunk. It was useless trying to complain to Damian about it. Emma was his girlfriend, she was expecting his kid, and it went without saying that he'd stick up for her.

'Make your own flippin' tea,' he'd said, though he hadn't used the word 'flippin' ' but another beginning with 'f'. 'And make your own flippin' bed while you're at it.'

'If that's the flippin' case,' Jason said, 'then I'm holding back me keep. I mean, what am I paying fifty quid a week for if it's not to have a decent flippin' tea made as well as me flippin' bed?'

Garth was convinced that Damian must have seen the logic of this. He didn't argue. In fact, he didn't say another word, but ever since a slightly better meal had been waiting when they arrived home and the beds had been made, if not as neatly as when Diana had done them.

The woman next to him on the train turned to another page of the *Echo*.

'Flippin' hell,' Garth gasped.

'Do you mind?' snapped the woman.

'That's me sister there, that is.' Garth pointed excitedly to a picture at the top of the page. 'That's our Di. Where does it say she is, missus?'

The woman looked interested. 'At a refugee centre in Winstanley Place off Cazneau Street. It says here that her name's Diana O'Sullivan and she works there.'

'That's right, that's our Di. I'll get the phone number on me mobile and give her a ring right now.'

'The number's here, lad. It asks for people to ring if they want to make donations or volunteer to work there.' She reeled off the number and Garth dialled it on his mobile.

It was Di who answered. Garth was so happy, so relieved, so flippin' *touched* to hear his sister's voice that he wanted to cry, despite being a tough, cynical seventeen-year old who'd forgotten what tears felt like. The woman with the newspaper was listening quite openly, nodding as if she approved of the conversation.

'Oh, but I left a note,' Di explained when Garth asked why she'd gone without telling them where. 'I put it behind the clock on the mantelpiece. It had me new address on.'

'We couldn't find a note, Di. We looked every flippin' where.'

'Don't swear!' Di said severely. 'I hope you're not all swearing your heads off just because I'm not there.'

'As if we would, Di,' Garth said virtuously.

Di asked after Damian and Jason and finally Emma. Garth assured her everyone was fine and asked when he could come and see her.

'Come whenever you like, luv. I'm in most nights.'

'Give us the address, Di, and I'll come tonight. We all will.'

All three lads came, leaving a scared and extremely anxious Emma behind in Coral Street. What if they persuaded Di to come back? This time, Di might not be so willing to be sidelined, not if she found out that Emma had been slacking a bit in the kitchen – well, more than a bit. It was a lovely kitchen to look at, but she wasn't exactly keen on *working* in it. Her sister, Sophie, had been to look at the house a few times and told Emma she was dead lucky – the father of *her* kids had walked out before the second had even been born.

'I wish I had a feller like Damian and a house like this,' she said enviously. 'And he treats you like Lady bloody Muck. When I had our Carly, I was working until two weeks before she was born, but you're not expecting until August and all you do is laze around the house all day smoking spliffs.'

'I come to see you, don't I?' Emma argued. Never the less, she resolved to pull her socks up and start watching cookery programmes on telly. She wasn't married yet. It mightn't be a bad idea to keep up the pretence of being interested in housework until she became Mrs O'Sullivan.

'The lads'll be along later,' Diana had informed Brodie as soon as she got in. 'Our Garth saw me photo in the *Echo* and rang up from the train. The day I left Coral Street, I put a note behind the clock, but Garth said they never got it. It must've blown away or something.'

'I hope this doesn't mean you're going back home,' Brodie said. 'I'd really miss you if you did.'

Diana assured her that she had no intention of leaving Chestnuts. 'I'm glad I came when I did. The lads are old enough to look after themselves. I know that from the centre; there's young people there who've been through some dead horrible stuff back in their own countries – and they haven't got a nice, warm house to live in. Anyroad,' she went on with a confident grin, 'it was about time I struck out on me own. I was dead miserable at first when me brothers didn't get in touch, but after a while I was enjoying meself too much to think about it.'

They were lovely boys, Brodie thought. Handsome and polite, glowing with health, they obviously thought the world of their sister. With a mother who'd walked out on them when they were still at school, brought up by a sister who wasn't much older than themselves, it was amazing that they'd turned out as well as they had. Diana ought to feel very proud.

Having entertained them on the piano with a one-fingered version of 'Yellow Submarine', Diana was now showing them around the garden. The youngest, Garth, had climbed a tree in an endeavour to capture the ginger cat.

'It's the gear here, sis,' he said peering through the leaves.

It made her wonder where she and Colin had gone wrong with their children; one a drug addict, the other wasting his time on failed business ventures. Yet they'd never gone short of money or attention or parental love. Colin had helped with homework; Brodie had kept them clean and warm and well-fed. Had they been given too much love, or not enough? Perhaps it would have done them good if life had been a bit harder.

The sounds of merriment coming from the garden were getting on Vanessa's nerves. She drove to Sainsbury's to buy groceries, hoping the visitors would be gone by the time she got back.

She wandered round the shop, gazing longingly at Battenbergs and chocolate biscuits, the cartons of fresh cream and the meat pies with crispy pastry that would taste delicious warmed up. She stacked up on thin-sliced low-calorie bread, cottage cheese and salad vegetables. It was an unappealing selection for a woman with a voracious appetite.

What she needed was to go on a sensible diet, the sort where you could eat a bit of almost anything, not leaves accompanied by stuff that tasted like cotton wool. The trouble was genuine diets were so *slow*. Vanessa wanted to lose weight quickly, imagining whole rolls of fat disappearing overnight like magic, except the more strictly she dieted, the more likely she was to be overcome with a hunger that she couldn't resist satisfying with something really fattening.

She walked quickly away from the food and looked at the CDs, the DVDs and the books, but nothing caught her fancy, mainly because they weren't edible. With an effort, she pushed the trolley towards the till. The female assistant looked at her sympathetically when she paid for her motley collection of unappetising foodstuffs.

'You'll get there in the end,' she said with a nod of encouragement.

'Get where?' Vanessa snarled. Sympathy was the last thing she wanted.

'You know where.' The woman smiled, not in the least put out.

For five days, Vanessa didn't leave the house except for an early-morning walk along the sands. She spent a lot of time lying on the bed staring at the ceiling and thinking gloomy thoughts, one of which was glum awareness that she had become the hopeless, helpless sort of person she'd used to loathe. Downstairs, the telephone in the kitchen rang frequently but, as it couldn't possibly be for her, she didn't answer. Sometimes, the doorbell went, but she didn't answer that, either.

Neither did Rachel, who was living in the next room with her baby. Vanessa had intended to complain if the baby cried a lot, but when it did she could hardly hear. She wondered why the girl didn't take the child into the garden. Weren't babies supposed to have plenty of fresh air?

It was unnerving to have such a quiet neighbour. She never heard Rachel go down to the kitchen, was only aware of it when she heard the click of the kettle being switched on, or the opening and closing of the fridge. The same with the toilet, which would suddenly flush, making her jump.

She hadn't much minded being the only person in the house once Diana and Brodie had gone, but there was something unnatural about two women living so close together, literally yards from each other, yet having no communication whatsoever. Only once had they come face to face.

Sometimes, late at night, Rachel would sing to her baby, her voice high and sweet. '*Rock-a-bye baby, on the treetop, when the wind blows, the cradle will rock . . .*'

Vanessa would shudder. There was something really creepy about it.

Late on Sunday morning, Vanessa was still asleep when Diana knocked on her door and shouted that she had a visitor.

'Who is it?' she shouted back. If it was one of her sisters, she wasn't sure whether to fling her arms around them or demand they go away. But the visitor was most unexpected.

'It's Mr Gosling from the shop. He said he's been telephoning you all week and he's called at the house twice, but there was no answer. He wants to take you out to lunch.'

Vanessa eased herself out of bed. 'Tell him I'll be down in a minute.'

'There's no need to hurry. I'll make him a cup of tea.'

She took pains with her appearance for the first time in ages, brushing her blonde hair until it shone, then screwing it into a bun at the back of her neck when she looked in the mirror and discovered she resembled a blown-up version of Marilyn Monroe with it loose. She put on her black top and trousers and supposed she didn't look so bad when she was ready.

But, oh, how she wished she were ten and a half stone again and about to go to lunch with William, wearing a smart blouse and the silver silk trouser suit that had cost £350.

The door to Diana's room was wide open. She must be proud of her ability to play tunes with one finger. When Vanessa went in, she was playing 'Night and Day' to Leonard and Brodie. They clapped when she finished and said, in a really friendly way, 'Hello, Vanessa.'

Vanessa's face cracked into a smile. She actually felt quite normal for a change, but knew it wouldn't last for long.

Half an hour later, Leonard was driving Vanessa to Southport in his elderly but beautifully preserved Morris Minor, Diana was on her way to Coral Street to have dinner with Emma and her brothers, and Brodie and her mother had met at Crosby station to catch the train into town to do some shopping. At least, her mother could shop; Brodie couldn't afford to and would just have to watch.

Rachel listened until the house was empty, then pressed the

keys on her mobile. 'It's all right to come now,' she said when it was answered.

She lifted Poppy out of the pram and held her very close. The baby's shape seemed to fit snugly against her neck and shoulder like the piece of a jigsaw. 'Daddy's coming, sweetheart,' she whispered. 'He won't be long. We'll look after you; don't worry. We won't let them take you away.'

*May–June 2006*

# Chapter 5

It had been Diana's idea for the centre to have a coffee morning once a week to which everyone, not just refugees, could come. 'Thursday would be a good day,' she said to Tinker. 'It's a way of raising funds. We can put signs at the end of the road, and have a bric-à-brac stall, too. If we don't charge too much for the coffee, it'll be somewhere for old people to come.'

Tinker reminded her that it wasn't in the centre's remit to provide for old people, but never the less agreed that Diana could go ahead. 'I'll leave all the arrangements to you, dear heart,' he said with his infectious grin. 'I like the idea of our clients and the local population getting together.'

So Diana made notices using a black felt-tip pen on white cardboard, and drew flowers in each corner merely because there was the space. She nailed one to each end of Winstanley Grove.

Ten women and two men came to the first event, not all of them old, and more than fifteen pounds was raised. Since then, there'd been another two coffee mornings and each had raised more money than the one before. Today was the fourth and at least twenty-five people had come. The lounge and dining room were crowded with local residents and people from all over the world chatting away to each other, even if some were only using sign language.

There was a lovely atmosphere, warm and friendly.

Everyone seemed very much at home. Tinker thought it important that the refugees who used the centre found it a happy place. 'Some have had a horrendous time getting here,' he said. 'It might have cost them all their savings, and they arrive and find themselves with nowhere to live. I want them to realize that life won't always be so black. "Look for the silver lining . . ."' he sang tunefully.

'I'm doing a roaring trade,' Megan, Brodie's mother, said when Diana passed on her way to the lounge with a tray full of coffees. Megan had felt at a bit of a loss when Brodie started work a few weeks ago, and now came to the centre regularly to give a hand. On Thursdays, she was in charge of the bric-à-brac stall, usually bringing lots of bits and pieces that she'd cadged off friends. There was more stuff that she'd found in the jumble in the basement.

'It's going really well.' Diana surveyed the depleted stall. 'How much have you taken?'

Megan looked pleased. 'I'm not sure, darlin'. Between thirty and forty pounds, I reckon.'

Tinker would be thrilled, Diana thought. 'What's that se-quinny thing?' she enquired.

'It's a blouse.' Megan held it up. It was black and truly beautiful, the material as fine as a spider's web, scattered liberally with gold and silver sequins. 'It's size thirty, darlin'. Much too big for you. You can have it for nothing.'

'I'd like it, please.' Diana had no intention of not paying for the blouse. She was scrupulous about such things and would give Megan the money later. She distributed the coffees and returned to the kitchen for more of the jam sponge cakes that she'd made with Brodie's help the night before. There hadn't been time for baking cakes in Coral Street.

'Diana,' Tinker said a touch distractedly when she went in, 'I'm in a desperate tizzy. Will you please try to get rid of your lot as soon as you can?' Tinker was in a desperate tizzy a lot of the time. He was by the stove stirring a giant pan of beans while slices of faintly brown bread popped out of the toaster. He pushed the bread back in, cursing. It was a hopeless toaster.

'My lot?'

'The coffee morning lot. Any minute, we'll have *our* lot in for lunch and there's nowhere for them to sit because *your* lot are taking up all the seats.' He ran his fingers through his red hair and it stood up on end, reminding Diana of a clown's wig. 'Next week, precious, ban them from the dining room and keep them in the lounge.' He began a vain attempt to tear his hair out by the roots. 'Actually, I'd better run this coffee morning thing by Mrs Banana. She might not like the idea of the centre being overrun with English pensioners when it's supposed to be for refugees.'

Mrs Banana was actually Mrs Bannerman. No one knew exactly what her job was. She seemed to be a sort of co-ordinator between the council, the government and various refugee agencies, and turned up at the centre from time to time to make sure things were running smoothly and that nothing untoward was going on, such as illicit coffee mornings.

Diana promised that next week she'd make sure *her* crowd left at half past eleven. Tinker kissed her on the cheek and thanked her profusely. 'What have I done to deserve a gorgeous girl like you, Di?'

'I don't know,' Diana said, blushing madly.

She blushed again when she took the sponge cakes into the lounge and saw Ahmed Rusafi. A doctor from Iraq, of philosophy not medicine, he was about forty and drop dead gorgeous. Women, young, old and in between, were enchanted by his exquisite manners and old world charm. Megan was one. The other day she claimed he was the spitting image of a film star called Clark Gable.

'I was crazily in love with him when I was a teenager,' she

said dreamily. 'My sister was, too. It's almost like meeting him in the flesh after all this time.'

'I thought you didn't have any brothers and sisters,' said Diana. She considered Ahmed better-looking than George Clooney.

'Of course . . . I didn't – haven't. What on earth made me say that?' Megan had got all hot and flustered. As Diana couldn't imagine why anyone would deny they had brothers and sisters when in fact they had, she'd not given the matter another thought. Megan had later said she had the DVD of *Gone With the Wind* starring the one and only Clark Gable along with loads of other old film stars and she'd bring it round one night and they could watch it together, adding, 'Our Brodie might like to see it, too. It's nearly four hours long, so it would be best if we watched it at the weekend and we can stay up as late as we like. I've seen it loads of times, but would love to see it again.'

'We could order a takeaway,' Diana suggested.

'And buy some wine.' Megan rubbed her long, thin, wrinkled hands together.

'And get dressed up, as if we're going to the theatre or something.'

'What a lovely idea, Diana.'

'Can we make it Friday?' She was meeting Leo Peterson on Saturday at his brother's twenty-first birthday party. Each time she saw Leo she told him she didn't want to see him again, but he talked her out of it. He was so nice and she didn't like to hurt his feelings.

'Friday's fine. I'm already looking forward to it.'

Diana was looking forward to it, too. She was enjoying life in a way she had never done before. Until recently, the lads had always come first, but now, although she still worried about them and always would, she was able to think of herself before anyone else. She really enjoyed being able to do what-ever she pleased.

Ahmed Rusafi came over, smiled into her eyes, and took a cake. She didn't like saying it was part of the coffee morning and he was supposed to pay for it.

'Have not got nowhere to sleep this night,' he said with a dramatic shrug and a devastating smile.

'Why not?' Diana was shocked. She had a feeling she might be in love with him as well as Tinker.

'Peoples who own house need my room for other peoples.'

'But that's awful! Can't you find a cheap hotel?'

He shrugged again, raising his shoulders and spreading his hands. 'No such thing as cheap when person have no money.'

'I'll lend you some—'

'No, no, no, no.' He shook his head, horrified at the idea. 'I manage somehow: sleep in park maybe, or shop doorway. Never take money off woman.'

'OK.' On reflection, Tinker would be cross if he found out. He had advised her never to get emotionally involved with the refugees. 'It'll tear your heart out, Di,' he'd said. 'Some have suffered really horribly and you don't want to suffer with them. Treat them with love, kindness and generosity, but try to remain detached.'

Tinker was so *wise*!

The coffee morning raised £55.37. Tinker was contemplating buying a six-slice stainless-steel toaster with the proceeds. Diana and Megan felt extremely pleased with themselves when they went home that evening on the same train. They got off at Blundellsands station and Megan went to collect her bike, while Diana commenced the walk home to Elm Road.

All in all, it had been a really satisfactory day.

Vanessa had spent the afternoon watching a horror film on television. It had made her flesh creep. It was still creeping while she contemplated what to have for tea, going through all the choices in her head. That morning, she'd gone mad and eaten the whole day's ration of butter on two poached kippers. The room still stank. How could something that tasted so nice smell so horrible?

Ham salad, cheese salad, sardine salad, omelette with salad . . . An apple for afters. Tea without milk she was slowly getting used to, but she couldn't acquire a taste for black coffee. She wondered if the day would ever come when she would find any of the choices tempting. They were fine for a snack, but a meal?

She sighed. She'd been living in Chestnuts for six weeks and the only weight she'd lost was the amount she'd put on since she'd arrived. A few times a week her willpower would desert her and she would rush out, usually late at night, and indulge in something ultra-fattening. The subsequent enjoyment was better than sex, but afterwards she felt ashamed and depressed.

Omelette and salad, she decided. It would be more filling than sardines, a lump of cheese or a slice of ham.

She opened the door to go down to the kitchen and found Diana outside about to knock.

'Hello, Vanessa,' she said shyly. 'I've brought you something. Today, we had a coffee morning at the centre and I found this on the bric-à-brac stall.' She held up a pretty lacy garment decorated with sequins. 'It's a blouse,' she explained when Vanessa looked nonplussed. 'It's size thirty. Is that big enough for you?'

'Yes,' Vanessa said in a cracked voice. She had a feeling that size thirty was the biggest you could get. Or was it thirty-two? 'Thank you.' She felt like wrapping the blouse around the girl's neck.

'Oh, and another thing: tomorrow night Megan and Brodie and me are going to watch *Gone With the Wind* in my room and I wondered if you'd like to come? We're having wine and a takeaway and we're going to get dressed up as if it was a film premiere or something. You could wear your new blouse.'

'I could, couldn't I?'

'That would be the gear. Do you think Rachel would like to come? We hardly see anything of her.'

'I don't know. You'll just have to ask her.' As the weather became warmer, the girl had begun to appear in the garden with her child in a pram. For some inexplicable reason, the sight of the tiny girl nursing the tiny baby almost brought tears to Vanessa's eyes. There seemed something very wrong about her being on her own. Where were her parents and the baby's father? She told herself it was none of her business. The baby was happy and seemed to be thriving, so there was no need to interfere.

Diana went away and Vanessa went down to the kitchen to make an omelette.

It was a stupid idea, getting dressed up to watch a DVD in your own home, Vanessa thought the next night as she watched the three women in the garden, each with a glass of wine. She'd been alerted by the music. 'Moonlight becomes you, it goes with your hair,' a man was singing in a frightfully posh voice. Perhaps they were waiting for the food to be delivered. She wondered what had been ordered.

Brodie was wearing an ordinary blouse and skirt made to look dressy with the addition of a white lace stole, and Megan a pink linen frock with a cherry-red velvet jacket. Diana actually had on a genuine evening frock, blue taffeta, very old-fashioned, the sort of thing women wore in wartime, with a little white fur cape. She looked utterly ridiculous. All three were giggling as if they'd already had too much wine. Or perhaps not. Vanessa gloomily remembered behaving in exactly the same way when she went out with her friends, laughing hilariously at nothing at all yet being perfectly sober. She couldn't remember the last time she'd gone out with friends, only that it was before William had dumped her at the altar.

She sniffed dejectedly as she pressed her face against the window. The scene outside was like something out of a play: the music, the women with their wine, the darkening trees casting darker shadows underneath as dusk fell, the light from the downstairs' windows shining on the grass. A single bird sang from somewhere inside the trees and the ginger cat was curled up on one of the chairs.

The doorbell went and Diana ran inside, holding her skirt with one hand and the wine glass with the other. She was wearing *diamanté* shoes with high heels, and managed to look graceful and awkward at the same time.

'Shall we go in?' Megan called to Brodie. 'We can't eat out here, the food will get cold.'

Vanessa turned away for a second to blow her nose. When she turned back the garden was empty except for the cat, which jumped off the chair and lazily stretched itself before strolling away into the shadows. The bird continued to sing, but mournfully now, or so Vanessa thought.

Then the light disappeared. Diana must have closed the window and drawn the curtains. Left with nothing but trees that were getting blacker by the minute, Vanessa drew her own curtains and settled down to . . .

What?

Watching television while thinking about food? It was all she had to do. She couldn't have read a book to save her life, having lost all powers of concentration. There'd been a time when she'd read a newspaper every day and knew everything that was going on in the world, but no longer. The television news was horrendous, nothing but people being killed. She'd brought her laptop with her, but what was she supposed to do on it? Play games when it had once been used for extremely important work.

She wondered if there were any messages on her mobile.

Seven, she discovered when she checked. She deleted the lot without reading them. Each time she looked there were fewer. The day would come when there'd be none at all and she would feel as if she had died and nobody was thinking about her any more. The thought made her blood run cold. She quite literally felt as if she were freezing. If she got any colder, she really would die.

Vanessa jumped to her feet and began to rub her arms, stamp her feet and shake herself all over in order to bring herself back to life.

This couldn't go on. For Christ's sake, she was only *fat*. And she'd been jilted by the manager of a video rental shop, who had earned less than half as much as she did. It wasn't the end of the world. She didn't have a deadly disease. She had relatives who loved her, a roof over her head, and plenty of money.

Why, then, did she feel more wretched and more lonely than she'd ever felt in her life?

She could hear the women in the kitchen, sorting out the food. She'd been invited to share that food, see the film and drink the wine, but had refused.

No, she hadn't: she'd accepted. She'd agreed to come and wear the second-hand, size thirty blouse that Diana had bought from a bric-à-brac stall in a refugee centre. Looked at in a certain way, it was an extremely thoughtful gesture.

Vanessa put on her black trousers and the sequinned top, which was miles too big – it felt quite heartening to put on something that was too big instead of too small – but looked very glamorous. She felt a tiny bit drunk as she brushed her beautiful blonde hair and left it loose, put on lipstick and a pair of sparkly earrings.

'Hello, darlin',' Megan gushed when Vanessa went into the kitchen where numerous cartons of Indian food were being shared out on plates.

'I'm glad you've come,' Brodie said. 'Pass us another plate

and I'll give you a bit of everything. There's loads here; we ordered far too much.'

'That blouse looks really pretty on you,' Diana said admiringly.

The film ended just after midnight. Vanessa was stuffed to the gills with cinnamon fried rice, horseradish bread, dahi ki dahl, egg curry, prawn curry with coconut, rogan josh, and finally steamed dessert dumplings, washed down with copious amounts of wine. The film had been lovely as well as the wine and the company.

Why, then, did she start to cry? Start to weep so intensely and so terribly that she felt as if her heart would break, literally break, into a dozen pieces, never to be put together again? Every part of her hurt with the sheer effort and energy she was putting into such tremendous weeping.

The women gathered around, patting and stroking her, murmuring words of sympathy and encouragement, telling her everything would be all right in the morning, that she might be just a little bit drunk and would feel better when she was sober.

They took her up to her room, helped take off her clothes, found her nightdress under the pillow and tucked her up in bed.

Vanessa waited until they'd gone. She got out of bed, looked for the scissors and stood in front of the wardrobe mirror. Bit by bit, she hacked off her hair until it was barely an inch long all over. She felt freer, lighter, younger, better.

Then she got back into bed and fell fast asleep.

The next morning, Brodie knocked on Vanessa's door. 'I've brought you some tea,' she shouted. If she didn't answer, she'd drink it herself. Poor Vanessa had been in a terrible state last night. Mind you, *Gone With the Wind* was awfully sad. Brodie could remember crying buckets the first time she saw it.

She was about to take the tea away when there was a croak from inside the room and Vanessa opened the door still in her nightie. 'G'morning,' she said grumpily, rubbing her eyes.

'You've cut your hair!'

Vanessa patted her head. 'It was getting too long. I thought I'd have it short for a change. What does it look like?'

Brodie searched for an appropriate word, one that didn't sound too tactless. 'Remarkable,' she said at last. 'Quite remarkable.'

'Anyway, thanks for the tea,' Vanessa said, almost smiling.

Vanessa closed the door, put the tea on the bedside table, and went to look at her hair in the mirror.

'Bloody *hell*!'

She screamed, but caught it just in time, jamming both her hands over her mouth. She looked *ghastly*. What on earth had possessed her to hack off her hair so carelessly, as if she didn't give a damn what it looked like?

Because she didn't give a damn, that's why. Because she didn't care what she looked like. Because life was shit and she wanted no part of it.

'You should see what Vanessa's done to her hair,' Brodie said when she went into the kitchen where Diana was cooking bacon, tomato and eggs. She leaned against the fridge-freezer to watch. 'It looks awful – Vanessa's hair, that is, not the food.'

'She must have done it when she was drunk.' Diana expertly turned over an egg. 'Would you like your egg fried both sides?'

'Yes, please. I hate them watery.'

Diana tipped her head sideways. 'If I'm ever stranded on a desert island, I shall shave me hair off. I'm told that if it's shaved, it can grow back curly when it used to be straight, or even a different colour.'

'That's probably an old wives' tale. If you were stranded on a desert island, you're unlikely to have a razor. Anyroad, our Josh shaved his head once and it grew back exactly the same.' She couldn't understand why Diana wanted different hair when the hair she had now was such a lovely colour, light-brown with streaks of gold, and very thick. Compared with Diana's, Brodie considered her own hair to be thin and tired-looking.

'Do you mind getting the plates out of the oven?' Diana gave the frying pan a shake. 'Shall we eat this in your room or mine?'

'Mine,' said Brodie. 'Yours is still in a state after last night. I'll help you tidy up when we've eaten this.'

'It's all right, honest,' Diana assured her. 'Just a few glasses and empty wine bottles, that's all. The leftover food's in the fridge. Don't throw any of the meat away, will you? I can give it to Kenneth.'

Brodie laughed. 'Kenneth is an awfully odd name to give a cat, Diana. What's his real name?

'I dunno.' Diana shrugged. 'He doesn't wear a collar. I don't even know where he lives. And don't ask why I call him Kenneth. It just came to me out of the blue. Would you like a piece of fried bread?'

'I would love a piece of fried bread more than anything I can think of,' Brodie said, noisily licking her lips, 'but I'd better not.' She pulled a face. 'It's probably the most fattening food there is.'

'I'm going to have two slices.'

Diana ate like a horse and never put on an ounce of weight. Brodie told her she was a truly horrible person. 'I hope you're not going to eat them in front of me.'

'You'll just have to close your eyes.'

Brodie put the warmed-up plates on top of the draining board. 'You know,' she said with a glance around the room,

'I'm beginning to get used to the colours – red and mustard. It's a strange combination, but very original, sort of oriental.'

'I think it's the gear.' Diana sounded a little defensive. She was probably still feeling guilty about the kitchen, though it had been Mr Peterson's fault, not hers, for going ahead without consulting Brodie.

They ate at the little table in front of the window in Brodie's room. It was a dull, damp May day. Even Diana, who loved the garden and sat under the trees whenever she could, felt disinclined to do so today.

Diana left straight after breakfast. Although she wasn't supposed to work on Saturdays, she often went into the centre to give this amazing Tinker chap a hand with whatever was happening that night: a pop concert perhaps, a social, some sort of party.

Brodie lay on the bed, really glad that it was Saturday and she had the day off. *She* didn't have to go to work today.

When she'd thought about getting a job, office work had seemed the obvious choice. At school, she'd learned to type and do shorthand. When she'd left at sixteen with five O-levels, she'd gone straight into a bank as a junior secretary to one of the senior clerks. It had been extremely boring, but she'd got on with everyone and had made friends that she still occasionally met.

Brodie had never planned on having a career. She was perfectly happy to leave the bank after four years and marry Colin Logan. Since that day she had never worked again, unless she counted the thousands of nappies that she'd washed, the mountains of ironing, the meals she'd made, the dusting, cleaning, shopping, gardening, mending, occasional decorating, and the multitude of other tasks that constituted being a wife and mother of two children. She'd always had a typewriter and later a computer.

So, the other week, when she'd been told, to put it brutally, it was time she earned her own money, she'd approached an agency and asked for temporary office work. She didn't want to commit herself to a full-time job just yet.

She'd spent the first week at Starks & Putney, solicitors, in Water Street down by the Pier Head, working for Robert Priest whose secretary was on holiday.

He was the most arrogant man she had ever met and she disliked him straight away. It didn't help that she was almost old enough to be his mother. He never thanked her once for the dozens of letters she typed each day, after having make sense of his scribbled, barely legible notes. It was even worse when he dictated whole jumbles of words at a hectic, barely discernible rate.

She and Robert Priest swiftly became mortal enemies. At night, she cried herself to sleep. It was Colin's fault she was in this position because she loved their daughter and he didn't give a damn. She was heartily relieved when the week came to an end and she could leave and transfer to another office.

This time she'd worked with five young women in the claims department of an insurance company over the water in Birkenhead. For five whole days she was barely spoken to. The women weren't being rude, they just weren't interested in a woman at least twenty years older than themselves who wore skirts that covered her knees, hardly any eye make-up, and didn't have a tattoo or a stud anywhere on her body. When the need to speak to the temp became unavoidable, they called her 'Erm'.

It was impossible to hide the fact that she was working from her mother. When Megan heard what Colin had said, she called him every horrid name she could think of and offered to give Brodie all the money she needed.

'It's only lying in the bank, darlin',' she said forcefully. 'It'll all be yours one day, and I'm not likely to need it, not at my age. You'll not catch me going into a home where they'll stuff me in an armchair and let me dribble meself to death.'

But Brodie flatly refused to accept her mother's money.

'I don't want Colin thinking I can't manage on my own. Any-road, Mum, it'll do me good to support myself for a change.' She really meant it. So far, she'd led a very easy life, especially when compared to Diana whom she admired so much.

The third week Brodie went to a different agency and enquired about being a cleaner. After all, she'd had more experience of that than office work. Hopefully, she would be left to her own devices. She made up her mind to refuse if she were asked to climb a ladder and clean upstairs windows or shift heavy furniture. She wasn't sure how she felt about cleaning lavatories, particularly if they were dirty.

But Mr Dougal was lovely to work for. He was in his eighties, very chatty, and could only walk a bit. Brodie found herself sitting for hours listening to stories of his time spent in the Navy during the war, then racing around the house to give it a bit of spit and polish when it was time to leave. Sadly it was only for a fortnight while his wife was in California where she'd gone to see her sister.

Home again, Nora Dougal had telephoned to thank Brodie for looking after the house while she was away.

'I didn't look after it all that much,' Brodie confessed. 'I spent an awful lot of time listening to your husband.'

'I know you did, dear. He drones on and on about things that young people have never heard of. You were very kind and patient with him. Should I ever go away again, is it all right to ask the agency if we could have you?'

'Of course.'

Now, lying on the bed the day after she'd watched *Gone With the Wind*, Brodie wondered what the next week's job would be like. She didn't like the uncertainty. She was neat in her ways and liked life to be the same: tidy and predictable. Next week, she was due to work for a Mrs Cowper in South-port and was looking forward it with a certain amount of dread.

★

Vanessa heard music in the room below. Diana was home and a woman was singing 'Every time we say goodbye, I cry a little'. She went down and knocked on the door.

'Come in, come in,' Diana cried.

'No, thank you,' Vanessa said stiffly, standing outside. 'It's just that when Leonard comes tomorrow to take me to lunch, will you please tell him I'm not feeling well.'

'Of course I will,' Diana said with a perplexed frown. 'But why don't you phone now and tell him yourself?'

'Because he'll try to talk me into it,' Vanessa said wearily. 'And I don't want to go, I really don't.'

'*Aren't* you well? Or is it because of your hair?' Vanessa winced and didn't say anything. The girl had no tact. 'Brodie said you'd cut it.'

She wondered how Brodie had described the hair to Diana. Right now, her head was covered with a scarf tied in a big bow. She looked a bit like Mammy in *Gone With the Wind*. She shrugged and looked numbly at Diana, not knowing what to say.

'Why don't you go to the hairdresser's on Monday, ask them to tidy it up a bit?' Diana suggested.

'Don't want to,' Vanessa said sulkily. They'd think she was mad. They'd be nudging each other, grinning and whispering, making fun.

'Would you like me to do it?' Diana offered, her blue eyes shining with kindness.

Vanessa winced again. The girl was too bloody nice by a mile. One of these days someone was bound to kill her.

'It doesn't matter.' She wished she didn't sound so sullen.

'Oh, but I'm quite good at cutting hair. I used to cut the lads' hair until I left home. I mean, all I'll do is tidy it. Come on in.' She made an inviting gesture with her head. 'I've got proper scissors. Sometimes I trim my own hair.'

'Oh, all right.' She still sounded sullen.

The blue taffeta dress she'd worn the night before lay on

Diana's bed. In an effort to be friendly, Vanessa asked where she'd got it from.

'From the refugee centre. I only borrowed it. I shall take it back on Monday. Tonight I'm going to a twenty-first and I'm wearing it for that.' Diana opened the door of the wardrobe and revealed a mirror on the other side. She placed a chair in front of it.

'It looked very nice on you.'

'And that blouse looked very nice on you,' Diana responded.

Vanessa supposed she'd asked for that. She sat on the chair and Diana draped a towel around her shoulders, then prowled around her, studying her hair and opening and closing the scissors with a loud clicking noise that Vanessa found vaguely threatening.

'It's a lovely colour,' Diana remarked. 'Is it natural?'

'Yes.'

'It's said that hair is a woman's crowning glory.'

'I know.' It had been the only bit of glory that she'd had left.

Diana stopped prowling. 'Have you ever had a fringe?' she enquired.

'Not since I was a little girl.'

'Well, I think you should have one now. You'd look better with it combed on to your forehead, it being so short, like.'

'Whatever.' In a way, Vanessa didn't give a damn about her hair, but didn't fancy giving herself a fright every time she looked in the mirror until it grew to a respectable length again, which would take months, years even. William had always loved her hair. He would run his fingers through it, saying it was her best feature.

Diana took ages, cutting off infinitesimal amounts so the hair began to look feathery rather than clumpy. 'We don't want it to look *too* neat,' she said, rumpling it with her fingers.

When she finished, Vanessa was despatched upstairs to

wash it. 'Do you have a hairdryer? I left mine at home,' Diana said. 'I keep meaning to go and get it.'

'I've got one – you can borrow it whenever you like.' It was the first kind gesture Vanessa had made since she couldn't remember when.

'Do you still not want to go to lunch with Leonard tomorrow?' Diana asked when Vanessa's hair had been washed and dried and didn't look too bad at all considering the damage she'd inflicted on it. It had the look of a crew cut on top, but the rest appeared neat and casual, much better suited to a woman with a fuller figure than the old style. In retrospect, it had made her appear a bit blousy.

'I'd still like to give lunch a miss this week.' At first, she'd enjoyed the lunches, but last Sunday Leonard had squeezed her knee and she'd had the horrible feeling that he might be making a pass. He was seventy-three and she was thirty-one, yet she'd actually felt a tiny bit flattered. It was essential for the sake of her pride that it never happen again.

It seemed odd to have nothing to do on Saturday. Early in the afternoon, the sun had come out and at tea-time Brodie was lying on the bed again feeling unnaturally idle and thinking about the garden. Very soon, the hydrangeas and rhododendrons would bloom. There was already blossom on the lilac tree and little red buds on the climbing roses. The grass was ankle-high and badly in need of cutting. It was wild grass and grew rapidly.

Mum was going to the theatre with friends. It had been arranged months ago, long before Brodie had left Colin. 'Otherwise we could have gone somewhere together, darlin'.' She'd looked worriedly at her daughter. 'I don't like the thought of you being on your own on a Saturday.'

'Mum,' Brodie had said patiently, 'you don't have to look out for me. I'm forty-three. I can read a book or watch tele-

vision. It'll be nice to have my own company for a change.'
And the evening would be George-free, which was a blessing.

'Even so,' Mum had said, 'it doesn't seem right.'

'It doesn't seem wrong, either.'

Brodie wasn't the only person on her own. Vanessa was, too. She scarcely ever left the house, just once a week to do some shopping and sometimes late at night when she was never out for more than half an hour. Brodie would have loved to know what she was doing in Chestnuts. Last night she'd been so distressed, crying as if the world was about to end.

Rachel and her baby were also upstairs. Surely a health visitor should be visiting Poppy regularly? She hardly ever cried. There were times when Brodie was tempted to report the situation to Social Services, but it might result in the baby being taken away and she would feel like a really horrible snoop. She'd tried to approach the girl a few times, take an interest in the baby, but Rachel just looked at her suspiciously and didn't want to know.

Tonight, Diana was going to Leo Peterson's brother's twenty-first birthday party wearing the blue evening frock and little white fur cape she'd worn last night to see *Gone With the Wind*. It seemed that Leo wanted them to get engaged, but Diana wasn't exactly keen. Brodie hoped she wouldn't let Leo talk her into it. The girl was too concerned with hurting people's feelings.

She got off the bed, wandered across to the window, opened it and went outside. A train passed and she could feel the ground shiver beneath her feet. There was a lovely fresh smell in the air and the birds had come out with the sun and were singing merrily in the trees.

It was very easy to wish that Diana, not Maisie, were her daughter, though Maisie had once been just as sweet and just as nice. Brodie walked through the moist grass, not noticing it was soaking her shoes. She remembered holding Maisie's hand as she skipped along beside her. She closed her eyes and could actually feel the small hand in her own and hear quite clearly the things that Maisie had said: 'Mummy, why doesn't the sun come out every day?' 'Mummy, where is heaven?' 'Do you love me, Mummy?' Brodie had picked her up, hugged her, told her she was the most loved little girl in the whole, wide world. She remembered a much older Maisie sitting on the swing, grinning widely, full of life. 'I plan my future here,' she'd said. Well, she wouldn't have planned on becoming a drug addict.

Karen Grant had telephoned about three weeks ago. She had nothing to report: there'd been no sign of Maisie. 'But I'm still on the case. I'll get back to you as soon as I hear anything,' she'd said.

Brodie sat on a bench, aware but not caring that it was damp. She heard the gate creak and Colin came into the garden. She felt so surprised she thought she was dreaming.

He said, 'I thought you might be out here, that's why I didn't ring the bell.'

'Why have you come?' Brodie asked. She still felt odd and dreamy. She noticed that his brown hair needed cutting and his sweatshirt hadn't been ironed. There were oil stains on his jeans: it being Saturday, he must have been working on the Triumph. He looked very young, hardly old enough to have two grown-up children. She realized that, despite everything, she loved him very much, but there was a barrier between them that neither he nor she could – or would – cross.

'I've come to cut the grass,' he said surprisingly.

'There isn't a proper lawnmower.' There was just a manual one, very elderly. It would take a week to cut the grass with it and she kept meaning to throw it out.

'I've brought the one from home. It's in the boot.' He aimed a kick at the grass. 'It'll go through this in no time.'

'That's very kind of you,' Brodie stood, suddenly aware

that her behind was freezing; the moisture on the bench had soaked through her skirt. 'But there's no need.'

'Of course there's a need,' he said huffily. Perhaps he was hurt that she didn't appear grateful. 'It looks as if it hasn't been cut for ages. I'll just go and get the mower.'

Their mower had a petrol engine. Brodie had never been able to start it, but Colin had no difficulty. It sliced through the long grass leaving a bright green flat ribbon behind. Brodie stood and watched for a while, then took a rusty rake from the shed and began to gather the cut grass into heaps.

Eventually, the whole garden was bright green. Brodie fetched plastic bags from the kitchen and held them for Colin to fill with grass, weeds and the few leaves that had fallen. It was the way they'd worked together all the years they'd been married, though the lawn in their old house had never been allowed to grow so long.

When it was finished, she thanked Colin and made him tea and a sandwich. They sat in her room and he started to mumble something about not having meant it when he'd suggested she go to work, but she cut him short.

'You meant it at the time,' she told him.

He went red. 'I'm sorry. It was a mistake. I don't mean it now.'

She didn't say that now was too late. She was determined to work and support herself, if only to prove that she was capable of doing it.

They sat in silence for a while. Someone upstairs, Rachel or Vanessa, had a television on, but the sound was very faint. At one point, Colin said, 'Will we get over this, do you think?'

'I've no idea,' Brodie replied.

They sat in silence again until Colin said he'd better get going. Brodie thanked him for cutting the grass. He nodded briefly and went home.

★

Russell Peterson's girlfriend wore a black leather dress that was extremely revealing at both ends, exposing most of her rather pimply breasts and only narrowly missing revealing her bottom. Most of the young women there were similarly attired, leaving only a few square inches of their bodily charms to the imagination.

By contrast, Diana's full-length evening frock looked very old-fashioned. She quickly became a favourite with the elderly women present, who could remember wearing similar frocks when they were Diana's age. And it wasn't just the older men who thought there was something awfully appealing and downright sexy about the young woman with the flushed face and radiant smile who was covered from neck to toe in blue taffeta. Leo Peterson was deemed an extremely lucky fellow.

The party was being held in a new hotel by the river. It was nearly over when Leo took Diana's hand and led her into the lounge, where it was much quieter and barely half full.

'Let's sit down a minute, Di,' he said. There was a tremor in his voice and perspiration glistened on his upper lip.

'But I was enjoying the dancing,' she protested.

'We'll go back and dance in a minute.' He swallowed nervously. 'I've got you a present.'

'That's nice.' Diana smiled delightedly. 'What is it?'

'This.' He produced a little black velvet box out of his trouser pocket, opened it, and showed her the contents. 'It's a ring,' he announced. 'An engagement ring.'

Early next morning, Sunday, Diana knocked on Brodie's door.

'Come in,' Brodie shouted. 'I'm nearly ready.'

Both women usually went to Mass together along with Megan, but Diana had come about something else. 'Look!' She held out her left hand. A solitaire diamond ring glittered on the third finger.

Brodie gasped. 'What's that?'

'An engagement ring.' Diana flared her fingers and wiggled them. 'Leo and I are engaged.'

'Really? Congratulations. When are you getting married?'

'I dunno. I said I needed time to think about it.' Diana looked faintly worried. 'He just bought the ring without telling me. Luckily, it fitted.'

'You didn't have to take it, love.'

'I did, really. I think poor Leo would have cried if I'd refused. He was already hurt because his mam and dad had paid through the nose for some group to play at the party, when they could have had the Little Dead Riding Hoods, Leo's group, for free. I mean, he's got these lovely sad brown eyes and I felt so sorry for him. I couldn't possibly have not taken it.' Diana stared critically at the ring, 'It must have cost the earth. It's a real diamond.'

It was Brodie's turn to be worried. 'If you don't mind my asking, Diana, do you love him?'

'A bit.' To Brodie's relief, Diana burst out laughing, putting her whole heart and soul into it as she always did, making her eyes shine as brightly as the ring. 'The thing is, since I haven't had the lads to think about, I seem to fall a bit in love with every man I meet. I quite fancy Tinker, even though he might be gay, and there's this Iraqi doctor at the centre who's really gorgeous. I love him as well.'

'So, if these men gave you a diamond ring you'd agree to marry them, too?' Brodie began to laugh, too.

'Probably.' Diana collapsed, still laughing, on the bed. 'Leo's mum and dad are dead pleased. Mr Peterson called me a "nice old-fashioned girl".'

'Well, you are!' Brodie said warmly. 'I'd be dead pleased if you were marrying Josh.' The only girlfriend of Josh's that she'd met had chain-smoked foul-smelling black cigarettes. She was glad when they'd split up.

'I really liked Josh, too.' They'd met briefly the first

weekend Brodie had moved into the house when Josh had come to Liverpool with his friend, Murdoch.

'Shall we go to Mass?' Brodie tucked a lace scarf in her handbag. It wasn't necessary to wear a hat in church any more, but old habits died hard and she felt undressed without one.

Diana said, 'On the way back, shall we go to that place opposite Leonard Gosling's shop and have coffee and a cream cake? I can tell him Vanessa doesn't want to go to lunch today – I think she's still a bit upset about her hair.' She grinned. 'Actually, I think I might be a little bit in love with Leonard, too.'

## Chapter 6

Brodie and Diana had gone to work when Vanessa returned from her morning walk along the shore and found a rusty Ford Cortina parked outside the house and a strange woman waiting by the front door. The woman was in her forties, with dyed blonde hair and bright orange make-up plastered on her hard face. She wore bright pink combat trousers with a lime-green T-shirt and said that she was Rachel Keen's mother and had been ringing the bell, but there was no answer. Although Vanessa didn't like the look of her, she had little choice but to let her in. Perhaps Rachel was still asleep.

'Rachel's in the upstairs room at the back,' she said. She wasn't thanked when she unlocked the door and stood aside to let the woman in.

She was washing at the sink in her room when an unholy scream rent the air. Grabbing a towel, she rushed on to the landing. There was another scream: it came from Rachel's room where the door was wide open.

'Just give her to me, girl,' a rough female voice was saying, not unkindly. 'Let your mam have her and come on home. You can go back to school again. It'll be the best thing in the long run, Rach, I promise.'

Vanessa paused in the doorway. Rachel, still in her night-dress, was standing in the corner holding Poppy tightly against her breast. Her mother stood threateningly in front of her, arms outstretched towards the baby.

'No,' Rachel screamed. 'I'm keeping her, she's mine, she's my daughter. How did you find out where I was?'

'Our Frances followed Tyler when he came out of school the other day. We had to find out, girl,' the mother said, a faint note of contrition in her voice. 'Women from the Social Services keep coming round asking about you and the baby, where you've gone, like. They're dead worried about you.'

'What's going on here?' Vanessa enquired. Poppy had begun to cry. It was an unpleasant situation and she tried not to sound as nervous as she felt. On reflection, she should have asked Rachel if she wanted to see her mother before letting her in. She might have deliberately not been answering the door.

'It's none of your effing business,' the woman snarled over her shoulder. 'Eff off.'

'I have no intention of effing off,' Vanessa said with as much dignity as she could muster. 'If no one's going to tell me what's going on, then I shall ring the police.'

It was Rachel who answered. 'She wants to take Poppy away and send her to be adopted.' She began to cry. 'But she's my little girl, *mine*, and I want to keep her.'

The mother said, without looking at Vanessa, 'Do you know how old she is? Hardly fifteen. The father's a year older. They only want to set up home together.'

'What's wrong with that? I'm sure it's been done before.' Vanessa took a step into the room. 'I think it's time you left. Rachel clearly doesn't want you here. If you don't go straight away, then, like I said, I'm calling the police.'

'Rachel shouldn't be here.' This time, the woman turned around. To Vanessa's surprise, she looked more upset than angry. Her mascara had smudged under her left eye. 'She should be at home living with her mam. I told you, she's only fifteen. Kids aren't allowed to leave home until they're sixteen.'

'That's not true.' Vanessa had no idea how she knew: perhaps she'd read it somewhere in the days when she'd read serious newspapers or watched serious programmes on TV. 'Children under sixteen are entitled to leave home if they don't get on with their parents, as long as they move to a safe environment. I keep an eye on the baby,' she lied, 'and a district nurse comes once a week.'

'If she keeps that baby,' Mrs Keen said a touch despairingly, 'it'll ruin her life. The same thing happened to me. And if she thinks the dad'll marry her when the time comes, she's got another think coming. She won't have a childhood, and she won't finish her schooling, either. She's a clever girl, wanted to be a teacher when she grew up.'

'She still can,' Vanessa said smoothly. She felt strongly that Rachel should be allowed to keep Poppy, despite her young age. She tried to lead Rachel's mother towards the door, then towards the stairs, without actually touching her, just standing behind and urging her along with her stomach.

When they reached the front door, the woman seemed to regret she'd given in so easily. 'I'll be back,' she promised, scowling. 'There's thousands of women who can't have kids and will give Poppy a much better life than our Rachel ever could. It's not fair on any child to have a mother who's only a child herself.'

Vanessa opened the door and practically pushed the woman out. 'That's open to question, Mrs Keen.'

The woman's expression changed. She looked pleadingly at Vanessa. 'You'll look out for her, won't you? And the baby?'

'Of course I will. And will you promise not to tell Social Services where Rachel is? I can assure you she's perfectly safe here.'

'I suppose so,' Mrs Keen said grudgingly. She lit a cigarette before getting in the car, and Vanessa closed the door with a sigh of relief. She was shaking, though pleased she'd managed to handle the situation as well as she had. At the same time, she wasn't exactly happy about having committed herself to look out for a teenaged mother and her baby. She couldn't help but wonder what had prompted her to do it.

'She's horrible.' Rachel was standing at the top of the stairs, still holding Poppy. Her face was pale and her eyes enormous. 'I hate her.'

'I think she loves you very much.'

'Well, she's got a funny way of showing it. When I told her I was expecting Poppy, she nearly burst a blood vessel. Then she rang up some place and told them I wanted the baby adopted. Women kept coming round to try and talk me into it. They said I was too young to be a mother.'

'Despite that, I still think that in her own way your mother loves you. I don't think she'll give you away to the authorities, not again, not now she's seen you managing so well.'

Rachel just shrugged. 'Perhaps.'

'Anyway,' Vanessa said as she climbed the stairs towards the girl, 'you are obviously a very good mother, but I do think you should let Poppy be seen regularly by a district nurse or a health visitor.' She knew hardly anything about motherhood. 'My sisters have children and I'm sure that's what happened when they were babies. I think they also went to a clinic and had injections for . . . things. We can soon find out.'

When Rachel pursed her lips and looked stubborn, she went on sternly, 'Look, I told your mother I was keeping an eye on you and Poppy, which isn't true. I also said the district nurse came regularly and that isn't true, either. I would feel very irresponsible if I let things continue the way they are. I think we should have a word with Brodie when she comes home. She's had two children and she'll know what to do.' She desperately wished Brodie were there now. 'By the way, who is Tyler?'

'Poppy's dad.' Her little face began to glow. 'He's

American and he goes to school in Waterloo. He comes most afternoons on his way home. We're getting married as soon as I'm sixteen.'

It turned out to be the day that things changed for Vanessa. Later on, after she'd showered and weighed herself, she discovered she'd lost four pounds. Her weight had been going slowly down in dribs and drabs, but this was the first considerable drop.

Then when Rachel announced she was going to sit in the garden with the baby, Vanessa said she'd better go with her. 'I think one of us should be with you all the time from now on when you're outside.' It was a kind gesture, particularly as Vanessa wasn't normally given to kind gestures.

So far, unlike Diana and Brodie, she hadn't felt inclined to sit in the garden despite the spring weather being really lovely – perhaps it was because she preferred to avoid the other women – but she remembered the canvases and paints she'd bought in Leonard Gosling's shop weeks before. They'd been stuck under her bed ever since. She took them out and carried everything outside. It was a warm day, but not as sunny as it had been. The clouds raced by, obscuring the sun for long periods.

Rachel was already there, her head buried in a book. Poppy was fast asleep in her pushchair underneath a big shady tree. Maybe the girl didn't fancy spending the afternoon in the company of a woman of thirty-one. She seemed to switch from behaving like a frightened, vulnerable child to a sensible young mother.

Vanessa wondered what to prop the canvas on. It measured about half a metre square. She needed an easel, but she wasn't in the mood to go out and buy one there and then. In the shed, she found an old wooden ladder that would do for now. She set it up beneath the largest tree and put the open box of paints on a chair – twelve tubes of different colours. The lid was a palette on which the paints were mixed.

What to paint? It was just an ordinary garden, if a bit bigger than most, and extremely untidy. Vanessa chewed her bottom lip and half-closed her eyes as she scrutinized her surroundings: the old trees, the swollen bushes just starting to bloom, the rundown shed with loose planks and a crooked door, the ginger cat sitting on the roof regarding her critically, the tightly grown laurel hedge at the back of the house and the crumbling brick wall between this garden and the one next door. Then there was the house itself, which had perhaps been built over a hundred years ago, with its old grey bricks and floor-length windows through which could be seen faded carpets with dark shadowy patches here and there. Lastly, Rachel in her blue jeans and red top, the invisible baby hiding behind the hood of her pushchair.

Everything! Vanessa wanted to paint every single thing. It *wasn't* just an ordinary garden; it was a thing of incredible beauty. She looked critically at it again and it made her heart lift.

She painted one of the trees as if she were standing inside it, as if she were the tree's heart surrounded by its leaves. Green leaves were boring, she thought after a while, so she made them red and blue, yellow and purple, pink and cream.

It was a wonderful feeling, imagining standing in the middle of the leaves, exciting, satisfying, incomparable to anything she'd known before: better than sex, better than *eating* . . . she didn't feel even faintly hungry.

'What's that supposed to be?'

'A tree,' Vanessa replied.

Rachel had put down her book and was lifting Poppy out of her pram. The baby sat on her arm and wriggled her feet playfully. Rachel poked her in the stomach: her eyes danced and she actually smiled. Vanessa didn't think babies smiled until they were about one. She couldn't help but smile herself at the sight of the baby shuffling about on her mother's knee.

'She looks healthy enough,' she remarked.

'I do all the things it says to do in the baby book. She has the right vitamins and stuff and I give her the right amount of milk, though I couldn't manage to breastfeed. It's time she had her injections, but I was scared to go to a clinic in case they took her off me. But,' she said, jiggling the baby up and down, much to Poppy's delight, 'I don't mind taking her now that you're coming with me.'

Vanessa couldn't remember offering to go with her to the clinic, but supposed she better had.

'Your painting's very nice,' the girl said. 'I must go and make Poppy her bottle.'

'Let me know if you need a hand, won't you?' Vanessa was still engrossed in the painting. She wanted to put dots on it somewhere, white dots.

Twice during the night she woke and could smell oil paint. Each time, she switched on the bedside light and admired the painting that she'd propped on a chair. Brodie had called it 'remarkable,' which she felt sure was the word she'd used to describe her hair after she'd cut it, and Diana said it was 'the gear': she loved the colours. Neither had recognized it as a tree. But Vanessa didn't care. Tomorrow – she remembered it was the early hours of the morning – today, she would go to Leonard Gosling's shop and buy more canvases, more paint, and an easel. From now on, she would paint every day. She would become an artist.

Leonard was genuinely pleased to see her. 'It's ages since we met,' he said joyfully. 'Diana said you've been feeling off colour. Are you all right now?'

'Absolutely fine,' Vanessa sang.

'You're looking extraordinarily well.' He said this with a little bow. 'You suit your hair short, if you don't mind my saying.'

'Thank you,' she said modestly. Diana had tidied her hair again and it looked as good as if she'd been to a top-class hairdresser – or so they told each other.

'Have you lost weight?'

'A tiny bit.' She couldn't recall hearing any words that thrilled her quite so much, not even when William had proposed, though on reflection, she had a feeling that she'd proposed to him. 'Yesterday, I did a painting,' she told Leonard proudly.

'Did you really?' He looked hugely impressed. 'Would you mind if I came to see it sometime?'

'Not in the least. I've called it *Tree*.'

She told him what she'd come for and he advised that she buy canvas boards rather than genuine canvases. 'They're made by Winsor & Newton and only cost a fraction of the price. Would you like a folding easel or the other sort?'

'What are the other sort?'

'The sort that collapse flat as opposed to folding into a smallish square. All the grand masters had the other sort. They are far more regal and suited to a *real* artist. I can't imagine our dear Queen having her portrait painted by an artist using a folding easel,' he said with enormous pomposity.

'In that case, I'll have the regal sort.'

'You have made a wise choice, Vanessa.'

After she'd paid for everything and it had been stowed in the boot of her car, Leonard asked if she would like coffee and a cream cake in the coffee shop across the road.

She accepted, but said all she wanted was black coffee. She thought how wonderful it was to be alive.

Brodie didn't like her latest job, but didn't exactly dislike it, either. It was just a job. She worked in an old people's home in Southport. It was called Five Oaks for the obvious reason.

She cleaned in the morning and helped with the laundry in the afternoon. Her favourite piece of equipment was the polisher. She'd never used one before and she always had the urge to waltz down the corridors with it while singing a Chris de Burgh song.

She had asked if she could work through the lunch-hour and go home an hour early. Mrs Cowper, who was in charge of the domestic side of things, had agreed. She didn't mind when the work was done as long as it was done properly.

Had Brodie had a lunch-hour, she might have been tempted to roam around the centre of Southport, a place where, year after year, she and Colin had brought the children in the summer holidays to play football and cricket on the sands, visit the fairground and the pier, and have fish and chips in the cheap little café that also sold mouth-watering Eccles cakes. She usually bought half a dozen to take home. She knew she would cry if she saw that café now.

Those days had been gloriously happy, but she hadn't been conscious of it at the time. If she was ever that happy again, she'd make sure she was aware of it, appreciate it more.

She was on her way back to collect her car from the car park, another day's work thankfully over, when a voice called, 'Brodie! Brodie Logan! Is it really you?'

A woman in a white top, white linen trousers and gold sandals with high heels was coming towards her with a wide smile on her perfectly made-up face. Her smooth black hair was rippling as she moved. When she reached Brodie, she grasped her shoulders and bestowed kisses on both cheeks. She smelled of very expensive perfume. Brodie smelled of Persil and fabric conditioner.

'How lovely to see you,' she cooed. Her lips twitched. 'You don't remember me, do you?'

'I'm sorry,' Brodie stammered. She had no idea who the woman was and wished she were wearing something smarter than an oldish cotton frock and even older sandals. She had no make-up on and hadn't combed her hair since she'd got up that morning. Although she'd never been keen on trousers, she was particularly taken with the woman's white ones.

'Polly Baker, as was. We lived next door to each other in Crosby when we were first married. We had two children around the same time, though I had the girl first and the boy second. How are your children getting on? And how is your husband? He was a teacher, wasn't he? Colin! He must surely be a headmaster by now.'

'He's head of English.' Colin had never had any ambition to become a headmaster. He loved teaching English. 'Our son, Josh, has his own business and Maisie's in her second year at university.' She wished she'd left work a few minutes earlier, or a few minutes later, and had missed meeting Polly Baker, who, in the old days, had seemed to live in jeans and her husband's old shirts and had her hair cut like a boy. She wasn't in the mood to reminisce about the past and tell lies about the present, yet wasn't prepared to tell the truth, either. 'And what about your children?' she asked dutifully. 'Your husband's name was Roger, I remember that.'

'Natalie works for a top advertising agency in London,' her ex-neighbour said boastfully. 'And Dylan decided not to go to university. He's a member of a pop group. Their latest single narrowly missed getting in the charts.'

'That's fantastic,' Brodie murmured. 'And Roger?'

'Oh, I got rid of Roger yonks ago.' She waved her long white hands with their long red nails dismissively. 'In fact, I'm Polly Michaels now. Edward owns a factory making pipes: exhaust pipes, drain pipes, stuff like that.'

'What are you doing here?' Brodie asked. She recalled having liked Polly during the years they'd lived next door to each other, but she didn't like her now.

'I come once week to see Roger's old dad,' she replied. 'His new wife's a bit of a cow and poor old Albert is sadly neglected. He's a dear old thing and I'm very fond of him.'

Brodie decided she did like Polly, after all. They exchanged telephone numbers and promised to meet up for coffee one day. She was glad Polly hadn't asked what *she* was doing there, as she wasn't sure if she was prepared to admit she was a cleaner, despite there being nothing shameful about it.

Driving back to Blundellsands, she wondered if Natalie really did work for a top advertising agency and if Dylan hadn't attended university because he couldn't get into one. She would never know, just as Polly would never know the truth about Brodie's children.

The encounter had shaken her, though. She'd never been one for keeping up with the Jones's. Fifteen years ago the Bakers had moved from the house next door to a much better one and she hadn't felt envious at the time, but now she envied Polly's obvious *cheerfulness*. Brodie couldn't remember when she'd last felt cheerful, apart from brief periods such as when they'd watched *Gone With the Wind* and made a night of it. They'd done the same thing last week with *Now, Voyager* starring Bette Davis and Paul Henreid: 'Why ask for the moon, darling, when we can have the stars?' Diana kept saying in a Bette Davis voice while pretending to smoke a cigarette.

Brodie smiled. Diana made her feel cheerful.

When she arrived home, she found Eileen, her mother-in-law, in the garden nursing Poppy, who was fast asleep in her arms. Brodie hadn't seen her since last October when she was about to leave the country to spend the winter in Goa and had come to Liverpool from London to say goodbye. Now she had come to announce she was back.

'I talked her mum into having a nice, relaxing bath,' she said, kissing Poppy's nose. 'She was very reluctant at first, but I managed to convince her that I was related to you, had four children of my own, no criminal convictions, and was extremely trustworthy. She's a sweet little thing. How old is she?'

'Do you mean Rachel or the baby?'

'Rachel.'

'Fifteen.' Brodie hadn't been all that surprised when Vanessa told her about Rachel's mother's visit to the house. 'You look wonderful, Eileen,' she said. 'Incredibly glamorous and the picture of health.' Her mother-in-law was in her late sixties, but could have easily passed for ten years less, even fifteen. She'd worn size twelve clothes since she was a teenager, something she was extremely proud of, and used just enough cosmetics to enhance her features, without looking like mutton dressed up as lamb. Her thick grey hair was streaked with silver. Like Polly Baker earlier, she wore white trousers, though with white sandals and a pink see-through blouse. Eileen was a lovely down-to-earth person with a colourful use of language. She was rarely seen without a cigarette in her mouth, though she was without one now as she nursed the baby.

'I feel wonderful,' she said in a heartfelt tone, 'particularly when I saw George and realized how fortunate I was to have left the miserable old bugger behind. But what's this about you and our Colin?' She looked genuinely distressed. 'Oh, Brodie, luv, you always seemed such a happy couple. I thought you had a perfect marriage. I can't even begin to imagine what went wrong. What do Josh and Maisie have to say about it – and why didn't anyone let me know?'

'I knew you'd find out about it when you came home,' Brodie said. 'It seemed silly to upset you until then.' Clearly, Colin hadn't thought to write and let his mother know their marriage was on the rocks. Was it on the rocks? Or was the present situation just a hiccup? Brodie had no idea. What did Colin think?

'Am I allowed to know the reason why?' Eileen asked. 'Or is it too personal?' Poppy sighed and Eileen stroked her white cheek. 'Poor baby! She sounds as if she has the weight of the whole world on her shoulders. Perhaps she will one of these days. I'm glad mine aren't young any more.'

'I'm surprised Colin didn't tell you why we've split,' Brodie said.

'I haven't seen Colin yet, only George. He was at your house working on that old car when I went round this avvy expecting to see you. His lordship told me sod all, only that you didn't live there any more.' Eileen snorted. 'He was kind enough to give me your address. I suspect *he* could be the cause of your difficulties. After all, I went halfway around the world to escape the bugger, didn't I, only for him to land himself on you. Is he there all the time, luv?'

'Not *all* the time, but he's there enough,' Brodie admitted. 'There've been occasions when I wished you were still around to keep him at home.'

'No such luck, I'm afraid. It seems I was living it up in Goa, while you suffered at home.' She regarded Brodie worriedly. 'Seriously, is George the reason you broke up with Colin?'

'I'll tell you later.' Soon, Rachel would come to retrieve her baby and Diana would be home. 'Have you met Vanessa?' she asked. 'She paints. Well, she has done for the past few weeks.'

Eileen's lively face brightened. 'Yes, I've met her. She was here when I arrived, and was doing this absolutely fabulous painting. I don't know what it was, but the colours were amazing. She's going to give it me when the paint dries.'

'You *liked* it?'

'I told you, it was fabulous.'

'They all look like a load of rubbish to me. Poppy could do as well if someone gave her a brush.' The ginger cat stalked by, eyeing them arrogantly. 'And Kenneth could do even better.'

'Brodie, luv, you have absolutely no imagination. And who's Kenneth?'

Eileen stayed until after tea. They ate – she, Brodie and Diana – in the old dining room where Brodie had eaten when she was child, but which the Slattery sisters had hardly used, preferring to live in the four big rooms that they'd turned into bedsits.

It was Diana's idea that they have a communal dining room. 'It's friendlier,' she claimed. She thought it unsociable that the four women should make their own meals, then take them to eat in their own rooms. And she thought the room should be called 'the snug'. 'I read a book once about a house having a room called the snug.'

'But we can't make our separate meals all at the same time so we can eat them at the same time,' Brodie pointed out. She thought it a lovely idea – she and Diana often had breakfast together – but a bit impractical.

'Then we can all have the same meal. I mean, take turns to cook for four,' Diana suggested. 'I make lovely scouse – least, the lads used to think so.'

'Yes, but what does Rachel do with Poppy?' Brodie said reasonably. Diana's often expressed desire to turn the house into a commune could be a bit of a pain. 'She'll never leave her upstairs on her own: we'd have to get a high chair. As for Vanessa, she's on a diet. Surely you've noticed the salad stuff in the fridge. She won't like sitting down to a lettuce leaf and a slice of tomato while we tuck into scouse. And she's not exactly a friendly person, is she? She'd probably far sooner eat by herself.'

'Probably.' Diana looked downcast. 'Anyroad,' she perked up a bit, 'everywhere Vanessa goes she smells of paint. It'd spoil the meals for us.'

'Exactly,' Brodie said, relieved that Diana had given in. 'But at least us two can eat in the dining room – I mean, the snug. We'll take turns making dinner and if the others notice and want to join us, then it's up to them.'

At this, Diana had been all smiles.

It was nice, though, eating together. They had a Marks & Spencer's chicken pie that Brodie had bought the previous weekend, accompanied by new potatoes and fresh peas. For pudding, they had stewed apple and custard that Diana had made. Eileen said it was years since she'd last had apple and custard, and that she'd forgotten how nice it was.

'I used brown sugar,' Diana explained earnestly, 'that's why the apple was a bit brown. It's so much better for you than white.'

'So I've heard,' Eileen said.

Afterwards, Brodie and Eileen went back into the garden while Diana took a heap of washing into the laundry room.

'You wanted to know why Colin and I aren't living together,' Brodie began. 'First of all, I must explain about Maisie . . .'

'Holy Mary, Mother of God!' Eileen gasped about ten minutes later when Brodie had finished describing, not just her daughter's plight, but Colin's reaction to it. 'Oh, Brodie, luv, it must have been awful for you. As for our Colin, he wants his arse whacking with a broomstick – I'll be tempted to do it the minute I clap eyes on him. Have you no idea at all where Maisie is?'

'Only that she was in London last time I heard.' She'd had another phone call from Karen, who still had no knowledge of Maisie's whereabouts, but had promised never to give up.

'London's an awful big place,' Eileen murmured. 'If you had a clue where she might be, I could look for her meself.' Very soon, she was going back there to live with her sister, Mary.

The phone rang in the hall and Brodie heard Diana answer it. A few minutes later, she came into the garden and announced that their Damian was coming in his car to collect her and she'd be gone for a while.

Brodie sensed trouble. 'Is everything all right?' she asked.

'Not really.' Diana pulled a face. 'I'll tell you later.'

'I'll wait up for you,' Brodie promised.

'Ta.'

'Have you adopted her?' Eileen asked when Diana had gone.

Brodie said with a wry smile. 'I was in need of a daughter and she a mother. We've sort of adopted each other.'


'Mum,' Diana said when she went into the house in Coral Street, 'are you all right?'

'Not really, Di,' her mother said tearfully, flinging her arms around her daughter. Damian, Jason and Garth were in various parts of the living room wearing frowns that ranged from the sceptical to the plain fed up. There was little love in their hearts for the mother who had abandoned them seven years before. Of Emma, there was no sign. 'I've left Warren, luv,' her mother sobbed. 'He's got another woman. She's nearly twenty years younger than I am.'

'Where are Shaw and Jude?' Her stepbrothers were only five and three. They were really adorable little boys.

'I've left them with Warren, luv. He loves his lads. He won't harm a hair on their heads.' Michelle nestled her own head against Diana's shoulder. 'Oh, luv, I thought we could sleep together in the double bed. No one told me you'd gone away and this Emma girl had moved in. I've got nowhere to sleep, luv. Damian said you're living in this lovely big house and there might be room enough there for me.'

'I said no such thing, Mam,' Damian snapped. 'I said you could sleep here in the box room like our Di did before she left. There's a single bed in there. I only went and fetched Di because you insisted.'

'I don't know what's going to happen to me,' Michelle wailed loudly. 'I've no longer got a home to go to.'

Diana and Damian exchanged glances: this was quite

obviously true. The Coral Street house had been bought by their father and Diana supposed, in law, it belonged to Mam. On the other hand, Diana and the lads had paid the mortgage for the last seven years. It was all very confusing.

Damian said, 'If Warren's been unfaithful, he should be asked to leave the place in Nottingham and you can live there. I'll go and see him at the weekend if you like, Mam.'

Michelle sniffed disconsolately. 'I don't want to be stuck in Nottingham all on me own.'

'You'd have Shaw and Jude,' Garth pointed out. 'Or are you going to walk out on them like you did with us?'

'I told you, Warren loves his lads.'

'But will his new girlfriend love them?' Garth persisted.

Everybody looked at each other, but it was a question only the new girlfriend could answer.

'I feel so *sorry* for her,' Diana said tragically to Brodie much later that night. Brodie had made her cocoa to calm her nerves. 'I mean, the lads were awful short with her, but she can't help the way she is, can she?' They were talking about her mother, who'd been left to sleep in the box room of the house in Coral Street.

'No, but if you carry that way of thinking to its logical conclusion, then you could say the same about Hitler.' It was the sort of argument that Colin would have enjoyed.

Diana, however, completely ignored it. 'You know what I did? I took me engagement ring off before I went because I didn't want her asking to meet Leo's mam and dad. Isn't that horrible? She looked so sad, poor thing, as if she knew. Would you go back and live at home if you were me?'

'No, I would not,' Brodie said firmly. She didn't want to lose Diana. And she wasn't just being selfish, but thinking of the girl as well. 'Where would you sleep?' she asked, 'with your mother in the box room.'

'That's a point.' Diana spoke as if she hadn't given a thought to the sleeping arrangements. They'd been unsatisfactory when she'd left and would be even worse with another person on the premises. 'She asked if she could come and live here.'

'I hope you told her that she couldn't.' Having her mother on the premises, probably expecting to be looked after, would be disastrous for the girl. 'Really, Diana, your mother's not an old woman. How old is she?'

'Forty-five.'

'She's only two years older than me.' Brodie would have liked to give Diana's mother a piece of her mind. 'She's well old enough to look after herself. And she has a nerve, turning up after all this time and expecting her children to take her in.' Colin would have said exactly the same thing. 'Remember the day we met? You were so unhappy. But since you moved in here, you seem to enjoy having a life of your own.'

'Do I?'

'Yes.' Brodie nodded. 'And now your mother's talking about walking out on two more of her children, even younger than your brothers were when she left. What are their names?'

'Shaw and Jude. Y'know,' Diana said, 'I used to imagine our lads leaving home and Mam bringing the little ones for me to look after until *they* left.'

'By which time, *you'd* be around forty-five! No, Diana.' Brodie shook her head so hard it gave her an instant headache. 'It's about time you put your foot down and told your mother to grow up.'

'I'm not much good at putting me foot down,' Diana said in a small voice.

'I know you're not, dear, and that's just one of the things I like so much about you. You're too soft-hearted by a mile.'

When Diana arrived home from the centre the next day, she was annoyed to find her mother, dressed like a teenager in a red mini-dress over footless tights, in the garden talking to Brodie's mother.

'I've had a terrible hard life,' she was saying. 'I've suffered more than any woman should.'

'You poor thing,' Megan said sympathetically.

'Six kids I've had – *six*!' Her mother spoke as if six children were a terrible affliction.

At this, Megan looked desperately sad. 'I only had the one, I'd've loved to have had six.'

Diana's mother didn't quite know what to say to this. She changed the subject. 'I must say, our Di's fallen on her feet. This is a lovely house to live in. Does it belong to you?'

'No, it belongs to Brodie, my daughter.'

So far, neither woman had noticed Diana was there. When they did, she sensed that Megan was relieved. She excused herself immediately and said she wanted to start making Brodie's meal. 'She's going to be late today. There's a tea party at the home and they asked her to stay and help.'

She disappeared into the house, leaving Diana and Michelle alone together. 'How did you know where I lived, Mam?' Diana asked. It was a truly horrible thought to have about your own mother, and she felt dead ashamed for having it, but she would sooner she hadn't come to Chestnuts. Her presence took the shine off the place. There wasn't such a pleasant atmosphere.

'I asked that Emma girl.' Her mother looked outraged. 'I could tell she wanted me out the way. You'd never think it was *my* house. What on earth prompted our Damian to get tied up with her? You won't catch me at the wedding, I'll tell you that much,' she finished spitefully.

'Shall I make us a cup of tea, Mam?' Diana offered. 'Afterwards, we could go back to Coral Street on the train and have something to eat there.'

Her mother sighed heavily. 'I was expecting to be given me tea here.' She sighed again, even more heavily. 'But never mind, eh? I know when I'm not wanted, but I never thought it'd be by me own daughter. It would appear I'm not wanted anywhere.'

Ashamed, Diana quickly made scrambled eggs on toast followed by tinned peaches and a spoonful of Cream of Cornish ice-cream – she and Brodie had bought a carton between them the week before. She and her mother, who had become strangely quiet, sat by the little table in her room to eat.

'I think I'll go back to Nottingham tomorrer,' she said when they'd finished.

Diana gasped. 'But what about Warren and the other woman?'

'I might have got hold of the wrong end of the stick. The woman might've just been giving him a lift home from town. She only lives in the house opposite. Sometimes, her little boy plays with our Jude.'

Diana got the distinct impression that the whole thing had been a lie: that Warren hadn't been out with a much younger woman; that her mother had just felt like a break and the cheapest place to have it was in Coral Street. She wondered how much Warren knew about it. 'What time will you be leaving, Mam?' she enquired.

'Oh, I dunno, luv. I suppose you'll be only too glad to see the back of me,' she said bitterly. All of a sudden, she looked old and tired and desperately forlorn. 'No one wants me.'

'Don't be daft!' Diana put her arm around her mother's shoulders and squeezed them. She wondered what sort of star her mother was chasing and if she would ever catch it and be happy. 'I thought I'd ask my boss if I can take an extra-long lunch-hour,' she said. 'We can meet in town, have something to eat, then I'll come with you to Lime Street station and see you on the train.' She had a wonderful idea. 'Oh, and it's your birthday next month. If we've got the time, I'll buy you a little prezzie. You'll find an Argos catalogue at home in the cupboard under the stairs. Have a look through the jewellery and see if there's anything you like up to about thirty pounds.'

They had a lovely three-course lunch in an Indian restaurant in Bold Street, after which they went to Argos and Diana bought her mother a pretty mother-of-pearl and marquisite ring.

'I'll treasure it for always,' Michelle said tearfully. 'Oh, Di, I was beginning to think you didn't love me any more.'

'I'll never stop loving you, Mam.' Diana felt just as tearful. She'd learned a hard and painful lesson: that no matter how much you loved someone, it didn't mean you wanted that person to be part of your everyday life.

Brodie had a need to satisfy. On Saturday, she caught the train into town and went to T.J. Hughes's, a well-known Liverpool department store that sold goods at amazingly cheap prices, and bought a pair of white trousers. She'd been thinking about them all week. She also bought gold sandals and a lovely gauzy Indian top. The whole lot cost just under twenty-five pounds.

After paying for the things, she went into a cubicle, got changed and went to meet her mother for a coffee, feeling like a million dollars.

# Chapter 7

Sometimes there was violence in the centre and Tinker had to call the police if he wasn't able to control it, or if Alan, with his boxer's fists, wasn't there to control it for him. It was usually a fight, always between men: over money, over women, or if someone was suspected of cheating at one of the games. Sometimes arguments between refugees from different countries, tribes or religions would turn ugly. Knives had been flashed but, so far, no one had been hurt.

In their homeland, some refugees had feared for their lives or been tortured. Women had been raped, their husbands killed and sometimes their children. Even worse, the children had just disappeared and couldn't be found anywhere. These sad women came to Britain for a better life, a peaceful one, a genuine refuge from the life they'd had before.

It was these women that Diana felt the most sorry for. They seemed lost and bewildered, with no one to turn to if their application for asylum was turned down, which often happened, though it seemed monstrously unfair. An expert in asylum law came to the centre one afternoon a week to offer advice.

One morning, a few days after Diana's mother had returned to Nottingham, four young women ran screaming into the centre, not stopping at reception to register as they were supposed to. (Tinker only asked for a person's name and their country of origin. From then on, they were expected to sign in and out whenever they came again so he would know exactly who was on the premises.)

Diana and Tinker looked at each other. Without a word, they left reception and raced after the women, catching up with them in the virtually empty restaurant, where they stood in the middle of the room not quite knowing what to do.

They were only girls, Diana realized. Two looked no more than thirteen or fourteen and weren't even fully grown. The other two weren't much older. They were pale-skinned with light-brown hair except for the smallest who was blonde.

Alan and Rosa were in charge of the restaurant that morning and Rosa was already trying to calm the girls, who were clearly terrified. 'What's wrong, darlings?' she was saying, patting them tenderly.

'We run away,' one of the girls cried shrilly. She was excessively thin with huge, haunted eyes and hollow cheeks. Some of her teeth were missing. 'Him leave open door so we run away, but him follow. Please hide us.'

Diana approached the girl and took her arm. 'Who are you talking about?'

'Hide us! Hide us, please!' the girl begged. The other three clung to her, as if she were their leader. Or perhaps she was the only one who could speak English. She shrank back, screaming. 'No, no, now is too late.'

Two men had entered the room. The first was huge and menacing with the grimmest face Diana had ever seen. His black hair was short, curly and full of grease and his dark eyes were filled with anger. With a growl, he threw himself at the girls, grasped two by the hair, and began to drag them out of the room. The girls yelled in agony.

Alan threw a punch at the big man's jaw. It had an effect, making him jerk his head sideways, but he didn't release the girls, who continued to yell and thrash about. Alan threw another punch, but he was twice the man's age and no longer had the strength to land a knockout blow on someone so obviously powerful. The only other occupant of the room, an elderly Asian woman, aimed a kick at the man's ankle, but she might well have hit him with a feather for all the notice he took.

Without any idea of what she was doing, Diana picked up a teapot off the table. It was full and felt very hot. The lid fell off and she threw the liquid into the man's face. He howled with a mixture of rage and pain, and released the girls. Rosa shepherded them into the kitchen and locked the door. Tinker had tackled the second, much smaller man, and they were rolling about on the floor. Alan was doing his utmost to fell the big man, who was still howling and holding his giant hands over his face. By now, other people had appeared out of the lounge. For a brief moment there was silence, apart from the sound of children singing in the playgroup upstairs.

'I've phoned the coppers,' someone said.

As if this were a signal, the second man aimed a violent kick at Tinker and managed to scramble to his feet. He dragged his companion out of the room, along the corridor and through the front door. Not a soul felt tempted to stop them. They stood, transfixed and silent again, until the sound of the police siren could be heard and everyone began to talk at once.

By lunchtime, things had calmed down, but those involved still felt shaky. The least little thing made Diana jump, and Tinker, who had a massive bruise on his shoulder, had drunk at least half a dozen cups of strong coffee. Rosa and Alan had gone to the pub for something even stronger and the girls had been transferred to a woman's refuge in Everton Valley where they would be interviewed by women police officers once an interpreter had been located.

'They were here legitimately,' the police sergeant said. 'The country they're from is part of the European Union, but they thought they were going to be models or actresses or something just as daft. Instead they got stuck in a brothel. The place is only just across the road. That's how the girls knew where to come; they could see the centre through the windows.'

'But they were so *young*,' gasped an appalled Diana.

'The youngest is thirteen, the oldest sixteen,' the policeman said. 'They were kept prisoner twenty-four hours a day, weren't given a penny of what they earned, weren't even fed properly, poor kids. I'd've given me eye teeth to get me hands on them two bastards,' he made a gesture with his hands as if he were snapping a neck, 'and the others that were running the bloody place, but the house was empty by the time we got there. From what we could tell, there must have been more girls, but they'd gone, too.'

After the policemen had left, promising to come back in the afternoon to take more statements, Diana went down into the basement and searched through the rack of women's clothes. There were loads of T-shirts and she picked four of the nicest, plus some jeans and summer skirts.

In her lunch-hour, she walked as far as Marks & Spencer where she bought two packs of women's briefs. She'd never minded wearing second-hand clothes, but had always balked at the idea of wearing other women's knickers. The young girls in the refuge deserved no less.

Brodie and Megan were horrified when Diana described the events of the morning.

'It must have been *awful*.' Brodie shuddered. 'And it must have taken some courage to chuck boiling hot tea in the man's face.'

'I just picked up the first thing that came to hand.' She looked troubled. 'I hope I haven't blinded him.'

'Why should you care?' Megan snorted.

'Even though he was really horrible, I'd hate to think it was my fault someone lost their sight.'

Vanessa, smelling of oil paints, came into the kitchen and

took a bottle of water out of the fridge. Brodie couldn't resist telling her about Diana's adventures that morning. Vanessa's appalled reaction was only to be expected, as was Rachel's when she came to make the baby's bottle later. Diana smiled half-heartedly. She was glad the men had been stopped from taking the girls, but throwing the teapot was playing on her mind. Vanessa said this was a typical female attitude to violence.

'We can't bring ourselves to hurt people even when they're hurting us. If women were stronger than men, the world would be a much more peaceful place,' she said, somewhat illogically.

It amazed Vanessa that she didn't miss the outside world, not a bit. Yet she'd always been a terrifically busy person. Every minute of every day had been taken up with some activity or other. Her job required non-stop action: she was either on the phone, on the computer, or at a meeting. At lunch she ate at her desk, took a client to a posh restaurant in Liverpool town centre, or was taken to one herself. Even when she was alone in the flat, which happened very rarely, she was making notes about the work she had to do the following day or the following week.

Evenings and weekends, she and William had gone out together, sometimes just the two of them, at other times with friends. Often, they drove down to London to see a show and stay the night in a hotel, spending Sunday wandering around the shops and markets.

But now Vanessa rarely left the house except for her early-morning walk on the shore, the fortnightly visit to the clinic with Rachel and Poppy, and calling at Leonard Gosling's shop for more painting materials. The narrowness of her life didn't bother her. Her horizons had widened just a little in that she no longer spent all the time in her room. If the weather was fine, which it usually was – the lovely warm spring having given way to a brilliant summer – she spent hours in the garden painting. She'd begun eating in the little dining room downstairs. One day, Rachel had found her there and they'd begun to have some of their meals together. A few times, Vanessa had given Poppy her bottle. It was a strange experience holding a tiny human being in her arms. She found it hard to describe: there was something almost mystical about it.

She didn't bother about an awful lot of things that had bothered her before. She no longer read newspapers or watched the news on television, so had little idea what was going on in the world outside Chestnuts, whether another war had broken out somewhere, or peace had broken out somewhere else.

It was a lovely feeling, being ignorant. It left her with absolutely nothing to worry about. She felt sorry for Brodie and Diana who had to leave the house every day. Diana's experience with the men who'd invaded the shelter and their young victims had shocked her to the core.

She was thinking about it the next morning when she stood in the garden in front of the easel. Rachel's window was wide open and she was singing to Poppy. She could hear the squirrels moving through the trees. Occasionally, they would appear and chase each other across the grass. Bees hovered around the flowers that bordered the garden, and she could hear the strange noise that grasshoppers made – Megan said they were scratching their legs together. Every now and then a train would pass on the other side of the grassy bank.

The idea for the painting had come to her when she closed the curtains before getting into bed last night. It was all she could do not to start it there and then.

There'd been a three-quarter moon and the sky was a glorious inky blue splattered with stars no bigger than dust-mites. The slate roof on the house opposite looked silver in the muted light and the trees, silhouetted as they were against the dark, gleaming sky, were smudges of black. The grass was the darkest of greens and the garden furniture hardly visible against it.

Vanessa had gone to bed with the image in her mind and it was still there when she woke the next morning when the sky was pale and milky and everything in the garden was bright and full of colour.

She set up her easel in the usual place amidst the trees and began to paint. She painted swiftly, hardly pausing, wanting to get the scene out of her mind and on to the canvas. For some people, the silver roof might have been a problem, but Vanessa used shiny black paint streaked with brilliant white and was perfectly satisfied with the result.

Excitement began to gather in her breast as she neared the end. She could hardly wait to see what her latest work would look like when every single centimetre of the board was covered with paint.

'Hello, I thought I'd find you here.'

Vanessa looked up. Eileen, Brodie's mother-in-law, had come into the garden. She really admired Eileen, who'd walked out on her monster of a husband after forty years of marriage. It was also flattering to know that Eileen considered Vanessa's paintings absolutely fabulous.

'I won't interrupt,' Eileen said, sitting at the wooden table. 'When you've finished, I'd like to talk to you about something.'

'I'm nearly finished.'

'Then would you like me to make some coffee for when you do?'

'Please. Mine's black, no milk or sugar.' She no longer bothered to weigh herself, but could tell by her clothes that she was growing thinner.

'OK. I'll do it now, shall I?'

Vanessa didn't answer. She was only half-conscious of Eileen going into the house. When she emerged with two mugs on a tray, the painting was complete and Vanessa was standing thoughtfully in front of the easel, her head on one side, not judging her work, or admiring it, just satisfied that it was finished and she'd got it out of her system.

'Can I see?' Vanessa nodded and Eileen came for a look. 'It's fabulous,' she breathed. She said the same thing every time. 'Absolutely fabulous. I can understand why you made the moon so incredibly big, almost as if it can be touched.' She looked imploringly at Vanessa. 'Can I please have it?'

Vanessa had no idea why she'd painted the moon so large – she hadn't realized she had until Eileen had pointed it out. 'Of course you can have it,' she said. She was generous with her paintings, mainly because she was no longer interested in them once they'd been done.

'I wish you'd let me pay for it,' Eileen said. 'This is the third I've had. You say you won't take money, but I'd love to at least buy you a prezzie before I go back to London at the weekend. Is there anything in particular that you'd like?'

Vanessa concentrated hard, but couldn't think of a single thing; she didn't want jewellery, make-up, perfume or clothes.

'Would you like a book on painting?' Eileen asked.

'I can already paint.' She didn't want to know about technique or scale or balance or perspective or how to mix paint properly or what to mix it with.

'I didn't mean it like that!' Eileen rolled her eyes with embarrassment. 'Of course you can paint, and you do it beautifully. I meant, would you like a biography of Picasso or Van Gogh or some other painter?'

'It's awfully nice of you to offer, but no. I'm flattered that you like my paintings and you can have as many as you want. I don't want anything for them.'

'Oh, Vanessa!' Eileen said emotionally. 'What a lovely person you are! I'm just so thrilled to have met you.'

'Why, thank you.' It must have been the first time in Vanessa's adult life that she had blushed.

'Anyway,' Eileen lit a cigarette and they both sat down, 'what I wanted to say is that I think you should have an exhibition.'

Vanessa choked on the coffee. 'Don't be daft, Eileen,' she spluttered.

'I'm not being daft. There are people like me who love having original paintings. Not only that, yours are *original* originals. I mean, it wouldn't enter the head of any other artist to paint that one you've just done – at least, not in the way you've done it. It's so . . . so natural and down to earth. Your work shows enormous imagination. And it's got *body*.' She was so wholly sincere, so obviously speaking from the heart, that Vanessa was touched. 'I'm sure your pictures would sell like hot cakes. If you don't want to take money for them, then give it to charity – Diana's refugee centre, for instance.'

'And where would I hold this exhibition?' Vanessa asked. 'The Walker Art Gallery? The Liverpool Tate?'

'Here,' Eileen said, glancing around the lovely garden. 'Let the *Crosby Herald* and the *Liverpool Echo* know about it. They'll turn it into a news item if they know it's for charity. Diana will organize it for you, and Megan and Brodie will help.'

'I'll think about it,' Vanessa promised. 'It would be best to wait until I had more paintings.' She didn't want her name or photograph appearing in the paper for William and her family to see. Once Eileen had gone, Vanessa could quietly forget about an exhibition.

It reminded her that Brodie was throwing a party for Eileen before she went away. She might well stir herself enough to go into town and buy something new to wear.

'What was your father like, Diana?' Brodie asked as they were finishing their dinner in the dining room one night. (She referred to the meal as 'dinner', but Diana had *her* dinner at lunchtime and the evening meal was tea.) The sun was shining blindingly into a corner of the room, separating the light from the dark as if a knife had sliced through it.

'Me dad?' Diana leaned both arms on the table and cupped her face in her long white hands. She'd recently taken to painting her nails strange colours and today they were ice-blue and badly in need of re-touching. 'He was lovely,' she replied dreamily, half closing her eyes.

'How old were you when he left?'

'Nine. He was brown-haired, like me, and quite tall. His name was James but everyone called him Jim. Sometimes he had a beard and sometimes he didn't, because he never shaved while he was away – he was a merchant seaman. He was lovely,' she repeated. 'Soft and gentle – too soft with me mam, that's for sure.' She paused, as if contemplating whether or not to trust Brodie with a further confidence. 'She used to have other men in when he was gone,' she said, making a face. 'Me, I didn't see anything much wrong with it at the time. I suppose I should have, but when you're only nine you think your mam and dad are perfect.'

'Where is he now?' Brodie laid her hand on Diana's arm. 'Don't answer if you think I'm being nosy, it's just that the four of us have been living together for over three months and we know very little about each other.' Vanessa was the most mysterious of all. Leonard Gosling apart, she'd never had a visitor, and if she had a mobile phone then it had never been heard to ring. Nor had she received a single letter.

Rachel was more forthcoming. She had two brothers and a sister, and Poppy's father was called Tyler and went to school in Waterloo. He called at the house on his way home from school and could occasionally be seen leaving on his bike at around half-past five. He sometimes came on Sundays and stayed upstairs with Rachel and Poppy. No one had ever spoken to him, but Vanessa had said he was American. She and Rachel had formed a friendship of sorts.

'I've no idea where me dad is,' Diana said. 'No one does. He divorced Mam and no one's heard from him since. What about your dad? Do you remember him at all?'

The sun was slowly moving across the room, leaving only a small slice of brilliant yellow. Very soon, it would disappear altogether and the whole room would be in shadow. For some reason, this made Brodie feel sad.

'He died when I was ten months old,' she said in answer to Diana's question. 'I only know what he looked like from photographs and all mine are at home.' This was her home now, she realized, though it didn't feel permanent.

'What was his name?'

'Louis. Louis Sylvester.' The other girls had been envious of her name at school: Brodie Sylvester. Her best friend, Wendy, said it was a film star's name. 'Me, I'm Wendy Lott,' she'd said disgustedly. 'When I become a film star, I'll have to change it.' Wendy hadn't become a film star. Instead, she'd married a builder called Timothy Houghton and gone to live in Australia.

'My dad was born in Ireland,' Brodie said to Diana. 'He and Mum met on a boat – a liner – sailing from New York to Liverpool. They got married soon afterwards.'

'It sounds dead romantic.' Diana edged her chair into the very last of the sunlight. Her untidy hair turned from brown to a tangle of gold. 'What was your mum doing in New York? I've always wanted to go there.'

'Nearly everyone does. Mum had an aunt over there who was on the stage. Don't ask what her name was because I've no idea: she was only in the chorus.' At junior school, some children had taunted Brodie for not having a father, but she was too sensible to care. It wasn't *her* fault he had died of pneumonia when he was only thirty-nine.

'He had a weak chest,' her mother told her many years

later. 'His family back in Ireland were dirt-poor and he hadn't had the proper nourishment when he was a child.' But he'd been brilliant at figures, Brodie's father. He'd actually gone to university and become a forensic accountant, able to charge fantastic fees.

The sun disappeared altogether and it was as if a black cloud had settled on the room. Brodie got to her feet. 'Shall I make a drink and we'll take it into the garden? It's sunny out there.'

Diana stretched her arms tiredly and nodded.

'Tea or coffee?' Brodie asked.

'Whatever you're having.'

'Then it's coffee.'

When Brodie said she was throwing a party for Eileen before she returned to London, Diana asked Tinker if he would like to come. Leo wasn't very pleased. 'But I'm your boyfriend,' he protested. 'Your *fiancé*. You shouldn't be asking other men out.'

Diana laughed. 'Don't be silly. Tinker's just a friend. I'm not asking him *out*, just to the party.' If the truth were known, she sometimes forgot she and Leo were engaged, which wasn't exactly fair. He was awfully nice and would make some girl a wonderful husband.

'Mum and Dad are taking us to Ormskirk at the weekend to look at houses,' he announced. 'They're building a new estate there.'

'Really?' She kept hoping he would go off her, but he showed no sign of it.

Brodie said she was silly to let the engagement continue. 'The longer it goes on, the more difficult it will be to extricate yourself and the more poor Leo will be hurt. Before you know it, you'll be walking down the aisle, and when the priest asks if anyone knows any reason why the two of you shouldn't be joined together in Holy Matrimony, I'm going to shout, "*She doesn't love him, Father.*"

Diana giggled. 'Oh, you wouldn't, would you?'

'I would,' Brodie said sternly. 'I just hope you see sense before it gets that far. And I'm not being funny, young lady, but deadly serious.'

It wasn't the least bit funny, Diana thought now. Leo's parents had offered to put the deposit down on a house for their wedding present and now Leo was inviting her to *view one!*

How was she going to get out of it?

Brodie switched on the computer every morning to see if there was an email from Karen Young. She would check again each evening when she got home from work and again before she went to bed, though she knew, if it was really important, Karen would telephone. There'd been a time when she'd used the computer every day, mainly to search Google for information that Colin wanted or send emails of her own. Now she only turned it on hoping for news of her daughter.

'What a coincidence!' she murmured the night after her talk with Diana about fathers, to find an email from Karen, not about Maisie as she'd hoped, but concerning Brodie's grandfather, Thomas Ryan.

'I kept forgetting to look him up on Google,' Karen wrote, 'but when I eventually did it was very interesting. There's loads of Thomas Ryans, but your one is called Thomas Edward Ryan and there's actually a photo of him. There's still no news of Maisie, I'm afraid, but I feel confident that I'll find her soon.'

Brodie sighed. The day couldn't come soon enough. She brought up Google, typed 'Thomas Edward Ryan' and, within seconds, a sepia photograph, faded at the edges, appeared on the screen. It must have been taken at a passing-out parade or something similar. It showed Thomas Ryan from the waist up wearing an old-fashioned policeman's uniform with a high collar and loads of brass buttons, his domed helmet held stiffly underneath his arm, his hair cut unnaturally short. She found herself smiling at the young, extremely handsome face. He looked terribly serious, but there was something about his eyes and the way his lips curved slightly that indicated he was extremely pleased with himself.

'Hello, Granddad,' she whispered, tears coming to her eyes. Why hadn't she done this before? She'd never dreamt she'd find her own grandfather on the internet.

Growing up, she'd never known another relative: no grandparents, aunts or uncles, no cousins, just Brodie and her mother.

She began to read the text accompanying the photograph. She knew her grandfather had been killed in 1930, that he'd disturbed two men who'd broken into a bank and one had shot him.

But as she read on, Brodie's jaw dropped further and further and her eyes grew rounder and rounder. 'I've been lied to all these years,' she said to the photo. 'Why?'


As Brodie had expected, Diana threw herself wholeheartedly into the preparations for Eileen's party, which was to be held in the garden if the weather was good or in the house if it wasn't. It turned out to be a perfect late-June evening with the setting sun a blazing ball of yellow in the sapphire-blue sky. An air of expectancy hung in the air, as if the garden itself was looking forward to the party.

Diana had been hard at work. Dozens of white balloons had been tied to the trees, and candles were burning on the iron table, on the headless statue where the head should have been, and in other places where it was deemed safe to put them. Earlier, she'd been in the middle of drawing up a list of games to play when Brodie assured her there was no need.

'It's not a children's party. Adults only want to stand around and talk.'

'Won't they want something to eat and drink?'

'And that as well. Everyone's been asked to bring wine, and Mum and I are doing the food. You can help if you like.' Colin would be there, as well as his two sisters and his brother and their partners, plus their grown-up children if they could find babysitters for *their* children – Eileen had three great-grandchildren. Brodie wasn't sure if George was coming: she hoped not.

'Can I be in charge of the music?' Diana asked eagerly.

'Of course you can.' Brodie was awed by her enthusiasm.

At seven o'clock, she stood in the kitchen waiting for the guests to arrive. She was wearing her new white trousers and gauzy top. Diana was re-arranging the little three-cornered sandwiches into a cone-shaped mountain. She had borrowed a long black skirt from the clothes donated to the refugee centre and a dark-green silk blouse that had a cape reaching as far as her elbows.

'You look like a character out of a Jane Austen novel,' Leonard Gosling said. He was the first to arrive.

Vanessa had gone all the way into town to buy something befitting a 'late-night garden party', as she called it, returning to say the sales had started and showing Brodie the floaty cream dress she'd bought. 'I'm down to a size twenty,' she said with a pleasurable sigh.

Rachel appeared in the jeans she seemed to live in, but Poppy, who was growing rapidly, wore a poppy-coloured frock that was all frills. 'Her daddy bought it for her,' Rachel said. Tyler arrived soon afterwards, a tall, beanpole of a young man with matchstick-thin limbs and a slightly withdrawn manner. Brodie reckoned he was shy.

'How do you do, Mrs Logan?' he said when they were introduced, but she insisted he call her Brodie.

'This is a lovely set-up you've got here,' Eileen said at some time during the evening. Ella Fitzgerald had just started to sing 'Every Time We Say Goodbye'. 'I cry a little,' Eileen sang.

Brodie raised her eyebrows. 'Set-up?'

'This lovely house and lovely garden.' Eileen waved her glass at both. 'Diana, Vanessa, Rachel with her pretty little baby. I'm almost reluctant to leave. But our Colin's terribly unhappy.' Her eyes turned to her son, who was standing moodily on his own clutching a bottle of beer. 'Have you spoken to him yet?'

'I did when he first came, but only for a minute.'

'He loves you, you know,' Eileen said soberly despite appearing to be just a little bit drunk, as were most of the people there, Brodie included.

'I love him,' she said, 'but I can't *live* with him while he thinks the way he does about Maisie.'

'I understand. I'd probably feel the same.' She half smiled. 'Did you know he smoked cannabis at university?' Brodie shook her head. 'I told him the other day he was a hypocrite. Mind you, a lot of the students used to do it and there's a big difference between that and cocaine or heroin.' Suddenly, for no apparent reason, tears began to trickle down her cheeks. 'Thank you for my party, Brodie. It's been a fabulous, magical evening.' She turned away, saying she wanted someone to dance with. 'It's a pity George didn't come. That's one good thing I can say about him, he was a fantastic dancer: still might be for all I know. Who's that drop dead gorgeous young man over there? I really like the look of him.'

Brodie watched as she made her way over to Tinker, who was talking to her mother. Mum was taking quite an interest in the centre and now went two or three times a week. Tinker bowed gallantly when Eileen approached. Next minute, they were waltzing on the grass, along with Diana and Leo and Colin's sisters and their husbands.

The night air was becoming dusky, making the candles

seem to glitter more brightly. The earthy evening smell was mixed with that of melting wax. Balloons drifted silently to and fro on the trees like ghosts. Kenneth was stretched on a branch, coolly watching the goings on below. Every now and then someone would reach up and feed him a titbit. Ella Fitzgerald sang 'Someone to Watch Over Me'.

Brodie went over and asked Colin if he would like to dance. He didn't say anything, just took her in his arms and rocked her back and forth on the spot.

'Is this dancing?' Brodie asked.

'It's the best I can do under the circumstances.'

'What circumstances?'

'I'm missing you badly, I'm as miserable as sin, I'm not sleeping properly, I'm out of clean shirts, I've had too many beers . . .' He stopped rocking and looked into her eyes. 'Are those circumstances enough?'

'I suppose so,' she conceded. It felt as if they were young again and hadn't long met. There was a slight turbulence in her breast.

'I'm enjoying holding you.' He held her closer and buried his head in her neck. 'When are you coming home, darling?'

The 'darling', and the touch of his lips on her ear, really got to her. She gasped. He was her husband and she loved him. She couldn't bring herself to snap at him, say, 'When you change your attitude to our daughter, that's when.' Instead, she mumbled, 'I don't know.'

He whispered, 'Can I stay tonight?'

And Brodie whispered, 'Yes.'

Poppy was a long time settling down. She wasn't used to being made a fuss of by so many people. Brodie could hear Rachel's light footsteps as she walked to and fro across the floor, probably trying to lull her to sleep before laying her in her cot.

Vanessa had a bath, then came downstairs to make a drink.

She was humming softly. She had clearly enjoyed herself tonight. Mind you, Eileen had given her a tremendous build-up when introducing her to her family. 'This is the artist I told you about,' she'd said. 'She's absolutely fabulous. One day she'll be as famous as Picasso.'

In the next room, Diana giggled. Someone was in there with her, a man. It could only be Leo. Brodie wondered if they'd made love. Although she would soon be twenty-five, Diana seemed too young to have sex. I hope she doesn't fall pregnant, Brodie thought, and *have* to marry Leo.

She said to Colin, 'Would you like some tea?' They were lying on the single bed, both stark naked, having just made love themselves. The time before had been months ago and this time they'd been greedy for each other. It had been better than ever, but now she felt embarrassed and was wondering how she could bring herself to cross the room with nothing on to get her dressing gown from behind the door.

Colin sighed. 'I'd like a ciggie.'

'You can't have a ciggie: it's bad for your health.' They'd both smoked when they first met in Waterloo delivering Labour Party leaflets prior to the 1983 election. They'd de-livered the rest together, taking them to alternate houses, which was a very inefficient way of doing it.

Then they'd gone to the pub, had a ciggie each and a drink – Brodie a medium sherry and Colin half a pint of best bitter. They'd both known that this was 'it'. A year later they were married. Another year later she was expecting Josh. Maisie had arrived eighteen months afterwards.

'Would you like tea?' she asked again. 'Seeing as you can't have a ciggie.'

'I'd love some.'

She steeled herself, got out of bed and went to get her dressing gown from behind the door, doing her best not to hurry. She tied the belt around her waist. When she turned around, Colin was watching.

'You're very beautiful, Brodie,' he said. His voice was strangely tired.

'You're not so bad yourself.' She tried to sound light-hearted as she went to make the tea.

When she got back with the drink in two mugs, Colin was sitting moodily on the bed fully dressed. He got to his feet. 'I don't think I'll bother with that, thanks. I'm going home.'

'But why? What's wrong? It was all right . . . before, wasn't it?'

'It was more than all right; it was bloody marvellous.' He glowered at her. 'But how long will it be before it happens again?' He ran his fingers distractedly through his hair. 'Come home with me,' he pleaded.

'What about Maisie?' Brodie asked.

'What about Maisie?'

'I can't be bothered explaining,' Brodie said. She felt exhausted. She put the mugs on the table and sat heavily in a chair. 'You know what I mean.'

'I'll never agree with you about Maisie.'

'In that case I shall never come home.'


Two of the candles were still burning in the garden. Brodie opened the window and went to blow them out. There was very little rubbish scattered about: people had been very good about leaving the place tidy.

Back in her room, she turned on the computer and pressed the keys until she found her grandfather.

'Hello, Granddad.' The young face regarded her impassively. 'I've been meaning to discuss you with your daughter, Megan,' she told him. Earlier, Mum had demanded to talk to *her*, but she'd been too busy serving food. 'Later, Mum,' she'd said, but her mother had gone home early. Brodie had got the impression she was in a huff.

'But not in as big a huff as *I* am,' she told her granddad.

*July–August 2006*

# Chapter 8

The black van was parked in Cazneau Street, its bonnet jutting forward just enough for the young man behind the wheel to see down Winstanley Grove and the front of the refugee centre where his brother, Rudi, had lost his sight. The young man, Jagar, wore a baseball cap pulled down as far as his eyebrows.

Although no doctor had confirmed it, Jagar was convinced that Rudi would never see again. The trouble was he couldn't be taken to any hospital in the country. Police records would show what had happened that morning almost a month ago and hospitals would be on the alert for a big foreign man who spoke broken English and had had boiling liquid thrown in his face. Since then, all Rudi had done was sit in front of a television that he couldn't see because a bandage covered his eyes. His shoulders were hunched and he rarely spoke. Every now and then Jagar would remove the bandage, but so far all his brother had done was shake his head.

Those four little bitches who'd got away would have provided a good description of Rudi and himself, along with names, places, and other information that was making living in this country a much riskier operation than it had been before.

Jagar didn't know which way to turn. These days, Rudi was helpless, a mere shadow of the powerful, dominating individual that Jagar had always known, that the whole village back home had known.

It had been Rudi's idea to bring the girls and set up business here. The money had come rolling in and they were well on their way to becoming millionaires. The plan was to return home in a few years and build a palace for their mother, though Jagar had other ideas. He wanted to live in London in a luxury apartment and run a couple of girls of his own. He'd wear gold chains around his neck, buy designer clothes and have sex whenever he felt like it. Until now, it was this, the sex, that he'd appreciated most; a selection of young women, every single one at his disposal to do with whatever he chose. Jagar licked his lips at the thought of it.

The two men who'd come with them were fools, incapable of lifting a finger without Rudi's instructions. But now it was up to Jagar and he honestly didn't know what to do. The girls they still had were missing Rudi's iron hand and getting restless. They were different from the four who'd got away. Older and more experienced, they had a used look about them and weren't nearly so appealing to the clientele. Most men preferred young bodies and were willing to pay more.

Jagar worried that everything was falling apart. The new place they'd found was within sight of the Catholic cathedral and it made him feel uneasy that the holy building could be seen from the front windows. He didn't know how to advertise the services they had to offer. In the past, Rudi had cards printed and had taken them round clubs and bars. Jagar had done the same, but in the first bar he'd gone to he'd been told to fuck off so many times he'd given up.

'You're in the wrong place, mate,' one man had said. 'This is a respectable pub. And while we're at it, why don't you go back to your own country?'

Jagar had fled. He'd never be as good a businessman as his brother.

He'd been watching the refugee centre all afternoon, taking

in every person who went in and out. It was past five o'clock when *she* appeared and he recognized her straight away.

She walked towards him, accompanied by a much older woman. In some secret part of his brain he recognized that she was very lovely, but his prime thought was how much he hated her for what she'd done to Rudi.

'I get you, lady,' he swore as she walked past, skirt rippling, shoes clicking delicately on the pavement. Her arms were bare and brown and her hair had streaks of gold. She was the reason for his and Rudi's misfortune, his bad luck charm, the reason why their amazing, unbelievable life had come to an end. 'One day I get you for what you do to my brother.' The girl would pay. It was only fair.


Brodie hadn't seen her mother since Eileen's party. She'd rung a few times, but had been fobbed off with various excuses; she was tired, had letters to write, had promised to decorate a cake for a raffle.

'For goodness' sake, Mum,' Brodie had said that afternoon when she'd called her mother at the refugee centre and she'd said she was washing her hair that night, 'leave your hair for now and come to tea. Anyroad, don't you possess a hairdryer? I've got fresh salmon, your favourite.'

She grudgingly agreed. Brodie hadn't got the salmon, but bought some on her way home from work, along with some cherry tomatoes and other bits and pieces for a salad. Tonight, Diana was going straight to Coral Street for Garth's eighteenth birthday party so she and her mother could have their tea together in the snug and perhaps Mum would divulge exactly why she had such a cob on.

The table was already set when her mother arrived with pursed lips and unsmiling eyes. Brodie wasn't prepared to sit through the meal in stiff silence. 'What's eating you, Mum?' she demanded before they sat down. 'It's ages since we spoke to each other, so what's wrong?'

'You may recall,' her mother said in the icy voice she reserved for occasions when her daughter had annoyed her, 'that I tried to speak to you at the party, but apparently you were too busy.'

'I *was* too busy. I was seeing to the food.' It wasn't like her to be annoyed over something so petty.

'It seems you had plenty of time to speak to other people, though – Eileen, for instance. Why was *she* told that Maisie had become a drug addict, yet you couldn't tell your own mother?'

Was that what it was about? 'Eileen was worried I'd left Colin because George was always in the house,' Brodie said patiently. 'She felt guilty, thinking it was her fault. I felt obliged to tell her the real reason I'd left was because Colin hasn't an ounce of sympathy for Maisie and all we did was row.'

Her mother contemplated this for several seconds. 'I still don't understand why I couldn't be told the truth about Maisie,' she said in an aggrieved tone. 'She's my granddaughter, the only one I'll ever have.'

Brodie reached for her mother's hand and squeezed it. 'I didn't want to upset you, Mum. I didn't want you knowing there was anything wrong with Maisie.'

'Do you think I'm an idiot, Brodie?' The icy voice returned. 'Maisie hasn't been home for six months or more. She used to come at least once a month. I haven't had a single letter or phone call, or even a card at Christmas. Of course I knew there was something wrong. I expected you would tell me when you were ready, but it seems everyone in the world knew except me.'

'Eileen was the only one who knew, Mum.'

'Even so, I'm very hurt.' She pulled out the chair and sat down.

Brodie's heart sank. It looked as if this was going to be one of the rare occasions when forgiveness wasn't easily forthcoming. She would have to wait a few days until her mother decided she'd been punished enough. Then she remembered that *she* had a bone to pick. 'Come in here a minute,' she said. The food could wait; it was only salad.

'Where?'

'My room.'

In the room, Brodie switched on the computer, then waited silently for the machine to start.

'What's this all about, Brodie?' Her mother was sitting on the bed.

'Wait and see.'

The machine was ready to use. Brodie typed in her grandfather's name, Thomas Edward Ryan, and his photograph appeared on the screen.

'Do you recognize him?' she asked.

Her mother put her head on one side and studied the screen from across the room. 'No, but the picture looks very old.'

'It's your father – *my* grandfather.'

'Holy Mary, Mother of God!' Her mother put a hand to her throat and went as white as a ghost. 'Is it really me dad?' she asked in a young voice, like a girl's. She looked quickly at the screen, then away again.

'Yes, Mum.' Brodie knew she was being rather brutal, but it served her mother right for being so unreasonable.

'Is he wearing his police uniform?' she asked.

'Yes.'

'I've never seen that photo before. We lost all our photos, see, when our house off Scotland Road was bombed just before Christmas in nineteen forty. The Christmas presents went at the same time as well as Mam's clothes, the money she'd saved, everything.' Once again she looked at the picture, but this time didn't look away. 'I wonder where this one came from. Perhaps it was on the police files or something.' She got up, crept across the room, sat in front of the computer and closely studied her father's face. She kissed her forefinger and placed it on his firm lips. 'He was a lovely man. I was dead proud of him. I'd forgotten how handsome he was. But Brodie,' she said in the little girl's voice, 'what on earth is me dad's photo doing on a computer?'

'You told me he'd been killed in the line of duty,' Brodie said, 'and when I mentioned this to a policewoman in London, she thought he might be on the Internet.' She waved her hand at the computer. 'And he is.'

'And what does all this writing say? Will you pass me my bag, darlin'; it's got my glasses in.'

Brodie fetched her bag from the dining room. She stood by the window and looked out on the garden. Vanessa was half-hidden behind a tree, wearing a straw hat and that awful stretchy tracksuit, painting one of her weird paintings. How strange that Eileen had liked them so much.

She heard her mother search through the bag for her glasses. There was silence while she read what was on the screen.

'Ah,' she sighed when she'd finished. She was still pale when Brodie turned around. 'There's a saying, isn't there? Your sins will find you out. I suppose the same goes for lies. I never dreamed that one day our family history would be there for the entire world to see.'

'It says Thomas Ryan had *four* children. You claimed you were an only child. Does that mean that somewhere in the world I've got aunts and uncles and cousins that I would love to have known when I was growing up?' She would still like to know them.

There was an air of defeat about the way her mother nodded. 'They're in Ireland. In a little village called Duneathly, but I suppose they could be all over the place by now.'

'How can I find them?' Brodie was bubbling over with questions, but there was only room right now for the really important ones. 'Are the other three children younger than you or older? What sex are they? And Mum,' she added indignantly, 'why have you been telling me all these years you were an only child?'

Her mother retreated to the bed and sat down. 'Could we leave this till another time, Brodie, luv?' she said shakily. 'I'm not in the mood to explain things just at the moment.'

'Well, I'm not in the mood to wait any longer.' This was something Brodie should have known all her life. It was a while since she'd found her grandfather on the Internet and she'd been trying to think of how she could broach the subject with her mother without upsetting her too much. It was for the same reason that she hadn't told her about Maisie. She was fed up trying to be tactful and understanding. 'I'd like to know why all this,' she waved her hand at the computer, 'was kept from me – and I'd like to know *now*, not one day when you feel in the mood.'

'Can I have a drink?' her mother asked pathetically.

'Would you like tea or wine?'

'Both, please.'

While Brodie waited for the kettle to boil, she uncorked a bottle of *rosé* wine and put it on a tray with two glasses. She fetched the salads out of the dining room and put them in the fridge, by which time the water had boiled and she made the tea. She carried everything into her room where her mother had returned to the computer and was sitting, gazing at her father's face.

'He's awful good-looking, isn't he?' she said softly. 'His hair was always cut very short. What is it people say nowadays? – drop dead gorgeous. I was only four when he died.'

Brodie put the tray on to the little table in front of the window. 'Which would you like first, the tea or the wine?'

'The wine, please. Oh, it's *rosé*, my favourite.' She picked up the glass and took a hefty mouthful. 'I was the eldest,' she said in a rush, as if the wine had already given her the courage to tell all. 'Brodie came next, then Joe, and finally Tom. He was born after me dad died. You were called after Brodie,' she said when her daughter looked surprised. 'I used to bully her something awful. I won't explain every little detail right now, but I'll tell you why I cut her, Joe and Tom out of my life — and Mam, too.'

Brodie picked up her own wine and prepared to listen.

'I was nineteen when the war finished,' her mother began. 'We lived in Duneathly and I was engaged to this chap called Richard O'Rourke who worked in a bank. We planned to get married on my twenty-first birthday. Anyway, right after the end of the war Annemarie came to see us. She was our auntie and she'd spent the last twenty years in America.'

'I know who Annemarie is,' Brodie said, interrupting. 'It says on Granddad's website that his wife, Mollie — your mother — was the sister of Anne Murray, the famous Broadway star. I looked her up on Google; her real name was Annemarie Kenny. She was incredibly pretty, but you said she was just a chorus girl.'

Her mother flicked away the interruption as if she were swatting a fly and took another long swallow of the wine. 'Anyway, Mam, Brodie and me went to stay with Annemarie in her apartment in New York. We were there for over a month. We'd only been there a few days when Brodie went to St Patrick's Cathedral on Fifth Avenue for some reason — she was always in and out of church, our Brodie; lighting candles, praying for this and that, doing the First Fridays. I used to tell her she should have been a nun. Hours later, she brings a young man back for afternoon tea.' Her voice was soft and husky, her eyes dreamy. Her face, so white before, was now pink. She looked very different from the mother Brodie had always known. 'He was beautiful, truly beautiful; tall, with dark wavy hair and remarkable blue eyes. Very Irish.' Her lips twisted in the briefest of smiles. 'He was, of course, your father, Louis Sylvester, and he and Brodie seemed quite smitten with each other. I was insanely jealous, having fallen head over heels in love with him on the spot.'

Brodie visualized the scene. Mum at nineteen, Brodie, who for some reason had a saintly halo around her head, two years younger, her grandmother, Mollie, who would have been about forty, all at Annemarie's Manhattan apartment, which she imagined being terribly smart, full of fine furniture and carpets you could lose your feet in.

Her mother finished the wine and re-filled her glass. 'I was determined to steal him off her,' she said grimly. 'I did every single thing I could to make him aware of me. Brodie, poor innocent Brodie, didn't notice, but Mam did. She said if I succeeded she'd disown me. I'm not sure if she meant it, but I didn't care if she did. I loved my family, but I loved your father more. I was besotted and determined to have him.'

Brodie was beginning to feel very slightly embarrassed, but she'd asked for an explanation and was getting one. She poured tea for herself – her mother was monopolizing the wine.

'I didn't manage it until we were on the boat back to Liverpool – of course, I didn't meet him on the boat like I've always told you. Anyroad, he'd been staying with an American friend from university. He changed his passage home so he could sail with us. He and Brodie weren't engaged or anything, but it was understood that one day they would get married. I suppose you could say I seduced him,' her mother said thoughtfully. 'I won't go into the intimate details,' her daughter breathed a sigh of relief, 'but by the time the boat reached Liverpool, he realized it was me he was in love with.'

'What happened then?'

'Like craven cowards, the minute it docked we got off and ran away.' A strange look passed over her face, as if she could still feel the guilt and the crazy passion of the time. 'I even left some of me luggage behind on purpose so no one would realize for a while that we'd gone. A week later we got married by special licence. From that day on I didn't look back. I resolved never to contact my family again; I was too ashamed. Your father bought this house and we settled down. I thought that fate was taking revenge when I started losing my babies. When I had you, it was your father who insisted we call you Brodie. But you know, darlin',' she said, smiling radiantly and looking very young again, even it if was only for an instant, 'despite everything, I've never regretted a thing. For some people, love isn't easy. Haven't you and Colin just discovered that for yourselves?'

'The thing is, Colin, *I* regret it, even if Mum doesn't,' she said two hours later after she'd driven her mother home because she was too drunk to ride her bike. She'd desperately wanted to talk to someone and Colin was the only person she could think of. She'd called him and he'd come straight away. 'According to her website, Anne Murray – that's Annemarie – didn't die until nineteen ninety when she was eighty-one. I could have written to her, gone to *see* her in New York. And Mum had a sister called Brodie and two brothers, all younger than her. They're probably still alive. And I might have loads of cousins.'

'Are you going to try to track them down?' Colin asked.

'Oh, I don't know.' She sighed. Her grandfather was watching from the screen, his steady gaze directed on her. 'I was all for it earlier, but it happened sixty years ago.' Her voice trailed away.

'Would your mother mind?'

'She hasn't objected. Anyroad, I'm not sure if I'd care if she did. She had no right to keep my extended family hidden from me.'

'No one would bear a grudge against your mum after all this time, surely. They might be really thrilled to see her again – and to meet you,' Colin said encouragingly. He was being so nice and helpful that she wondered why she was living in one house and he in another miles away. She supposed she'd only have to mention Maisie and she would find out. 'Would you like me to do it for you?' he offered.

'How? You haven't got a computer.'

'I've bought one. I needed to find out all sorts of things for work and you're no longer there to do it for me. It seemed time I learned to do it myself.'

Unreasonably, Brodie felt a bit put out. She preferred to think of him being unable to cope without her. 'How are you getting on?'

'Quite well, actually. It's easier than I thought. There's a new teacher at school who lives quite close. She's coming round tomorrow night to show me how to set up an email address.'

*She*? Brodie felt even more put out.


'Hello.'

Vanessa looked up from the easel, but could see no sign of who had spoken. It had sounded like a child. She willed the voice to go away, but it didn't work.

'Hello,' it said again. 'I'm over here, next door.'

It *was* a child – with short red curly hair, exceptionally rosy cheeks and a good scattering of freckles. Vanessa couldn't tell if it was a girlish boy or a boyish girl. And he or she must be standing on something, or else they were about seven feet tall, as the crumbling brick wall was at least six feet high and he or she was resting his or her freckled arms on it.

'What are you doing?' the child enquired.

'What does it look as if I'm doing?' Vanessa asked testily. 'I'm painting.' She hated being interrupted while she was working. It was the best time of the day, morning, not long after Brodie and Diana had gone to work and before Rachel and Poppy appeared on the scene. There was a slight haze lingering in the trees and the air felt damp, but she could tell it was going to be another lovely day. She was loving this summer with its endless sunny days. She felt lucky that this was the year she'd become an artist. She couldn't remember another summer quite so fine, but then she'd been stuck at work without time even to look out of the window.

'I can see that you're painting,' the child said a trifle haughtily. 'What I meant was, *what* are you painting?'

She felt tempted to tell the little sod to mind his or her own business. She wasn't too sure what she was painting that morning; she'd just felt like daubing colours on a canvas and seeing what she ended up with. 'I'm experimenting,' she snapped, wishing the child would go away.

But it seemed he or she had no intention of doing anything of the sort. 'It looks a very nice experiment,' it remarked. 'I'd like to do one, too.'

'Well, no one's stopping you.' That was a horrible way to speak to a child. 'Shouldn't you be at school?' she asked a bit more pleasantly.

'I'm not well.'

'You look well enough to me.' He or she was the picture of health.

'I've got a tummy ache. It hurts really bad.'

'Then you should go and see a doctor.' The red cheeks might be the sign that the child had a fever.

'Will you take me?'

Vanessa snorted. 'I'll do no such thing!' How on earth did she get landed in this situation? It sounded awful, refusing to take a sick child to a doctor, but she'd never set eyes on the child before and it wasn't exactly her responsibility. 'Where are your mum and dad?' she asked.

'Dad's at work, Mum's in the Army. They're divorced. Mum told him she wasn't cut out to be a wife and mother.'

'And your dad just went to work knowing that you were sick?' She felt outraged. Some people didn't deserve to have children.

'He'd already gone by the time I got up and realized my tummy was aching.'

'Had he now?' What the hell was she supposed to do? As the only adult in the vicinity she supposed she'd better do something. 'Have you had anything to eat this morning?' Should the child eat if it had a tummy ache? God, she was hopeless at this sort of thing.

'I haven't had anything to eat, no.'

'What about a warm drink?'

'I haven't had a drink, either.'

'What are you standing on?'

'I climbed up the wall; it's got bricks missing.'

'If you'd like to climb over, I'll make you some warm milk.' It was the least she could do, though she was as averse to children as she was to cats and dogs.

'Can I bring my paints with me and we can both paint a picture together after I've had the milk?' the child asked eagerly.

'I suppose so,' she replied, teeth gritting, heart sinking, longing to refuse, but it would have made her feel like the Wicked Witch of the West. It looked as if today was going to be ruined. 'What's your name?' At least she'd know if the child was a boy or a girl.

'Charlie. I'll just get my painting set.'

He disappeared and reappeared more quickly than one would have expected from a child with a tummy ache. Back again, he climbed on to the wall with a paint box, a cheap sketchbook, and a rag doll with unnaturally long legs tucked underneath his arm. Vanessa lifted the small, slight figure down, dismayed to see he was wearing a brief denim skirt and red tights.

'What's Charlie short for?' she asked.

'Charlotte.'

'That's a nice name.'

'I hate it. What's your name?'

'Vanessa.'

'I don't like that, either.'

'I'm sorry about that.' As it happened, Vanessa had never cared much for her name.

'I think we should be able to christen ourselves and change our names every five years. I used to want to be Stacey like the girl in *EastEnders*, but now I'd sooner be Angelina.'

'That's not a bad idea, changing your name every five years,' Vanessa agreed. She'd always fancied being something Shakespearean like Olivia or Rosalind. 'How old are you, Charlie?'

'Seven, but I'm old beyond my years – my mummy used to say so.'

The same thing had been said about Vanessa when she was a little girl, though much good it had done her. It hadn't stopped her from being jilted at the altar by William Lunt. 'So, would you like some warm milk?' she enquired.

'Yes, thank you,' Charlie said gravely. 'It will be good for my tummy.' She put her assorted possessions on the metal table and accompanied Vanessa into the house. 'I haven't got a thingy to stand my painting on,' she complained.

'You mean an easel? Well, you're just going to have to do without one, aren't you? I didn't have one straight away.'

'It's nice in here,' she said when they entered the kitchen. 'I like the tiles. Did you paint them?'

'No.' Vanessa filled a mug with milk and put it in the microwave.

'You're a woman of a few words, aren't you?' she said with all seriousness.

'You talk too much,' Vanessa riposted.

'My mummy used to say that, too.'

While the milk was warming, Vanessa made coffee for herself. She stole two chocolate biscuits out of the fridge, having no idea who they belonged to, and gave them to Charlie. 'I hope they don't make your tummy worse.'

'Oh, they won't. Anyroad, it's beginning to feel just a little bit better. Maybe it's the thought of the milk.'

Vanessa was beginning to doubt she'd ever had a bad tummy. She looked too well and acted too chirpy. 'What does your father do?'

'He's a whiz with computers,' Charlie answered proudly. 'He's invented loads of games and has his own business on Kirkby Trading Estate. I can play them all, even though they're much too old for me.'

She was probably one of those nauseating kids who went to university at twelve and emerged a few years later with half a dozen first-class degrees.

Vanessa said, 'Shall we go back into the garden? Here, take these biscuits and I'll carry the milk.' She felt rather pleased with herself, a little bit saintly, as if she were being awfully nice taking this odd, clearly lonely child under her wing. If she ever came across the father, the computer whiz, she'd have a few words with him about leaving his daughter on her own when she was ill.

For the rest of the morning, Charlie lay on her bad tummy on the grass behind Vanessa, copying every stroke of her painting. The doll, whose name was Gwendoline, was draped around her neck. Kenneth, the cat, strolled into the garden. Charlie said she had no idea who it belonged to, but tomorrow she'd like to paint it.

'Shouldn't you go to school tomorrow?' Vanessa reminded her.

'It depends if my tummy ache is *really* better.'

'You must tell your father about your tummy ache tonight so that if you still have it he can take you to the doctor's in the morning.'

'Mmm,' Charlie said vaguely.

Vanessa gave her a sharp look. 'If you don't attend school, your father will get into trouble.'

'It won't bother him.' She shrugged carelessly. 'He's too busy inventing these awesome computer games.'

'He can be sent to *prison*,' Vanessa stressed.

'Honest? Shouldn't it be me who's sent to prison? After all, I'm the one who's not going to school.' She sounded as if she quite fancied a spell behind bars. 'I could write a book about it. I've already written a book; it's called *The Curse of the Crypt*. Would you like to read it?'

'It doesn't exactly sound my cup of tea.' Now she felt churlish again; she just wasn't used to conversing with children. 'Perhaps I could have a little peek at it one day.'

At around midday, Rachel arrived in the garden with Poppy – sometimes, it took all morning for the girl to get herself and her baby ready for the world. Poppy always looked as if she was ready to be entered in a baby show and would have been a credit to any mother. Today she wore a pink embroidered frock, pink socks, and a pink ribbon in her freshly washed fair hair.

Rachel said that at this very moment Tyler was flying to New York to spend a few weeks with his mother, his parents being divorced. 'They're going to some place called The Hamptons where his grandmother lives. He's dead pleased his stepfather's staying in New York because he doesn't like him very much.'

'He doesn't like his stepmother in England, either,' Vanessa commented. Privately, she wasn't very keen on Tyler, whom she considered an arrogant young man. But there was no denying that he adored Rachel and Poppy and was extremely protective towards them.

'He doesn't dislike his stepmother as much as he does his stepfather,' Rachel explained. 'The truth is, he didn't want his mam and dad to get divorced.' She reminded Vanessa it was clinic day. Vanessa had forgotten all about it, but promised to be ready to leave by two.

Charlie had abandoned her painting to admire Poppy. 'It's

an amazing name. I wish my mum and dad had called me that. Gosh, she's pretty. Can she walk and talk yet? Well, what *can* she do?' she asked exasperatedly when Rachel shook her head.

'She's only six months and she can sit up by herself.' Rachel spread a blanket on the grass and laid Poppy on her tummy with her rattle. The baby beat the hell out of the blanket, then rolled on to her back and regarded her mother with a beatific smile.

'She's beautiful,' Charlie breathed. 'I'd like to have a baby like Poppy when I grow up.'

Vanessa wasn't quite sure how it happened, but all of a sudden Rachel and Charlie were playing tick, climbing trees and kicking an old collapsed football they'd found in the bushes to each other. Of course, Rachel was still a child, she remembered. She was incredibly brave; leaving home, insisting on keeping the baby and looking after it all on her own. Vanessa felt a surprising lump come to her throat. She wasn't sure if she would have had the courage to do the same thing at Rachel's age. It would probably do the girl the world of good to let herself go like this.

Poppy fell asleep on the blanket so Vanessa picked her up and nursed her until the girls finished playing and collapsed, giggling excitedly, on to the grass.

When she'd recovered her breath, Charlie announced she was hungry and was going home to see what was in the fridge, but Vanessa told her not to bother. 'I'll see what we've got here. Would you like something?' she asked Rachel.

They ate in the dining room, which Diana called the snug, where the sun had turned the top of the polished dining table into a mirror. She made Welsh Rarebit, which William always made for breakfast on Sundays when they got up late. It had filled a corner until they went out to lunch. Today, they had a carton of fruit yoghurt each for afters. None of the food was hers; after she'd been to the clinic, she'd call in the supermarket and buy replacements.

Of course, Charlie asked if she could come with them to the clinic. 'Aren't you worried someone from school will see you and you'll get into trouble?' Vanessa said.

'I go to this stupid girls' school in Southport so no one's likely to see me, are they?' She looked terrifically annoyed about it. 'That's why I never have anyone to play with; none of the girls live round here. Anyroad, I only didn't go to school because I've got a tummy ache, didn't I?'

'How does it feel, your tummy?'

'Middling.'

'What does that mean?'

'It could be worse and it could be better.'

Vanessa didn't believe her for a minute.

Poppy was thriving. The nurse in the clinic was all smiles and couldn't find a single thing wrong. The baby was the right weight and progressing normally. As often happened, she seemed to think Vanessa was Rachel's mother and Vanessa didn't bother to disabuse her. It saved Rachel being questioned about her ability to manage on her own.

'You've got a lovely family,' the woman behind the till in the supermarket said when Vanessa paid for the groceries. Poppy was sitting in the trolley propped up with a pink organdie pillow, queen of all she surveyed, while the girls helped load it. Far too much food had been bought. Vanessa, used to shopping so carefully, always keeping an eye on the calories, had just flung stuff in without a care.

On the way home, she wondered what William, her parents, her sisters, or anyone from Siren Radio would think if they could see her now, steering a pushchair with a baby in it, Rachel and Charlie each side clinging to the handle while sucking strawberry Cornettos. The groceries were piled in a tray underneath. No one would believe it was her; they'd think it was a double.

She paused to cross the road. 'Be careful,' she murmured just in case one of the girls shot into the traffic. There was a strange feeling in her throat or in her chest, possibly in her stomach. She couldn't work out exactly where or what it was.

Happiness, she realized after a while. At that particular moment in time, she felt utterly weary, excessively moidered and, for some strange, unaccountable reason, purely and supremely happy.

## Chapter 9

Diana had hardly been at work five minutes when the telephone rang. 'Di? Is that our Di?' an agitated voice demanded.

'Damian!' she cried. 'Yes, it's me, Diana.'

'Can you come to the ozzie straight away, sis. Something's happened.'

'Have you hurt yourself? Oh, Damian, what's wrong?' Diana's heart beat like thunder in her breast.

'It's not me: it's Emma. She's had the baby. It came earlier than expected, at least a month. Oh, Di,' Damian sounded as if any moment something would snap, 'come quick. I think I'm going round the twist here.'

'I'll be there straight away.' Diana turned to tell Owen Hughes, a volunteer who was almost ninety and had been manning the office until she arrived, that there was an emergency and she had to leave. 'When you see Tinker, tell him I'll be back as soon as I can.'

'Be off with you, girlie,' Owen said. 'I couldn't help but overhear. I hope everything's all right. Shall I ring for a taxi?'

'Please.'

Diana had virtually told the taxi driver her entire life story by the time they reached the maternity hospital.

'Well,' he said, when he stopped, 'I hope Emma's baby is all right, kiddo. Give Damian my congratulations. Say they're from Tony.'

'Thanks, Tony. Oh, look! There he is outside.'

Damian, wearing odd trainers, no socks, and tattered jeans, was marching up and down outside the hospital entrance as if he were on guard. He virtually dragged his sister out of the taxi. 'What am I going to do?' he demanded croakily.

'What about? Oh, Damian, please tell me what's the matter?'

'It's the baby,' he paused.

'What's wrong with the baby?' Diana rarely had violent thoughts, but she felt like beating him to death with her handbag. 'Is it a boy or a girl?'

'A boy and there's nothing wrong with him: it's just that . . .' Another pause.

'*What*?' Diana screamed.

'He's not white.'

'Shit,' Tinker said later that morning when Diana arrived back at the centre and told him. 'What's Damian going to do?'

'He doesn't know what to do.' Diana still hadn't got over the shock. 'He doesn't like to chuck Emma out, not with a baby. But he isn't really in love with her and doesn't want her back in Coral Street. They met in the Job Centre when she came looking for a job and he asked her out. Then she came to live with us because she told him she was pregnant and said it was his. They were going to get married one day.' She'd been really proud of her brother for behaving so responsibly, but look where it had got him! She'd like to bet Damian thought he was the first man in Emma's life, but he couldn't have been more wrong.

'Shit,' Tinker said again. 'What does Emma have to say for herself?'

'Nothing. She and Damian haven't talked about it. She was nursing the baby when he was allowed in to see her, but they both ignored the fact that he wasn't white. If Emma does leave,' Diana went on, 'I hope the lads don't expect me to go back and look after them. I really like living at Chestnuts. You liked it, didn't you, when you came to Eileen's party?'

'I adored the place, darling,' Tinker gushed. 'I can't wait to go again. As for the lads, I should imagine they're big and strong enough to look after themselves. Anyway, you and Leo will be getting married soon, won't you?'

Diana ran her fingers through her already untidy hair. 'No . . . yes . . . oh, I don't know,' she stammered.

'I like a girl who knows her own mind.'

In her lunch-hour, Diana bought a mobile phone. Damian had rushed Emma into hospital at around four o'clock that morning. 'If you'd had a . . . a stupid *mobile*,' Diana reckoned he'd really wanted to use a much stronger word than stupid, but knew she'd disapprove, 'then I could have phoned you, but I didn't want to wake up the whole house by calling the one in the hall. I would have liked you with me earlier, Di,' he'd said pathetically.

'I desperately wish I'd been there for you.' Diana squeezed his hand. Emma was a truly loathsome individual for tricking him into believing it was his baby she'd been carrying.

Tinker made her swear she wouldn't sign a contract for the mobile. 'Knowing you, you'll get tied up for some ridiculous monthly amount for the next ten years or something. Just buy a Pay-As-You-Go. They're the best if you're not going to make all that many calls.'

'All right.' Diana had no intention of making many calls once she had a mobile. Sometimes, on the bus or train, people would be on their mobiles for the entire journey, leaving them with no time to think. Diana loved thinking.

After leaving work, she met Damian in a coffee shop by Central Station to work out what he should do next.

'All I can do is dump her,' Damian said gloomily. 'But that seems awful. I mean, where will she and the baby go? Yet there's no way I'm having her back in our house with another bloke's kid. I mean, just imagine what the neighbours would say! I'd look a proper idiot.'

'Maybe she thinks you won't mind – or you haven't noticed.'

'Well, I *do* mind. I mind very much. And I noticed straight away.'

They sat there for a further half-hour, but couldn't think of a way out that didn't hurt the completely defenceless baby. In the end, Damian went to talk to Emma. Before parting from his sister, he said the baby was an amazing little chap, a real charmer. He just wasn't *his*.

As Damian had said last night, it was obvious for the whole world to see that he wasn't the baby's father. He'd suggested quite nicely and rather sadly that Emma make other arrangements.

She couldn't go home – she didn't *want* to go home. Her mother was an out-and-out bitch and her stepfather a pig. It was why she'd left the minute she'd finished school at sixteen and got a job. And she couldn't bring herself to live in her sister's shitty flat in Walton Vale. Besides which, there wasn't the room.

But she knew what had to be done and it nearly broke her heart. She loved Damian, and the house in Coral Street, especially the kitchen, and had genuinely thought the baby she was carrying was his.

After two nights in the hospital, Emma was discharged. With the baby – she still hadn't thought of a name for him – in one arm and small rucksack in the other, she caught a taxi outside the hospital and asked the driver to take her to The Shining Light restaurant in St Philomena's Street by the Pier Head.

The place was still closed, but when she looked through the window she could see the staff getting the tables ready for lunch. She banged on the door. Someone shouted at her to go away, 'We're not open yet,' but she banged even harder and eventually an elderly Indian gentleman wearing a turban opened the door.

'Is Ravi here?' she asked, praying that he hadn't gone back to India as he'd often said he might. When the man, who she was pretty certain was one of Ravi's numerous uncles, nodded courteously, she said, 'Tell him Emma's here to see him.'

The post arrived – Vanessa heard the postman open and close the rusty iron gate. She settled in front of the easel. Charlie, lying on the grass behind, waited for her to start painting so she could copy it stroke for stroke. The school in Southport had closed for the summer holidays so she now had a perfectly legitimate excuse for being at home. Vanessa thought it disgraceful that her father didn't appear to care that his young daughter would be alone in the house for the entire seven weeks.

She picked up a tube of white paint and squeezed out a quarter on to the palette, and so did Charlie. She softened the paint with the brush and out of the corner of her eye saw Charlie do the same: it was like having a miniature shadow. She was wondering what colour to use next when a shrill scream rent the air. It came from the open window of Rachel's room.

As one, Vanessa and Charlie made for the back door, which was usually kept open during the day. Rachel's mother must have got in somehow, Vanessa thought, determined to have another go at getting her hands on Poppy.

Charlie reached the top of the stairs first and flung open the door of Rachel's room. When Vanessa arrived, there was no sign of Rachel's mother. Poppy was lying in her cot clutching her feet and giggling, completely oblivious to Rachel's distress, while Rachel was waving a sheet of paper in the air.

'It's from Tyler,' she screamed. 'He's not going to marry me. He said his mother won't let him. And she's not letting him come back to England, either.' She collapsed face down on the bed. 'I'm never going to see him again.'

'Oh, dear,' Vanessa said, somewhat inadequately. Tyler's mother clearly hadn't known about Poppy until he arrived home and told her. She didn't suppose his father did, either.

Charlie burst into tears of sympathy and threw herself on to the bed with Rachel, the baby continued to giggle and Vanessa hadn't a clue what to do. She went downstairs and made a pot of tea, as much for herself as anyone.

When she got back with the tea on a tray, the girls had quietened down somewhat. They were sitting up in bed reading Tyler's letter. Charlie said, 'He's spelt maintenance wrong. He mustn't have a spell check on his computer.'

'What does he have to say about maintenance?' Vanessa asked, sitting on the edge of the bed and handing out the mugs – both girls took loads of sugar.

'That he'll send a cheque every month,' Rachel said thinly.

Vanessa frowned. 'I think we'd better see a solicitor about that, have something drawn up legally.'

'Can I come with you?' Charlie asked eagerly.

'I expect so.' She couldn't imagine going anywhere without Charlie for the foreseeable future. 'Can I read the letter?' Rachel handed it over with a sigh. The letter was typed and, although Vanessa didn't say so, she got the impression that Tyler's mother or another adult had written it, not Tyler. It was full of stiff phrases, such as: 'I am too young to take a decision that will last a lifetime'; 'I will be too busy with further education for many years to properly fulfil my role as a father'; 'I regret having behaved so irresponsibly and hope you will forgive me.'

Crap, crap, crap, she thought. It was all crap. The letter finished by saying a cheque for $200 was enclosed and a similar cheque would be sent monthly from now on. More crap. The letter was signed. 'Yours sincerely, Tyler Carter Booth', and the cheque came from Mrs E. Carrington.

'Two hundred dollars won't go very far,' she told Rachel. 'In fact, it's peanuts – roughly a hundred pounds. It's important we see a solicitor very soon.' She'd find out about one later.

Simon Collier was one of the names Vanessa was given by the Citizens Advice Bureau. He specialized in Child Support and similar matters and agreed to see them that afternoon. He was shocked to learn that Rachel wasn't in receipt of any benefits from the State. 'There's housing benefit, child benefit and other allowances. Would you like me to claim them for you?' he asked kindly. He was a nice young man, anxious to please, who looked much too young to be a solicitor specializing in anything. He had baby-blue eyes, a snub nose, and a crew-cut. He told them to call him Simon.

'Until now I've never needed benefits: Tyler always paid for everything,' Rachel explained. 'He left me plenty of money before he went away. His dad gave him loads of pocket money – Tyler called it an allowance.' She lowered her head and said in a small voice, 'I thought he really, really loved me.'

'Perhaps he does, Rachel.' Simon picked up Tyler's letter between finger and thumb, as if he was worried he'd catch something. He gave it a look of disgust. 'This might have nothing to do with Tyler. I wouldn't be at all surprised if it came from his mother – or *her* solicitor.'

'That's what I thought,' Vanessa put in.

'Ah, great minds think alike.' He smiled. 'What do you think, Poppy?' Poppy, who was sitting on Vanessa's knee, just waved her arms and smiled back. 'At this stage,' Simon went on, 'I think I can treat the case on a Legal Aid basis, so there are some forms for you to fill in, Rachel. If we do them together, then it will be much quicker. Vanessa, would you like tea or coffee while you're waiting?'

'Coffee, please.'

'And what about you, Charlie? There's always fruit juice in the fridge.'

'I'd prefer coffee, please.' She could be exquisitely polite when the situation called for it.

'Like mother, like daughter, eh?'

'Oh, but I'm not . . .' Vanessa began, but before she could finish the sentence, Charlie said loudly, 'We nearly always like the same things.' She beamed at Vanessa, but there was a sadness in her green eyes, a look of longing, as if she desperately wanted to belong to someone. Vanessa felt a lump come to her throat. Lumps were forever coming to her throat these days for all sorts of different reasons, but being taken for Charlie's mother and Charlie wanting her for a mother made the biggest lump yet.

The white paint was like a little hard worm on the palette. It hadn't been touched since Vanessa had squeezed it out yesterday morning. By now, she'd gone off white and reached for a tube of red instead. At that exact moment, the gate creaked and seconds later the front doorbell rang. She put the paint back. She wouldn't open it until she felt sure everything was going to be all right.

Charlie said, 'I'll go and see who it is. Perhaps it's the postman with a parcel.' She came back seconds later saying it was a man to see Rachel. 'She opened the door and let him in as if she was expecting him.'

'What did he look like?'

'He was tall and thin with big spectacles and a funny accent.'

'I wonder if it's Tyler's father?' Vanessa mused.

'I wouldn't be surprised if it was,' Charlie said in her grown-up way.

Once again Vanessa picked up the tube of red paint: once again she paused and stared at the open window of Rachel's room. She could hear a man talking, but couldn't make out his accent. Then, as she'd almost anticipated, there was a scream, followed by, 'Vanessa, *Vanessa*!'

With one accord, Vanessa and Charlie streaked into the house and up the stairs. The door to Rachel's room was open and she was in exactly the same position as she'd been when Vanessa had found her months ago the day her mother had come to take Poppy away: standing in the corner like an animal at bay clutching the baby to her breast.

'It's Tyler's dad and he wants Poppy,' she wailed. 'He thinks he's entitled to her because he's her grandfather.'

'I didn't put it quite so bluntly. I was trying to be reasonable,' Tyler's father said in an unemotional, dry-as-dust voice. He was tall, thin and bespectacled, exactly as Charlie had described, with pale receding hair, pale eyes and a prominent Adam's apple. His clothes were casual – cotton trousers, check shirt, beige linen jacket, cream leather loafers – but Vanessa could tell they'd cost a bundle, as had the wafer-thin gold watch on his knobbly wrist.

'What is there to be reasonable about?' she asked. 'Poppy is Rachel's baby; you can't just come in here and demand she be handed over.'

'Hear, hear,' Charlie said supportively.

'Who are you?' Tyler's father asked, looking at Vanessa and entirely ignoring Charlie.

'Vanessa Dear. I'm Rachel's friend.'

'And I'm Charlie Ormerod.' Again, the little girl might well not have spoken for all the notice the visitor took of her.

'Is this a lesbian household?' he enquired.

Vanessa laughed. '*No!*'

'What's a lesbian?' Charlie enquired.

'You'd better ask your father that,' Vanessa told her.

'I only learned yesterday from my ex-wife that my son had fathered a child.' The man spoke irritably, as if he resented having to explain himself. 'I found this address with a mobile number on his pad at home.'

'He rang this morning and asked if he could come.' Rachel crept out of the corner and sat on the bed. Poppy regarded the newcomer gravely. 'I didn't realize he wanted to take Poppy away.'

'I don't want to take her away.' Any minute now he'll stamp his foot, Vanessa thought. 'As the child's grandfather, I would like access: at weekends, say, or during the holidays. My wife and I plan to visit her relatives in Ireland soon, and she would like to take the baby with us.'

Rachel gave a little scream and Vanessa said, 'In other words, you *do* want to take Poppy away?'

'Only for a few days,' he said.

'Do you honestly think you can come here and expect Rachel to hand over her baby, if not today then tomorrow or next week or something? That's *stupid*.' The man flinched. He clearly didn't like being called stupid. '*Really* stupid,' Vanessa emphasized, rubbing it in. 'I suggest you see a solicitor and find out how the law stands on access. Oh, and talking about the law, it's a crime in this country for a man to have sex with a minor. Rachel was only fourteen when your son made her pregnant. That makes him a criminal, Mr Carter Booth, no matter how old he happened to be at the time.' So put that in your pipe and smoke it, you horrible man, she wanted to add, but didn't. Anway, for all she knew, she might have been talking nonsense.

Tyler's father had gone. Vanessa said she'd take Poppy into the garden while Rachel had a bath to calm her nerves. 'Something horrible seems to happen every day,' she complained.

'Not *every* day,' Charlie argued.

'*Nearly* every day then.'

'Did I run up these stairs earlier?' Vanessa asked when she, Charlie and Poppy were about to go down.

'Yes, and you did yesterday, too, but not as fast as me.

Though that's not surprising because I'm only seven and you're much older.'

When she'd first come to the house, she'd lumbered up the stairs, Vanessa recalled. Thinking about it now, she felt much lighter. The new dress she'd bought for Eileen's party was already a bit loose around her hips. 'I might go into town and buy some clothes one day next week,' she said.

'Can I come with you?'

'Naturally. We can have lunch.' She'd see if Megan, Brodie's mother, could come to the house for a few hours while she was out to ensure Rachel was all right. The girl was badly in need of bodyguards.

Emma telephoned Diana and asked if she'd mind fetching her things from Coral Street. She'd come to the centre and collect them after Diana finished work. 'I don't like asking your Damian or one of the lads,' she said. 'The suitcase I brought with me is under the stairs.'

Diana couldn't bring herself to be cross with the girl she'd expected to be her sister-in-law. She said she'd do it that very night and gave Emma her mobile number, 'Just in case you need to get in touch one day.' She loved her new mobile and had given the number to everyone she knew.

That night, she went to Coral Street and found only Damian in. He was lying on the settee watching an old James Bond DVD and said he was pleased she'd come for Emma's stuff. 'I'd been expecting her to come herself and wouldn't have known what to say. But you'll never guess, sis, I'm missing her a bit,' he said gruffly. 'In a way, I'm missing being a dad, too. I'd been expecting it to happen any day soon.'

'Never mind, luv,' Diana said consolingly. He was a lovely-looking young man and the day would soon come when he'd find another girl, hopefully one much nicer than Emma. She made him a cup of tea and a jam butty. 'It's about time you did some shopping,' she reminded him. 'You're short of virtually everything.'

'Emma always did the shopping. I'll have to start doing it on the way home from work.'

'Make Garth and Jason take their turns, too. If you like,' she added generously, 'I'll come round on Saturdays and do the shopping for you.'

'You'll do no such thing,' Damian said, shaking his head. 'It's about time us three learned to look after ourselves. You've got a life of your own to live, Di, and so have we.' He said he wouldn't help her with Emma's things, it would only upset him, but she knew where they were. 'And after you've packed them, I'll take you back to Blundellsands in the car.'

When Diana emerged from the centre the following night, Emma got out of the passenger door of a large grey car parked across the road and came to meet her. The driver was a handsome young brown man. There was a middle-aged woman sitting in the back.

'Ta,' Emma said when she took the suitcase.

'Where's the baby?' Diana asked. She longed to see him.

'Ravi's mother's got him in the car. Would you like to see him? We're calling him Umesh.' Emma seemed much happier than Diana had expected. Somehow, in some way, things had turned out well for her.

'Is that Ravi in the front?'

'Yeah. I was going out with him before I met your Damian. I never realized he'd put me in the club.'

An Indian woman in a lovely green sari with a red caste mark between her eyes, beamed and opened the rear car door when she saw Diana approach. 'You want to see my beautiful, beautiful grandson?' She pulled the shawl down from the baby's face. 'This is Umesh.'

'He *is* beautiful,' Diana agreed.

The baby had smooth light-brown skin, long black lashes, and a head of thick black hair. He was fast asleep, unaware of the turmoil his birth had caused.

The woman closed the car door. Emma walked round to the back and opened the boot. 'I expected Ravi to tell me to get lost,' she whispered. 'But he was dead pleased to find he'd got a son, and his mam and dad were over the moon, though they insist we get married straight away. The thing is, Ravi hasn't got any brothers and both his sisters are married and they've only got girls. Umesh is their first grandson and they said it was the best dowry a girl could have, though I'm not sure what a dowry is. I didn't know Ravi lived in this amazing big house in Princes Park. Even so, Di,' she smiled wistfully, 'I still wish it was your Damian's baby that I'd had.'

Brodie was falling in love with her own grandfather! She kept his picture on the computer screen whenever she was in her room, glancing at it frequently. Every now and then it would disappear and she'd click the mouse to make it come back again.

'Goodnight, Grandad,' she would say when she switched off the computer and went to bed. There was no need to try to imagine what he would have looked like as an old man because he'd never had the chance to grow old. A few years after the photo had been taken he had been killed by a random act of violence. It didn't say on the website what had happened to the man who'd shot him. She hoped he'd been executed, a thought so disturbing that she telephoned Colin to discuss it.

'I've always been opposed to capital punishment,' she said, 'we both have, yet I hope the man who shot granddad was hanged by the neck until he was dead – isn't that what the judge used to say when murderers were sentenced?'

'Something like that.' She imagined him shrugging at the other end of the line. 'It's not sensible to guage something like capital punishment if we're emotionally involved. Every now and then someone in Parliament has tried to bring it back, but it's always been overwhelmingly rejected.'

'I know,' Brodie agreed. 'It's what separates civilized countries from the more backward ones. I suppose my head's telling me one thing and my heart's telling me something else.'

'*Because* you're emotionally involved you're assuming whoever shot your grandfather was a cold-blooded killer. But say if he left his house that night without any intention of killing anyone? Say if the gun was just bravado, that he panicked, that he didn't know it was loaded? And Brodie,' he said gently, 'isn't it just a little bit weird to be getting all worked up about your grandfather when he died seventy-six years ago?'

Brodie thought it was more than weird: it was unhealthy, unnatural. 'The thing is,' she said, 'until we got married and I became your wife, I didn't have a single other relative apart from my mother. There were no photographs, either, only ones of Mum and my father and me when I was little. You've no idea what it feels like to see my grandfather's photograph. If he hadn't been murdered he could still be alive.'

Colin guffawed. 'He'd be well over a hundred.'

'Well, it happens,' Brodie protested. 'On the news the other day they said that more and more people are reaching a century.'

'I heard that, too, darling, but I'm afraid you'll just have to get used to the fact that your grandfather was a remarkable man who was destined to die young.' There was a pause and in the background she could hear the introduction music for BBC News 24. 'Have you seen the news? They're still bombing the hell out of Lebanon.'

'I haven't seen the news today.' These days, she avoided watching if she could, though it was often on in the home where she worked. She and Colin had talked about little else but politics in all its various forms, but it had never been a topic of conversation in Chestnuts. There was so much else to talk about: the refugee centre, Diana's brothers, Emma's baby, Rachel's troubles . . . Then there was Charlie, the delightful little girl from next door who had a perfectly awful father according to Vanessa, who kept her own secrets tightly to her chest. And, of course, there was Maisie, of whom there was no news whatsoever. Karen Young still telephoned or emailed from time to time. Last time they spoke, she wondered if Maisie had moved away from London and told Brodie that she'd sent her photograph to other forces throughout the country.

Brodie was upstairs looking through cupboards and drawers in the unused rooms for bits and pieces that could be sold on her mother's stall at the refugee centre. Mum behaved as if the stall was an important career move and was taking it very seriously.

The house was very quiet. There were no sounds at all coming from Rachel's room, and Vanessa's television was on low. Diana was out with Leo, which accounted for the lack of real noise. Brodie missed her.

There were four spare rooms about a quarter of the size of the ones that had been let. They were darker, the windows smaller, the decoration untouched for many years. When Brodie had lived in the house as a child she couldn't remember the rooms having been used for anything except storage of old furniture and cardboard boxes full of mysterious stuff.

There was some sort of unwritten law about the more space you had, the more it would be filled. At their house in Blundellsands, she and Colin were forever having clear-outs. Old bedding would go, along with frayed towels, worn shoes that weren't worth being mended but still had some wear in them, books that had been read, toys that were no longer played with, clothes that were no longer worn or had been grown out of, broken gardening implements, odd dishes. Everything would be piled in the garage waiting to be taken to charity shops or the corporation dump. There wasn't room in their brand-new house to keep anything that wasn't strictly necessary for everyday living. Here, there were even two spare beds and a wardrobe that took up almost an entire wall.

She wondered why her parents had bought such a large house, but remembered mum had wanted a big family. Perhaps her father had, too: she must ask one day. These small rooms might have been destined to become nurseries, painted blue or pink for the babies who would have been her brothers and sisters.

To her relief, apart from the odd glove and occasional coathanger, the drawers and cupboards were empty. She hadn't fancied coming across some of the Slattery sisters' old underwear or other personal items.

The boxes were an altogether different matter. The first she opened was full of ghastly ornaments, such as plaster birds painted hideous colours, brass candlesticks that would make ideal murder weapons, giant ashtrays that looked equally dangerous, and plaques with reassuring messages such as, 'There's no place like home' and 'Home is where the heart is'.

She thought there was a good chance that Mum and Diana would enjoy sorting through the boxes so decided to leave the task to them. She wasn't in the mood.

There was one room that hadn't been investigated. When she opened the door she was greeted with a familiar smell – oil paint. Of course – Vanessa had asked if she could store her paintings there. They were stacked against each other on the floor in three rows. Brodie counted one row and there were twenty, so that meant sixty altogether, and there might be more in Vanessa's room. What did she intend doing with sixty or more hideous paintings? They were being produced at a rapid rate. Some days, she finished one, occasionally two, and would start on another. Others took days and days to complete. Vanessa must have the patience of Job.

Eileen, Brodie recalled, had suggested Vanessa hold an exhibition in the garden.

Diana would enjoy getting involved. She loved organizing things. Brodie would mention it the next time she saw her. If she waited up long enough they could have a cup of cocoa together when Diana came in.

Vanessa was trying on dresses in John Lewis and Charlie was outside the cubicle waiting for her to pull back the curtain and ask her opinion on the latest model.

'What do you think of this?' she asked, showing off a bright red fitted number with a fluted skirt and flared sleeves.

'I like that one best of all,' Charlie said approvingly. She had dressed for the trip to town in a pink cotton frock, a fluffy pink beret, old-fashioned leather sandals – the sort that Vanessa had worn as a child – and a white plastic handbag trimmed with plastic flowers. 'You suit red.'

Vanessa had always worn what she called 'business colours': greys, browns and blacks, with a pastel blouse when a blouse was called for. 'I think I like this best, too.'

'I liked the green one as well and the white one with cherries on. I think you should buy them all. My mummy used to get me two or three dresses at a time because it meant she wouldn't have to go shopping again for ages. Me, I love shopping,' she added in an aggrieved tone.

'I only want to buy the one. I'm hoping to lose more weight and whatever I get will be too big.'

'I think you're perfect as you are, Vanessa.'

'Why, thank you, Charlie.' She closed the curtain, removed the red frock and put the old cream one back on. Not that it was all that old, only about four or five weeks. She had been in Chestnuts for four months and for a large part of that time had been losing weight at the rate of approximately two or three pounds a week. On the last occasion she'd been down to less than sixteen stone. She was now beginning to look plump rather than fat.

But not *just* plump. Vanessa looked at herself in the mirror, half closing her eyes so that her reflection was slightly misty. Her hair was mussed after trying on the dresses, not that it ever looked tidy these days. She'd been wearing it long her entire adult life and had forgotten how curly it used to be when short. It was time she asked Diana to give her another trim. In the old days, she'd gone to the very best hairdressers to have it highlighted, cut and blow-dried. It had cost the earth, but now Diana did it for nothing and Vanessa blow-dried it herself.

She rubbed her hands over her cheeks. They'd never used to be so rosy – and her face was brown. Her arms and legs, too, due to the outdoor life she led these days, painting in the garden day almost every single day. With her wild hair, fuller figure and red cheeks she looked a little bit . . . *wanton*!

Vanessa felt herself go hot and cold and hot again. She quite liked being this brown-skinned unexpectedly *wanton* person.

'What are you doing?' Charlie shouted.

'I'll be out in a minute.' She slipped her bare *brown* feet into old mules. In bygone days, the only time she hadn't worn tights was in bed. She came out of the cubicle a minute later as promised. 'I'll just pay for this dress,' she said, 'and then we'll have lunch.'

'Where *is* your mummy, Charlie?' she asked while they waited for the meal to arrive. They were in a new, very modern restaurant behind St John's Market. It had white walls, white furniture and a bright red carpet. Carpet apart, it looked extremely hygienic and would make an ideal place to have an appendix out, or a similar operation.

'Iraq. She divorced Daddy because she wanted her independence, but he said that was silly as the last place to find independence was in the Army and she'd be pissed about something awful. He also said that she looked horrible in the uniform, though it went with her eyes.'

'When did this happen?'

'Three years ago when I was four. I cried an awful lot when Mummy went, but I never cry now,' she said stoutly. 'I've got used to the situation, you see. Daddy said you can get used to anything if you try hard enough.' She was extremely practical for such a young child. Her father didn't sound a pleasant character, but Vanessa had thought that right from the start.

'Do you think my burger will be in a bun?' Charlie asked.

'It might be. I didn't notice what it said on the menu.' The waitress had taken the menu away.

'Do I have to eat the bun if it is?'

'Of course not. You shouldn't eat anything that you don't want to. The burger should be nice: it said they're home-made.'

'Then why aren't you having one?'

'I prefer a salad.'

Charlie wrinkled her nose. 'I *hate* salad.'

'Well, I don't, which is why I'm having one and you're having a burger.'

She noticed a couple on the far side of the restaurant were staring at her – a wishy-washy woman accompanied by an even more wishy-washy man. The man stood and came towards her. Vanessa swore underneath her breath. She didn't know him from Adam.

'Vanessa?'

There was something about the way he pronounced her name that was familiar. '*William*!' she gasped unbelievingly.

'You look wonderful.' There was awe in his voice.

'You don't look so bad yourself,' she said, lying through her teeth. Was this really the man she'd cried so many tears over, the man who had caused her to put on so much weight? Had he always been so wishy-washy, his hair the colour of dirty water and his eyes lacklustre, or was she seeing things in a different light? He even looked smaller than she remembered.

'Where are you living nowadays?'

She waved a vague hand. 'Oh, Crosby way.'

'I understand you gave up your job. What are you doing now?'

Vanessa threw back her shoulders and looked squarely at the man who had once been her fiancé. 'I paint,' she announced. 'I'm a professional artist.' Eileen had offered to buy three of her paintings and had suggested she have an exhibition – Brodie had brought up the subject only the other day. Vanessa made up her mind there and then to go ahead.

William – was this *really* William, or merely a pale imitation built by scientists in a laboratory? – looked flabbergasted. 'But you never used to paint!'

'No, I didn't, did I? But I've discovered I have a vocation. Now I paint all the time.'

The waitress arrived with their food. William said goodbye and returned to sit by the pale woman across the room. Was she his girlfriend? Were they getting married? Vanessa silently wished them all the luck in the world. They deserved each other.

# Chapter 10

By the time she and Charlie turned into Elm Road, Vanessa was feeling pretty satisfied with herself. She was pleased with her new frock, impressed with her new image and would never forget the look of stunned admiration on William's face when he'd seen her across the restaurant. The improvement in her fortunes had seemed to have happened overnight – no, that afternoon – and was taking some getting used to. But the sight of Brodie's mother, Megan, waiting outside Chestnuts looking terribly worried, slightly lessened her feeling of satisfaction.

'I hope everything's all right,' she murmured, concerned that someone else had turned up wanting to lay claim to Rachel's baby. She waved at Megan and began to hurry. Charlie was holding her hand and skipping along beside her.

As they got nearer, a man emerged from the house adjacent to Chestnuts – Charlie's house. He was tallish, slim, wearing black jeans, a T-shirt and knee-high boots. His thick black hair fell in an untidy fringe on his forehead and the rest was secured in a ponytail at the back of his neck. He scowled and folded his arms – there was a tattoo of a bird on his right forearm – and watched them approach.

'What the hell do you think you're up to, Charlotte?' he demanded angrily when they got near. He had a broad Lancashire accent. 'I've been out of me mind with worry. Mrs Fuller called me at work. She wanted to know if your grandmother was looking after you for the entire holiday or just part of it? Was she to expect you at any time or not? I had to confess I hadn't a single clue what she was talking about and she said I'd sent her emails about it.'

'What did you tell her, Daddy?' Charlie asked meekly. She hadn't let go of Vanessa's hand. In fact, she was holding on to it more tightly.

His scowl deepened. 'What I *didn't* tell her was that you haven't got a grandmother alive in this world because I didn't want her knowing I had a daughter who's the biggest liar on earth.'

'Not the *biggest*, Daddy.' Charlie attempted a roguish grin.

'Don't be cheeky with me, Charlotte Ormerod,' he thundered. 'I phoned here, but there was no reply. I called your mobile, but there was no reply to that, either. By then, I was in a right old state, I can tell you. I came home straight away, but found the house empty. Luckily, there was a lady next door who told me you had gone off to town with another lady, who has apparently kidnapped you for the entire school holiday.' He turned to Vanessa whom he had so far ignored. 'You are desperately irresponsible, whatever your name is. It's a good job you arrived home when you did: I was about to call the police.'

'Huh!' Vanessa scoffed, equally angry. 'And say what? That I'd kidnapped your daughter when she's standing right outside your very own house? As for anyone being reported to the police, it should be you for abandoning poor Charlie for weeks on end. You don't give a damn whether or not she's being looked after. One morning, she felt so sick she urgently needed to see a doctor. And where were you?' she asked more shrilly than she had intended. 'At work, that's where. You didn't even know she wasn't at school.'

'Sick?' His jaw dropped and he looked horrified. 'When were you so sick and needed to see a doctor? Charlie, my darlin' girl, come on here.' He held out his arms. Charlie released Vanessa's hand and flew into them.

'I love you, Daddy,' she sobbed into his neck. 'I love you with all my heart.'

'I know you do, sweetheart. And I love you.' He picked her up and carried her tenderly into the house. The door closed and Vanessa felt surprisingly and terribly alone, as if something very important had gone out of her life.

'Come in, Vanessa, dear, and I'll make some tea.'

'Yes, oh, thank you.' She'd forgotten Megan was still there.

'He came round earlier in a terrible state,' she said when they were in the kitchen. 'He thought Charlie was at some holiday club place in Southport, but the little madam had only written to the woman on her daddy's computer to say her gran was staying for the summer and looking after her. Then she was supposed to go to the holiday club with another girl in her mother's car, but she'd written to her, too, and cancelled the arrangement.' She smiled. 'I can't help but admire her nerve. I think I might have done the same thing at her age. And isn't her daddy a sight for sore eyes? He's as dishy as a rock star. Sixty years ago and I'd've been drooling.'

Vanessa hadn't noticed anything faintly attractive about Charlie's father. She took the tea into the garden and listened by the communal wall in case he was beating the living daylights out of his daughter, but couldn't hear a thing.

Diana was in her element organizing Vanessa's art exhibition. Leonard Gosling had designed a large poster to put in his shop window and had another fifty copies made. It was no use having one in Chestnuts; with it being at the end of a *cul-de-sac*, nobody ever walked past. Colin, Brodie's husband, offered to put one in his window, so did Megan, and one went on the noticeboard in the refugee centre and another in the house in Coral Street. All three lads promised to come for their sister's sake, though they were convinced it would be as dull as flippin' ditchwater.

On the Sunday before Diana's twenty-fifth birthday, poor Leo, who had intended taking her across the water for lunch at a posh restaurant, instead found himself driving around all the shops and pubs in the vicinity of Blundellsands and waiting in the car while Diana persuaded people to take a poster. Most did. After all, it was a bit up on the jumble and car boot sales that they were usually asked to advertise.

'All the money is going to charity,' Diana explained, 'every single penny. There'll be refreshments and music and it's on Saturday and Sunday of next week between twelve o'clock and four.' It was Diana who had decided to hold the exhibition on two days because it meant more people would be able to come.

Vanessa had agreed to be interviewed by the *Liverpool Echo*, the *Crosby Herald* and *Bootle Times*. She was unrecognizable in the photo that was taken in which she wore the grey babygro, a giant straw hat and sunglasses. She told the reporters she wished only to be known by her initial, D, and refused to reveal her first name. The *Echo* referred to her as the 'mysterious artist'.

The exhibition was being held in the garden, weather permitting, though it had been a beautiful summer so far and the long-range weather forecast didn't mention rain. The paintings – by now there were seventy-five – were to be hung from the branches of the trees or attached to the trunks. Leonard Gosling had arranged for a friend to look after his shop on Saturday and was put in charge of the exhibition arrangements – which paintings would go where, attaching a tiny label to each indicating the price, and collecting the money when they were sold. The paintings were priced at £25, £35 and £45 depending on their size.

Brodie and Megan were organizing the food. Diana was

sorting through her CDs and trying to decide what sort of music was suitable for an art exhibition.

On Saturday morning, Diana woke early. Leaping out of bed, she pulled back the curtains, opened the windows and stepped outside in her bare feet. The very air sparkled and the sky was powdery blue with little white threads of cloud. The garden was at its very best, surrounded by bushes and clumps of glorious flowers of every possible colour. She sniffed deeply: the scent was intoxicating. Brodie's Colin had been the night before to cut the grass on the gently sloping lawn so that it was velvety smooth. She wriggled her feet in it. It was wet and cold, but she loved the feeling.

'Good morning.'

'Oh, good morning.' She hadn't noticed Vanessa half-hidden behind a tree, paintbrush in hand. 'What are you painting?'

'A flower, a big one. I don't know what it's called. It's maybe a hydrangea, a peony or a rhododendron.'

'I don't know, either. I hardly know the names of any flowers, just roses and daffodils. I can't remember what else.'

'Buttercups and daisies, I bet.'

'Yes, buttercups and daisies. I'd forgotten about them. And the ones with faces – pansies. Can I look at what you're doing?'

'Of course.'

'It's a lovely dark pink,' Diana said, studying the painting. She couldn't exactly see where the flower was.

'I visualize myself being inside the flower,' Vanessa explained.

Diana closed her eyes and tried to imagine the same thing. 'I think I understand what you're getting at,' she said triumphantly, and Vanessa looked pleased. Diana said she was badly missing Charlie. 'She's such a lovely little girl. Will she be around today, do you think?'

'I don't know. They've been away, her and her dad. There's been no sign of anyone in the house for a fortnight. I say, Diana, if I were you, I'd change out of that thin night-dress into something a bit less revealing. Leonard Gosling has just arrived and you'll have the poor man all in a flutter.'

Diana went indoors and put on an old pair of jeans and a sweatshirt for now. When she returned, Leonard Gosling, in well-pressed jeans and a pastel flowered shirt, was studying the notes he'd made about where to hang the paintings.

Brodie threw open the windows of her room and came outside to join them. 'I thought I heard voices. Isn't it a lovely morning?'

Everyone agreed that it was outstanding.

'Hello!' Rachel poked her head out of the window and said that she thought Poppy had started teething. 'She cried a lot last night.' Everyone denied having heard a thing, though they all had. They didn't want Rachel to feel uncomfortable about it.

Not long afterwards, Colin arrived and unloaded half a dozen folding garden chairs and a little round table out of his car. For the life of her, Diana couldn't understand why he and Brodie had separated as they got on perfectly well together and were clearly madly in love.

Megan came, and she and Brodie went into the kitchen to make dozens of tiny scones. 'We'll do just a few sandwiches until people start coming, otherwise they might be wasted,' Megan said. 'If the scones aren't used, they can be eaten tomorrow. And if they're not eaten tomorrow, I can take them to the refugee centre on Monday.'

Diana went over to Vanessa, who was deeply involved in painting the pink flower and didn't seem aware of the efforts being made all around her for the exhibition of her work. 'I hope you won't be disappointed if not many people come,' Diana said. Until now, it hadn't entered her head that the day might not turn out to be a great success.

'I won't be disappointed, no. It's nice of everyone to do all this,' she waved her hand around the garden, 'but if no one comes I won't care. You see,' she explained carefully, 'all I want to do is paint. What happens to the paintings afterwards doesn't bother me. Do you understand, Diana?' she asked, smiling sweetly. Vanessa had become much nicer since she'd first moved into the house.

'Yes.' Diana wasn't sure if she did. 'But I worked out that if we sell every single painting, we will have raised over two thousand pounds for the shelter,' she informed her.

'Good,' Vanessa said vaguely, continuing to paint.

Diana went into the kitchen where Megan was rolling out the scone mix on the breadboard and turning it into little frilly circles with a cutter. Brodie was transferring the circles on to a metal tray with a fish slice. The room was warm with heat from the oven.

'Eileen's just been on the phone,' Brodie said. 'She and her sister Mary are driving up from London tomorrow. She wants some of Vanessa's paintings for Christmas presents.' She put her head on one side and said thoughtfully, 'I wonder how I'd feel if I was given one of Vanessa's paintings for Christmas?'

Megan poked her daughter in the ribs. 'You would thank the person politely and pretend to be grateful, darlin'. That's the way I brought you up.'

'You're right, Mum. Of course I would.'

'I'd love a painting for a present,' Diana said.

Brodie looked dismayed. 'Oh, I wish you'd said that before, love. It was your birthday last week and didn't I go and buy you a bottle of perfume?'

Megan wiped her brow with the back of her hand. 'And I got you a box of chocolates.'

'Oh, I'm not complaining,' Diana said hastily. 'It's lovely perfume. I'll be putting some on later – I'm keeping it for best. And the chocolates were lovely, too.' *Too* lovely. She'd eaten the entire box in one go and made herself sick. 'I'll buy a painting for myself.' She'd have the one Vanessa was doing at this very moment of the inside of a hydrangea, a peony or a rhododendron.

Tinker, Alan and Rosa were also coming to the exhibition tomorrow, as well as Leo and his mum and dad, and her brothers, who were going to see a footy match today.

Only thirteen people turned up on the first day. A couple with two children – a boy and a girl of about eight and ten – were the first. As they walked around the garden viewing Vanessa's paintings, the girl kept saying in a loud voice, 'I could do these standing on my head, Mum.'

They left without having a cup of tea or anything to eat, even though the refreshments were free. The man and woman looked rather strained and the children were giggling madly.

After a long gap, an elderly couple arrived. Brodie suggested that she, Diana and her mother go inside leaving only Leonard in the garden, rather than stand around gawping at everyone who came and making them feel uncomfortable. 'Leonard will tell them where the refreshments are if they want any.' Apparently, the elderly couple didn't because when Diana peeped outside they'd disappeared. She changed the music from very new to very old, just in case Jakatta's loud, persistent beat was putting people off. They might prefer something by Cole Porter.

By now, it was almost two o'clock, Vanessa and Rachel had taken Poppy to the shore. Brodie made yet another pot of tea and they ate another sandwich and another buttered scone. They stood in the kitchen, not saying much, until the relative silence was disturbed by the sound of shrieks of laughter.

Diana shot outside to find out why people felt the need to make such a racket at an art exhibition and found four scantily dressed young women walking from painting to painting, pointing at them, gasping in turn, 'Look at *that* one!' 'And look at *THAT* one!' One actually fell down on the grass in a fit of hysterics.

She was amazed that when they finished laughing they bought two of the smaller paintings, handing over a fifty-pound note.

'I hope it's not a forgery,' she said to Leonard when the girls had left. He assured her that it was real.

'Correct me if I'm wrong, Diana,' he said in his courteous way, 'but were those young ladies wearing only their under-wear?'

'It looked like underwear, but in actual fact it's the latest fashion.'

'In my young day, those sort of lacy things were called camiknickers.'

'They're called dresses now.' She would never have the courage to wear such a dress herself. Anyroad, at twenty-five she was too old.

Just before four o'clock two women turned up but hardly stayed a minute. Then a man came who said he was an art teacher at a school in Chester. He studied each painting in-tently, eventually buying one that Vanessa explained was the underside of a mushroom. 'It's got something,' he said. 'I'm in a hurry right now, but I might come back tomorrow and buy more.'

'Well, it wasn't a *complete* failure,' Diana said to Leonard as together they took down the paintings. 'We made seventy-five pounds.'

'Eighty-five pounds. That last painting was thirty-five.'

'I feel awful,' she confessed, 'putting everyone to so much trouble. I know it was Eileen's idea, but it was me who in-sisted on going ahead with it.'

'You must absolutely not feel awful, Diana.' He patted her bare arm – he had a habit of patting women's bare arms whenever he could. 'It is better to have tried and failed than not to have tried at all – I'm sure someone like Shakespeare must have said something like that. If he didn't, he should have. And it might be quite different tomorrow.'

It was different. If anything, the weather was even better than the day before: the sky bluer, the sun warmer, the air even more dazzling, like bubbles in champagne. Between forty or fifty people came. Diana, wearing an orange jumpsuit decorated with sequins, was the only person who bothered to count and she lost track after a while. At one time, there were at least twenty visitors sitting or standing around with a drink and a plate of refreshments, many of them friends or relatives: Diana's brothers, Brodie's mother-in-law Eileen, who was smoking like a chimney, and her sister Mary, Leo Peterson and his mum and dad, Tinker, Rosa and Alan from the refugee centre. Rosa, who had never had children of her own, was making a big fuss of Poppy.

Inside the house, Brodie and Megan were making sandwiches like nobody's business, and Colin was despatched to buy another three loaves. Soft, romantic music came from the open window of Diana's room, adding to the slightly unreal, almost dreamy quality of the afternoon.

At least half the paintings were sold. If the purchaser didn't want to take their painting straight away, then Leonard self-importantly put a little red sticker in the corner to indicate the picture was no longer for sale. 'It's what they do in *proper* art galleries,' he whispered to Diana.

More than a thousand pounds was raised for the refugee centre. Tinker tried to make up his mind what to spend it on: making the restaurant more attractive, for instance, with chairs and tables that matched; another snooker table; more toys for the playgroup; a carpet in the lounge; a new computer . . .

Neighbours came to see what was going on, astounded to

find there was an art exhibition in their very own road. Some stayed and bought paintings.

'Do you actually *live* here?' a woman asked Diana. 'How lucky you are,' she continued when Diana agreed that she did. 'It's a little oasis, so quiet and peaceful, like being in the very heart of the countryside. You can hardly hear the trains at all.'

Vanessa couldn't help experiencing a feeling of elation as she watched people hand over good money for her paintings. She'd told Diana she didn't care what happened to them once they were finished, but she was wrong. She hadn't realized the pleasure it would give knowing that people would hang them on the walls of their homes. Eileen actually bought five, saying, 'I want them for presents, but I reckon I'll end up keeping the lot.'

The art teacher from yesterday returned and bought another two. 'They've *got* something,' he said to Vanessa after asking to meet the artist. 'I don't know what it is, but they've definitely got *something*.'

Could it be that she really had talent? That her desire to get down on paper the corner of a roof, half a window, the inside of flowers and trees, strange patterns, the rusty gate, a patch of sky, Charlie's red hair – just the hair, nothing else – Poppy's little foot or the back of her pushchair actually *meant* something? She must take care in future not to think about people's reactions and the saleability of a painting before she started it.

There was a gentle tug on her skirt and a little voice said, 'Hello, Vanessa.'

She looked down, and had never been so pleased to see anyone before in her whole life. 'Hello, Charlie,' she said, a lump instantly forming in her throat. She suppressed the urge to cry and hug the little girl to death. 'Where have you been?' She guessed the white T-shirt she wore with the letters NY on the front in red and gold provided a clue.

'To California with Daddy,' the little girl replied, starry-eyed. 'There was an exhibition of computer games and his company had a stall. I played loads of games and we've brought even more home with us. When it was over, we went to Disneyland and then to New York where Daddy has some friends who took us out to dinner every single night.'

Vanessa smiled. 'There's no need to ask if you had a good time.'

She sighed blissfully. 'I had a *marvellous* time, and so did Daddy.' Her hand seemed to creep inside Vanessa's. 'But I kept wishing you were there with us.'

'I wish I had been, too.' She wondered if the father had always intended taking his daughter to America, or if she would have been left with the woman who ran the holiday club in Southport if Vanessa hadn't told him a few home truths. 'Where is your daddy?' she asked.

'He's here somewhere. I think Brodie's making him a cup of tea. He was surprised when he saw what was going on next door and said he was glad we'd got home in time to come.' She rubbed her face against Vanessa's arm. 'And so am I.'

Four o'clock approached and gradually people began to go home, until only close friends and a few relatives were left. Diana's brothers had more important things to do and Tinker, Rosa and Alan were expected at a concert. Leonard took the paintings down, put them in the house, and went home: Sunday was his chess night.

The sun continued to shine as warmly and as brightly as ever. Frank Sinatra sang 'Come Fly With Me' and 'Nancy with the Laughing Face'. Charlie's father and Colin were in deep conversation about cars. It would seem Colin had an old Triumph he was restoring and the other man was anxious to see it. He was dressed as he'd been when Vanessa first saw him, all in black, though this time his dark hair wasn't tied back, but sticking out all over the place as if he'd been dragged through a hedge backwards. She would have expected him to have ginger hair like his daughter, but Charlie must take after her mother.

Leo's mum and dad had gone, but Leo stayed, his eyes following Diana in her orange jumpsuit as she darted like a firefly all over the place, never pausing to rest. He was so much in love with her that it was painful to watch. Vanessa could understand Diana finding such devotion hard to resist.

Rachel and Charlie were playing with Poppy on a blanket under the trees where it was shady. 'I didn't see a single baby in New York,' Charlie was saying.

Brodie revealed that there was wine in the fridge. 'Who'd like a glass?'

'Me!' Eileen put up her hand. 'I'd like two glasses: any colour, dry or sweet.'

'I would, too.' Megan had collapsed in a deckchair. She wasn't a young woman and had had a busy day.

'How about you, Vanessa?'

'Yes, please.' She was sitting on the grass, glad that the afternoon was almost over, only conscious now that it had been a bit of a strain.

Almost immediately, Charlie's father came and sat on the grass beside her. 'I want to thank you for looking after Charlie,' he said. 'And apologize for what I said the other week. I was a pig. I hadn't realized Charlie had been emailing all over the globe cancelling the arrangements I'd made. I hadn't realized she was so unhappy, either, being looked after by all and sundry instead of her dad.' He held out his hand. 'Reggie Ormerod – or Reg, but definitely not Reginald. There's no need to ask who you are: Vanessa Dear, the famous artist.'

'Not exactly famous,' Vanessa said modestly as they shook hands.

'The time will come, I'm sure of it,' he said, smiling brilliantly. He *was* dishy, as Megan had said, and *did* look like a rock star. He also had buckets of Lancashire charm.

Normally, Vanessa didn't like men with long hair and tattoos, and couldn't stand the name Reginald in any of its various forms. Perhaps she was going through a personality change because she quite liked Reggie Ormerod, though in an entirely unromantic way. Soon, she thought, there'd be nothing whatsoever left of the woman who'd come to live in this house in March, On second thoughts, she wasn't entirely sure if her liking for him was all that unromantic.

'I want to ask you something,' Reggie said. 'Charlie still has a fortnight to go before she goes back to school. Can I leave her with you? It's what she wants. If it's inconvenient, I can always make other arrangements.' There was something quite touching about this dishy individual being so concerned about his little daughter.

'I love having her,' Vanessa assured him. 'We all do, particularly Rachel and Poppy – that's the young girl with the baby. You can leave her with us whenever you want.'

'Thanks, I really appreciate it.'

It had all gone wonderfully well, Brodie thought as she went round with the wine, far better than expected. It was astounding to think that people were willing to hand over more than a thousand pounds for Vanessa's paintings. How did the old saying go? A fool and his money are soon parted.

Oh, that's most unfair of me, she thought, ashamed. Just because *she* didn't like the paintings, it was silly – no, not just silly, but arrogant and condescending – to expect other people to think the same. The day might come when Vanessa's paintings would be worth ten times, a hundred times as much as they'd gone for today, and Brodie would have to eat her words – thoughts – and wish she'd bought half a dozen as an investment when she'd had the opportunity, just like Eileen.

'I'll buy one later,' she vowed. 'No, I'll get two, one for Diana.' She wondered if her mother would like one.

She returned to the kitchen for a glass of wine for herself and wished she'd thought to buy a few bottles of beer for Colin and Charlie's father, Reggie, who didn't look the sort of person who was into wine. Mum, bless her, fancied the pants off him, and Brodie didn't exactly find him unattractive, either. He and Vanessa had been talking for ages. Wouldn't it be great if they got together? She imagined another day like today with Vanessa and Reggie getting married in the garden.

Colin came in and she remembered what had happened the last time they'd had a party: they'd made love afterwards. Would it happen again tonight? She'd be very easy to persuade once she'd got a few glasses of wine down her.

'Any beer?' he asked.

'Sorry.' She grimaced. 'I didn't think about it until a few minutes ago.'

'It's all right. Reggie's got a six-pack in the fridge. He said he'd go and fetch it if we had none here. Is that your mobile, Brodie?'

'Yes.' One of the Brandenburg concertos was being played at a furious pace in her room.

'I'll get it for you, darling.' He came back a few seconds later. 'I answered it. Someone called Karen wants to speak to you.'

Karen Young, the policewoman she'd met in London. Brodie grabbed the mobile. She listened intently, hardly speaking, just the occasional 'yes'. When she'd finished, she switched the phone off and laid it on the kitchen unit beside the wine. She was shaking.

'Who was it?' Colin asked tensely.

'Karen is the policewoman who's been looking for Maisie.' Brodie didn't know whether to laugh or cry. 'She's been found. She's not very well, though, and Karen is driving her home. She's already come a bit of a way and thinks she'll be about another three hours.'

'She's coming here?'

228

'Yes, here.' All the antagonism that had built up between them when they'd lived together returned with a vengeance. 'Not the house in Crosby, that's for sure,' she said coldly. 'We both know she's not welcome there.'

He punched the fridge so hard that she wondered if he'd made a dent in it. 'For Christ's sake, Brodie, let her come to her real home, please, and we can both look after her.'

'You don't want to look after her.' Hot tears came to her eyes. 'You've said all along that the drugs are all her own fault, that she doesn't deserve pity – certainly not yours.' She walked into her room and he followed. 'I don't want you near her, Colin,' she shouted over her shoulder. 'I'm not having you accusing her of letting you down and all sorts of other rubbish.'

'As if I'd say that.' He was red with frustration. 'She's my daughter, for Christ's sake.'

'Huh! You've changed your tune, I must say. You didn't think like that before. You virtually disowned her.'

'Then I was wrong, OK?' His hands became fists and he stuffed them into the pockets of his jeans as far as they would go. 'It was the only way I could think of dealing with the situation. You leaving me taught me the error of my ways.' He glared at her belligerently. 'Now I'm sorry and I want to help.'

Brodie tossed her head. 'I can manage on my own, thank you.'

'Where will she sleep?' Colin demanded in a different tone, more practical.

'In here with me.'

'But there isn't the room: it's only a single bed.'

'There are more beds upstairs. I'll put another single in here.' She made to leave through the French window. 'I'll ask Reggie Ormerod to give me a hand.'

He grabbed her arm. 'Don't be so bloody stupid. *I'll* bring one down.'

'You can't do it on your own. It needs two people.' She thought for a moment. 'OK, let's both do it. If I ask Reggie, my mum and yours will want to know why I need another bed downstairs. If they know Maisie's coming home, they'll make a huge fuss, and I'd sooner it was kept between the two of us for now.'

They went upstairs where there were two single beds. Both felt quite comfortable, but the more modern one, which was merely a hollow base with a mattress on top, would be the easiest and lightest to carry.

'This one, I think,' she said. 'The headboard is simple to take off and put back on again.'

Quarter of an hour later, the bed had been erected next to the single bed already in Brodie's room. She looked for bedding in the wardrobe drawer. 'Damn! I've only got one duvet,' she swore. 'I'd forgotten.'

'Shall I go home and fetch one?' Colin asked.

'Thank you. Bring the one from Maisie's bed, and the pillow and the bottom sheet as well.' She pushed the new bed further from her own. Maisie might prefer them not to be too close. Brodie resolved not to smother her with love when she might not be ready for it. She might even prefer to be left alone. If she wanted a room of her own, then she could have this one, and Brodie would sleep in one of the little rooms upstairs.

After Colin had gone, she collected her wine and went into the garden, otherwise someone would be bound to come looking for her. Karen had said she expected to arrive around ten o'clock and it was gone half past seven now.

'Are you all right, darlin'?' her mother enquired.

'I'm tired, Mum, that's all.'

'If that's the case, you'd be better off with tea or coffee, not wine. It'll only make you more tired.'

Brodie merely smiled and tried not to appear irritated. She wasn't in the mood to be told what was best by her mother.

And Eileen was getting on her nerves, talking too loudly and drinking and smoking far too much. Her sister Mary, who looked quite sober, seemed to sense Brodie's disapproval and shrugged slightly, as if to say there was nothing she could do.

Reggie Ormerod went home with Charlie, and Rachel took Poppy upstairs, saying she hoped she wouldn't keep anyone awake that night crying. 'I'm sure she's teething,' she said again. 'Her gums look very red.'

'Have you got stuff to rub on them?' Eileen asked.

'Oh, yes.' She was an admirable young girl, Brodie thought. Poppy couldn't have had a more dedicated mother.

Diana and Leo had disappeared into another part of the garden. Vanessa sat in a deckchair close to sleep. It was gone eight o'clock and the sun was setting behind the trees, making long shadows on the grass. Brodie heard Colin return. She went into her room through the window and closed it surreptitiously behind her, hoping no one would notice. Then she opened the front door for Colin.

'I've brought a few other things,' he said, coming in, his arms laden with bedding and a black plastic bag. 'I've got her dressing gown from behind the door, some slippers, and a few clothes out of her wardrobe, including a couple of night-dresses.'

'Thank you.' He was being very thoughtful.

He helped make the bed for their daughter. After they'd finished, he said, 'Surely we should be doing this together, darling? Not just making beds, but looking after her, sharing the responsibility.'

She looked at him impatiently. 'You must have lost your memory. It wasn't long ago that you wouldn't even discuss Maisie. It's the reason I left, because I couldn't stand your indifference.' She was aware she was merely making the same point in another way.

'I've already told you I didn't mean it. I was confused.' He groaned and rubbed his forehead with the back of his hand. 'I don't seem to be able to get through to you.'

She sat on the bed. 'Oh, Colin,' she said, 'I feel terrible.'

He sat beside her and tenderly put his arm around her shoulders. 'In what way, darling? Are you ill?'

'No. But it's been a lovely day. I've really enjoyed myself and hardly thought once about Maisie.' Then it had only been in passing, some swift memory from the past. By now, she'd completely forgotten whatever it was.

'If you let yourself worry about something every minute of every day, you'd very soon go mad,' Colin said soothingly.

She relaxed against him, hating him, yet loving him so much. 'I wish my mother and yours would go home,' she said. 'They make me feel all on edge. I desperately want both of them to be gone by the time Maisie comes.'

'I'll tell mine that our Stephen has a meal ready, shall I?' Stephen was Colin's younger brother, and Eileen and Mary were spending the night in his house. 'I'll offer to take her and Aunt Mary there.'

Brodie gnawed her lip. 'If your mum leaves, mine will only come and see what I'm up to. No, offer *her* a lift home. There's no way she can ride a bike, not in her condition: she's drunk far too much wine. When you come back, you can try to get rid of Eileen.' She was being awful, but could imagine the women following Maisie when she came in, commenting loudly, offering advice, perhaps even shedding a tear or two. Eileen might give her a cigarette, mum would offer to make strong tea with loads of sugar, her remedy for virtually everything.

'I'll see to it,' Colin said. He left and minutes later Brodie could hear him in the garden asking her mother if she'd like to be taken home.

Mum must have agreed. 'I'll go and get my bag,' she said.

The bag was on the table in Brodie's room. 'What on earth is another bed doing in here,' she imagined her mother saying if she came in. She took the bag into the garden and gave it to her mother there. She took ages saying goodnight, what a wonderful day it had been, and fancy raising so much money for the refugee centre. Tinker must be thrilled to bits.

She'd hardly been gone a minute, when Eileen and Mary went through the same routine. Then Vanessa yawned and rubbed her eyes and said she was going straight to bed. Rachel and Poppy had already gone, leaving Diana and Leo the only ones still around, though they were nowhere to be seen.

Brodie breathed a long sigh of relief and returned to her room. All of a sudden, the house and the garden were silent. She wanted to be the only person about when her daughter came home. If Karen wanted a drink, then Brodie would show her the kitchen and suggest she make it herself while she concentrated on Maisie. There were still some sandwiches and scones left over – it felt as if the exhibition had happened a week ago, not that afternoon.

By now, it was quarter to ten and the night was dark. She made the tea she'd been on the point of making for the last half-hour.

Her mobile went. It was Colin to say her mother had been delivered home safely. He wanted to know if his own mother was still there. If not, did Brodie want him back or was he to take himself home?

Brodie suggested he came tomorrow. He was doing his best to be helpful and it would be silly to keep turning him away.

She sat in her room with the tea. At one point, she got up, turned on the computer, and sent Josh an email telling him his sister was on her way home. Afterwards, she brought up the photograph of her grandfather and sat looking at that until she heard a car stop outside.

'I suppose your legs are stiff,' Karen was saying gently as she helped Brodie's daughter out of the back of her car. 'Here, lean on me.'

'Let me help.' Brodie turned on the porch light and ran down the path. It was hard to believe that this was really happening.

'Here's your mum,' Karen said.

Maisie was having difficulty getting out of the car.

Brodie gasped, 'Maisie, oh, sweetheart.' Karen was holding Maisie's right arm and Brodie took hold of the left. It felt as thin as a stick.

'Hello, Mum,' Maisie mumbled. She stood up at last, clumsily, unsteadily, and took a step forward so that she was fully illuminated by the light from the porch. It was only then that Brodie saw that her daughter was heavily pregnant – at least seven months, perhaps more.

# Chapter 11

Brodie's mobile rang. It was Colin. 'I take it Maisie's there by now?' he said quietly.

'She arrived about half an hour ago. But Colin . . .' she began, then paused, finding it hard to continue.

'What?' he asked.

'She's pregnant. Seven, maybe eight months gone.' She also looked awful, like a like a walking corpse, and smelled sour and unwashed.

'Jesus Christ! Did she say who the father is? Does she *know* who he is?'

'We haven't had a chance to talk,' Brodie said tiredly. 'Karen found her in a place in Islington, a rehabilitation centre for drug addicts. She hadn't long been there, only a few days.' She swallowed hard and tried to hold back the tears. 'Karen thinks she's going to be all right.'

'Thank God,' Colin said. 'What's she doing now?'

'She's asleep. When she got home, she just went straight to the toilet, then threw herself on the bed fully dressed. She's very restless. I'm in the garden, actually. I left the window open in case she wakes up and wants something.' She sighed. 'I wish I smoked: it might help me relax.' It seemed to help people like Eileen.

'Why not have a glass of wine?' he suggested.

'I've already had too much. I'm not exactly sober at the moment.' And it hadn't helped. The wine had made her feel nervy and on edge. It was why she'd come into the garden, to walk around, get some fresh air. 'What I need now is a strong cup of tea with loads of sugar – Mum would make it for me if she were here.'

'Would you like me to come over and make it?' He seemed anxious to help and had apparently got over the feeling of antagonism he'd had for their daughter.

'No thanks. I'll do it myself in a minute.'

'But I can come in the morning like you said?'

'Of course, Colin, Any time.'

Despite everything, it was pleasant in the garden. The only illumination came from the window of Diana's room where the curtains hadn't been drawn and the light was spread fan-shaped on the grass. The night-time scent of flowers was much stronger than during the day and the trains sounded louder, making the earth tremble. The trees were black against a sky made dull orange by the lights of the city, as if a giant spotlight had been directed on Liverpool from outer space. There were a few barely visible stars. Shuffling and scrabbling noises came from the bushes, as if little animals were having a party.

Kenneth came and rubbed himself against her legs, tail erect, purring loudly. She bent down, stroked his furry back, and lifted him on to her knee. 'What are you doing out so late?' she asked. 'I hope you're not a stray.' The cat responded by making itself comfortable on her knee and purring even louder.

Diana opened the window and said in a stage whisper, 'Would you like a drink, Brodie?'

'Oh, tea, please, very strong. Thank you.' She'd forgo the sugar. By now, the thought of sweet tea made her feel sick.

'Won't be a mo.' The window closed.

She was a diamond, that girl, Brodie thought. She and Leo had come in from the garden as the same time as Karen

Young had arrived with Maisie. Poor Leo had been sent home on the spot and Diana had taken Karen into the snug with a drink and something to eat. While Brodie had been stroking her daughter's head, trying to calm her jerky, troubled sleep, she could hear the subdued, earnest voices of the two women.

Then Karen had knocked softly on Brodie's door to say she was going back to London.

Brodie came into the hall, closing the door behind her. 'Are you sure you wouldn't like to stay the night? My mother has a spare bedroom; she doesn't live far away.'

'If you don't mind, I'd sooner go now while there's hardly any traffic, and sleep tomorrow,' Karen said. Her young face glowed with health and she didn't look even faintly tired after the long journey. 'I've left some leaflets in the kitchen that will help you understand what is happening to Maisie.'

'Would you like to sit down?'

'No, thanks. I'll be sitting down all the way back to London.' She cleared her throat. 'She's only been at this rehab place in Islington a few days. For weeks, she'd been taking smaller and smaller doses of the drug – it's heroin by the way. She took the last dose the other day and she's been in agony ever since – that's when she went into rehab because she needed some support. Now she's almost over her addiction.'

'That was quick! Is that all that was needed to get over it, a few days?' Why hadn't she done it before? Maisie cried out in her sleep and Diana had turned the television on or was playing a CD. Strains of highly dramatic music were coming from her room.

'Yes, but you have to make the decision to quit,' Karen said earnestly, 'that's the biggest hurdle, then be able to stick to it. The thinking at the centre is that Maisie has given up because of the baby, which is really good. She's shown the most enormous willpower and courage. There'll be another three or four weeks of her feeling pretty rotten: pains in the joints, panic attacks, nightmares, and so on. Try not to let her out on her own, just in case she weakens and goes looking for a hit.'

'We'll be careful,' Brodie promised. 'But what about the baby? I've heard that babies of drug addicts can be born with withdrawal symptoms.'

'That's not likely to be the case with Maisie. She wasn't a heavy user. She never injected, just smoked the stuff. Never the less, make sure she sees a doctor as soon as possible.' She held out her hand. 'I'll be off now, Brodie. I hope everything goes well with Maisie – and with you and your husband.'

Brodie ignored the hand and threw her arms around the girl. 'Thank you so much for finding her and bringing her home.' She would never cease to be grateful. 'I'll keep you informed as to how she's getting on.'

Karen left and Brodie returned to sit by Maisie and try to calm her troubled sleep. Images kept passing through her mind of Maisie as a baby, a toddler, starting playgroup then school, and so on until the day she'd left for university. In all the images, her daughter shone like a light: bright-eyed, glossy-haired, creamy-cheeked.

She thought about Josh and switched on the computer, turning the sound down first. There was an email from him: 'Is Maisie all right? Give her my love and ask when I can come and see her.'

Brodie didn't email back straight away because she didn't know what to say. She'd reply to him tomorrow.

Maisie had settled down, and it was at that point that Brodie went out into the garden and Diana had brought her tea. 'I'm going to bed now,' she whispered. 'I'll see you in the morning.'

'Goodnight, love.' She caught the girl's hand. 'And thank you.' Diana had known Brodie had a daughter – so did Vanessa and Rachel – but they hadn't known that she was a drug addict.

Diana's window closed and the curtains were drawn. Minutes later, the light went out. Now there was no light at all except from the sky. It was only then that Brodie allowed the pent-up tears to stream down her cheeks. She cried quietly, the tears falling on Kenneth's back, thinking about the daughter she'd once had, and the one she had now.

At quarter past four, Maisie woke up and began to moan. 'I'm hurting,' she whined. 'I'm hurting all over.'

Brodie, in her own bed by then, reached out her hand and rested it on Maisie's shoulder. 'What's wrong, sweetheart? Can I get you something?'

'I'm hurting so much. My bones are aching.' She sat up suddenly and Brodie's hand was knocked away. 'Have you got any tablets? Headache tablets? Aspirin?'

'I'll get some.' There was Paracetamol in the cupboard in the kitchen.

'Who are you?' Maisie asked rudely. 'Where am I?'

'It's Mum, sweetheart, and you're at home.' She reached for the bedside lamp and switched it on. 'There,' she said in a bright, unnatural voice. 'Don't you recognize me?'

Maisie stared, stared and stared, until her eyes glazed over and her face looked as if it was about to fall apart. 'Mum,' she said brokenly.

Brodie didn't know whether to hug her or not. She blinked back the tears that threatened to return and said, 'Would you like me to make you a drink, sweetheart? Tea or coffee? Or hot milk? You used to love a mug of hot milk before you went to bed, remember?'

'Milk would be nice. Thanks.' She leaned back against the pillow. 'I feel awful,' she groaned.

'I'll fetch those tablets,' Brodie promised.

They sat up in their beds, mother and daughter, drinking the milk. Brodie couldn't have described how she felt. The situation was so totally unreal. She wasn't prepared for it.

Between sips, she made innocuous remarks: what a warm night it was, what a lovely summer it had been, how Josh was still setting up businesses that always failed. Now he'd bought an old van and had started to do removals. 'I expect that will fail like everything else.' She thought about Diana's brothers. Garth, the youngest, had done well in his A-levels and was going to Manchester University in October, yet there hadn't been a parent in sight to offer support. Was it possible, she wondered, to offer too *much* support? Perhaps that's where she and Colin had gone wrong.

Maisie started to shiver violently. Brodie had never heard anybody's teeth rattle before. 'Would you like to have a bath?' she asked. She'd always considered baths to be a miracle cure for virtually everything, just as her mother promoted sweet tea. Colin used to make jokes about it. 'The water will still be hot.'

'All right,' Maisie said, somewhat surprisingly.

Brodie got out of bed and began to fuss around, collecting the dressing gown Colin had bought, a nightdress, slippers. 'Dad brought these earlier,' she said.

'Dad? Where is he?' Maisie, still shivering, glanced around the dimly-lit room. 'This isn't Crosby. Why isn't Dad here?'

'This used to be Gran's house, now it's mine. You've never been here before. I'm just staying here for the time being, that's all. Dad's coming tomorrow.'

She was pleased when Maisie didn't question this, but finished the milk and climbed out of bed. Brodie was glad she'd agreed to a bath. It would get the smell off her.

They went upstairs. Brodie ran the water, adding tea tree bath foam. Maisie just stood by the door, watching. 'Is that enough?' Brodie asked when the water was six or seven inches deep and covered with a froth of bubbles.

Maisie sniffed and nodded. Her long brown hair was hanging partly over her face in greasy clumps. She'd removed her cardigan and the T-shirt underneath was a shade between grey and black. Her jeans looked as if they hadn't been washed in months. In the gap between the T-shirt and the jeans, the skin on her stomach was stretched so tightly it was almost blue.

'There's shampoo here if you're going to wash your hair. Oh, and the pink toothbrush is mine if you want to use it. I'm afraid I haven't got a new one for you. I've hung your dressing gown and nightie behind the door and the clean towels are on the stool. Well,' she said, slightly breathless, 'I'll leave you to get on with it, shall I?' She hadn't been allowed in the bathroom with her daughter since Maisie was ten.

'Please.'

'Don't bolt the door. Oh, and take as long as you like – I'll be right outside if you need me.'

'All right, Mum.'

The 'Mum' held a touch of normality and was rather comforting. As quietly as she could, Brodie fetched a dining chair with a huge padded seat out of one of the small bed-rooms and placed it close to the bathroom door. She didn't want to disturb Vanessa or Rachel and Poppy – that's if they hadn't been disturbed already. It had never been the sort of house in which people took baths at half-past four in the morning.

It was a good half an hour before Maisie appeared, looking almost human again, almost like the old Maisie in her lemon towelling dressing gown and white nightie. She'd washed her hair and combed it back off her face. There was a spot, almost a boil, on her right cheek and another on her forehead. 'I fell asleep,' she said.

Brodie had been fighting sleep the whole time, worried she'd fall off the chair. 'I'll dry your hair,' she said, 'and then we'll go back to bed.' She felt as if she could sleep for a week.

Maisie's hair was pitifully thin compared with how it used to be. When it was dry and she'd crawled into bed, she said sleepily, 'I feel better. Don't wake me up if Pete calls.'

'Is Pete likely to call?' Brodie asked. 'You'd better let me have your mobile. Does he know where you are?' If so, he could turn up at any time.

After a pause, Maisie gave a rather rusty laugh. 'I forgot: someone pinched my mobile and even *I'm* not sure where I am.'

'Who is Pete, sweetheart?' Brodie asked.

'My boyfriend.'


At half-past eight the next morning Maisie was dead to the world, there wasn't a sound coming from upstairs and Brodie was in the kitchen waiting for the kettle to boil. She hadn't slept a wink after going back to bed at around five. She'd kept asking herself questions to which she couldn't possibly have known the answers.

She'd heard Diana leave for work. Much too late, it dawned on her that *she* should have left for work by now. It was Monday, the start of a new week. Under the circumstances, she couldn't possibly go. In a minute, she'd telephone Mrs Cowper at Five Oaks and tell her she was leaving – no, had already left. It was an awful thing to do, she was badly letting the woman down, but had no choice.

How quickly life could change, she thought, sometimes for the better, sometimes for the worst. This time yesterday, she'd been in this same kitchen with her mother and Diana. They'd been standing around wondering if the art exhibition would be more successful than it had been the day before. And of course it was.

Now Maisie was home, life had changed for the better. She had her daughter under the same roof and was able to look after her. The trouble was, life felt worse. No, not worse, she reflected, just more troubling, more of a problem, more *real*. She had to worry about Maisie in a different way, no longer from a distance.

The bell on the front door made its strange buzzing sound

and she hurried to answer it. The woman outside looked about forty, and was smartly dressed in a business-like black suit and low-heeled shoes. She carried a shorthand notebook in one hand and a pen in the other, and a sensible black handbag over her shoulder. Her black hair was cut in a stern fringe and heavy, horn-rimmed spectacles helped give the impression that in another life she could have been a concentration camp guard. She gave Brodie – in her denim skirt, check blouse and flip-flops – a disparaging look. Brodie noticed and the instinctive dislike she'd felt took a turn for the worse.

'Yes?' she enquired politely.

'I'd like to see Rachel Keen,' the woman demanded in a peremptory tone and without so much as a 'please'.

'She's not here.' Rachel and Poppy were no doubt asleep upstairs, but as far as Brodie was concerned the woman could go and jump in the lake. She didn't feel in the least bit accommodating.

'When will she be here?'

'I've no idea.'

'Does she actually live here?'

'Yes.'

'What sort of house is this?'

'A brick one.' She lost her patience. 'What do you mean, what sort of house is this? It's not a doss house, or a house of ill repute. It's just a house and I'm the owner.'

'I see.' The sarcasm was completely lost on the woman and she wrote something on the pad. 'And what's your name?'

'Hillary Clinton.' Brodie was beginning to enjoy herself.

'Is that Mrs?'

'It is indeed.'

'You must have some idea of when Rachel will be in.'

'I think she might be on holiday.' It was time *she* asked a question. 'What was it you wanted to see Rachel about?'

'We understand,' the woman said grimly, 'that Rachel is an

under-aged mother and concern has been expressed that the baby is not being properly cared for.'

Brodie wondered if the person who had expressed concern was Rachel's mother or Tyler's father. Vanessa had reported that the father was a pretty revolting piece of work. She said, 'I know for a fact that Rachel attends the baby clinic every week without fail accompanied by a very concerned adult. She is a far better mother than I ever was and a fine example to mothers of any age. Now, I'm afraid I am very busy. Goodbye.'

She closed the door and stood leaning against it feeling triumphant. She'd certainly won *that* battle. After a while, she began to feel ashamed. The poor woman was only doing her job. She opened the door, but there was no sign of anyone and she could hear a car driving away.

'I'm sorry,' she said to the road in general. 'Really sorry.'

She stepped outside and took a deep breath. It was another lovely day. This was the best summer she could remember. If global warming got no worse than this, then she was all for it.

In the kitchen, she boiled the kettle again, made tea, and took it into the garden. To her surprise, she found Rachel and Charlie squashed together in a deck chair reading a magazine, and Vanessa seated on a bench nursing Poppy, who was chewing madly on a rattle. Kenneth was draped over a branch of a tree like the fur neck thing her mother used to have – she thought it was called a tippet and it had been brown, not ginger.

'What a scene of domestic bliss,' she called as she approached the group. Everyone, including Poppy, looked up and smiled. She decided not to tell Rachel about the visitor. It would only worry the girl and the woman might not come back. She'd have a word with Vanessa next time they were alone together.

'Poppy's got half a tooth,' Vanessa announced.

'Aren't you a clever little girl?' Brodie cried. 'When did that appear?'

'Sometime last night,' Vanessa replied on the baby's behalf. 'It definitely wasn't there before she went to bed.'

'About last night,' Brodie said, 'my daughter, Maisie, arrived very late and had a bath. I hope she didn't disturb anyone.'

Rachel denied she'd heard a thing.

Vanessa merely said, 'I wondered who it was.'

'Maisie's expecting a baby,' Brodie went on. 'She thought she'd like to have it at home – I don't mean on the premises, but in Liverpool.'

'When's it due?' Rachel enquired.

'She's not absolutely sure. In about six weeks, she thinks.'

Vanessa didn't say anything. Brodie got the impression that she wasn't exactly pleased. Perhaps she'd guessed that Maisie wasn't there because she was pregnant and that there was something else, something that might interfere with the tranquil life she'd led since she'd come to live at Chestnuts. As if to prove this might be the case, a piercing scream came from the house and Brodie rushed inside. So much for a tranquil life!

Maisie was standing in the middle of the room, her arms wrapped across her breasts, looking utterly distraught. The spot on her cheek had bled during the night and the red stain had run as far as her chin.

'There's insects in the bed.' she screeched. 'Spiders! Loads and loads of spiders.'

Brodie pulled back the bedclothes. 'There's nothing there, sweetheart,' she said. 'Look, it's empty.'

'But I could feel them crawling all over me.' She shook herself frantically and rubbed her arms and legs as if she were brushing the insects away.

'Honestly, Maisie, there are no spiders anywhere.' Brodie was just as terrified of spiders as her daughter. Colin had always had to come to the rescue when a spider had been found in the house in Blundellsands.

'Don't kill it,' Brodie would plead. 'It's unlucky.'

'Particularly for the spider,' Colin would say with a grin. The spider rescue kit, as he referred to it, consisted of a sheet of cardboard and a little red plastic bowl. After some complicated manoeuvres, the spider would be caught and transferred to the garden, where, as he pointed out, it was at risk of catching a cold.

Maisie gingerly approached the bed to check that it was completely free from the dreaded creepy crawlies, as she'd used to call them.

'See!' Brodie said with a cheerfulness she definitely didn't feel. 'Now, would you like some breakfast? There's eggs, toast, all sorts of cereals.'

'Is there any ice-cream?'

'Yes, we've definitely got ice-cream.' It was a strange thing to want for breakfast. There was a carton of Cornish in the fridge that belonged to Diana: she wouldn't mind if some was used. 'While I'm gone, perhaps you could get dressed? Dad brought some clothes and they're hanging outside the wardrobe. I'm afraid he didn't think to bring shoes. Oh, and unpack that bag of yours in case there's stuff that needs washing.' The filthy clothes in which she'd arrived were presently in the washing machine.

In the kitchen, she rang Colin in the hope he was still there and she could ask him to bring shoes. To her horror, George, her father-in-law, answered and said he'd left ten minutes before.

'How are you keeping?' Brodie felt obliged to enquire.

'Not so bad. How are you?' It was probably the first time in many years he'd shown interest in her health. He even sounded as if he meant it.

'OK. How's the Triumph coming along?' The Triumph could fall to pieces as far as she was concerned: she didn't give a fig about it. Then she squirmed. What a truly horrible person she was being this morning. The car meant a lot to her husband and his father.

'Very well,' George said. 'Really well.'

'I must come and have a look at it some time.'

'That's a good idea, Brodie. It's almost ready to go on the road.'

Brodie rang off. It would seem she was on far better terms with George than she'd ever imagined. She remembered she'd come for ice-cream and spooned some into a bowl.

'Dad only brought dresses,' Maisie said, allowing herself be guided across the room with the ice-cream to the table in the window. She was wearing a pretty blue flowered thing with frilly sleeves and *broderie anglaise* trim at the hem that was too tight over her tummy. 'It's ages since I last wore a dress. I'd sooner wear jeans.'

'I'm pretty certain you took all your jeans away with you, Maisie,' Brodie said. 'Dad probably just grabbed things out of your wardrobe. You look really nice in that,' she lied, 'even though it's not a maternity dress.' In fact, she looked painfully thin, her knees all knobbly and her anklebones like golf balls. She wasn't in a good state to have a baby.

Maisie wriggled uncomfortably. 'It feels funny.'

'Well, it doesn't look funny. I tell you what, shall we go into town later and buy you some new jeans and tops?'

'All right,' Maisie sighed. A couple of years ago she would have clapped her hands and jumped for joy at the idea and asked if they could have lunch while they were there, but Brodie was glad to have got a positive reaction. She had imagined having to care for someone who was virtually an invalid. That Maisie was willing to go shopping was quite unexpected. Perhaps Colin would come with them, make it a family outing, though without Josh. She recalled she'd vowed to email her son that morning. She'd do it as soon as she had a minute to spare.

The curtains were still closed. Brodie pulled them back. Vanessa and the children were still in the garden. If Maisie noticed, she didn't ask who they were.

There was a knock on the door: it was Colin. He looked tired, too, as if he hadn't slept much. 'Can I see her alone?' he whispered.

'Why?'

He frowned. 'Why not?'

Brodie frowned back. 'You're not going to say anything, are you? Tear her off a strip or something like that?'

'I'm not going to do any such thing.'

'It wasn't long since you were saying things like, "she's made her own bed and she must lie in it," ' she reminded him.

'I know that, but now I've stopped.' He rolled his eyes impatiently. 'I was in a state, not thinking properly.'

'Oh, all right.' She stood aside to let him in, then went into the kitchen, wondering what he had to be in a state about.

'Dad, oh, *Dad*!' she heard Maisie cry, and felt hurt that she hadn't been afforded such a warm welcome.

'Shall we all go out somewhere today?' Vanessa asked. 'To town, say?'

'Go out? But we never go out anywhere except to the clinic and the supermarket,' Rachel said.

'Me and Vanessa went to town the other week to buy her a new dress,' Charlie pointed out a touch smarmily. There was a small amount of rivalry between the girls and Vanessa had to make sure she treated them exactly the same.

'We could go on the train; it's much easier than using the car,' she suggested. She didn't feel herself today. She'd already had a strong suspicion that Brodie's daughter was into drugs – or trying to recover from them – when she'd heard the bath running at about four or five o'clock that morning. There was something about the false way Brodie spoke to the person having the bath – she didn't know then it was her daughter – unnatural, like a grown-up to a child, or a nurse to a patient.

Earlier, when Brodie had come into the garden and said, unconvincingly, her daughter had come home to have a baby, it had only strengthened Vanessa's suspicions, and that awful scream had confirmed them. It rather clouded the house's lovely atmosphere.

The reason she'd been awake so early that morning was nothing to do with someone having a bath, but because she'd felt terribly restless. Something awful had happened: *she no longer wanted to paint.* It was Eileen's fault for suggesting an exhibition, then Diana's for carrying it through.

The exhibition had been like a grand finale, the final overture, the last page of the book. Too much attention had been paid to her; her privacy had been invaded. From now on, people would be *interested.* It was something she preferred to do completely alone.

It was only a few weeks ago that she'd been congratulating herself on the improvement in her fortunes, but now, in the middle of the night, with the trees in the garden swishing in the breeze and the sound of police sirens in the distance, Vanessa's thoughts were distressingly dark. It was nothing to do with William, with being jilted at the altar, putting on weight: it was to do with there being no point to life, not having an aim or something to look forward to. She'd thought painting was all she'd ever want to do, but she'd been wrong.

In the next room, Poppy gave a little cough, and the sound reminded her that people relied on her, at least for the time being. But they wouldn't always. Rachel was convinced Tyler would soon be back from America. Next year, she would be sixteen, there would be no reason for anyone to take Poppy away and she wouldn't need Vanessa's protection any more. As for Charlie, she would be back at school in a week or so.

'I'd love to go to town,' Rachel was saying. 'I'll make Poppy some bottles to take with us and pack some nappies. Oh, and I'll change her nappy before we go.' She scooped Poppy off Vanessa's knee and went into the house.

Charlie said she was going home to get ready. 'But you look perfectly all right as you are,' Vanessa told her. She wore cotton shorts and a striped T-shirt.

'But I need a hat and a handbag,' Charlie insisted. 'Aren't you going to put your red dress on?'

'Why not?' There was no need to make herself even more miserable by going out looking a sight, wincing every time she glimpsed her reflection in a shop window. 'While you're in there, Charlie,' she shouted as the little girl climbed over the wall into her own garden, 'telephone your father and tell him where you're going, please. I don't want him shouting at me again.' She felt convinced that if anyone so much as raised his or her voice, she'd burst into tears.

They got off the train at Central Station, then caught the bus down to the Pier Head where they watched the ferries sail to and fro across the Mersey. It was a bit of a palaver getting on and off trains and buses with two children – she counted Rachel as a child – a baby and a pushchair, but if other people could do it, then so could she.

She sat on a bench and gave Poppy her bottle while the girls went to buy ice-creams – both appeared to have plenty of money. When the ice-creams were finished, they chased each other around the bench. Anyone watching would never have guessed that one was the mother of the baby, who was clapping her hands and screaming with delight while she sat on the older woman's knee.

They walked slowly back towards town, called in at British Home Stores so Rachel could buy Poppy half a dozen pairs of stretchy leggings, then wandered as far as Central Shopping Centre where it was agreed that they stop and have something to drink. They took the lift to the first floor where there was a restaurant within a circle of shops.

'Do you mind if I look in that clothes shop?' Rachel asked after she'd finished her Coke. Poppy had fallen asleep in the pushchair and Vanessa was barely halfway through her coffee.

'Of course not.' She couldn't very well stop Rachel from doing anything.

'Can I go with her?' Charlie finished her drink and jumped to her feet.

Vanessa shook her head. 'I'd sooner you stayed here with me. You're too young to go wandering off on your own.'

Charlie looked outraged. 'But I wouldn't be on my own; I'd be with Rachel.'

'I'll keep hold of her hand, I promise,' Rachel said.

The shop was only about ten feet away. 'Oh, all right, but don't go anywhere else, just that one place. We'll go to St John's Market later where there's loads of shops.'

She watched until they seemed to melt into a crowd of mainly young women shoppers, still holding hands. For some reason that would always remain inexplicable, she began to cry: not noisily, in fact not making any sound at all, just conscious of the tears running heavily down her cheeks, dropping into her coffee, making tiny plopping sounds.

She closed her eyes, first putting her hand firmly on Poppy's tummy in case someone made off with her while she wasn't looking. Everything seemed so bleak. In the not too distant future, the year in Chestnuts would come to an end. What would happen then? Where would she go? She imagined never seeing Rachel, Poppy or Charlie again. They had their whole lives ahead of them and Vanessa would just be a person they'd once known. They might forget about her completely and she wouldn't even be a memory.

'What's up, Picasso?' a male voice enquired.

Vanessa's eyes snapped open and saw Reggie Ormerod in the seat opposite. His black hair was in its usual state of disarray and his shirt was urgently in need of ironing. He had quite nice eyes, she noticed, very dark grey, and they were watching her with an embarrassing measure of concern. 'Nothing,' she replied. 'Absolutely nothing.'

'Liar,' he scoffed good-naturedly. 'No one cries over nothing.'

'*I* do; it's a habit of mine.' She sniffed and wiped her nose on a paper napkin. 'What are you doing here?'

'Charlie rang earlier and said you were coming into town,' he explained. 'I asked her to phone once you'd got here. I had a meeting with these two American guys this morning in a hotel in Lime Street. I thought that maybe we could catch up with each other.'

Did he mean catch up with Charlie or catch up with her? Vanessa wondered, before deciding she didn't really care, and then deciding that she did, very much so, and she hoped it *was* her. It would do her ego the world of good. 'Charlie's in that shop behind you,' she said.

'I know, I saw her go in.'

That meant he must have been watching her cry for a good five minutes. In similar circumstances, most men would have run a mile. Poppy woke up, grinned at them both, and went back to sleep. At the sight of the grin, Vanessa just couldn't help it: she started crying again. 'I keep thinking the day will come when I won't see Poppy any more: she and Rachel will disappear out of my life, Charlie, too.'

'Charlie and I aren't thinking of moving,' he said gently. He put his hand over hers and a little frisson of something passed between them. Vanessa felt an odd sensation in her breast, as if her heart had skipped a beat.

'But I'll have to move,' she said. 'Brodie will probably sell the house next year. I've no idea where I'll go then.'

'Haven't you got any family?'

'Loads,' she said. 'Loads and loads. But if you're unhappy,

you can't always fall back on family. In the end, you have to be able to manage on your own.'

'You don't have to be quite so hard on yourself, Picasso.'

The name reminded her of the main reason she was in such a state. 'I don't want to paint any more,' she said wretchedly. 'I don't know why, but after yesterday I've lost all interest.'

'Don't be daft,' he said flatly. 'In fact, I was going to ask you to do a painting for my office.'

'What sort of painting?' she asked with a tiny pinch of interest.

'Anything you like, as long as it's colourful and at least two metres long. I don't fancy something white with a little dribble of black ink that's supposed to mean something vastly significant. Just throw loads of paint at the canvas and mix it up. That's the sort of painting I like.'

'OK,' she said slowly. Ideas were already racing through her head. She'd buy some paints while she was in town: no, she wouldn't, she'd buy them from Leonard tomorrow along with a really big canvas.

'Daddy!' Charlie came running up. 'I didn't know you were here. I've bought a new top.' She took a blue frilly T-shirt out of the bag and showed it to him.

'Very nice,' Reggie said approvingly. 'Very nice indeed.'

'And what have you bought, Rachel?' Vanessa asked when the girl arrived, not wanting her to feel left out.

'Just some red jeans and a T-shirt.' She sniffed and made a face. 'Poppy needs a clean nappy. There's a changing room somewhere . . .' She wheeled the pushchair away.

Charlie shot after her. 'I'll come with you.'

'This is great,' Reggie Ormerod said with a happy sigh as he watched them go.

'What is?'

'I don't know, but whatever it is it's great.'

★

In another part of Liverpool, in another restaurant less than half a mile away, Maisie Logan was clinging to her mother's arm. 'Get me something,' she was saying in a gritty voice. 'Anything, something to chew. Toffees. Get me something *now*.'

'I'll do it.' A panicky Colin jumped to his feet. 'Do they sell sweets downstairs with the food?' They were in Marks & Spencer. Brodie nodded.

'I need a fix,' Maisie said, licking her lips. 'I really need a fucking fix.'

Brodie swallowed hard. 'All right, sweetheart. Dad's gone to get you some toffees. Would you like to drink some of your coffee?'

'*No*. Can you smoke here? Have you got any cigarettes?'

'I'm afraid you can't smoke anywhere in Liverpool these days.' The hand tightened painfully on her arm. 'Anyway, Maisie, you're pregnant. It would be very wrong to smoke when you're expecting a baby.'

'Don't fucking lecture me, Mum.' She gave Brodie a look of what could only be described as hatred.

Two women on the next table glanced at each other. One tut-tutted and shook her head. Brodie tried not to take any notice, but couldn't help but feel ashamed. How would she feel if she were one of those women and heard a young woman swear at her mother like that?

And she'd thought coming shopping would be like old times, a family outing. Instead, it was a nightmare.

'It's all right,' Maisie was saying. Her grip loosened on her mother's arm. She began to breathe deeply, noisily. 'I'm all right now.'

'Of course you are, sweetheart,' Brodie crooned, putting her arms around her daughter. 'Very soon, everything will be all right.' She only wished she could believe that.

*September–October 2006*

## Chapter 12

Tinker told Diana that her happiness showed in her eyes. They were sitting on either side of the desk in the stuffy little office supposedly having a 'staff' meeting, although they were the only official members of staff, the rest being volunteers. The room was lined with battered metal filing cabinets, and an ancient fan whirred away in the corner. It was an exceptionally warm day. Tinker chewed the end of his pen and looked at Diana oddly.

'What's that for?' she asked.

'What's what for?'

'The funny look.'

'It was an admiring look. You're a sight for sore eyes, d'you know that, Di? Where did you get that outfit from?' She wore a flowered corduroy frock with a lace collar, a nipped-in waist, and an ankle-length flared skirt.

'Out of the clothes in the cellar. Rosa said it was called the New Look and came into fashion right after the Second World War. It ponged a bit and I had to wash it twice to get rid of the smell.' She wished she'd worn something lighter as she was sweating cobs. 'I always put money in for the things, Tinker,' she assured him. 'I pay more for them than they'd get if they were sold on the stall.'

'I know you do, Di. I wasn't suggesting you didn't. You look very sweet.' He winked. 'Why exactly are you so happy?'

'I dunno.' She sighed blissfully. 'I expect it's because life's so perfect. I love this job, I love where I live, I love everything.' She waved her arm as if to include the room, or it might have been the city of Liverpool, or possibly the entire world. Upstairs, the click of snooker balls could be heard, the playgroup was on the point of packing up and children were shouting excitedly over something, the telly was on in the lounge, and one of the young men on the stairs was playing a guitar and singing something terribly haunting and beautiful. This cacophony of sounds only served to remind her why she loved the place so much.

'When are you and what's-his-name getting married?'

'Leo. I don't know.' Her face fell. At least once a week poor Leo suggested they set a date for the wedding, but she kept putting him off. She didn't think it was terribly nice always to think of him as 'poor'. Once she'd said jokingly, 'We'll get married on my fiftieth birthday,' and he'd got really, really upset. 'Why did you ask?' she said to Tinker.

'Because if you ever decide to dump the bloke, I'd like to be the first to know.'

'Why?'

'So I can marry you meself before another bloke appears on the scene.'

'Honest?' She felt herself blush.

'Honest to God.' He had a smile on his lips. 'Are you surprised?'

'I thought you were gay,' she told him.

The smile turned into a laugh. 'Did you now? Well, I'm not.'

'Do you perm your hair?'

He touched the mass of tiny red ringlets. 'No, it's natural.' He put the pen down, frowned and crossed his eyes at the same time. He wore little gold hoop earrings and a sweater that was purple on one side and green on the other. It made him look like the star of a pantomime. 'So, you thought I was gay with permed hair, eh? I bet you thought it was dyed, too. And here's me thinking you found me desperately attractive.'

'Oh, I do, I do.' She'd been a little bit in love with him since she'd first come to work at the centre. He was a really lovely person with a sunny disposition who really cared for the refugees. Unless you counted the desperate tizzies he was inclined to get into from time to time, he never properly lost his temper. He was also enormous fun. Being married to Tinker would be much more enjoyable than being married to poor Leo, who was so intense about everything. Diana felt as if she had to tread on eggshells all the time in case she hurt his feelings.

'If I give you my card,' he said, 'keep it in your handbag and give us a ring on my moby if you and Leo decide to break up? I doesn't matter if it's in the middle of the night. Any time, and I'll pop the question straight away.' He handed her his business card. It said 'Anthony Taylor', and had the refugee centre address and telephone number and his mobile number underneath. She wondered if he'd been nicknamed Tinker because his surname was Taylor.

'All right,' she promised, keeping a straight face. 'I'll let you know.' She wasn't sure if he was joking or not. She hoped not.


On the train on the way home she showed Megan the christening gown she'd found in the cellar. 'Isn't it lovely? It's pure silk. I know it looks cream, but Rosa thinks it should be white. She's going to find out what to wash it with so it won't get damaged. She thinks it must be at least eighty years old.'

'It's beautiful, Diana. Is it for you?' Megan enquired, fingering the fine lace trimming.

Diana looked at the woman as if she were mad. 'It's a *christening* gown. It'd never fit *me*,' she snorted.

'You silly idiot,' Megan snorted back. 'I meant, is it for you because you're pregnant?'

'No, it's for Maisie. I don't think she's got any baby clothes. D'you think she'll like it?' Diana wondered how she'd feel about being pregnant. It was an impossible state to be in as she was still a virgin.

'She might.' Megan couldn't imagine her granddaughter liking anything much at the moment. She had been at Chestnuts for a week and the only person who could get anywhere with her was her father, which was ironic considering the circumstances. Brodie was being as kind and understanding as it was possible to be, yet Maisie was being perfectly horrible back. Sometimes she used really disgusting four-letter words.

'It's the drugs,' Brodie had said only the other day. 'She doesn't know what she's saying.'

'No, darlin',' Megan had argued. 'It's the *lack* of drugs. She's having withdrawal symptoms. Has she been to see a doctor?'

'She flatly refuses to see a doctor.' Brodie sounded tired to death. 'Anyway, Mum, what do you know about it?'

'I watch television like everyone else. I read the papers. I probably know as much about drugs as you do.' She made Megan feel like a silly old woman. '*My* daughter never went near them, I'm pleased to say.'

Brodie's face crinkled into something that was either a smile or a pained expression, Megan couldn't tell. 'I never led that sort of life. I suppose it's a combination of London and university that did it.'

Since Maisie had come home, Megan felt in the way at Chestnuts. Brodie kept watching whenever she went near the girl, as if she expected her to say something desperately tactless. She was glad there was the refugee centre where she could occupy her time doing things that were worthwhile and interesting. She had friends, but although most were younger than she was, they weren't very active. Their idea of entertainment was to play bridge, preferably in the afternoon, rather than visit the pictures or go shopping. At night Megan felt just a little bit lonely.

'Are you coming with us?' Diana asked when they got off the train and Megan went to collect her bicycle.

'No, dear. I think I'll go straight home tonight.' Megan would have far preferred to go with Diana.

'Ah, come on and have tea with us,' Diana said persuasively. 'I'm going to make sausages and mash with onion gravy. Afterwards, we can watch a DVD. Have you seen *Pride and Prejudice* with Keira Knightley? I bought it the other day. I love Shakespeare, don't you?'

Megan was about to correct her, tell her that *Pride and Prejudice* had been written by Jane Austen, but held her tongue. She suspected the girl had sensed her loneliness. What did knowledge of English Literature matter when compared to having a really kind heart? 'I love Shakespeare, too,' she said.

Brodie stared at the computer screen and wondered where Maisie was. She'd gone to the lavatory and had been heard coming out. Perhaps she was exploring upstairs or was in the kitchen. She really, really wasn't in the mood to go looking for her. She glanced through the window in case she was in the garden, but there was no sign: just Charlie throwing a ball to Poppy in the hope that she might catch it and Rachel reading a book. Vanessa was painting, a really big canvas for a change.

The computer played a little tune to indicate an email had arrived. It was from Colin and said: 'The other day, I emailed the post office in Duneathly, Ireland, the village where your mother lived as a child, and asked if there were any Kennys or Ryans there. I'm forwarding you an email that came back today from a woman called Roseanna Ryan who claims you are her aunt.' There was a document enclosed and when

Brodie brought it to the screen she saw it was a complicated family tree with dozens of names. She didn't want to look at it right now.

The front door opened and Diana came in. She wasn't alone. Brodie winced when she heard her mother's voice. She wished Mum would keep away. She wasn't doing Maisie any good, kept saying the wrong things.

Diana shouted, 'Hello, everyone,' but Brodie didn't answer.

Seconds later, Diana and Mum appeared in the gardens – followed by Maisie. Brodie stiffened. The window was closed so she couldn't hear what was being said, but there was a great deal of laughter. Diana took something out of a bag – it might have been a blouse – and gave it to Maisie. Rachel and Charlie came over for a look. Then Maisie flung her arms around Diana's neck and the two girls clung together for several seconds before they laughed and broke away.

Brodie sat glued to her seat as she watched this strange drama being acted out. Her mother and daughter, with Diana, returned to the house and went into the kitchen. Maisie sounded quite normal, quite like her old self. 'I've got eight sausages,' Diana was saying, 'so that means we can have two and a bit each. I hope no one minds Smash instead of real potatoes. I'll open a tin of peas.'

'Yummy!' said Maisie.

It was hard to think of a more unhealthy meal: sausages, dried potatoes and tinned peas. Brodie had been feeding her salads and fresh fruit since she'd come home and she was looking the better for it: her skin and eyes were clearer and her hair had acquired a sheen. She even looked as if she'd put on some weight.

Diana asked if they would please keep an eye on the sausages while she got changed. 'The belt on this dress is slowly cutting me in two. I was daft to wear it on a day like this. Oh, by the way, where's Brodie?' she enquired.

'She must be having a little lie-down,' Mum said. 'It's probably best if we don't disturb her.'

Brodie immediately got up and went to lie on the bed, feeling as if she'd been given permission. She wouldn't be missed: no one would expect her to come out. The minute her head touched the pillow she was aware of how tense she was when her neck and shoulders began to throb, as they did so often these days.

The last week had been really unpleasant. Most of the time, she found it hard to relate to her daughter – or perhaps it was the other way round. Brodie thought she was being extremely patient and tolerant, but Maisie seemed to think the opposite.

'Don't bug me, Mum,' she would say, shying away if Brodie so much as touched her or suggested she did something sensible like going to see a doctor.

And what was galling, really galling, was that Maisie and her father got on like a house on fire, yet Maisie was only home because Brodie had gone to London and met Karen Young. It was Colin who'd discovered that Pete, the boyfriend, had been a drug addict, too, that they'd met at university.

'I bet it was him who introduced her to drugs,' Brodie had said bitterly.

'No.' Colin shook his head. 'It was the other way round. She took them first, then he did. But he was sensible enough to recognize what a bad idea it was and gave up. He's been looking after Maisie the best he could ever since, but she kept disappearing.'

'Doesn't it seem strange', Brodie murmured, 'that we're sitting here talking about drugs and our Maisie?'

They'd been in the snug at the time. Maisie was asleep in Brodie's room. Colin got up and began to walk around the table. He looked on the verge of tears. 'She first took the heroin at a party, our little girl. She was just about to sit her first year exams and she says it helped focus her mind: she could see things much more clearly. It also made her feel extraordinarily happy. She liked the feeling so much that she got more. Within a matter of weeks, she was desperate for it, looking for dealers, spending all her money.' He shrugged. 'She was hooked.'

'And what about Pete?'

'He tried to stop her, then he took it just to keep her company, then he got scared and stopped.' He paused by the window. 'Diana's coming. What on earth is she wearing?'

Brodie didn't bother to look. 'I don't know,' she said. The front door opened and Diana came in.

'Whatever it is, she must think life is one long fancy dress party.' He turned back to Brodie. 'They're funny, drugs. Some people can take them or leave them. Others get hooked after a few doses. Is that what you call them, doses? Or is it fixes?'

'I don't know,' Brodie said for the second time. 'I take it Pete is the baby's father?'

'I haven't asked her straight out, but I expect he is. She was lucky to have had him. He's stuck by her as best he could. He must love her very much.'

'I'm home,' Diana shouted.

'We're in here,' Brodie shouted back.

Diana came into the room wearing an extremely smart dark-green taffeta dress. She beamed. 'Hello, you two.'

'Hello, there.' Brodie smiled, and thought for the umpteenth time how much nicer it was talking to this young woman than it was to her daughter.

'I'm off to make me tea,' Diana said. 'I could eat a horse.' She went singing into the kitchen.

'It's a cocktail dress,' Colin said when the door closed.

'What?'

'What Diana is wearing is a cocktail dress. Until now, I've only seen women wearing them in films.' He sighed. 'At least *she's* happy.'

'She's always happy.' Brodie returned to the topic under

discussion before Diana had appeared. 'Does Maisie have any idea where Pete might be? Is he likely to turn up one day?'

'He's either in London or he's staying with his folks. They live in Exeter. In Devon.'

'I know where Exeter is,' Brodie snapped.

'There's no need to bite my head off,' Colin said mildly. 'Anyroad, she's got his mobile number should she want to contact him, which apparently she doesn't right now.'

'I see.' Brodie groaned. 'I can't get through to her. Why is it you can and I can't? Why does she open up to you when she won't to me? Oh!' She dropped her head into her hands. 'It's so *frustrating*.'

'I think you ought to lighten up. Just talk to her normally. Try not to be so gentle and understanding. It makes her feel uncomfortable – guilty.'

'Has she said that to you?'

'No, it's something I worked out for myself. I know I was being much too tough on her before and it's one of the reasons you left. I'm sorry about that, Brodie. Now you're being too soft.' He stood behind and put his hands on her shoulders. 'I think you should both come home, darling. It's where you belong. Maisie would feel happier sleeping in her old room in her own bed.'

He'd suggested that before and she'd been adamantly opposed to the idea. She still was. 'The holidays are nearly over and you'll be back at school on Monday,' she reminded him. 'It means Maisie and I will be stuck in the house, just the two of us, all day. Here, there's all sorts of people she can talk to – young people. She hasn't asked to go home, has she? She and Diana get on really well and she loves Poppy. Oh, and this is such a lovely garden, Colin, compared to the one at home.' She glanced out of the window, but all that could be seen from the front were the chestnut trees that shielded the house from the road. 'I'll miss this when the time comes for us to leave,' she said.

Now, as she lay exhausted on the bed, shoulders throbbing, feeling as if she was gradually sinking through the mattress, Brodie remembered that Josh was coming on Sunday. He would have come last weekend, but had had too much work on.

Work! She hadn't thought her son would ever mention the word.

On Sunday morning Megan had hardly been home from Mass a minute when there was a knock on the door of her flat in Burbo Bank Road. She opened it to find a woman outside who was somewhat younger than herself. Her hair was light-brown and she wore a white frock with a pattern of green leaves and a green linen jacket. She had pink cheeks, blue eyes, and a face that was only moderately wrinkled.

'Yes?' Megan said after a few seconds, having established in her mind that she'd never seen the woman before in her life.

'Hello, Megan,' the visitor said in a strong Irish accent. 'It's Brodie.'

'*Brodie*!' Megan took a stumbling step backwards and nearly tripped over the doormat. '*Brodie*!'

'Yes. Jaysus, Mary and Joseph, sis, don't go and faint on me.' She came in and grabbed Megan's arm. 'Where's the sitting room, the lounge, the parlour, or whatever it is you call the damn place?'

'The living room. I can get there on me own, thank you.' She pulled her arm away and walked unsteadily into the room. Brodie followed. *BRODIE*! Her sister, *Brodie*. How long was it since they'd seen each other? Sixty years. 'What are you doing here?' she croaked when they were both sitting down. She could easily have had a heart attack.

'The other day, Duneathly Post Office received an email from a gentleman called Colin Logan who said he was your son-in-law and wanted to know if there were any Kennys or Ryans living in the village.' She spoke swiftly and brightly

266

and, from the grin on her face, seemed to find the situation desperately amusing. Her legs were crossed neatly at the ankles and her hands clasped together on her knees. It was a pose that Megan remembered well. She had a feeling she'd used to make fun of it. 'Look at Little Miss Prim and Proper,' she would say, or something like that. 'The email was passed to us and Roseanna sent an answering email: she's our Tom's granddaughter.'

'Our Tom?' Megan whispered. He'd been the image of their dad.

'Our Tom and our Joe both still live in Duneathly. Me an' all. There's a whole tribe of us in the area. Didn't our mam have a sister and three brothers? They're dead now except for Uncle Aidan, but they had twenty-three kids between them and every single one got married and has kids of their own. Annemarie's side of the family all live in America, but you'll know that, won't you, Megan?' She looked slyly at her sister. 'Weren't we staying in Annemarie's apartment in New York when I met Louis Sylvester in St Patrick's Cathedral? I brought him back and introduced him to you and Mam.'

'I do remember, yes,' Megan agreed. Her throat had gone as dry as a bone. 'Would you like a drink?' she wheezed. 'Tea, coffee . . .?' She was desperate for a glass of water.

'A little drop of the hard stuff wouldn't go amiss, although you look as if you need it more than I do. Have you got any alcohol on the premises?'

'I've got sherry – oh, and there's some brandy left over from Christmas,' Megan recalled. 'I keep it for when I feel a chill coming on.'

'Brandy, then. If I were you, I'd have a double.'

'Well, you're not me, are you?' Megan said crossly. 'I don't need a double. I'm perfectly all right. I admit I was more than a bit knocked back when you showed up on me doorstep, but that's only understandable. I'm not made of stone.'

She took the brandy out of the sideboard. She'd intended

having a mouthful in the kitchen, but Brodie followed and stood in the doorway, watching while the glasses were taken out of the cupboard and the drink poured – exactly the same amount in each glass, plus water for herself.

They carried the drinks back into the living room. 'It's nice here,' Brodie said. 'I love the view of the River Mersey. Is this where you lived with Louis?'

'Of course not,' Megan replied, annoyed that Brodie should think she and Louis had spent their married life in such a poky little flat. 'It's much too small. We had a nice big house not far from here. My daughter's living there just now. Her name's Brodie, too.'

'I know, Roseanne said. It was in the email.' Her blue eyes twinkled with amusement. 'I'm terribly flattered that you called her after me.'

'You don't look flattered,' Megan said sourly. 'You obviously think it's a great big joke.'

'Let's say I suspect you called your girl Brodie because either you or Louis had a fit of conscience. Or perhaps you both did.'

Megan ignored this. 'How did you know where I lived?' she asked. 'Did Colin give you this address?'

Brodie chuckled. 'We've always known where you've lived, Megan. I knew you didn't live here with Louis. I just said that to get up your nose. The nice big house you mentioned is Chestnuts and you hadn't been in Liverpool all that long before you moved in.'

'How on earth do you know that?' Megan gasped.

'You were in the Liverpool telephone directory, darlin'. Remember Nona who worked in the Post Office? She looked you up for us. We knew exactly when Louis died, because the entry changed from his name to yours.' Her voice softened and so did her smile. 'Many's the time I thought about ringing the number, but I wasn't prepared to lower meself. I thought to meself, she's the one who ran off, let her do it first.'

'So, what made you do it now?' Megan wondered if her face was as pale as it felt. Did she look as if someone had just landed an extra-hard blow to her solar plexus?

'Well, sis, you're eighty, I'm seventy-eight, and I reckon one of these days I'd look in the directory and your name wouldn't be there any more. Either that, or I wouldn't be around to look for it. When we heard from your son-in-law, I didn't care about lowering meself: I just hopped on a plane and flew over.'

Megan stared at her knees. 'You're not lowering yourself,' she muttered. 'I'm really glad you came. I've often wondered how you all were: you and Joe and Tom. Did you get married, Brodie?'

'I did indeed,' Brodie said heartily. 'I married a fine gentlemen farmer called Gerry Flaherty. He only died last year. We had three children – two girls and a boy – and they're just as fine. They're all married and we – oh, did you keep saying "we", sis, when your dear husband passed away when you should have been saying "I"? – I have nine grandchildren and six great-grandchildren. Two are twin boys and the liveliest pair of rascals you're ever likely to meet.'

'Three of my babies died,' Megan muttered. 'Brodie was the only one who lived.'

'Ah! Sometimes the Lord can be very cruel. I'm sorry,' Brodie said softly, looking for the first time like the kind, gentle Brodie that Megan remembered from six decades ago. 'That was something your son-in-law didn't tell me. Look, sis, I hope I don't sound rude, but I'm virtually gasping for a cup of tea. I'll make it meself if you're not up to it.'

'Not up to making a cup of tea!' Megan said indignantly. 'Do I look like an invalid or something? I've already admitted that I was more than a bit taken aback when you turned up, but I'll have you know I'd just ridden to and from Mass on me bike. And I work several days a week at a refugee centre in town. I'm as fit as a blooming fiddle.'

'Sorry, sis,' Brodie said meekly. 'In that case, I'll just sit and wait for the tea. By the way, what's that thing on the wall?'

Megan followed her gaze. 'It's a painting, of course.'

'What's it a painting of, if you don't mind my asking?'

'It's the inside of a chimney. See that blue bit in the middle? That's the sky.'

'And did the artist actually lie with his head in the fireplace while he painted it?'

'The artist is a woman and she just used her imagination,' Megan said, adding tartly, 'It's what artists do.' She paused at the door. 'Tell me, do you dye your hair? It's not natural, that brown colour, on such an old woman. And have you had that Botox stuff injected in your wrinkles? There's not as many as there ought to be on someone of your great age.'

Brodie confessed that she had her hair tinted once a month. 'But as for the Botox, I've never touched the stuff. Is it not made out of rat poison or something similar?'

'I do believe it is. Look, after we've had the tea, we'll go round to Chestnuts for our Sunday dinner. My Brodie will be thrilled to bits to meet you.' Megan rubbed her hands together, thrilled at the way things had turned out. It was lovely to be back in touch with her family after all this time. 'Oh, and me granddaughter will be there, Maisie. She's having a baby, but the father's nowhere to be seen.'

'Well, that's the way of the world nowadays, is it not? Our Tom's youngest lad has been divorced twice and is already on his third wife. Can you imagine in the old days, Megan, a Catholic getting divorced?'

'But you can't get divorced, can you, when you've been married in the eyes of God?'

'Gerry – that's our Tom's lad – managed to avoid that predicament by getting hitched in them heathen register offices, so he was never married in the eyes of God in the first place.'

'It's almost as if he knew he was going to get divorced before he even got married,' Megan said.

'Exactly,' Brodie agreed. 'And then didn't he go and do it twice!'

'I'll make that tea.' Megan disappeared.

Left by herself, Brodie stared at the river, glimmering like molten silver in the late August sunshine. Joe and Tom would be pleased to know that she'd been to see Megan. In fact, she'd give them a call on her mobile later on in the day.

Her mobile! That was just one of the ways in which the world had changed since she'd last seen her sister. Now people carried telephones – rare enough in houses in those days – around in their pockets or their bags. Then there were computers and motor cars all over the place, aeroplanes – people had actually walked on the moon, for God's sake. There was a fellow from Duneathly who'd actually had a heart transplant.

She got up and went to stand at the window, wondering if Megan had enough room for her to stay the night. Tomorrow, early, she'd quite like to go for a walk by that silvery water.

Megan had worn well, she thought: tons of wrinkles, but her back was straight and there wasn't a sign of stiffness about her. She wouldn't tell her sister that there'd been no need for her to go running off with Louis Sylvester the minute the boat had docked in Liverpool in 1946. It hadn't entered Brodie's head that Louis would want to marry her and if he had she'd have turned him down flat. He was a nice enough fellow, but not a bit her type. If Megan had been thinking she'd stolen him away from her sister, then she could go on thinking it.

They caught a taxi to Chestnuts, stopping at a supermarket on the way to buy two large roasted chickens, two packets of pre-roasted potatoes and piles of salad stuff.

'It's no wonder young women these days don't spend much time in the kitchen,' Brodie marvelled when they were back in the taxi. 'I mean, spuds already roasted – bought on a Sunday an' all. What do you do with them – heat them up in the oven?'

'I expect so. Me, it's the first time I've ever bought them. And what about disposable nappies?'

'And disposable torches, of all things! They sell them in the supermarket in Duneathly for a euro each.'

'You mean there's actually a supermarket in Duneathly?' When Megan had lived there there'd been just a few little shops, which didn't only close on Sundays, but on Wednesday afternoons, too. 'And I forgot they don't have pounds any more in Ireland.'

'We joined the euro years ago,' Brodie said somewhat proudly. 'We didn't shilly-shally around like the UK.'

Brodie hadn't even started on the lunch when her mother and her aunt turned up laden with food.

'Aunt Brodie!' she gasped, stunned, hardly able to believe her eyes when they were introduced.

'It's lovely to meet you, Brodie,' her aunt said with a really sweet, rather mischievous smile.

A larger than usual lunch had already been planned: Colin and Maisie were there, and Josh had arrived early that morning, having driven up from London in a large white van. Now there would be two more guests at the table.

Brodie went to see Vanessa, who was painting in the garden, to say she hoped she wouldn't mind if the snug was monopolized at lunchtime. 'I don't normally have people to lunch, but today there's six of us. An aunt has turned up that I never knew I had until quite recently. Her name is Brodie, too.'

'How amazing,' Vanessa commented, adding that she didn't mind at all. 'Rachel, Poppy and I are going next door to have lunch with Charlie and Reggie. He's ordered an Indian takeaway.'

'I hope you enjoy yourselves.' Brodie lightly touched the woman's arm. She had a feeling that she could become great friends with Vanessa in the course of time.

'I hope you do, too.'

'Do you know what Diana is doing?'

'I invited her to come with us, but she's going to Southport with Leo.'

'That's good.' The girl couldn't have been left to have lunch on her own.

In the past, there'd only been her mother, her husband and their two children. But today there was also a pretty, elderly aunt with a soft voice and a lovely accent, who talked about her uncles Joe and Tom and loads of cousins and nieces and nephews with names like Kerianne and Bernadette and Eoin and Finbar.

'You must come and stay with us soon,' the new Brodie said — she preferred that to being called the 'old' Brodie. 'You're all invited. We'll throw a party for you.'

Brodie couldn't wait. 'As soon as Maisie's had the baby,' she promised. If it arrived before half-term, then she and Colin could go together. Mum was returning to Duneathly with her sister for a while.

'I'd love to come,' Josh said.

Colin looked at him in astonishment. 'But I thought you were too busy with your new business, son?'

'I am, but I wouldn't want to miss a party like that. I mean, it would be a once-in-a-lifetime thing, wouldn't it? Even people with their own business have to have holidays,' he said importantly.

Brodie looked proudly at her son. She would sooner he had aspired to be a doctor, say, or an artist of some sort, but Josh had only ever wanted to have his own business and it appeared he was successful at last. Having bought a large van for a few hundred pounds, he was in great demand in London. As he had explained earlier, 'When people move from one flat to another, all they have are tellies, DVD players, computers, books, clothes, and stuff like that. An ordinary car is too small and a furniture van is much too big. My van is just the right size.'

What's more, Josh and his van were available at any time of the night and day. No one was obliged to take a day off work when they wanted to move. He would turn up at the crack of dawn if they wanted, at tea-time, or in the middle of the night.

She hoped he wasn't losing too much sleep. He looked tired, she thought, but happy – and pleased to see his sister looking much better than he'd expected.

In fact, today everybody looked particularly happy, including Colin and Maisie. Her mother, who'd seemed a bit down recently, was smiling fit to bust, as was the new Brodie.

It was during the meal that Brodie decided she would sell Chestnuts when the year it had been let for came to an end. She had no idea what she and the other women in the house would do then. The money from the sale she would divide into three: a third between her and Colin, and a third each for Maisie and Josh. Josh could buy himself a brand-new van and use the rest as a deposit on a property in London – she doubted if he would ever live in Liverpool again, which was sad, but you couldn't expect your children to live close to their parents for the rest of their lives. Maisie could do whatever she liked with her share.

And she was fed up being a housewife. She would train for something – how to use a computer properly, for instance, or study for some A-levels – or try to get a job in a hospital; she'd always fancied working in a hospital.

'A penny for them, Brodie,' Colin said.

She laughed. 'Oh, they're worth much more than that.'

'I hope this lovely weather never ends,' Megan remarked from her chair underneath what Diana called the 'plate' tree, with its big flat leaves. It was late afternoon and the lunch guests had moved into the garden.

'It's global warming, Gran,' Josh reminded her. 'It could be a sign that the world is about to end. Next year, it'll be even hotter and so on and so on until we all frazzle to death.'

'There were nicer summers during the war,' the new Brodie said. 'But some of the winters! You'd think another Ice Age had started.'

'Now the ice caps are melting,' Josh said gloomily.

'Sure, 'tis a terrible thing for young people to look forward to: the end of the world. I'm glad I won't be alive long enough to see it.'

'Me, I never want to die,' declared Megan.

'If the world ends, you'll not have any choice in the matter,' her sister pointed out.

Brodie made tea and Colin opened a bottle of wine. 'Parties in the garden are getting to be a regular event,' he said. 'Let's hope Diana comes back soon and we can have some music.'

Diana turned up just after five o'clock bringing Leo with her. She opened the window of her room and a melancholy voice began to sing 'The Mountains of Morne'. 'It's a CD of Irish songs,' she told the company, as if they didn't know.

Alerted by the sound of activity in the next door garden, Charlie and Rachel appeared with a sleepy Poppy, followed shortly afterwards by Vanessa and Reggie, who both looked a bit subdued.

'That's Vanessa, the artist who did the painting in me flat,' Megan told her sister. 'There's loads more upstairs if you'd like to buy one. The money goes to the refugee centre where I work.'

'I wouldn't mind one or two to take home with me. I'll have a look at what you've got later. I must say,' the new Brodie remarked, 'there's a remarkably charming crowd of people living in this house. I can't remember when I last enjoyed meself so much. But I still haven't exactly worked out in me mind who exactly lives here and who doesn't.'

'I'll explain later,' Megan promised. 'There are times when I'm not quite sure meself.'

The air felt slightly colder as the night grew darker. Cardigans, shawls and jackets were fetched, and Diana lit candles for the tables and the window sills. Kenneth came and jumped on to Brodie's knee. She'd be sorry to leave him when she left the house. But then she'd be sorry to leave the house too and it would be awful if she never saw any of her tenants again.

She gave the cat a little hug. 'I'll make sure you're not a stray before we leave,' she told him. 'If you are, wherever I go I'll take you with me.'

Her new aunt had really made herself at home. She'd given an exhibition of Irish dancing and had taught Diana how to do a reel. Mum looked happier than she'd done in ages. Brodie had the uncomfortable feeling she'd been sidelining her mother more than a bit, worried she might upset Maisie, whereas it was Brodie herself who seemed to upset Maisie more than anyone. Nothing she could say was right.

She glanced at her daughter, who was nursing her swollen tummy and looking as if she was enjoying herself. She still flatly refused to see a doctor, no matter how hard Brodie pleaded. Colin had joined in with the pleading, but to no avail.

'All I have to do when it starts to arrive is go to hospital,' Maisie insisted. 'They're not going to refuse to deliver it because I haven't registered with a doctor, are they?'

'Well, no, but there might be something wrong,' Brodie

would argue – they'd had the conversation more than once. 'The baby might be feet first, or your blood pressure could be too high – or other things,' she finished lamely.

But Maisie said she wasn't in the mood to see a doctor. 'I just know that everything's going to be all right. If I thought it wasn't, then I'd see one straight away.'

And that was the way the matter had been left.

It was gone eleven o'clock and Vanessa was sitting alone in the garden. She didn't think anyone had noticed she hadn't gone indoors when they did. The lights were on in all the rooms except her own. Only Diana hadn't closed the curtains and she could be seen draped over a chair reading a book while the television was on. Vanessa wouldn't be at all surprised if her CD player wasn't on, too. Diana was the sort of person who liked noise coming at her from every direction, as well as being in the company of loads of people. Perhaps it was something to do with growing up in a small house with three brothers: she wasn't used to silence or being alone.

She stared at the orange-lit sky with its faint sprinkling of stars and a slice of lemon moon on the wane. She was in love with Reggie Ormerod and all she wanted to do was sit alone in the dark and savour the feeling of bewilder- ment 'Bewitched, bothered and bewildered' was how the song went.

It was a feeling that she'd never had before and certainly not for William with whom she'd thought she was in love. There was another song she remembered: 'This can't be love because I feel so well . . .' She felt marvellous! As if she were walking on air.

She had no idea if Reggie felt the same, though she hoped so, naturally, and one of these days it would be important to find out.

'Don't worry about it, Vanessa,' she told herself. 'If it's going to happen, it'll happen. Go with the flow, as they say.'

She stared at the sky for another few minutes, then went inside.

# Chapter 13

Someone was pressing the doorbell so persistently it was obvious they weren't prepared to stop until the door was opened.

Vanessa rolled off the bed and crash-landed on the floor. She stared bleary-eyed and slightly stunned at her watch and saw it was only quarter to seven. Downstairs, she heard Brodie shout impatiently, 'I'm coming, I'm coming.'

The door opened, footsteps bounded up the stairs, a fist hammered on Rachel's door and Rachel called, 'Who is it?'

'Tyler,' was the terse reply.

Rachel screamed, 'Tyler! Oh, Tyler! I just knew you'd come.'

Vanessa hauled herself to her feet, struggled into a dressing gown and staggered on to the landing. Rachel's door was open and she peeped inside to see Tyler – tall, deeply tanned and bespectacled – with one arm around Rachel's shoulders and Poppy in the other. He and Rachel were crying, and Poppy was gleefully pulling her father's sun-streaked blond hair for the very first time, but probably not the last.

Vanessa, who'd once considered herself a cynic to her bones, burst into tears. 'It's so *touching*,' she sobbed when Brodie came upstairs.

Brodie had a peek and began to cry, too. '*Isn't* it?'

Diana came out of the bathroom wrapped only in a towel.

'What's going on?' Her face dropped. 'Something awful's happened, hasn't it?' she croaked when she saw the two women in tears. 'Is it Maisie's baby?'

'No, love,' Brodie assured her. 'It's nothing bad. In fact, it's marvellous news. Tyler's come back to Rachel.'

It turned out that Tyler had never actually left Rachel except to go on holiday. His mother had been scandalized when told about the little family he'd acquired back in England. Rachel's age was questioned, her social position found wanting – she wasn't even remotely related to royalty – and her morals were impugned. Tyler was whisked off to the Carter Booths' isolated summerhouse in Cape Cod to stay with his sick grandmother. His mobile just happened to get lost and he didn't know the number of Rachel's so he couldn't ring. He did, however, write regularly, 'two or three times a week', and left them in the tray by the front door for his mother or one of the servants to post. He had assumed Rachel had received them.

'But I never got a single one,' Rachel told Vanessa and Brodie when they were having breakfast. By then, Diana had gone to work, Maisie was having a lie-in, and Tyler was upstairs getting to know his daughter better. 'His mother didn't post them, apart from the one she wrote herself pretending to be Tyler and saying that he'd dumped me. Even me mam wouldn't be *that* sneaky,' she said, her little face a picture of indignation. 'He was worried *I'd* dumped *him* when he didn't get any letters from me. When he said he wanted to come back to England, he was told his grandmother was likely to die any minute. Oh, and that's why Simon Collier, the solicitor, never got a reply: the family weren't living in their apartment in New York. Is it all right if Tyler stays here sometimes?' she asked Brodie.

'The more the merrier,' Brodie said.

★

'I hadn't noticed until this morning, but Rachel's grown a few inches since we first met in March,' Vanessa said to Brodie later when they took Poppy in her pram for a walk on the shimmering sands. Although it was gloriously sunny, there was quite a nip in the air, a signal that winter was on its way. Vanessa had offered to take Poppy, assuming that Rachel and Tyler would like to be alone together for a while and preferring not to be in the house, not even in the garden, while they were. Anyway, she was badly missing Charlie, who'd gone back to school on Monday, and was glad to have something to do.

'It must be strange to fall in love and have a baby when you're only fourteen,' Brodie mused. 'I was such a child at that age. I'm pretty certain I still played with dolls.'

'All I cared about was tennis. I had designs on Wimbledon, but I wasn't even good enough to be in the school team.' Vanessa glanced at the sleeping baby and wondered what lay in store for her. Perhaps a life in America beckoned – it would certainly be a life of affluence if Tyler stuck by Rachel. She hoped the boy would be strong enough to defy his mother, who, it would seem, had other plans for him.

'I used to like playing tennis. Perhaps we could have a game one day?'

Vanessa laughed. 'I don't think I can run any more, let alone hit a ball at the same time.'

'Shall we walk as far as Leonard Gosling's shop and have coffee and a cream cake in that little café opposite?' Brodie suggested. 'Leonard can come with us and keep an eye on the shop from over the road.'

'I'd like that.' She'd lost so much weight it wouldn't hurt to have a cream cake for once – a little treat to celebrate Tyler coming home to Rachel.

'You don't seem to be painting as much as you used to, though you still spend a lot of time in the garden.'

'I'm thinking instead,' Vanessa explained. 'I suppose you could say I'm painting in my head.'

Brodie chuckled. 'Well, you won't sell your thoughts for twenty-five pounds each. What happened to that big painting you were doing?'

'It was for Reggie. It's hanging on the wall of his office. He said people keep asking about it. They like it.' She'd divided the canvas into twelve squares and done a little painting in each, all quite different. 'He wants me to do another for the house.'

'Are you going to?'

'I'm only waiting for an idea. That's what I've been thinking about.' And one or two other things concerning Reggie, too.

Leonard Gosling, a picture himself in pale grey and turquoise, was only too pleased to see them. 'I miss your mother,' he said to Brodie. 'I miss popping into her flat for a little gossip now and then. How's she getting on in Ireland? I've had a postcard, but it didn't say much.'

'I get the impression she's having a marvellous time,' Brodie said.

Megan had hurriedly packed a bag and flown back to Ireland with her sister. She intended to stay a month and get to know all her relatives. Ever since, she'd been on that thing she'd read about but had never experienced before – an emotional roller-coaster. Sometimes it was going too fast and became much too emotional when she came face to face, first with her brothers, Joe and Tom, who'd been in their teens when she'd last seen them, and the cousins that she'd lived with during the war, and also the ones who hadn't been born when she'd left for New York with her mother and Brodie after the war had ended. There was even an uncle still alive, Aidan, who'd only been four when Megan was born.

The oldest cousin, Patrick, she'd fallen in love with when

she was very small. In fact, she remembered telling her mother that she intended marrying him when they grew up. She tried to tell Patrick the story now, but he was a curmudgeonly eighty-one and very deaf. He refused to wear a hearing aid, so the story remained untold. For some reason this really depressed her.

'Old age is a pain,' she said to Brodie after a few days in Ireland.

'It's better than dying young,' Brodie replied.

They were in her sister's neat little bungalow on a modern estate on the edge of Duneathly. The sleepy little village had expanded greatly since she'd left and there were loads of foreigners around, mainly Americans who worked in factories making computers, according to Brodie.

Megan didn't like the bungalow, its unblemished, characterless newness, and loathed the view of similar bungalows across the road, as well as the road itself with its smooth black Tarmac and clean, perfect pavements. The residents all appeared to be elderly – two cousins lived in the same road – though Brodie said it wasn't a retirement area.

'You're right, growing old is better than dying young,' Megan agreed, sniffing gloomily. 'I probably think the way I do now because I haven't watched all these people become old. It's as if it has happened behind my back – oh, I know it's me own fault,' she acknowledged when Brodie opened her mouth to argue. 'Even so, it's really depressing and a terrible shock to see everyone so desperately ancient – with walking sticks and hearing aids – when I've always thought of them as sixty years younger.'

In her mind, time had stood still, yet in Ireland it had been marching steadily onwards and the years had taken their toll. Even Brodie's daughters and her sons were well into their fifties with grown-up children who had children of their own. Brodie actually had six great-grandchildren.

'I must admit,' Brodie conceded, 'that when I knocked on

your front door I half expected a twenty-year-old Megan to open it. Instead, there you were, all silver-haired and your face as wrinkled as a dried old prune.'

'Do you mind?' Megan said frostily. 'You never used to be so offensive.'

'I was scared of you, that's why. You used to bully me something awful. I'm getting me own back after all this time.'

'In that case I'm dead sorry. I honestly didn't mean to bully you.'

'Apology accepted.' Brodie grinned.

'I don't think our Joe and Tom's wives like me,' Megan said fretfully. 'They look upon me as an intruder.'

'Oh, that pair! They used to hate each other once, but as they've grown older they've formed a witches' coven.'

'I hope they don't put a spell on me.'

'They're probably very inefficient witches and won't know how.'

Megan shuddered. 'I think I'm glad I missed that sort of thing. I mean, having relatives that I didn't get on with and all the backbiting that goes with it.'

'It's all part of being a family, Meg. There's a hundred and sixty-three Kennys around and it'd be a miracle if we all liked one another.'

'A hundred and sixty-three!' It was a terrifying thought having to meet so many people. Uncle Aidan would be eighty-five at the weekend and a party was being held at a grand new hotel on the other side of Duneathly to which every single Kenny had been invited, young and old, including those from the United States and Liverpool. Megan was the only Liverpool relative to attend as Maisie's baby was expected any minute, and two of the young boys in the States were fighting in the Iraq war. If it hadn't meant hurting Brodie's feelings, Megan would have gone home early in order to avoid Uncle Aidan's party. Fancy having an uncle when you were eighty! But she'd promised to stay a month and a month she would stay.

In Liverpool, the weather continued to be fine and warm, but the nights were drawing in, growing dark while the women were still in the garden. Lights were switched on in the house and curtains left undrawn to provide illumination. Diana supplied plentiful scented candles, so that the garden looked like a scene from a fairy tale and smelled delicious. Vanessa felt inspired to paint the way the light made the grass look silver instead of green and the effect it had on the golden leaves that had started to fall from the trees and made crunching noises under foot.

The shops were suddenly full of Christmas decorations. Brodie was disgusted. 'Summer's hardly over,' she complained, but nevertheless started to make lists of presents to buy. 'Will we have our Christmas dinner here or at our respective houses?' she wondered aloud one Saturday morning when they were all having breakfast outside. '*Al fresco*,' Diana said it was called.

'I haven't got a respective house,' Vanessa pointed out. '*This* is my home.'

'Neither have me and Poppy,' said Rachel. Tyler was at school playing rugby. His father wanted the three of them to move in with him and his new wife, but Rachel had refused.

'I'd sooner have Christmas dinner in Chestnuts. I can have me tea in Coral Street with the lads,' Diana said.

'My mother would expect to come, naturally, and Maisie. Would you mind if I invited Colin?' Brodie asked the group. She supposed there was a chance that Josh would be home.

'Not if you don't mind if I invite Reggie and Charlie.'

'Oh, Vanessa, that would be lovely. We can let the leaves out on the table and there's loads of chairs upstairs. I must start making another list of what to eat: a menu of sorts. I'll get chicken, turkey and pork.'

'Make sure the chicken and the turkey are free range,' Diana reminded her. 'We'll all pay our share towards it.'

Brodie shook her head vigorously. 'You'll do no such thing. It's the only Christmas dinner you'll ever have in this house and it'll be on me. Oh, and I suppose we'd better invite Leonard Gosling. I think that makes eleven.' She rubbed her hands together excitedly. 'I'm really looking forward to it.'

Maisie's baby was likely to be born any minute if her huge size was anything to go by. She had no idea of the date of her last period and still hadn't seen a doctor.

'Don't you think you should at least contact the hospital so they'll know to expect you?' Brodie said late one night when she was tidying the kitchen. She was finding it hard to keep her patience with her daughter, and felt convinced Maisie was refusing to see a doctor out of sheer perversity. Brodie heartily wished she'd go and live with the father she thought so highly of, let *him* have the worry of the baby arriving in the middle of the night and rushing her to hospital.

'Do you seriously think the nurses in a maternity hospital will get in a panic if a woman turns up unexpectedly about to have a baby?' Maisie said with a curl of her lip. She looked infinitely better than when she'd first arrived, almost the old Maisie, except for her figure. 'That's the very reason for their existence, to deliver babies. And it could be any woman from anywhere. She might be on holiday in the area or visiting someone and her name is down at another hospital. They're not going to turn her away, are they? They're not going to turn *me* away.'

It wasn't the words that Brodie found were the last straw, but the curl of the lip. She didn't mention, as she had done several times before, anything about blood pressure, which was supposed to be checked throughout the pregnancy as well as the blood itself, which might be lacking iron or something, or that the baby might not be in the right position. Instead she threw the teapot she was holding across the kitchen so it shattered against the wall, landing on the floor in dozens of pieces along with three teabags.

'Sod you, Maisie,' she yelled. 'You're behaving like a total idiot. When the time comes for you to have your baby, then make your own way to the bloody hospital. Don't expect me to drive you there and have to explain why you've never been near the damn place, yet you only live a few miles away. They'll think *I'm* the irresponsible one, not you.'

'And is that all that matters to you?' Maisie said with another curl of the lip. 'People you've never met and are never likely to meet again thinking you're irresponsible?'

Brodie picked up the teabags, contemplated throwing them at her daughter, but put them in the rubbish bin instead. 'No, Maisie,' she said, very coldly and very deliberately, 'that's not what I'm worried about. What I'm worried about is my first grandchild having a difficult birth, perhaps even being permanently damaged for one of the reasons I've already explained. But you, you're so bloody arrogant and full of yourself you don't care.' She took the dustpan and brush out of the sink unit and began to brush the pieces of teapot off the floor. Fortunately, there'd hardly been any tea left so the floor was only slightly wet.

When she looked up, Maisie had disappeared. Brodie put the kettle on. Tea, tea, she badly needed more tea. There was another teapot in the cupboard, a metal one. At least it wouldn't break should she ever feel like throwing it against the wall.

'Oh, all right,' a voice said from the door. 'You can take me to the hospital in the morning.'

'Thank you,' Brodie said tartly. 'Thank you very much.' Until recently, she'd felt nothing but sympathy for her daughter, but now she was fed up with pussy-footing around, being incredibly nice because Maisie was having a baby, when all she did in return was sneer and be outrageously rude. There were some parents who would refuse to have their pregnant, drug-addicted daughters back in the house, but Maisie didn't appear to be the tiniest bit grateful that she'd been allowed to return without a single word of criticism for the disgraceful way that she'd behaved.

'She's made her own bed, so let her lie in it,' Colin used to say. 'She's let us down.' While Brodie didn't exactly feel the same as he once did, she was sorry now that she hadn't given the girl a good telling-off.

'It might have done us both the world of good,' she said to herself. She felt better for having lost her temper, and wondered if Maisie might feel better for having witnessed it.

The tea made, she looked in her room: her daughter was lying on the bed fast asleep or pretending to be. She quietly closed the door. It was too cold to sit into the garden – Vanessa had come in quite a while ago – so she sat in the snug instead. She was still shaking – it wasn't often she lost her temper – and would have really welcomed someone to talk to. It was a relief when the front door opened and Diana came in.

'Hello,' Brodie called.

'Oh, hello.' Diana poked her head around the door. 'I wondered why the light was on.'

'Where have you been?'

'With Leo to see *The Bourne Conspiracy*. It's very good. I really like Matt Damon.'

'The kettle's not long boiled if you fancy a cuppa,' Brodie said invitingly. 'And there's some nice chocolate bikkies in the fridge.'

'Goody! I won't be a mo. Do you fancy another cup?'

'Thanks, but I've still not finished this one.'

Diana returned with a mug of tea and two biscuits on a plate. She put the things on the table and threw herself into a chair with a sigh. 'On Saturday, I'm going to tell poor Leo I can't see him any more and give him his ring back,' she announced glumly. 'He keeps on at me to get married, but it just wouldn't be fair.'

'On you or him?' Brodie asked. This was just the sort of conversation she needed to take her mind off her own problems.

'Oh, on him, poor thing. I mean, I don't love him, do I?' The girl looked moidered to death. 'If I give him up, he'll get over it, won't he?' she asked anxiously.

'I think you can definitely count on that, love. And don't blame yourself. Leo has been awfully pushy – and his parents put pressure on you, too.' She squeezed Diana's hand. 'You're a catch, that's why.'

'Tinker's asked me to go out with him. I really fancy going.'

'If you do, I hope you won't agree to marry *him* until you're quite sure you're in love.'

Diana nodded solemnly. 'Don't worry, I won't.'


It was ages before Brodie fell asleep. She kept going over the row with Maisie in her head while listening to her daughter's steady breathing. She hoped the baby would arrive during the daytime or, even better, at the weekend when Colin was around.

It felt as if she'd only been asleep a few seconds when Maisie groaned. Brodie was alert straight away, particularly when Maisie sat up and began to scream.

'Oh, Mum, I've got this really terrible pain. Oh, fuck, it's killing me.'

'Where is the pain, sweetheart?' When she thought about it afterwards, this seemed an incredibly stupid question to ask.

'In my stomach. Oh, Jesus, Mum, it's agony.' She screamed again.

'It sounds as if you've got contractions. I think we'd best get you to hospital.' Brodie got out of bed and began to throw on some clothes. 'Where's the suitcase with your things?' She remembered it was on top of the wardrobe and went to fetch it. 'Come on, sweetheart, put your dressing gown on. I'll ring the hospital and let them know we're on our way. We'd better leave straight away.' Her recent anger was entirely forgotten.

'I can't, I couldn't. I can't walk.' Maisie began to kick the bedclothes away. 'Oh, fuck, Mum, the baby's coming. I can actually feel it move.'

'Jaysus, Mary and Joseph.' Brodie opened the door and screamed, '*IS THERE ANYONE IN THIS HOUSE WHO KNOWS HOW TO DELIVER A BABY?*'

There was silence for what seemed like an extraordinarily long time, then a door opened and Rachel came running down the stairs in her bare feet, her white nightie flowing out behind her.

'I do,' she said. 'The nurse taught us how to do it at school. Have you rung for an ambulance? If you haven't, ring straight away, then fetch some clean towels. I'm going to wash my hands.'

Diana had come out of her room. 'I'll ring for the ambulance, Brodie,' she said. 'You get the towels.'

When Brodie went in with the towels, Rachel was kneeling at the foot of Maisie's bed. 'Are there any problems I should know about?' she was asking Maisie. 'Do you know if the baby is in the breech position?'

'She has no idea,' Brodie said.

'I've got to push,' Maisie screamed.

'Try not to,' Rachel said calmly. 'Pant instead. Like this.' She began to pant like a little engine. Maisie made an attempt to do the same. 'Brodie, put the towels underneath her bum and help me spread her legs. I think I can see the baby's head,' she said a few seconds later.

'Already?' Brodie said frantically. 'Isn't that dangerous? Isn't it too soon?'

Rachel didn't reply. She said to Maisie, 'It's time you pushed.'

'Holy Mary, Mother of God,' Brodie screamed. 'It's coming!'

'Brodie,' Rachel said sternly, 'you aren't helping. Please go outside, make some tea or something, and ask Vanessa to come in if she's there.'

Holding on to the wall, Brodie limped out of the room. 'She wants you,' she whispered to an anxious Vanessa, who was standing in the hall with an equally anxious Diana. Vanessa went straight into the room and Diana said, 'An ambulance is on its way. It shouldn't be long.'

'Thank the Lord.' Brodie clasped the girl's hand. 'I think I'm going to die.' Together, they walked up and down the hallway, eight steps one way, eight steps the other – Brodie counted them. She felt as if they'd done this for several hours, but was told later it was a mere twenty minutes, when she heard a baby cry, just one little, rather pathetic cry.

Vanessa opened the door looking exuberant. 'It's a boy,' she cried, 'and he's gorgeous. Do you know, I wouldn't have missed that for anything. You can come in now.'

The baby had been wrapped in a towel and was lying on his mother's breast. Maisie was like a wild woman, her hair all over the place, but her face was relaxed and quite beautiful. Her arms were folded over the baby, who had an enormous amount of brown curly hair and looked rather bemused by his recent experience.

'I've got a son, Mum,' Maisie said.

'I know, sweetheart.' Brodie laid her hand on her grandson's back. He felt warm and solid. 'He looks enormous – about nine or ten pounds.'

'I've checked his mouth and nose are clear,' Rachel said, 'but the cord hasn't been cut – they can do that at the hospital – and the placenta hasn't come yet. I'll wash my hands again and go back to bed. If Poppy's woken up she's probably wondering where I've got to.'

'Thank you,' Brodie stammered. 'Oh, Rachel, thank you.'

'I like living here,' Diana said to Vanessa after the ambulance had taken Maisie, the baby and Brodie to hospital. 'It's dead exciting.'

'I like it, too.'

The women smiled at each other and went to bed.

Vanessa couldn't sleep. It was a relief when a glimmer of light appeared around the curtains and she felt justified in getting up. The house was completely silent. When she went downstairs, the door to Brodie's room was wide open, so she went in to see what sort of state Maisie's bed was in and found only the towels were full of blood. She took them into the laundry room and loaded them into the washing machine.

Back in Brodie's room, she made the beds and tidied up. She pulled open the curtains and saw that a fine mist hung over the garden. The sun wasn't visible this early, but she could just tell it was gearing up to be another lovely day, if not as warm as it had been.

She was about to make coffee when she heard a soft knocking on the glass in the front door. Some thoughtful person didn't want to wake the entire house by ringing the intrusive doorbell. She recognized who it was through the stained-glass panels: Reggie Ormerod.

Vanessa was conscious of the fact she didn't look exactly appealing in her old dressing gown, but didn't care. It wasn't the sullen, hopeless not caring that she'd felt when she first came to live there, but an acknowledgement that this was how she looked when she got up in the morning and hadn't combed her hair or had a wash.

'Hi,' Reggie said when they came face to face. He'd actually made an effort with his own appearance and his hair was combed for once. He was dressed in his usual black. There was no doubt about it: Megan was right to call him dishy, with his tough, yet sensitive face and dark-grey eyes. 'I was still up when the ambulance came last night and I wondered if everything was all right.'

'Everything's fine.' Vanessa could actually feel herself glowing. 'It was Maisie having her baby.'

'I thought that might be it. What did she have?' He looked genuinely interested.

'A boy. Look, come in, if you've got time. I was just about to make some coffee.'

'I'd love some coffee.'

She stood aside to let him in and he followed her into the kitchen. 'Did she actually have the baby here?'

'Yes.' She turned to him, wanting to convey how the birth had affected her. 'I was there, helping, and it was truly wonderful. I've never known anything like it before. Maisie was screaming and shouting and all of a sudden there was silence and this gorgeous little baby slid into the world.' She felt tears trickle down her cheeks and rubbed them away with her dressing-gown sleeve. 'I'm not crying because I'm sad, but because it was so moving. It was a miracle. Let's have these in here.' She carried the coffees into the snug and closed the door. 'I don't want to wake anyone. Oh, and I haven't told you: Rachel actually delivered the baby. She was wonderful too, so level-headed. She didn't panic a bit. Poor Brodie was in a terrible state.' She paused, out of breath. He was watching her with a strange expression. 'I'm sorry, I'm going on more than a bit.'

'I don't mind,' he said. 'Go on as much as you like.'

'I can't – you've made me feel embarrassed.'

'I'm sorry.' He picked up her hand and kissed it, picked up her other hand and kissed that, too, and held them both against his cheeks.

Time seemed to stand still. A train passed: it sounded miles away. Birds sang, somewhere a dog barked. Vanessa could have sworn she could hear the leaves outside falling from the trees and the flowers opening up to the sun. Then Reggie Ormerod kissed her again, on the lips this time, and everything seemed to fall into place.

Before, her life had been one long plan of action, but she would never plan anything again. From now on, she would do things first and think about them later, which was why she kissed Reggie Ormerod back.


'We've got a grandson,' Colin chuckled. It was four o'clock in the morning and he was driving Brodie back from Liverpool maternity hospital. Their first grandchild had been washed, weighed, inspected, and was now fast asleep in a crib beside his exhausted mother. 'A big, beautiful, healthy grandson, who looks as if he'll make a first-class rugby player.'

'Thomas!' Brodie breathed. 'Maisie doesn't realize she's called her son after his great-great-grandfather.'

'Will Maisie and Thomas live with you when they come out of hospital?' he asked tightly after what seemed to Brodie to be a slightly awkward pause. His mood had changed in an instant.

'There isn't room in Chestnuts,' she said. 'The unused rooms are awfully small and they all need decorating.'

'In that case, will they be coming home? I mean *real* home, where you and I used to live together and where our children were raised?' He was doing his best not to sound bitter.

'I don't know. I feel as if I should be with her . . .' She broke off, not knowing how to continue. It was probably silly, but she felt a certain amount of loyalty to what felt like her other family in Chestnuts. She didn't want to leave them in the lurch.

'There's no question that you should be with your daughter,' Colin said so sharply that she felt annoyed. 'It so happens there's a double bed in the house I just mentioned that has room for someone else – a wife, for example. Maisie's bed-room is nicely decorated. And there's room for the cot I bought that's waiting to be put together. By the way, I'm no good at that sort of thing. I need some assistance.'

He'd bought a cot! Brodie couldn't resist it. She said, 'Why don't you ask your father to help?'

'I haven't seen him for a week or two. He's courting.'

'*What*?'

'Her name's Blanche. She's just moved in next door – to him, that is, not us. With Dad out of the way,' he said impatiently, 'perhaps you could review your position about coming home?'

'It wasn't just your father. It was the way you felt about Maisie, the things you used to say.'

'I feel very differently about Maisie now,' he pointed out. 'How many times do I have to tell you?'

'So it would seem, but you were no help when we first discovered she was a drug addict. It was me who went to London and met Karen Young, the policewoman who brought her home.' She turned towards him as they drove through the silent streets. 'Do you mind if we have this argument another time? I feel very tired and I'm not in the mood.' She'd go back to the house in Crosby right now and stay for a few days, help Maisie settle in, but would sleep in Josh's bed, not with Colin. She wasn't in the mood for that, either.

She woke in Josh's room just after half-past eight. It was a beautiful morning and the room was filled with sunshine. Colin had already left for school. Downstairs, she found cornflakes in a cupboard in the kitchen and a fresh carton of milk in the fridge. It felt odd, not quite right, eating in this kitchen and not the one in Chestnuts.

When she finished, she rang Josh on her mobile to tell him he was an uncle, then her mother in Ireland.

'So, I'm a great-grandmother!' Mum sounded thrilled. 'I'll book the earliest flight and be home later today.'

'There's no need for that, Mum,' Brodie protested.

'Oh, darlin', there is,' her mother said in a heartfelt tone. 'Now I've got a marvelous excuse to leave. On Saturday, Uncle Aidan is eighty-five and all the Kennys in the world are expected to be there. I hate the very thought of it. Maisie's baby has arrived at just the right time.'

Brodie dug out the underwear Maisie had left behind when she went to university and a few other items of clothing that might be useful. The cot that Colin had bought would need bedding: she'd go into town that afternoon and buy some. She imagined the pleasure she would get out of choosing a baby blanket – perhaps blue and white stripes. She'd get something nice for Maisie at the same time: perfume, maybe, or some jewellery.

Her car was in Blundellsands. She decided to go on the train, see Maisie now, make sure she was all right, then do some shopping. She would collect the car later.

Maisie already had a visitor, a young man with a lovely, open face and brown curly hair. His eyes were a slightly darker shade of brown and he was nursing Thomas with all the pride and dewy-eyed emotion of a brand-new father. This could only be Pete. She was pleased he looked nice, so wasn't sure why her heart dropped like a stone.

'Mum!' Maisie cried when Brodie approached. She looked radiant. 'This is Pete, Thomas's father. He's just arrived from London. I phoned him from the hospital last night – well, early this morning.'

'How do you do, Mrs Logan?' Pete said shyly, half standing. He had a touch of an accent, Welsh, she thought, and was too scared to let go of the baby to shake hands.

'Call me Brodie, please. What do you think of your new son?'

'He's awesome.' He sat down again. 'This has all turned out much better than I imagined.'

Brodie frowned. 'What do you mean?'

'Well . . .' he began, but Maisie interrupted. 'What he means is I've been behaving like an out and out pig. I left where I was living without telling him, so he's had no idea where I've been for ages. I've put him through hell this last year.' She put her hand on Pete's knee. 'I'm sorry.' She held out her other hand to Brodie. 'And I'm sorry, Mum. I've been a double pig with you. I don't know why, but I wanted to blame people for things that were no one's fault but my own.' She threw back her shoulders and laughed. 'I feel myself again for the first time in ages.'

'I hope you stay that way, sweetheart.' She wanted to ask her daughter what had prompted her to take drugs in the first place, but wondered if there would ever be a right time.

'Are you going home now, Mum?' Maisie enquired.

'After I've done some shopping. Why?'

'I'd like you to bring some of my stuff back here with you: my black coat and boots and I think I had two pairs of decent jeans. The rest can be chucked away – or Diana might like it for that stall of hers in the refugee centre.'

It was then Brodie realized why her heart had sunk like a stone; she must have sensed something like this was about to happen. 'Does that mean you're going away?' she asked, trying to keep her voice steady.

Maisie's eyes shone. 'We're going back to London in the morning in Pete's car. He's got this great bedsit in Muswell Hill and a really good job as a researcher for the Green Party. In a few months, I can leave Thomas with a childminder and get a job myself.'

Brodie's heart began to hammer in her breast. 'Do you think it's all right for two adults and a baby to live in one room?'

'Oh, it's a really big room. Isn't it, Pete?'

'It's massive, Mrs . . . Brodie. Really massive.' Pete assured her. 'There's space for a cot and everything.'

She wondered if they already had a cot. She couldn't bring herself to say that Colin had bought one. He could tell them himself later on.

She was no longer in the mood to go shopping. Anyroad, she didn't know what to buy. Instead, she caught the train home. Despite the tension between them early that morning, she badly wanted to talk to Colin, tell him that Maisie wouldn't be staying in Crosby or Blundellsands. It was the last thing she had expected. She'd been looking forward to their grandson being around for a while at least, not to be whisked away from under her nose when he was scarcely two days old. Was Maisie so insensitive that she didn't give a thought to her mum and dad's feelings? When had she become like that? Or had she always been that way? And, out of interest, who had been supporting Maisie during the time when she and Pete hadn't been in touch? It was something that she, Brodie, would never know.

In Chestnuts, she found Vanessa in the garden staring dreamily into space while holding the handle of Poppy's pushchair, jogging it slightly from time to time.

'She's a bit restless this morning,' she said when Brodie joined her at the table. 'I think she might be cutting another tooth.'

'Where are Rachel and Tyler?' Brodie asked.

'They've gone to the fairground in Southport. They were going to take Poppy, but I offered to look after her so they can be kids for the day instead of parents.'

Brodie imagined the young couple with ice-cream cornets wandering hand in hand among the rides. She noticed Poppy was wearing a little padded jacket. It depressed her, the fact that summer was so obviously over and everything was about to change.

Vanessa enquired about the new baby. 'Has he got a name yet?'

'It's Thomas and he's fine. He weighed nearly ten pounds.'

'I'm longing to see him.' She looked genuinely excited. 'After all, he's the only baby I'm ever likely to help deliver. Would it be all right if I went tonight? Or will Maisie be coming home soon?'

'I'm afraid Maisie's going back to London tomorrow. I'd go tonight, if I were you: it might be the last opportunity you'll ever have. Diana and Rachel, too.' She prayed Mum would arrive home from Ireland early enough to see Thomas, otherwise she'd be desperately upset.

Diana came home, full of beans. Apparently, she and Megan had been exchanging text messages all day and had planned to get dressed up and watch a film on Friday night.

'*Singin' in the Rain*,' Diana announced. 'It's one of my favourites. I thought we could buy some wine and order a takeaway. I'm going to make a trifle. Have I ever told you I make the most fantastic trifles?'

'No,' Brodie conceded. She was so pleased to see the girl she wanted to cry. Diana would never let anyone down. 'What do you put in your trifles?'

'Everything,' Diana said with her glorious smile. 'The last time I made one we all got drunk.'

Only Diana could have turned watching a more than fifty-year-old film in the house into a grand occasion. Wine was bought, pizzas ordered, the ingredients purchased for the trifle – cider seemed to play an important part. Christmas decorations were already in the shops and Diana came home on Thursday night laden with tinsel.

By then, Maisie, Pete and Thomas had returned to London, but Brodie didn't feel as hurt as she might have done had she not had the film to look forward to. She went shopping, not for baby bedding as originally planned, but for a Per Una skirt and blouse in autumnal colours from Marks & Spencer. Mum had bought a couple of outfits in Ireland and planned on wearing royal purple.

'Oh, it's so lovely to be home,' she said to Brodie on her first night back. 'I feel quite young again. In Ireland, I felt as old as the hills. And thank you for the flowers in my flat. They're beautiful.'

'The flowers were Diana's idea,' Brodie told her.

Friday dawned bright and chilly. Colin rang early before he left for school to ask how she was feeling.

'Not so bad at all,' she assured him. 'How about you?'

'All right, I suppose,' he said gloomily. 'Tomorrow, I'm going to have to take this bloody cot back.'

'I'll come with you,' she offered. 'We could go for a meal.'

'What are you doing tonight?'

She explained about the film and he asked if he could come, but she told him no. 'It's for women only. You can come and sit in the kitchen and we'll feed you scraps. Or you could go next door and have a drink with Reggie Ormerod. Charlie's coming to see the film with us seeing as she hasn't got school tomorrow, though she's not being allowed any trifle.'

He rang off, saying he might well come later.

At five o'clock, Brodie draped the tinsel around Diana's room. Upstairs, Vanessa and Rachel were getting ready. Mum arrived on her bike with a bag full of fairy cakes. The telephone rang in the hall and Brodie answered. It was the worst call she'd ever had. It would be a long time before she was able to answer the phone without a feeling of dread.

'What on earth is the matter?' her mother asked seconds later when Brodie replaced the receiver, having hardly uttered a word. 'You've gone as white as a sheet.'

Vanessa was coming down the stairs followed by Rachel and Poppy. Perhaps there was something in the atmosphere, or perhaps it was Brodie's white face that made them stop and stare.

'What's wrong?' Vanessa whispered.

'That was Tinker,' Brodie said. 'Diana was knocked down outside the centre by a hit and run driver.' She burst into tears. 'I can't believe it. Diana's *dead*.'

# Chapter 14

There were a good fifty mourners at the church for Diana's requiem Mass. A report of her death had been in the *Liverpool Echo* and the Bootle and Crosby papers along with a photograph, alerting people who otherwise wouldn't have known: neighbours from Coral Street who'd known her all her life, for instance, the call centre where she'd used to work, and girls she'd been at school with. There was a whole crowd from the refugee centre, who found it hard to believe such a thing could happen in a civilized country.

Not everyone came back to the house for refreshments: just Diana's immediate family, Megan, Leonard Gosling, Tinker and Eileen, who'd been dreadfully upset by the news and had insisted on coming all the way from London. She and Brodie's mother couldn't stop crying, and seemed to be vying with each other to see who could drink the most wine. There were also one or two people Brodie had never seen before. Colin had been at the church, having taken a few hours off school. He'd since returned and wouldn't be seen again until later.

Diana's brothers were standing in a circle, arms around each other, heads bent, joined together in their grief. Leo was standing helplessly nearby and the circle was broken to allow him to join.

'Poor Leo,' Brodie whispered, recalling that had Diana

lived another day she'd intended telling Leo she didn't want to see him again. At least he'd been spared that.

Why had she been killed? Why had Diana, who wouldn't have hurt a fly, who was one of the sweetest people on earth, been mown down by a stranger in a black van?

'It was intentional,' Tinker said. He'd told that to the police. 'I came out of the centre only minutes behind her and the van quite deliberately mounted the pavement and came straight at her.' He'd managed to make a note of the registration number. The police had a good idea who it was, but weren't prepared to reveal details until they were certain.

It was another beautiful day, the garden a fabulous riot of golden trees and fallen leaves. Brodie wasn't sure if this miracle of nature made the day more, or less sad. She half expected Diana to come bursting out of the house wearing a dramatic hat with a black spotted veil, the star of her own funeral, flinging her arms around everyone in sight.

People had brought their refreshments outside. Michelle, Diana's mother, was absolutely distraught. Her mini-skirt hardly covered her behind and her lacy tights were snagged in numerous places.

'No woman could have wished for a better daughter,' she wept. 'And thank you for paying for the funeral, Brodie; it was lovely. I'd've had to borrow if it had been left to me. I'm not one of those sensible types who takes out insurance and stuff like that.'

'It wasn't me who paid,' Brodie told her. 'It was my mother. She was especially fond of Diana.'

Megan was desperately angry about Diana's death. 'It's not fair,' she raged. 'All those old people back in Ireland with seventy and eighty years on the clock, me included. What are we doing alive when Diana's dead?'

'There's nothing fair about life, Mum. There never has been.' She was glad her mother was home, having missed her far more than expected.

Diana had lain in a white coffin in a white dress, blood-red rosary beads threaded through her long fingers. Brodie and Megan had gone to the funeral parlour every day to say prayers and watch the lovely, untroubled face, eyes closed for the final time. They shed tears until they choked on them.

Vanessa came up. She wore bright green – none of the women were in black, not for Diana's funeral. 'I didn't like her, you know,' she said. 'Not when we first met. I remember she brought me a hideous glittery blouse from that stall in the centre. I felt obliged to wear it. It was the night we watched *Gone With the Wind*.'

'It was also the night you cut all your hair,' Brodie reminded her.

'Diana tidied it up for me. I still didn't like her. She seemed much too bossy, as if she wanted to organize all our lives.'

'She had the biggest heart in the world,' Brodie said soberly. 'All she wanted was to help people, to make them happy.'

'I realized that after a while.' Vanessa nodded. 'The other day I thought we could all watch *Singin' in the Rain* tonight, but that's a terrible idea, isn't it?'

'Absolutely terrible.' Brodie scrunched up her face. 'We'd cry ourselves to death. In fact, I'll never watch that film again if I live to be a hundred.'

Charlie arrived cuddling Kenneth; the cat was asleep in her arms. 'He's missing Diana,' the little girl announced, 'just like me.' She'd been allowed to come home from school at dinnertime for the wake.

'Do you know that man who's talking to the lads?' Brodie asked Vanessa. Tall and gangly, he was about fifty with fair hair turning grey at the sides. He bore the weather-beaten, slightly weary air of someone who'd travelled a lot and was looking for somewhere to rest. His outfit was informal: jeans, a grey sweatshirt and shabby trainers.

'I've no idea. He's not bad-looking for an older man, is he?'

Vanessa said with an approving click of the tongue. 'I expect your mother would call him dishy. Oh, look, he's coming over. I'll see if anyone would like more tea or coffee and leave him to you.' She patted Charlie's head. 'Come along. You and Kenneth can help.'

'Hello.' The man's eyes were a familiar blue and were surrounded by mesh of wrinkles, as if he'd squinted too much at the sun. He held out his hand and Brodie shook it: it felt warm and rough. 'I'm Jim O'Sullivan, Diana's dad. I apologize for the clothes, but I left most of my stuff behind; it wasn't worth fetching home.'

'Di's father!' Brodie was stunned. 'Where have you been all this time?'

'All over the place,' he answered in the sort of voice that made her think he hadn't exactly enjoyed it all that much. 'I understand your name is Brodie and you're in charge here.'

'I'm Brodie, yes, but I'm not in charge. This just happens to be my house.' They were still holding hands. She squeezed his. 'I'm so sorry about Diana,' she said fervently. 'She was a genuinely nice person. She lived here, you know, with us, and we all loved her. But how awful for you to come back just when she died.'

'I have a mate in Bootle. We write to each other now and again, about once a year. He managed to contact me when he read about Di in the paper.'

'It must have come as a terrible shock.' Imagine getting a message like that when you were in some far-off country.

He sighed. Brodie wondered how many miles he'd come over the last few days because he sounded extremely tired. 'I kept hoping one day I'd come back for her wedding,' he said.

'She was engaged – did you know that? Except she intended breaking it off the day after the accident.'

'I've just been told she was engaged – to that young man with the lads, Leo – but not that she was about to break it off.'

He looked surprised and his eyes blinked wearily as if even being surprised was an effort.

'I might have been the only one who knew. Look, when did you arrive in Liverpool? Have you had anything to eat? Anything solid, that is.' He was holding a plate of dinky sarnies.

'The plane from Amsterdam touched down this morning at about ten. I managed to get to the church just before the service finished.'

'That's where you've been working, Amsterdam?'

'No, Ecuador, in a little village about a hundred miles from the nearest airport. Amsterdam was where I changed planes.' He smiled. It was a gentle, sweet smile, just like Diana's, but without the sparkle. 'I'm afraid I'm not much good at sleeping on planes.'

'Would you like to sit somewhere quiet and comfortable for a while?' she asked. 'And I could make you some soup. It might make you feel better.' She put her hand on his elbow, led him inside and sat him down in the empty snug. 'What about the soup?' she asked. 'It'll only be tinned, but a bit more nutritious than what you've got there.'

He perked up. 'Soup sounds great.'

'After you've eaten, you can have a rest in my bedroom. When you come out of this room, it's the second door on the left. I'll look in on you at about four and wake you if you're asleep. You won't miss much. Most people are likely to be here all day.'

'You're being very kind.'

'Well, you're Diana's dad, aren't you? She would have expected me to look after you. In similar circumstances, she would have done the same for me.'

As the afternoon progressed, the atmosphere in the garden lightened, just a little, as wakes often do. The person who had died, no matter how beloved, had gone for ever, and those left behind had to get used to it, as well as feel glad that they were still alive and in a position to enjoy life, even if some didn't have all that many years left.

Brodie noticed that Tinker had been missing for ages. She found him in Diana's room, which was still laced with tinsel, where he was lying face down on her bed, his eyes red from weeping. He wore a hand-knitted cardigan with multi-coloured stripes.

'I loved her, you know, Brodie,' he said brokenly. 'She was a glorious girl. Her brain never stopped working and thinking up new ideas.' He sniffed and, as an afterthought, almost laughed. 'There were times when she drove me crazy.'

'She drove us all crazy. Have you noticed the ghastly walls and tiles in the kitchen? Diana chose the colours.' Mind you, she'd got used to them ages ago and they no longer bothered her.

'I've always really liked your kitchen,' Tinker said wanly.

Tyler and Colin came straight to the house from their various schools. Reggie Ormerod arrived home from work and Brodie saw him pull Vanessa behind a tree. She could only assume they were kissing. She felt enormously pleased and also envious, remembering how thrilling and exciting it had been when she'd first met Colin and they'd begun to fall in love.

Michelle left to go back to Nottingham. Before she went, she asked Brodie if she knew where Jim was so she could say tara. 'He seems to have disappeared.'

'He's in my room, probably asleep.' She'd forgotten to wake him as promised. 'Do you want to tell him that you're going?'

'No, ta, luv. Leave him be for now. Poor chap, he's been travelling for days. He's planning on staying around for a few weeks, so I'm bound to see him again.' She hunched her shoulders and made a face. 'I suppose you think I'm daft, letting a husband like Jim go?'

'Of course I don't. I hardly know him.' Or you, she wanted to say.

'He's a lovely chap, a real diamond.' Brodie vaguely remembered someone using the same word to describe Diana – it might have been herself. 'But I drove him away. I didn't realize which side me bread was buttered. He was a merchant seaman in those days and used to say I needed one of them chastity belt things when he left me behind.'

Brodie could only imagine what she'd got up to. Thinking about it, of the four O'Sullivan children, only Diana bore any resemblance to Jim.

It was nearly midnight. In the snug, Brodie and Colin, Vanessa and Reggie, and Jim O'Sullivan were sitting around the oval table finishing the day with the remainder of the wine. Everyone else who didn't live there had gone home, apart from Charlie, who was fast asleep in Vanessa's room until her father took her home. Rachel and Poppy had gone to bed ages ago. Brodie had no idea if Tyler was with them.

The conversation ranged from greenhouse gases, to the war in Iraq, the rate of inflation, the education system, the health service and, of course, Diana.

'She was nine when I left,' Jim said with the smile that reminded Brodie so much of his daughter. 'I'd swear she had an older head on her shoulders than did me wife. She used to write out the shopping lists and help the lads with their schoolwork.'

'It was a bit irresponsible to walk out on your family, wasn't it?' Colin growled. 'Leaving a wife who couldn't cope and four children under nine.' This wasn't the first critical remark he'd made. It was obvious he didn't like Jim. Nor was he exactly pleased to discover that Brodie had said he could stay in Diana's room while he was in Liverpool. It was also obvious that he wasn't prepared to go home until Jim had gone to bed.

'I didn't say Michelle couldn't cope, but I admit I shouldn't have walked out,' Jim said steadily. 'It's just that things were happening that *I* couldn't cope with. Seven years ago, if I'd known Michelle had left the kids to live on their own, I'd have come back straight away.'

Colin snorted. Brodie wanted to remind him that he hadn't exactly stuck by his own daughter when she needed help, but the atmosphere was already unpleasant enough. In the end, she wished everyone goodnight and went to bed herself. Soon afterwards, she heard Colin drive away and Jim enter his daughter's room.

'Goodnight, Diana, wherever you are,' she whispered as she laid her head on the pillow.

'I'm glad today's over,' Vanessa said when she and Reggie were the only ones left.

'I liked Diana.' Reggie slid his arms around her and kissed her ear, 'Though she had a lousy dress sense.'

'It's the first time in my life that someone of my own age has died – someone I've known, that is.' She was enjoying having her ear kissed, the feel of his arms, and the lemony smell of the aftershave he used.

'Will you come back with me tonight?' he whispered.

'Yes.' She'd slept in the house next door for the last five nights. So far, Brodie hadn't appeared to notice – not that it was any of Brodie's business – but Vanessa felt just a little bit uncomfortable about it. 'Charlie doesn't seem to mind my being there, does she?'

'Charlie's as pleased about it as I am.' He turned her face towards him and kissed her full on the lips.

Vanessa had read of women wanting to swoon in similar situations, but it had seemed a daft idea and she'd never thought it would happen to her. Now it was happening all the time. She gasped when they came up for air. 'Wow!' she said huskily.

'You can say that again.' Reggie tenderly stroked her cheek. 'Is this the right time to ask if you'd consider moving next door permanently?'

'It's the right time and the wrong time,' Vanessa said seriously. 'I will come and live with you, but I can't say when. I promised Brodie I'd be here for a year. I don't want to leave when we've only just lost Diana.' She wanted to spend the rest of her life with Reggie and Charlie Ormerod more than anything she'd ever wanted in the world, but there were other people to consider. 'Do you mind?'

'I mind about as much as it's possible to mind. But I understand,' he said with a grin. 'It's a question of sisterhood.'

'Is it?' She'd never thought of herself as belonging to a sisterhood.

'Isn't it?'

'I suppose it must be.' In a way, she felt closer to the women in Chestnuts than she did to her real sisters.

A train passed, the sound audible in the thick silence that had fallen over the house. Upstairs, Poppy gave a little cry in her sleep. Downstairs, Jim O'Sullivan coughed. Vanessa could hear herself breathe.

'Shall we go?' Reggie asked in a low voice.

Vanessa nodded. 'I need to collect some things from my room.'

'And I need to collect my daughter.'

It was early when Brodie woke. All she could hear was birdsong. She felt as if a great weight was pressing down on her and just knew something bad had happened. Then she remembered: Diana was dead.

She sat up and wished she had one of those machines that made tea at the press of a button. For the first time in months it was cold in bed: she needed a thicker duvet. Maisie's duvet had been put away in the wardrobe drawer and Colin had taken the bed she'd slept in back upstairs. It reminded her that Maisie hadn't sent flowers to the funeral, even though Diana had been incredibly generous and helpful while Maisie had been staying in the house. She'd thought they were friends. On the day Thomas had been born, Diana had gone into town in her lunch-hour and bought half a dozen little white vests as a gift. Brodie wondered what had happened to the lovely christening gown that had come from the refugee center. Had Thomas even been christened yet? Surely Maisie would have invited her parents if he had.

Brodie didn't think she would ever get used to the extent her daughter had changed. It was as if the sweet little girl she'd always known no longer existed. Something had happened, perhaps it was the drug-taking, that had hardened her heart. She'd wanted her mother while Thomas was being born, but maybe that was because Pete hadn't been there. 'You'll just have to get used to it,' she told herself. 'You can't let it get you down for the rest of your life.'

The funny thing was that Josh, who'd hardly known Diana, had sent a beautiful bunch of chrysanthemums tied with a bright green ribbon. 'For the girl with stars in her eyes,' his card had said.

'I know we only met the twice,' he said to Brodie when she'd rung and told him about Diana, 'but to tell the truth, Mum, I really fancied her. I'm sorry now I didn't ask her out, though I suppose it would have been awkward, her being in Liverpool and me in London.'

It had been done before, Brodie thought. Courtships even happened between couples on opposite sides of the world. For a while, she entertained herself with the lovely idea of Diana being her daughter-in-law, until she could stand the cold no longer. She leaped out of bed, fetched the other duvet and flung it over the bed, then got back in and pulled both duvets up around her shoulders.

'That's better,' she muttered. Very soon, she'd have to collect some warm nightdresses and her fleece dressing gown from home. When she was a child and had lived in Chestnuts, she recalled the house had been very chilly in the winter: the central heating was totally inadequate. Since those cold, far-off days, she'd become accustomed to living in a much warmer atmosphere.

Anyway, did she really want to stay there until next March? She had no intention of getting someone else for Diana's room, nor did she intend looking for another job. If necessary, she'd borrow from her mother if she needed money. Eventually, she would go on a course, acquire a skill, start a career, preferably in something medical.

She stiffened when she heard the front door open and footsteps, very faint, go upstairs. The door to Vanessa's room opened and closed. She must have spent the night with Reggie. Brodie sniffed. Lucky thing!

If she didn't have some tea soon she'd die. She got out of bed again, stuffed her feet into sandals, and put a padded jacket on over her thin nightie. In the kitchen, she shivered violently as she ran water into the kettle. The temperature must have dropped about a hundred degrees overnight. The thought of having a shower was unbearable. She tried to remember how the central heating worked, but couldn't. Later, she'd ring her mother who would know.

She was about to go back into her room with the tea when the door to Diana's room opened, giving her such a fright that she narrowly avoided dropping the cup. Jim O'Sullivan appeared, looking much more awake than the day before. She'd entirely forgotten he was staying there.

'Sorry,' he said apologetically. 'I gave you a scare. I was trying to be as quiet as I could. I was hoping you wouldn't mind if I made myself a drink.'

'Of course I don't mind. I'll do it. Would you like coffee or tea?'

'Coffee, please. No milk or sugar.'

'Did you have a decent sleep?'

'Despite everything, I had a great sleep, but the first thing I thought about when I woke up was Diana.' He smiled his sad, sweet smile. She noticed he was in need of a shave: silvery hairs bristled on his chin. His mouth was wide and slightly full, like his daughter's. Brodie thought she must be going mad when she visualized kissing it. Like most women, she had flights of fancy from time to time, but they were usually concentrated on characters who could have been from another planet – George Clooney, for instance, or Antonio Banderas – not real flesh and blood men who were actually within reach.

She gulped. 'As it happens, I thought about Diana as soon as I woke up too.'

The coffee made, she said, 'Would you like to have it in my room? The snug will be rather chilly and the chairs aren't too comfortable.' She didn't like to send him back into the room on his own, though he might have preferred it.

He followed her into the half-dark room and she pulled back the curtains. 'Sit down.' She indicated one of the chairs by the little round table.

'You've got squirrels!' he remarked when the garden was revealed.

'Just the two – at least, I assume it's always the same two. Diana loved them. She used to buy them nuts.' The squirrels were chasing each other up and down the trees. 'Are you warm enough like that?' she asked. He wore jeans and a short-sleeved T-shirt. His sunburned feet were bare.

'I don't feel the cold, or the heat – except when they're extreme. I apologize for my feet. Would you like me to put socks on?'

'Oh, for goodness' sake,' she snorted. 'I've seen a man's bare feet before. I've been married for twenty-three years.'

'To that chap who was here last night – Colin?'

313

'Yes.' She supposed an explanation was necessary as to why they were on speaking terms, yet not living in the same house. 'We're separated at the moment,' she told him.

'And he's not very pleased about it.'

'What makes you say that?'

He shrugged. 'It was obvious. He couldn't keep his eyes off you, for one thing.'

'Oh, it's a long story,' Brodie sighed.

'When we get to our age,' he said rather bitterly, 'we've nearly all got a long story or two to tell.'

The sun had appeared in the furthest corner of the garden. Kenneth arrived, jumped on the table and began to give himself a thorough wash. Squirrels raced through the branches at the tops of the trees and leaves floated to the ground. There was what looked very much like frost on the grass. The birds continued to sing.

'It's nice and peaceful here,' Jim said.

'Everyone thinks that,' Brodie told him. She sipped her tea. There was something peaceful about him, too, a dignified quietness. She felt totally relaxed in his presence and could have sat there for ever, listening to his quiet voice with just a hint of Liverpool accent. She couldn't imagine him being angry. He might disagree with something, even argue, but wouldn't get worked up about it.

'Would you like some breakfast?' she asked.

'It's great of you to put me up, but you don't have to feed me,' he protested. 'I'll go and buy some bread or something and make toast.'

Brodie hooted, conscious she sounded just like her mother. 'Oh, don't be ridiculous! As if I'd let you go hungry. You're Diana's dad. We have bread here as well as butter and jam. There's also bacon and eggs in the fridge and loads of cheese and other stuff.'

'A cheese sarnie would go down well. Thank you, Brodie.'

There were sounds upstairs. Someone was having a shower.

Brodie was conscious of the air being slightly warmer; the thought of a shower was no longer quite so painful. Someone else came downstairs and went into the kitchen.

She said to Jim, 'Vanessa lives upstairs. She's spent most of the time here painting in the garden. She wasn't very happy when she first came, but now she's become friendly with Reggie, who lives next door, and I'm really pleased about it.' Kenneth stopped washing his face for a moment and hungrily eyed a bird that was perched on a branch directly above him. 'Rachel's in the other upstairs room,' she continued. 'She's only fifteen and has a nine-month-old baby, Poppy. Tyler, Poppy's father, stays with us some of the time. He's still at school.' She stood and reached for his empty cup. 'I thought I'd let you know who your neighbours are while you're here. Here, let's have that cup and I'll make you more coffee while I toast the bread for that sarnie.'

At about nine o'clock, her mother turned up. It seemed she'd promised to take Jim to the refugee centre so he could see where Diana had worked. Later, they were going to lunch in town.

'He's a very nice young man,' Megan opined.

Brodie raised her eyebrows. 'Hardly young!' She resented Jim O'Sullivan being taken away.

'Once you reach eighty, the whole world seems young. Do you intend to go and see your relatives in Ireland?' her mother asked curiously.

'One day, not just now. I've too much on my mind.' Soon, she and Colin would have to go and see their grandchild, even if they weren't invited. She doubted if it would ever cross Maisie's mind to bring him to Liverpool.

'I bet one of the things on your mind is how to keep this place warm in the winter,' her mother said. She touched the radiator in the hall which Brodie knew was stone-cold. 'I noticed how chilly it felt when I woke up this morning and

315

thought about this house. It's a bugger to heat. It probably needs new central heating.'

'It would cost the earth and it hardly seems worth it when I've made up my mind to leave in March then sell the place.'

Her mother gave her an affectionate push. 'I'll pay for it, you know I will, but you're right, it doesn't seem worth it. If it's put on the market, a developer will snap it up, the house will be demolished, and a block of expensive flats go up in its place. This land is worth a small fortune, darlin'.'

Brodie stood at the window watching Vanessa in the garden. Clad in a thick grey cardigan and tweed skirt, she was painting an extra-wide canvas, the one for Reggie's house. It was only a few weeks since she'd told Brodie about it, but since then Diana had died and the world seemed a vastly different place. One day, Vanessa might move next door permanently – she might even want to do it now, but feel obliged to stay for the whole year.

And hadn't Rachel said that Tyler's father wanted her, Tyler and Poppy to go and live with him and his new wife? When they'd refused – well, Rachel had – he'd offered to buy them a house close by. If things went a certain way, Brodie could be the only person left and the problem of keeping the house warm would be solved. She could go and live in Crosby with Colin, and Chestnuts wouldn't require heating of any sort.

But was living with Colin what she wanted? She remembered meeting Diana and the girl explaining that there was nowhere for her to go, that she wasn't needed any more, that she felt superfluous. Now Brodie felt the same. Her children were managing perfectly well without her and she wasn't sure how she felt about Colin – or how he felt about her.

There was a shuffling noise outside and Rachel shouted, 'Brodie, it's me. Will you open the door, please?'

'Oh, my goodness, she's walking!' Brodie gasped when the

door was opened to reveal Rachel holding Poppy's hands and the baby girl standing quite firmly on her white-socked feet. Brodie dropped to her knees and held out her arms. Poppy took a few tentative steps forward, still holding her mother's hands, and fell into the older woman's arms, chuckling loudly.

'You little darling!' Brodie felt the urge to weep until there was no tomorrow, although she had no idea why.

'She did it just now,' Rachel said proudly. 'I was holding her by the waist and she walked a little bit. I'll just take her out and show Vanessa.'

'You'd better put shoes on her first,' Brodie advised. 'The grass will still be damp.'

'I'll get some from upstairs.'

'I'll mind her while you do.'

She sat on the bed with the little warm body on her knee, stroking the silky hair. Memories poured in of doing the same thing with her own children. Rachel came in with a pair of tiny blue shoes and Poppy regarded her feet with interest when they were put on.

'She's never worn shoes before,' Rachel explained.

There's a first time for everything, Brodie thought. Pretty soon, Poppy would walk unaided. In time, she would learn to ride a bike, start school and so on, until she got married and had children of her own. And how would Rachel feel then?

'Oh, stop it, you stupid woman,' she said out loud. Rachel and Poppy had gone. 'Stop being so maudlin.'

She watched Rachel show off her baby daughter's walking prowess to Vanessa, who scooped the baby up in her arms with a delighted smile.

Right now, what would I like more than anything in the world? Brodie asked herself. It didn't need much thinking about: she wanted Jim O'Sullivan back so they could talk again. She put on her coat, drove to the supermarket and bought the ingredients for a chicken casserole, along with enough apples to make a pie, and a carton of double cream.

She'd make him a really nice meal and tonight they could eat it in her room, just the two of them.

She wasn't trying to seduce him or anything: she wasn't that sort of person. At least, she didn't think so.

Her plan went awry when her mother returned with Jim and showed no sign of leaving. Brodie couldn't very well ask her to go home. Then, at about five o'clock, Colin arrived and she couldn't bring herself to ask him to leave, either, though she'd be really cross if he was nasty again.

The four of them ate in the snug and she made a big bowl of rice so the casserole would go further. Colin behaved very well and it turned out to be a very pleasant evening, if not quite what Brodie had in mind, though had she been asked exactly what she'd had in mind, she wouldn't have known.

Her mother had turned on the central heating in the airing cupboard in some mysterious way involving switches and dials that Brodie didn't understand. The antique radiators became barely lukewarm and made strange gulping noises. Jim, who appeared to be a jack of all trades, had a look and said the system was so old-fashioned he doubted if it could be repaired.

'I reckon the parts won't be available any more,' he told her. 'If I were you, I'd get a proper plumber in. See what he has to say.'

The proper plumber said the pipes were probably blocked. 'You need new pipes throughout. As for that boiler, in my view it's highly dangerous. It smells as if there's a slight leak. It's too old to be fixed; you need a brand-new one.'

'How much would new pipes and a new boiler cost?' Brodie enquired.

'For a place this size? I imagine somewhere between eight and ten thousand smackeroos, possibly more. Would you like me to work out a proper estimate?'

'No, thank you,' Brodie said faintly.

On Sunday, four days after Diana's funeral, Jim hired a car and drove to see Michelle in Nottingham. 'I won't be there for long,' he told Brodie. 'We're going out for a meal for old times' sake.'

'That's awfully nice of you,' she said. He'd told her why he and Michelle had got divorced, and that he knew for certain none of the lads were his. 'They've got dark hair and I'm fair,' he'd confided. 'Their eyes are brown and mine are blue, and I'm an inch or two taller than all three of them. The lads aren't stupid and I'm pretty sure they've guessed the truth. But Diana did a real good job with them and I couldn't be prouder than if they really were me own.'

'Michelle couldn't help it,' he said now. 'She wanted more from life than I could give her. Mind you, I still don't think she knows what it is. A good time, I suppose. Maybe all she wants is to be happy, but doesn't know how to go about it.' He grinned. 'Like us all.'

Brodie felt edgy all day without him. She'd got used to him being there. She watched an old film on television and jumped when there was a knock on the door. It was Vanessa asking if they could eat their dinner together.

'Tyler's taken Rachel and Poppy to see his father and stepmother and I'm feeling a bit lonely on my own,' she explained.

'What about Reggie?'

'He's at work – there's a rush job – and Charlie's spending the day with a girl from school whose birthday it is. I've got a steak and onion pie in the oven that's big enough for two and can bake a couple of potatoes in the microwave.'

'That sounds lovely.' Brodie had forgotten all about eating. 'Shall we have it in here, in my room? I'll get the table ready. It's freezing in the snug.' It was freezing everywhere. She'd bought some plug-in radiators for the big rooms, but they hadn't had much of an effect.

'Actually,' Vanessa said when the meal was over and they were finishing a bottle of wine that Brodie had forgotten she had, 'I wanted to discuss something with you.' She cleared her throat. 'I wondered if you'd mind if I went to live next door with Reggie? I wasn't going to mention it until after Christmas – remember we planned to have dinner together on Christmas Day, about a dozen of us? But the other day your mother mentioned you were thinking of getting new heating put in and it was going to cost the earth. I didn't want you to have it done on my account.'

'Well, I *was* thinking about it,' Brodie agreed, 'but that's all. I hadn't made up my mind.'

'Another thing,' Vanessa went on, filling up both their glasses until the bottle was empty, 'Rachel and Tyler have gone to look at a house that Tyler's father wants to buy for them. He doesn't approve of them living here. He's a real nerdy guy. Tyler's a bit like him, but Rachel hasn't noticed. Anyway, there's just a chance they'll want to move out soon.'

Brodie sighed. 'Diana's dead, the summer's over and everybody wants to leave.'

'Nothing lasts forever, Brodie,' Vanessa said wryly. 'The house seems darker without Diana and much too quiet. The life's gone out of it. Would you stay living here on your own or get new tenants in?'

'What would you do if you were me?'

'I don't exactly know what you mean by that, whether you're just referring to the house or to your life, but I'll guess.' She put her hand on Brodie's and squeezed it. 'If I were you I'd sell this house or rent it to someone else, then go back to your Colin and live happily ever after.'

Brodie heaved a sigh. 'I see.' She wasn't sure if that was the advice she'd wanted, though the 'happily ever after' bit sounded good. 'Oh, look,' she cried, 'there's Kenneth outside all by himself.' She sprang to her feet and opened the window.

'Here, puss, here.' She rubbed her fingers and Kenneth came prancing across, his tail erect. He walked gingerly into the room and toured the furniture, sniffing, until he jumped lightly on to the bed and fell asleep.

Vanessa said, 'Charlie claims he's missing Diana. I was wondering if he'd come and live next door with us, but the other day I saw him washing himself in the window of the first house in the road. He looked very much at home.'

Leaving Kenneth behind would be a wrench, Brodie thought. He had played a part in the lovely summer that had come to such an abrupt and ugly end. She began to clear the dishes off the table. 'Later, would you like me to help take your stuff next door?'

'I wouldn't dream of going yet!' Vanessa protested. 'I'll stay until you're ready to move, or until the end of the year.'

'That's awfully nice of you, Vanessa.' Brodie was touched. 'But you don't have to.'

'I'd sooner stay,' Vanessa said awkwardly. 'We're friends, aren't we, and that's what friends are for.'

After the dishes had been washed and Vanessa had gone upstairs, Brodie did what she always did when she had something on her mind: she rang Colin.

'I was going to come and see you soon,' he said when he heard her voice.

'For any particular reason?' she asked.

'A perfectly good reason — to see *you*. What can I do for you, darling?'

She explained about the central heating. 'The plumber said that to have a completely new system installed would cost between eight and ten thousand pounds.' Actually, he'd said 'smackeroos', a word she'd never heard before.

Colin gasped. 'Jaysus! But you've got tenants, Brodie, and one is a baby. You can't expect them to live in a freezing cold house. You need to have something done, even it just means radiators in a few rooms.'

'I've bought some radiators that plug in, but they're hopeless. I was wondering what to do next when Vanessa told me she wants to leave and she thinks Rachel will too in the not-too-distant future.'

There was a pause while he took this in. 'I hope you're not thinking of living in that big house on your own,' he said eventually.

'I don't know.' She didn't know anything any more.

There was another pause. 'If you like,' Colin said, 'I mean, if you're really keen on staying, we could sell this house, pay back the mortgage, and get Chestnuts completely modernized with what's over.'

It was then Brodie realized that he truly loved her. To think that he would sell their nice, square house in Crosby with its nice square rooms, the garden that was his pride and joy, and the tidy garage in which he kept the Triumph that he was so lovingly restoring to its former glory. He was willing to give up all these things for Brodie, his wife.

She could go back to the nice, square house and 'live happily ever after' as Vanessa had suggested, but she still wasn't sure if it was what she wanted.


A policeman and policewoman came to see Jim. They were in the snug for almost an hour. Brodie made them tea and apologized for the cold. They thanked her gravely.

'I understand there was an incident at the refugee centre a few months ago,' Jim said after the police had gone. 'Two foreign blokes came chasing after some young girls.'

'That's right.' Brodie remembered it well. 'Diana threw tea in the face of one of the men.'

'The police said the black van that ran her down was the one the blokes escaped in. They expect to make an arrest any minute.' He looked angry and puzzled. 'It would seem our Di was killed just so somebody could get their own back.'

The next morning, Brodie rang an estate agent who offered to come round there and then to provide a valuation when she gave him the address, but she told him she didn't want him until two o'clock, when Vanessa and Rachel took Poppy to the clinic.

In Diana's room, Jim was sorting out his daughter's things. Tinker was having her clothes for the refugee centre and Jim was giving the rest of her possessions to her mother in Nottingham. 'She'd really appreciate that little telly and all the DVDs and CDs,' he said. 'Is there anything you'd like, Brodie, as a memento?'

'I don't need a memento. I'll never forget Diana.' The memory of his shining, gentle daughter would always be like new in her mind.

Not long afterwards, Brodie was in the kitchen giving it a superficial clean, when Jim came in with a plastic carrier bag. 'I found these at the bottom of the wardrobe,' he said. 'They're obviously Christmas presents. There's a little white frock with poppies embroidered round the hem, a knitted patchwork scarf – and this.' He handed her a small cardboard box that contained a brooch made from tiny white and gold enamel flowers forming the letter B. 'It can only be for you, Brodie.'

'Will you be going back to Ecuador?' she asked later when she'd made them both coffee and were drinking it in her room. He was leaving in a week or so.

'I've had enough of South America.' He didn't give the impression he'd given the matter much thought. 'This time I think I'll go to the Middle East. It's been a while since I worked on an oil rig.' He'd worked on a farm in Ecuador, driven a bus in Australia, repaired cars in Canada.

'Oh, but it's dangerous in the Middle East right now!' Brodie gasped, alarmed.

'Not everywhere.' There was a note of hopelessness in his voice.

'Why don't you settle down somewhere in this country?' she suggested gently.

'I'm not ready to settle down just yet.'

'What's to become of you?' She felt achingly sad. 'You should get married and have more children.'

'Should I?' His lips twitched slightly in a smile.

'I can't bear to think of you being unhappy.' She couldn't believe she'd said that. But it was true.

'Thank you, Brodie,' he said gravely. 'I'll always remember that.'

Had he touched her then, she would have willingly responded. She was trembling, her throat thick with excitement and fear at the thought of making love with a man other than her husband.

But Jim merely smiled and went back to Diana's room, saying that he had a letter to write.

Brodie relaxed and studied the garden, empty for a change. Was there really a letter to write, or had he somehow sensed how she felt and had made his escape?

Afterwards, when she was herself again, she was glad he'd gone when he did. She would have hated herself for ever had she been unfaithful to Colin.

Which more or less seemed to settle things. At least now she knew where she stood.


It seemed to happen all of a sudden. A property company offered to buy the house for a sum of money that made Brodie's head spin.

Then Rachel told her that Tyler's father was in the process of buying them a house. 'Tyler's stepmother is really nice, though Tyler claims he doesn't like her. She's only thirty, but can't have children. I'm going back to school after Christmas and she's going to look after Poppy. I'm looking forward to it in a way, school. I always wanted to be a teacher. By the time I'm properly trained Poppy will be at school herself.'

'When are you going?' Brodie asked.

'Well, they're getting a room ready for us in their house because ours will take a few weeks to buy. In a few days, I expect.' She looked uncomfortable. 'I hope you don't mind, but it's been awful cold here lately, even with the radiator turned full on. I've been having Poppy in bed with me to keep her warm.'

'Gosh!' Brodie swallowed hard. She was a hopeless land-lady. Perhaps, without realizing it, she was trying to drive everyone away. 'I'll miss you and Poppy terribly.'

'And we'll miss you – and that lovely cool garden.'

With Brodie and Charlie's help, Vanessa had begun gradually to move her stuff into Reggie's house. Colin had now taken it for granted Brodie would move back to Crosby and asked if he should start moving hers.

'Not yet,' Brodie said, though she didn't know why. She felt restless and dissatisfied, though she knew the reason for that.

'You're not going to change your mind, are you? You always said you'd give Josh and Maisie a big chunk of money when Chestnuts was sold. You're not going back on your word?'

'I didn't tell *them* that, did I?' she snapped. 'What sort of person do you think I am?' There would also be enough money for her to buy a flat of her own and Colin could go and jump in the lake, but was it unreasonable to expect the husband who loved her never to make a stupid remark?

'I'm sorry,' Colin said humbly. 'There are times when I speak before I think. It's just that I'm worried that I'll lose you.'

'You won't lose me,' Brodie said with a sigh.

Rachel and Poppy had gone with the promise they would all meet next door on Christmas Day, Brodie's family, too, when Vanessa would make dinner. 'I'll have to go on a crash cookery course,' she said. 'I've never made Christmas dinner before.'

On a breezy Monday morning, the last in October, Vanessa moved the remainder of her possessions into Reggie's house and put her head around the door of Brodie's room to say goodbye. 'I'm off now,' she announced.

Brodie was sitting on the bed feeling lost and watching the leaves outside swirl around like snow in a paperweight. 'Are you going to look for a job when you've settled in?' she asked.

Vanessa blushed slightly. 'I already have a job. I'm an artist, but I'm going to become a housewife, too, look after Reggie and Charlie, and try very hard to have a baby – several babies.'

'I envy you,' Brodie said thoughtfully. 'Me, I've done the housewife and baby bit; now I want to train for a career.'

'Good luck, then, Brodie.'

'And good luck to you, Vanessa.'

Vanessa had hardly been gone a minute when Jim came back, having been to the shops on Crosby Road. He was travelling to Heathrow that afternoon and catching an overnight flight to Saudi Arabia. Brodie went into the hall to meet him.

'I'm sorry,' he said when he saw her. 'Are you waiting for me to go so you can go yourself?'

'I suppose I must be.' Her heart twisted at the thought that, after today, they might never see each other again.

'I'll just shove these things in me bag. I've just bought meself a new toothbrush and soap and stuff.' He went into Diana's room where his rucksack, already packed, lay on the bed.

In the hall, Brodie rubbed her forehead distractedly. 'I don't want you to go,' she said, but only to herself.

He came out of his daughter's bedroom, the rucksack suspended from his right shoulder, a lonely traveller, wandering the world without wanting anything solid or permanent out of life – certainly not her. He might not have had any of the peculiar and outlandish thoughts she'd been having about him. 'I've promised to stay in touch with the lads,' he said gruffly. 'If you ever need anything, you can contact me through them.'

'All right,' Brodie said. She wondered if she ever would.

He squeezed her shoulders. 'Tara, girl,' he said, grinning now. He shook her hand and kissed her cheek, both at the same time.

'Tara, Jim.'

She looked into his blue eyes for the final time, then turned away until the door had closed. He'd gone. The sound briefly echoed through the house until everything became quiet and the house seemed to be ticking over like a giant clock. She picked up the bag containing the last of her things and counted up to a hundred so there'd be no sign of Jim when she left.

She opened the door, went outside and stood there blinking, with the feeling that she'd just stepped out of a dream and all the strange emotions she'd been experiencing recently were being blown away. She looked at the intensely blue sky and the fast-moving clouds and laughed for the first time in ages. Her mind was completely clear.

The wind had loosened a piece of ivy and it flapped in front of her face. She was about to tuck it behind the trellis attached to the wall, but paused. Something was shining softly through the dark-green leaves. She moved them carefully to avoid the thorns and found a rose nestling inside. It was a luscious cream, in full bloom and utterly perfect, the smooth petals looking as if they were made of velvet.

'Oh!' she gasped. For some reason she thought of Diana. She felt tempted to pluck the flower, but then it would only live for a few more days. Left to itself, it would die naturally as

Diana never had. She touched it with her finger: it felt surprisingly cold.

The last rose of summer.

Brodie threw back her shoulders. She was ready to go home to Colin.

She couldn't wait.